TRILOGY IN G MINOR

TRILOGY IN G MINOR

Dorsey Butterbaugh

Baltimore, Maryland

Cover photograph and photo of Dorsey Butterbaugh by Tim Collins of TC Inspirations Photography, Salisbury, Maryland.

ISBN-13: 978-1494888558
ISBN-10: 1494888556

Dedicated with love and thanks to SB and AB.

Acknowledgements:

Thanks to all those who read the manuscript and gave their unbiased comments, hard as they were to sometimes take. A special thanks to Frank Minni, President of the Rehoboth Beach Writers' Guild, who never seems to tire of my stories and provides well-needed and welcome feedback.

Thanks also to Steve Robison for his assistance with proofreading and line editing the manuscript, for the cover design, and for producing the paperback and ebook versions of this book.

WATER WILL RUN DOWNHILL
ONLY IF GIVEN A HILL
DOWN WHICH TO RUN.

Late April

1

Meteorologists called it one of the worst spring heat waves to engulf the east coast since such records were kept. A Bermuda high was trapped between two smaller systems, and showed no signs of moving. The system extended from Florida to New York, and midway along the Gulf coast. For over a week, the daily high broke one hundred degrees in many areas. The nighttime temperatures remained elevated as well. Except for an occasional scattered shower, it had not rained in over a month. Forecasters could only sit back in their air conditioned offices and watch as the history making weather pattern remained stationary. There had been few April showers. There certainly would be no May flowers. It was joked that to try to get the Bermuda high to pass, many meteorologists resorted to an unproven, but often times effective method of weather science: they went to the roofs of their respective buildings and did a rain dance. To the layperson who did not fully understand the peculiarities of the weather, it was simply hot as hell. To many, it had never been hotter.

Such was the case for April Blackstone. In her twelve plus years, she could only recall being hotter once in her life, and that was when she had a high fever. She remembered the shivering that followed as much as the fever itself. She had never been so cold—so cold she could not get warm regardless of how many blankets her mother laid atop her. She remembered thinking that once the fever broke she hoped she would never be that cold again. She decided now, the feeling might not be so bad.

Short and frail in stature, the kids at school called her squirt. She could never tell if it was an insult, simply a nickname, or a compliment. April told her mother about this once, to which the elder Blackstone replied, "You are kind of puny for your age. But don't you worry, that'll change soon enough."

That night April took a long look at herself in the mirror that hung on the back of her mother's door. She realized her mother wasn't being nasty, just telling the truth. April was a short skinny little kid, who to many always looked on the verge of starving; unbeknownst to them, sometimes she was. She kept her long blonde hair pulled in a ponytail and in spite of the heat, refused to let her mother cut it. Her hair was the one feature that made her proud. She had deep blue eyes. Her face was a bit sunken yet still pretty and she almost always carried a smile. In spite of the lack of formal dental care, she was blessed with remarkably straight teeth. Her arms were long and lanky, as were her fingers, yet her arm muscles were well developed. She was much stronger than she looked, partially due to the many hours of hard work in and outside their trailer, and partially due to the many hours at the piano. Her chest and stomach were totally flat. Her legs were mere twigs upon which the rest of her body balanced. So yes, if April gave it a thought, she was a skinny little girl. But was she really a squirt?

Her sleeveless cotton top was soaked as perspiration rolled down her face. She attempted to wipe her brow with her forearm. It was debatable, however, which of the two body parts was wetter. She dried the last of the dishes and stacked them away in the cupboard. As the water drained from the sink, she hurriedly wiped down the countertop. Just as quickly, she scurried around the trailer, straightening up as she went. In spite of the temperature inside the old trailer approaching 105, she worked with determination. She was hot, yet had grown accustomed to the heat. She lived in the Deep South all her life without air conditioning so she had never known summer to be anything else. Her only complaint was that summer had arrived early. Besides, she much preferred the heat to the cold of winter. Heat didn't make her fingers go numb. The cold also made the already out of tune piano sound even worse.

Yes, she'd take the heat any day over the cold. Thinking like that was one way she tolerated the environment in which she lived. Simply ignoring it was another. After all, it was only one of the many things she'd grown to accept during her short life. Besides, like her mother always said, "Why worry about what you can't control?"

The trailer was old, and from the outside barely looked livable. Inside, the dwelling was spotless, in spite of the open windows letting in dust. The walls, light pine paneling, were wiped clean every week; the floors scrubbed twice as often. The furniture was tattered and worn, especially the couch which had a broken leg propped up by an old phone book. It was a good use for the book as they had no telephone. She and her mother considered themselves lucky to have running water and inside plumbing, although both were a source of contention at times between April's mother and the landlord who owned the farm where the trailer rested. The water pressure on occasion was almost non-existent. Her mother didn't complain too much though. It was all they had. While they didn't own the trailer, only the meager furnishings inside, it was home. And while it took a lot of work because of the never ending dust, the place was clean. April was determined to keep it that way so her mother would be proud when she got home from her weekend job the next night—Sunday.

April rose with the sun in order to beat the heat and quickly finished her chores. After a visual inspection to make sure everything was in place and there was no dust to be found, she sat down at the small kitchen table to have her breakfast—two slices of stale bread, an apple, a pear and two glasses of water. There had been milk the day before, but she finished that the previous evening. It was the last thing left in the old Frigidaire so she had shut off the power to save electricity, and to keep the appliance from adding heat to the trailer. There was a small fan, but that was run only at night to help with sleep. While they were poor, a well thought out plan allowed them to survive with a lot less suffering than one might expect. Her mother was fond of saying, "Things could be worse, you know. We could be back in that shack with your father." The thought had both good and bad points. Her father had always been kind and caring towards April. Towards his wife, it was a different story.

So mother and daughter survived, hiding from the past, living the present day to day, with little thought about the future. What they lacked in physical needs, they made up for in other ways. In spite of leaving her daughter every Friday to work for the weekend, Elizabeth Blackstone was a good mother. April disliked being left alone three days each week, but she understood there was no choice. Work was slim in the area. Besides, the money was good and there was always plenty to eat for the first few days of the week. Often there was a present such as a new piece of music for April to learn. While life was lonely at times, it was bearable.

April stared out the kitchen window, slowly chewing a crust of bread. The trailer sat on a barren piece of land at the bottom of a hill a quarter mile or so from the main farmhouse. The small yard surrounding the trailer was parched. The grass had died even before the official start of the heat spell. With unpredictable inside water pressure and a back-up well of unknown capacity, there was no water to spare on luxuries such as grass. They had planted a few flowers in an attempt to brighten the outside, but the heat as well as the drought discouraged any further green thumbs. Beyond the yard, the spring corn planted by the owners of the farm was threatening to succumb to the heat also. April correctly deduced the crop had only a few days left before it would have to be plowed under.

The farmhouse sat atop a small knoll across the long narrow field. April had never been inside, but her mother said it was the same as the man and woman who lived there—dirty and in disarray. The farmer and his wife had three boys, all around April's age. April saw all three in school and they looked clean enough. They acted normal as well, and wore the usual dress code for kids in the area—tee shirts, jeans and tennis shoes. Their hair was always at least semi-combed although often in need of cutting, and they never smelled, so April figured they were okay. They never said much to her because she and her mother weren't locals, and non-locals were frowned upon in these parts. That they weren't here by choice mattered little.

She let her thoughts wander back to the past. While in some ways she did miss her father, she didn't miss him beating up on her mother. She thought time would help, but time—the alleged healer of all wounds—wasn't doing too good a job on this one. April had the same mixed-up feelings as before. On one hand, she loved him. After all, he was her father. On the other, there was a deep hatred for all he had done to her mother. She just hoped one day the feelings would straighten themselves out.

Hope was a hook to hang your hat on—a reminder that someday the future might be brighter. One of the last nights before she and her mother ran away, her father had come in to kiss her good night. It was one of the only times April had seen him sober in weeks. He sat on the edge of her bed and gave her a back rub, something he often did before his drinking became out of control. As she dozed off to sleep, he leaned forward, kissed her gently on the cheek and whispered, "Things will be better one day, April. You'll see."

Her last friendly words to him: "I hope so, Daddy."

While hope was alive, it weakened with each setting sun.

Her mother continued to say they shouldn't complain. Things could be worse. Even with the farmer charging an excessive amount of rent, and even though they were not the friendliest bunch, they were not mean. The woman did give them an occasional quart of milk and some vegetables now and then. She even brought over an occasional chicken, one time saying, "Only because everyone's belly is full, including the pigs." Then she winked and added, "Just don't tell my old man. He'd kill me if in he knew I was a giving away food to people like you." April often wondered what she meant by *people like you*. She knew not to ask.

With each visit, April's mother would shower the woman with praise and thanks. Once the woman was halfway home, she would add, "Bitch." She was especially vocal after the chicken delivery visits. "Because everyone's belly is full, including the pigs," she mocked just the week before. As she watched the farm woman walk away, she added, "Someday April, you and I will be eating better than her whole goddamn family, including her pigs. Fuckin' bitch… 'xcuse my language."

"When?" April had asked. The thought of not living from day to day made her quickly forget about her mother's profanity, something she seldom failed to correct. That, and her smoking.

"When what?" Her mother fumbled in her pocket for a cigarette.

"When will we eat better than them?"

"I'm workin' on it, April. By God, I'm workin' on it."

"How?"

"Don't you mind that. Just get to those vegetables. Feel like chicken soup?"

April nodded her head vigorously. Soup always made her stomach feel full. Her mom pulled the one sharp paring knife from the drawer and slid it across the counter to April. "Then get a peeling, girl." The soup lasted three days—three days in a row without even a twinge of hunger.

A man picked her mother up every Friday afternoon and brought her back Sunday evenings, sometimes early Monday mornings. Her mother said she worked as a waitress in a fancy restaurant about a hundred miles away, and that it paid real good, too. Plus, she felt it was safe from April's father, as he would never be caught in such a place. That was all April knew. That was all she was allowed to know. Anytime she inquired more, her mother quickly changed the subject. And since her mother did come home with food and presents, April was appeased. The young girl just wished she wasn't left alone so much. But she kept busy, using the time to get her homework done and do her chores. It also gave her ample time to practice the piano.

April brought her thoughts back to the present. This week there had been no chicken, and only a few tomatoes and one squash. Again, the milk was gone and the bread, made two days earlier, was already stale. She just hoped her mother got back home tomorrow evening instead of Monday morning. Although April had grown accustomed to being alone, she did miss her mother a lot, and April knew her mother felt the same. It was a rough way to live, yet they were surviving, and doing so in relative happiness. Times were tough, yet things could always be worse.

April drank another glass of water and went into the living room. She did a visual inspection making sure everything was in its place. Satisfied, she plopped down on the old couch that also served as her bed during the week. On the weekends, she was allowed to sleep on the mattress in the one bedroom. While not any more comfortable, April did feel closer to her mother there—comforted by the stale smell of her mother's cigarettes.

There was a stack of old magazines on the coffee table (two planks held up by concrete blocks), but April had read each several times. Her school books were there also, but she had already finished her homework. A straight-A student, school came easily to April. Besides, she found most of the stuff in school boring, not because it wasn't interesting. They just moved so slowly through the material. Her eyes traveled to the far corner of the room where the old upright piano stood. The original color was black and showed the scars from the many moves. It still shined, however, from the polish April applied on a regular basis. Except for a couple of keys that liked to stick now and then, it worked okay, even though it was out of tune.

No one seemed to mind because no one was around except her mother. Naturally, her mother thought April's playing was superb, praising and gloating over her all the time. That was why April saved most of her practicing for the weekend. For April, praising was fine. Gloating was a bit much.

True, the piano had seen better days, but when April Blackstone played, the instrument seemed to awaken and gather long lost energy. Her mother recognized her daughter's talents early on. While never able to afford formal lessons, she did see that April had music to play. She often came home from her weekend of work with a new music book stuffed in the bag of food. She also knew enough to bring a variety of songs as well as books on fingering exercises. In the beginning, April whizzed through the books. When her mother started bringing home difficult classical pieces, the pace slowed, but the older Blackstone was still amazed at how quickly her daughter picked out the notes. Elizabeth Blackstone never claimed to be an overly religious person, but she told her daughter God had given her two gifts in her life. First was being able to escape from her husband, second was her beautiful and musically talented daughter who gave her a reason to live.

April stared at the piano. She tried telling herself it was too hot to practice. She knew, however, her fingers worked better in the heat, even when her sweat sometimes made the keys slippery. Besides, her mother's birthday was only two weeks away and April had yet to finish the song she was making up for her. There was no money for physical presents. There probably wouldn't even be a cake. But not all gifts came in a box.

She rose from the couch and went over to the instrument. She sat down on the bench and adjusted her posture slightly. She poised her fingers above the keys, making sure her finger position was the way she had learned from the books she studied. They were the only music teacher she ever knew. She took a deep breath and closed her eyes. A moment later the sounds of scales filled the dense humid air. She started with the C scale, first an octave—then two—then three. She played a transition chord and repeated the pattern in C#. She continued the process in all twelve chords. She then played the scales in their minor versions, then augmented them. As the muscles in her hands loosened up, her fingers moved faster and faster. She never lost her touch however, and remained focused on the tone as well as the technique. "The piano sounds like the keys are touched," one of the lesson books preached. "A key that is banged sounds like a bang. A key that is caressed sings like a bird."

Other finger exercises followed, all memorized from a book by Czerny that now remained closed inside the bench. Besides touch, she worked on dexterity. Some exercises required intricate fingering. Others required an expansion of her reach. Still others incorporated both. Faster and faster she played until her fingers were at times a blur. While not perfect, there were few errors. Once the exercises were completed the way they were designed, she started through the series again, only this time she varied the rhythm and speed. The exercises were no longer just a series of notes. They now gave the impression of a song. She made birds sing.

After an hour of uninterrupted play, she took a break for a glass of water, and to wipe the sweat from her face and arms. Returning to the piano, she worked on a couple of new songs her mother had brought her. They were three southern folk ballads, all soft and with slow melodies. They were simple yet beautiful. Next, she worked on the song she had written for her mother. It, too, was in the form of a ballad. There were no words, just the delicate voicing of the instrument as the harmony of the chords filled the air. April called it *Happy Birthday Bouquet*. If you closed your eyes, you could imagine a field of beautiful flowers. There was also wind, sun and much happiness in the piece. It was the latter of the three effects April strove for the most. She knew her mother hadn't had much happiness, and April wanted to do everything in her power to fill the void.

The young girl's concentration was tremendous when she played. She forgot about the humidity, the heat, and she easily lost track of the time. She forgot about being hungry, the empty cupboards, the skimpy wardrobe and the school shoes that were worn and too small. She forgot about her mother leaving on Fridays and coming back on Sunday evenings (hopefully), and how much she missed her during those lonely hours. She forgot about the trailer, the high rent, the mosquitoes that circled her head at night and the welts found the next morning. She forgot about the snide remarks of the farm lady, the stares of her classmates at her old clothes and their snickering behind her back. She forgot about the fact that they were living—hiding out—in one of the poorest sections in Louisiana, stashed away like some unwanted dogs.

She forgot how much she missed her father, in spite of everything. She forgot she had not seen him in over four years, the last time being when the police took him away after he beat her mother because she would not give him any more money to buy booze. She forgot that he threatened to kill them both as soon as he got out of jail and forgot the hope that was raised just a few nights before his arrest when he gave her a back rub. She forgot about her and her mother sneaking away that same night, loading up their old pickup with the help of neighbors, running and hiding for the next six weeks, crossing state after state. She forgot about the truck breaking down in No-Where-Louisiana, no money for repairs and little money left for anything else. She forgot about the farmer agreeing to take the truck as collateral for the rent of an old run down trailer, the trailer that was still their home. She forgot that the farmer had since sold the truck for a hefty fee, keeping the money himself in escrow in case they failed to pay the rent. She forgot about the loneliness, the isolation, the lack of friends, no family, no pets, no entertainment, no pretty dresses, no shampoo, no new underwear and no bed to call her own. She forgot there was still a sense of fear in her mother that one day her father would find them and carry forth his threats.

She forgot about it all when she played. The piano was her one true escape. It was where reality turned to fantasy. It was where nightmares turned to dreams, where painful fresh memories turned to vague distant recollections, where heartaches in the past turned to wishes for the future.

As such, she played often and she played with vengeance.

Today was no different. Three hours after she started, completely soaked in sweat, short of breath and with fingers aching, she stopped, rose from the bench and went outside to get some fresh air. She walked around to the shady side of the trailer where she tried to keep a small flower garden. She pulled a few weeds and made a mental note to water the struggling plants later. She then tended to a single rose bush that was crawling up the side of the trailer. The garden, in spite of the heat, seemed to be doing fine. And in spite of her mother's weak protests, there were always fresh flowers on the table when she returned from her weekend excursions. April planned for this ritual to continue. April told herself she should say a little prayer that it would indeed be tomorrow night and not Monday.

And so she did.

2

It took April's several trips to the well on the far side of the trailer to get enough water for the flowers. She took her time as the sun approached its peak. Already sweating from her work inside, the sun beating down on her skin made her pores open wider. She didn't mind, however. There was a healing effect to being outside. Hearing voices during the last trip, she stopped and glanced over her shoulder, wiped the sweat from her brow and brushed a loose strand of hair from her eyes. She recognized the three brothers who lived in the farmhouse.

The oldest was Jake. He was fifteen, the tallest of the three. He was also the most muscular, shouldering many of the routine chores around the farm and seeming to love every minute of it. April often watched him work in the fields. He always had a cheery manner about him, and even spoke to her occasionally in school. Although he was nice enough, there was a part of him April could not quite understand—a side she couldn't trust. John was the middle boy. April guessed he was thirteen or fourteen. He was two grades ahead of her in school. He was a few inches shorter than his older brother and not quite as muscular. Except in school, he was always at his brother's side. Jack was the youngest and in April's class. He seemed the opposite of his brothers in many ways. He was short, heavier and had blond hair verses the brownish color of the other two siblings. April very seldom saw him outside, and when she did, he never looked as happy as his brothers. April reckoned he simply didn't like farming. Even though they were in class together, he seldom spoke to April. Matter of fact, April never saw him speak much to anyone. He just liked to stare at the girls, usually sending chills up their spines. While the girls all gossiped that they thought Jake was handsome and cool, they all thought John and Jack were sort of weird.

April figured the boys were heading to the stream that ran through the woods behind the trailer. It was narrow with a few deep spots, and even pooled in one area almost like a small pond. April had wandered back there on several occasions herself, never venturing in more than to get her feet wet. She remembered the placidness as the cool water rushed through her toes. She remembered wondering from where the water came, and where it went. She thought of the stream like one giant rain drop, striking the earth at one point and slithering downhill until reaching its destination somewhere in the distance. She wondered why it chose a particular path—a bend here in one direction, there in another. What controlled the stream, and what would happen to the water if there were no hill down which to run? The unexplained elements of nature stirred a strong level of curiosity in the child. Then again, she was curious about a lot of things in life.

She watched the brothers as they neared the trailer. Boys were one of nature's elements she decided she'd probably never understand. One minute they could be sweet as pie; the next like buzzards, circling high overhead. When asked about this, her mother simply said that all men were a waste, and strongly recommended April do everything in her power to avoid them. However, her mother always left open the possibility that one day the right boy would come along, quickly adding that day was a long way off.

As they drew closer, Jake spotted her and stopped. He watched her a moment before speaking. "Where's your mother?"

"She's workin'," April said.

"What kind of work she do?"

"She's a waitress," April responded.

"Where?"

April shrugged her shoulders. Her mother would never tell her the name of the town.

"What's the name of the restaurant?"

April hesitated. Again, she did not know. There were more glances and more snickers.

She had overheard several conversations in school—other kids talking, claiming her mother was more than a waitress. April was unclear what that meant, but she didn't dare ask—the other kids or her mother. She just stuck to her story that her mother was a waitress somewhere in a near-by town. After all, that was all her mother ever told her and she had no reason to believe otherwise.

All three boys were grubby looking today, bare chested and bare footed. They each wore an old pair of denim cut-offs. Thank goodness they looked better in school, April thought. There they were clean and mostly combed. They wore shirts and shoes, too.

"How old are you?" John asked, continuing to watch as she moved toward the well.

"Twelve," April said. "Be thirteen soon." She felt three sets of eyes burn into her body. It suddenly felt even hotter. Even though she had little to cover up, she instinctively crossed her arms in front of her chest.

"You don't look twelve," John said.

"Looks more like eight, maybe nine at the most," Jake inserted. This time their laughter was louder.

"Well, I am," April insisted. "Believe it if you want. Don't if you don't. Makes no difference to me." The latter point was a bit of a lie. She did want them to believe her so they would be more apt to talk to her sometimes. Being ignored was as bad as being eyed by buzzards. While she had no special interest in them individually, she longed for someone to talk to other than her mother. On the surface, she and her mother had a good relationship. April could talk to her about school, about music and about things surrounding their life. However, as soon as she ventured into more personal territory such as the nature of boys, her mother always found an excuse to cut the conversation short. It left April with a void called loneliness. "I gotta finish my chores," she said as she reached the well. She filled up a bucket to take to the few pots of flowers she kept inside.

Jake stepped forward. "I'll get that for you," he said, reaching out with his hand.

April was quick to realize his intentions. "No, but thanks anyway," she said firmly.

"It's no bother."

"No!" No one was allowed in the trailer when her mother was away.

It was a rule April wasn't interested in breaking, even if it meant the conversation, although brief, would end.

Jake stopped his forward movement and shrugged his shoulders. "Just tryin' to be neighborly." He saw his two younger brothers were getting antsy. "Well, you gotta do chores. We gotta go swimming. We're goin' over to the stream. Water's real cool 'spite the heat."

April let her mind wander to the stream. The thought of the cool water flowing through her toes caused a surge of jealously.

"Come on, boys." Jake started to lead his brothers away. He stopped after a few seconds however, looked over his shoulder and said, "Wanna come along?"

"No!" the two boys objected simultaneously.

"Shut up, you jerks."

"But Jake, we…"

The glare in his eyes was the stimulus for obedience. "How 'bout it?" Jake encouraged.

"Can't," April said after a moment's hesitation.

"Why not?"

"Like I said, I got chores to do."

"Do them later."

"I can't."

"Your mama won't be home till tomorrow night at the earliest."

"How'd you know that?" April demanded. Then she remembered. The noisy truck was hard to miss. "I'd better be getting back inside," April added. Having filled her pail, she headed toward the front door.

"Come on and go with us," Jake said almost pleadingly. "Water in the stream is nice and cool. Ain't that right, boys?" The younger siblings nodded and mumbled something in support of their brother's comments.

April again hesitated. Her mother's rules came into mind. "No one in the trailer and don't wander too far on the outside."

No one was going into the trailer but she never said just how far was *too far*. After all, April had been back to the stream before and the thought of having someone to talk to was tempting. Besides, it was awfully hot and the image of cool water through her toes again captured her imagination. The lure of the dream was too powerful to ignore.

"I'll just be a minute," she said.

3

April lay in bed, her body very still, her mind racing like a chicken being chased by a fox. While it was now late in the evening, the images continued flashing through her mind, the same pictures over and over. She was lying in the damp ground. She was nearly naked. Every joint in her body ached. She tasted vomit in her mouth. Her mother was standing over her, looking down. She was yelling, only April could not make out what she was saying. The dream—the nightmare—repeated like a song stuck in her head.

The screaming grew louder until she awoke with a start. Her eyes snapped open. Her heart thumped in her chest as adrenalin flowed through her bloodstream. She let her eyes grow accustomed to the darkness. She remained still so her other senses could awaken as well. She slowly realized she was not on the cold ground. Nothing was happening to her. She was alive. She was lying in her mother's bed. The scent of cigarettes verified that. Her sense of relief was abbreviated by the realization that, like in the dream, she was naked except for her underclothes, and every joint in her body did ache. In addition, she had a throbbing pain in the back of her head. She vaguely remembered falling and hitting her head. Other details were a blur at first. Then her memory started to return. The pain in her head heightened in intensity. She cut the remembrances short. She dozed back off. The dream returned. The yelling continued. The voice pulled her awake again. It took a moment, but April was finally able to discern what her mother was saying.

"You shouldn't have gone down to the stream with the boys."

Only she did.

She did, and in spite of what she might think or want, there was nothing she could do to change the past. It was another event to be burned in her memory, to be buried in her soul.

She tried telling herself maybe she was making too much out of it. Was it really all that bad? After all, nothing really happened, did it? Almost maybe, but almost didn't count in this case—did it? She was afraid. She was confused. She began to question what really did happen. She had hit her head. She knew that much. So was her memory really clear?

It didn't matter. The *almost* was enough.

Then she thought about the boys. She gasped for a breath. Her pulse quickened. What would she say to them? What would they say to her? What would they say to her mother?

"Oh God," she mouthed. If only she had listened and stayed close to the trailer. What was she going to do? She said a little prayer.

There was near total silence as even the mosquitoes were too hot to buzz about. She prayed again. Silence again.

Then she heard it. The sound she so anxiously awaited every Sunday evening. *It* being the sound of tires on the gravel as the truck brought her mother home. It was the same tires, the same engine noise, the same truck. April was sure. She sat up in bed. A wave of joy shot through her veins. This was replaced an instant later by a surge of panic. She jumped to her feet. It was only Saturday. The panic rose. How did her mother find out so fast?

April flicked on the light and hurriedly made the bed. Thank goodness the rest of the trailer had already been straightened up. A moment later, her mother burst through the door.

"April, I'm home."

The young girl stood in the bedroom door. She waited for the wrath that was sure to come. She noted her mother wasn't carrying any bags which also meant there was no food or presents. That added to the young girl's anxiety. Tears welled up in her eyes. Her knees weakened. Her mother proceeded further into the room. April prepared for the assault.

"Come and give your mother a big hug," the woman commanded.

April did as she was told, knowing it was the calm before the storm. The hug was long and warm, just like usual.

"I missed you," her mother said with a smile.

"I missed you, too," April returned, hiding her confusion.

"I have a surprise for you," her mother said. She separated her body enough so she could look into her daughter's eyes.

"You do?" More confusion.

"Yes, sweetheart, I do. How would you like to blow this joint?"

"What do you mean?"

"I mean, we're getting out of here."

"Moving?"

"Yes," her mother said. Her smile widened.

"Where?"

"Ohio."

"Ohio. What's in Ohio?"

"To begin with, your new stepfather and my new husband, or rather husband-to-be."

April just stared as it took a few moments for the words to sink in. There was a lot of confusion. There were a lot of questions. "When?" was the first thing that came to mind.

"Tonight."

"We're leaving tonight!"

Her mother nodded.

More questions. More confusion. One thing was certain though, her prayers from a few moments before had been answered.

4

The computer monitor went blank for an instant. The words CONTROLLER FAILURE flashed in the lower right corner. "Press F1 to continue, F2 to abort." The message was accompanied by a shrill beep. Jennifer Blackstone squirmed in her seat, cursed beneath her breath and hit the F1 key as directed. The screen again went blank, the hard drive spun and buzzed, and the words "CONTROLLER FAILURE. Press F1 to continue, F2 to abort," again appeared.

"I just did that, stupid," the young woman said, louder this time and with plenty of emphasis on the word *stupid*. "If you're not going to let me boot up, then why tell me to hit F1?" She paused, waiting for the machine to reply. The message did not change. She reached down to the computer sitting beside her desk and hit the power button. The screen went totally blank. She waited a few seconds and turned the power back on. The indicator lights flashed, beeps beeped, and the hard drive again started to spin.

"CONTROLLER FAILURE. Press F1 to continue, F2 to abort."

"Come on, Bertha," she pleaded with the terminal. She turned the power off, this time with much more force than was necessary. "Just what I need."

The computer was an old Pentium with tons of memory along with a lot of other bells and whistles. It had been built by a friend who designed and built computer systems on the side. In real life, he was a fireman. The two career combination didn't make a lot of sense to Jennifer. Then again, who cared? The computer had operated flawlessly for over four years, until lately when Jennifer noticed it acting a little weird. For one, it was slower and took longer to boot. For another, it often rebooted itself with no apparent reason. However, until today, it always worked. She tried to think what might be wrong, only nothing came to mind. She ruled out a virus. It wasn't connected to the Internet. She used this computer for her writing only. The more modern Dell laptop sitting on the floor was for business.

"Bertha baby, you need a face lift, maybe even a heart transplant," Jennifer said to the blank screen. "I'll call and make an appointment with your doctor in the morning, unless you think you need to go to the emergency room."

Again, she stared as if waiting for a response. She let out a long sigh and pushed away from the desk. She rose to her feet, saying, "Bertha, you're just like me, a blank mind." She wanted to add, "Crazy at times too," but she didn't want to insult the machine even more, especially since Bertha was also the name of the cook in her parent's restaurant below her apartment. She made a mental note to call Harry the fireman in the morning. He did most of his work while on duty at the firehouse. Okay, if you can get away with it, Jennifer guessed. She shouldn't be critical though. A lot of people had weird combinations of professions and hobbies. She was an emergency room nurse who also wanted to be a writer. She had been working on her book for over two years. It was a collection of short stories about people's experiences in an emergency room. The people were fictional. The experiences were real. The book was titled: *ER Anthologies*. The writing had been going well until the past couple of months when her ability to create characters hit a brick wall. It was a wall she was having a hard time scaling. Her mind mimicked her computer— controller failure!

She grabbed her sweater from atop the TV, and with her free hand, turned it off. At least something around here works. She patted her pocket to make sure she had her keys and headed out of the apartment.

Outside, she paused to let her body adjust to the sudden heat that smacked her in the face. It was like she was opening an oven door. She wiped a bead of sweat that immediately formed on her forehead. At five-nine, she was the tallest person in her family. She was all Blackstone though—prominent cheekbones, prominent chin, beautiful brown eyes that matched her shoulder length hair. Her extremities were long, her body thin and firm. She was well kept and could have easily worked as a model or a cocktail waitress. (She did fill in at her parent's restaurant at times.) Tonight, she was serving as hostess. She wore one of her favorite cocktail dresses, a knee length pale blue satin material that was cut moderately low in the front and very low in the back. The dress nicely accentuated her well-formed figure. As the sales lady at Nordstrom's told her, it teased without taunting, although her mother would no doubt disagree with that.

Jennifer surveyed the surrounding area from the steps on the landing to her apartment. Since it was one of the tallest buildings in Annapolis, Jennifer enjoyed a panoramic view of the harbor. The sun was setting rapidly in the west, sending fingers of yellow through the low lying clouds. There was no wind so the multitude of boats anchored in the harbor pulled little on their moorings. All the slips at the city dock were full and, in spite of the ungodly heat, people were already out for their evening strolls. She again wiped sweat from her brow. It was some of the hottest weather she could remember for this time of the year. She contemplated throwing the sweater back inside, but remembered the day before when the air conditioning had been turned down to a level where the restaurant felt like an igloo.

She shaded her eyes and focused on the bulkhead running up toward the inner harbor. She found the boat she was looking for, an old Chesapeake Bay skipjack, but was unable to see any movement on the old boat's deck. She made a mental note to check on Old Man Hooper, the boat's skipper. He never complained about the heat. She knew, however, it was getting harder and harder for him to get along in any type of weather, much less this latest heat wave. The radio and TV were full of warnings for people with pulmonary problems to avoid the heat and stay inside, but inside for Old Man Hooper meant the boat's cabin which was even hotter. The possibility of him going elsewhere, even for a few days, was out of the question. Jennifer had given up arguing with him about that long ago. He had been a full time live-a-board since retiring eight years ago. He had no plans to move anywhere else. Still, she was worried about him. He was more short of breath all the time. She wished he'd stop sucking on those old cigarettes, and without filters no less.

She glanced down at the parking lot to the left. The spaces were already beginning to fill, meaning the restaurant would have a busy night. Her stomach grumbled as the aroma of homemade oyster stew made its way up the steps. The hunger pains intensified as she realized this would probably be one of the last weeks for local oysters, especially with the weather having turned so hot so early. Then they'd go through what they went through this time every year—trying to find oysters elsewhere at a reasonable price. Her mother's oyster stew was demanded and served twelve months a year. Jennifer's stomach growled again. She told it to hush. "Don't worry; Mother will certainly save you a bowl."

The *Riverboat Inn* sat atop a hill along the north side of the Annapolis harbor. One side of the property ran alongside Spa Creek, the south edge bordered the municipal parking lot in front of the City dock. The western side edged up against a line of small specialty shops and the back contained several undeveloped acres of land that the Blackstones owned and allowed the city to use as a park. The restaurant itself was in the shape of an old Mississippi riverboat—or rather the front third of such a boat. The first two decks were the actual restaurant and lounge—a large spacious area decorated in the same motif as the restaurant's name. The boat's pilot house served as Jennifer's apartment. Her parents had talked for years about expanding the restaurant back into the undeveloped property. However, up until now, that had only been talk. Only talk because it was unclear just how to expand the restaurant and because previous attempts by her father to obtain the necessary permits had been held up by bureaucratic red tape. Not wanting to cause any trouble in the community, her father never pushed the issue, saying, "There's always tomorrow."

Jennifer thought about going in early to see if there was anything her mother needed. She decided against it, telling herself a walk would help clear her mind. At the same time, she asked herself who she was kidding. Like Bertha the computer, her mind was a crashing motherboard. On the surface, she portrayed everything to be okay. Beneath the surface, her life was in turmoil. Like her computer, she needed an overhaul. The creative portion of her mind that allowed her to write—her one and only hobby—was simply a...

She struggled to find the right words.

"Controller failure." She laughed at the thought.

There had to be something she could do to jumpstart her mind. She'd sit down at the computer and go totally blank. Like Bertha, it was as if her brain wouldn't boot up. She knew it was writer's block, and she had it bad.

She enjoyed writing from an early age. She dabbled in poetry in elementary school, progressed to short stories in middle school and wrote her first long story her junior year in high school. It was about a young girl's dream of becoming a nurse. While not an autobiography, it did follow her own progression from an early interest up to her acceptance at Hopkins School of Nursing. There, she had to take several electives in the humanities, always choosing some sort of writing. While she was never the most flamboyant student, her stories and poetry did impress her professors. She aced every course. She always told herself that while she might someday become a fulltime writer, she first had to pay the bills. So for now, she kept her writing as a hobby, and a way of relieving stress.

She strolled down along the waterfront to check out the boats. Born and raised in Annapolis, she was a true blue Annapolitan. She loved the water and loved living around it. Her parents had a boat when she was younger, a small runabout they used for cruising up and down the Severn River with an occasional fishing trip out on the bay. They were fun times, especially when she could get her father's mind off the business for a few hours. As the restaurant got busier and she herself had less and less time to go out, the boat was sold. An era had passed. She missed all that now, thinking time out on the water might help clear her mind. She recalled many an hour just sitting anchored in a favorite cove on the Severn, soaking up a tan and thinking about absolutely nothing. Now it seemed her mind was in constant motion, thinking about too many things at once.

Her thoughts returned to her writer's block. "You're in denial," she said aloud. She didn't want to face up to the fact that her life was a mess—professionally and personally. Her parents were putting pressure on her to take a more active role in the restaurant. "We're not getting any younger, you know," was a commonly heard phrase from her mother. It was a scenario everyone working at the restaurant expected, but it was a situation Jennifer was not ready to accept.

Her parents wanted their only child to study the food and beverage industry in college, but they finally acquiesced and paid her tuition at Johns Hopkins School of Nursing. She was a good nurse, too, and loved working in the emergency room at Annapolis General Hospital. There she learned the true meaning of empathy. She also learned how to separate her personal feelings from the wants, needs and demands of her patients. Like many state capitals, Annapolis had its share of both wealth and poverty. This brewed a wide mix of people coming into the emergency room. It also supplied Jennifer with true-to-life stories for her book.

Not a bad gig, she reminded herself frequently.

She had taken well to the position of nurse manager, a promotion she'd received the year before. She made the transition with ease, and except for the seemingly endless amount of paperwork, enjoyed the challenge. Her mother, however, noticed a gradual change and insisted Jennifer was burning out. Jennifer argued the restaurant business was just as draining as health care. Her father rebutted that if you provide poor service in a restaurant, the food gets cold and the customer complains. If you provide poor service in an emergency room, the customer may not live to complain. Jennifer acknowledged her father, but she knew the problem wasn't from the clinical side of medicine. It was the stress related to the hospital being in financial trouble. The administration's prescription was unrealistic budgetary cuts across all departments. Jennifer and other managers argued the reason things were even worse was because previous cuts kept them from hiring and retaining good staff. She argued that Johns Hopkins was world famous, not because of the facilities, but for the people who worked there.

The continuing budget battle provided a spark of hope. Things were coming to a head and everyone expected the problems to be resolved soon. Several department heads had written the CEO an anonymous letter expressing their concerns. Surely, he would see it their way.

She turned and headed toward the inner harbor. Ego alley, the narrow channel off Spa Creek, was so named because of all the Cigarette type boats that liked to cruise the narrow waterway. The guys and girls were always good looking, and the boats always noisy. The narrow pier was already crowded with boaters and tourists. Jennifer had to stop several times to let people by. She recognized a couple of customers from the restaurant and returned their greetings. One guy asked her aboard for a drink. She laughed and said maybe another time. She had no doubt he'd be in the bar later searching her out, which was fine with her. He drank a lot, bought a lot for others and was an above average tipper. In short, he was good for business. Her rule with customers was simple: tease, but don't touch. She expected the same from them. It didn't keep them from trying, though.

She ignored the slow pace along the pier. It was too hot to rush. Her thoughts turned to the personal side of the multi-sided coin known as her life. The image of Dr. Daniel Baker came to mind. He was Chief of Staff at Annapolis Memorial Hospital and one of the most respected (and successful) plastic surgeons in the area. He was forty-one. She was twenty-six. They had been going together for almost two years. She dreamed of getting married, settling down, having a bunch of kids and writing bestselling novels. He claimed he wanted the same. There was only one problem, and it was not the difference in their ages.

He had a wife.

"If you hate her as much as you say you do, why not just file for a divorce?" She had asked the question just the night before.

His reply was always the same. "The timing isn't right."

Because she loved him and was convinced he felt the same, she bought into the excuse. The hospital rumor mill had picked up the story soon after they started seeing one another, but only a couple of people knew for sure. Her mother even confronted her about the issue after overhearing a conversation at the *Riverboat Inn* one evening. Jennifer just laughed it off. Her mother knew, however—they always do. Those that did know for sure thought she was nuts. Her mother would have undoubtedly agreed. And maybe they were right, but…

"But what?" she said loud enough for others to hear. She ducked her head and told herself not to blush.

She was starting to have doubts of her own. Was everyone else right? Was she crazy waiting for him to make up his mind, to find the right time, to make a commitment to her? No one questioned her messing around with a married man. What they all focused on was her foolishness in believing he was going to leave his wife. He was not only a well-respected member of the medical staff, his wife was also important to the hospital. Her social connections kept him supplied with women who wanted their bodies augmented in one way or another—women who listened to the beautifully proportioned Mrs. Daniel Baker, who assured them instant beauty if they paid her darling husband a visit.

Annapolis General Hospital was surviving for several reasons, one of which was the revenue generated by Dr. Daniel Baker. His operating room schedule was the heaviest of any physician on staff.

But what, Jennifer repeated, this time silently. She didn't have answers to remaining doubts that added additional stress to an already overloaded set of brain cells. It was no wonder she was experiencing writer's block. There wasn't any room left in her skull for creativity.

Writing was more than a hobby. It was a way for her to release the tension built up from her work. ER nursing was not only physical, it took its toll emotionally. The daily stress of seeing people's lives suddenly changed by one uncontrollable event was a lot to take. An emotional person herself, Jennifer struggled as she watched the emotions of others come forth during these tragic times. Some say that people who work in medicine get used to the good and bad, the sick and the healthy, the life and death. No, Jennifer thought, you don't get used to it. You just learn how to hide it, and you learn ways to release the pressure. For her, it was writing.

Writing also helped release the frustrations built up by her affair with Daniel Baker and the pressures being put on her by her parents regarding the *Riverboat Inn*. Her characters took on her feelings, good and bad. Her characters felt happiness when she was happy. They felt pain when she felt pain. They dreamed when she dreamed. They even showed signs of confusion. Now, however, they were showing nothing. She was unable to write. Her characters were unable to live. As the frustrations in her life continued to build, it was a wonder she didn't explode. It was controller failure for sure.

At the end of the dock, she stepped down to the concrete walkway. She passed a couple of large boats moored against the bulkhead. One was a tour boat offering half and full day excursions out on the bay. The other was a private yacht offering nightly dinner cruises up the Severn River. Since both were in dock, Jennifer figured they weren't booked for the night. That meant both crews would be up at the bar later creating more noise than desired. That problem, however, was countered by the money they spent.

She slowed at the next boat, the old skipjack she had eyed from her window. Her name was *Windskater*. While it had been many months since she had cut through the waters of the Chesapeake Bay, in her day, she was one of the fastest skipjacks around. The solid oak mast was set well forward, and reached sixty plus feet. The boom, also solid wood, carried one's eyes along the deck and off the stern. Above the water line, she still looked seaworthy. Her lines were pure, her decks, clean. The evening sun reflected sharply off the polished metal air intakes. The freeboard, while showing a few stains, glistened as well.

Jennifer smiled as her inspection continued. The bar backs at the restaurant were doing a good job of keeping her cleaned and polished. The smile faded a bit. She just wished the wood below the water line was in as good a shape.

She scanned the deck for Old Man Hooper, the owner and proprietor. He was always good for a little small talk, the kind that got one's mind off other things in life. He was also good for advice, especially to those he liked. Jennifer was one of his favorites. He was old and wise. He was an expert at sizing up a situation, whether you wanted him to or not.

"What would he say about this?" Jennifer wondered aloud. Another faint smile crossed her face. He'd first listen intently. Then he'd think a bit, all the while sucking on a cigarette. Then, while rubbing his hand across his poorly kept beard, he'd say, "Sounds like things can't get no worse, don't they?" After she agreed, he'd add, "Then I reckon that means things can only get better." Her smile widened, anticipating the conversation before it occurred.

The smile disappeared. He wasn't on deck. She contemplated knocking on the side, but didn't want to awaken him. Besides, she had already seen him earlier in the morning when she brought him his daily sampling of her mother's oyster stew. He was fine then, cantankerous as ever.

"No matter, I know what he would say anyway," she muttered.

In reality, however, she was wrong. He would never suggest waiting around for things to get better. He was a proponent of addressing problems in the then and now. "Very seldom can you run from a storm," he'd say. "They come up too unexpectedly and too quickly. You just have to turn into them nose first and ride 'em out." In her particular case he might add, "Sounds like you have a couple messes on your hands you need to deal with head on. If not, things may even get worse for ya."

She stuck with the things-will-get-better story and turned back towards the *Riverboat Inn*. She glanced up at the sky. There was still no sign of rain, although the clouds to the south had thickened. It could be the sign of a storm developing, but Jennifer doubted it. Why should today be any different from the recent past? She glanced at her watch. She had just enough time to get into the restaurant and freshen up. She was glad she brought the sweater. In spite of the heat, she knew the restaurant would be freezing. Hot outside and freezing inside—symbolisms she chose to ignore.

5

As predicted by the experts and anticipated by those sweltering from its effects, the heat wave extended into the next week. The entire east coast remained on a full day siesta. Electric utilities were implementing organized brownouts as they were not ready for this level of demand so early in the season. To help, most local governments closed early. Private businesses were encouraged to do the same. Schools had already closed for the week, and a few systems were discussing ending the school year early if the crisis persisted. One astute sixth grader interviewed by a local news reporter referred to being out of school, "like having a snow day without the snow." The heat wave was so unusual for this time of year, the major networks were covering it as part of their regular news updates. One network even did a special on the aberrant weather pattern, with one expert calling it a sign of the future. According to Baltimore's most popular radio talk show host, the heat was all anyone wanted to talk about.

Well, not everyone.

Cliff Davidson sat quietly with his feet dangling off the end of the pier, his toes barely touching the water. The tide was on its way up, so he would soon be able to dunk his whole foot in. But so what? The water was as hot as the air. Even a dip would be little relief from the heat. Cliff glanced over at his uncle aboard *Rose Bud*. Bent over with his head down, the man worked slowly yet diligently on the array of crab pots stacked three deep on the roof of the boat.

Rose Bud was a 33 foot all white Chesapeake Bay work boat. She was designed for one purpose and one purpose only—to harvest crabs and oysters from the bay. She sported few amenities. There was a small cabin forward to protect the navigation and steering instrumentation, and the crew in extreme weather. The rest of the craft consisted of open deck space. There was a roof that came three quarters of the way back offering protection from the sun. It also served as additional storage space for the crab pots.

Rose Bud was wider than most bay boats. Cliff's uncle had her built that way for added stability. While the boat was used every day during crabbing season, the vessel was spotless. The hot sun reflected brightly off the fresh coat of white paint that was only a few weeks old.

"Three things are important in life, boy," Cliff's uncle often orated. "A clean home, a clean mind, a clean body." Even though he had been a widower for many years, he still followed these rules and expected Cliff to do the same. The boat was immaculate like the large Cape Cod style home nestled atop a small hill overlooking Middle River. The man himself was tall, lean and fit. His hair was windblown and bleached from the many hours exposed to elements. His face, one time smooth and tight, was wrinkled beyond his fifty-two years. He had a moustache that was kept short, and a chin that stuck out more than normal. His arms were larger than most men his age, developed over the years while serving as human cranes. His legs were proportional in size. His hands were weathered and scarred. The left pinky finger was missing the tip, courtesy of a crab's claw many years before. While the style was always the same, work shirt and coveralls, his clothing was always fresh and clean. He was always clean shaven as well. And as far as Cliff knew, the man was also pure of mind. He spoke badly about no one. He didn't smoke. He drank only an occasional beer or two, and except for the tirade of curses on the occasion of a missing crab pot or one being damaged by a pleasure boat, Cliff never heard any foul language.

"Need any help, Uncle George?" Cliff called out. While not a clone, he was obviously a close relative to the man on the deck of *Rose Bud*. Many assumed Cliff's uncle was his father.

Falling below his ears, the boy's curly blonde hair was badly in need of a cut. It could have also used a comb. His messy hair aside, he was a good looking kid. His cheeks were full, his green eyes prominent, and his body much stronger than it should have been for his age. With minimal investment by his uncle, his teeth were perfectly aligned. He had a wide smile, and it took little to get him to laugh. It spite of the tragedy of having lost his parents at an early age, his disposition was upbeat. He had nary an enemy anywhere.

"Nope, I'm just about done here," his uncle replied. "Thanks anyhow."

Cliff wasn't disappointed in the response. He was still tired from the morning's run. They had left several hours earlier at the crack of dawn, partially because that was their normal time and partially to try and beat the heat. They had worked over a hundred pots, and while Cliff considered himself to be in shape, he was worn out from the past two days on the water. The unexpected heat drained the best of men. Besides that, the haul was unusually low—only a few bushels of small crabs. This accentuated the fatigue factor even more. There was never a sense of tiredness when the catch was good.

In spite of the hard work, Cliff loved crabbing with Uncle George, especially this year, being the first time his uncle had let him take *Rose Bud* out alone. At fifteen years of age, Cliff Davidson was a boat captain—or at least that's what he considered himself when out on the water alone. It didn't matter if they were working pots or were simply out for a ride, Cliff loved the water. No excuse was too small to take *Rose Bud* out for a spin. Still, Cliff was hot and looked forward to the sun passing its high point of the day. Maybe he could even waggle an overnight stay at their next door neighbors. They had air conditioning, and sometimes invited Cliff over for the night—Uncle George too, but he always refused.

Looking over in that direction, Cliff said, "Where're Ralph and Betty?"

"They had a crab feast to go to this afternoon."

"Another one? Didn't they just go to one last weekend?"

"Don't complain, boy. Crab feasts keep you and me in business."

"When will they be back?"

"Later this evening, I suspect." His uncle tossed a few old pieces of bait over the side. "Why you so interested in them? You figure on sneaking over there for the night?"

"No," Cliff quickly injected. He didn't sound too convincing.

"Couldn't blame you if you do. If it gets any hotter, I might even come over for a visit."

Cliff knew it was hot when his uncle started talking like that. Uncle George thought air conditioning was a waste of perfectly good electricity, and thus a waste of perfectly good money. The heat never seemed to bother him, although he had made a few negative comments of late. He said while they were out earlier that if the bay water got any hotter, they could just throw Old Bay (a popular Maryland seasoning) into the water and steam the crabs in their natural environment.

"You can always sleep outside with Chessie," Uncle George suggested. Chessie was Uncle George's Chesapeake Bay retriever.

Cliff laughed at the thought. While the dog liked to sleep with Cliff, that only made things hotter. Cliff often joked that Chessie always seemed to have a fever. On cue, the large dog came up to Cliff and plopped down beside the boy. She rolled over on her side, ready for a belly rub. Obliging, Cliff laughed. "You heard your name, didn't you, girl?" The dog failed to respond. She just lay there looking at Cliff, her eyes half closed, her tongue hanging out, panting as if she couldn't get enough air. Cliff felt the heat radiating from her body. "Maybe I can sneak you in next door with me," Cliff said.

Overhearing the conversation, his uncle responded, "That'll be your last night there."

Cliff continued to laugh. While their neighbors were great, and even looked after Cliff at times when his uncle had to go out of town, they didn't like animals in their house or in their yard. The only thing Cliff ever heard Uncle George and Ralph argue about was the dog. While it usually seemed to be in fun, Cliff often wondered if there was more to it than that. Uncle George often came back from a visit next door shaking his head and muttering beneath his breath, "How can anyone live on the water and not like dogs?"

Regardless, they were more than good neighbors. They were good friends. Over the years, Betty had kept an eye on Uncle George to make sure he was doing the right things by the boy. She was satisfied overall, although she did make an occasional comment about one thing or another—usually related to Cliff's hair. "You could buy the boy a comb, you know?" was one of her favorites.

"He gets an allowance," was the normal response.

Betty couldn't argue about setting a better example because she knew her long time neighbor was doing everything he could for his nephew. She had known Cliff's parents well, and was just as devastated as everyone when they were killed in an automobile accident when Cliff was only four. He'd been living with his uncle ever since and was turning out to be a fine young man. He was always polite, courteous and helpful. While he never came home with straight A's, he did well in school. While his hair might not be cared for in the manner she wished, he was clean, properly clothed and always sported a positive attitude. Her husband, one of George's closest and oldest friends, always liked to add, "You don't see no tattoos or metal hanging from any body parts either." His reference was toward a teenager across the street who recently came home with a ring in her navel.

Cliff was also proving to be an excellent artist. Betty loved it when he came over to show her his latest drawings or photographs. Many were taken while working the pots, and most were spectacular.

One hand rubbing the dog's belly, Cliff pushed the hair from his forehead with the other. "What you going to do after the pots?" Cliff called out.

"Count my money, I reckon."

"You ain't got no money," Cliff pointed out.

"Then I'll go count what I wish I had."

It was their standing joke. Whenever Uncle George wanted to take a nap, he always said he was going to go count his money, even though he told Cliff he never had any. When asked why he never had any money, he'd say the price of crab is too low and the price of gas was too high. "Takes every penny I have just to keep ole *Rose Bud* here afloat."

Cliff had even asked him once why he didn't select another line of work, especially if crabbing' was so bad.

"I didn't say it was bad, son. You just don't always make a lot of money. Most important thing in life is to do what you like. Besides, it's what my college degree's in."

Truth was, George Davidson was a crabber because he was raised a waterman. He was the third generation to work the Chesapeake Bay, and he was the third generation to live in the house his grandfather had built during the depression. The house was named *Loafer's Glory*. According to legend, Cliff's grandfather loved to do two things in life. One was to crab. The other was to sit around and do nothing with his feet propped up on a favorite stool. One hand would be behind his head, the other held a bottle of his favorite spirit. While the original *Loafer's Glory* died many years before Cliff was born, Uncle George kept the memories alive with frequent stories of days-of-old, often times copying the legend's pose on the porch, but without the spirits. His uncle's beverage of choice was nothing stronger than iced tea made with the tea bags soaking too long.

To George Davidson, there was nothing finer in life than simply being on the water, and there was no finer water to be on than the Chesapeake Bay. Cliff knew this because his uncle said more than once that he hoped the boy would be the fourth generation waterman at *Loafer's Glory*. Cliff never had the heart to tell his uncle he had other ideas about his future.

"Well, Uncle George, you go count your money, and I'll stay here and make sure no one steals *Rose Bud*." This was Cliff's message that he too was interested in a nap and would stretch out on the pier.

"I'd keep an eye out if I were you," his uncle warned.

"An eye out for what?"

"Thunder boomers."

"A storm—it hasn't rained in days."

His uncle glanced up at the hazy sky, then up towards the shore. "Yeah, but that don't mean it won't today."

Cliff knew better than to argue with his uncle who was better than the pros at predicting the weather. "They don't have to work in it if they're wrong," Uncle George often remarked.

Cliff followed his uncle's vision trail. The sky looked the same as it had for the past few days—hazy and sunny. Then he noticed a subtle change in the leaves on the big oak tree that sat between the house and the water. The leaves had turned outward slightly. The tree was thirsty, and in anticipation of what might be coming, was opening its multiple mouths.

"I'll keep an eye out," Cliff promised.

Finished with the crab pots, his uncle stepped off the boat and made his way toward the house. Cliff again glanced at the sky. Uncle George liked to say that nature played tricks on people regarding the weather, but there were always clues.

Cliff turned back toward the house. His uncle was already halfway up the path. "He wants to count his money pretty bad," the boy said to Chessie. The dog's mouth widened and she grunted in agreement. Cliff caught a whiff of the dog's breath. "You need to brush your teeth more, girl," he said. He made a mental note to pick up a box of the special dog biscuits the vet said were good for her teeth.

Satisfied with her belly rub, Chessie rolled over, inched forward and dropped her head over the side of the pier. She stared at the water and then glanced over her shoulder at her master. "Go ahead and jump in," Cliff directed. The animal didn't need to be coaxed and was in the water the next instant. The water she splashed up over Cliff was even warmer than he expected. "It's like a bath, isn't it, girl?"

The dog shook her head in agreement. Cliff watched as she swam around a few minutes. It was so hot, she even ignored the few ducks that swam by. When she was either refreshed or had decided the water was too warm, she climbed up onto the floating work platform tied to the pier. She shook the excess water from her fur before plopping down onto the planks for a rest.

Cliff leaned back, his arms folded behind his head. He sat up quickly as the head of a nail, heated well above the air temperature, burned the back of his shoulder. He rubbed the area and settled back again, this time making sure to avoid the hot spot. His eyes weren't closed for more than a minute when he heard the sound of a motor starting up. He rolled up onto his arm and watched as a red Mastercraft boat pulled away from the pier two houses up. As he expected and subconsciously hoped, Robin Thomas was at the helm. Even though she was two years older, she was always friendly. She waved every time she passed. Cliff always waved back as he looked at everything but her wave. She was the hottest girl in school. She had also become somewhat of a friend.

Her father was also a waterman and a good friend of his uncle's. In fact, Uncle George was her Godfather. She never took to the life of a true waterman. Instead, she used the opportunity to water ski and to have fun. She even took Cliff out on a regular basis. Uncle George never refused to let Cliff go with her, but his last words were always the same.

"Watch yourself 'round those older women, boy." Cliff always blushed, only to regain his composure just as she pulled up to the pier.

She saw him on the dock, waved and turned the craft toward the shore. When she was close enough to be heard over the engine, she shouted, "Hey, Cliff. Wanna to go for a ride?"

"You goin' skiing?" Cliff said, ignoring the heat for the moment.

"If we can find someone to spot for us."

Cliff looked up toward the house. He thought about letting his uncle know where he was going. Cliff figured, however, his uncle would already be snoring loudly. He looked down at Chessie. "Tell him if he comes looking for me that I went out with Robin, okay?"

Appearing to fully understand the command, the dog rose to her feet and barked twice.

Cliff jumped up and stepped onto the boat just as it approached the dock. Robin pulled the gearshift into reverse and the boat slid away.

Chessie barked again as if to say have fun and be careful. Cliff waved back in response.

6

Once the boat cleared the pier, Cliff moved forward and sat on the back of the companion seat. Robin pushed the throttle forward and the boat took off with a lurch. Cliff held onto the top of the windshield. Normally, the breeze would feel good. Today, however, it only made things hotter

"What you been up to?" Robin asked.

"We went out this morning," Cliff said. "Didn't do too good."

"Water's too hot for this time of the year," Robin said. "Crabs don't know whether to come out of hibernation or dig deeper."

"Everything's too hot."

"You can say that again."

By now the boat had come up on plane and rapidly picked up speed. They both knew any further attempt at conversation was futile as the noise of the engine overrode any spoken words. Cliff turned his attention to the water ahead. He noted there were only a few boats out and about. One was a large cruiser heading up river. As the vessel passed, Robin turned the bow of the runabout into the wake and pulled the throttle back. Even with the maneuver, there was still a heavy sheet of spray over the bow. Normally this would feel good, even chilly. Today, however, it was simply hot and sticky wet.

Picking up speed again, they soon passed the red flasher marking the mouth of Middle River. They bore left towards an area called Miami Beach. Unlike the community of high rises in Florida, Maryland's Miami Beach contained a mixture of middle class housing from an array of eras. The water was shallow and the bottom sandy, making it a favorite spot for daytime anchorage. Because the shoreline was directly on the bay, there was normally a breeze as well. Today, however, the flotilla of pleasure boats was noticeably absent, as was the breeze. There were a few beach umbrellas scattered about. A couple of children splashed in the water along the shore, closely watched by their parents. The life guard chair sat empty. In a few weeks the beach would be packed from sunrise to sunset.

Robin slowed the boat and turned perpendicular to the shoreline. Shading her eyes, she said, "Get the binoculars, will you? I want to see if Jamie's home. She can spot for us."

Taking the binoculars from Cliff, she pulled the throttle to neutral. Scanning the horizon, she found the house she wanted and said, "I have my cellphone, but don't remember her number. I don't suppose you know it, do you?" She turned and winked at Cliff. Jamie and Robin were two of the more popular girls at school, and much of the talk was about them. While Cliff liked listening to all the gossip, he was not a spreader of the same. This, on top of his genuine skill of being a good listener, made him popular with the girls at school.

Robin's reference to his knowing Jamie's number related to the two having spent a lot of time together recently. The rumor mill had it the two were getting together. The truth—Jamie was using Cliff as her therapist to get over a recent breakup. Robin also knew Cliff didn't mind the attention. She had seen him eying Jamie on several occasions. She also caught Cliff doing the same to her. Robin was not one to hide her God-given features. Just like today, she wore a bright red bikini covered only by a thin tee shirt. It could have been skimpier, but not by much.

Robin looked a few more moments before lowering the binoculars. Handing them back to Cliff, she nudged the throttle forward and turned the wheel hard to port. "I don't see her car, so she's probably not home anyway. Let's take a ride over to the cut and see if there's anyone over there we know."

She was referring to what was once a series of three low lying islands near the mouth of Middle River that several years before had been converted into a man-made land fill for the sludge dredged from the bay to deepen the channels. There was a big fuss over the project when it was first announced, but the Army Corps of Engineers did create a nice beach and anchorage area for the boating public. The area had always been popular in the past. It was even more so now, especially since it gave additional protection form the weather. The Chesapeake Bay was known for sudden storms.

Cliff thought back to the tree leaves a few minutes before.

The boat proceeded across the surface with little effort and few bumps. The water was like a sheet of glass, even out past the mouth of the river. The cut came into view quickly as visibility was good. The Eastern Shore, some seven miles away, was as clear as the banks of Middle River. Cliff let the breeze fluff out his hair. He stood up straight and made sure his shoulders were pulled back. While already a nudge above 5' 7", he wanted to appear as tall as possible next to Robin. The wind felt good against his bare chest. He ran his hand across his shoulder to the earlier burn from the hot nail. The spot was still tender. He then scratched an area of sunburn starting to peel. It seemed funny to have that problem so early in the season. He knew, however, that issue would be short lived as he would soon be deeply tanned. While modest in general, he too was not afraid to show off his body. Not God-given like Robin, his physique resulted from hours of hard labor at his uncle's side. A vegetarian diet did not hurt either. His uncle had been a partial vegetarian all his life, eating only fish and other seafood. When he came to live with his uncle, Cliff easily adopted the regime.

Thinking of appearances, he glanced over at Robin. While no one ever called her muscular, her arms and thighs showed the effects of her passion for water skiing. It was well known she skied whenever possible. The only requirement was an air temperature safe enough for a wetsuit and someone willing to drive the boat. It was not uncommon to see her buzzing around the river in the middle of winter. Maryland had weird weather like that. Cliff was often at the wheel, although his temperature requirements for taking the plunge were a bit higher than Robin's.

Robin spent winter vacations and most of her summers in Florida at a ski school. Cliff asked her one time why she just didn't move there. She answered jokingly, "I like to snow ski, too." Her answer was in response to the previous winter when they were actually water skiing while it snowed.

Her sun bleached blonde hair was shoulder length and pulled into a ponytail. A few loose strands flowed across her face, pushed about by the wind. Her face was smooth, unblemished, and tanned to perfection. Her nickname at school was 'Goldie' because regardless the time of year, her tan never faded. Cliff kidded her once that maybe the real reason she went to Florida in the winter was to work on her tan. Winking, she said, "I certainly don't ski with a sweatshirt on."

Becoming aware of his stare, she turned her head in his direction and gave him another wink. Embarrassed at being caught, Cliff snapped his head forward. A chill went up his spine. It was the same sensation every time she gave him that look. He knew she was just playing with him—after all she was just a friend. Still, the youthful fantasies were enjoyable. To keep from embarrassing himself further, he turned and looked out over the stern of the boat. He watched the waves of water roll off the transom. There was little wake as the boat was a high performance ski boat.

His eyes moved to where the two wakes met. His mind filled with the image of Robin skiing. He had watched her many times, and had never lost interest in driving or spotting for her. Not only was she beautiful, she was a great skier. Her figure came into focus somewhere deep in his mind. She was leaning heavily to one side, pulling hard on the tow line to make the next buoy, creating a giant rooster tail of water behind her. Even when straining against the G forces, she always managed a smile. Cliff had never seen her unhappy, and only seldom without her smile. No wonder she was so popular. He was glad they were friends.

Before that time, he often sat on the pier watching her ski. It was on one such occasion when her spotter had to go home early. She saw him sitting alone, drove over and asked him if he wanted to fill in. Naturally, he jumped at the chance. Soon he was a regular on the boat. As they spent more time together, his attention level increased, driven by his hormonal changes and her physical development. During this time, she taught him how to ski. By the end of the first summer, his skills didn't match hers but were above average.

They often skied across the bay to Tolchester where they'd lunch on one of Ms. Virginia's famous crab cakes. One would ski over, the other back. Robin claimed that anyone could learn how to ski. All they had to do was settle their fears, hang on and let the boat do the work. Besides being competitive herself, she also enjoyed teaching others and was quick to praise Cliff for how rapidly he advanced. "You listen good," she'd say. "Especially for a guy."

This was true of Cliff in general. He had the ability to stay focused on the task at hand and thus learn quickly. This allowed him to do well in school and to advance in his own area of interest—art. According to his teachers, he was very gifted with a lot of potential. He won numerous awards for drawings as well as photography. Whenever there was an art show in the area, his works stood out. He never focused on how good he was or wasn't. He just knew he liked it.

Lately however, during the time he was supposed to be concentrating on his art, he caught himself drifting more and more into dreamland, with Robin or Jamie often the center. While he was naïve in *the ways of the world* as his uncle called it, his fantasies often expanded beyond reality. His uncle noticed the change. "She's a real looker," he'd say, catching Cliff's wandering eye.

Cliff blushed the first time his uncle caught him starring as Robin skied past. "Does she sweat you?" Uncle George asked.

Cliff had been surprised his uncle knew such terminology. Then again, Cliff was often surprised at his uncle's grasp of modern issues. "Yeah, she's hot," he replied.

"She'll boil your juices, boy."

"Don't worry, Uncle George, we're just friends."

"Things can change, you know. Remember, things ain't always as they look."

Cliff turned back around and looked at Robin. She was staring ahead, the inevitable smile in place.

Just friends, Cliff thought.

The boat slowed as they neared the island. It loomed up like a large sand dune in the middle of nowhere. Cliff saw why there were only a few boats out and about. They were all here. Too hot to do anything else, he figured. There were at least a hundred boats, mostly runabouts, with a few larger vessels mixed in. Clusters of people stood in the water. A few were up on the beach.

He looked around and found a vessel that looked like a floating out-house. It was named *Bull on the Bay*. It was really a floating grill that sold pit beef sandwiches, snacks and soda. Cliff remembered people laughing at the idea when it showed up the summer before, but few were laughing now. Word was the owner had hit pay dirt. Cliff was surprised, however, to see it already heading back towards Middle River. It was still early in the day. A moment later, he realized people were starting to climb back into their boats. Others were already pulling up anchor.

Robin also noticed the increased activity. "Somebody must know something we don't." She scanned the horizon. Visibility was still good with very few clouds. The only issue was due south. Visibility in that direction was cut off by the height of the island.

"A storm coming in?" Cliff offered.

"Maybe, but the marine weather only called for a slim to none chance of rain." Both boaters knew, however, that the Chesapeake Bay did not always behave as predicted. The leaves from the old oak tree came to mind again.

"Where's your hand held?" Cliff asked, referring to the VHF radio Robin kept aboard. It would allow them to pick up the marine weather.

"It got wet the other day," Robin said. "I took it into the shop to make sure it was okay. I didn't bother picking it up because the weather's been so…shit!"

They both saw the dark clouds break over the island at the same time. The clouds were tall, black and moving fast. "Now we know where everyone's going," Cliff said. There was no excitement in his voice. He was used to the sudden changes in the bay's weather.

"Yeah," Robin agreed. "But I'm not sure that's the best thing to do."

Cliff did not argue.

Robin continued. "We're on the lee shore, so we'll be protected."

"To a point."

Robin responded with a hearty laugh. "Touché there. I don't think even I can outrun this baby." While her boat was one of the fastest in the area, the storm had caught them by surprise. Flight was not a safe option. "A lot of people are going to get caught with their pants down," she added.

"More are trying to join the party," Cliff added, motioning to even more boats pulling up anchor.

"What do you say we stay put and party right here?" She laughed again, this time with a wink.

"Sounds like the safest thing to me," Cliff agreed.

Neither spoke for the next several minutes. Once Robin maneuvered closer to shore, Cliff pulled out the boat's two anchors and jumped over the side. He took one up to the beach, burying it in the sand. He walked the other twenty or so yards from the stern and set it on the bottom. When finished, he climbed back aboard and helped Robin pull the cover up over the deck. It would be hot, but both decided that would be better than getting pelted with rain.

As the storm closed in, the winds built quickly. Just as the last clasp was snapped on the cover, the clouds let loose. Thunder and lightning filled the air. The winds increased even further. The boat, while pulling hard on the anchor lines, held firm. Cliff doubted few if any of the boats that left the protection of the island made it back to port in time. While he had been in numerous storms with his uncle, he didn't want to think about being *a kite without a string* as his uncle liked to call small boats caught in a storm.

Robin pushed the antenna down on her cellular phone and put it back in its case. "I got a hold of my mother. She's going to call your uncle and let him know what's up. I told her it looked like it was going to be a bad one."

"Good thing we stayed put," Cliff said.

A loud clap of thunder interrupted their conversation. By now the storm was directly overhead. The lightning and thunder were in unison.

"I wonder what she's so mad about," Robin said, shouting over the wind.

"Who?"

"Mother Nature."

"Uncle George would say her bladder is just really full."

Robin laughed. She moved a bit to rearrange her torso on the floor. They were lying in the space between the rear seats and engine box. "You got enough room?" she asked. Their bodies had never been closer.

"Not really," the youth responded. "Why don't we move up to the bridge?"

"Smart ass." She laughed.

Each adjusted their position and settled back to wait. It was bouncy, but the anchors held. Cliff knew there was no use trying to look outside. Visibility was nil. He also realized he was now hotter than ever. Wiping the sweat from his brow, he stole a glance at Robin. She was moist as well. "I bet once this passes, it'll be just as hot as before," he predicted.

"Certainly can't get any hotter," Robin acknowledged.

Cliff listened as the storm continued. Gusts of wind pushed at the boat, which responded with jerky motions. "I'm really glad we stayed put," he said. "We would have been floundering around like a wet noodle."

"We're doing a pretty good job of that right now," Robin responded. "But you're right, I'm sure those who left are getting it a lot worse." She rolled up on her side and faced him. "I don't make too many bad decisions," she teased.

Cliff looked in her direction and realized just how close she was. His eyes were staring almost directly into her chest. "What's your guess on how long this will last?" Cliff asked, trying to make conversation regarding topics on the outside of the boat.

"Long enough," she replied.

"Long enough for what?"

"To get a buzz on. Didn't we say we were going to party?" She raised her eyebrows. "You get high?" She reached into a side pocket of her seat and pulled out a small plastic bag. Cliff watched as she pulled out a joint and lighter. She put one end in her mouth and touched the flame to the other. She pulled in a deep breath and held it for a few seconds. She released the smoke in a narrow stream. She handed it to Cliff. He hesitated a moment before following her lead. The smoke burned his lungs, but he refused to cough. His eyes did widen, however, as he began to feel the effects of the drug. He opened and closed his eyes a few times in an effort to keep them clear. It was his first time smoking pot. He emptied his lungs.

Robin was looking at him, a wide grin across her face. Taking the joint from him, she pulled in another drag. She passed it back to him and he repeated the procedure. Again the smoke burned. His eyes blurred. His mind clouded. He became immune to the noise and motion around him. He blinked rapidly as he handed her back the joint.

Exhaling a moment later, she asked, "What are you staring at?"

Cliff's eyes snapped up to meet hers. While he successfully fought off the cough, he failed to keep his face from turning red. "Didn't mean to stare," he apologized meekly.

Her eyebrows raised a bit. "I'm not complaining. I'm just asking, that's all."

"Asking what?"

She broke into a loud laugh. "You're feelin' good, huh?"

"Oh…" His mind tried to send a warning of caution to his mouth. He reminded himself of a common Uncle George saying: loose lips sink ships. He realized he was about to wander into uncharted waters and had to be especially careful. Only that was an incorrect thought—he was already in such water. While his mind screamed not to, his tongue started to move. "I was watching you move up and down as you breathed."

"Cliff Davidson!"

The realization of what he had said went through him like a bolt of lightning. His face reddened more deeply. He was thinking about apologizing when she took a deep drag on the marijuana cigarette. Without exhaling, she leaned toward him and pressed her lips against his. He felt her tongue pry open his mouth. His mind spinning out of control, he obliged. She wrapped her hand around his neck and pulled to tighten the seal. She exhaled slowly, filling his lungs with smoke.

He felt the effect immediately. Any guard or concern he may have had was now totally destroyed. He was no longer concerned with his own lips. He focused instead on those touching his. She let him pull away long enough to exhale, then they kissed again. This time her tongue reached in deeper. Yes, without a doubt, he was in uncharted water, only he didn't care. The burning in his lungs subsided. His breathing grew heavier, his arms weaker. His head spun out of control. He held onto Robin tightly so he would not float away. She responded and pressed into him. Sweat jumped from his pours as the heat beneath the canvas intensified. He tried to think his head clear, but all he accomplished was the urge to continue the journey.

Somewhere in the distance he heard thunder.

"Relax," she said.

And so he did.

7

Predictably, soon after the storm passed, the temperature rose back to its high of the day. The humidity, if possible, was heavier than before. Except for a few lingering clouds, the sky was clear. The sun bore down on them with an intensity that made Cliff's sunburn

burn. In spite of this, he wished the trip home to take an eternity. Reality, however, dictated otherwise. The boat was fast and Robin was pushing it to the maximum.

Because of the noise, there was no opportunity for conversation, which was probably for the best. Cliff had no clue what to say anyway. His mind, however, was spinning, not from the effects of the marijuana—that had worn off an hour before—but from the effects of the residual activities. His brain cells were working full force, cranking out emotions and questions. What had just happened was quite clear. Where it happened was a surprise. Why was still a mystery. Was the whole thing spontaneous, or had she planned it? Had he somehow planned it? He struggled to remember the details; not the event itself, but the minutes before. Had the whole thing been induced by the marijuana? Did he force himself on her? Had she done the same to him? He was not one to give into peer pressure, he knew that. While he admitted to liking beer—his uncle even let him have one now and then—he was far from a regular indulger like some of his friends. He certainly had never smoked marijuana before. Although the opportunity had presented itself on several occasions, it was just something that never interested him—that is, until today. Today, when Robin offered him the joint, he didn't hesitate.

A smile crossed his face. It had just happened spontaneously. There was no force from either party.

Either party…What a party!

He decided the marijuana had had some effect, but was not the culprit either. A lecture from his uncle came to mind. "You do something, the consequences are yours. Whatever road you take in life, take responsibility for your actions. Do that, and you'll seldom go wrong."

Well, it had happened. No problem accepting the responsibility. However, he wondered about the consequences. What was going to happen now? What was he going to say to her when they got back home? What about in school? How would he act? How would she act towards him? Would they still be friends? He cautioned himself not to over-analyze. He was often criticized for being too intense, for thinking too deeply. On the other hand, his art teacher claimed one of the reasons he was such a stand out artist was because of his ability to see past the surface so well. He was able to bring out an emotion, even from an inanimate object. His friends told him to lighten up. His art teacher told him to dig deeper.

With all due respect to his teacher, he figured his friends' advice wasn't all that bad at the moment.

It had happened, and it had felt good… still did for that matter. His mind wandered to the pleasurable side of the experience. Her kiss. Her touch. Her smell. Her explosion. His own. To paraphrase a comment by Robin afterwards, "Damn!"

He stole a glance in her direction as they sped towards Middle River. She was saying nothing. Except for the inevitable smile, she had a nothing look on her face. She was just looking straight ahead. What did she feel? What was she thinking? What did she think of him? When would they do it again… they would do it again, wouldn't they?

He was about to turn his head when she turned his way. Their eyes met. She smiled. She winked. Then she blew him a kiss.

His heart skipped a beat. His knees went weak. It was his turn to look ahead. He wished the ride home would take an eternity.

As they passed the buoy marking the no wake zone, Robin pulled back on the throttle. The boat came off plane and the rear wake washed forward. The motion rocked the boat hard and Cliff inadvertently leaned into the driver. "Sorry," he said.

The boat rocked again in response to the secondary wake. This time Robin leaned towards him. Her chest pressed against his arm. "Sorry," she teased. Another smile, another wink.

He felt a stirring in his crotch. "Steady Duke," he silently quoted from his favorite book, *Voyage*. His body listened. His mind, however, continued to swirl with questions. He had no answers, but who cared? He was in seventh heaven. He looked skyward hoping to see the storm returning. They had enough time to get back out to the island, didn't they? His eyes again returned to her. Her hair was matted from the rain, her face streaked with dried sweat, but she was still beautiful. She had put her tee shirt back on, but he could still see the outline of her figure. Images in his mind were no longer fantasies. Dreams were no longer dreams. They were now realities. He felt a burden from what happened. The burden was not bad, however.

If anything…

His train of thought was broken by the sight of his house up ahead. He didn't realize they were home so quickly. Robin slowed the boat to a crawl, gently guiding it towards the pier. Cliff looked at her. Their eyes met again. There were many feelings he wanted to express, many thoughts he wanted to convey, many questions to ask. He wanted to say something, but his tongue was tied in knots.

"Watch the piling," she directed, pulling the gearshift into reverse.

"Sure." He climbed up on the pier and held the boat off with a foot.

She smiled. "Later," she said.

And with that, all his questions were set aside. For that statement gave him the hope he was seeking. The most pressing question of all dealt with the future, and *later* was the answer. There would indeed be a future for them. With that, nothing else mattered.

He gave the boat a gentle push and watched as Robin pulled away. "Later," he mouthed softly.

He watched until she was well clear of the pilings. One last wave before he turned and headed up the pier. He glanced around for Chessie. She was nowhere to be seen. Passing *Rose Bud*, he noticed the crab pots were all in disarray. He figured the storm was pretty bad here as well. He thought about straightening them out, but first he wanted to let his uncle know he was back. He half-skipped, half-ran up the path to the house. Bursting through the back door he shouted, "Uncle George, I'm back. Did Robin's folks call and tell you we were okay? What a storm, huh?" He turned the corner into the living room and was about to say something else when he came face to face with Robin's father.

"Oh, hi," Cliff said, sliding to a halt. The expression on the man's face made Cliff's heart sink. His chest filled with pressure. Where was all the oxygen all of the sudden? A wave of guilt flowed through his suddenly icy veins. How could the man have known? After all, they did have to anchor. And Robin did call her mother.

Cliff took a step back and glanced around the room. Another neighbor from up the street was sitting on the couch. Robin's mother was standing off to the side. He saw Ralph and Betty along with a couple watermen they sometimes worked with. Chessie was lying in the middle of the floor. She slowly rose to her feet and headed toward Cliff.

Cliff focused back on Robin's father. The man hesitated, meeting the boy's stare. Finally, "Cliff, I have something bad to tell you." During this time, Cliff realized his fears were unfounded—Robin's father wasn't mad. He wasn't upset that they had anchored. He couldn't know anything else. Cliff exhaled slowly. Oxygen was restored.

But only for a moment as his mind repeated what Robin's father just said. "Something bad to tell you." He stared down at Chessie who was now at his side. It was the dog's lack of energy that told Cliff something was amiss. His eyes darted around the room looking for his uncle. The heaviness that had just been lifted returned with vengeance. He remembered the messed up crab pots.

Robin's father continued. "There's been an accident, Cliff. Your uncle was struck by lightning while out on the boat."

Cliff's mind digested the words quickly. "Struck by lightning. But he came into the house to take a nap."

Robin's father slowly shrugged his shoulders. "It must have been too hot so he went back outside."

The pressure increased further. "Well, where is he? Is he okay?"

Cliff got another answer, one he didn't want to hear.

8

Cliff awoke in a state of confusion. It took him a moment to get his bearings and realize he was lying across the transom of *Rose Bud*. He opened his eyes, wiping away the crust that had formed while he slept. It was dark. The sky was clear. A few stars sent down light rays, but the moon was absent. He felt the faint hint of a breeze. He wondered about the time. He could tell nothing by the temperature as it was still awfully hot. He started to rise, but there was a pounding in his head. He pressed his hand to his brow. The pain eased a little. The confusion cleared. Memories slowly returned. Sweet ones at first—Robin. Then Robin's father. Which was a dream? Which was not? He took in a couple of deep breaths. He closed his eyes and told himself to wake up again. Only there was no *again*. The memories came into clearer focus. They were both true.

He sat up quickly. His uncle! He rolled to his feet. The movement caused the pounding in his head to worsen. He ignored it. He jumped up on the dock and headed toward shore. He had a sudden need to find his uncle. Approaching the house, he saw the lights were all still on.

More memories. More questions. Wrong answers. He slowed his pace and walked around to the front. The driveway and street were lined with cars. He recognized a few. Others he did not. He walked up onto the front porch. The main door was opened, the screen door charged with keeping the mosquitos at bay. He heard talking, soft low conversation. He couldn't make out specific words, but something was missing in the tone. It took him a moment to realize it was laughter. So many people and no laughter.

Loafer's Glory held a reputation for some of the finest parties in the area. There was always an open house at Christmas and an egg hunt at Easter. During Halloween, the property turned into one of the scariest around. The annual crab feast was perhaps the most famous. His uncle put it on every Labor Day. All the neighbors were invited, and usually they all came. There would be long tables of food. Kegs of beer flowed freely. It was the only time he saw his uncle really indulge. The water would be filled with children swimming, and boats would come and go to pick up the next set of skiers.

There was always a lot of laughter.

It was one of Cliff's favorite times. Normally, *Loafer's Glory* was a quiet home. Life was relatively simple compared to many modern day households. For Uncle George, the day consisted of work, overseeing Cliff's homework and *counting his money*. For Cliff, it was school, homework and a few chores. But near the time for parties, their routine changed and other activities took precedence. There was a change of pace, a variety from the norm. Cliff never complained about either.

Now, the laughter was gone. The image of Robin's father came into focus. His voice filled his ears. "Something bad to tell you." Cliff turned his back to the door, jumped off the porch and ran out the front gate. His legs carried him away from *Loafer's Glory*… away from the people, their voices, the lack of laughter…away from the parties that would be no more… away from the memories…

Heading down the street, he slowed to a walk. His heart pounded. His head did, too. His shoulders drooped. He stared down at the road. His mind raced, struggling to find answers. When he looked up, he was in front of Robin's house. Like his uncle's, it was an old summer cottage that had been added to, built up, and insulated to make a year round home. Several junk cars sat in the back yard in various states of repair. He made his way past an old rusty Chevy Camaro and moved up to the porch. The outside of the house was dark. There was, however, a light on in the living room. While he had been tongue-tied earlier and unable to express his feelings, he now felt the need to empty his soul. After all, she had said, "Later." A lot had happened in that short period of time.

Cliff was about to knock when he heard a sound. It was laughter. He recognized it as Robin's. He took a step forward and peered through the screened door. His silhouette was hidden by the darkness. He could see nothing. He could hear, though.

"I missed you this afternoon," he heard her say. Cliff took a step back. He was contemplating a response when he heard a different voice, deeper in tone.

"I missed you, too." Cliff did not recognize this voice. He leaned forward to better hear. There was some soft giggling. "Where were you? I tried calling you all afternoon."

"I got stuck out in the storm," Robin answered.

"In your boat?"

"No silly, in my underwear." More laughter followed.

"Were you alone?"

"Lonely for you." She did not even hesitate in her response.

"I wish I was there with you," the stranger said. "We could have screwed all afternoon."

"Uhmmm."

"What say we make up for lost time?"

Robin laughed. "Not here silly. My parents might walk in."

"Lock the door."

"You ever hear of the word *key*?" More laughter.

"Let's go out back."

"You lead the way."

Cliff heard the rustling of bodies followed by hurried footsteps. Then there was silence.

The pounding in Cliff's head worsened. His heart skipped several beats. More grief. More confusion. More questions. More pain. An inner voice in his head told him to turn and walk away.

Which he did.

9

Cliff lay staring at the ceiling. His body demanded sleep. His mind refused to cooperate however, cluttered from all the activities of the past week. In addition, the emptiness deep inside continued to suck any sense of reason from his soul. He had always been one to think straight. Life, while it did indeed have its ups and downs, was relatively simple. Decisions were the same. Sure, he felt emotions, hopes, dreams and the typical fantasies of a teenage boy. Sure, he was exposed to all the temptations of one who grew up in the environment of the times. But with his uncle's gentle yet firm guidance, Cliff managed to survive basically unscarred. While he thought about his parents often, he never really knew them. He was young when they died in the car accident. There was a never ending pain, but it was a feeling he'd been able to keep buried. Now, however, that all changed thanks to one Chesapeake Bay storm. The storm had been no worse than he had experienced in the past. The outcome however…

The funeral was over. The obligatory mourners had been greeted; words of comfort offered, accepted politely and with dignity. Emotions, for the most part, were held in check. After all, the waterman community, having been toughened by years of unexpected tragedies, looked not to the past, but to the future. These *farmers of the sea* always looked ahead with the belief that the next season would be better. This religious-like conviction helped many through tough times, Cliff included. That, however, was *pre-storm* era. *Post-storm* was another matter. While the grieving process had already begun, the course was tumultuous. First, there was denial, then anger, then fear, then back to anger, and denial again. And through each phase, one theme remained—guilt. While he was out with Robin smoking pot and losing his virginity, his uncle was losing his life—a bolt of lightning right into the boat—an explosion—crab pots everywhere—his uncle sleeping through it all, never to awaken. Words of comfort were of little value.

"A swift death."

"Quick."

"Painless."

"He didn't suffer."

"A real tragedy."

"Such a good man."

"If you need anything…"

"We're so sorry, Cliff."

"He never felt any pain."

"We're so sorry…"

Cliff rolled over and pulled the pillow over his head. It was his fault… all his fault. His uncle had probably gone out to the pier looking for him. Robin's mom said he never answered the phone when she called. He was out on *Rose Bud* waiting for his nephew to come home, worried that Cliff was in trouble.

No pain, yet so much pain… and so much guilt. If only Cliff had thought about his uncle instead of himself. He should have taken the time to let his uncle know where he was going, and with whom. Then Uncle George might not have worried as much. Or at least maybe he would have stayed in the house when the storm hit.

If only…

Cliff pulled the pillow down tighter.

10

Silence filled the room for what seemed an inordinate amount of time as the two occupants remained locked eye to eye. Jennifer Blackstone—Annapolis General's emergency room nurse manager—pressed her fingertips hard into the highly polished desk as a way to keep her hands from shaking. She counted her breaths as a method to help control her respirations. Her heart pounded against her chest wall. Beads of sweat trickled down her back. She was determined she would not be the first to look away. She knew she was as tough as her opponent. She just had to prove it. She had run the ER with a tight rein the past eighteen months. She was firm yet fair with her staff. She was the same with the patients, many indigent, who wandered through the doors. Modern day emergency rooms saw a combination of true emergencies, pain medication seekers, work-slip seekers and others simply using the system for their routine health care. The result was often a potpourri of humanity all gathered into one overcrowded waiting room. The problems were enormous as demand continued to grow. Jennifer, however, was quite skilled at the juggling act necessary to ensure the truly sick were treated appropriately and the others were treated in such a way no laws were broken. Only to succeed, she needed good staff. To hire and retain good staff, she needed money. And money was what this meeting was all about.

Her opponent was Samuel Robertson, the hospital's President and CEO. He was without a doubt a better negotiator than Jennifer. He obviously had the skills necessary to run a hospital in today's environment, and he knew all the tricks of the trade necessary to succeed, or *have it his way*, as he was so often accused. After all, few doubted Annapolis General would have survived the past two years without him. High costs, poor quality of care that was more than a perception and a public image that was worse than bad— Annapolis General needed a miracle.

A seasoned hospital administrator, he had been brought in to provide that miracle. He quickly assembled a management team—Jennifer Blackstone included—and went to work. With a firm hand that pounded the table often, a tongue that struck out like a whip and a brain that neither forgot nor missed a trick, he set out to salvage the sinking ship. But there was a great price to pay. While his title was indeed the #1 administrator, many felt he'd fit better in the kitchen. He quickly earned the nickname *the butcher*. He lived up to the reputation well. If he saw something to cut, the hatchet fell. However, there were cuts, and there were *cuts*. Long term thinking and prudent management were not phrases used to describe him. Jennifer chose to avoid thinking about descriptions that did fit.

However, he weathered the storms well. Proving his critics wrong, the hospital survived. With various, and at times painful, cuts and through assistance from local and state government in the form of a controversial bond issue, the financial drain stabilized. He cut staff to a minimum and squeezed wage concessions out of everyone. At the same time, job descriptions were expanded. The phrase: *that's not my job* was actually posted around the hospital with a line drawn through it. His management style fit the micro mold. He had his nose in everything. The hospital sported a very flat organizational chart and there was a lot of what he liked to term MBWA—management by walking around. He could be found roaming the hallways all days of the week, all hours of the day. And he expected to see his managers doing the same. Samuel Robertson was a ship's captain who never looked back. *Full steam ahead* was a commonly heard expression.

Physically, he was lean and mean looking as well. At fifty-six, he was just starting to turn gray above the ears. One spent little time looking at his hair, however, because you were immediately drawn to his eyes which spewed malice, arrogance and confidence. His stare was legendary. It was often all it took to get what he wanted from his employees and the medical staff. While not able to get to the gym as frequently as he'd like, he still maintained his weight and kept his percentage of body fat below twenty. As he never smoked or drank heavily, his cardio-respiratory condition was intact. Rumor had it his gray was worse than he revealed. Rumor also said he had a newly diagnosed ulcer. He was seen popping what looked like Zantac in the cafeteria one day, and there were occasional traces of whitish, chalk-like material around the edges of his mouth, an indication of guzzling Maalox.

Jennifer didn't always agree with his particular methodology, but she had no complaints with what he had done so far. She started her nursing career at Annapolis General when times were tough. Low morale and concern over job security were common topics of lunchtime conversation. Times were still tough, only now in a different fashion. Progress was being made and discussion about job security was seldom heard unless you were on the critic list. So yes, she liked Samuel Robertson—that is, until he sent out a memo announcing a hiring freeze and pay reduction for all employees. "An unfortunate but necessary action to ensure the long term survival of this institution," the memo read.

Naturally the impact was immediate and severe. Everybody felt things were getting better. Employees had already made both willing and unwilling concessions in benefits as well as salaries. Now they were being asked to sacrifice more.

No, they were not being asked. They were being told.

A new generation of critics was born. Several of Jennifer's nurses quit on the spot. More threatened to resign if the memo was not rescinded. Consultation with fellow managers showed the emergency room was no different than other units. During this time, secret meetings were held, a few including supervisors and middle managers. Jennifer was one such manager.

At first, she was uncomfortable being involved in these covert gatherings. They went against all she had been taught about managing. On the contrary, not to get involved would mean she'd have no voice, and that wasn't good either. Finally, the urge to know overshadowed her sense of loyalty.

Besides, she was starting to lose faith!

The consensus of the group was that something had to be done before Robertson did more damage. A lot of questions were thrown about. Had he gone insane? Was something else going on in his life that caused him to lose focus? Was there a hidden agenda? Robertson reported at the last management council meeting that things were looking better. So why such a change now?

Jennifer went home that night to study the issues. She showed the memo to her father, a prominent Annapolis businessman in his own right in that he (and her mother) ran the most popular restaurant in town. It took him only an instant to draw an opinion.

"He's trying to make the books look good in the short term," her father said.

"Why?" Jennifer said, surprised at her father's quick response.

"There's really only one reason you do that in the business world, and that's if you're contemplating selling."

"Selling… like selling the hospital?"

"It's happening all over the country. Merger, merger, merger—that's all you read about in business these days."

"Why Annapolis General?"

He shrugged his shoulders. "For many reasons. But I'm sure Samuel Robertson is taking care of himself."

"You mean like… what's it called?"

"A golden parachute?" her father replied. "In spite of what you may believe sweetheart, to the people with the real money in this world, health care is just another business."

Jennifer went to a meeting the next day and forwarded the ideas brought forth by her father. The others in the room were stunned. This was not one of the options they had considered.

"Who would want to buy this place?" someone asked, partially in jest, partially with sincere curiosity.

There was more debate, some focused, some off the wall. The discussion, however, kept coming back to the same question: what to do? An idea finally surfaced. They'd write Robertson an anonymous letter demanding a meeting with the entire staff, and threatening to unionize if denied. Although Jennifer was very anti-union—an attitude developed from working in her parents' restaurant—she wondered if it was the only way to force Robertson's hand. The letter was sent. They all hoped it would bring things to a head and force a peaceful settlement. Two weeks went by. Nothing was said. No changes were made. Then without warning, Jennifer was summoned to the CEO's office.

The staring continued. Then to Jennifer's surprise, Robertson looked away. For a moment Jennifer thought she saw a streak of pain cross his face—a weakness perhaps? But that was only for a moment. His eyes again hardened and his agitation poured forth. "So you all are threatening to bring a union in here?" He motioned her to take a seat. He did the same. His mouth puffed out as if needing somewhere to spit. "Now that's a real creative solution." His sarcasm was hard to miss. "And please don't give me a lot of crap about you not knowing anything about this." He pushed the letter towards her.

She contemplated reading the letter, but decided otherwise. "How did you figure out I was involved?" she asked instead, a sense of defeat creeping into her voice.

Robertson turned and stared out the window. On the south side of town, the hospital sat directly on the water. The view was out across the peaceful setting of Back Creek. Quite a contrast to what was happening inside the glass. He turned back toward her. A smirk crossed his face. "I didn't figure it out. It was just an educated guess."

Jennifer's mouth opened and closed several times. "And I just confirmed it."

The smirk disappeared, replaced by a smile. "Don't worry. You saved us both a lot of time. I would have figured it out eventually."

He was right about that. Still, she was mad at herself for letting him trick her. Worse, what advantage she and her colleagues may have had was now gone.

Unless she could regain control quickly.

Their eyes locked together again. Her face remained expressionless. Inside her skull, however, her mind whirled like a tornado. She had to think of something, and something fast. A phrase her father liked to use came to mind. *When in Rome, do as the Romans do.* It was risky, but what did she have to lose? Aloud, she said, "How much are you personally going to get when you sell the hospital?"

Robertson's mouth dropped open. His smile disappeared. "How did you come to that far out conclusion?"

"I didn't conclude anything. It was just an educated guess."

His head cocked to the side. The hint of a smile returned. "And you think I just confirmed it?"

"That's exactly what happened."

With only a brief pause, Samuel Robertson took the initiative. "I'm not going to lie to you, Jennifer. The board and I are considering merger possibilities with another hospital group. Any independent hospital CEO in the country would be lying if he wasn't at least thinking about the same. The environment is such we have no choice. Bigger is better. The principles of economy of scale have indeed penetrated the health care industry. As such, change is inevitable. And the driving force behind all this change is the insurance industry's determination to control cost. As competitors for these health care dollars, hospitals are forced to do the same. As administrators, we're forced to focus on dollars versus diagnoses, media image versus medicine, board of directors versus tumor boards. Today, many once thriving hospitals are struggling to survive. Healthcare as a whole is going through—"

He stopped suddenly. "But you know all this already…"

Yes, she had heard the arguments before. She agreed changes needed to be made, but not at the expense of patient care. Health care was a business, and as a business, it needed to keep up with the times. In the end though, the patients were the ones who suffered the most.

He interrupted her train of thought. "And this talk about unionizing." She watched him turn red as his veins begin to bulge. "I'm not going to deny that unions have done some good things for the people they represented throughout history. However, unions always mean increased cost to the company. In our case, it's a cost we can ill afford."

It was Jennifer's turn to interrupt. "Are you sure it's a cost you choose NOT to afford?" She paused to let her question sink in. As she did, her own anger continued to rise. She agreed there was room, maybe even a need, for some cost cutting, and had even supported the measures in the past, but this time the butcher had gone too far. If anything, he should start cutting at the top with administrators' salaries, not at the bottom with nurses and others who provided the direct patient care. After all, there were few administrator jobs that sat open very long. On the contrary, some of the nursing positions had gone unfilled for over a year. It was like war, Jennifer thought. The generals who directed the battles lived the life of luxury and reaped the benefits of victory. Those without the power, without a voice, paid the ultimate price.

"Yes, Jennifer, it is a cost we choose not to afford," Robertson responded. "But choices have to be made." He took a sip of coffee. "Surely, you understand all about unions, don't you?"

Strike one, she acknowledged with her silence. His reference was to her parents' struggle with unions several years before. Some employees wanted the union in. Others did not. The vote had been close, but her father's wishes prevailed. It didn't hurt that he also threatened to close the place the instant a unionized waitress set foot through the door. He felt he paid his people well, treated them even better and offered them a demanding yet pleasant atmosphere in which to work. He successfully argued that a union would destroy the relationship he and Mrs. Blackstone had developed with their staff over the years, and would also destroy the restaurant's reputation. After all, it was one of the finest and most popular in the area. It was also the most successful.

"Health care is a lot different than the restaurant business," Jennifer argued aloud.

"Oh, is it really?"

She failed to think of a quick response. Strike two, she conceded. She reminded herself she had not been 100% in favor of the threat of a union in the first place. It was just a way of posturing in their position. She decided to get back to an earlier point. "Not all mergers are working. That Washington-Baltimore group isn't doing too well."

"They are a well-run organization, and in time will do just fine."

"If they survive that long."

"They will."

"How can you be so sure?"

"They will soon be the largest health care organization in the region. The impact on the community if they went under would be enormous. As such, the government won't let them sink."

Jennifer hesitated. He said something a moment ago that she had yet to comprehend. She sensed another light about to flicker. In the meantime she continued, "The Titanic was the largest passenger liner ever to set sail. Economies of scale didn't help her, did they? When the big boys collapse, people will find other ways to get their health care."

"Only the big boys aren't going to collapse," Robertson spouted.

Suddenly, the light came on. "Because you're going to be part of the crew, correct?" she said.

Their eyes again locked, but only for a brief moment. She realized it wasn't about saving the hospital. It was about saving, and even improving, Robertson's career. She wondered whether this wasn't his plan when he came to Annapolis in the first place. Her anger, which had started to subside, began to boil again. Yet, she knew any further discussion was worthless. She did voice one question though, one last glimmer of hope. "What about the hospital board?"

"I've been called a lot of things, but I've never been called stupid," he said. "I have their full support. I expect to have yours and everyone else's as well."

Jennifer looked away. It was obvious this conversation was basting his ego. She wondered if he was even having fun playing with her.

The CEO continued. "You've developed into one of my best department heads, Jennifer. You were a good nurse when I first met you. Now, you're a good manager as well. Your desire to keep Annapolis General an independent community hospital is commendable. But that's all it is. It's now time for you to get back on track with the program. You're too good to do otherwise."

She looked back at him. "Maybe I'm not as good as you think." She rose to her feet, turned and walked away. She had avoided strike three.

Or so she thought.

11

The cafeteria was packed with the usual lunchtime crowd—a combination of staff, visitors and attending physicians. Jennifer never understood why the various nursing units didn't stagger their lunch breaks. The result was a thirty minute lunch break consisting of a twenty minute wait in line with ten minutes of food gulping—certainly not a positive influence in reducing one's stress or rejuvenating one's energy level. However, at least these people got lunch. Her ER staff was lucky some days if they found time to pee.

Jennifer sighed and got in the sandwich line. Trying her best to be casual, she glanced around the large room. As planned and expected, Daniel Baker was sitting alone in the far corner. She watched him slowly chew on a chicken salad sandwich. She knew it was chicken salad because it was the only thing he ever bought there. He complained about the food, arguing he could trust the chicken salad because it was the only thing not made on the premises.

Twenty minutes later, Jennifer collected her change and headed for the far corner. She sensed eyes following her—the visitors, because she was one of the best looking people in the room, the doctors, because they all had fantasies of her sitting with them. The rest of the staff watched because they not only knew where she was headed, they also knew where she had been. They were looking for signs of what happened. She had no doubt rumors were already spreading. Annapolis General was small; the rumor mill was large.

She sat down across from him, her counterpart in attractiveness and eye snatching looks. She made a face at the mayonnaise dripping from the toasted rye bread but said nothing. She was his mistress, not his mother. She opened a package of light Italian dressing and poured it across her salad. A half of a turkey breast sandwich sat on the side.

Daniel Baker looked down at the pile of lettuce. Normally, he'd make some comment about the age of the wilting pile of greens. Today, however, he kept his mouth shut. He feigned a happy hello as he pushed a bite of sandwich into his mouth. She feigned back a similar greeting.

She picked at her meal a minute or two, trying to pretend she was enjoying the flavors teasing her palate. However, the only thing she could taste was the bile that kept erupting into the back of her throat. She pushed the salad away. Her actions did not go unnoticed by the eyes around the room.

"If you want to talk about it we can," Daniel said.

"Really isn't much to say," Jennifer countered. She tried to keep the hurt, the anger and all the other emotions she was feeling from her voice. She glanced around the room. Her sweeping eyes were enough to cause others to return to their own business. "He knew about the letter and that I was involved."

"Does that surprise you?"

She shrugged her shoulders.

He paused. "I'm sorry, really sorry."

She looked up and stared him in the eye. "Did you know the hospital was for sale?"

His look gave Jennifer the answer she hoped not to see. She didn't bother asking why he never said anything to her. He could at least have warned her.

Or did he in a way? He strongly advised her not to get involved in any covert operations, as he liked to call it. He was adamant from the beginning that she should simply keep her mouth shut and do the job for which she was hired. He basically told her that in spite of what might or might not be going on in the executive offices, her job was secure—so long as she toed the line. He told her that on more than one occasion, too. But no, she was too stubborn to listen.

Staring down at her food, she realized it was all a moot point. She had just gone on an unsuspecting suicide mission. There was no doubt in her mind her career at Annapolis General was over. One of the things Samuel Robertson emphasized during her interview for the nurse manager's position was his requirement of total loyalty. There was ample opportunity to voice concerns. He had an open door policy which meant anyone could go to him at any time to discuss anything. Many did, including Jennifer on occasion. Lately, however, while the door was still open, his receptiveness to their concerns had changed. That had been the onus for the letter in the first place.

Yes, it was a very moot point.

The thought threatened to add tears to the raw taste in her mouth. She loved Annapolis General. She loved what she did. She loved the people she worked with; and most of all, she genuinely cared for her patients.

Yes, they were her patients. She ran the ER with a fair, yet tight set of reins. She set high expectations for herself and for her staff. While officially, the physician group was a separate contracted organization, for all intents and purposes, they answered to her as well. She had the power and she used it to make life better for everyone. Only now, she had abused that power. She had taken it too far, crossed the line with failed loyalty. In doing so, she not only failed herself, she failed her staff.

She felt sad. Before the past couple of weeks, her life was controlled chaos. She thrived on this lifestyle. Her two careers, one as a nurse, the other working in her parents' restaurant, were both going well. The pressures from her parents to get more involved in the *Riverboat Inn* were still there, but she was able to handle the assault with the *maybe soon* defense. The two main aspects of her personal life were also buzzing along smoothly. Her relationship with Daniel Baker was progressing to more than a simple affair. She knew she was in love with him. She had few doubts he felt the same about her, in spite of his own failed commitment. Her writing had accelerated to the point where she was staying up late at night to clear her head of the thoughts and ideas that had accumulated through the day. Only lately, things had come to a screeching halt. It was like her brain had run out of lubricant. The words were there; only they wouldn't surface. Instead, they swam around aimlessly. Controller failure! It wasn't fun.

She was a classic type-A personality. The stress of always being under the gun served as her endorphin. However, that euphoria slowly spiraled downward when the rumors started floating around concerning the CEO's additional cost cutting measures. Daniel Baker was supportive of the measures, and as Chief of Staff, waved the banner with the rest of the senior administration. (They were loyal.) Even though he and Jennifer were determined not to let this conflict interfere with their personal relationship, it did. They had never fought before. Now, nothing-issues often caused sharp words.

Yes, she was feeling awfully sad. She refused, however, to let pity enter the picture. There was no one else to blame. She had gotten where she was in all aspects of her life because of her efforts, good or bad. In the past, the good far outweighed the bad. Her future now, however, looked mighty bleak.

She watched Daniel Baker shove the final piece of sandwich in his mouth. "It's a wonder your coronaries have any room for blood to flow," she said.

She looked down at her food. Her appetite was gone. She rose to her feet, telling herself she should leave before she said anything she might regret. She headed toward the tray disposition area. Eyes were on her but she made eye contact with no one. It wasn't the answer they were seeking.

12

Jennifer hesitated, not because she wondered if he was home, but rather wondering if he would answer the door. After all, their time earlier in the day had been anything but cordial. Their parting in the cafeteria had been even less so—and in front of so many people! Tensions were high lately, directly proportional to everything going on at the hospital. They tried to keep a wide boundary between work and their personal lives, but the task was growing more and more difficult. She had noticed a definitive change in their relationship the past few weeks. She was taking longer and longer to answer his calls. He was leaving fewer and fewer messages of sweet nothings on her answering machine. They were both pros at hiding their emotions. They were also both experts at seeing though the armor of others.

She initially tried to blame the change on the maturing of their relationship—something all couples go through. The human body is a bag of emotional charcoal. The fire may start slowly, or it may start quickly, depending on the amount of ignitable fluid one dedicates in the beginning. With time, the fire becomes fierce and hot. More time, and things settle to a soft glow. Unless more fuel is added, the fire starts to die out. The challenge is to find the extra fuel. The challenge is also not to let it rain on the fire—something Jennifer believed was happening to them in the form of hospital storms.

Realizing she was messing around with a married man, especially one married to such a powerful woman as Diane Baker, Jennifer initially had no long term expectations. There were wishes, hopes, dreams and fantasies maybe, but not true expectations. She was too seasoned, too smart for that. She did, however, fear the end. Without him, she'd be lost. "I'd go nuts," she told him on numerous occasions. Over the past several months, however, her expectations changed. She initially denied she was falling in love with the man, but as the days passed she could no longer ignore how she felt. The key now was to keep the feeling strong, to keep the fire burning, to wait for the *maybe soon* to arrive.

But how?

With that thought, she closed the car door and walked the short distance to the house. Daniel called it a cottage on the water. Jennifer thought it more like a mini-mansion—a spacious six bedroom home overlooking the Severn River. It was set like a castle high up on a bluff, the water some thirty feet below. The driveway ran from the street through the garden that in the summer was full of daffodils, tulips and other colorful flowers neither she nor Daniel could ever name. Once past the gardens, there was a tennis court on the left and a swimming pool on the right. This led onto the circle at the front of the house where one was greeted by tall white pillars and a walkway guarded by a pair of lion heads. The entire two story structure was painted white which gave one the impression of an old plantation home.

It was because of the resemblance to the southern architecture that Diane Baker did not particularly like the place. She was a New York City girl, Manhattan more specifically. Any place outside any city limits was a no-no for her. She only honored the estate's presence when it was a convenience to her, meaning some charitable function she was hosting, and then only in the summer. The rest of the time, she barely gave it a thought. The location was thus an excellent rendezvous point for two lovers.

Jennifer rang the doorbell. It seemed he answered before the ringing stopped. She felt a glimmer of hope. That was the way it used to be.

"Hi, Jen," he said, stepping aside to let her in. His tone of voice gave her additional hope.

The foyer was large, the floors marble, the ceiling rose to the top of the second floor. A large chandelier filled the air. Two winding staircases were set against each wall. She knew each bedroom upstairs was exquisitely decorated, clean and ready for immediate occupancy—by whom she did not know in that Daniel had few visitors—or so he claimed. The downstairs consisted of an office, large kitchen, formal living room, and dining area. There was a family room that contained a large pool table and big screen TV. She saw it as lot of room for so little use. His two children, both in college, did not want any part of a place that didn't have stables for their horses.

"Hi," she returned, handing him a bottle of French Merlot, one of his favorites. He took the bottle with a smile. He was dressed in a blue turtleneck and khaki pants. His hair was still wet, indicating he had just gotten out of the shower. The scent of the shampoo stimulated her olfactory nerve. As she leaned forward to kiss him, she also smelled the fresh cologne. It was one she had given him the previous Christmas—another good sign. Most importantly though, his upper lip was moist with perspiration—a sign he wanted her—a sign that had been missing of late. He was barefoot with a tea towel draped across his shoulder, signs he had shed the day's stress.

As he approached his fifth decade, he was still a handsome man, his eyes dark blue, his teeth straight, his smile wide. At 6' 2", he was the ideal weight of 180 pounds. In spite of his feigned nonchalant attitude about diet, his caloric intake was balanced with a very structured exercise program. His physique was nearly perfect, exactly what one would expect from the area's most popular plastic surgeon, and the husband of Diane Baker. However, Jennifer knew that behind the superficial covering of perfection, fatigue was starting to emerge. A careful look showed faint crow's feet in the corners of his eyes. A slight hint of darkness circled his orbits. Yes, the strain was starting to show, and Jennifer knew it would only get worse.

"You look good tonight," he complimented, barely pulling his lips away.

"You smell good," she returned.

She caught a look at herself in the mirror hanging near the left stairwell. She had to admit, she did look good tonight. Her shoulder length dark brown hair was pulled back into a ponytail. A yellow bow held the strands in place. She wore a pale red lip gloss and had only a touch of color to her cheeks. Her face was long and the features near perfect, or so she was told by Daniel. Then again, he should know. He was an expert in the area. A yellow sweater showed off the curves of her figure. Her breasts were properly portioned and well-shaped. And yes, they were all natural in spite of Daniel's offering of help. Her stomach was flat and her thighs were firm. Tight white pants curved across her backside and outlined her thin, well-shaped legs.

Brushing a moist strand of hair from his forehead, she said, "You look tired."

"I've no reason to be," he responded, a sharpness to his voice.

She scolded herself for setting him up so he could show his cynicism, the one trait that bothered her. He never missed an opportunity to display a sharp defensive tongue. She learned over time not to give him the opportunity. As with most cynics, he only attacked if given the chance.

She quickly changed the subject. "It's a beautiful night. What do you have planned?" She knew he had something planned. He always did. He was the most prepared person she had ever met. Every second of every minute of every day was a predetermined event. Heaven help anyone who caused him to fall behind in his schedule, including his wife and his mistress.

"Nothing," he said.

"Nothing!"

"Not a thing," he repeated. "You always say I have our time together planned to the T. Well, tonight I've decided to play like Burger King and let you have it your way."

She laughed at his reference to the fast food chain. Besides chicken salad dripping with mayonnaise, another vice was his passion for fast food burgers, the greasier the better with as many condiments as possible.

"That's a surprise, and a switch," she said.

"That I did plan." He led her into the living room. A large fireplace sat empty, surrounded by white marble stone. Above the fireplace was a Picasso. She had been told it was from the artist's blue phase. She had been told several others things as well, but had forgotten. The only thing that really interested Jennifer—it was an original. He told her that one night when she asked where he found such a good copy.

"It's not a copy," he had said nonchalantly.

She responded with the obvious follow-up. "Then what is it?"

"An original."

She didn't know much about art or Picasso, but she did know original Picassos were not commonly found hanging above fireplaces in one's second home. If the intent had been to impress her, it worked. He went on to explain he bought it at an auction in London several years before while attending a medical conference. He happened by the auction house during an evening walk. Needless to say, a couple of hours later and many pounds lighter, he had made his first and last investment in art.

"So?" he questioned.

"So, what?" she repeated.

"What do you want to do?"

Jennifer walked up to the painting and gave it a closer look. "Are all of Picasso's paintings so erotic?"

"Do you think it's erotic?" Daniel said, stepping up beside her.

"Sometimes."

"When is sometimes?"

She laughed as she turned and faced him. She brushed another strand from his face. "When I'm horny, I guess."

"Is the painting erotic tonight?"

She laughed again. "Most definitely." They quickly embraced, his arms much too strong for the delicate fingers of a plastic surgeon. He pulled her tightly to him. His lips touched her forehead. His tongue traced a path to an earlobe. She purred softly as his moist caresses swept the earlier tension away. An excitement took its place. She glanced up at the Picasso and wondered if the blue distorted figure was watching. The possibility sent a chill down her spine.

Jennifer was not an inexperienced woman when she first met Daniel Baker. At the same time, she wasn't casual about her intimacies. She had several relationships over the years, each ending when the newness evolved into a mundane repetitiveness. With Daniel, it was different. The newness had worn off and the stress had indeed increased, but the fire was still there. There was always something fresh, something exciting, even if their time was limited. From the anticipation leading up to their visit, to the initial greeting and small talk, to the first touch, to the ascending passion, he made her feel her fire.

Tonight was no different. In spite of everything, the coals were burning.

13

Jennifer remembered many of the details of the dream. She was with Daniel. They were someplace far away, a mystical place with lots of people. Life was good. There were no problems. There was no sorrow. There was only happiness and beautiful people. It was the perfect dream. Only it was just that, a dream.

She awoke with the images fresh in her mind. Normally, she would have been disappointed. Finding out such a dream did not come true would disappoint anyone. On this particular morning, life indeed was good. There were still problems, but they were no longer hers to solve. And any sorrow she felt was covered over by the memories of the night before.

They made love several times until each was spent. Then they talked, a definite missing factor from their current relationship. Daniel told her not to worry about the hospital. It and she would survive, even without each other. Life went on. He even suggested she might be better off away from the place. He suggested more strongly, *they'd* be better off. Of the many issues related to her leaving Annapolis General, the one that loomed the largest was her relationship with Daniel. Of all the fears, their potential break up topped the list. His reassurances and last night's lovemaking all but eliminated those fears. Her dream just now… well, that added icing to the cake.

Yes, life was good.

When the phone rang, she thought it was him. A smile crossed her face. A chill went up her spine. He used to always call her the morning after they'd been together. "Good morning," she chirped, picking up the receiver.

"Jennifer?"

Jennifer sat up straight. It wasn't him. "Yes."

"Jennifer, it's Sally, Sally Thornton." Sally Thornton was the ER's daytime charge nurse.

"Oh hi, Sally." Jennifer couldn't believe she was calling her about a problem in the ER.

"Listen, Jennifer," the charge nurse continued. "I'm sorry to bother you. I know what went down yesterday, and I'm sorry… truly sorry. But I knew you'd want to know."

Sally's voice, normally cool and controlled even under the most trying circumstances, was quivering.

Jennifer's thoughts spun like the wheels on a slot machine, trying to figure out who Sally was going to tell her about. She eliminated anyone in her family as she would have already known about that. It must be someone at work. But then why was Sally having so much trouble talking. The wheels stopped on Old Man Hooper. She jumped out of bed and went to the window. She looked out across the harbor. It was a beautiful Annapolis morning. The sun was already well off the horizon. Many boats in the anchorage were in the midst of heading out for a day on the bay—a *hot* day on the bay, she corrected. Her eyes moved up the walkway and stopped at *Windskater*. She squinted to see if he was up on deck. She saw no one. Then again, nothing else looked out of the ordinary.

Sally finally gained control of her voice. "He came in with chest pain. At first we didn't think much of it. After all, we all know his dietary habits. But the second EKG... there were changes. Then..."

Jennifer felt the blood flow from her head. She sank to the floor. Poor Mr. Hooper, she thought. Poor Mr. Hooper. "Then what? What, Sally?"

"He went into V fib. We worked on him for over two hours, but..."

It was the sentence all relatives in the ER feared. *We worked on him for some time frame*, then the most feared word of all... *but*.

Sally didn't have to say any more. There was never any more to say after the *but*.

There was a long pause. Then Sally said, "I just hope your last time together was a happy one."

Jennifer tried to remember. They were. They weren't. No, she never saw him yesterday. He wasn't up on deck the first time she went by. She never stopped for the second.

A wave of guilt flooded over her. Had she stopped by to check on him, she would have seen... she would have noticed something was wrong. While he was a very private man, and didn't say a whole lot to anyone, he did talk to Jennifer. She would have known something was amiss. The feeling of guilt thickened.

"Poor Mr. Hooper," she said softly. "Poor Mr. Hooper."

There was a pause on the other end of the line. "Mr. Hooper? Jennifer, who's Mr. Hooper?

Another pause. "That's who you're calling about, isn't it?" Jennifer said. A glimmer of hope filled her heart.

Yet another pause. "No, Jennifer. That's not who I'm calling you about."

Jennifer felt a sense of relief. "Then who?"

"Daniel... Daniel Baker."

The name crashed down on her like an anvil from the sky. Air escaped her lungs as if sucked out by a vacuum. Her chest hurt. She needed oxygen. Where was all the oxygen? Her thoughts returned to the earlier dream. Everything was perfect. There were no problems. There was no sorrow. Life was good.

Except for the inevitable *but*. There was always a *but*.

"The dream... the dream," she said softly. Luckily, she was already on the floor as the last ounce of blood drained from her brain. She told herself she was going to faint.

And then she did.

Early May

4 Years Later

14

The school bus bounced extraordinarily hard as the front right tire dropped into a deep pothole—a pothole that could have been avoided, but was not, or so April believed. She started to mutter "bitch" under her breath, but caught herself in time. Her mother used too much profanity and April promised herself she wouldn't become dependent on the same vocabulary. Instead, she inhaled a deep breath before bending down to retrieve the books that had slipped from her grasp. She held onto the seat in front of her as the bus came to a screeching halt at her stop. She almost lost her books again, only this time she anticipated the movement.

The bus driver was Mrs. Smyth… Mrs. *R.* Smyth as the old lady insisted on being called. No one knew what the *R* stood for, nor did anyone really care. Everyone did know the driver had no love for April. Few cared about that either. It did bother April, however, not fully understanding the reasoning for the woman's attitude. Surely, Mrs. *R* Smyth didn't blame her for being fired from her stepfather's plant way before April ever arrived in town?

Regardless, April cleared her mind and stepped forward. Mrs. *R.* Smyth was glaring at her in the large rear view mirror. Her facial expression's message was clear. "Hurry up you little brat." Instead, April did just the opposite, taking her time to reorganize her books. At the front of the bus she stopped and examined her hair in the mirror. Then she carefully made her way down the steps leading to the pavement. She glanced over her shoulder. As always, the bus was empty. Hers was the last stop, so she wasn't holding anyone up except the driver. With an afterthought, she turned and faced her antagonist. She smiled as if to say, "Have a nice day." She almost verbalized the words, but remembered a lesson from her mother. "The spoken word is a precious commodity. Don't waste them on people who aren't worth it."

She stepped onto the curb and was just out of reach of the closing doors when the bus pulled away with a lurch. The gears ground together as if the driver was in a hurry, which April knew was indeed the case. It was the same scenario every day. A slowpoke ride to school because of the hangover from the night before, and a fast jerky ride home in the afternoon as the desire for a drink set in. Everyone knew she was a drunk, but she never drove impaired. In fact her driving record was excellent—not one major incident in over twenty-five years. She claimed it was because she was a good driver. Others figured everyone simply got out of her way when they saw her bus approaching.

Stepping up to the sidewalk, April headed for home. The community was spacious, the landscaping meticulous and clean cut. Every house had at least a front and side garden. Most had huge gardens in the rear as well—many surrounded oversized pools. Every unique customized house had at least one tree in the front yard.

Just like the people that live inside, April thought. So different from their trailer on the farm. The town and surrounding area were named Worthington Valley. The specific community where April lived was Worthington Valley East, one of the more exclusive developments in Ohio.

Still curious about the overall environment into which she had moved four years earlier, April talked little about it for fear of being asked in return about her past. The only exception was her stepbrother, Danny. Once he got used to having someone else in the house and they became friends, he asked enough questions for three busloads of kids. Once she got used to him asking and he started actually treating her like a real person, she answered as honestly as possible—within reason, of course.

At sixteen years of age, April had grown into an intelligent young lady. She came to Worthington Valley with little understanding of the real word outside of their trailer and her school in Alabama. She did well in her new school, however, and made up for lost time by spending many extra hours in the library. She was sharp and picked things up quickly. She adjusted to her new surroundings with few stumbles. Just like her mother taught, she kept her mouth shut and listened carefully. Initially, she focused only on her music, her mother and school. With time, she began to take more of an interest in other things. Time also drew her closer to her stepbrother. Danny oriented her to Worthington Valley. He agreed with her initial assessment that most kids were aloof and stuck up—not all, but most. April saw that he played the game when he had to in school, but away from that environment he was down to earth. She had grown to like him.

Her stepfather, however, remained somewhat distant. He accepted April as part of the package when he married her mother. He was polite and firm with both children, but there was a lack of warmth towards both April and Danny. He was just the opposite with his new bride. There, he was like an octopus with too many hands. That didn't bother April, however. He wasn't mean towards her, and he was kind and affectionate to her mother. That was good enough for April. Besides that, they no longer lived in the dusty old trailer, and there was always plenty to eat.

Her stepfather was Samuel Adams Worthington, the fourth to be exact. The huge farm to the east of Worthington Valley had been in his family for generations. The family's long term plan was for that to continue. He saw matters differently. When he inherited the property, Sam Worthington was quick to find an interested developer and cash in on his fortune. Of course, part of the deal was the choicest lot and biggest house for himself. After all, the president of Worthington Industries had to show everyone he was the biggest and the best. Besides his land dealings, he was also one of the area's most successful businessmen. With part of the profits from the land sale, he bought a small windshield manufacturing company located south of the town. Through additional expansion and acquisitions, the company grew into one of the biggest part suppliers to Detroit, and was now one of Ohio's largest private employers.

So while April felt no real attraction towards Samuel Worthington, there was a certain level of respect and admiration. She knew not to complain either. She lived in a big house and had most everything she wanted. She had her own bedroom, her mother was happy and there was a grand Steinway in the living room. The piano was Samuel Worthington's gift to his new stepdaughter the day he married her mother. It also served as another symbol of his success. April was so surprised, so thrilled, she was almost late getting ready for the wedding. She remembered what he said as the delivery men wheeled the large instrument through the door. He may not have been warm, but he was very wise. "April, you never have to make excuses for who you are, or where you came from. You are you. You have good points and you have bad points. Overwhelm people with the good and they'll ignore any bad."

She did just that with her piano playing. The important people in the community soon accepted the new Mrs. Samuel Worthington. After all, she was a real charmer, a looker and knew how to host a fine party. In addition, the new Mrs. Worthington had a fine daughter who knew her manners, and who could play the piano like no one they'd ever heard. The same went for the important people's children. April was accepted by her peers because she was quiet and kept to herself. She wasn't cocky like most expected when they heard Sam Worthington was remarrying someone with a child. She was just the opposite. And while she was pretty in her own right, she dressed down compared to the other girls, so she was not seen as competition for the boys. She was also Danny Worthington's new stepsister; and because Danny was one of the hottest guys in school, another straw was raised in April's favor. So even though Mrs. R. Smyth may not like her, so what? There were others who did. And that didn't really matter all that much either. April and her mother were happy. They were out of the trailer. They were safe.

The sound of a honking horn broke her train of thought. She glanced in the direction of the street. Inching along beside her was Eddie Richmond in his bright red sports car. She knew little and cared even less about cars, although she had to admit, this one was pretty. She wasn't sure of the make, but the name *Mustang* did come to mind.

"Hey, babe, want a ride home?" he called, leaning over toward the passenger's seat.

He always called her babe, and she hated it. Mainly because it wasn't her name, but also because it was what he called all the girls in school. He was a tall handsome boy with dark blue eyes and a head of curly blond hair. He was well built and muscular, and played on both the football and lacrosse teams. He was the hottest thing going in school, or so the other girls claimed. A date with him was like a trip to paradise. He was also her stepbrother's best friend.

"So cool," was a commonly heard expression.

"A real six pack."

"He sweats me all over."

"So stuck up," was April's common response.

"Yes, but he is the star quarterback, and his father is the Sheriff of Worthington Valley."

"So what?" April would exclaim.

Her classmates would just shake their heads and laugh. "You're so gay," they'd tease. At the same time, they knew she was the one fish, in spite of many attempts, Eddie had yet to catch. They also knew it was just a matter of time.

Eddie pulled a few feet ahead of her, stopped the car and pushed open the passenger door. "Get in," he said in a commanding yet polite voice.

April started to say no, but remembered she promised her stepfather she'd be nice to the sheriff's son. There was always a lot of traffic through their house of *very important people*, of which the sheriff was one. At the end of each visit, the sheriff always made a point to suggest that his son and Sam Worthington's stepdaughter ought to get together sometime. Mr. Worthington always responded with a promise to look into the possibility, and then request of April that she at least be nice to the boy. In which case, stepdaughter Worthington always promised to try.

So she tried now, and in spite a deep down but sequestered desire to ride in this particular car—just to see what all the hype was about—she declined the invitation, arguing that it was a wonderful day and she needed to walk for her exercise. She followed this with a friendly smile.

Eddie didn't pursue the issue. While he was eager to win her over, he also knew, like in any sport, patience was a virtue. Instead, he said, "Have you made a decision about the spring dance?"

The question caught her off guard because she thought she made it clear the other three times he asked her to the spring dance. "Thank you, but I'm not going," was her repeated response.

"Why not?" was always his rebuttal.

"Because."

"Because why?"

"Just because." In truth, there were many reasons. The top two were fear and the fact that she did not know how to dance. She acknowledged the two were probably related. "Because is good enough," she added.

"For you, but not for me."

"That's your problem, not mine." She usually ended the conversation there.

This time however, she decided to be a bit more forceful. "Eddie, I appreciate you asking, I really do. However, I'd also appreciate if you'd stop asking."

"I will, soon as you say yes."

"No."

"Then I'm not done asking."

Her face turned red, a combination of embarrassment and anger. By now she was at the corner of her street. She shifted her books to the other arm, took a deep breath and headed up the cul-de-sac.

"See you tomorrow," he called out as he gunned the engine and drove away.

April refused to turn and look, even though her curiosity was aroused by the car.

Catching the direction of her thoughts, she self-scolded aloud, "Don't even go there."

15

Those at the west end of the mall headed east. Those at the east end headed west. The result was an inevitable gridlock of people in and around the mall's center court—an acre or so of space already filled with mini-carts and vendors displaying a variety of arts and crafts. The art display, part of the mall's tenth anniversary celebration, was highly publicized, as were the sales in most of the shops.

To no one's surprise, the rest of the mall was crowded as well. To many people's surprise, the art show itself was also doing exceptionally well. The crowd was charged and cash registers were ringing. Naturally, back in the management offices, each of the various departments was taking credit for the weekend's success. Truth was, the weather deserved most of the credit. The long cold winter was over. The daytime temperatures were approaching 70's. The final snow plows had disappeared. The final pile of snow had melted. People who had been secluded for several weeks were free to venture out. Cabin fever collided with spring fever and the inevitable occurred—mankind went to the mall.

The ad campaign promoted the event as a large variety of arts and crafts, and it was exactly that. There were metal sculptures, tee shirt painters, a photo-on-a-cup display and a candle maker. There were flag makers, pillow makers and wood carvers. If a craft was invented, it was there.

And then there was Cliff Davidson, Chesapeake Bay seascape artist *extraordinaire*.

He didn't have a mini-cart, but rather a series of easels set in a semi-circle displaying a variety of seascape works of all shapes and sizes. There were several full oil canvases with ten or so small ones. There were drawings, some in charcoal, others in colored pencil. There was also a large array of photographs. All were unique, all were originals. *Everything original* was his hallmark.

The artist himself sat on a stool before a partially completed painting of the Chesapeake Bay Bridge. The view was from the north looking down the bay. The two spans loomed large through the middle third of the canvas. While the range was less than half a mile away, the scope was wide angled. The bright silver steel beams were juxtaposed against the deep blues of the bay's water. The sun, setting to the right, shot streaks of orange light radiating across the scene. The water was calm. As such, the resulting shadows and sparkles set the entire piece off in a brilliant array of colors. Again, the scope was large, but the details were meticulous—every geometrical angle precise. In addition, there was no land in sight, giving the impression the structure sat in isolation.

Cliff sitting and working on this painting was a tremendous marketing tool. Nearly everyone venturing by paused for a look. Many blatantly gawked, making comments about the quality of this young artist's work. The stopping was what the piece was intended to do. Once stopped, the people then gazed at the other items on display. Many made purchases immediately. Others returned later. Through all this, the artist remained focused on the canvas before him. From the many hours of working such shows, Cliff had learned the *art* of concentration. The only things of importance were the brush in his hand, the canvas before him and the image in his mind. Unlike the other proprietors who aggressively hawked at the crowd in a style best described as *polite confrontation*, Cliff did nothing personally to market his wares. He remained silent unless spoken to directly.

A poster board sign leaning against his stool was the only hint that Cliff was even interested in moving product.

Chesapeake Bay Seascapes
By Cliff Davidson

Smaller print emphasized the features of his work.

All works of the Chesapeake Bay.
All by Cliff Davidson.
All originals—no prints or copies.
Feel free to browse.
Most pieces for sale.
Feel free to ask questions.
Feel free!!

While he usually did well at these types of shows, this weekend was proving to be especially successful—successful to the point he was concerned about his inventory. He was never one to come with cases and cases of material, believing that quality, not quantity, helped set him apart from the others. However, on this weekend, his back up supply was already depleted. Everything he had for sale was on display. It was a good news/bad news scenario. He was glad he was doing so well, but wished he had been more diligent about his portfolio. He wasn't going to complain, however. Running out of inventory was a nice problem to have. It boded well for the future when he cut the final cord to be totally on his own—an experiment to see if he could survive as an artist. The time was coming soon—in less than twenty-four hours to be exact.

Ever since his uncle's death four years earlier, Cliff was determined to someday make it on his own as an artist. It was a long term dream, helped by the events surrounding his uncle's death. His uncle's will was read two weeks after the funeral. The question naturally came up as to Cliff's future. Where would he go? Where would he live? Who would look after him? While mature for his age, he was only fifteen at the time. There were endless possibilities thrown about. His uncle's lawyer suggested a family member. There were none. He had inherited all his uncle's assets, but nothing else. He and Chessie were alone. Several neighbors said he could live with them. Cliff balked at that, however, making it quite clear he wanted to stay at *Loafer's Glory*. After all, that was his home. But he could not live there alone.

Or could he?

Throughout the years, his uncle had made many friends, on the water, in the community and in politics. One just happened to be a local circuit court judge. He took a personal interest in Cliff's situation and had the case assigned to his docket. The day of the hearing on Cliff's future, a variety of interested people showed up in the courtroom. Cliff, his uncle's attorney, and Ralph and Betty had already been briefed on the judge's decision. All others were surprised at what the big man in the black robe said.

Strolling into the courtroom like a king approaching his throne, the judge took his seat on the bench. He glanced over at Cliff, gave a nod and proceeded to speak in a deep voice. "This court has been assigned a difficult decision—that is the future of a young man, Cliff Davidson. Now, everyone is aware that I know Cliff personally—have known him most of his life. His uncle was a wonderful man, and Cliff appears well on his way to being the same. The question is how to ensure this road to maturity is not interrupted. It appears to me Cliff needs three major things in his life. First is our undivided love and support. George Davidson's death was a tragedy to us all. To Cliff, it is beyond words. Second, Cliff needs to have as little other interruption in his life as possible. He is doing well in school and needs to continue with that. He is also turning into an exceptionally talented artist. Now, I am certainly not an art expert, but I will tell you this: Cliff Davidson is good." The judge took a long breath. "Finally, Cliff needs a father figure to look out for him, to guide and protect him."

"So with that, the decision is really quite simple. There is only one person who has the ability and who I can trust with this responsibility. As such, I hereby order the guardianship of Cliff Davidson, personal and financial, be assigned to Walter Donnelly."

A hush came over the crowd as the various participants digested what they had just heard. Walter Donnelly was the judge himself.

Walt Donnelly had been to *Loafer's Glory* on numerous occasions and often wished he had such a place to live, instead of Towson where his wife insisted they reside. After all, a judge and high flying interior designer had to live where the action was. The judge, however, preferred the calmer more subdued lifestyle of the waterfront. He preferred it, and he understood the desire and need for it. So, when hearing Cliff's desperate wishes to continue living at *Loafer's Glory*, the judge sought a solution. However, there was no one he could ask or trust to move there with the boy. One day while sitting on the end of the pier with Cliff and Chessie, he came up with an idea. He would become Cliff's legal guardian. At the same time, he would allow Cliff to live on his own, with close supervision from himself and Cliff's neighbors. Judge Donnelly knew Ralph and Betty through Cliff's uncle. He was convinced they were good people. The judge discussed the idea with several people he knew in social services. All thought the idea a bit strange, but quite possible. He threw it past his own Chief Justice who saw through the plan immediately. "You just want an excuse to go down there all the time." Then she smiled and added. "It's a brilliant idea so long as you add a contingency that you can change your decision if it doesn't work. I'd keep a close watch on how he does in school—that'll probably be the best indicator." Neither spoke about Judge Donnelly's longing for a son of his own. His wife was too busy with her career for children.

Walter Donnelly took the suggestions and discussed it with the trust attorney, who agreed to manage Cliff's finances. "I've had my share of bad investments," the judge said. "But I know that an investment in Cliff today will pay great dividends in the future."

So Cliff remained at *Loafer's Glory*. He stayed in the same school with his same friends, and he continued working on his art. Much to his wife's dismay, Judge Donnelly was forced to make frequent visits to *Loafer's Glory* to check on his assigned son. As promised, Ralph and Betty kept their end of the bargain too, watching over the boy. Betty often teased that *Loafer's Glory* was simply a standalone bedroom—an extension of their own house.

This arrangement helped Cliff get over his grief and guilt, and to get on with his life. Good or bad, he never saw Robin again after the funeral. Her parents sent her to Florida to live with relatives so she could focus on her skiing. Of everything that happened the day of the storm, getting over Robin was the hardest. He felt used, a tough pill for anyone to swallow, much less a young teenager with no one to confide in. No one else knew what took place that afternoon.

One thing the adults worried about was how quickly *Loafer's Glory* would fall into disarray. Cliff quickly put those concerns to rest. He proved very versatile, keeping up with all the minor repairs as well as most of the major ones. Naturally, Judge Donnelly was there when needed, as were Ralph and Betty.

Besides his art, Cliff focused on school. The next fall, he took extra courses, with a plan to finish high school a year early. He made a deal with the judge that he could start working full time as an artist once he completed high school. When Cliff got the idea to try to graduate a year early, the judge shrugged his shoulders and said, "I made the deal. I'll stand by it."

Cliff took extra courses during the summers, and the effort paid off. He was able to complete all the requirements a year early. At the commencement ceremonies, it was announced that Cliff Davidson was the youngest person to graduate from Bowleys Quarters High School. He also received several awards for his art work, was voted by his classmates as most likely to succeed and received a standing ovation when he was awarded his diploma. It was said Walter Donnelly had tears in his eyes for the first time in years. He, along with everyone else in the auditorium, had no doubt Cliff had the talent to make it as a professional artist. They just hoped Cliff would get the necessary breaks every young artist needed.

Over the ensuing months, Cliff prepared for the time when he would cut the umbilical cord and venture out on his own. This was the eve of that journey. If the present art show was any indication, it was a future filled with promise.

Cliff worked on the painting for the next hour, pausing only when purchases were made. He contemplated putting the brushes down and working on his drawings, maybe even getting a few completed he could sell, but instinctively knew sitting at the easel was his best marketing tool. It didn't matter that the painting was basically complete.

So he continued until the next interruption.

"Excuse me, young man," a voice said from behind. At the same time he felt a tapping on his back.

Brush in mid-stroke, Cliff turned toward the barely audible sound. He noticed nothing unusual at first until he looked down and saw a short elderly lady standing at his side. She was leaning on a cane and appeared mildly short of breath. Atop her head sat a way out of style, flowery hat. She was bent forward as if carrying a tremendous load, which in a way she was. She wore a heavy full length mink that nearly swept the floor.

Cliff found her eyes beneath the hat. She was squinting directly at the painting. "May I help you?" he asked, careful not to stare at the oversized coat.

She said nothing as she continued to examine the painting. Cliff was about to repeat the question when she said, "How much for that one?" She lifted her cane and pointed to the painting.

"This one?" Cliff said, motioning with his brush to the one he was working on.

"That's what I said."

Cliff cleared his throat. "Well, ma'am, this one isn't finished yet."

"Nonsense. You haven't done anything to it in over an hour. You're just sitting there looking pretty." The sharp tone of her voice softened. "Now there ain't nothing wrong with that mind you, but you can't bullshit a bullshitter." A faint smile crossed her face. "So then, how much?"

Cliff shrugged his shoulders and leaned closer to the woman so others wouldn't hear. "To be honest with you ma'am, I haven't thought about that yet. You're right, it's almost finished and I'm just adding a few final touches. Besides that, I haven't given it much thought. It may not even be for sale."

The smile disappeared and her head tilted to the side as if to eye him up. He was wearing jeans, Docksiders and a long sleeve polo shirt.

"You rich?" she asked.

"Pardon me?"

"Don't ever accuse old people of having a hearing problem." The volume of her voice increased. She drew out the words as well. "Are… you… rich?"

"Not by a long shot," he replied without considering the nosiness of the question.

"Then the painting's for sale. How much?"

He started to protest again, but stopped. He smiled and let out a soft laugh. "I haven't a clue."

"Least now you're talking straight. There ain't nothing worse than someone who can't shoot straight. You know what I mean? You shoot straight in life, son, and you'll get along real well." Her head tipped in the direction of the poster board. "You are Cliff Davidson, aren't you?"

"Yes ma'am, I am."

"You don't look like an artist, especially one that does paintings of the ocean."

"Thank you… I think," he responded. "But I must tell you, the painting isn't of the ocean. It's the Chesapeake Bay. See, the bridges are the Chesapeake Bay…"

"It's water, isn't it?"

He hesitated. "Yes, it's water."

"All the same to me."

Cliff wisely chose not to argue.

She continued. "My granddaughter's getting married soon and I want to get her a painting."

"That's nice. Do they like nautical things?"

"He… the one she's marrying… is a cowboy. He hates the east coast. He hates everything about this area, especially the water. That's why I want a picture of the ocean."

Cliff laughed louder this time.

"When will it be finished?"

"It can be finished now if it has to be. It just needs to dry some."

"When will it be dry?"

Cliff glanced at the canvas. "This one's in acrylic, so by the end of the day."

"That's plenty of time for the wedding." Rummaging around in her oversized purse, she took a pen and filled out a check. "I guess if you can't decide on the price then I'll just have to do it for you." Ripping it off, she folded the check in half and handed it to Cliff. "My name and address are on the top. If it's enough, send the painting to me UPS insured. If not, I'd appreciate you sending me the check back. I do hope I get a big package next week and not a small envelope."

Cliff took the check and put in his shirt pocket.

"You make sure you insure it, you hear?" the lady directed.

"Yes ma'am."

"Now, you better get back to work… if that's what you call sitting in front there like a dummy." A faint smile crossed her face. "Sold me, though."

16

Hearing the bells chime as the front door opened, Robert Granger looked up from the cash register where he was adding up the day's receipts. It had been an exceptionally good day so the task was taking longer than normal. No complaints, however, as the first quarter had started slow. While they were still behind the targeted sales, the weekend's success showed promise for the future. *Granger's Galleries and Art Supplies* had been in Middle River Mall since the mall opened ten years earlier. Business was good at first, but with the passage of time and that fire spitting dragon called competition, sales growth had dropped to where it had been flat the past several years. He and his wife were still earning a comfortable living, but the hours were long and the stress formidable. Retail had always been tough. Lately, however, tough was not a strong enough adjective.

As expected, Cliff walked through the doors a few minutes after closing. "Hey Cliff," Robert said, closing the cash register drawer.

"Hi, Mr. Granger," Cliff replied.

"All loaded up?" Robert asked.

"All loaded up," Cliff replied. "What's left, that is."

"Word is you did pretty good today."

"Word is?"

The art store proprietor laughed. "The last time we checked on you, your inventory was a might low."

"I didn't see you guys."

"We didn't want to bother you. You were either too busy with someone or had your nose stuck in that painting. Did you finish it?"

Cliff lifted a package wrapped in brown paper up onto the counter. "Here it is."

"It's done?"

Cliff nodded.

"Why is it all wrapped up?"

"I need a favor."

Robert tilted his head to the side as if to say, "Go ahead."

"I sold it, but I need to deliver it—or rather have it delivered. I was going to ask you to help with that."

"You sold it! I thought you said it wasn't going to be for sale?"

Cliff pulled the folded check out of his pocket and dropped it on the counter. He chuckled a moment. "I really didn't have a choice." He went on to explain about the encounter with the little old lady. "Once the check clears, send her the painting, although I doubt there will be a problem."

"Never be so sure about that," Robert cautioned.

"Well, if the little old lady is a scam artist, she deserves the painting for free."

Robert shrugged his shoulders. "Whatever." He wanted to ask the amount of the check, but knew better. His curiosity would be satisfied in due time anyway. Instead he said, "So tell me, how did the sign work?"

"The sign?"

"The poster board Carol made you."

"Okay, I guess."

A third voice broke into the conversation. "No one said anything?"

Both male heads turned in response to the female voice. Carol Granger, Robert's wife and business partner had come from the back of the store where she was taking inventory of the weekend's activities. Unlike her husband who was tall and starting to show a bit of a pot belly, she was short, dyed blonde and still very attractive. Near daily visits to the mall's gym didn't hurt any either.

Robert laughed. "No honey, no one made any comments about your poster board. Don't be hurt. The focus wasn't on the board, but what the board said."

"The part that said *most pieces for sale*." She was referring to the line her husband added as an afterthought when she was first designing the poster.

Robert smiled broadly. "People want most what they think they can't have."

Carol gave her husband a flirting look. Turning her attention to Cliff, she said, "What's this about a little old lady?"

Cliff quickly filled her in on the details.

"Sounds like she knows good art when she sees it," Carol commented.

"She didn't know the difference between the ocean and the bay," Cliff said.

Carol said, "Well, I'm happy for you, but sad for me."

"How's that?" Cliff inquired.

"I watched you work on that all weekend," Carol explained. "I was thinking about getting that one for Robert and me. I just hope you didn't sell it too cheap."

"I really don't know," Cliff said, shrugging his shoulders. "I have a lot of trouble with pricing my work. Who can really say what art is worth? The lady had her opinion about the piece. Anyway, if I knew you wanted it, I would have saved it for you."

"Don't be ridiculous," Carol replied.

"Carol can get one another time," Robert suggested.

"Maybe." Carol forced a laugh. While she was indeed happy for Cliff, she was sad for herself. She had planned on giving the painting to her husband for their anniversary in a few weeks. Robert always said he'd like to have one of Cliff's early paintings for himself, "before he gets too famous and the price gets too high."

The couple had taken a liking to Cliff from the first moment he set foot in their store a few years earlier. He was youthful, handsome, muscular and had a head full of sun bleached hair. If there had been a recent attempt to run a comb through the hair, it had been a weak one. He was dressed in jeans and a sweat shirt. While his appearance had only changed by adding a few subtle years to his looks, the rest of him was the same—except his hair was better cared for and his clothing matched. He came in the first time looking for art supplies. He had a display set up—almost exactly the same place as now. He was part of a high school art show, a *filler* event designed to fill the time between Christmas and New Year's. The Grangers were judges for the show. Visiting the various displays, they were genuinely impressed with the overall talent.

High schools from all over were represented. There were drawings, black and white, and in color. There were photographs and paintings. There were even a few sculptures. The art was remarkable and judging proved to be more difficult than anticipated. That is until they came upon a large pencil drawing of an old man dressed in coveralls leaning over the side of his work boat. A crab pot could be seen half in, half out of the water with several crabs crawling up the side. Overall, the design of the drawing was simple, uncomplicated and uncluttered. However, the details of each image were breathtaking. The work was titled: *The Old Man and the Bay*.

They thought the play of words was cute and imaged the figure even looked a bit like the original Spencer Tracey. Neither spouse had a trace of talent themselves regarding art. They did, however, have an exceptional eye for recognizing the talent of others. They were constantly in search of young undiscovered artists hoping someday to feature them in their store. As in most professions, there were many talented people who only needed a chance.

They had obviously just found one such person.

They were friends with the art teacher at the artist's high school and sought him out. He beamed when they asked about the drawing, claiming the boy was one of the most talented he had ever seen in someone so young. Soon, they were introduced to the artist himself. It was the same boy who had been in their store earlier—same hair, too.

Cliff returned to the store later that evening bearing the gift certificate that was part of the prize package for *Best of Show*. He had been in many times since and the trio had become friends. While Cliff had Judge Donnelly looking after him in general, the Grangers took him under their wings as an artist. They helped him battle the demons of self-doubt as he continued to work through the grief of his uncle's death. He also told them early on that his goal was to succeed creatively and financially. So subtly, they went to work. They *un-roughened* his physical edges. They taught him basic customer service tactics, and they encouraged and supported him in his practice of selling only original pieces. In any field of business, the major goal in marketing was to separate the product or service from the competition. *Original only* was a most unique trait in the art world. Most local artists earned the majority of their income by selling prints. Cliff, however, stood firm, and so far was successful with the tactic. Many people liked the idea that they had a painting, drawing or photograph that would never be duplicated. Cliff was a quick learner and absorbed the advice with enthusiasm and appreciation.

"So, she thought the bridge was across the ocean?" Robert said.

"I guess so," Cliff replied. "I didn't push the point."

"Smart man," Carol injected. "I guess she knew what she wanted and went after it, even if she had the *it* a little confused." She pointed to the folded check lying on the counter. "So what's a Cliff Davidson original going to cost me these days?"

"I don't know," the artist said. "I haven't looked at the check."

"You haven't?"

Cliff shook his head. "The lady told me to look at it and make up my mind, but I'm going to send her the painting regardless." Cliff tapped the check with his fingers. "She trusted me. I should do the same for her."

"Gallant, but dangerous," Robert scolded with a snicker. He wondered if Cliff's marketing hat was on crooked.

Cliff shrugged his shoulders. "Not any more dangerous than anything else I'm about to do. Besides, didn't someone I know tell me that sometimes you have to take a chance in business?"

Robert looked at his wife. Maybe the hat was on straight after all. "You'll be just fine," Carol encouraged.

Cliff laid the folded check on the counter. "Anyway, can you deposit this for me?" He ran his fingers gently across the paper covering the painting. "Also, can you drop the painting off at the Postman Plus next door? They're going to ship it for me."

"Be glad to," Carol said. She picked up the folded check. "You really don't want to know?"

Cliff hesitated. "You look and then decide."

Carol unfolded the piece of paper. "Holy mackerel," she exclaimed. "Cliff, this check is for a thousand dollars!"

"No way," Cliff said.

Robert looked over his wife's shoulder. "That's what it says."

Cliff leaned forward and took a look himself. He was at a loss for words.

"She must know something we don't," Carol said softly.

"She must," Robert said. "Congratulations, Cliff."

It took Cliff another moment to respond. "A thousand dollars for one painting? I've never charged more than $500 for anything, even large canvases."

"Well, Cliff, you're in the big time now… at least it's a start," Carol said.

Cliff continued staring at the check.

"Speaking of starts," Robert said, "how's everything going for tomorrow?"

Cliff pulled his mind away from the check. "I did take time to call the boat yard," he answered. "Everything's ready as planned. I just hope the weather holds out. It's supposed to, but you never know."

"Last report I heard calls for partly cloudy and temperatures in the mid 60's," Carol offered.

"That's what I heard, too," Cliff said. "I just hope there's some wind."

"Not too much," Robert offered as a caution.

"That's why she has a motor," Cliff returned. The trio laughed.

"I thought you weren't planning to put up the sails for a few days anyway?" Robert said. He hid his nervousness over what Cliff was about to undertake.

"That's the plan, but she's still a sailboat. I'll have to see how things go," Cliff said. He pulled a slip of paper from his pocket. "I do need a few things." He laid the shopping list on the counter.

"Go ahead and help yourself while we finish closing. Then we can go get something to eat." Robert slid the paper back toward Cliff.

"I'll buy," Cliff said.

Robert impulsively started to argue then hesitated. "Yeah, you got the big check today." They all laughed together.

The Grangers focused on closing out for the night as Cliff made his way up and down the aisles, gathering armfuls of supplies as he went. As the pile on the counter grew, Robert commented, "Are you sure you have storage for all this?"

"I hope so," Cliff said, eyeing the pile with concern.

"I just hope you're doing the right thing," Carol said. Her mothering instinct was taking over as one of her cubs was about to leave the den.

"He is," Robert insisted.

Cliff hesitated. In his heart he felt the answer was affirmative. While he had his doubts, he was enthusiastic over what he was about to do. Surviving on his own as an artist had always been a dream. Tomorrow was the first step toward that goal. It was now less than twelve hours away and… there was no turning back. He had signed the papers the previous Thursday. *Loafer's Glory* had been sold.

"I'll find a place for everything," he insisted.

Carol eyed him a moment and then returned to the back room.

"Don't mind her," Robert directed. "She's just worried about you, that's all."

"I appreciate that," Cliff said.

"You have a good head on your shoulders. There's no reason to think that'll come unscrewed now."

Cliff smiled. "Thanks." He made the last trip to the counter. "I think that's everything."

Hearing the cash register start to run, Carol came out from the back. She was carrying a small box. "Don't know what all you got, but I'll wager you forgot this." She handed the box to Cliff. It was a mechanical pencil sharpener. "Electricity will be a little scarce while you're at sea."

"I'm going to be out on the bay," Cliff laughed. "Not lost out in the ocean."

"All the same to me," Carol said.

"You sound like the little old lady," her husband teased.

"Behave," Carol cautioned.

Robert put his arm over his wife's shoulder. "Cliff will be just fine, honey." The reassurance was directed at himself as well. "You want this put on your account, right?" Robert said, pulling off the long strip of paper.

"That's fine," Cliff said.

"We know you got money," Carol teased.

"The check hasn't cleared yet," Cliff pointed out.

"I'm sure it will," she said encouragingly.

Cliff thought a moment about the check. A thousand dollars! A twinge of much needed confidence flowed through his veins.

17

There was a soft hiss and a click as the disc jockey's voice blared from the radio speaker. "Good morning, Baltimore. We're back for the five o'clock hour. It's going to be a beautiful spring day here in Charm City. Highs today will be in the mid 60's, low tonight in the 50's. Tomorrow we warm up with highs in the 70's. Winds on the bay both days will be light and variable at 5 to 10. Right now it's 48 degrees. I'll be back with the rest of the news right after these messages."

Cliff reached over and smacked the off button on the alarm before the first commercial started. He rolled over and looked at the time. 5:01 am. "Why do you have to be so accurate?" he muttered.

He climbed out of the sleeping bag, yawned and stretched to loosen his joints. He didn't mind the sleeping bag. The hard floor, however, took some getting used to. The movers had been in the day before and cleaned out the house. Most of the furniture had been sold at auction. Some he donated to charity. The only things left were his personal effects. Cliff shuffled out to the kitchen to make coffee. Filling the pot, he glanced out the window. While it was dark out, one of the two spot lights lit up the oak tree in the front yard. The leaves were still asleep. No wind so far, he thought. He decided that was both good and bad.

Chessie strolled into the room just as the flame came up on the front burner. Cliff poured a bowl of dry dog food and set it down on the floor. He filled another bowl with water. The dog was more hungry than thirsty.

"Today's the day, girl," Cliff said, leaning over to rub the animal on her side. "Today's the day," he repeated, this time with trepidation. His mind turned to the property's new owners. He met them at settlement earlier in the week—a newly married couple in their late 20's. This was their first home, and in spite of the husband's inflated ego, they both seemed nice enough. Both were very excited about the whole ordeal. Cliff imagined their enthusiasm would dwindle quickly with the reality of owning a home on the water. Cliff had kept the place up over the past four years, thanks in part to his own abilities and the help of Judge Donnelly. The real estate agent claimed *Loafer's Glory* was one of the best waterfront properties in the area. Cliff doubted her at first, but when the place sold within a week and at full price, Cliff realized his efforts had paid off. Still, there was always something to be done. Just like Cliff, the new owners were about to embark on a journey of unclear destinations.

At first, Cliff balked at selling the property. Judge Donnelly argued it was a big step, but a necessary one. While the value of the property would continue to grow if kept up, it would also continue to require a great deal of maintenance. Besides, the economy was good and real estate values were up substantially from the year before. It didn't hurt either that there was talk of aggressive waterfront development further up Middle River. The Judge also subtly suggested that if Cliff was going to start anew, the boy should have as few things as possible to worry about. Finally, the sale of *Loafer's Glory* allowed Cliff to pay cash for his next *home* with plenty to fall back on if his experiment as a self-sustaining artist failed.

The coffee ready, Cliff poured a mug and strolled through the house for a final inspection. It was his final sojourn through what had been home for most of his life. The fact there was no furniture didn't bother him. What did have an impact was the lack of memorabilia sitting round on the various tables, shelves and what were now bare walls. *Loafer's Glory* had always been filled with memories of the past. Pictures of friends and acquaintances were everywhere. His uncle, in his dry, often unrecognized sense of humor, had even bought a few picture frames several years back and left the pretty photographs of the professional models in place. (Distant relatives, he claimed.) The walls also held many items of their life, from framed old charts of the Chesapeake Bay to many of Cliff's works. When Cliff's parents died, his uncle took him in without hesitation. The only condition was that Cliff paid rent. The fee was one piece or art—either a painting, photograph or drawing—a month. Subtly, it was a tremendous compliment, and Cliff always labored long and hard over whatever happened to be that particular month's rent.

Now, however, there was nothing but bare floors and bare walls. The place looked strange. It was cold and damp. The air even seemed stagnant. He felt the same sensation in the pit of his stomach—cold, damp, empty. His eyes swelled with tears. He quickly wiped them away with the back of his hand.

He finished his inspection and returned to the kitchen. There he emptied the coffee pot and put the last few kitchen items in a box. He went back to the bedroom and cleaned up as well. He had planned to take a shower but decided otherwise. *Loafer's Glory* was no longer home. He wanted to leave as soon as possible.

A short time later, the van was packed. He whistled for Chessie and climbed in behind her. Hands on the steering wheel, he glanced at the house one last time. Then he looked ahead. "Eyes forward," he muttered aloud, quoting from his uncle's chest full of sayings. As the van pulled away, Cliff's thoughts turned to the rest of the quote. "Remember boy, it's okay to look back now and again. Good memories are good, and we learn from the bad ones. But, if you look back too much, you won't see where you are going and you're liable to trip."

He stared straight ahead, keeping his eyes fixed to the road. After all, he didn't want to trip too soon.

18

Dawn was just beginning to break as Cliff made the final turn onto Ruby Lane, appropriately named after the marina owner. Cliff slowed the van to a near crawl as the tires fell into the first defect in the road's dirt surface. Frequent visitors to the facility preferred the name Pothole Boulevard. Ruby Kelly, the marina's proprietor, claimed the defects were on purpose. "We don't have speed bumps," he responded to anyone who complained. "We have speed dips." Many insisted the road had not been graded in over twenty years. Others questioned why anyone would speed to get into the place in the first place. Cliff smiled at the concept of speed dips as his teeth banged together after the van went through another deep hole. When does a pot hole become a sink hole, he wondered?

He drove through the run-down gate, itself so old, it often was left open at night. He immediately noticed the change in road conditions. The ride was now smooth because the travel lift which hauled the boats in and out of the water would never be able to navigate around defects in the road's surface.

The yard was full of boats that had been pulled the previous fall. Some were covered in tarps, some were shrink-wrapped in white plastic and others were left exposed to the elements. While the boats themselves were lined up in neat rows, the ground beneath was unkempt. Railroad ties, concrete blocks, and angled pieces of wood used as shimmies for blocking up the boats were scattered about the ground. The yard's maintenance shop was an old wooden building to the left that looked like it had received its last coat of paint about the same time as Ruby Lane received its last manicure. An old trailer served as the office and sat in the shadow of the building. The marina itself was off to the right. A few boats were left in the water during the winter, but most slips were empty. The piers were old with many planks warping up at the ends. The pilings themselves, weathered from many changes of seasons, stood crooked and frail. The joke among the slip holders was that if the speed dips didn't get you, the piers would.

No doubt about it, a ride down Ruby Lane was indeed a ride into nostalgia. In spite of this, the business was successful. The marina sat at the head of Middle River, protected on three sides by land. The water was deep and the service provided by Ruby and his staff was impeccable. There wasn't anything related to boating they could not do, fix or replace. The yard was also a Mecca of spare parts, many considering it the finest junk yard for boats on the entire Chesapeake Bay. Ruby Kelly was a character all his own. And yes, his name was Ru*by*, not Ru*dy*. He had been teased his whole life about having a girl's name. He took the ribbing in stride and always came back with an appropriate response. A few years back, a group of his friends even went so far as to buy him a ruby necklace for Christmas. The story goes that he put the necklace on that day and had yet to remove it. He explained to anyone who'd listen that his mother really meant for him to be named Rudy, but the person who filled out the birth certificate made a mistake. Instead of having the birth certificate corrected, his mother kept the name.

Ruby was no polished gem, that's for sure. He was more like the name of his own personal boat *Ruby In The Rough*. He looked, dressed and spoke like an old lumberjack. He was either smoking a cigarette, lighting his pipe or puffing on an old cigar. When he wasn't smoking tobacco, he was chewing it. Sometimes he did both at once. In spite of his outward appearance, Ruby had a heart of gold and a business mind of platinum. In contrast to the owner's appearance, *Ruby In The Rough*, a forty-two foot Owens, was one of the best kept, sharpest looking wooden boats on the bay. The boat was docked at the end of the gas pier and served as a marquee for what Ruby and his crew could do with an older wooden craft.

Ruby was especially popular among the watermen, many claiming he was the best mechanic around. So what the marina lacked in aesthetic appeal, it made up for in its reputation as a top notch boatyard. Cliff knew Ruby through his uncle and spent hours strolling the grounds of the marina while *Rose Bud* was being attended to by the boat doctor, as his uncle called the man. Over the years, the place proved to be a Mecca of opportunities for Cliff. The dilapidated boats and grounds gave the young artist many images to work with. He even did a painting of one of the oldest known boats in the area. It sat rotting in skids, neglected by its owner for several years. Ruby never removed it, claiming so long as the man paid the dry dock fee, the boat would remain in its place. "Besides," he told Cliff, "it gives the place some character. And we certainly need another character around here, don't we?" He always followed with his famous deep throat lumberjack laugh.

It was only natural that when Cliff decided he wanted to buy a boat he could live and work on, he turned to Ruby for help. Cliff smiled, remembering the initial conversation eight months earlier.

"You want to buy a WHAT?" Ruby bellowed.

"You heard me," Cliff returned, not surprised at the mariner's response.

"Did you fall and hit your head or something?" Ruby had yet to smile.

"No."

"You sick then?"

"No!"

"A sailboat! Why a sailboat if you don't mind me asking?" The frown had disappeared, but still no smile.

Cliff was prepared for the question, having asked himself the same many times. "Costs less than power. Good living space. Stable, so it will be a good working platform. Plus, cheaper to operate than a power boat."

"But you gotta know how to sail."

"I'll run under power till I learn."

"So slow." A large spit of tobacco landed between the boy and the man.

The ability to chew tobacco was a skill Cliff never mastered. He had tried twice and vomited vehemently after both. "Why do I have to go fast?"

"You've been down to the sailboat show and some sleazy salesman's got his fingers wrapped around you, ain't he?"

As anyone with any knowledge of the water knows, sailboats and powerboats do not mix well. The same was often true of their skippers. The rag haulers, as those depending on the effects of the wind were so politely called, complained about the noise and the wakes of their counterparts. Gas hogs, the term given to powerboats, complained about the sailboats' speed, or lack thereof. Powerboaters were especially bitter over the fact that sailboats had the legal right of way.

Uncle George sided with those adding value to the major oil companies, at least when conversing with his watermen cronies. In private, however, he often commented that sailboats added a beauty to the water unmatched by any other manmade structure. His uncle also pointed out that sailboats gave powerboaters something to complain about and that sailboaters ate crabs, too.

During these times, Cliff was indoctrinated into the mindset of anti-sail. That is until one day when a friend took him out on a small day-sailer and he experienced the thrill first hand. From that day on, he was a *twinner*—someone who went both ways—power versus sail that is.

"Can you help me or not?" he pressed of Ruby.

Another glob of tobacco landed beside the previous one. "The correct question, boy, is not can I, but will I? And that one you shouldn't even have to ask." This time a smile did form. "Even if you have lost your cotton-pickin' mind."

Once Ruby made the commitment to help Cliff, he dove in with both feet, learning everything he could about sailboats, and about the sailboat market. It took time, but he insisted Cliff was worth it. Besides, he admitted during one of his weaker moments that he was considering adding sailboats to his brokerage service. "There's a lot more *twinners* around here than you think," he said. "Besides, this place could always use a little more character."

Cliff pulled his thoughts back to the present. He drove through the marina until he came to the travel lift at the water's edge. He shut off the engine and leaned forward across the steering wheel. The stern of a large sailboat took up most of the view as it hung in the slings, its winged tipped keel only inches off the ground. She was a 34 foot Hunter, ten years old and in excellent condition. She was rigged so that both the jib and mainsail could be managed from the cockpit—one of the main prerequisites Cliff had for a boat. The freshly waxed hull glistened in the early morning light; the bottom held a fresh coat of anti-fouling paint.

Cliff and Ruby debated a variety of makes, models and sizes before deciding on the *Mona Lisa*. Big enough to offer protection in the unpredictable weather of the Chesapeake Bay, yet not too big she couldn't be crewed alone. Good condition. Not too pricey. And again, the boat could be handled completely from the cockpit. Cliff had been aboard several times but he had never seen her out of the water. She looked huge.

As he had done many times since deciding on this boat, he questioned whether he had gone too big. After all, this was his first boat; and again, he was inexperienced regarding the art of sailing. Ruby argued that docking and undocking would be done with the motor on, and that a sailboat under power was simply a powerboat with a big antenna. He also said that the only way to learn to sail was to get out there and do it.

Cliff felt well prepared. He read everything he could find in the library on sailboats. He had also been out a couple times on a friend's sailboat, and felt he had the bare basics under control. While he acknowledged he had much to learn, he felt he could at least set the sails without too much embarrassment. And as Ruby reminded, there was always the motor.

Ever since he had been out on the day-sailer, Cliff thought he'd like to try it again sometime. It always looked so peaceful, so serene. It was definitely a lot quieter. At the same time, there was a sense of excitement. Cliff often watched sailing on TV, especially the big events such as the America's Cup and coverage of the Whitbread, the around the world race. He wondered what it would be like to sail around the world. Heck, he'd be satisfied with a short excursion out in the ocean, or even an overnight stay.

While the ocean part wasn't going to happen any time soon, staying overnight was just a sunset away.

Cliff climbed out of the van and stepped aside as Chessie jumped out and ran up to the boat's keel. She sniffed the fresh paint. Then she turned and looked at Cliff, barking twice as she sat back on her hindquarters.

"Yes, girl, that's her all right." Cliff looked up at the name painted across the stern. "That's the *Mona Lisa* I've been telling you about."

The boat would never win a race, and she'd never sail around the world, but she was Cliff's—or soon would be, once he signed the final papers.

"I just hope I'm doing the right thing," Cliff muttered aloud.

"What'd you say there, chap?"

The voice at his back startled the boy. He turned and saw Ruby standing a few feet off his shoulder.

"Morning," Cliff said, ignoring the question. "You know, you shouldn't sneak up on people like that," he teased.

"If you weren't having a fine ole conversation with yourself, you'd a' heard me a' coming. I ain't no tippy-toe kind of a person, you know."

Cliff smiled as he turned and accepted the outstretched hand. "I wasn't talking to myself, I was talking to Chessie here."

"That's okay then… so long as you don't start expectin' ole Chessie to answer you back." Ruby reached into his pocket and pulled out a dog biscuit. Handing it to the eager animal, he said, "So Chessie, what do you think of Cliff here falling over the edge and going for a sailboat instead of a real boat?"

Chessie wisely chewed her treat without comment.

"Smart animal," Ruby laughed.

As usual, the man was dressed in overalls, a dirty tee shirt, no jacket in spite of the cool weather, and work boots. His head was capped with an old hat sporting the marina's name and logo of a Chesapeake Bay work boat. His hands were as aged as the marina itself, scarred, calloused and not many areas without dirt. He held a large Styrofoam cup of coffee in one hand. With the other, he motioned toward the hanging boat. "She's all ready," he said. "I was afraid it wouldn't warm up enough yesterday to paint the bottom, but we had a two hour window in the afternoon, so we got her done."

"Everything else finished?" Cliff inquired. There had been a list the marine surveyor recommended and the insurance company thus required. Most of the repairs had to do with the inside of the cabin. The surveyor, an avid sailor himself, also recommended a couple of changes in the rigging to make it easier for Cliff to handle everything single handed, including the installation of a roller furling on the jib.

"Yepper. We even got the door to the head glued back on tight." He took a long sip of his coffee and glanced over his shoulder. "If you repeat this, I'll tie an anchor to your waist and drop you overboard." He leaned in closer. "I think you got a real good boat here. She'll do you well."

"Even if it's a sailboat?"

"Even if it's a sailboat." Ruby draped his arm around Cliff's shoulder. "I might even let you invite me out for a ride one day."

Cliff laughed loudly. "Now who's fallen and hit their head?"

The marina owner smiled. "Fair 'nough... Fair 'nough." He finished the coffee and crunched up the cup before tossing it into a nearby barrel. "If you want to come up to the office and finish signing some papers, I'll have Andy drop her in the water. I want to leave her in the slings for at least thirty minutes to make sure the stuffing box is tight enough and there aren't any other leaks we don't know about. Then you can be on your way."

Cliff smiled. While Ruby spoke in a sincere and polite fashion, the message was clear. The boat may be Cliff's, but Ruby was still in command until he was sure everything checked out. It was not a new attitude, and had served Ruby well over the years. Only once, many years ago, did a boat owner argue with the marine owner and insist on deciding when he would take his boat away. Story goes the boat never made it past the mouth of Middle River before sinking from a sea cock being left open by the previous owner. Ruby was more than happy to salvage the vessel, and was more than happy to personally present the man with the bill covering the activities. The man, a well-known local business owner, wrote a check the moment he was handed the bill, and for the next twenty years, preached the gospel of Ruby Kelly, always ending with the statement, "The man saved my life, he did."

When anyone would inquire just how Ruby saved his life when all he really did was salvage the boat (the man actually swam to shore on his own), the man would add, "because if he hadn't gotten *Ms. Betsy* a running again, my wife would have killed me for sure."

"Okay," Cliff said. "I'll be up in a minute." As Ruby walked away, Cliff stood quietly a long moment, staring at the boat's transom. The letters in the boat's name blurred, came into focus and blurred again. Cliff wiped his eyes and dropped them to Chessie's head. The realization that the goal he'd set for himself was about to be reached slowly set in. A few more papers to sign and he'd be there.

"Come on, Chessie. Let's go sign our life away."

As if comprehending the statement, the dog turned and headed toward the trailer.

19

Forty minutes later, Andy and Ruby helped with the lines as Cliff guided the *Mona Lisa* away from the travel lift. Cliff nudged the throttle forward and turned the wheel to starboard. The *Mona Lisa* responded willingly. Andy claimed handling the *Mona Lisa* under power would be no problem for Cliff in that she behaved like a single engine trawler. The only thing missing would be the lack of power bursts used for docking. Cliff had been taught the bat-out-of-hell docking method—the waterman's way of doing business. This was not an option with the *Mona Lisa*. "Treat her like the beautiful woman she is," Ruby instructed. "Gentle and with tender loving care."

As the stern of the vessel cleared the last piling, Cliff eased the throttle forward. The noise increased as the prop dug into the water. Cliff looked back and saw the trail of water "At least you got a wake," he said aloud.

Chessie, who had been below deck staking out her quarters, climbed out of the galley way. She watched her master a moment and barked as she saw the marina shrink further into the background. She turned and climbed up onto the gunwales and made her way forward. She stuck her head under the bow rail and looked down at the water. She barked again before flopping down on the anchor hatch and burying her head in her paws.

"Glad to see you're so excited," Cliff shouted, laughing at the dog's nonchalant attitude. "Just wait till I put up the sails and we heel over."

They cleared the break water at the marina's entrance and throttled up to 2800 rpm. Cliff steered to port so the bow was headed directly for the red nun buoy marking the mouth of the creek. Once past the marker, they made a forty-five degree turn to starboard and headed out Middle River. By now, the morning was at full light and the thin layer of mist that protected the river from the night had burnt off. Visibility was so clear, Cliff could pick out the tree line of the Eastern Shore across the bay. He also noticed yet ignored a slight south-easterly breeze.

Chessie rose to her feet and made her way back to the stern. She propped her front paws up on the gunwale and tipped her head back.

"So what do you think about this here motorboat with curtains?" Cliff asked, reaching over and patting her on the head. The dog turned and looked at him. Her eyes said, "Too early to tell."

To reassure her, Cliff said, "Don't worry, ole girl. The *Mona Lisa* is going to be a pure powerboat for a while… at least till we get used to everything." Just as he finished speaking, a gust of wind crossed the port rail as the breeze picked up a knot or two. "It's going to be a beautiful day!"

Cliff made sure the boat was headed straight, checked the compass and flipped on the autopilot. He stood beside the wheel making sure the autopilot had not only engaged, but was awake enough to stay on course. It seemed to be working fine. He took a 360 degree sweep with his eyes. His was the only boat in sight. He climbed up on the foredeck to check the rigging, or so he told himself. The truth, he wanted to make sure he remembered just what all the lines, halyards and sheets were called, and to what they were connected. Surprisingly, his memory was good. His studying of a sailboat's anatomy had paid off. He just hoped he'd remember it all when the time came to put up the sails.

He draped his arm across the boom and glanced about. Yes indeed, it was a beautiful day. He smiled as the call of the breeze crossed his face. As the river widened, the wind picked up another couple knots. The call of the breeze continued. He hesitated, but only for a moment. With an extra snap to his step, he made his way to the mast and started unbuttoning the boom cover. He looked around the thick aluminum pole and shouted to Chessie, "Change of plans, girl. Prepare to set the sails."

20

The perfectly round sun dropped toward the tree line on the western shore of Worton's Creek. The afternoon breeze had subsided, leaving the air temperature nothing to do but drop as well. Cliff took bearings by sighting across the mast. Satisfied they had not drifted, he checked the anchor line one last time. He glanced skyward and saw the anchor light was visible. Allowing his eyes to focus further in the distance, he spotted an early star shining through the evening sky. He knew there'd be more to follow. It had always been a favorite pastime of his and his uncle's—watching the stars come out for the first time at night. While he knew the names of many, his uncle always knew more, and would often preach, "Even though we're in the bay, you should learn celestial navigation. You'll never know when you'll be blown out to sea."

"That's kind of hard in the upper part of the bay," Cliff always argued.

"Don't ever underestimate the weather," was always the reply.

Cliff was always amazed that man could navigate across the oceans using small specks of light that were light-years away. While he never bothered to learn the details of celestial navigation, he did understand the message buried in his uncle's comment: never underestimate mother nature.

Thinking of the weather, he refreshed his memory of the latest marine weather report. Winds would remain calm and the temperature would drop to the low 50's. He had already cranked up the alcohol stove, turning it up just enough to take the chill off the air. Otherwise, it was an ideal first night on board. They were in Worton's Creek, a popular Eastern Shore anchorage in the summer. Tonight, there was only one other boat in the creek, and Cliff was actually surprised to see that. It was a sailboat about the same size as the *Mona Lisa*, and from what Cliff could tell, was occupied by a man and a woman. He contemplated calling over to say hello, but decided he wanted to be alone his first night out. He pulled his collar tighter as he felt the temperature dropping with the sun. He finished tucking the *Mona Lisa* in for the night, checking the jib sheets and the mainsail cover. Almost forgetting, he tied the halyards off so they wouldn't clang against the mast if a breeze did come through.

He smiled, remembering his earlier struggles to fold the mainsail on top of the boom so the cover would fit. From the moment he decided to set the sails, the day had gone without major problems. Except for one unintended jibe, he made all the appropriate turns necessary to keep from running into the Eastern Shore. The wind was perfect and remained steady most of the day. He practiced what he had read, often repeating a particular move to gain the experience. There was plenty of space, few ships and only an occasional pleasure boat, so he was able to experiment at will. He quickly learned how the

Mona Lisa handled, and what she would and would not do. By the end of the day he felt he might even pass as a true rag hauler—a beginner, but still a sailor nonetheless.

Again, things went well until it was time to bring down the sails. The jib was no problem as it was on a roller furling. Pull a small line that ran along the starboard gunwale and the sail rolled itself right up. Ruby claimed it was one of the smartest devices ever invented for a sailboat. The mainsail, however, was the true test, and there Cliff failed miserably. He didn't remember reading that the sail was supposed to come down on top of him. After several minutes however, he managed to show the mainsail who was boss. It was his first day and he already learned that the worst part was *unsailing* the boat.

Satisfied the *Mona Lisa* was secure for the night, Cliff stretched out on the bow to watch the changing of the guard. It was his uncle's description of the sun setting and the darkness of the night taking over. It was their favorite time of the day. They would often take *Rose Bud* out to the mouth of Middle River and watch the fireball drop from the sky. It was a fascinating and peaceful sight. While some sunsets were more beautiful than others, tonight's was one of the best. He rubbed the top of Chessie's head. "Yeah, girl, we've seen prettier, but never from a more beautiful spot."

Chessie let out a soft moan in agreement.

Cliff had made a Swiss cheese and pickle sandwich earlier and now picked at the cheese falling off the bread. He held out a piece for Chessie who raised her head and took the offering without hesitation. Because of the excitement of the day, Cliff had eaten very little. Now that they were settled in for the night, he realized he was famished. He chewed slowly however, and concentrated on the phenomenon before them. As the sun completely disappeared, the sky changed from bright yellow to deep orange. Blues and grays soon took over as darkness further engulfed the area. The remaining light intertwined with low-lying clouds. The overall scene gave the appearance of a living kaleidoscope. Normally, this would have stimulated the artist into action. This evening, however, was different. This picture was for Cliff, and Cliff only. It was an original scene never to be duplicated. After all, there would never be another first night aboard the *Mona Lisa*.

With the changing of the guard nearly completed, Cliff turned his attention back to his sandwich which he finished except for the last bite. He offered it to Chessie, who didn't hesitate. "I know, girl," Cliff said, rubbing the dog behind the ears. "You want more than a bite of pickle flavored cheese. I'll feed you in a bit." The animal seemed satisfied with the response and settled her head onto her paws. She, too, was enjoying the moment.

The scene in front of Cliff blurred as he washed down the last bite with a swallow of Coke. He had no doubt selling *Loafer's Glory* and moving aboard the *Mona Lisa* was the right decision, but he still wondered about the sanity of it all. The work would be hard, the hours long and there'd be many lonely times. However, it was what he needed to do to succeed.

He had dreamed about being a live-aboard artist for a long time—a Huckleberry Finn so to speak, exploring the great Mississippi. Only instead of a river, there was place called the Chesapeake Bay. While he was happy the dream had come true, he was saddened over the cause that led to the effect. While many suns had set since his uncle's death, his heart still yearned for the times they spent together. He missed the noise. He missed the people. He missed the laughter. He missed his uncle.

Yet in many ways, his uncle was still with him. The man's voice rang out loud and often. As this particular day's end drew closer, his voice had grown even louder. "Doubt yourself once. Doubt yourself again. Then put the damn word away and just do it."

It was a similar theme passed on by Judge Donnelly and others. Cliff just wished he had the same confidence as everyone else. But like the mountaineers who yearned to climb Everest, Cliff knew he would never be satisfied until he tried.

His mind flashed back to Robin, to the boat, to the island... the storm... inside the boat. And later, rushing up into the house, nearly colliding with Robin's father. He remembered few details of the following week. He was at the funeral home several times. How he got there was unclear. He remembered little of the funeral itself, but he did remember being at the grave site, especially when a seagull landed on the grass a few feet away from where people had gathered around his uncle's casket. Uncharacteristically, the seagull was not spooked by the mass of people. It simply cocked its head to the side, looked at Cliff and nodded before flying away. It had come to pay its respects.

Cliff remembered people in the house afterward. There was a lot of talk about what was going to happen to *Loafer's Glory* and to Cliff. The conversations were all in whispers, but Cliff had good ears. He remembered having the same thoughts, silently asking the same questions. He remembered the reading of his uncle's will. There was no surprise that most of the estate, including *Loafer's Glory*, was left to him. His uncle had always told him that. The only exception was *Rose Bud* which had been promised a long time ago to St. Michael's Maritime Museum. Cliff knew that, too. *Rose Bud* was the last bay boat built by the St. Michaels Boat Works before the business closed. The only stipulation in the will was that Cliff had to care for Chessie for the remainder of her life. Cliff knew about that stipulation as well, not to ensure Cliff doing his part, but to ensure finances were available for the dog. Cliff's uncle wanted the estate's trustees to know that Chessie was important, also.

A nudging beneath his arm broke Cliff's train of thought. He reached down and patted Chessie atop the head. "You hear me thinking about you, huh?" The animal purred in agreement. His tongue licked at Cliff's hand.

"I know," Cliff acknowledged. "You need something more to eat." The dog lapped at the outstretched hand again. Cliff rose to his feet. "Well, you want dinner or dessert?"

Chessie barked twice.

Cliff laughed. "Dessert it'll be."

A few minutes later both were sitting in the cockpit munching on Oreo cookies and peanut butter. Even before his uncle's death, Cliff had always watched his own diet as well as that of the dog. He was even more cognizant as his body changed from boy to young man. Except for seafood of course, he remained a vegetarian. He knew watching their diet was especially important with both being cooped up on the boat. But tonight he decided to splurge. He dunked an Oreo cookie into the peanut butter and held it out to Chessie. She wasn't thinking much about her diet either.

One more cookie apiece and Cliff tightened the lid on the jar of peanut butter. He leaned back against the forward bulkhead. The temperature continued to drop with the darkening sky. It would be a good night for sleeping, he thought. He rubbed Chessie along the spine. She let out a cat-like purr.

The sound of ducks overhead broke the ambiance as four birds flew low across the water. They circled the *Mona Lisa* once before landing in perfect unison about fifty feet off the stern. Chessie rose to her feet and barked at the intruders. They ignored her warning and started swimming toward the vessel. "M R ducks," Cliff said, quoting from a famous Ocean City eatery. Chessie sounded the alarm again but to no avail. Realizing her efforts were fruitless, she disappeared below deck and returned with a loaf of bread pinched between her teeth. Cliff chuckled as he accepted the package. "You getting wise in your old age? Fatten 'em up before you attack." The ducks didn't seem to be worried about their diet as they made quick work of the broken pieces of bread. When their bellies were full, they swam away, disappearing into the darkness. Cliff looked out across the creek. The only thing that could now be seen of the other sailboat was her anchor light and a faint light coming from the cabin. The changing of the guard was now complete.

Cliff made one last check to make sure everything was intact before heading below for the night. He filled Chessie's food bowl, made sure she had water, flipped on the overhead light and partially closed the galleyway hatch. He moved forward to the V berth and pulled out the duffle bag containing his clothes. He looked around and smiled. Carol Granger had been right, there wasn't a lot of room left.

The *Mona Lisa* was 34 feet long. She sported a wide beam, giving her extra room below deck. Forward, the V berth was designed to sleep two, or in this case store all of Cliff's personal belongings and extra food. Next was the head that included a stand-up shower—a prerequisite as Cliff reviewed various cabin layouts. Across from the shower was a small sink and mirror. A narrow walkway led to the main salon. A sitting booth occupied the starboard side. The surface area of the tabletop gave Cliff plenty of room to work. A narrow couch lined the port wall and would serve as Cliff's bed. The galley was in the rear of the salon right below the steps leading topside. It included a two burner alcohol stove, double sink and a large ice box. The walls above the galley were lined with cabinets, small but adequate. The aft cabin was a double bed, although the ceiling was low because of the cockpit floor above. This was where Cliff stored his camera gear and art supplies. A series of bungee cords held everything in place.

Cliff cleaned up the galley, grabbed a soda and slid into the booth. He pulled a sketch pad from a folder setting on the overhead shelf. The book was full of drawings in various stages of completion. He opened it to an unfinished drawing of the shore lines on Middle River. He tried working underway earlier, but while his enthusiasm was real, his ability to concentrate wasn't. He found himself constantly looking up. He figured once he became more comfortable with the boat and once he developed faith in the autopilot, he'd be better able to work under sail. His plan was to do photographs and rough sketches during the day and finish the drawings at night. His ability to paint would be dependent on the temperature and humidity. It was a well thought out plan. The question was how easily could fantasy become reality?

He sharpened a pencil and started shading in the water beneath a pier. He told himself to concentrate. His mind focused on the drawing before him. He worked steadily as the reality of the situation settled in. He was indeed living his dream. He was a live-a-board artist. Everything was perfect except he missed his uncle.

Chessie, who had curled up beneath the table, stuck her head up between the seat and table top. Cliff swore the dog winked at him as if to say, "Don't worry, I'm still here." It reminded Cliff of another popular saying of his uncle. "Just because you can't see something, doesn't mean it's not there."

The wave of sadness faded. Chessie inched her head forward and nuzzled a cold nose against Cliff's leg. He patted her on the head and said aloud, "Yeah, I know, girl. I miss him, too." He looked toward the rear hatch which was partially open. Lowering his head, Cliff could see a few stars in the distance. They too seemed to be winking. "But he's here with us, I know he is," the artist added. "Aren't you, Uncle George?"

And so he was.

21

While the night proved chilly as anticipated, Cliff took it all in stride. The alcohol stove proved more than capable of keeping the cabin warm. Cliff never minded the cold when crabbing with his uncle, but that was physical work and if anything, the cooler the better. Working on his art, however, was different.

He worked without pause until after 1:00 am. He was tired when they first anchored for the night, but he quickly caught a second wind. By the time he stopped he had finished several drawings. He was never one to rush his work, but he knew from the past weekend he had to do a better job of keeping up his inventory. Climbing into his sleeping bag, he reminded himself he would have to work long and hard to do so. It was a challenge he was ready to tackle.

Cliff expected he'd have trouble sleeping the first few nights, especially being anchored instead of tied to a dock. He was wrong as he was fast asleep in five minutes. The next thing he heard was a flock of geese overhead. He opened his eyes as sunlight poured in through the side porthole. He sat up, almost banging his head on the ceiling above. He yawned and stretched, and went up on deck. The other sailboat had already left. He checked the landmarks on shore. Their own position had not changed. The anchor held true. He stretched again and smiled. He could already feel the air warm as the sun lifted off the horizon. The sky was totally clear as a gentle breeze swept through the cove. It was going to be a beautiful day.

Chessie followed Cliff topside. She walked around the gunwales as if to see for herself that everything was okay. She stuck her head over the side at several spots and looked into the water. Back in the cockpit she looked up at Cliff, who laughed saying, "You got two choices, girl. You can swim ashore or do you want me to make you up a litter box like a cat?"

The retriever tilted her head to the side as if insulted. She barked, climbed down to the swim platform off the stern and jumped into the water. Cliff watched as she swam ashore. Shaking out her fur, she sniffed around before finding a satisfactory spot. Soon she was back in the water swimming toward the boat. To her surprise, the four ducks from the day before landed between her and the *Mona Lisa*. Chessie barked and started swimming harder. Like yesterday, the ducks ignored her and headed for the boat. Cliff had already gone below to make coffee. He came back up with a fresh cup and a loaf of bread. Chessie chased the ducks around the boat a couple times, but they refused to leave. If she got too close, they'd simply fly a few feet ahead. They even got wise and split up so the poor dog didn't have a chance. Watching the action, Cliff wondered if the dog was actually trying to catch them, or was just having fun. He guessed the latter.

Their bellies full, the ducks picked an imaginary runway out the creek, took off and disappeared over the trees. Chessie swam to the back of the boat and climbed up onto the platform. Shaking out her fur, she slopped down to catch her breath. Cliff looked over the side and said, "You didn't have a chance, girl. They can fly." He laughed. Chessie just panted.

Cliff went below for more coffee. He contemplated fixing breakfast, but decided on a breakfast bun instead. He was anxious to get underway. He chuckled softly. Ruby would have a fit if he knew Cliff was already preparing for his *second* day of sailing. Fifteen minutes later, the *Mona Lisa* was headed out of Worton's Creek. The mainsail and jib were both up, and surprising for this time of day, full of air. As the distance from shore to shore widened, the wind picked up. The breeze came out of the north, but Cliff knew that was likely to change as the day progressed. Soon the *Mona Lisa* was heeling to port. Cliff looked over his shoulder. The sun was now breaking over the tree line. Long thin rays of rainbow colors bounced off the water's surface as sparkles of light glistened off the sandy beach. It was a very picturesque scene. As he already had a camera draped around his neck, he checked to make sure all was clear ahead before snapping off a quick half-roll of film. He didn't realize it at the time, but the photographs would lead to the first full drawing ever done aboard the Mona Lisa. It would also be a gift for a couple of dear friends.

Photo op completed, he turned his attention forward. He had no specific agenda except to improve his sailing skills while building up his portfolio. As for specific destinations, he had no plan there either. Where the wind blew is where they would go. His uncle used to say that crabbing was farming the sea. Cliff figured he was in a sense farming as well. His only desire was to see as many ports-of-call as possible to ensure a variety of work.

He turned the wheel to starboard to make sure he cleared the red can buoy marking the entrance of the creek. A gust of wind caught the mainsail and the boat heeled over. "Woo baby," Cliff cautioned as he fought the vessel's urge to fall off course. The gust passed and the *Mona Lisa* came back upright. Looking down at the buoy, Cliff saw the tide was already ebbing heavily. He estimated at least two knots of current down the bay.

Chessie laid her head back over the port side rail. An occasional splash wet her face. She would bark softly and shake her head as the cold water stung her skin, all the while waiting for the next splash.

"Chessie," Cliff said. "Which way you want to go, girl? Tide's running out, so we'll make better speed if we head south." Another spray of water splashed across the dog's face. This time she barked even louder. "You like that, huh? We'll stay on this course then."

So south they went. Cliff spent the next several hours experimenting with sail settings and boat direction. His comfort level rose as did his confidence. Noon found them just three miles north of the Chesapeake Bay Bridge, the same set of bridges depicted in the painting he had sold to the little old lady two days earlier. He had been down here several times on *Rose Bud*, but seeing the bridges come into view the first time aboard the *Mona Lisa* was something else. Never had the two bridges looked so ominous, and never had the steel towers supporting the main spans looked so close together. He reminded himself the target was much bigger than it appeared and lined the bow up with the center of the north span. He knew the only way to convince himself of his ability was to actually sail through. After all, if it was a wide enough area for a large ship, certainly the *Mona Lisa* could squeeze through. Cliff chuckled at the thought, mouthing aloud, "I'd rather be at the helm of a large ship right about now."

A gust of wind knocked them off course. He righted the boat and redirected the bow. "Settle down and concentrate," he muttered.

Three miles equaled nearly a half hour sailing. Still, the minutes passed quickly as the steel structures loomed larger and larger. There were additional gusts of wind, and even a subtle change in the wind's direction. This was an expected occurrence in this section of the bay and Cliff took it all in stride. As they reached the north bridge, Cliff's heart started beating faster. He gripped the stainless steel wheel as tight as possible, but it still seemed slippery. Traffic overhead was light, so there was little noise to distract him. With a blink of the eye, shadows passed overhead and they were under the first span. He adjusted course, took aim and passed beneath the south bridge a short time later. When he looked back, the bridges looked more like the dimensions he remembered. A broad smile crossed his face. "We did it, Chessie. We did it."

Chessie, asleep on the foredeck beneath the shadows of the jib, had been oblivious to the whole experience.

Cliff turned down the bay before again looking back over his shoulder. The sunlight reflected off the steel beams like rays from a space gun. He held his hand over his eyes as his pupils dilated in response. He looked again and realized that while the light was indeed very bright, the resulting shadows spreading out across the water were awesome.

Another spur of the moment decision and he yelled up to Chessie to prepare to come about. Awakened from a sound sleep, the dog took a moment to get her feet beneath her. Regaining her sea legs, she made her way back to the cockpit where she waited to see just what Cliff meant by his command. She recognized the words from the day before. Each time it resulted in a lot of noise, her master pulling and cranking on a lot of lines and the boat suddenly tipping the other way. She never remembered all this hoopla on board *Rose Bud*.

The tack was accomplished with minimal difficulty, and soon they were running parallel to the bridges. "Keep a close eye out on traffic," Cliff told Chessie. "Especially big stuff," Cliff added. Chessie wagged her tail at the directions. She still didn't understand, but she was smart enough to pretend. Satisfied all the commotion was over, she made her way forward where she took her position of watch.

They spent the next two hours sailing back and forth parallel to the south bridge. A third hour was spent between the two spans, and an additional hour on the north side. During this time, Cliff shot several rolls of film and sketched out a dozen or so *partials*— rough drawings outlined only to depict the basic concept of the work. The finer details, including the addition of color if used, would be added later.

With the aging of the day, the sun started its trek towards the western horizon. The cloud cover increased and the light changed such that Cliff was no longer satisfied with the available shots. He guided the *Mona Lisa* back through the center spans, this time without any noticeable anxiety. He bent his head back for one last look at the massive steel structure just as the mast cleared the span. He was about to look ahead when he caught a flicker of movement. He squinted as he shaded his eyes. There was someone up there!

As if he had been doing it all his life, Cliff came about and headed back toward the bridges. At the last moment he tacked and set a course parallel to the structures. He pulled out his Nikon with the telescopic lens. Looking upward, he saw a lone figure sitting on a beam. The man was dressed in coveralls, his feet dangling nonchalantly over the side. He had a cigarette in one hand while painting with the other. He looked down at Cliff as Cliff looked up at him. Cliff watched the workman until the scene brightened as a cloud overhead cleared the sun. He quickly snapped off several shots. He saw the figure nod and wave his brush hand. Cliff returned the greeting. The artist wondered how long the man had been up there. Cliff hadn't seen him earlier. He guessed the man had been watching him. One artist watching another. The only difference was the size of the canvas.

Another nod, another wave and Cliff turned due south, setting the sails accordingly. He figured he had a couple of hours to decide where to go for the night. He told himself not to worry and to enjoy the rest of the day. After all, the guard was just starting to change.

22

They rode in silence as April stared out the side window and watched the luxurious homes pass by. Each was architecturally unique, but to April, they were all similar piles of brick mortared together in an ornate fashion. While true, her own residence was included in this mix, the Worthington home did not seem to be as fixated on protrusions, intrusions, angles and dangles of brick like the others. On top of this, all the houses seemed to be jammed together. Even their trailer, as old and rundown as it was, had plenty of room around it.

The car bounced hard in response to a small but strategically placed pothole. Instinctively, April brought her eyes back forward. She bit her lower lip out of nervousness and locked her fingers tightly in her lap. Eddie Richmond was driving way too fast for her taste. She didn't know if this was his normal pace or if he was just showing off. She guessed a little of both.

As he did on a near daily basis, he pulled up beside her right after she got off the school bus. The question was always the same: did she want a ride? Her response was always the same: no, thanks. Except for today, when she impulsively said just the opposite. Her response shocked the Richmond boy as much as she surprised herself. He recovered quickly and took off down the street as soon as she was buckled in.

April did steal a glance around the inside of the car. It was all black including the leather seats. The sun was shining so there was a glare off the polished dashboard. Like the outside of the vehicle, the inside was very clean. No surprise there as the car was as meticulously cared for as the driver. Besides being naturally handsome, Eddie was well *cropped*, as the girls in school called it. His blonde hair was cut stylishly short. He was clean shaven, and when in the right frame of mind, could throw a grin at you that traveled from ear to ear. A gold necklace surrounded his neck, although the well developed muscles threatened to challenge the jewelry's circumference. He wore a maroon dress shirt without a tie, and khaki pants. For a jacket, he wore his varsity sweater, a big *W* sewn across the left pocket area. Like April's stepbrother, Eddie was a jock, only unlike Danny Worthington, Eddie wasn't shy about living up to the meaning of the word.

Music blared from the radio, a rap song April had heard many times before coming from her brother's room. She did not recall the name of the artist, but the vocalist was one of the popular ones, especially among the boys. Much of April's world centered around music. She still failed to understand the attraction to this style of poetry with a beat, she called it. She had to admit the car's stereo system was certainly superior to the CD player in her bedroom. She wondered what it would be like to listen to classical music on such a system—Beethoven's Fifth Symphony perhaps.

Barely slowing at a stop sign, Eddie said over the blaring of the alleged music, "You are going to go to the dance with me on Friday, aren't ya?"

April turned her head toward him. "What?"

He turned the radio down a few decibels before repeating the question, this time adding, "What time do you want me to pick you up?"

She was stunned at his forwardness, although not really surprised. After all, he might be the biggest star in school, he was also the most obnoxious. While all of the girls in April's class *just died* over him, she found Eddie quite nauseating and disgusting. Unfortunately, his feelings toward her were quite different. He had been overheard saying in the hallway just that afternoon, "She's just one hot cherry waiting to be plucked, and I'm going to do the plucking."

His boasting got back to April, and perhaps the reason she got in the car with him was simply to prove him wrong. She was not going to be plucked, by him or anyone else.

"You're a jerk," she said. The second surprise of the afternoon was her ability to say such a thing.

He smiled, pleased to have at least gotten some response from her. "You know, babe, you don't know how lucky you are. I've got girls lined up waiting... no, begging me to take them to the dance. Friday's lacrosse game is the state championship, and once we kick South Western's ass... what a dance and party it will be. You don't want to miss that, do you?" Besides football, he and Danny were both stars on the lacrosse team.

April turned her head toward him and said, "What makes you think you'll beat South Western?"

He laughed loudly before his expression turned serious. "All my old man has ever wanted was for me to win a championship. And by God, no piddle school like South Western is going to get in the way."

"What do you want?" April challenged. Danny had confided in her that what really motivated Eddie was a passionate desire to please his father.

"It's what I want, too," Eddie responded. He gave her an ear to ear grin. "And I always get what I want."

April's fine ear in music also gave her the skill to pick up subtleties in the spoken word. She wasn't convinced with the first part of Eddie's response. The second part frightened her.

Her mother always told her to look for something positive in a person. She had tried numerous times with Eddie, always coming up empty. Today was no different.

Or was it? Did he just show her a vulnerability she never before noticed?

She stared in silence, her mind swirling with questions. Was there more to Eddie than the *chick magnet* sitting beside her. There was a piece of the puzzle missing, but what was it? More importantly, how could she go about finding it?

A thought developed... a scary thought. She broke off eye contact when she realized he was not watching the road. He whipped into her court and came to a screeching halt in front of her house. She struggled for something to say. Just a moment ago, she wanted to put him in his place. Now, she wanted to ask questions, personal questions restricted to close friends.

And she and Eddie certainly didn't fall into that category.

She decided silence was the best comment. She gathered her books and pushed open the door.

"I like the silent type," Eddie said.

She hesitated, her mind still searching for something to say. Again, her lips remained sealed.

He called out as she started to walk away. "Since you can't decide, I'll pick you up at 7:30. Wear something sexy, too. Okay?"

She stormed into the house, her irritation at his arrogance rising. She told herself not to be angry. She told herself not to obsess over him. He wasn't worth the effort.

Or was he? The earlier thought continued to develop.

A chill went up her spine. The thought of such an occurrence frightened her. At the same time there was a sense of curiosity, a sense of enjoyment. After all, the ride home had been nice for a change, for no other reason than it was different. She had never been on a date. There wasn't anyone interested in her that she knew of. Sure, boys talked to her, but it was usually to ask about homework. She was number one in her class. They seldom talked to her otherwise. She didn't have many girlfriends, unlike everyone else who seemed to have tons. April wasn't close to anyone except Danny. She did feel close to him. She was leery about saying too much to him, however. They were close, but not that close. The last thing she wanted was to cross some imaginary boundary that would damage what they had.

She thought about asking her mother. It seemed, however, the new Mrs. Worthington had little time for her daughter of late, especially with all her social engagements and club activities. She had even taken up golf, and from what April's stepfather said, was getting quite good, too. April also recognized her mother was getting good at other aspects of her new life—aspects not all that favorable in April's opinion. She was smelling alcohol on her mother's breath more and more. At first, April shrugged it off to the excitement of a new husband and new environment. As time passed, however, the newness wore off, but her mother's method of showing her excitement continued. No, April didn't feel she could depend on her mother's advice.

Her stepfather was out of the question in that he was already biased. The pressure from him to go out with Eddie was subtle, yet put forth at every opportunity. Heaven help her if he found out she had actually been in the car with the boy. He'd probably throw a celebration party. He had thrown parties for lesser reasons.

She considered Sally, Danny's girlfriend, and decided it was not a bad idea. Sally had taken her under her wing when she first came to Worthington Valley. She introduced April around and gave her the scoop on who was hot and who was not. The problem there, Eddie was on her hot list, along with Danny, of course. Subsequently, April questioned her ability to be objective.

Her thoughts returned to Danny. Even though he was Eddie's best friend, could he give her straight advice? Why not, she asked. After all, he also helped her when she first came to town. Besides, of everyone she knew, he had his head screwed on the straightest. He had other interests besides impressing and pursuing the opposite sex. For one, he took his schoolwork seriously. For another, he loved to spend time outdoors, up in the mountains behind their community. He had even started taking April along and teaching her *the ways of the wild*, as he called it.

But there was still the risk…

She dropped her books on the foyer table. Instead of following her usual routine of heading into the living room to practice the piano before starting her homework, she ran up the stairs to see if Danny was even home yet. Risk or not, she was anxious to talk to him.

She heard loud music as she approached the second floor landing. He was in his room. Practice must have ended early. Her enthusiasm built. She paused to catch her breath before hurrying toward the doorway at the end of the hall. She passed her room and glanced in. She saw the maid had been in. Her bed was freshly made and the sheets turned down. She smiled at the sight of two mints lying a top her pillow. It was a small yet thoughtful gesture, and April looked forward to the weekly treat.

Her room was quite spacious, at least in her mind. Danny's, however, was huge, taking up the entire area above the three car garage. Mr. Worthington had put him up there the year before she and her mother arrived as a way of buffering his loud music from polluting the rest of the house.

Reaching the end of the hall, she knocked on the door. Simultaneously she turned the knob and walked in. She took two steps before coming to a sudden halt. Her eyes widened at the sight before her. Sally and Danny were naked on the bed. Danny was laying back, his arms holding onto the headboard. Sitting at his side, Sally was bent over him, her head buried in his groin.

The girl did not realize they had a visitor. Danny, however, saw the door open and saw his stepsister come into view. He was as startled as she. The color drained out of her face. His reddened like a long day in the sun. April stared a moment, then turned as bile crept up into her mouth. She ran down the hall. The earlier excitement was gone; earlier questions were ignored.

"April," she heard him call. She ignored him, her mind telling her legs to keep moving. And so they did.

23

April sat with her arms wrapped around her legs, her chin resting on her knees. She pressed her back against the cool wall of the tree house as the late afternoon breeze crept through the boards. While the structure was sturdy, there was ample motion of the branches. She pulled her sweater over her knees. She was tired and drained of energy. She was hungry and she was thirsty. All sensations, however, were ignored. She stared straight ahead, trying to empty her mind of the thoughts swirling around her. While they were distorted and out of focus, they were clear enough to be recognized.

Naked bodies, all boys, all faceless, arms outstretched, coming at her—dark dreary figures circling like vultures. She screamed, which startled them, allowing her enough time to escape, but not before falling and striking her head. Then a sudden change of scenes. More images—one girl facing away, one boy facing forward, both oblivious to anyone's presence. What was she doing to him?

Disgusting!

Why was she doing it?

Even more repulsive.

The boy's face came into focus. It was Danny. He was looking at her. His lips started to move as if trying to say something. She listened closer. He was calling her name. "April… April… April."

April shook her head and blinked several times.

"April… are you okay?"

She focused into the near darkness. Danny's head was poking through the floor of the tree house. She turned her head away and swallowed. The urge to scream competed with the urge to vomit. She buried her head in her arms.

Danny climbed the rest of the way into the tree house and sat in the corner across from her. He pulled a box out from beneath a pile of blankets and soon a lantern lit up the small space. They sat in silence as the heat from the lantern slowly took the chill off the air. Finally, she sat up straight. "How'd you know I was here?" she asked.

"If you were a fox, a hound would have you in a heartbeat."

"Well, it isn't as if I was running away or anything," she said defensively. "If I didn't want you to find me, you wouldn't have."

"Maybe," he conceded. The thought sent a spark up his spine. He pulled a bottle of water from his coat pocket and handed it to her along with an energy bar. She hesitated before accepting the two items. Over the past couple years, he often took her with him into the mountains outside Worthington Valley. He always loved the outdoors, even as a young boy. The older he became, the more time he spent in the woods—hunting, exploring, tracking and hiding.

Hiding was his favorite. He hid from no one in particular, but just to see if he could avoid being followed. If he came upon someone else, he'd follow them. Stalking was a type of hiding, he said. He learned how to survive in the wild by reading extensively, and by trial and error. He learned what to eat, what not to eat and how to purify water. He even learned how to find water when there was no apparent source. He loved the concept of living totally off the land. Regardless of the season, regardless of the weather, he spent part of most weekends in the mountains. It was his way of escaping the pressures of the world down in the valley—Worthington Valley.

He initially took April along after making a deal with her that she'd be quiet and stop asking so many questions about what he did with his free time. To his surprise, April took an immediate liking to the outdoors. While resistant to her tagging along at first, his reluctance diminished when he discovered she was a quick learner, and was in far better physical condition than he initially thought. On top of that, she never imposed herself on him when she sensed he really wanted to be alone. She was the first person he knew who seemed genuinely interested in the physical and mental advantages of being outside. Danny was able to deal with the many rigors of growing up in Worthington Valley because of his time in the mountains. Not that he was a total loner—he could party with the best of them—but he also liked the solitude that came with dating nature and liked the challenges of surviving in the woods. He liked the adventure, albeit it many times imaginary.

As April grew more astute in the ways of the woods, Danny was able to leave her alone. It became fun having someone to play *fox and hound* with, a game he designed to further hone his tracking and evading skills. He had to admit, she was getting quite good at both sides of the game. The previous weekend, it took him nearly a half a day to find her.

He built the tree house when he was in middle school. It took over two years to haul the lumber the mile or more up the mountainside behind their development. The tree he selected was a large pine situated well off the main fire path. It was buried in a group of other trees, yet it was tall enough he could see a hundred yards or more in every direction. When it was finished, and camouflaged properly, no one standing on the ground could tell there was a manmade structure buried in the branches. Danny used it as a base camp for weekend excursions deeper into the forest, and once old enough, spent nights there as well. He always called his father from his cellphone to let him know he was okay, simply saying he was somewhere on the mountainside. The tree house was his private place that no one knew about except April.

April fell in love with the hideaway the first time there. To Danny's surprise, she did nothing to change the decor, which consisted of an old piece of carpeting covering the floor, a couple crates for tables, and an ice chest used to store dry goods. A waterproof trunk stored extra clothes and sleeping bags. She thought it was fine just the way it was. It was not uncommon for him to come out and find April already there, usually reading or doing her homework. Even in the summer, it quickly became her favorite place to go. As long as she kept the place a secret, and was able to travel up the mountain without anyone following her (except him, of course), he didn't complain. Deep down, he was thrilled to have someone to share his love for the outdoors. Fishing and hunting were beneath his friends at school, including Sally who didn't want any part of anything that might mess up her nails.

"If you weren't running, why are you here?" Danny said.

"Same reason as always."

"You don't have any books with you, so it can't be to study."

April started to say something, but realized it was fruitless.

"What were you doing home so early?" Danny asked.

"School was out."

"You got home earlier than normal."

"Eddie gave me a ride from the bus stop," April said nonchalantly.

"He what?"

She looked up for the first time. "I said he gave me a ride home."

Danny could not keep the surprised look from his face. He was able to bite his tongue before he said something stupid. Instead, "That was nice of him."

"He bugs me every day. I did it just to get him off my back."

Danny shrugged his shoulders.

April hesitated. "He keeps bugging me to go to the dance with him, too."

"He's really not a bad guy once you get to know him. He's like ice cream with that magic chocolate sauce you like—hard and crunchy on the outside, but all sweet and soft on the inside."

"Ice cream is cold."

"You get my point."

"Yeah, I get your point. What I don't get is why he just doesn't leave me alone."

"You're a challenge," Danny said. "You're the only fish in the sea who hasn't been caught."

"What do you mean *caught*?"

"Hasn't been caught by the lure of Eddie Richmond."

"What's there to catch?" April said.

"In reality, probably nothing. In the fantasy world all us teenagers live in, who knows? Sometimes you can't define it. It's just there, like a fad, like a magnet drawing you in before you even realize what's happened."

"Like drugs?"

"I really wouldn't know… Nice try though, Sis." He always called her Sis when he wanted something.

April ignored this and remained focused on her thought process. "How about…" She hesitated.

"How 'bout what?" Danny encouraged.

Her voice softened more than usual. "Sex—is that a fad?"

His mouth dropped open and he cursed under his breath. While they had spent many hours together talking about many things, the topic never turned personal. He never asked her details about her past and she never quizzed him about life before his mother died. With the exception of superficial comments about Sally, they definitely never talked about each other's relationships—or lack thereof, in April's case.

He closed his mouth and swallowed hard. "April…" That was all he could get out.

"Is it really all it's made up to be?" April asked.

"Is what?"

"You know, what I just said."

"Sex?"

Danny thought a moment, making sure his words were organized and appropriate. "It can be, with the right person."

"How do you know who's the right person?"

"You just know."

"There are certainly a lot of *right persons* floating around Worthington High," April mocked.

"Maybe some don't fit into what I'm talking about," Danny conceded.

"How 'bout most?"

"Whatever."

"I'm not like those other girls," April said softly.

"No one said you were."

"I thought Sally and I were… well, I'm not like any of them. I don't do those sorts of things. I'm not a…"

"Sally's not either," Danny snapped.

"I didn't mean…" At a loss for words, April started to cry.

"Just what are you then?" Danny said a little too sharply. The tears increased. "April!"

She stared him in the eye. "I'm April Blackstone, period. Is there anything wrong with that?"

She left her sitting position and crawled to the hole in the floor. She made her way down to the bottom of the ladder. A four foot drop and she was on the ground. Pulling the sweater around her neck, she headed toward the fire path. She heard Danny hit the ground a few moments after he turned out the lantern. There was a pause as he pulled the ladder up into its hiding place. Then his footsteps could be heard behind her. She increased her pace, but he caught up with her a hundred feet or so down the trail. He reached out and grabbed her arm. She knew any attempts to pull away would be futile. After all, while her strength and stamina had improved, she was still no match for one of Worthington High's star athletes. She slowed her pace. Coming up beside her, he draped his arm over her shoulder and gave her a squeeze. "Come on Sis, let's go home. I've got studying to do."

"Bullshit," she muttered.

He laughed loudly at her uncommon use of profanity. "But I do. Coach gave us a whole pile of new plays to learn by practice tonight. Besides, I know you haven't practiced the piano yet. What's that new piece you've been working on?"

Her tears stopped with his inquiry. "Which one is that?"

"I don't know the names. You know, the song they play for the airline commercial. I think it's United."

She chuckled. "That's *Rhapsody in Blue*, you dimwit."

"Funny name for a commercial jingle."

"Double dimwit." She couldn't help but laugh at his ignorance about music, at least real music.

They made their way down the mountain in silence. Shadows were lengthening as darkness was already starting to engulf the area. Even though they had made the trip many times, each step was taken with care. Like Danny preached, a sprained ankle in the wilderness could be deadly. There were many more questions April wanted to ask—the same questions she had been thinking about for a long time. In the past, she had been able to subdue such thoughts, telling herself what she had just told Danny: she was different from the others. Her surplus energy was directed towards her music. That was the focus of her life. Lately, however, she found herself thinking more and more about other things, things she had never really thought about before, things she had never experienced before, things she thought repulsive.

The image of Sally and Danny in bed together came into view. It was repulsive, wasn't it? A twinge of curiosity, a twinge of jealously shot up her spine. Her knees suddenly felt weak. She snapped her thoughts back into focus. Now was not the time to be losing her concentration. Another time, she decided. Then reconsidering, she said aloud, "Do you think I should go to the dance with Eddie?"

24

April lay staring up at the ceiling, her hands folded behind her head. The only noise in the room was the hum of her electric clock and the sound of her own breathing. Earlier, a few decibels of her stepbrother's music filtered beneath the door, but that had ceased many minutes before. No doubt Danny was sleeping soundly like he always did after a hard day's practice. She thought he would have been more anxious with the big game being only two days away. However, when he got home from the evening practice, he was calm and nonchalant as usual. He sat in the living room and finished his homework while listening to her play the piano, something she noticed he had been spending more and more time doing of late. He claimed it was simply because he liked her music. She knew it had to be something more. She didn't pursue the point, satisfied with his interest. Besides, she always felt she played better with an audience.

She tossed and turned for over an hour. It was most uncharacteristic for her in that once she went to bed, sleep usually came quickly. Tonight was different. Tonight, in spite of her best efforts, sleep had yet to arrive. The events of the day kept flowing through her mind. First, the ride home with Eddie, next the discovery of Danny and Sally, then the trip to the tree house and subsequent walk home. Initially, she told herself she should be angry. Once the shock wore off, her anger was short lived. The fact that Danny came up to the tree house to find her showed he cared. Any negative emotions were erased. In a weird kind of way, she felt closer to her stepbrother than ever before. She wondered if he felt the same.

She continued her stare. A figure seemed to form on the ceiling. It was blurry at first before slowly coming into focus. The figure was a female. She was dressed in a long silvery gown. Her hair was curled and piled atop her head. She had a broad smile across her face and her makeup—her makeup was minimal as there was little need to enhance her natural beauty. Pearl earrings hung from each earlobe and a matching necklace circled her neck. The gown was cut low and showed the figure off nicely—a bit too nicely, April thought. She concentrated back on the image's face.

She looked away and sat up in the bed with a start. She rubbed her eyes. Had she been dreaming, or just imagining? It didn't matter, the results were the same. The figure was her.

Or was it? April would never dress up like that, nor would she ever have a reason to. While she never downplayed her looks, she never dwelled on them either. Her mother always told her how pretty she was. While the woman was careful never to make promises, she often talked about the day she'd be able to buy her daughter pretty dresses. April had dreamed of the same. Yet now that the dream was possible, she continued, as her stepbrother teased, the same *plain Jane* look. Baggy tops, jeans and tennis shoes were the norm. She seldom wore make up or jewelry except earrings on occasion.

Her attire represented her personality, or at least the personality she wanted to convey. On the surface, she was plain, simple and uncomplicated. While she was clean and lived healthy, flashiness was not part of her picture. Her energies focused on her music and school. She had been a straight A student before moving to Worthington Valley. That had not changed, much to the chagrin of some classmates. At Worthington High, straight A's were not cool. Since the move, she was exposed to much more than she ever dreamed. Opportunities for change were rampant. Actual change was minimal. She was afraid to venture too far for fear of anything interfering with the one love in her life—the piano.

At least that was the excuse she hid behind.

Even with the pressures of her new life, she had no real complaints. Things were going well. Her grades were good and she was pleased at the progress she was making with her music. The social side of the coin still needed some work. While she might appear naïve about a lot of things, she knew much more than people thought. She just didn't go around discussing it the way other girls did. It bothered her that, just because she was quiet, people thought her socially stupid and without feelings.

Still, what change there was had not been easy. From the moment her mother came home from work that Saturday and told her they were going to move, to the lavish wedding some six weeks later, there was little time to get used to anything. There was barely time to pack what few belongings they had. April's mother never belittled their situation, other than to complain occasionally about the rent and their lack of food. She was very upbeat after the announcement. She never talked about their future in specifics before, content with the *one day at a time* philosophy. Now, there was talk about what lay more than a week ahead. She talked to April about things the young girl only fantasized about—a big house, her own room, clothes that fit, plenty of food, and on and on and on. Throughout it all, April's mother focused on the material things. She never mentioned the emotional aspect of the change either, for herself or her vulnerable daughter. She said little about her new man—soon to be April's stepfather, except that he was well off and lived in a large house. And, oh, by the way, April was going to have a stepbrother.

When April asked how her mother met this man, the only explanation ever offered was they met at work. April thought it odd that such a man would come to a restaurant down in Alabama. Her mother explained that away with the comment that he had to travel a lot on business. Her mother went on to add, with a twinkle in her eye, it was love at first sight. April didn't understand love in its simplest form, much less how anyone could fall in love so quickly. But that was for another time. They were moving and that was final. April had little to say in the matter except for the many questions which her mother handled with great vagueness. While April knew she would miss the trailer and the little garden on the side, she had no reservations about moving. After all, along with everything else, she'd be leaving behind the farm boys, and the memories they evoked.

She rolled over to again try and sleep. However, her mind continued to scroll through the images screaming for somewhere to go... Sally on the bed with her brother... April at the stream with the boys... the figure on the ceiling overhead. Like a broken record, the scenes spun around and around.

She squeezed her eyelids tighter. "Stop it," she scolded. "Just stop it."

If only her mind would listen.

25

The next day at school, the Wednesday before the dance, April finally answered the question she had been asked so many times in the past. She found Eddie at his hall locker, surrounded by a crowd as usual. She overheard him boasting about how they were going to kick South Western's butt on Friday. They beat them in football in the fall. They were going to beat them in lacrosse in the spring. Since his eyes never stopped surveying his surroundings, he easily caught her approach. He locked in on her, his mind searching for something to say. Only instead of the normal smart aleck remark, he wanted to say something nice, something less offensive. After all, she did get in the car with him yesterday. "April babe, how's it goin'?" he said. His cronies all turned to stare at the target of Eddie's comment.

She startled everyone by stopping and answering in a congenial voice. "Fine, thanks. And you?"

"I'm okay, thanks," he said.

April continued. "I just wanted to answer the question you asked me yesterday."

Eddie glanced around at his buddies, a puzzled look on his face. Other faces followed suit. "Refresh my memory, sweetheart," Eddie said.

This time her congenial voice was laced with a sprinkle of lemon. "You can refresh your own memory, but the answer is yes. Seven-thirty is fine. Just please be on time."

After a moment for the comment to sink in, the puzzled look on the boy's face was replaced by one of astonishment. Again, his normal habit would have been to say something trite and smug, but for once he thought before he spoke. "Seven-thirty it is... and I'll be on time."

April turned to leave.

"By the way," he said, causing her to pause. "What color is your dress?"

She turned and looked back at him. "Why do you want to know that?" she said defensively.

"Flowers… I need… I want to get you flowers… they need to match." It was the nicest thing he had ever said to her.

She blushed. Her embarrassment deepened when she realized she did not know the answer. "Huh… I'll let you know."

"Good."

She again started to walk away.

"And, Babe… I mean, April…"

She looked over her shoulder.

"I'm looking forward to it. Thanks."

She blushed again. This time she turned, started away and did not look back. She ignored the cheers and whistles that burst forth as everyone in the crowed realized just what happened.

She announced her plans to her family at dinner that night. She was not surprised by the immediate and enthusiastic support given by her mother and stepfather. She was surprised, however, at the reaction from Danny. He obviously had not heard the news. He choked on his food, sat back in his chair and looked at her as if she'd lost her marbles. He thought from their conversation the day before she had decided against such a move. He recovered quickly, however, and after a stern look from his father, joined in on the family celebration. April was going on a date!

Plans were quickly made for a trip to the mall after school the next day. Hair and make-up were discussed, or rather her mother talked and everyone else listened. April tried to downplay the whole thing and convey a nonchalant attitude. Inside, however, her excitement began to build, especially seeing her mother paying so much attention to her for a change. Her stepfather, also showing more enthusiasm than normal, offered to get them a limo for the evening. Danny interjected, however, and said he would talk to Eddie and they would double date. He glanced at April and saw an immediate look of gratitude. He reassured everyone he'd make sure everything went okay, only he turned the statement around as if the need was to protect Eddie. There was laughter from three of the four people at the table.

April excused herself before dessert, claiming she had a lot of homework to do. While that was not a lie, she really wanted to get away so she could think. Had she really made the right decision? Sure, there was excitement. There was also a lot of apprehension. The latter, however, had been blunted greatly by Danny's announcement that they'd be double dating. In spite of what she had seen in his bedroom the day before, she felt confident he'd never let anything happen to her, at least not anything she didn't want to happen. She blushed at the thought. She scolded herself for even thinking about such things. She told herself that regardless, the decision was made. There was no turning back. She allowed the positive side to come forth. She was going on a date! She was going to the big dance! She looked at herself in the hallway mirror. She leaned in closer, checking her complexion to make sure no unwanted blemishes were threatening to break out. She survived adolescence so far without a major skin problem. She stepped back to examine her silhouette. She straightened her back, checking her posture and pushing out her chest. She blushed at her actions. She never thought much about her figure. For all she knew, no one else did either. While her mother always told her she was pretty, April never hear the word beautiful. She always thought her mother was beautiful—tall, thin, long blond hair and very buxom. She wondered if she would turn out like her mother. While there was some family resemblance in the face, other more specific areas were lacking. She didn't really care though. Until now.

Her self-assessment continuing, her mind began to wonder if she was good enough for Eddie Richmond. She scolded herself for asking such a question and turned the issue around. "Is he good enough for me?" she said aloud. She blushed again, this time at her own conceit. She told herself it was okay to be a little conceited. It was okay to be excited. Friday was going to be a big day at Worthington Valley. She even considered going to the game, although what she knew about football and lacrosse combined could be engraved on the head of a pin. While she was not one to get caught up in the tidal wave of emotions that flowed through Worthington High, she knew that besides the big game, she'd be the center of the story the next day.

She looked straight into the mirror. "How do you feel about that?" she mouthed.

It didn't take her long to decide she liked it.

26

Eddie picked her up right on time, his freshly polished car squealing up to the driveway at exactly 7:30 pm. He also kept his promise about flowers. Since April forgot to tell him the color of her dress, he took the advice of the florist and chose a white gardenia wrist corsage. April forced back tears as he slid the corsage over her hand. Except for the bouquet she carried at her mother's wedding, it was the first time anyone had given her flowers. Danny was already there with Sally. Both boys were decked out in white tailed tuxedos. Sally wore a long flowery dress that was cut low in the back as well as the front. April selected a more conservative plain long red gown. While showing off April's own petite figure, it was not cut nearly as low at the cleavage. The dress was simple in design, yet complex in the emotions it drew forth. While both girls were pretty in their own right, April was absolutely stunning. Not one to lack words, even Eddie stammered at first when April made her entrance down the spiral stairway. The town's Sheriff just happened to be at the Worthington's for dinner that evening. Trained to conceal his emotions, even he was taken aback when he first saw his son's date.

Looking down from the top landing at everyone looking up at her, April could only glow. This was her moment.

The two couples tolerated the obligatory picture taking session that followed before hurrying to the waiting car. Eddie even held the door for April, making sure her dress was inside before slamming the door shut. April told herself to relax. Everything was going to be all right. Eddie was being a pure gentleman. Besides, Danny was in the back keeping a close eye out. As the car pulled away, April allowed a smile to cross her face. The thought crossed her mind that two weeks earlier she would have never believed she'd be where she was now, dressed in the most expensive piece of clothing she had ever worn, looking the best she had ever looked and feeling better than she had ever felt.

She hesitated at the last part of the thought. Sure, she had gotten all dressed up for her mother's wedding, but that was different. She wore a nice dress and had her hair done, but she looked nothing like she did tonight. Her mother's wedding day was her mother's day. This was April's day. Her smile widened. Yes, this was the best she'd ever felt.

A hundred yards from the house, however, April sensed a change in atmosphere. Eddie let out a long sigh and said, "Phew, am I glad that's over. I didn't know my old man was going to be there."

"You knew he'd want to check out the chicks," Danny teased from the rear.

"You guys did just fine," Sally said, snuggling up against Danny. "Didn't they, April?"

The front seat passenger hesitated. "I guess. I didn't think it was all that bad myself."

"That's because you were the star, Sis," Danny said, poking her gently in the back of the head.

"You were that," Eddie reinforced. "But that's over and it's now time to…"

All but April chimed in together, "Party… party… party!"

"After the game we had today, we certainly deserve it," Danny said.

In the excitement of getting ready, April forgot about the game. Thank goodness, Worthington Valley won.

"The game we had," Eddie injected. "It's more like the game you had. If you hadn't scored that goal right at the end."

"It was only because of your assist," Danny insisted.

"Okay, you two," Sally laughed. "You both deserve the credit."

"Yeah," both boys said simultaneously.

April stared out the side window, trying to keep a positive attitude. She had missed the game and now felt a twinge of guilt, but she wanted to practice the piano and get started on a book report she had to do over the weekend. Besides, her mother had arranged a hair appointment.

Eddie sped up as he made the last turn out of the community. April told herself to ignore his driving and just enjoy herself. It was a recommendation earlier in the day from her stepfather. The same quote came later from her stepbrother.

Her excitement rose as they drew nearer the school. She had purposely avoided the gym during the day where there'd been a bustle of activity decorating for the dance. She wanted to be surprised tonight. She sensed the traffic picking up as they made the turn onto the road that passed the school. She sat up straighter. For the first time in her life, she seriously worried about her appearance. She hoped her make up was okay. And her hair, what about her hair? Was it still in place? She reached behind her head to feel if all the pins were intact. She had never had her hair piled up on her head like this. She wore it long at her mother's wedding.

She realized what she was doing and giggled softly. Eddie heard her and looked over. He laid his right arm across the top of her seat. His fingertips sat softly on her shoulder. To her surprise, she didn't mind the intrusion into her space. She looked up ahead and saw the lights from the school. The parking lot was already jammed with cars. The line waiting to park was backed up into the road. She wondered if Eddie would drop them off at the front door. While the heels of her shoes were low, her feet were already starting to object at the new shoes her mother insisted she get.

To her surprise, however, Eddie whipped around the line of cars and drove right past the school. "It's early yet," he said. Nobody in the rear objected, nor did April as she was too stunned for the moment.

"Where are we going?" she finally asked.

Eddie's arm came down from the back of the seat and patted her leg. "It's early yet, babe. Things are just getting started."

"Yeah," Sally said. "The boys want to make sure everyone's there before they make their grand entrance." Everyone but April laughed.

April gently removed Eddie's hand from her leg. "Aren't you supposed to have two hands on the wheel?"

Eddie laughed again. "Whatever you say, babe. It's your night too, ya know." April thought she saw him wink at her.

The school quickly disappeared as the car sped down the road, past the last house and made a gradual slow turn to the left. Darkness loomed ahead. In spite of the lack of visibility, April knew they were headed up into the mountains, more specifically the backside of the same mountain containing the tree house. Eddie pressed down on the accelerator and the car responded with a powerful thrust forward.

April told herself to calm down. They were just going for a ride to kill time before making their grand entrance. She closed her eyes to better imagine just what that would be like. Her mind returned to the days her mother read to her at night. Her favorite stories were from an old book of fairy tales. April liked *Cinderella* in particular. She often dreamed of being a princess and going to a grand ball. Tonight, that dream was coming true.

Remembering something, she felt a sudden twinge of fear. She did not know how to dance! Her skin broke into a cold sweat. Her hands started to shake. The blood drained from her head. What was she going to do? Surely, Eddie was a great dancer and would expect her to dance with him. What if I make a fool out of myself, she thought. What if I embarrass Eddie… or Danny?

Her eyes opened and she looked toward Eddie. She had to tell him. But before she could say anything, he snapped the steering wheel to the right and veered off the main road onto a partially hidden dirt road. Caught off guard by the action, the momentum caused her to lean into him. He was apparently ready, and before she realized it, his arm was again behind her, this time gripping her shoulders tightly. "Hello," he said with a grin.

She tried to see ahead, but all she could make out were the headlights bouncing up and down. She wanted to ask where they were going. Her mouth became dry; a sudden pain in the pit of her stomach shot a warning to her brain. She tried to sit up, but Eddie's grip was too tight. Another quarter mile or so and Eddie hit the brakes. As they came to a halt, April reached out and braced herself against the dashboard.

Eddie shut off the engine and unsnapped his seat belt. She felt his fingers dropped between them and her own snap was unbuckled. He leaned over and glanced into the back seat. "Everybody okay back there?" The only response were muffled giggles.

April's mind raced as she tried to figure out what was happening, or so she told herself. She knew what was happening. They'd come to *Point-To-Point Overlook*, a peak midway up the mountain. It was a popular spot for hikers during the day and other rumored activities at night. She had been there several times with Danny. On a clear day, the view was spectacular out over Worthington Valley. The name *Point-To-Point Overlook* came from the ability to see from the northern tip to the southern end of the township. The town itself sat a thousand feet below and to the right. Acres and acres of farmland spread out to the left. Her stepfather's factory could be seen in the distance. It was a favorite spot for her and Danny to stop and have lunch. Danny would sit on the rocks that hung out over the mountainside and dangle his feet in the air. He insisted that once April was able to do that, she would be well on her way to conquering any other fears she might have in life. It had taken a couple of trips, but she finally did it. She had to admit, it was an uplifting experience.

However, she had never been here at night, and never with anyone except Danny. But wasn't Danny here with her now? She wanted to look over her shoulder to make sure that was true. Noises from the back seat warned her that would not be a good idea. Instead, she looked straight ahead. All she could see were the lights below, which told her they were awfully close to the edge.

Eddie pulled his arm away, kicked open his door and stepped out. "Sit tight," he ordered. He went to the rear of the car. April heard the trunk lid open and close. He came back carrying two sets of cans wrapped in plastic. April may have been naïve, but was able to realize the can she was handed was a cold beer. Her heart raced as she continued trying to figure out what to do. Her mother had insisted she have a good time. Her stepfather had ordered the same. And her stepbrother had promised he'd look after her.

Her thoughts were interrupted by Eddie taking the can from her hand and replacing it with his own—one that he had already opened. "Drink up," he encouraged gently. "It'll help you relax." She watched stunned as he opened her can and drained it with only a few gulps. Magically, another appeared.

Not wanting to displease him, she lifted the can to her lips. The sensation was cold and bitter as the foam reached her palate. She fought the urge to lower the beverage. Instead, she tipped the can back further. The liquid was cold as it passed down her throat. It was weird tasting, but she was able to get it down without gagging. An instant later, her head began to spin.

She heard a lighter click. Her nostrils filled with the pungent odor of smoke. She recognized it as the same smell she occasionally noticed in the bathrooms at school. She had overheard conversations that pot was a common, if not required, companion to beer.

After Eddie inhaled deeply, the marijuana cigarette was offered to her. She shook her head. She was relieved her date did not press the issue. She guessed he figured the beer was enough. It certainly was for her. In hopes of appeasing him, she took another small sip. She watched as Eddie took another drag on the joint before passing it back. He exhaled and took a long sip of beer, emptying the second can. She desperately wanted to look around and talk to her brother. She knew the energy would be wasted. The sounds of passion in the cramped rear seat were quite clear.

She stared out the passenger window and tried to clear her head. While she had only swallowed a couple of sips, the alcohol was having an effect. She blinked to focus her eyes, which were burning in response to the smoke that filled the car. When would they be finished doing whatever it was they were doing? When were they going to go to the dance? She wasn't afraid, at least not yet. That particular emotion was lingering in the background, however.

She was about to say something when Eddie opened his door and jumped out again. He slid the driver's seat forward. Danny and Sally piled out with Danny saying that they'd be back in a few minutes. A moment later, Eddie was back in with the door closed. She felt his arm around her shoulders. He pulled her to him.

"What do you think so far, babe? You having a good time? You need another beer or something?" His hand slid up to the back of her head and he leaned into her. The pungent aroma of his breath burned her nose as his face approached hers. She tried to turn away, but his grip tightened. She knew what was coming. It was not the way she had dreamed.

"Enjoy yourself," Danny had said.

"Enjoy yourself," her stepfather ordered.

"Lighten up and have a good time," her mother coached.

Eddie's lips converged onto hers. The pressure was gentle at first. Then he pulled her tighter to him. His tongue forced her lips apart. She struggled not to jerk away. She struggled not to gag. She struggled to lighten up. She struggled to enjoy.

She let her lips part and his tongue entered her mouth. The tension in her shoulders relaxed as the nervousness was replaced with a new excitement. She felt her heart start to pound in a way never before experienced. Her legs felt weak. Her arms went numb. She quickly decided that once you got past the beer and smoke, the kiss wasn't all that bad. Matter of fact, it was…

Suddenly, she felt something at her side. It was his other hand, pressed smoothly against her waist. The hand was moving upward, slowly, yet definitely in a direction new to her, in a direction she had not anticipated, in a direction she did not want. Her body began to quiver. Eddie misinterpreted this for a positive response. The hand continued to move upward. She broke out in a cold sweat. Her throat tightened. She tried to say something. Nothing would come out. She tried to lift her hand. He somehow had them pinned. Her dress, it was going to get messed up. And her hair…

The quivering accelerated to visible shaking. Her head began to spin faster and faster. He was pressing his tongue into her mouth deeper and deeper. The earlier lingering-in-the-background emotion took over. Fear was replacing her joy at being on her first date and having her first kiss. She had looked so nice. Her hair, her makeup, her dress… She told herself to relax. Maybe it wasn't going to be all that bad. Maybe they'd be leaving soon. Oh, how she wished she could move time forward.

27

Eddie broke off the kiss and buried his head in her hair. "You smell good," he whispered. April wanted to tell him he didn't. He smelled good when he first picked her up. Now, however, the cologne was gone, replaced by the odor of beer and pot.

She tried pulling away but his strength was too great. Her fear heightened as his hand continued its journey upward. He paused a moment right below her chest and before she could protest further, his hand squeezed her breast. An attempted protest was hindered by his mouth again pressing into hers. She struggled, but he held her firmly in his grip. All she could focus on was getting him away from her. What a moment ago had been the newfound pleasure of a kiss had now turned into a bad dream. She finally managed to get one hand free and pushed at his shoulder. She broke her lips away and found she was now able to speak. "Get off me, Eddie," she pleaded.

The tone of her voice caused him to stop. He sat upright and removed his hand from her chest. "What's the matter, babe. Don't you like it?"

"No!"

He laughed. He reached down on the floor and picked up another beer. Flipping the tab with his free hand, he emptied the can in three long gulps. "Sure you don't want another *brewsky*? Night's still young." He laughed and tossed the can on the floor. He turned and faced her again. "Now, where were we?" He leaned in to kiss her again.

"I said get off me." This time April's tone was not as polite.

Eddie laughed again as his lips pressed into hers. He had eased the pressure behind her neck to the point she was now able to turn away. She pulled a hand free and reached over for the door handle. She heard the click of the electric lock and knew she was too late. Her fear rose as he grabbed her again. Where earlier he had acted the true gentleman, all civility had been crushed by the combination of beer, marijuana and raging teenage hormones. She wanted to scream, but knew that would be useless. She wanted to cry. She knew that would be a waste as well. His hands clawed at her dress, his fingers digging into her skin. Her mind raced for a way out. Her head continued to spin. Her stomach started to turn. She felt herself becoming sick. She turned to tell him she needed to get out of the car. However, it was too late. Her stomach emptied like an angry volcano.

It took Eddie an instant to realize what happened. When he did, his own anger erupted. "Shit," he said, pushing away in response to the pungent odor. "Damn you! Look what you've done."

His eyes stared into hers. April saw a look never before experienced. Her level of fear rose. She felt her heart begin to race harder than before. Fear turned to panic. Her bad dream was now a nightmare. She told herself she had to keep control. Danny always said when confronted with a dangerous situation, you had to keep control.

Memories of being at the stream with the boys flashed into her mind. They were coming at her… wet… naked… aroused. The scene switched to Danny's bedroom. He was lying on the bed naked, Sally at his side. She was…

April felt her stomach starting to erupt again. She swallowed hard, not wanting to make the situation any worse. She closed her eyes to wish the images away.

When she opened her eyes, all control was lost. She did not know from where it came, but Eddie was now waving a pistol at her. "Now bitch, you and me, we're going to come to a little understanding here."

Her eyes widened. He leaned into her, his tongue hanging grotesquely from his mouth. She froze and he was on her in an instant. She tried pushing him away. Again his weight was too much. He didn't have her head, however, and she was able to slide her lips to his cheek. His free hand was in her hair. He jammed the pistol into her side. She stopped struggling.

"Now, that's better," he said, easing up on her hair a bit. "Nobody has to get hurt here, you know."

She knew that was a lie. "Okay… Okay," she said, forcing her tone to be soft. Her tongue darted out and licked his cheek. The taste of his sweat caused her stomach to churn yet again. She bore down and closed her throat.

It took him a moment, but she felt him relax a bit. "That's better," he said. He pressed the side of his face against her mouth. She let her lips part slightly. His tension eased even more. Her lips opened more until her teeth touched his skin. Her tongue lightly teased his cheek.

"Ahhh," he said.

She bit down as hard as she could. He yelled in pain and tried to pull away, but she held her jaw closed. She felt the gun come away from her side. She saw his arm rise above his head. His other hand freed her hair and struggled to push her away. Just as the arm holding the gun started to fall, she let go with her mouth, arched her back and pushed off with all her strength.

Her actions again caught him off guard. He instinctively reached back with an arm to catch himself. While he was able to get his hand onto the floor, he could not keep the rest of his body from sliding off the seat. As his eyes caught hers, his expression was one of fearful expectation. It was then April realized what was in the hand that had reached out for the floor. An instinct of her own told her what was about to happen.

And so it did.

28

Danny felt the heat build inside Sally causing his own sensations to heighten. She screamed out in delight. Her vocalization encouraged him to push faster, harder and deeper. He felt her fingers dig into his back, pulling him tighter to her. Even running on genetic instinct, he was able to press his fists into the ground to keep from collapsing on top of her. He felt her juices starting to boil. His own fire approached the same.

"Almost," he said through clinched teeth.

"You're going to feel me!" she said.

Then instead of feeling it, he heard it… the explosion.

He snapped his head back and looked to the side… one way and the other. Sally heard it too, stopping her motion as the noise echoed off the side of the mountain. Danny's arms weakened and he rolled to the side. He came to a sitting position. "What the hell was that?"

"I don't know," Sally said.

"Sounded like a gunshot," Danny said. He felt the blood flow from his head. While the effects of the couple of hits he had taken on the joint were minimal, he was feeling the effect of the three beers he guzzled earlier.

"Who's out here shooting this time of the night?" he said to the darkness. He rose to his feet and pulled up his pants. He looked around trying to locate the bearing of the sound that had so rudely interrupted his time with Sally.

He caught a movement from the corner of his eye. He turned his head and focused on the faint silhouette of the car. A figure seemed to be stumbling out of the passenger's side. He opened his eyes wider to improve his night vision. The figure turned in a circle as if confused or looking for something before heading towards the edge of the woods. The figure… the figure…

He opened his eyes even wider.

The figure was wearing a long dress.

"Oh, shit," he said, feeling a nightmare coming on.

29

Danny slowed to a trot as he approached the base of the mountain. He pulled in a few deep breaths to slow his respiration rate. While he was sure-footed, the darkness threatened his confidence and increased his level of caution. A few more steps then he stopped to check his bearings and to listen. He turned his head in all directions, holding his breath to further increased his concentration. Except for the gentle wind rustling the trees, he heard nothing. On many nights, he would simply stand and listen to the silence. It was a phenomenon of nature that always amazed him. One place on the earth there would be near total silence; a few miles away was a town bustling with activity at an uncomfortable decibel level.

He started up the firebreak, eyes scanning the horizon as he made his way forward. Pushing the illumination button on the side, he looked at his watch. It was nearly 10:30. A hundred and fifty minutes had passed since he'd heard the gunshot, time he could only describe as a living nightmare.

How could one go from near ecstasy to hell so quickly? From watching the paramedics working feverishly on Eddie, to sitting in the back of the police car as it ran interference for the ambulance, to the time in the emergency room, to giving his statement to the police (modified somewhat), to going home and changing clothes, to heading back up to the overlook, to finding the search was already on for April.

It was all a blur. He wished he'd wake up from this most disturbing dream. But he knew it was not a dream.

When he got back to the car after hearing the gun fire, he found Eddie slumped over in the driver's seat, his head against the steering wheel. His right hand was reaching across the seat as if trying to grab for something. His other hand was bent behind his back. Danny froze a moment, not wanting to believe what he was seeing. The hand behind his back was holding a pistol. Where the hell did that come from, Danny wondered. He had no time for an answer as a wave of panic filled his throat. When he realized April was not in the car, he remembered the figure he had seen running away. He turned quickly and saw April disappear into the woods. She seemed to be moving okay. He remembered thanking God before he turned his attention back to his best friend. There was a strong smell he later learned was vomit. Besides a cellphone, Eddie's car was also equipped with a CB radio—old fashioned to many, but still very useful in the more rural areas of the country. Making sure Eddie was breathing, Danny put out a call for help. By now, Sally had caught up to him. He grabbed her and pulled her away. They held one another and waited. He was torn between going after April or staying put. Experience told him April would be okay. Besides, Sally was gripping him so tight, he'd have trouble getting away. As for Eddie, he wasn't okay.

It seemed like hours before Danny heard the first siren.

Danny brought his focus back to the present. He was making good time up the mountain and soon saw the clearing ahead marking where he needed to turn off the fire break. The thought crossed his mind that maybe he needed to cover his trail, but that would take time. Besides, he had just been up here two days before so his footprints were already all over the place. The search party would be coming from the other direction anyway.

His mind filled with the image of what he saw when he returned to *Point-To-Point Overlook* after the shooting. There were police cars everywhere. Every deputy in Worthington Valley had already been on duty because of the dance. Now, instead of monitoring the activities at the school, they were up on the side of the mountain. In addition, there were a couple of state troopers plus a few in plain clothes with shiny badges around their necks. It the middle of it all sat Eddie's car. The realization set in that this was not going to be a game of fox and hound. This was the real thing.

He slowed his pace near the base of the tree house, coming to a stop a few feet away. He stooped low, listening and looking for any unusual activity. Several minutes passed. Except for a raccoon running across his path, there was nothing. The stillness continued. He stared up into the tree. It was too dark to see anything. A sixth sense, however, told him she was there. After all, where else would she go? The only question: did she have enough time to get up over the mountain to the tree house? He contemplated the possibilities. Normally, it was a three and a half hour trek from the tree house to *Point-To-Point Overlook*. But that was casual hiking without any sense of urgency. The trip was also made during daylight hours. He waited another minute before proceeding. He wanted to wait longer, but he knew time was becoming an issue. He had to find her before…

He refused to let his mind complete the thought.

He glanced around one final time. Fresh footprints on the ground indicated she had indeed been there. However, there were other footprints as well. The urgency of time increased its intensity. Not wanting to take the time to pull down the ladder, he used the hand and foot holds he had carved into the tree several years before and made his way up to the first heavy branch. From there he pulled himself up several more branches. Muscle memory took over and he climbed the rest of the way up without incident. He pushed his head through the opening in the floor. He swept the room with a small flashlight. She was hunched in the corner, her arms wrapped tightly around her knees. She was rocking back and forth ever so slightly. Her hair, which looked beautiful a few hours ago, had fallen and was matted against the side of her head. Her face was dirty and he could see scratch marks on her cheeks. Her dress was filthy and torn in several places. Her breathing was hard and fast.

Her eyes were staring directly at him, yet it appeared as if she did not see him. The rocking motion continued. Stooping down to assure the safety of his head, he approached her slowly. "April," he whispered. "It's me, Danny."

She said nothing.

"Are you okay?"

She said nothing.

He realized the stupidity of the question. Rephrasing, "April, are you hurt?"

Her rocking stopped suddenly. Her eyes locked onto his. A surge of fear ran up his spine. He had cornered many animals in his life. He felt he had a good understanding of their fight or flight mechanism. Now, however, he was caught off guard by the biggest animal he ever faced. He told himself to hold his ground. He had to be strong for her.

The muscles in her neck relaxed. Tears formed in her eyes. "I never touched the gun," she said softly.

"What did you say?" he asked.

The rocking motion stopped. "I never touched the gun," she repeated, this time with more volume.

Danny let the words register. Answers to yet unasked questions flowed forth. Danny remembered Eddie bragging in the past about carrying a pistol in his car to scare away bears, but Danny always shrugged the claim off as another one of his friend's bullshit stories.

"Why are they after me?" April pleaded, her voice breaking his train of thought.

His pulse quickened when he remembered the other footprints around the tree. He answered by asking, "Who's after you?"

Her eyes widened in fear. "I don't know, but they were here. When I left the car, I didn't know what to do. I couldn't find you. I couldn't find Sally. I was afraid. I just knew I wanted to get home. I figured the quickest way was up over the mountains. I was about half-way up the first side when I heard someone behind me. I started backtracking hoping it was you. But as I got closer, I heard voices—two of them, and they weren't yours. So I hid in the bushes. They were two of the deputies in town. They stopped right in front of me. They didn't see me, but I could hear them talking." There was a brief pause. "One of them said, 'That bitch has to be around here somewhere. She couldn't have gotten far.' The other one then said, 'We just need to remember what the sheriff said, he wants her alive, but if she resists.' Then they both laughed." April paused again. "And then one of them said, 'It's been a long time since we've had a murder in Worthington Valley.'"

April started crying harder. "Danny, I never touched the gun. I swear."

Danny fought for something to say of value. "I believe you," he finally said.

However, there was a more pressing point at hand. Having climbed the rest of the way into the tree house, he moved over to April and put his arms around her shoulder. "April, I believe you, but I need to know what happened with the deputies."

She wiped her eyes on her arm. "They went on ahead. I guess when they came to the point where I backtracked, they stopped. In the meantime, I took off. I tried to be quiet, but I fell once and they must have heard me because they were soon on my trail again. I started running, which only made matters worse. I did, however, get here in time and just barely got up into the tree house when they caught up. They were right below me, Danny. I heard them say what they were going to do to me when they caught me… It was awful."

Again, Danny had empathy. Again, however, he had to get her refocused. "I understand… Just tell me what happened next."

She regained her composure. "After rummaging around a few minutes, they decided I must have become lost and headed back up the mountain. So that's the way they went. They also said what they might have heard was a deer or something like that."

"Are you sure?"

"I never heard them again."

Danny didn't voice his concern that in reality, it was two of the deputies who were most probably lost, which made them even more dangerous. At least the tree house had not been compromised, and their thinking that they may have been chasing a deer was a positive point. Regardless, there was still a search party of at least two roaming around on this side of the mountain. Danny had no doubt the number would grow. His mind again returned to the scene at *Point-To-Point Overlook*. The whole picture made for a very dangerous situation. He shook his head to clear the questions swirling around in his brain.

He told himself not to focus on the past. He had to think about the present and put on his survival cap. The first order of business was to get April off the mountain and buy some time. Forcing himself to concentrate, a few ideas began to form. All the while, there was the sense of urgency. Sand was falling through the hourglass way too quickly.

Finally, he said, "We've got to get out of here. You sure you're not hurt?"

April shook her head in the negative.

"Good, so let's go."

"Where are we going?" she asked.

"I don't know. I just know we've got to get out of here… and I suspect we need to do it in a hurry."

She didn't argue the point.

He went first and helped her down through the series of branches. It was slow going as her dress kept getting hung up on the branches. At the base of the trunk, they crouched low and waited in silence. She was starting to shiver so he put his coat across her shoulders. He gave her a squeeze to let her know he was there for her. She didn't resist his offer of support. Instead, her knees seemed to weaken as he held her.

Danny tried focusing on the environment, but had great difficulty. His mind kept wandering to Eddie lying across the car seat. He looked so grotesque in that position. Danny had started to move him to see if he could help, but the local 911 operator told him that as long as he was breathing and had a pulse, it was best to leave him alone. Danny now wondered if that was the right advice. He decided it probably wouldn't have mattered either way. Danny just hoped Eddie didn't suffer too much.

Danny cut the thought off and turned his attention back to April. He knew he had to get her off the mountain. He also knew he had little time to do so. "Come on, let's go," he said.

She simply nodded.

One of the things that always impressed Danny about his stepsister was her common sense. His father, whose compliments were few and far between, told Danny even he thought April had her head screwed on straight. And the older Worthington thought just the opposite of most young people. Danny just hoped her screws remained tight tonight.

"I want to backtrack first, then we'll divert over to the north," he said. He choose north hoping and guessing that if the deputies were indeed lost, they'd head south, or more on a downhill trek.

"Why backtrack?" April asked.

"To get the trail away from the tree house. I don't want any association between you and me. I don't want anyone to know I've found you."

He watched her digest the idea a moment. "People don't think a whole lot of me, do they?" she said.

"That's not true," he said with encouragement. He picked up a couple of broken branches and started wiping away any traces of human footprints. He reached into his pocket for the box of skunk pellets. They were designed to throw off their scent for any dogs that might be in the area. While he had not seen any when he first returned to *Point-To-Point Overlook*, he had no doubt they'd be out soon. If nothing else, the sheriff's old dog, Bullet, would be in the hunt.

He followed her up the hill, careful to cover up their new markings as they went. They traveled a hundred yards or so before coming to an especially thick series of trees. Danny saw April and the detectives had tried to cut right through the trees before going around. He had April walk around the trees a few more times to leave plenty of prints, wanting to show confusion before backtracking April's previous trail. When they came to another tree similar to that of the tree house, he cut off both their trails before heading across the slope of the mountain. He dropped a couple of skunk pellets just in case. He made sure he eliminated even the smallest clue of their presence. He wanted anyone tracking April to think she had turned back towards *Point-To-Point Overlook*.

They traveled a half-mile along the side of the mountain before heading for the base. The moon was out and the trees were heavy with leaves. Visibility was a problem. It was also a benefit. If they couldn't see, neither could anyone else. Danny kept the use of his flashlight to a minimum, using it only to check landmarks. He knew the area well, but it still changed from season to season. He also kept a close eye out for any other lights that might be visible. He figured any search party wouldn't be worried about noise or light.

When they finally reached the bottom of the mountain, April came to a sudden stop. She looked up at Danny. In spite of the darkness, he could see tears still rolling down her cheek. She spoke softly. "What am I going to do, Danny? What am I going to do?"

"We'll figure something out," Danny said. He emphasized the plurality of his remark.

He took her arm and nudged her forward. She hesitated before responding to the pressure.

"Thank you," she said softly as the pair continued their journey.

Danny said nothing. He was already feeling guilty for getting April in this mess. And now she was thanking him.

This wasn't a game, he reminded himself.

30

At the bottom of the mountain, they came to a large open field. There was a little known dirt road that ran between the woods and the field that was mainly used for access to the fire break that cut through the mountain range. The field showed early signs of hay growth, so visibility in all directions was excellent. Danny handed April a granola bar and an apple. "This is where we part ways for now," he said.

"What do you mean, part ways?" April responded, her previous panic returning.

Danny wanted to get home in order to eliminate any ongoing suspicion. When the police asked him earlier where April may have gone, he played dumb, saying she was probably hiding somewhere near *Point To Point Overlook*. After all, it was dark, and how far could April Blackstone get in such conditions? For all the deputies knew, she was a plain

Jane girl who did little except study and practice the piano, which was just the way Danny wanted it. It would keep the search area small. If the deputies got any inkling she might be with him or that he knew where she was, all bets would be off. He refused to let his thoughts go any further.

"Just what I said," he repeated. "You're going to stay here, or near here until tomorrow night. By then I'll have a better feel of what's going on and what we should do."

"I'm staying here… by myself!"

"I'll be here tomorrow an hour after dark. That'll be around nine o'clock. I want you to go back into the woods about a hundred feet or so. Cover your tracks real good, too. There's a thick clump of trees you can use for protection. It's dense enough even in the daytime that no one can see in but you can see out. There's a stream to your left… that's your left as you're looking down towards the road. The water's not the best, but it's safe to drink.

April remembered the stream from a trip the year before. The water was cold and very irony. She also remembered… "Isn't the mountain pretty steep over there?"

"Exactly! No one will expect you to be messing around up there. It'll also protect your rear."

It was a trick he had played on her on more than one occasion during their fox and hound games. Go steep and slow versus flat and fast. Early on in her indoctrination, April always figured speed was the most important factor in escaping capture. She quickly learned finesse was as important.

One of the fascinating features April discovered about her stepbrother was his ability to change from this low-keyed, laid back, let's-get-our-feelings-in-touch-with-nature sort of guy to a fierce competitor who focused not only on the game, but on winning. She told herself to hope and have faith that the latter was the side of the person she was now seeing. After all, her future was dependent on it. While this gave her some comfort, it also made her uneasy. There was this question of trust floating near the surface of her brain. "What if someone comes up here?" she said.

"I doubt if anyone will even expect you to be on this side of the mountain," Danny replied. "Regardless, we can't be too careful. So except to get a drink, I want you to stay put. You'll have a good view of the road and field, and you'll hear anyone coming toward you from behind. Once daybreak arrives, I especially don't want you moving around."

She certainly didn't like the idea of being left alone even though she understood the importance of Danny getting back to town. She took a deep breath. She liked that he had used the word *we* a moment ago. It helped bury the question of trust a little deeper. "Tell my moth—"

"I plan to say as little as possible in case I let something slip by accident," Danny interrupted. "Once I find out what's going on, I'll have a better feel for what we should do and who we can talk to." He paused. "When it gets dark, come back down to this spot and hide behind those bushes over there." He pointed to the area in question barely visible in the darkness. "I'll drive by slowly in my pickup and have the door partially open up so you can jump in. I don't want to stop completely in case anyone sees my lights. Remember to cover your tracks."

"What if you can't make it?"

He started to say he would, and then realized he had not planned for the unexpected. "If I'm not there by nine-thirty, go back up to the trees and wait until midnight. I'll be here soon after."

"What if you're not?"

He hesitated. "I don't know."

She accepted his honesty without comment. "What happens if I have to move away."

He was pleased at her ability to think through the scenario so carefully. He let a faint smile cross his face. "I'll find you."

"Maybe," she said matter-of-factly.

"I'll find you," he repeated.

He slid the watch off his wrist and handed it to her. "You'll need this." He gave her a hug. She felt good in his arms, although she was shivering slightly. He knew her ability to handle the elements so he knew the reaction wasn't from being cold. He started to say something in hopes of calming her down. He decided against it, knowing a little fear would help keep her alert.

He released his grip, turned and made his way out onto the road.

31

Danny fought the urge to look over his shoulder. He also fought the self-doubt about the adequacy of his plan, although he was comfortable with the spot he had chosen for April. She could hide and remain relatively protected from the elements. The weather forecast called for mild temperatures with only a slight chance of precipitation. It was the latter part of the forecast he was most concerned with. Rain left the ground muddier, which meant foot tracks that were harder to eliminate. It also meant for a less comfortable experience. April had nothing but his jacket, but at this particular time, there was little choice.

Thankfully, his father and stepmother weren't home. He figured they were at the hospital or over at the sheriff's house offering whatever support they could. It always amazed Danny that someone's death generated so much immediate activity. Suddenly, there was so much to do—arrangements to be made, phone calls to make, and on and on. His mind wandered back to his mother's funeral. She was sick—some sort of cancer— and in spite of everyone being prepared for her death, it still came as a shock. And then all the above mentioned activity started. Just when he wanted to be left alone, his house turned into total chaos. The worst were the relatives who showed up from everywhere. He knew their intentions were good, but...

It was the first time he went up into the mountains.

He expected the same was going on at the Richmond's house right now. Next to Danny's father, Sheriff Richmond was the most powerful person in the community. The man had been sheriff for over twenty years. While he no doubt made a few enemies along the way, he also had many friends. And since he never lost an election, his friends far outnumbered his enemies. Danny knew the words *high profile* were going to be attached to this case rather quickly, especially with the disappearance of April. It was the opposite of what he wanted at the moment. It was also the opposite of the way he liked to live his own life.

Danny certainly didn't mind the perks of being the son of Worthington Industries's owner and largest employer in the region. The cost, being the excessive public attention, he could do without. One reason he spent so much time up in the mountains was to get away from it all. The animals there didn't give him a second look. They didn't care who his father was.

Danny did a quick search of the house to make sure he was indeed alone before packing some clothing and gathering some food. He went into April's room where he hesitated. Everything was so clean and in its place. If only her life was the same. It did make finding what he wanted easy, however.

Loading up the truck, he fought the urge to go back to April. He knew it was imperative there be no question of his knowing her whereabouts. She had to stay a fugitive, at least until he figured out a plan. Sure, he worried about her. He also knew she'd be okay. While she might present herself as shy and naïve on the surface, Danny knew beneath that she was anything but. From what little he knew of her past, she had already proved herself a survivor. One night alone out in the woods was going to be a piece of cake. It was what followed that would be the real challenge. The only question: what would that be?

"The *only* question," he mouthed.

Another question: what should he do now? He didn't want to talk to anyone. At the same time, he wanted everyone to know he was not with April. He mulled over his options, deciding the best thing was to make an appearance at the sheriff's house and join in the chaos.

He was about to go out the front door when a set of headlights caught his eye. He peered out through the bay window. A patrol car passed slowly by. It stopped at the end of the driveway and the car's spotlight hit the back of his truck. Danny just hoped no one came up to the door. His wish was granted as the light was extinguished and the patrol car pulled away. No doubt, a report would be made to the sheriff and to his parents that he was home.

The *what to do now* question was repeated. There was no longer a need to go to the sheriff's house. With the desire not to talk to anyone continuing, he went to bed. With some rest, he could get an early start in the morning.

Contrary to what he may have thought, sleep came easily. He was exhausted.

32

Danny awoke the next morning feeling refreshed and energized. A smile crossed his face. His mind replayed the scenes from the day before. They had won the lacrosse game in Worthington High fashion—a goal in the last few seconds. What a victory! A hectic couple hours of celebration followed before the dance.

And then he remembered. They never made it to the dance.

He sat up with a start. The want-to-be memories were quickly erased. The smile disappeared. The truth returned as reality came into focus. He thought of April. Was she okay? Had she survived the night? Was she…? He cut the thought off. He had other things to worry about.

He had a sudden urge for knowledge. What was going on in town? What was happening up on the mountain? His heart skipped a beat. Had April been found? He quickly dismissed that idea. He would have heard about that.

Wouldn't he?

He jumped out of bed and went down the hall. April's door was open, the bed empty. It was the same as he left it the night before. He looked down the end of the hall towards his parents' room. That door was shut. He wondered what time they got home. He had heard nothing. He decided it didn't matter. They were still asleep, which was fine with him. He wasn't ready to play twenty questions. He had done enough of that the night before at the police station. He told the truth then, which was easy. Now though, he'd have to lie.

He dressed quickly, left a note on the kitchen counter and exited the house. As he drove toward town, he thought about who he could go to for advice. He quickly decided the answer was no one. There was no one he could trust.

He spent the morning riding around looking for anything that might tell him what was going on. It seemed everyone was holed up in their homes as if a plague had enveloped their town. The streets were virtually empty.

He thought about giving Sally a call, but decided against it. It would only get him angry again. She had been upset over the whole ordeal, which was to be expected. She was even hysterical at times, also to be expected. The surprise, however, came when Danny took her home. As they said good night, she dropped yet another bombshell on what was already a bomb-laden evening. She said she wanted to break up. She claimed she had this planned even before Eddie was shot. It was also something she had been thinking about for a long time. Danny claimed she was just upset. She claimed it had nothing to do with Eddie. He claimed she was a bitch for dropping this on him now. She claimed he was a bastard for not understanding. He admitted he didn't. He was too shocked to carry it any further.

He drove out to *Point-To-Point Overlook*. Eddie's car was still roped off and there was a single police car nearby. He turned around before being spotted. Heading back into town, he flipped on the CB radio. The usual chatter about the weather, things going on at his father's plant, ambulance runs and fire calls the night before were noticeably absent. The talk was all focused on the big event. Danny listened closely as several people participated in the conversation. He learned the command center for the search had been moved back to the sheriff's office and that so far nothing had been found. They had been on April's trail earlier but had lost it. Seems she doubled back toward *Point-To-Point Overlook*. Everyone assumed she was nearby—either hiding, hurt or both. Confidence was high, however, they'd find her soon. Danny ignored the specific comments about his stepsister, even fighting the urge to get on the radio and let his own feelings be known.

He was about to turn the CB off when the conversation switched to the sheriff himself. Seems he left with Eddie's body sometime in the early morning hours. No one was sure where he was headed. He told his senior deputy he was taking his boy far away from Worthington Valley. People thought that a little strange, as did Danny; although, Danny figured the sheriff didn't want to be around all the chaos either. One good thing though, the sheriff was out of town for the time being.

Finally, Danny figured it was safe to head out of town himself. Besides, he wasn't going to get any more information anyway. He called home and left a message that he was going for a drive. He headed east—the opposite direction of the mountain. He stopped once for fuel and another time to get a sandwich before pulling into a rest stop to await darkness. At the same time, he kept an eye out to make sure he wasn't being followed. While April flashed through his mind on a regular basis, he refused to let himself worry.

"She's a survivor," he said aloud.

33

While Danny slept, April stayed awake like a frightened kitten. She was too afraid to do anything else. Except for an occasional bird, an owl that seemed to think it was a cuckoo clock and a rabbit digging for food, the night remained quiet. Just before dawn, she made her way to the stream where she quenched her thirst and tried to wash some of the grime off her face. While the water was cool and sent a chill down her spine, it felt good against her skin. Back in the bed of pine needles, she ate the apple, saving the granola bar for later. She started to feel better as the fruit absorbed some of her hunger pains. Having made it through the night and her hunger appeased, her fears subsided somewhat. She lay back and closed her eyes. Even though she was tired, she told herself to stay alert, but her fatigue quickly won the battle over fear.

She slept soundly until late in the afternoon when she was awakened by a loud thumping sound overhead. She lay very still, too paralyzed to move. She finally let out a breath once the noise of a helicopter passed overhead. The realization of where she was and what had recently transpired brought her fully awake. The worst part, she was being hunted—by land and by air. She sat up and looked around. She saw nothing of concern. She yearned for a cool drink of water but remembered Danny's instructions to stay put during the day. She did as she was told, lay down, and fell back asleep.

The next time she awoke it was near total darkness. She looked at Danny's watch. It was nearly six-o'clock. It would be another three hours before he would be there. She sat up, ate the granola bar and waited a few more minutes before moving from the trees. She went to the stream and quenched her thirst. She took her shoes off and dangled her feet in the water. It was cold and she was chilled, but the sensation was pleasant as she felt the blood flow back to her extremities. She leaned over to take another drink when she heard the rotors of a helicopter. She froze an instant before quickly putting her shoes back on. She half ran, half stumbled, back to her hiding place. She stayed in a sitting position so she could see through a crack in the bushes. Her eyes adjusted quickly to the light and she was able to see past the tree line. She realized it wasn't as dark as she thought. She cursed herself for being so careless.

This time, instead of simply flying overhead, the helicopter came to a hovering pattern over the field. April's heart pounded as she watched the craft land and the rotors slow to a stop. She considered her options, deciding she'd be best if she stayed still. Two figures emerged from the helicopter. One was a town deputy she recognized. The other was the pilot who she did not know. The deputy made his way to the edge of the field and came to a halt directly in front of her. He took a couple steps onto the road before stopping again. He was less than a hundred feet away. April held her breath.

He called back to the pilot, who had remained in the field. "It's too dark in there. I can't see a God damn thing. I told them we needed lights. And even with those, I doubt we'd find anything. This is way out of the search area."

"The perimeter's been expanded, remember?" the pilot shouted back.

"Whatever," the deputy returned. "What say we come back here in the morning at first light? If she's up there, she ain't going nowhere in the dark. It's too steep."

"What are you going to tell the command center?"

"The truth—we ain't seen hide nor hair of her all day. Besides, like I said earlier, she isn't on this side of the mountain." The deputy turned and headed back toward the aircraft. "The bitch—why'd she have to go and shoot him? Fucked up my whole weekend."

April fought the urge to shout out that she didn't do anything… she didn't shoot anyone.

"You're the boss. I'm just the pilot," the second man said.

"Let's get out of here," the deputy directed.

Several minutes later the rotors were turning and the vehicle lifted lazily off the ground.

April stayed in among the trees until it was time to move down the road. She did so with great caution. While her footsteps were quiet, she feared the pounding of her heart would give her away. The next minutes were some of the slowest she had ever experienced in her life. She prayed that Danny would be there, and be there on time.

Her prayers were answered.

34

April nudged the water temperature up a couple degrees. The steaming liquid felt good against her back. She shampooed her hair a second time, using up the soap in the small give-away bottle. She scrubbed her body a second time as well, making sure any lingering smell from the past two days was gone. Until she got in the shower, her nostrils still held a sensation of stale alcohol. She just wished she could wash the memories down the drain as well. She knew that was impossible. Memories, especially certain types, were awfully hard to erase.

The initial shock from the past couple of days was starting to wear off. In its place was an even scarier scenario—reality. While she had yet to organize all the details of what happened, she had the big picture in her mind. As Danny termed it so bluntly, they were in big trouble. Only, she insisted it wasn't a plural situation. Danny had done nothing wrong. Regardless, Danny insisted he was not going to leave her.

She shut off the faucet, grabbed a towel and stepped out of the tub. Danny's voice from the other side of the door startled her as she was drying off. "I brought your bag in out of the truck. I hope I got the right things. I brought you a pizza like I promised. I'm going to get some ice—be back in a minute."

She waited until she heard the door close before exiting the bathroom. The motel room was small and dimly light. The furnishings were from the 60's, if not earlier. Danny said it was used mainly in the winter by hunters. When she asked what the place did the rest of the time, he said it was a hideout for fugitives. She didn't think the joke was funny, and told him so. He apologized. Regardless, the room was clean and it wasn't the woods where she spent the night before. It was also many miles from Worthington Valley.

She unzipped the canvas bag sitting on one of the two double beds. To her surprise, Danny did seem to get everything she needed, including a favorite blue sweatshirt. She finished drying off and dressed quickly. She wrapped her hair in a towel, brushed her teeth and then turned her attention to the pizza on the dresser. She was accustomed to going long periods of time without eating. She tended to skip breakfast in the morning because she always seemed to be in a rush, and lunchtime at school was often spent practicing the piano in the music department. Now, however, she was famished. She attacked the food with gusto. Danny came back a few minutes later with a bucket of ice, poured them each a soda and dove in himself. The eight slices disappeared in a matter of minutes.

"You act like you didn't eat yesterday either," April said.

"I didn't," Danny replied.

"Why?"

"I was too busy. Besides, I knew you didn't have any food."

April tilted her head to the side. "I had an apple and a granola bar, remember?"

"That's about all I had," Danny said. He forgot about the sandwich.

"That's so sweet." As an afterthought, "A little stupid though."

"I really wasn't hungry."

"Heaven help you if I ever have a baby. You'll have labor pains right with me."

Danny looked at her, a curious expression covering his face. "That'll be your husband's job. But if you need me, I'll be there."

She stared back at him, trying yet failing to hold back the tears. He didn't have to ask. This time he thought he understood. He sat down next to her. "It'll work out, April. Somehow, it'll work out." He resisted the urge to add, "I promise."

Silently, Danny prayed for his statement to come true. Except for April's close call with the helicopter earlier, they had made it this far without incident. He wondered how long their luck would last. He had yet to decide on the next step. However, like a wild animal caught in a corner, their options were few. From the rhetoric he'd heard on the CB radio, April going back was out of the question, at least for the time being. He also ruled out anyone he could trust for advice. So he and April were on their own. He had little doubt they'd be okay, at least for a couple of days. School had already been canceled for Monday because of the shooting. That gave them a little more time. The question was what to do with this time?

One thing, good or bad, time gave him the opportunity to question his judgment. Was this indeed the right thing to do? Were they running just to run? Was there really a need? Could she go back? And assuming he was making the right decisions, was he good enough to outfox the sheriff's deputies? Or were they smarter than one might think? Danny reminded himself there were others involved in the search as well—others better trained, with better equipment and better organized. They already had helicopters in the air! Fortunately, the sheriff himself would be out of the picture for a while.

Danny was able to subdue many of the feelings threatening to cloud his thinking. However, there was one issue that kept surfacing—he should have never let April go out with Eddie in the first place. He knew Eddie's reputation. He also knew the reputation was well founded. Eddie was a hormone raging male who dated hormone raging females—and if the girls weren't raging in the beginning, Eddie would stir things up by the end of the night. Worthington High's star athlete was a player on and off the field.

April's voice broke his train of thought. "How's my mother? Did you tell her…"

"I haven't seen or talked to anyone since I left the emergency room… except for Sally."

"Oh," April said. She so much wanted to talk to her mother and tell her it was all an accident. "How's Sally?"

"Upset like everyone else." Danny turned away and stared into space. "But I guess she feels better in some ways."

"Some ways?"

"We broke up."

"Broke up! What do you mean you broke up?"

Danny looked back at his stepsister. "Just what I said. She broke up with me last night."

"Oh, Danny. I'm so sorry. It's all my fault." April started to cry again.

"On the contrary, it's not. She said she had it already planned even before the night began."

The tears stopped and April stared. "Why didn't she tell you earlier?"

Danny hesitated. "She wouldn't have had a date for the dance, I guess." He didn't add that she probably also wanted one last…

He cut the thought off. No need to be vulgar. No need to be mean. He had bigger things to worry about than Sally. He knew April's physical and emotional status were very precarious. She was holding up, but it wouldn't take much to push her over the edge. He cursed himself for even saying anything about Sally. At the same time, he had to admit it felt good to talk about it, even if the talk was only a sentence or two.

"Everyone hates me," April said, reinforcing Danny's concerns from a moment before.

"That's not true," Danny said, struggling to find something positive to add.

"They all blame me."

"No they don't."

"Then why are we running?"

Danny told himself to tell the truth. "I'm not sure."

The eye rain increased in intensity. "What am I going to do, Danny? What am I going to do?"

He took her in his arms. He wanted to tell her everything would be okay… she would be okay… Eddie would be okay. He wanted to tell her it was all a bad dream and when they woke up in the morning, everything would be back to normal.

Only they were all lies. Reality was just the opposite.

She pulled away and threw herself across the bed, burying her face in the pillow. After a few moments she rolled up onto her elbow. "Why are you males the way you are?"

"What do you mean?"

"You know what I mean. You all have a one track mind. You all think with the wrong… How do you say it? … You think with the head in your pants instead of the head on your shoulders."

It took Danny a second to understand what she was talking about and additional time to recover from the surprise at the statement itself. April was not known for her candor.

"It does take two to tango, you know," he finally said.

"Shouldn't both parties be willing participants?"

"It helps."

"That's just the point, it helps… but if help's not there, you push on anyway."

"We all don't push on," Danny insisted. Images he had so far been able to subdue rose to the surface—images of what happened in the car right before the gun went off. He tried denying what intuition was telling him, but he knew it was just that—denial. He looked down at her. She still shook as sobs flowed through her body. He decided it was a nightmare he never wanted to visit. "I have never forced myself on anyone," he said.

April's eyes filled with fear as she remembered. "He had a gun, Danny. He pointed it right at me."

"He may have been drunk and high but he would have never forced you to do anything you didn't want," Danny defended. "I'm sure he was just having fun." More denial flowed forth.

"It wasn't fun for me. It was my first date. It was my first dance." She paused. "We never got to dance."

"I know."

"I didn't touch the gun, Danny."

"I know," he repeated.

April wiped her eyes with the back of her hand. "I still don't see what's so special about it all."

"Special about what exactly?"

April hesitated. "About sex—is it really all that great?"

Her candor again surprised him. As he seemed to be doing a lot tonight, he chose his words carefully. "With the right person under the right circumstances it can be."

She wiped her eyes again. "Was it for you on Friday?"

Her stepbrother blushed.

"I'm sorry I ruined it for you… and for Sally."

"You didn't ruin it for anyone. Eddie did."

She looked away. "Maybe I shouldn't have resisted. Maybe I should have…"

Danny set the palm of his hand across her mouth. "Drunk or not, pretending or not, Eddie shouldn't have done what he did."

She pushed his hand away. "Maybe that is true, but still…"

"You did nothing wrong, April," Danny said sternly.

He looked deep into her eyes. How did he really feel about her? He wanted to feel sorry for her, only he knew that would be wasted energy. She wouldn't respond to pity. He wanted to feel sorry for himself. There was no value there either. Besides, he wasn't the issue here. April was. He felt close to her; and at this particular moment, closer to her than anyone else. That bond was even stronger with Sally out of the picture. They could talk about most anything. They had fun together. She liked being in the outdoors with him. He was even beginning to like her music. If nothing else, he realized just how good she was at the piano. If nothing else, he realized just how special she was. If nothing else…

He reminded himself she was his sister… his stepsister.

His eyes moved down her body. Until the night of the dance, he never realized how beautiful she was. Her complexion was the envy of many her age. She was a little tanned, yet not overly done. Her eyes looked dark in the dimly lit room. Her face was round, surrounded by long brown hair. She had smooth lips and near perfect teeth. Her arms were long and thin, as were her fingers. He knew there was ample strength in all her extremities. Even being skinny, she was quite stunning. And even now with her hair all wet, no makeup, her body dressed in a tee shirt and jeans, she looked good.

He began to see her in a fashion never before imagined. He remembered the several times he had hugged her over the past couple days. She had always responded positively. Was it out of need, or was it out of…

Her voice broke his train of thought. "Well."

He refocused his mind. "Well what?"

"Why is everyone so hung up on sex?"

"Everyone's not hung up."

"You know what I mean."

He started to argue the opposing side, but stopped. "I guess I really don't know… except that it feels good."

She rolled over to her side. He was now staring down at her chest, covered only by the thin material of a tee shirt. "Does it really?" she asked. There was a hint of desperation in her voice.

His mouth opened and closed without a sound.

April looked away. "It did feel good when he kissed me the first time."

"You let him kiss you!"

Her eyes snapped back. "Was that okay?"

"Sure, sure," he quickly reassured. He paused. His mind flashed the word *caution*. "How did that make you feel?"

She giggled softly through her tears. "I did feel tingly all over. I don't know if that was from the beer or from…" It was her turn to hesitate.

"For it to feel good, both people have to want it," Danny said. "The kiss felt good because you both wanted it. Whatever happened next didn't feel good because…"

Her eyes started to water again. "Why can't I be like everyone else?"

As the meaning of the question sank in, Danny's voice became stern. "Because you're not, April, and that's good enough. In spite of what you may think, not *everyone* does it." He hoped she didn't ask him to name someone in that category because he'd be hard pressed to do so.

"Still…"

"Still what?" His softness returned.

"I wonder…"

While their conversation was getting uncomfortable for him, Danny realized April needed to talk. According to Sally, he was never a very good listener, but he always could listen to April. When she spoke, it was different. She didn't bitch and complain all the time like most of the girls he knew—ex-girlfriend included. He tuned out Sally because listening to her meant listening to who did what to whom. April, on the other hand, never said a negative word about anyone. Nor did she gossip—a rarity in the Worthington High community. She was different, so very different. She had a depth about her far beyond her physical beauty.

April continued. "I often wonder what it would be like to be with someone free of fear. Someone I want to be with; someone who wants to be with me because of me, not just because I'm a girl."

"When that time comes, you'll know it," Danny said. He felt a knot form in his throat. He wanted to take her, to hold her, to give her the answers she was seeking, to tell her everything was going to be okay, to show her what it was like, how nice it could be, how good it felt. Only, he couldn't. The already cloudy issues became even more confusing as his own emotions came into play. He often questioned his feelings towards April. He caught himself many times wondering about her in inappropriate ways. At first he wondered if he was a pervert or something. After all, she was his sister. However, as he matured, as their relationship drew closer, he realized she was someone special and that his feelings were genuine, therefore okay… at least to a point. His father once told him that thinking was fine. It was what you did with your thoughts that got you in trouble. Maybe that's what happened to Eddie. He lost his thinking control. The alcohol, the pot, his raging hormones… all added to the problem. The bottom line, however, Eddie lost control. Eddie was wrong.

April's voice broke his train of thought. "You know, Danny, you're the only friend I have."

He started to argue, but realized her statement was probably true. He wiped a tear away with the back of his hand. Yes, she was special, and now she was in trouble, reaching out to him for help. So far he'd been okay with what they had done, escaping off the mountain and hiding out here in the motel. He knew, however, that was only a temporary fix to a far more complex problem.

Her voice again broke his train of thought. "You are my friend, aren't you?"

His eyes refocused. "I'm more than a friend."

Her eyes widened ever so slightly at the sincerity in his voice. "More than a friend?"

Danny realized his tongue had gotten ahead of his brain. *Caution* again flashed before his eyes. "You're my sister."

"Oh."

Throwing caution to the wind, he continued. "It may seem weird, and please don't take this the wrong way, but sometimes I think about you in other ways… nothing bad, mind you… just in other ways."

"Why would I take it the wrong way?"

He shrugged his shoulders.

"You mean you think of me as…"

His face turned red. "In spite of what you may think, April, you are a beautiful person, inside and out."

The tears stopped and a hint of a smile crossed April's face. "I guess that's a compliment, huh?"

Again his shoulders moved up and down. Danny turned his face away.

She reached up and touched his cheek, pressing till their eyes again met. "It's okay, Danny. It's okay."

His mind swirled. Here he was trying to comfort her and suddenly the tide had turned. What was he thinking even admitting such thoughts, especially at a time like this? Staring into her face, he had to admit there seemed to be no ill effects. On the contrary, she seemed to be calmer, at least on the surface. Maybe his opening up made it easier for her to do the same?

The bed shook slightly as she repositioned her back. He refocused, saying, "Everything's not okay, but it could be worse."

"How?"

"It just could be."

"What would make it better?" she asked.

Her inquisitive mind never ceased to amaze him. "You're asking a lot of questions."

"Then make me shut up," she challenged.

They had the same exchange many times in the past, usually when she was intrigued by an idea or topic that needed a lot of questions. While they never wrestled rough, he usually tried putting a hand or pillow across her mouth. This time, however, he approached her lips with something else. He paused a few inches above, watching for a sign of discomfort or rejection. He always did that the first time he kissed someone, just in case they didn't want to. There was no such sign however, and the gap was closed an instant later.

35

His actions caught her completely off guard. She had no doubt he'd try and put something over her mouth. He always did when she told him to make her shut up. She never expected that something to be a kiss. The connection of their lips lasted only an instant. When it was over, Danny seemed as startled as April. They stared at each other. Finally, Danny's lips parted to say something. It was April's turn to cover his mouth, only she used her hand. "You don't have to apologize," she said. "It was just… it was just a kiss." She hesitated. "It was nice, too."

He looked at her startled a moment. "Really?"

She nodded.

He allowed a thin smile to form. The smile disappeared a moment later. "We shouldn't let things get any more complicated than they already are."

"Can they get any worse?" April asked.

"Sure. When both people don't want something."

"I don't really know what I want," April said.

"Don't think you're unique there," Danny directed. "Before we decide what we want, we need to decide what to do. We haven't solved that problem yet, remember?" He rolled over to his side. "I'm gonna take a shower and work on it some."

He scooted out of bed and made his way into the bathroom where he undressed quickly. He turned the water on as hot as he could stand it. He wanted steam—lots of steam. Steam was good. Fog in the bathroom was like trees in the forest—a good place to hide, a good place to get his thoughts together. His mind was racing with contradictions leading to a sense of urgency to get his feelings under control. "She's my sister… my stepsister," he said aloud. "You shouldn't have kissed her."

He was about to continue the lecture when he heard the bathroom door open. He froze, trying to hear above the sound of the water. He heard the door shut. "I was lonely out there," a voice said.

He didn't want to believe his ears, yet the list of options that the voice belonged to was rather short. He said nothing.

"Should I leave?"

He sensed regret in the voice. "No… no… it's okay," he said.

"You sure?"

"Yeah… yes."

"Like I said, I was lonely… No that's a lie. I was afraid."

"Of?"

"Everything, I guess." There was a pause. "Mostly about the future."

He could understand that, he thought. Aloud, he said, "What do you want the future to be?"

"In the perfect world, I want to rewind time a few days."

"Life isn't perfect, is it?"

"I guess I found that out the hard way."

"We all do," he said, trying to sound reassuring. At the same time, he tried to ignore the awkwardness of the situation. "You just have to make the most of whatever life tosses at you."

"Well, it's tossed me a big pile of shit, hasn't it?"

Again, he was surprised at her use of profanity. At the same time, he had to laugh.

"What's so funny?"

"You never cease to amaze me."

"*Everything* never ceases to amaze me," she countered. There was another pause. "So, how do you make the most of this mess?"

"My grandfather used to tell a story about coal mining," Danny started. "He said that after a cave in, you will never find a dead coal miner's lunch box with his dessert left and the sandwich gone. He said coal miners always eat their dessert first in case the next moment is their last. It's sick, I know, but there's a message there somewhere."

April laughed. "What does that have to do with fixing this mess?"

"Maybe we can't fix it," Danny said. "Maybe the cave in is coming and there isn't anything we can do about it."

"Maybe the cave in has already happened."

"Good point," Danny acknowledged.

"So you're saying make the most of it, huh?"

"Never leave the dessert in the lunch bucket."

The shower curtain pulled back slightly. "Can I come in?" April said softly. Their eyes met for only a second before a cloud of steam obstructed their view. He could hear both the eagerness and the caution in her voice.

"Only if that's what you want," he said.

She hesitated. "To be honest, I'm not sure what I want, except that I want to know more."

"Know more of what?"

"What it's like to be with someone… on mutual terms."

Her candor continued to take Danny by surprise.

"What do you want?" April asked.

"For you to be okay," Danny replied. Fighting the urge to look at her body, he kept his eyes focused on her head. Somewhere during their conversation she had undressed.

"What about you?" she said.

His shoulders shrugged. "I'm a survivor."

"And I'm not?"

"There's a hell of a challenge ahead."

"Do you really think the cave in is yet to come?"

He gave a short laugh. "A good analogy."

She stepped over the tub's edge. He reached out and took her arm to make sure she didn't slip. In doing so, his head moved downward. The darkened silhouette of her figure cut through the fog. He gasped. She was more beautiful than he had ever imagined. She looked up as she stepped towards him. Her chest pressed against his. They embraced. She sought out his mouth with hers. He put an arm around her shoulder to steady her, and to steady himself as his knees threatened to buckle. He pulled her into him as their kiss deepened.

She reached down for his free hand and raised it to her breast. The tissue was firm, her nipple hard. "Touch me, Danny. Help me to understand what it's all about."

And so he did.

36

Deputy Chief Willard Clusterman was only halfway through the pile of paperwork when the phone started ringing. He was always a person who left the end of his shift with a clean desk. What needed to get out, got out. What needed to get done got done. Since the shooting, however, things had slipped. Other than running home for a quick shower and a change of clothes, he'd been on the job continuously. Since the shooting, everything else in the department had come to a halt, including the never-ending reports that went along with the business of law enforcement.

When he transferred from Pittsburgh five years earlier, he did so because he wanted to spend more time on the street and less time behind a desk. That goal was easily accomplished. Sheriff Richmond was adamant in his belief that crime prevention was far more valuable than crime solution. While you might be able to solve a crime from behind a desk, you could not prevent one. Thus, the majority of the force's time was spent on the street. Even with that, there was still so much damn paperwork!

There was also much more to understand. In Pittsburgh, crime was high; caseloads were heavy. However, you knew the game; you knew the rules. For the most part, the crimes made sense—at least in the mind of law enforcement. In Worthington Valley, the rules were clear as well. He and his colleagues called it the *Richmond Doctrine*. Simply put, you did as you were told. The problem: what you were told did not always make sense. Like the night of the prom—Clusterman suggested they station a patrol car up at *Point-To-Point Overlook* to make sure none of the kids went up there before the dance. Hell, he even suggested a roadblock to make sure they didn't go further up the mountain. It was a good idea. Others thought so as well. The sheriff, however, insisted he wanted all the cars in town around the school.

If only the sheriff had listened!

It didn't make sense.

Like after the shooting when the sheriff simply disappeared with his son's body. No one knew where he was. No one knew when he was coming back. No plans for a viewing. No plans for a funeral.

More confusion. More to understand.

The deputy cursed under his breath as the ringing persisted. Someone must have forgotten to turn on the answering service. He let it go two more times before snatching the receiver from its cradle. "Hello," he said abruptly, quickly adding in a softer tone, "Sheriff's department."

"Who's this?" the voice on the other end demanded.

Exhausted from the long hours, the deputy hesitated as his auditory nervous system transformed the sound into a recognizable voice. "Sheriff Richmond! How are you, sir?"

"Willard?"

"Yes, sir."

"You don't sound yourself."

"Must be the connection," the deputy suggested. He didn't explain the connection referred to that between his mouth and brain.

"You got the late watch?" the sheriff inquired.

"Ah, yes, sir." The deputy chief failed to explain he had canceled all watches and simply put everyone in the department on call until the situation was resolved.

"Then what are you doing in the office?"

"I just stopped by to get a cup of coffee and try and get a little paperwork done."

"Paperwork," the sheriff snorted. "Documentation is the French word for let's see how many trees we can kill."

"Anyway, how you doing, sir?" the deputy inquired.

"I'm okay." The response was unconvincing.

Clusterman never knew what to say at a time like this. It was an uncomfortable situation. He could not imagine losing his wife or any of his kids. To do both… well that was too much. The deputy was not one to express a lot of emotion. In this case however, he felt true empathy towards his superior. While the older man could be a real son-of-a-bitch at times, he was always fair—with his employees as well as with their *clients*, as he liked to label Worthington Valley's criminal element. While the deputy wanted to help, the sheriff would have none of it. He had rejected everyone's approach. Hell, they didn't even know where he was. Clusterman thought the attitude strange, even for a man like the sheriff. At the same time he attributed the sheriff's reaction as emotional defense mechanism—a trick of the trade in an already lonely man's life.

Something else to understand.

The sheriff's voice broke the deputy's train of thought. "I just called to see if there was any news."

The deputy's hesitation gave his boss the answer. "You sure you don't want one of us to come and stay with you, sir?" Clusterman said.

"No!" the sheriff replied. "Thanks anyway. I'll be back in a couple of days."

"Call if you need anything."

"Just find the girl." Again, the *Richmond Doctrine*—do what you were told and don't ask a lot of questions.

The line clicked dead. The deputy stared at the silent receiver. He decided again, there was something peculiar about this whole thing. He focused back on the report in front of him. It concerned one of Worthington Valley's finest drivers, a young man who received his third ticket for speeding through the center of town in as many weeks. When he was pulled over the third time, it became a major issue. That was two days before the dance. Now it didn't seem so important. Still, the report had to be done. The boy was scheduled for court in the morning.

A few minutes later, the phone rang again. This time the deputy only let it ring once before answering. "Sheriff's office."

"Yeah, Willard, I think we have something." It was one of the newer deputies on the force. The man was young, cocky and overzealous at times, but so far had proven to be an asset to the department.

"What have you got?" Clusterman listened as the question was answered. "Where are you now?"

"I can pick you up in twenty five minutes."

"Make it fifteen."

"Yes sir!"

The line clicked off again.

37

April stared at the ceiling, thinking, trying to put everything into perspective. She had hoped Danny would offer some answers. Instead, the picture was now even cloudier. There were more questions without answers… answers her body ached for. She wanted to know more… to feel more… to experience what she had yet to experience.

The shower had been nice, once she got over her initial embarrassment, and Danny his. There were gentle caresses, gentle kisses, timid explorations. They washed one another, letting the hot water wash away some of the memories, some of the pain. Her curiosity was aroused, as were other senses in her body. Danny, however, refused to allow things to go too far, claiming he did not want to do anything they would later regret.

"We won't regret this?" she asked, both teasingly and with sincerity.

He hesitated. "I don't think so." He was right.

After the shower, they lay in bed together, naked, hugging, continuing the kisses, continuing the exploration. She had never been this close to anyone before, especially in this condition. (With the boys at the stream, there had been a chase, but no catch.) Danny's touch was soft and gentle, almost teasing like. What embarrassment she felt initially was erased by her curiosity as she did the same to him. But touching and kissing were all they did. Danny again urged caution. A side of her was relieved, another disappointed. She tried to focus on what had happened. She wanted to step back and analyze her body, her feelings, her emotions. Why wasn't she satisfied? Why did she still want more? What was left?

While she knew the answer, she avoided the issue. That would only make her more…

More what, she wondered? More… more… She struggled for the right word.

She told herself she should be ashamed. She told herself she was bad. She called herself several more superfluous names; but with each, the desire to throw caution to the wind only heightened. She rolled up on her elbow and looked at him. There was enough light to see his silhouette. He was lying on his back, one arm behind his head, the other reaching out in her direction. He was asleep, a soft smile across his face, his chest rising and falling with each breath. What was he dreaming, she wondered. She hoped about their time together a short while ago.

She touched her fingertip to his. He did not pull away. She pressed harder. There was still no reaction. She leaned over, her lips approaching his. She was about to kiss him when suddenly the room became much brighter. A red flash ran across the ceiling. It disappeared only to return a moment later. Startled, she sat up, her legs falling over the side of the bed. It took a second to get blood flowing to her head. She rose to her feet and made her way to the window. She peered out through the curtain. She blinked once, twice and the blood drained away.

She fell hard against the bed. The jolt brought Danny away from his dream. "What's the matter?" he demanded, wiping the sleep from his eyes.

The red light returned. Danny jumped to his feet and looked outside. "Shit! A fuckin' deputy's car—they must have found out where we were."

"How?" April said, having recovered from her fall.

Danny looked at his truck parked in the middle of the lot. "They're either real lucky or someone ratted"

"Who would rat?"

There was a moment's hesitation. "Then I guess they were lucky." Danny started getting dressed.

April filled with panic. "What do we do?"

"Give me a minute to think. In the meantime, get dressed." Danny looked out the window again. He could not see anyone in the patrol car, so he reasoned whoever was there had gone into the office to wake up the night clerk. They may have found his truck, but still did not know which room they were in. Another thought came to mind. He continued his thinking aloud. "They know I'm here. They don't necessarily know you're here. That gives us a chance… a slim one, but still…"

April finished dressing and gathered up her belongings, stuffing them in the backpack Danny had brought her. She didn't have to be told to get rid of all traces of her presence. She also didn't have to be told that certain traces were irremovable. Danny looked outside again to make sure no one was coming and disappeared into the bathroom. "Come here," he called out.

She followed his directions, and found Danny had already started taking out the screen of the small window. "I don't care how you do it, but you need to squeeze through this," he said. "The ground is lower in the back, so be careful when you drop down. This motel is backed up against a mountain. It's part of the same range that runs behind our house. Head straight out behind the motel. When you come to the top, head north. That should take you back towards home."

"I don't want to go back that way, do I?"

Danny hesitated. "You need to get into country you're familiar with."

"What about you?"

"I'll stay here and stall them somehow."

She looked around the room. "How?"

"I'll tell them I was here with someone… someone other than you, and that she already left."

"Here with who?"

He cocked his head to the side. "Jesus, it doesn't matter. I'll think of someone. Just go." He picked up her backpack and tossed it out the window. "Hurry up."

As she squeezed through the window, she paused and looked at him. There were so many things she wanted to say, so many things yet to do, yet to discover. Their eyes met. Time skipped a beat. "Go on," he directed.

She dropped to the ground and grabbed her backpack. He leaned out the window and handed her some money and a plastic card. "That's my bank card. The password is *stud*."

While she wondered about the value of this gesture, she made no comment. She stuffed the plastic and money in her pocket and moved away from the motel. She was just clear of the rear yard when she heard a loud knocking coming from the front of the building. She forced herself to ignore the sound as she broke into a run. She told herself she had to put as much distance between herself and the motel as possible. She also told herself she had to bury what just happened between her and Danny deep in her mind. There was no time to think about that. She had to focus on what lie ahead.

She looked up. All she could see was darkness. Her night vision had yet to kick in. "Time is wasting," she said aloud. "Look ahead, not behind."

38

April ran until she came to the edge of the woods. There she slowed to a fast walk to ensure she kept her footing. Danny taught her haste made waste, especially if you broke your leg in the process. Once in the woods, she collected her bearings and headed up the mountainside for several hundred yards. There was no definite path to follow, but the underbrush was relatively thin. She stopped to listen for any unusual sounds. Hearing none, she decided to backtrack as a way of covering her trail and to give anyone searching for her the impression she was lost and confused. A chuckle escaped her throat at the irony of her actions. Back at the original spot where she entered the woods, she went along the tree line, this time covering her tracks. She had a couple of skunk pellets in her backpack, which she laid down as well. She refused to let the thought of dogs cross her mind. After a half mile, she headed back up the mountain. Her pace was slow as she took the time to cover her trail. She kept her mind on her work, refusing to think too much about the future, or reminisce about the past. Her whole focus was on getting away—again—and to do it in such a way no one would be able to find her.

No one. The definition of the term lurked in her mind. She brushed the thought aside, reminding herself to stay focused.

Halfway up the mountain, she stopped again for a well-deserved break and to listen carefully for any activity. With her night vision now intact and some light from the moon, she had a good view of the field below. So far, she saw nothing of concern. She could barely make out the lights of the motel off in the distance. She saw nothing there either. She wondered if that would change soon, or if the deputies would believe Danny, whatever story he came up with. It didn't matter. She had to assume the worst.

When her breathing slowed to near normal, she continued her journey upward. At the mountain's peak, she searched for an area where she could see out. A surge of panic shot through her as she realized she wasn't sure where she was.

A faint smile crossed her face as Danny's words came to mind. "Always remember, you are never lost. Look down and you will see where you are. Look up, and you will always see where you're going. The only question is what's ahead, and that will only be answered with patience." While the advice wasn't all that helpful in reality, the words did help soothe her anxiety.

She figured she had three choices. She could head north along the mountaintop, which would take her in the direction of Worthington Valley. She could go south along the peak, or she could go down the far side. Her thirst told her that whichever direction she choose, she needed to find water. She compromised and took an angle downward and to the south. Her hope was to cross one of the many streams that ran through the mountain range.

Danny said that a good outdoors person could smell water. That lesson proved true on this night. A short time later, she smelled the humidity in the air first, and then she heard the faint sounds of water running across rocks. Had she not slowed her pace out of caution, she would have actually fallen into a stream that was hidden below the foliage on the ground. She followed it downward for a hundred feet or so before it broke free. There she was able to get safely down the muddy bank. She tasted the water first, swirling it around in her mouth, checking for any signs of impurities. Sensing none, she cupped her hands and hurriedly quenched her thirst. There was nothing like the taste of cold mountain water.

She sat on a large rock protruding from the stream and listened. She heard only the faint hoot of an owl and the inevitable sounds of crickets calling crickets. A heaviness fell over her. She suddenly felt very tired. Every joint in her body ached. She realized she was stiffening up. She told herself she should get up and get going, yet her mind did not respond to the pleas from her body. Instead, she focused on a recurring thought.

The idea was simple. No matter how much Danny talked a good story, no matter how good his actual intentions, no matter how supportive her parents might be, she could never prove what really happened in the car. It was her word against the opinion of the town. The only one who could set the record straight was Eddie, and he was dead.

Her eyes filled with tears. She sobbed softly. Life as she had known it the past few years was over. She could never go back. The question of what to do haunted her. It didn't take long for an answer to surface. The choice was simple. She had to get away from Worthington Valley, not head back toward it. She had to get away from the people, the memories, the sheriff. She had to get away from her parents, and from Danny. She had to escape it all. There was no alternative. That thought wasn't really as troubling as she might have imagined. Her mother, while still warm and caring, had distanced herself from April's daily activities. After all, she now had a whole lot of other things on her calendar. While April never vocalized any objection to this change of behavior, silently it bothered her. She even considered the real reason she had agreed to go to the dance with Eddie was to regain some of this attention. It seemed to work too, that is, until—

She stopped the thought process.

She would also be leaving Danny, the one person who had filled in some of the voids since she had been in Worthington Valley. He had become much more than she could ever had hoped from a stepbrother. He was a confidant, a friend and a teacher. Over the past couple of hours, he had also become a…

She was unclear just how to complete this thought. Even now, sitting on a cold rock, atop a cold mountain, she yearned to complete the journey they had started earlier. She had always been attracted to him in a brotherly kind of way. A new set of feelings now skewed the picture.

The heaviness in her chest increased. Looking out through the darkness, she realized she was at another major turning point in her life… just like when she and her mother had snuck away from her father… just like when she and her mother left the trailer in Alabama. She knew her mind wasn't working as well as it could because she was tired and thirsty. She also knew she had to make a decision, good or bad.

The earlier sought after definition became clear. *No one* meant just that. The realization slowly set in that the best thing for everyone was that she disappear so no one could find her… *no one*!

39

Danny circled the area a second time, carefully making sure he left no new traces of his presence. He stood still and listened, slowing his breath until his heart stopped pounding in his ear. Satisfied with what he heard and saw, he made his way to the base of the tree. Taking one last glance around, he quickly climbed the trunk. He poked his head through the floor of the tree house. His heart skipped a beat. The place was empty. He had been right—the ground in the area had not been disturbed since the last time April and he had been there. He glanced at his watch. Over twenty-four hours had passed since they parted at the motel. She should have been here by now.

Right before he stole away into the woods, he checked in on the CB radio. By now the whole area was swarming with law enforcement officers from all over the state. They had even called out a few dogs, and while they had picked up her scent a couple of times, it was quickly lost. Everyone was still convinced she was hiding near *Point-To-Point Lookout*. The police were baffled, yet not discouraged. The more time passed, the more determined they became.

As for the scene at the motel the night before, Danny easily convinced the two deputies he had been there with another girl. He said she left about fifteen minutes before their arrival. When they pressed him for a name, he hedged, saying he did not want to get her in trouble. It was obvious to the deputies that a fling had occurred in the room. The conclusion was quickly reached that April was not involved. She was not that kind of girl.

With each passing moment, April's failure to make it back to the tree house became more and more bothersome. Danny's mind raced through a spectrum of possibilities, each one worse than the last. He tried to stay objective and without emotions, and tried predicting what April was doing, or more specifically, where she was headed. While she had been gone twenty-four hours, he was confident she was okay. After all, he had trained her in the ways of the wild. She was a survivor.

He turned his attention back to the tree house. He had to do his best to protect the place from discovery. He had no doubt the area would be swarming with people sooner than later and wanted to ensure the place was safe. Besides wanting to protect that side of his life, he also wanted to protect the knowledge that April was an avid outdoors person as well, thus giving her an element of time… a very important factor in the game of fox and hound.

He left the tree house, carefully covered his tracks and headed down the firebreak. He had nowhere to pick up her trail from this side of the mountain. He'd go back to the motel and hoped he could pick it up there. A twinge of doubt flowed through his veins. He felt confident that if something really happened to her, he'd find her sooner or later. If on the other hand, she did not want to be found—he wasn't so sure. Her abilities both pleased and scared him.

"She's good," he muttered aloud.

40

Sheriff Richmond sat at his desk staring blankly into space. It was the first time he had been back to his office since the shooting. In the past, he had always been excited about coming to work. He looked forward to the challenges of the day. After all, being Worthington Valley's sheriff required a fine balance between law enforcement and politics, what was best for the community versus what was best for the individual. While he was always a *get tough on crime* kind of guy, he also understood the need for a certain amount of crime to justify his budget. This was true in any society. The key was finding an acceptable balance. That was probably his greatest forte—he was always able to find that balance. To have succeeded politically and professionally for so many years was the ultimate test of his ability. He was not only a great law enforcement officer, he was also a good politician. He could smooth talk with the best of them. He never lost an election. He lost very few court cases. It was said that if it would benefit Worthington Valley, Sheriff Richmond could sell chicken shit to a chicken farmer.

That had all changed, however, with one phone call—one phone call telling him his boy had been shot. Enthusiasm and confidence were traits of the past. He wasn't sure what he could do now. More importantly, he wasn't sure what he wanted to do. He had always been a dedicated, hardworking individual. If anything, he was driven by the pressure confronting him in the job. Even when his wife died, he was able to continue functioning once he went through the appropriate stages of grief. He had a young boy to raise and he needed the job to survive. The pay was good, the benefits fair, and the perks even better. The workload wasn't really all that bad. Worthington Valley was a small town with small town criminals, most of whom he knew. The balance was easily maintained.

Before the shooting, he never once regretted what he did. He was a driven man, driven to help his community. Now, however, all bets were off. His whole attitude had changed. The only drive left was the burning desire to find the girl. He hid behind his grief so others would not see his true feelings. While he grieved for his son, his hatred for the girl was far greater. The sheriff had never been a vengeful person. He was known for his fairness in the treatment of prisoners under his care. Strict but non-judgmental—that was the rap on Sheriff Richmond. He was even known to show compassion at times. He felt differently now, however. There was one criminal on the loose who presented no room for compassion.

"Focus on her, not Eddie," he told himself. He reached down and rubbed the dog's head lying at the side of his chair. "I know I promised you could retire soon, Bullet, but we got one more job to do."

The old animal pushed to his feet and shook out his fur. He stretched to loosen his stiff limbs and walked to the office door. Remembering hunts from the past, his sad demeanor suddenly shifted as his face pulled into a mean snarl. He growled and barked once. It was his way of telling the sheriff he was ready. He sat on his hind legs and waited for the next command.

A smirk crossed the sheriff's face. If none of his men could find the girl, he'd just have to do it himself. He had to admit, he had a weapon no one else possessed. He rose to his own feet. "If you find her, Bullet, she's all yours."

The sheriff bestowed the name on the German Shepard when as a pup, the dog proved to be very fast. Bullet could run down a rabbit with the best of 'em. While the breeder's papers claimed the dog was pure breed, the sheriff believed the animal had some Greyhound in him as well. As time passed and the dog's training progressed, the sheriff's confidence in that fact grew.

The sheriff corrected his earlier thoughts about his *clients*, as he liked to call them. Yes, he was compassionate to those criminals who obeyed him. Those who did otherwise were fed to his number one deputy. He smiled at the thought of the last person Bullet ran down. It was a young punk in a stolen car. Instead of exiting the vehicle with his hands raised as the sheriff had instructed, the man decided to back into the patrol car and then bolted on foot. The sheriff, mad as hell that his new patrol car had been damaged, counted to ten before letting Bullet out the rear door. The sheriff took his time catching up to the animal, which had caught up to the man within a hundred yards. Over the next several years, the would-be-thief had several surgeries on his left leg. His doctors said there were several more to go.

"One more good hunt, boy. That's all I ask." The sheriff realized this would probably be his last hunt as well.

41

Danny pulled into an empty parking space and shut off the engine. He glanced in the rear view mirror. The town square was empty. It reinforced his earlier sense that the whole town had come to a stop. He understood the concept of the community needing to mourn. Only it seemed to him the town had gone even further. There was a sense of fear—fear over the impact the shooting would have on one of Worthington Valley's top citizens—Sheriff Richmond.

Over the years, the community had become very dependent on its sheriff. The people of Worthington Valley, regardless of their economic status, basically had it good. Crime, while present, was lower than most communities. Taxes were tolerable and the people in general were friendly. The public schools had an excellent reputation, not only for the education provided, but for the lack of major behavioral problems. The percentage of students in private schools was one of the lowest in the country. Private schools were reserved for students with strong religious beliefs.

So things were good. Until now, when a single incident suddenly transformed everything. Danny realized that while people did feel real pain for what happened to Eddie, they were also concerned over what was going to happen to *them*. This concern, as well as concern over the community's reputation as a whole, intensified with each passing day April was at large. Danny always felt the citizens of Worthington Valley possessed an unusually high level of self-centered behavior. That theory was proving to be very true.

Danny couldn't really blame them. They had indeed grown to depend on the sheriff. In many ways, he was more than the town's senior law enforcement officer, Sheriff Richmond also wore the unofficial hat of mayor. This was fine with the community in that it saved them from having to pay for such a person. Officially, decisions affecting Worthington Valley were made by the town council, a group of individuals elected every four years along with the sheriff. Unofficially, the town council followed the *Richmond Doctrine*—they did what they were told. Those that wavered were usually defeated the next election. Danny realized long ago the sheriff was adept at making people need him. The man was like a dealer getting their victims addicted to drugs. The more you had, the more you wanted.

Danny closed the truck door and walked toward the bank machine. He kept his head low and shoulders hunched forward. While people were polite, there was still a sense of distance being kept. In the past, he was often approached by someone wanting to talk to him. Now, it was if he had the plague. While the attitude hurt, he really didn't care. If anything, leaving him alone let him focus more on the task at hand—finding April. The problem, he had no clue where to begin. The trail had come to a dead end. He went back to the motel the day before and trailed her into the woods. However, the trail was lost as darkness fell. He blamed it on the darkness so as not to bruise his own ego.

He bought a map of the area and tried to predict what April would do, where she might go. The options were many. He just hoped she was okay. While he had seen nothing to leave him thinking otherwise, he knew the dangers increased with each day she was alone. One thing he did suspect, she never headed back toward Worthington Valley. She was probably afraid to reenter the perimeter that had been established around *Point-To-Point Overlook*. The general consensus from the chatter on the CB was that she remained in the area. There was more and more talk that she was seriously injured, or even dead. The deputy sheriff leading the search was convinced of this. His overconfidence was getting in the way of his judgment. But Danny wasn't going to complain because it was this poor judgment that let him talk his way out of the motel situation several evenings before.

Danny walked up to the bank machine and reached for his wallet. He looked over his shoulder to see who was around. The town square was still empty. He opened his wallet and went to pull out his bank card. It wasn't in its normal slot. It took a second before remembering he had given it to April. A sense of sadness enveloped him.

First Eddie, then Sally, and now April. It was like his whole world was crumbling in around him.

His thoughts turned to Sheriff Richmond. What was he thinking… feeling… doing? Danny felt a surge of sympathy for the man. He remembered when Eddie's mother died. That was hard on everyone, but through it all, the sheriff remained strong. But now to lose his son, too! Danny just hoped he didn't go off the deep end. That would be bad for the sheriff, and for the citizens of Worthington Valley. But hadn't the sheriff already gone off the deep end? After all, he whisked Eddie's body away in the middle of the night without anyone having a chance to pay their condolences. Strange, to say the least.

Danny wondered about April's mother. The woman was amazing in that she had adjusted to her new life so smoothly and quickly. And she did it with such grace and poise. April told him her mother had attended charm school as a young teenager. But now he suspected that charm would fade away. All she ever wanted was a good life for herself and April. He never heard her ask for anything else. In return she had become a wonderful wife for his father, whose own dreams focused on building a company and raising a son. But those dreams were shattered with one moment of time.

Danny brought his focus back to the present. There were a lot of things he could think about at the moment, including how he, himself, was dealing with these shattered dreams. But there was only one thing he needed to focus on, and that was April.

If only he knew where she was!

42

She had been at it for over two days. Or was it three? Her muscles ached, her feet screamed in pain from blisters. Her hands, chapped and cut from the underbrush, often times hung limply at her side. Her shoulders were raw from the straps of her backpack. She had long ago tossed aside the walking stick she had picked up to help with her balance on the uneven slopes. She was so weak from hunger she began to question how much longer she could go on. Initially, she had tried to keep track of how far she had gone. Danny taught her basic land navigation and how to estimate distances based on time and speed of travel. However, once her hunger pains became the center of focus, all other issues became less important. She even became less prudent about covering her tracks. She figured if someone got on her trail this far away, they'd probably catch her simply because she was too weak to stay ahead of them. She knew if she did not find food soon, she'd collapse. She had survived on various roots, berries and grasses, and while they did take the pain away and provide an occasional boost of energy, the benefit was short lived. Because of the large amount of energy she was expending hiking through the mountains, calories expended far exceeded calories consumed.

She tried fishing in a couple of larger streams she passed, but she saw nothing. Besides, the one thing she failed to bring was matches. While there was the risk of being spotted with a fire, the benefits were now worth the chance. The ability to cook would also increase her food options. However, this was not a planned trek out into the woods like she and Danny usually made. This was an unplanned excursion for which she was ill prepared. She scavenged what she could to eat and made sure she kept her hydration level high. One good thing, there were plenty of streams running through the mountains.

She continued her journey, up one mountain and down the next. Each slope upward seemed steeper and steeper. The downside of each seemed more and more treacherous. Except for the many birds, an occasional deer and other smaller animals scurrying about, she saw nothing. She was alone in the world of the forest—a forest that so far provided the protection she needed. Although, she did wonder at times what would happen if she never made it out of the woods. She never realized how big the mountain range was behind their house.

She was now hungrier than she had ever been in her life. Even during the worst of times on the farm, she could ignore the hunger pains by doing something around the trailer or playing the piano. And none of these activities required the calories of mountain climbing. However, the will to distance herself from Worthington Valley, to distance herself from the past, gave her energy she never knew she had. She was determined to continue the journey until the well ran dry. So up one side of a mountain and down the other she continued.

As she neared the base of one hill, she thought she sensed the smell of water. It was a stronger sensation than that put off by the smaller streams. She also heard birds chirping, and thought she even heard a duck's quack. She told herself to be careful. While she was delusional at times, she still had enough sense to realize one of her greatest enemies was her own imagination. Just in case her mind wasn't playing games, she quickened her pace down the hill. A bigger body of water might mean additional food sources. She ignored the increased objections from various parts of her body. She stopped a hundred feet from the bottom where she was able to see through the trees. A large body of water did lay before her. She tried to think what lake or river this might be. She could not recall ever seeing anything on a map; then again, she never paid much attention to maps anyway. She did know she had never been here before, by foot or by car. She began to wonder just how far she had traveled. How many mountains had she crossed? How many days had passed? The bottom line: where was she? She looked up at the high noon sun. One thing for sure, she was still heading away from Worthington Valley.

Wasn't she?

Ignoring the pain in her legs, she hurried to the water's edge. While she wanted to look for food, she reminded herself water was still the priority. She found a spot where she could safely get to the water without the fear of falling in. She was now able to get a better look of what lay before her. It was much larger than she originally thought. She could not see an end either left or right, and the opposite shore was at least a mile across. She watched a flock of birds swoop low over the surface. She heard the quack of a duck again. Shielding her eyes, she saw the bird swimming alone a short distance from the shore. It looked lost, too.

She glanced down at the ground to check her footing. While she was hot, and started to sweat as the day grew warmer, she knew getting wet could be disastrous. It was chilly at night. She took off her shoes and socks, and rolled up her pant legs. She carefully made her way into the water. The bottom was soft and muddy. She quickly sank in above her ankles. The water felt cool against her skin. Satisfied her footing was secure; she glanced around before leaning over to quench her thirst. She drank quickly and was on her third mouthful when she suddenly heard a noise. Instinctively, she looked up in the sky. How did they find her, she wondered? Recovering quickly, she made her way back to shore, slipping and almost falling to her knees in the process. She cursed herself at being so careless. She climbed back up on shore and ran toward a thick set of bushes, ignoring the underbrush tearing at her feet.

In among the bushes, she rolled to a sitting position and pulled her knees up to her chest. Wrapping her arms around her legs, she tried to make herself as small as possible. It was also a good position to prevent movement—a trick Danny had taught her. She slowed her breathing and tried to do the same to her heart which was threatening to jump out of her chest. Except for her eyes, which continued to sweep the sky, she remained very still. The sound persisted. A minute or more passed. She realized the sound was not coming from above, but from the water itself. Another minute passed and a small rowboat came into view from her left. She watched it carefully as it made its way past.

Suddenly, something else caught her eye. Her shoes and socks were sitting on the edge of the shore. While she had small feet, her tennis shoes never looked bigger. She cursed herself again—another mistake. She had no choice but to wait and hope. She focused back on the boat. The row boat was old. A small outboard engine hung from the stern. While it made a lot of noise, the boat's progress was painstakingly slow.

There was a man in the back steering with the handle attached to the motor. Another man sat up in the front. Fishing rods hung over the side. She saw two large ice chests sticking out between the seats. She refused to think about the food they might contain. She glanced down at her shoes. So far, both men were looking straight ahead. She held her breath as the boat continued its slow progress.

After what seemed an eternity, the boat finally passed from view. Realizing she was barely breathing, April sucked in some fresh air. The noise slowly abated. She waited another minute before retrieving her shoes and socks. She also hurriedly took in a few more mouthfuls of water. This time, however, she remained on shore. Back behind the bushes, she examined her feet. There were a few scrapes and superficial cuts, but no real damage. She told herself her recent carelessness was due to her weakness and hunger. She knew she had to find more substantial food.

She stood up and stretched, trying to work the stiffness from her joints. At the same time, she contemplated what to do next. Her thirst was satisfied for the moment.

However, the hunger pains continued gnawing at her stomach. Gnawing at her mind was the thought that she had almost just been seen. She again scolded herself for being so careless. She had to stay alert, regardless of what her body was telling her.

She put on her shoes and socks, and explored the area along the water's edge. She found a few wild blackberry bushes. She ate some of these along with a few handfuls of grass. She was careful not to eat too much. She didn't want to get sick. For the moment, the hunger pains were satisfied. She knew, however, that would not last for long. She still had to find more substantial nourishment. The other issue was what to do now? The body of water stood between her and the direction she was heading. She would either have to change course or find a way across. She wracked her brain trying to remember anything Danny may have said about such a place. While he did at times talk about distant locations, when he referred to the mountains, all conversation was local. Even when they were out for long periods of time, they never ventured far from Worthington Valley. April did not know how far she had come. She knew she was well outside that perimeter. She was getting further and further away from Worthington Valley, and that was the only thing that mattered.

Her thoughts were interrupted by a wave of nausea. Her stomach contracted and her mouth filled with bile. She spit out the liquid and leaned against a tree. Her body wasn't used to the raw foods found on the mountainside for this long a period of time. She made her way back to the previous clump of bushes. She made a bed out of pine needles and lay down. Every joint in her body ached; every muscle screamed in pain as stiffness set in. Fatigue, however, overrode it all. She closed her eyes and was asleep within minutes.

She slept soundly as exhaustion won the battle over the impulses of discomfort. She was not one to fantasize when awake. Asleep, however, her mind easily traveled into the world of make believe. She dreamed often, and she dreamed vividly. Today was no different. As she entered the dream state, images formed of her own bed. The stuffed animals hanging above her headboard came to life, surrounding her, comforting her, rubbing her sore muscles. She dreamed of the school dance, of being the center of attention, of she and Eddie being crowned Princess and Prince of the dance. She dreamed of living happily ever after, of a life filled with joy, children, family and friends. There the picture suddenly changed. She dreamed of a noise… a loud noise… a shot… and suddenly she was no longer the Princess of the dance. Her gown had been replaced by torn jeans and a tattered sweatshirt. She was running through the woods, strange woods, someplace she had never been. She ignored the pain in her lungs as they screamed for air. She ignored the pain in her face as tree branches smacked her on the cheeks. She ignored the pain in her legs as her feet, still encased in glass slippers, twisted and turned in response to the irregular ground.

The scene changed again. This time she was back in school, in math class. Mr. Hopkins, one of her favorite teachers, was at the front of the room, writing a formula on the board:

$D = ST$

"Remember, it's like an address. You live on D Street. Distance equals speed times time." He took a big piece of chalk and started circling the word distance over and over and over, repeating the phrase, "Distance equals speed times time." The scene faded without further clarification. She passed through the dream state as her level of unconsciousness deepened further.

The sun was below the trees when she awoke. She remained still a few moments to get her bearings. Her joints ached. Her mouth tasted foul. She sat up. A wave of nausea filled her stomach and her head began to spin. She lay back down and swallowed to keep from vomiting. When the nausea passed, she sat up again, this time more slowly. Her head felt better, but the hunger pains were still present. She stood up, stretched and listened. The sounds of the forest were all she heard. She went down to the water's edge and rinsed her mouth, swallowing only a small amount. She picked a few berries and chewed them slowly. They were sweet and the sugar helped settle her stomach. After a few minutes, she took a few more sips of water. Re-energized, she began working the stiffness out of her limbs.

She looked out over the water. Danny always told her that water was a good way to break up a trail. The question was how to get across. Her stomach growled. The berries were only a tease. Food would have to come first. She ate another handful, but stopped short there. She didn't want the nausea to return. The image of the coolers in the boat came to mind. What she wouldn't give to have a look inside one of those.

A thought struck her. The row boat contained two men. They were obviously heading somewhere. She assumed they were headed home after a morning of fishing. She also remembered they were close to her side of the shore. Did that mean home was on her side? She knew the prudent thing to do was head in the opposite direction. Her stomach, however, told her to head towards the coolers.

She went back to the bushes and eliminated any signs of her presence. She started along the bank of the lake—in the direction of the coolers. She realized she was now traveling perpendicular to her desired path, which meant she was no longer adding distance to the equation.

She traveled a mile or so when she broke out into a less dense area of the shore. She stopped, looked and listened. She stayed low and carefully moved into a field. By now the sun had set so darkness was encircling the area. In addition, the night sky had clouded over, blocking out any light the moon might be tossing her way. The field was about a hundred yards wide with a tree line on the opposite side. In the distance she saw what looked like a man-made structure. As she drew closer, she saw her vision had been correct. It was a small one story cottage sitting back off the water's edge. She could barely make out a small pier jetting a short distance out into the water. A row boat similar to the one she saw earlier was tied between two of the pilings.

Her speed slowed, her senses heightened. She moved to the very edge of the tree line and stooped low, slowly scanning the area around the building. She saw a narrow dirt road that led up to the house. There were no cars or other vehicles in the yard. All the curtains were pulled on the windows. April stayed put for a full fifteen minutes, watching and listening. She saw nothing. She heard nothing.

She contemplated her options, deciding her hunger was far greater an issue than anything else. She moved in slowly and pressed up against the side of the building. She completely circled the building, stopping at the front porch. A couple of dog food bowls sat empty on the front porch. In particular, she noticed the water bowl was dry. She took that to be a good sign. She stepped up on the porch. The wood creaked. Hearing nothing else, she tried the door. The knob turned and the door swung open. The inside of the house was dark. She waited a full minute before stepping across the threshold. Still hearing nothing, she moved forward a few steps. She used the faint light coming in through the door for guidance. While the room was dark, Danny had trained her to be patient while her eyes adjusted to the situation. She made her way through the room to a doorway in the distance. As she hoped, this led to the kitchen.

She found the refrigerator and started to open the door when the inside light came on. She quickly shut the door, but it was too late. Her pupils had constricted in response and her night vision was ruined. She cursed beneath her breath and opened the door again. There was a loaf of bread and a half filled quart of orange juice. Otherwise the space was empty. She left the door open a crack so she could better see the kitchen cabinets. She opened several before finding one containing food. There were several packs of cheese and crackers, a box of Pop Tarts and a few cans of soups.

Her mouth watered and her stomach growled in anticipation. She contemplated her options and finally decided to take two packages of Pop Tarts, along with half the cheese and crackers. Anything else would be too noticeable as missing. Her temptation was high, but her discipline prevailed. She had enough to get through a couple more days. Besides, she was feeling guilty about having broken into someone's home.

She was about to close the refrigerator door when another thought came to her. Again leaving the door propped open, she looked around on the counter tops. They were clean and empty. She opened several of the drawers and finally found the junk drawer. Two books of matches sat on top. She took one. She was out of the house an instant later, deciding to exit before her night vision fully recovered. She didn't want to overstay her welcome.

She ate one of the four Pop Tarts and one package of crackers. Her hunger pacified and her blood sugar on the rise, she felt more adventurous. She decided to explore the area around the cottage to see where the dirt road led. She stayed on the grassy edge, making sure her silhouette blended into the background. The road wound to the left about a quarter mile before coming to a dead end at another dirt road. This one was wider, and from the deep ruts, showed a lot more wear. She contemplated which direction to head and finally decided away from the mountainside. She passed several sets of mail boxes which meant houses with permanent addresses. Her senses on high alert, she continued to make her way along the road. From the direction, she figured she was heading parallel to the water. The road was long and she had traveled for over fifteen minutes when she heard a distant sound. She stopped and hid in the bushes. She cocked her ear in the direction of the noise. It grew louder at first before fading away. She waited a few minutes and the sound was repeated. The third time, April realized the noise came from the grinding of truck gears. This meant there was a major road nearby, which meant a possible way across the water. Her journey along the road continued. The only problem, the road took a turn and headed in a steep incline back up the mountain. She again debated her options and finally decided the possibility of a highway overrode everything.

She did eventually come to the intersection of the dirt road and a four lane highway. One side continued up the mountain side. The other headed downhill towards the water. She watched a few minutes and saw that the traffic was steady, but light. More debate followed. The road would make travel much easier. She could cover a lot more distance in a shorter period of time. In the same instance, the risk of discovery was much higher. However, the urge to put distance between herself and Worthington Valley, and the possibility of a bridge across the water won out. She stepped out onto the road and headed down the hill.

She half-walked, half-ran along the gravel shoulder. She had plenty of time to skirt into the underbrush when she saw lights coming toward her. She had just come out of the bushes past a sharp turn when she suddenly froze. She saw light, but was confused. Before she realized what had happened, a large truck whizzed by her. It had come from the other direction and had been rolling down the hill on gravity, thus the engine noise was quiet. She dove into the bushes, but it was too late. The head light lit her up like a frightened deer.

She rolled to a sitting position and froze. She listened for a change in the truck's sound and heard nothing. It continued its journey and disappeared around the next bend.

It took several minutes to get her pulse and breathing under control. She wondered if the driver had seen her, but that didn't really matter. The truck kept on going. She debated her options and finally decided to continue down the road. She just had to be more careful. She left the security of the bushes, this time with frequent glances over her shoulder. Several more cars passed and another truck came down the mountainside. Each time she was able to get into the underbrush without difficulty. Her confidence rebuilt, she increased her pace. She knew she was getting close to the water. The thought of how she was actually going to get across the bridge crossed her mind. She allowed a thin smile to cross her face. She'd cross that bridge when she came to it.

She wanted to make the most of the darkness. Feeling more energized than she had in several days, she broke into a trot. She rounded two more bends and was just thinking about emptying her bladder when a voice almost did it for her. "Hey, sweet thing. What are you doing out here on a night like this?"

She turned in a full circle, trying to figure the direction of the voice. A tall thin figure emerged from the bushes, which happened to be her only way of escape as the opposite side of the road was too steep a drop. She said nothing.

The figure took a few steps forward. Through the thin light of the moon, she saw it was a man—tall, thin and dressed in a plain white tee shirt and jeans. His head was covered with a wide-brimmed hat and his feet were covered in cowboy boats. It didn't take too many IQ points for her to guess he was the earlier truck driver.

"Don't fret none, I ain't goin' a hurt you," he said with a southern accent. "On the contrary, I just want to make sure you're okay. You know, you shouldn't be walking out in the middle of the road like that. You could have gotten yourself squished real good?"

"Sorry," April managed to say.

"Well, be that as it may, you okay?"

"Yeah, I'm okay… thanks."

"It ain't none of my business as to why you're out here and all that. I see a lot in my travels, and I learned a long time ago to ask little and listen a lot."

April remained silent, her mind working feverishly for what she should do. At this particular moment, she did not see a lot of options.

"Anyway, like I said, I don't mean you no harm." The trucker hesitated. "I can offer you a ride if you want."

"A ride?"

"Yeah, my truck's parked around the next bend."

"A ride to where?"

"I got a load of vegetables I'm taking to Atlantic City. We'll be there by morning."

"Atlantic City?"

"Yeah, as in New Jersey… the east coast… the boardwalk… casinos. You have heard of it haven't you?"

"Sure, sure," April said quickly. She was surprised he happened to be going so far… so far away from Worthington Valley. A side of her started screaming objections. At the same time, other voices told her to go. Memories of the earlier dream returned. Mr. Archibald was again at the chalk board. "Distance equals speed times time." In this particular case, the focus was on speed. On foot, her rate was slow at best. In a truck, there would be speed and no scent for dogs to track or nothing for a helicopter to see.

On top of that, it was a way over the bridge.

43

In contrast to recent nightmares of her running from someone or something, this was a more pleasant dream. She was walking across the tops of clouds with an occasional dance step thrown in. She was coming from nowhere in particular. She was headed nowhere in particular. She wore a long white laced dress. She was barefoot and had flowers woven through her hair. She was smiling. She had no problems per se. Life was wonderful and she was happy.

Yes, it was a pleasant dream.

And then she felt it! The dream ended. The visual images went black. Something was on her leg. She awoke with a start. Her eyes snapped open. She heard a voice.

"Hey, sweet thing," the truck driver was saying. "We're here. Sorry to wake you, but I have to go to the terminal to unload and I can't have any passengers in the cab when I get there."

April sat up and rubbed the sleep from her eyes. The hand on her leg moved away.

A grin crossed the trucker's face. "Now, about payment for the ride."

April's eyes widened. "I don't have any money," she stammered.

"Well, there're other ways to pay for fuel." His smile widened. He leaned her way. He had that look in his eyes… That look… the same she had seen before.

April slid towards the door as fear filled her veins. Recent memories fired through her brain. However, before she could even begin contemplating what to do, the trucker straightened up. His hands flew up into the air. "Whoa there," he said. "It's a request, not a demand. I ain't into forcing someone to do something they don't want. Now, why don't you skedaddle out of here?"

And so she did.

44

The old lady rummaged through the trash barrel with a long pointy stick looking for empty soda cans. She had just inspected the same container an hour earlier and didn't expect to find anything new. To her surprise, however, she saw two Diet Coke cans. She speared them and put the cans in the pouch strung across her shoulders. The canvas bag was almost full. It had been a good morning so far. The day was warming rapidly. The morning news called for the temperatures to be in the 70's, about right for this time of year. Then again, whoever said the weather along the east coast was ever normal? The only thing normal was the weather's unpredictability. The old lady smiled. Wasn't that true of life in general?

The old lady didn't care though. The warmer the weather, the more sweat. The more sweat, the more thirst, all leading to more empty cans for her to recycle. Yes, the hot weather was definitely good for the can business. It was good for another kind of business as well.

Except for those staying in the casino hotels, most folks got up early. Those that had something specifically to do, did so. Those that did not hit the boardwalk. Over the years, she had divided *boardwalkers*, as she dubbed them, into several categories. First were the elderly who came to Atlantic City fantasizing about the past. They got off the tour buses dressed to the gills, only to realize dressing up was no longer the fashion. Second were the athletic wannabes who pretended they were jocks, and ran up and down the boardwalk like it was an athletic track. The old lady often had the urge to trip one of these runners as they ran by. As they hit the deck, their bodies would collect splinters. The old lady would yell out to them that this was a boardwalk, not a *boardrun*. The third type of *boardwalkers* were the tourists who were either taking a break from gambling or who had already lost all their money and needed to kill time before leaving their fantasy world of striking it rich.

And then there was the fourth type. They were the lost and lonely. They came to the boardwalk because they had nowhere else to go. They were the discarded leftovers of life—the empty soda cans of humanity. Now that's where you could make money in the recycling business, especially if you specialized in the young ones, which the old lady did. For reasons she never fully understand, Atlantic City attracted all types of people, including the runaways of the earth. In her sarcastic fashion, she reasoned this was as far east as one could go before having to swim. While the can recycling business was good, it was really an excuse to spend a lot of time on the boardwalk without raising a lot of questions. She played the part of a dumb old lady. In reality she was sharp, keen and had eyes of a feline predator. She could spot 'em a mile away.

She had spotted this target an hour or so earlier. The girl came from the north end. She looked tired, disheveled and lost. She walked slowly, stopping and looking in almost every shop window. She obviously had little or no money as she bypassed all food and beverage places until she came to Pollock Johnny's. It was the greasiest food on the boardwalk. It was also the highest calorie to dollar ratio. The old lady watched as the girl carefully counted her change. That action alone meant the girl was a hot prospect. The girl took her food to a nearby bench where she gobbled the sausage down as if there were no tomorrow. The old lady chuckled to herself. For many of these girls, that was indeed the truth. The odds of making it to tomorrow were about the same as winning at blackjack. It was hard to tell the girl's actual looks, but the old lady reckoned the girl probably cleaned up real good. Her age was a question, but that could be altered, too.

The old lady waddled over to the trash barrel next to where the girl was sitting. A closer look did not change her initial opinion. The girl's hair, pulled into a ponytail, was disheveled. Her face was clean, but there was a streak of dirt on her neck. Her sweatshirt was crumpled and dirty. Her jeans showed signs of mud around the bottoms and her tennis shoes were muddy. The old lady knew under normal circumstances a girl this age would never be caught dead on the boardwalk looking the way she did. Appearance was just too important for the younger generation. This told the old lady the girl had other priorities, at least for the moment.

Without looking directly at the girl, the old lady spoke quietly. "Who you are or why you landed in this God forsaken place is none of my business. It's obvious you need help. I got room and board real cheap, and if cheap's still too much, we can always work something out. I don't ask no questions either, except for maybe one… You are eighteen, aren't ya?"

The old lady continued rummaging in the trash can, waiting patiently for the response she knew would come. It always did, and it was always the same. "Yes," the girl replied.

The old lady chuckled aloud. "And really, that don't matter no how anyway. I can make you whatever age you want." She speared a can and put it in her sack. "Corner of Baltic and 25th. Big old white house. You can't miss it. I'll be there sometime after noon." She stole a glance at the girl. She knew the facial expression to expect. It was always the same. First denial, a no-I-don't-need-any-help look. Next, the how-do-you-know look. Finally, the we'll-see look.

The girl's facial expression did not disappoint her.

She'll come, the old lady said to herself. They always do.

45

April watched as the old lady walked away passing three trash cans before stopping to scratch her arm. She turned, looked at April, nodded slightly and disappeared between two tall buildings. April finished her sausage, wiped the grease from her face and drained her soda. She glanced around suspiciously, not sure what she was looking for. She did feel a sense of concern. Since being dropped off at a truck stop a mile out of town, she felt pretty good about her situation. The trip to the east had been uneventful. She slept nearly the whole way and the trucker seemed content to let her alone, which he did until the end when he started talking about payment for the ride. Thank goodness he backed off. Once she was safely on the ground, she said good-bye and thanked him. He laughed and thanked her for the company. He told her to go up onto the boardwalk and look around. She'd find plenty to see and do. The trucker told her to make sure she saw the place at night when all the lights were on.

April had her doubts at first. The walk from the truck stop toward the waterfront showed dilapidated houses lining streets in no better condition. Many were in worse shape than their trailer back in Alabama. However, once she broke into the casino district, the change was drastic—from poverty to posh in a block. April had never seen anything like it. While she had seen poverty and had experienced the better side of life, she had never seen such a drastic change in such a short distance.

That was not for her to worry about, however. Danny taught her to stay focused on the task at hand and not get all caught up in surrounding issues. The task at the moment, now that her hunger pains had been brought into check, was to come up with a plan. She was fearful at being around people. What if someone recognized her? What would she do? Where would she go? She was far away from the security of the mountains. Being in the mountains might spell hunger. The wilderness also spelled safety. Here on the boardwalk of Atlantic City, there were no trees. There was nowhere to hide.

Or was there? She realized she was still in the wilderness, only of a different kind. Instead of trees, there were people. Instead of bushes, there were buildings—casinos to be more exact, filled with even more trees, even more people. Like she and Danny used to blend in with the forest, she could blend in with the people of Atlantic City. Maybe it would work? Maybe she could stay here, at least for a little while.

She reviewed the old lady's remarks, mulling over in her mind what she said about not asking questions. It took April a while to realize the significance of the comment. She would not be able to get a job. She had no ID. And if she did, she certainly wouldn't want to show it. An unexpected problem suddenly surfaced. For the first time, April realized she not only had to get away from Worthington Valley, she also had to escape from April Blackstone.

She rose to her feet as she fought back the tears. She had seen a money machine earlier and decided to try and get some cash. After all, in spite of what the old lady said, room and board would not be free, and she already spent part of the money Danny gave her.

46

Once out of sight of the girl, the old lady picked up her pace until she came to a pay phone on the next corner. She lifted the receiver and banged the lever hard, trying an old trick to steal a dial tone. "Shit," she muttered as she reached into the pocket of her tattered dress for two quarters. Finally getting the sound she wanted, she dialed the number. She let the number ring three times then hung up. She repeated the action, this time allowing the ringing to occur twice before breaking the connection. The third time, the phone was answered before the first ring fell silent.

"Yeah," a voice said.

"I got one," the old lady said.

"Shit," the voice said. "You get one every week. Last three were flops."

"This one's hot," she insisted.

"They're all hot."

The old lady allowed her anger to build. "Well, if you don't want her, I'll just call…"

"Hold on, I didn't say I didn't want her."

"Then quit fuckin' with me."

"Now, listen here…"

The old lady, having gotten the ball successfully back in her court, interrupted the voice on the other end. "She'll need papers."

There was hesitation on the other end. Age, or lack thereof, worked both ways in this business—very positive and very negative. The trick was to balance the two. "Just how bad does she need papers?"

"Fifteen… sixteen at the most."

The voice on the other end exhaled. "That ain't too bad I guess."

"She's a looker, too," the old lady said.

"They're all lookers in your eyes," the voice said. "After the last one you sent me, maybe you ought to get your eyes checked."

"My eyes are just fine," the old lady argued. "I tell you, this one's hot. So much so, I want double my usual rate."

"Fuck you!"

"Fine. I'll just call…"

There was laughter on the other end. "Fine, send her over. If she's a keeper, you'll get double. Only, you pay for the papers."

The lady hesitated. She figured she had pushed him as far as possible. "She'll be there this afternoon."

"She better not be a dog."

"She ain't, I tell ya." The old lady hung up the phone. She waited to hear the click of the coins falling before checking the return slot just in case. She cursed under her breath. The old machines used to be forgiving once in a while and return the money. These modern day *phone slots* never paid off. She turned around and headed back toward the boardwalk. She'd pick cans for another hour or so, keeping a watchful eye out for anyone else who looked lost. She figured she would never be that lucky. She reminded herself that Atlantic City would be bankrupt if people really paid attention to the odds.

She turned her thoughts back to the girl. Probably more mature than she needed to be at this time in her life, she was still just a child. It was a pattern the old lady had seen over and over. Forced to mature faster than nature intended, these runaways always came with more emotional baggage than Samsonite had luggage. She felt sorry for them when she first started in the *recycling* business. Each had a different, yet similar story. All had one main reason for running away—to escape the environment from which they came. They all were in search of greener pastures. If they only knew the truth, she often thought.

She herself was a prime example. She'd left home at the ripe age of twelve to escape an abusive mother and alcoholic father. By fifteen, she was a hardened street girl, hooked on alcohol, drugs and the fast life. She landed in Atlantic City three years later and had never left the city limits since. She had no need. With hard work, determination and a willingness to learn the trade, she found moderate success in the recycling business of cans and girls. In her earlier days she was successful in other ways as well, only she seldom discussed that part of her life. While drugs were a thing of the past, and there wasn't much fast life left for someone her age, she still enjoyed a sip or two. Bourbon was her drink of choice.

Yes, the casinos had been bad for some people in the town. But for her, there was opportunity—something she'd always been able to use to her advantage. The casinos drew people in like bugs to a light. Above, the vultures, circling ever so slowly, waiting patiently for their prey to falter so they could swoop in for the kill. Whether it be the casino managers looking down onto the casino floor from their eyes in the sky or a little old lady prowling the boardwalk, they waited.

A vulture herself, she had learned the art of patience. She went through a few more trash cans before calling it quits for the morning. If her instincts were correct, the girl would be waiting for her return, sitting on the porch steps, biting her fingers, fidgeting around and looking constantly in all directions with jerky head motions.

Yes, human behavior was so predictable.

47

April saw the old lady coming from the left. She was bent forward from the weight of the bag she carried over her shoulder. Her gait was slow and shuffled; her eyes focused on the uneven pavement before her. The young girl rose to her feet as the woman approached.

The old lady looked up. Seeing the girl, she smiled. "Well, hello again."

April nodded.

"I'm glad you decided to stop by," the lady continued. "Come on in and I'll show you around." She dropped the bag of cans on the side of the house and led the way inside.

The house was a three story wooden building with a large porch and overhanging roof. Many coats of white paint tried to hide the building's age. The porch creaked with each step as they entered the foyer. The inside was dark and it took April's eyes a moment to adjust. She saw a living room to the left decorated with old Victorian furnishings. The foyer also passed a dining room decorated the same. They came to a large kitchen which was much brighter in that the window shades were up. In general, the decor was old, yet the place seemed well maintained. More importantly to April, the place looked clean.

The old lady went to the counter by the stove and picked up a pan of freshly made muffins. The smell quickly filled April's nostrils. "Hungry?" the old lady asked, pulling the paper off the base of the muffin and offering it to the girl. April took it with a nod of gratitude

"My name is Sally Richards. You can call me Ms. Sally." She took a muffin for herself.

"My name is April Bla—"

The lady's hand snapped upward. "First names are fine… April. Is that what you want to be called?"

April nodded. She broke the pastry in half and ate the top part first. Ms. Sally motioned April to a chair at the kitchen table. She pulled a container of milk from the refrigerator and poured two tall glasses. She sat across from the girl and watched her eat the rest of her food. "Like I told you earlier, I run a nice place here. Rent's cheap and even free if you're willing to work."

April's eyes raised in response to the last statement.

"This is a big place to keep up. We have a fair turnover of rooms. Some come here for a few days, others for a week or more. We even get an occasional college student who has come down for the summer. But I run a tight ship. No overnight visitors, no drugs and no loud noises." She broke her own muffin in half. "Those who work for me, I treat them right. You get a clean room with a comfortable bed and two hot meals a day. I make no promises, but if we have a good week, I even throw in a few bucks as spend money." She paused and tipped her head to the side. "But if you think you want something more, I may be able to help you there as well."

April hesitated as her mind nibbled on the bait Ms. Sally dangled in front of her. The girl shrugged her shoulders.

Ms. Sally continued. "I don't know all that much about it, but from what I do hear, the girls love it. It's exciting and glamorous, and you get to meet a lot of nice people." As she anticipated, the prospect of meeting a lot of people caused the young girl to withdraw. It was the same with all of them. They were afraid of being discovered. It was the reaction she wanted. It was how she set the hook. "I can't do much about anything if you stay here and work for me, but this other opportunity…" She looked around to make sure no one else was in the kitchen with them. "They can give you a whole new identity, with papers and everything."

The girl's eyes widened. The hook was set. The old lady rose to her feet and fetched the carton of milk. She poured April another glass. "Drink up, you look like you're half starved." She watched carefully as the girl wrapped both hands around the glass and raised it to her lips. She smiled. Yes, human behavior was so predictable.

"I'll tell you what," the old lady said. "Why don't you go upstairs and freshen up— bathroom's at the top of the steps. There's fresh towels beside the sink. While you do that, I'll make a phone call and see what I can do. For all I know, they may not have any openings." She watched as a look of concern flashed across the girl's face. She decided to let the fear of a missed opportunity linger on. "Go on now, and do as I say."

April finished her milk and started to gather up her glass and plate.

"That's okay," Ms. Sally said quickly. "Just leave them."

April did as she was told. She grabbed her backpack and headed toward the stairs.

The old lady waited until April was well on her way up the stairs before heading to the phone hanging on the far wall. She dialed and let the number ring three times then hung up. She repeated the action, this allowing the ringing to occur twice before breaking the connection. The third time, the phone was answered before the first ring—just like before.

"Yeah," the voice on the other end said.

"She'll be over this afternoon."

There was a pause. "Make it noon."

"She'll be there."

The line disconnected. She hung up the hand piece and walked to the table. She pulled a Kleenex from her pocket and grabbed the glass April had been drinking from by the rim. She lifted it high so she could see it through the light, squinting to get a better view. She saw what she wanted and smiled. She carried the glass to the sink and carefully put it in a plastic bag. She went back to the phone and dialed another number. This time she let it ring without interruption.

It was answered by a deep harsh voice. "Detective Moon here."

"Morning, Detective."

"Sally, you bird. How the hell are you? Been a long time."

"I've been good."

"Bullshit. You just ain't been caught." He let out a deep laugh. "Anyway, what are you doing calling this time of the day? Aren't you usually asleep by now?"

"I told you before, I've mended my ways."

"Ditto to the bullshit."

"I got a hot one for you," the old lady said, ignoring the detective's remark. At the same time she chuckled to herself. Maybe *mended* wasn't the right word. *Adjusted* her ways fit better.

"Is this another one of your wild goose chases?"

"When's the last time I sent you on a wild goose chase?"

The detective started to respond.

"Don't answer that," the old lady laughed. "I know you're going to bring up the college student last year."

The detective laughed.

"This time I got good prints, so it should be easy," Ms. Sally teased.

The detective's voice became quieter. "Same terms as always, if it's a hot one, we split the reward."

"Right down the middle. The bag'll be on the back porch as usual."

"Okay. I'll pick it up when I get off later." The detective's voice rose back to a normal tone. "You free tonight?"

Ms. Sally laughed. "I ain't never free. Besides, I said I mended my ways."

"And I said bullshit."

The old lady hung up the phone. She ran her hand through her hair. The possibility did intrigue her. After all, it had been a while since she'd had any, free or otherwise.

"We'll see how this plays out," she said aloud. She had a suspicion this one would play out very well—and pay out, too. She took the plastic bag with the glass out to the back porch where she gingerly placed it into an old milk box sitting in the corner. Back inside, she headed up the steps to see how her guest was making out.

Yes, she told herself. She had a good feeling about this one.

48

April held the piece of paper tightly as the stiff breeze tried to pry it away. She looked at the paper and up at the old dilapidated building in front of her. The address, 522 Ventnor Avenue, matched. It was not what she expected. The building was an old house, similar in style to Ms. Sally's, only the condition was much worse. A quick glance showed peeling paint, streaks of dirt and mold, and some areas of bare rotten wood. It looked like it hadn't received any outside attention for many years. Then again, little attention was paid to the area in general. Several blocks away were multimillion dollar hotels and casinos, where cleanliness was an expectation. Two ends of the human spectrum so close together, yet so far apart. It was a repeat of the impression April had when she first came to town.

She stepped up to the porch and knocked. The door opened and she was greeted by a young woman she guessed to be in her early 20's. She was tall, slender and dressed in a short bright green dress. She was holding a mug of coffee in one hand and a cellular phone in the other. "Can I help you?" She did not seem happy at having been bothered.

"I'm April, Ms. Sally sent me." April said.

The girl's demeanor changed as a wide smile crossed her face. "Hi April, I'm Patricia. You can call me Pattie." She stepped forward and looked up and down the deserted street. "Come on in. We've been expecting you."

She led April into a dark hallway, again similar to Ms. Sally's. The inside of the house wasn't in much better condition than the outside. The air was musty. There was very little furniture. What pieces were scattered around haphazardly didn't match and had probably been rejected by Goodwill. April did notice all the walls were bare. The floors, covered with scattered throw rugs, sported a half inch of dust.

She followed the girl through the dimly light walkway to a set of stairs that led to the basement. Here, the atmosphere was brighter. The walls were less dingy and looked painted within the last few years. Fluorescent lighting hung from the low ceiling. The spacious room was set up like an office, with several desks sitting against the walls. There were a couple file cabinets and each desk contained at least two telephones.

A middle aged man sat behind the desk furthest from the stairs. He was short, overweight and balding. Thick black glasses rode halfway down his nose. An unlit cigarette hung from the corner of his mouth. He had one telephone cradled to his left ear and was dialing a cellular phone with his right hand. Seeing the two women caused his focus to change. Without uttering a word, the two phones were set down. He eyed April with a slow sweep. April sensed the heat of his glare.

"She the one from Sally?" he finally said.

"Yeah," Pattie said. "Her name is April."

"April what?"

"Blackstone," April responded.

"Where you from?"

"Worth—"

"Since when did you start asking so many questions, Jerry?" Pattie interrupted.

The man glared at her. "Since whenever I damn well please."

Pattie turned her attention to April. "You'll have to excuse his manners. He's just being an asshole today. Then again that's normal for him." She looked back at the man. "You interested or not?"

The man's stare continued. "She looks awfully green. You wanna show her the ropes?"

"You paying a training fee?"

The man laughed. "You charge for everything, don't ya?"

"Just like you taught me, ain't nothin' in life for free."

"You work that out with your sweetie pie there. If you want her, she's yours."

It was Pattie's turn to hesitate. "Long as things stay slow."

The man shrugged his shoulders.

"What about the papers?" Pattie added.

"Get me a picture."

Pattie turned her attention to April. "I guess that's it. You'll be staying with me. I have a room at the Bradford Towers—that's right on the boardwalk. It ain't oceanfront, but hey… I'll take you with me the first couple of times and show you the ropes. Then you'll be on your own. I got some clothes you can borrow till you get your own—we're probably about the same size. Anyway, we have to be in the room every afternoon between two and four. That's when we get our assignments for the night. If we don't get a call, we're free to do whatever we want. But if the call comes in, you'd better be there."

"Asshole over here—his real name is Jerry—collects the fee directly from the client. We get to keep any tips. He pays the hotel bill. We pay for our own food, so I suggest you get a doggy bag whenever you can. You do your job and no one asks any questions. We don't really care who you are or where you're from. Anyway, in a day or so, you'll be a whole new person. Any questions?"

Trying to hide her confusion, April looked back and forth between the two people. "Just what is the job you're talking about?"

The man called Jerry laughed. "The old lady did it again. She didn't tell her nothing, did she?"

Pattie looked at April with her mouth half open. "You are green, aren't you?"

"If green means stupid about what's going on here, then yes," April admitted sheepishly.

"Least you're honest. That's more than I can say for most," Pattie said.

Jerry rose to his feet and walked a couple steps toward the two girls. "We're the biggest escort service in town," he boasted.

"Escort service?" April queried.

"Yeah… a dating service." He watched the confusion remain of April's face. "You are new to all this, ain't ya?"

April shrugged her shoulders.

Jerry continued. "But don't worry sweetheart. Everything we do here is on the up and up—well, almost everything. Anyway, it works like this. We get a lot of businessmen in town—some pretty high rollers. They're here alone and need company for the evening. So they call us and we fix 'em up. It's as simple as that. They pay us for our service. They tip you for yours."

A sudden wave of realization began to envelop April. Seeing her face turn red, the man held up his hand. "You're an escort… a date. That's all we arrange. That's all we expect. Anything else happens is entirely up to you. I don't care, and quite frankly, I don't want to know. Like we said a moment ago, we ask no questions. We're not Whore's R US. If you want that, you've come to the wrong place."

He watched April's face twist into an even greater expression of shock. Sensing he was about to lose his newest girl, he softened his voice. "Listen, you're new in town, you're lost or running from someone or something—again, it don't matter to me. You got nowhere to go except back to the old lady's boarding house. We can give you a fresh start here. See if you like it. There ain't no contract. You're under no obligation. You want out at anytime, you simply say so and move on. Not to beat a dead horse, but again no questions asked. And Pattie here will see you're taken care of, won't you, sweetheart?"

"Anything you say," the girl said with a smile. It looked genuine enough.

April digested the information. The whole idea was quite scary, even a bit revolting, especially after what she had been through recently. But, as negative as the whole idea seemed, there was a certain level of curiosity—most probably because it was so far from anything she had ever imagined. Plus, there was one aspect of the whole thing that kept her attention. "Can I ask a question?" she finally said.

"Shoot," the man said. He stood amazed as the blood drained from April's face. There was a clue there about her past, but he really didn't give a shit. It was still an interesting bit of information.

April realized her face had lost its color and quickly regained her composure. "What did you mean when you said I'll be a new person in a few days?"

"Just what I said. April Blackstone will be history. You'll have a whole new ID, and papers to prove it."

"How old… How old will I be?" April asked

"How old you wanna be?"

April shrugged her shoulders.

The man hesitated as he continued to eye her up. "With the right make up and clothes, you can pass for eighteen, no problem—any more will be pushing it. Long as you don't try and buy booze or gamble too much, you'll be okay."

April's eyes widened. The expression wasn't lost on either of the other two in the room. The previous hook was set even deeper.

49

The teenage couple strolled hand in hand across the town square. The boy held an ice cream cone which he offered to the girl. As she took a lick, he pushed it up into her mouth, smearing the vanilla/chocolate swirl over her face. The two laughed as she returned the favor by grabbing him by the back of the neck and giving him a big kiss.

The sheriff watched the scene another moment before turning away from the window. He tried telling himself the whole thing was disgusting. He knew that was a lie, that he was just envious—jealous—that his son would never walk across the town center again, much less hand in hand with a girl.

The sheriff's anger built. The last few days saw his behavior become more and more unpredictable. One minute he was calm, the next he was an angry volcano. His men, normally eager to Velcro themselves to his side, reacted by keeping their distance. They realized he needed to get through this on his own, and after having their offers of help rejected numerous times, they gave him his space. But it wasn't space he needed. He wanted the girl. So far, he and everyone else had come up empty. While his deputies insisted she was still within the search area, he was beginning to have doubts. He had been out in the woods all day with Bullet, who had taken to the task like a real trooper. It had been a long time since the sheriff had seen the dog perform so well. The animal's arthritis was starting to worsen. The sheriff guessed his lack of activity didn't help. As the hunt progressed, the animal showed some of his old spirit. Regardless, they found no trace of the girl. To the sheriff, if Bullet couldn't find the scent, there wasn't one to be found.

The sheriff picked up two Xerox copies lying on his desk. One contained a copy of the girl's yearbook picture. The second was a blow up of a fingerprint. He placed the two papers in the scanner sitting beside his computer. He logged onto the Internet, went to Google and typed in the word *bounty hunter*. The search engine came back with a list possibilities. He found the one he wanted and clicked on the web site. This web page was a private site used by law enforcement and others to search for missing people. The sheriff had success in the past using such a site. He hoped he'd have the same luck again.

Once the initial screen came up, he typed in his password and went to the main page. He clicked on *new data entry* and reached over and hit the scanner button. The next screen was where he could type in additional information. He wrote:

$10,000 REWARD LEADING TO HER WHEREABOUTS!!

He hit the command key that told the site he was finished, verified the information and logged off. He turned his attention to the letter on his desk. It was addressed to the City Council telling them he was going to be taking a leave of absence. He knew they would be concerned about his request—for their own sakes of course. He also knew they dared not deny him his due.

He finished the letter, put it on the corner of his desk where his secretary would see it in the morning, and rose to his feet. He leaned over and patted Bullet on the head. "Come on boy, we need to go home and pack. I suspect we'll be needing to travel real soon."

50

The ringing startled her as she was just walking past the desk with her first cup of morning coffee. A cigarette dangling from the corner of her mouth, she cursed under her breath. Who would be calling this early? She contemplated ignoring the intrusion, but decided against it. After all, she did rent rooms and she did have vacancies. She pushed the hair from her face, cleared her throat and picked up the receiver. "Aunt Sally's Boarding House."

"Mornin', Sally."

She recognized the voice immediately. She stood a little straighter and smoothed out the wrinkled apron wrapped around her unsmooth abdomen. "Why, hello, Detective Moon. To what do I owe the pleasure of this call… so Goddamn early in the morning?"

The detective laughed. "So good to hear your voice, too." Getting no response, he continued, "You got a hot one this time, Sally. Dangerous, too."

Sally's mind was still waiting for the coffee to take effect. "Help me out here, detective. Just what-the-fuck you talking about?"

"The girl, April Blackstone. She's wanted in a small town in Ohio, place called Worthington Valley. Seems she shot the sheriff's son the night of a big school dance. There are a few details missing—actually, I smell a lot of rotten fish with this one—but there's a ten thousand dollar reward for information concerning her whereabouts."

"Ten thousand!" The name along with the talk of reward quickly refreshed Sally's memory. She glanced around to make sure no one was listening. Boarders, especially the kind she attracted, usually had big ears. Determining the coast was clear, she said, "So, she is on the run. I figured as much. They almost always are."

"From home and the law."

"Then go and arrest her."

"That's one of the smelly fish. There isn't a warrant posted for her, least not yet."

"What does that mean?"

"There's no reason to arrest her."

"Isn't she a minor?"

"Sixteen."

Sally nodded. She had that part correct. "Pick her up for that."

"If I get officially involved, there's no reward money," the detective said.

Sally contemplated the thought without argument. She knew he could not accept reward money when acting in his official capacity. They had run across that problem in the past, but always found a way around it. She was sure this time would be no different. "How'd you find her?"

"On the Internet."

Sally knew not to ask for any more details. She knew she wouldn't get them anyway. She did know, from comments the detective had made in the past, that a lot of modern day police work was done through computers. She was not computer literate, but she knew enough to understand that their potential was hindered only by the limits of one's imagination.

The detective continued. "Anyway, where is she?"

"I'm not sure."

"What do you mean by that?"

"Just what I said, you dumb ass."

The detective laughed. Sally could curse with the best of them. The detective's tone remained serious. "Where'd you send her?"

"I fixed her up with someone."

"Someone! Who?"

"An agency."

"An agency. They'll scarf her up and heaven only knows what'll happen to her."

"Not that kind of agency. Just one of the local escort services."

The detective also knew not to press for more information. "Get in touch with her somehow and find out where she is."

"What are you going to do?"

"I ain't figured that one out yet. I need to reply to the Internet posting, only I'm not sure how to make contact. If I give them my number, it can be traced to the station here." He paused a moment. "Hey Sally, you still have that 800 number?"

"What are you talkin' about?"

"Don't bullshit a bullshitter. I know you used to have a number you gave out to special clients. You still have that?"

She hesitated. "800 numbers can't be traced. Can they?"

"Not as easily," he lied. "You need access to the phone company computers." He didn't add the various other sources available.

"What if I do?"

"We'll use it so they can't trace anything to me."

"You afraid or something? Is there something about this you're not telling me?"

"No… and it's not me. It's who I am. You should know that."

She did, but was just checking. "I still have it, but I don't have a phone plugged into that jack."

"Then…"

She quickly interrupted him. "I know, stick it in. That's what they all say."

The detective laughed. He wrote the number down as she recited it.

51

The Bradford Towers stood on 14th Street and the boardwalk. The hotel itself was not a casino, although it was right in the midst of several. The Towers was used mainly for overflow from the better known resorts. It also housed those who wanted to get away from the hustle-bustle yet still be close to the action. The atmosphere was more relaxed and a lot quieter. The décor was older than several of the other Casinos April had walked through. The main colors were purple with some deep reds mixed in. April thought the scheme odd until she realized the pattern allowed one to sit in the lobby without being seen.

She slowed her pace as she walked through the heavy gold trimmed doors, allowing her eyes to adjust to the darkness. As she approached the bank of elevators, she nodded to the bellhop/security guard who stood watch over the area. She learned her first day that no one was allowed near the elevators unless they were a registered guest or had a visitor's pass. Pattie told her the people who stayed here wanted their privacy protected. April had no problems with that.

She nodded to the young man, showed him her room key and pushed the elevator button. The door opened immediately and she walked into the empty box. She pushed the button for the 9th floor and stood back against the far wall. She glanced at her watch. It was five minutes before two. She was getting back just in time. She had spent the past two days sitting in the room for the designated hours. Each day the phone rang once to check up on her and Pattie. Yet each day, there was no assignment. She herself wasn't disappointed, but Pattie complained about the lack of activity, although she did admit it could be slow during the week. But this was Friday and April's roommate expected the activity to pick up. While April remained apprehensive about the whole ordeal, her curiosity level continued to rise the more she explored the various venues on the boardwalk.

While each casino sounded the same as far as the noise emitted, each had a different theme. One was a circus. One was very *Frenchy*. One seemed to be from turn of the century and another had New York as the main theme. In all though, the people were the same. They came, they lost their money and they went away happy. It was a phenomenon the young girl failed to comprehend. How could someone lose so much money so quickly? Pattie told her it was entertainment and the thrill of maybe hitting it big. April's analogy was more like a herd of buffalo not knowing any better as they followed the bright lights right off a cliff. Regardless, Atlantic City's gaming establishment was big business. She patted her left hand pocket where she now had a few dollars of her own. She had avoided the bank machine the first couple days, sensing someone was watching her. Today, she finally told herself to stop being paranoid. The two twenty dollar bills she had withdrawn from the ATM earlier in the day were still there. Her forty dollars compared little to what she had seen lost on just one roll of the dice. She shook her head. Atlantic City was proving to be a very good forest in which to hide.

When the elevator doors opened, she stepped out. She looked in both directions to make sure no one was in the hallway before heading towards her room. April had begun to feel more relaxed the past couple of days, but she knew she had a long way to go before the paranoia fully evaporated. As she entered the room, Pattie was coming out of the bathroom, a towel wrapped around her hair, the rest of her body uncovered. April turned her head away and quickly closed the door.

Pattie laughed. "Just how naïve are you anyway?" she asked, pulling the towel off her head and wrapping it around her body. She held up a hand and continued. "Don't answer that. I really don't want to know." She laughed again. "Training you's going to be a trip."

April moved to the window and stared out across the parking lot in the back of the building. "Sorry," she said, not wanting her roommate to see her blush.

Pattie walked over and wrapped an arm around her shoulder. It didn't seem to bother her that she was naked and so close to another person—a person she only knew for a couple of days. "Don't fret it none, girlie. I was just like you once, and not too long ago either. You learn real fast in this business or…"

She paused and stepped away. "Look April, I know this is all kind of sudden for you, but if you want to escape your past, you've got to change your identity as well as your lifestyle. Besides, like we've said, this is an *escort* service. Anything else is between you and your clients." She offered a reassuring smile. "I was scared at first too—"

The sentence was interrupted by the ringing of the phone. Pattie glanced at the clock sitting on the table between the two beds. "Christ, he's a minute early." She sat on the edge of the bed and picked up the phone. She said hello and listened. "Got it," she eventually said.

She turned to April and smiled. "We're in business, girlfriend. We have a dual assignment. Some bigwig's in town throwing a party on his private yacht. Seems his male to female ratio is out of balance and he needs us to help set the numbers right. I've done these type of things before and they can be a lot of fun. Besides, the food and booze are usually real good. You can make a lot of tips too, that is, if you want." She tilted her head to the side. "Maybe we'll meet a couple weirdoes who want to watch…" Thinking twice before continuing, she let the sentence fade away. She rose to her feet leaving the towel on the bed. "All in all, it's a good place for you to start." As she disappeared back into the bathroom she shouted. "By the way, I picked up a package for you this morning. It's lying on your bed."

April saw a large manila envelope sitting against a pillow. She opened the seal and poured the contents out onto the bed. There was a birth certificate, a New Jersey driver's license, a passport and a social security card. The name on all four documents was the same, April Whiterock. The documents showed the person to be eighteen plus a few months of age.

Pattie came back out from the bathroom. "I suggested they leave your first name the same—it's common enough. Whiterock is the opposite of Blackstone, so you shouldn't have a hard time remembering it. You just need to remember the information, especially the date of birth and your social security number… and remember, April Blackstone is no more."

April stared at the papers. Her hands started to tremble. Tears formed in her eyes as she realized she was making the final break from her past. Pattie, now clad in her bra and panties, came up and wrapped both arms around April's shoulders. Again, there was no concern over the physical contact being made. "I remember standing in a hotel room a while back feeling the same as you." She laughed aloud. "And I didn't even get to keep my first name. You're lucky there."

April's eyes darted up to her roommate's. "You're not—"

"No silly, I'm not."

April looked down at the papers on the bed. "April Whiterock," she repeated several times. "April Whiterock."

Pattie slid her arm down and pinched her in the side. "Come on, girlfriend. We gotta get you cleaned up. I'll do your hair. Now run on and hop in the shower." She pushed April toward the bathroom door.

With little hesitation, April Whiterock did as she was told.

52

Danny sat at his desk trying to concentrate on the words before him. He was trying to get a head start on his reading requirements for English. He didn't mind school and actually enjoyed certain subjects like math and English. He thought about journalism as a career, stimulated by the local coverage of the recent events. They did so in such detail, yet there were still huge gaps in the story. He just wished he could fill in those gaps, and fill them in with the truth. Now that would be a story. He was beginning to wonder if the truth would ever have a chance.

But since the shooting, things had changed. He no longer looked forward to school. He no longer looked forward to his treks into the mountain. As for Sally, they had not spoken since they broke up. Thinking about April took most of his energy. His interest in other things had gone down the tubes. He knew he could not let this go on much longer. A week was enough. He had to get on with his life—at least he had to get back to the basics, whatever that meant. He had to keep his head on straight in case something did come up about April. He had to be ready to move, physically and emotionally. He wished he had someone close to share his feelings. But there was no one. Sally was a thing of the past. April's mother had yet to sober up. Danny did try talking to his father once, but he was too wrapped up in April's mother and in trying to forestall the flood of negative publicity directed towards Worthington Industries.

So there was no one. Danny was alone in a town of tragedy struck people.

The whole town was still abuzz about the shooting. The name Worthington kept appearing in conversations, on the evening news and in the daily paper. In the past, the media had always been favorable towards Worthington Industries and the man who ran the company. Lately, however, everyone seemed to have forgotten just how important the business was to the town. Besides the five thousand plus actual jobs inside the boundaries of the plant, almost everyone else in town and in the surrounding communities was somehow or another dependent on the factory. In the past, it had been dubbed *the foundation upon which the town was built*. Lately, phrases such as the *town's albatross* were thrown about. Danny felt like his family was being attacked by a school of piranha on a wild feeding frenzy. He could handle it, though. Growing up in such a high profile family, he simply ignored the rhetoric. His father said that dealing with the news media was part of the business, and a part with two conflicting sets of emotions. "You can't live with them, and you can't live without them."

What also bothered Danny was the way his friends acted towards him. It was as if he had fallen off the face of the planet, and no one cared. He wanted to stand in the middle of town and shout that it was as tough on him as anyone else. However, like his father said over dinner one evening, real friends in life were few and far between, and only showed their true colors in times of need. He was hurt and disappointed, but he couldn't be all that angry. After all, Eddie had been one of the most popular, if not the most popular, boy in school. Now Eddie was no more. As was Sally. And for the moment, as was April. Danny lost three of the most important people in his life in one fell swoop, one millisecond in time, one blink of the eye. It was a tough pill to swallow.

Theories as to April's whereabouts were as rampant as the number of people who lived in the area. Most focused on her being dead or injured somewhere up on the mountain.

No one considered the possibility that she slipped past the search perimeter. There was even some talk of calling off the search in a day or so.

Danny had not given up hope. In fact, he was sure she was okay—injured maybe, holed up somewhere maybe, but alive. He never suggested to the sheriff or anyone else that perhaps they were simply looking in the wrong place. They had yet to make the connection between finding him in the motel and his stepsister. His father called it *looking outside of the box.* The search team had yet to do this, and thus had failed to consider the possibility that she had given them the slip. After all, they were experts in the woods. She wasn't, or so they thought. Again, had they looked outside the box…

His confidence level was high that she was okay, but he was still worried. He'd feel much better once he had confirmation she was at least alive. He decided he'd wait until the search was called off. An announcement was expected Saturday morning at a press conference scheduled for 9:00 am. That would take all the people out of the woods, giving him plenty of room to roam on his own. He still had to be careful of where he went so as not to throw any suspicion his way. While the sheriff's office officially left him alone, he sensed they were watching him closely. He told himself he was being paranoid. He also knew from experience in the woods, that paranoia was often a person's unexplained sixth sense coming into play. So he kept his activities to a minimum, claiming to be having a difficult time like everyone else. It was a story that made sense, and it was a story that kept people from probing too far into what he really thought. The line about having a difficult time adjusting wasn't all that far from the truth anyway. The more time passed, the more time he spent thinking about the whole scenario. He blamed himself. He also realized there was plenty of blame to pass around. He just wished he had someone to talk to. He wished he could write the story.

His train of thought was interrupted by a knock at his door. He knew by the firmness of the bang, it was his father. He also knew not to bother answering in that the elder Worthington would be entering regardless. Danny had stopped fussing at his father long ago for entering his room uninvited. The response was always the same. "It's my house, and I'll go where I damn well please when I damn well please." Danny knew from overhearing conversations of other people that the man ran his business the same way.

He watched his father inspect the room as he walked through the door. From the day he was able to understand the concept, Danny was expected to keep his room neat and clean. That started when he was a young boy and hadn't changed over the years. "My house will be kept the way I want it," was another favorite phrase. Worthington Industries was a very clean and efficient place to work.

The inspection completed, his father walked over to his son and laid a hand on the boy's shoulder. Seeing the book open on the desk, he said, "It's probably a good thing to get your nose back in the books." While his father wasn't up on many of the day to day issues of his son's life, he did keep a close watch on school related items.

"I have a lot to read over the next several weeks, so that's the plan," Danny responded.

"Only a plan?"

"I've read a few pages."

"Take the total number of pages you have to read and divide them by the number of days before everything's due. Make that your daily goal and it won't seem so bad."

"Okay Dad." Danny added no editorial comment.

"Dinner'll be ready in ten minutes," his father said.

"What are we having?"

"Lasagna."

Danny started to blurt out, "Again!" But he was able to capture his tongue in time. His father was obviously cooking as his wife was still in a stupor. At first, Danny was bothered by her behavior, but the more he thought about it, the more he decided it was probably for the best that she stayed drunk. Her own hysteria was kept subdued by the booze and tranquilizers her doctor ordered. Danny felt sorry for his father. He'd married her to help him entertain and for companionship, and now when he needed her most, she was useless. At least she wasn't making things worse. Their whole marriage had been puzzling. He never objected to the idea of his father remarrying. Then one day his father came home with this woman—a real looker too—and the next thing Danny knew, he inherited a new stepmother and stepsister.

He kept an open mind, and with time came to like having the friendship of his new sister. His stepmom was alright, too. She seemed to make his father happy, although Danny suspected the marriage was more out of convenience than true love. Danny guessed his father's whole attraction to her was physical, an easy assumption considering the amount of noise that came out of the bedroom at times. The one thing Danny did like was that she didn't try to play mother with him. She was content letting him define the extent of their relationship, although she did drop hints on occasion that if there was ever anything he needed or wanted, she'd be there for him.

That is, when she was sober.

"It's only the second time this week," his father said.

"Stouffer's?"

"Nothing but." Their eyes met. His father was trying hard, even though he didn't know quite what to do or say. The man was an experienced, seasoned manager. Public speaking was one of his fortes. However, since the shooting he'd been at a loss for words. Danny thought there was something else strange about his behavior as well, only was unable to get a grasp of it. He chalked it up to the stress.

Not wanting to add additional stress to the situation, Danny let his father off the hook. "I'll be down in a few."

His father nodded, patted the boy on the shoulder, turned and walked out of the room. He closed the door behind him, an unusual occurrence for Worthington Industries' president. Danny tried again to concentrate on the words before him. They remained a blur so he closed the book and turned to his computer. He was about to hit the icon for the Internet when he noticed he had an email. He clicked on the blinking envelope and his email opened. There was one from his bank. It was a reminder that his truck payment was due in a week. He clicked on the *go to* button and his checking account information opened a few seconds later. His truck and insurance payments were already preset and all he had to do was authorize payment by a click of the mouse. While his father gave him an allowance each month that covered the two items, Danny had to ensure the check was deposited and that the bills were paid. He was about to do so when he noticed the balance in his account. It was less than he thought the last time he checked. He moved the cursor and opened the page depicting his account summary. Scanning the page, his eyes froze on the last line—a debit card withdrawal earlier that day of $40. There were several things wrong with that transaction. First, he always made withdrawals in increments of $100. Second, he had not gone to the bank machine earlier. And third…

He started at the line again. The transaction had taken place in Atlantic City, New Jersey. The address was Baltic and the boardwalk. He was not one to get emotional with tears, but on this occasion his eyes became blurry. He glanced over his shoulder to make sure he was alone. Looking back at the screen, he said aloud, "She's alive!"

53

Less than three miles away, another Internet dialup was taking place. Sheriff Richmond, packed and ready to officially start his leave of absence, decided to look one last time at his favorite web page. He waited impatiently as the computer made the connection and the graphics filled the screen. He put in his name and password, and waited. Once in, he next clicked on the open file icon and several new cases came up on the screen. He scrolled down and stopped at the one he had posted the day before. Assuming there would be no response this quickly, he automatically started to close out of the site. However, there was an asterisk next to the case which meant there had been activity on the page. His hands started to shake as he moved the cursor to the appropriate spot on the screen. He clicked and the next window opened. It was an email from a person claiming to be a private detective. The message was short and simply stated that the detective had reason to believe the girl, April Blackstone, was nearby and he could help track her down. There was an 800 number to call and that was all. The sheriff wrote the number on a piece of paper and closed the main page. Next, he dialed up the FBI's main web page. He clicked the *law enforcement only* page. His name and another password were entered. (Well-placed favors over the years kept his account active.) A few more clicks of the mouse and he was into the computer that searched out various pieces of data, including addresses and phone numbers. He entered the 800 number and in less than a minute, a name and address appeared on the screen. The number was registered to a Sally Masterson in Atlantic City, New Jersey. The sheriff smiled. Two Sallys in the case so far, but only one April. He printed out the information and picked up the telephone. Halfway through the number, he paused. He looked down at Bullet who was sleeping on the rug beside the desk. As any good investigator did, he weighed the options. If he called, he may save a wild goose trip. On the other hand, the call may tip off April, or someone near her.

The other option, driving to Atlantic City, didn't bode too well either. What if it turned out to be a wasted lead? He'd have made the trip for nothing.

Only the trip wouldn't be for nothing. The girl had to have been there, or no one would have bothered to look up the bounty hunter site in the first place. And if she was there, then she did make it through the search net. He smiled to himself as he placed the phone back on the receiver. "Slicker than we thought," he muttered.

Bullet heard the words and looked up with one eye.

The sheriff continued. "Or so she thinks." He reached for his hat and plopped it atop his head. "Come on, Bullet. Let's go catch us a fugitive. We'll show her who's the smartest." He let out a sick bellowing laugh. "Time to start my leave of absence."

54

Pattie insisted they leave at least a half hour before they were due at the boat, claiming their clients did not tolerate lateness very well. Besides, she wanted to walk around the casino where the boat was docked. She denied being a hardcore gambler, but admitted a fondness for the craps tables. She wanted to scope out the place and see who was working. If the party was a bust, she'd have an alternative plan. She liked *velcroing* herself next to some half drunk gentleman and help him lose his money. Every so often she won. If not, she was usually able to convince the person to give the pit crew a hefty tip, some of which always managed to find its way back to her.

Dressed in near matching long bright blue evening gowns, the duo piled into a cab and made the journey through the city to *Harrah's On The Bay*. Pattie decided on the near matching look to ensure the two stood out from the rest of the crowd. She argued that anyone else at the party would be appalled if they were dressed similar to someone else. But that was the look she was after. "After all, in Atlantic City, a pair of aces beats a single," she said.

Harrah's On The Bay was much like the other casinos April had seen, a lot of lights and a lot of noise. Only this one was attached to a marina. April walked through the casino with Pattie. The floor was filled with people of all walks of life dreaming about hitting it big. The hour was early so the high rollers had yet to finish their complimentary dinners in their complimentary suites. Pattie was able to get the scoop as to who'd be working the craps games later. Eye contact was made, nods were exchanged and the alternative plan was set into motion.

At 7:45 sharp they exited the back of the casino and made their way down to the marina docks. There were boats of all makes and sizes, some sail and some power. The farther out the pier, the bigger the boats. April knew nothing about boats except what little she had seen on television. She had never been so close to such big ones before, and immediately started wondering just how large they could get. The answer came a few steps later.

April looked up as they approached the end of the dock. Taking up the whole T head was the largest boat April had even seen. It was pure white and shined like a piece of white glass. The aft deck alone was well above her head. She stopped dead in her tracks. "Oh my God, we're not going on that, are we?" she stammered.

"Why not? We've dressed the part," Pattie quipped.

April stayed put and pulled the front of her gown up. The dress was cut way too low for her taste. She had protested when Pattie first chose the gown, but her protests were ignored. "You're petite, but you've got a great body," her roommate and advisor said. "You look hot. Take advantage of it."

"I don't want to be hot," April had protested.

"Oh, yes you do," Pattie insisted. "Heat loosens up the wallet, and that means bigger tips."

April tried to protest, again to no avail. Pattie continued her directions. "Come on girl, we got to find the captain. That's who we report to." She grabbed April's arm and headed for the gangplank. They marched up the metal incline, the heels of their shoes clicking with each step. They were greeted at the top by a man dressed in a white uniform. Pattie did a quick look-over. Seeing the four bars on his epaulet, she said, "Captain Rogers, I presume." He was tall and well built. His curly blond hair didn't fit beneath the hat he wore. His skin was tanned and dry, his arms very muscular. His blood vessels were easily discernable and his posture was as straight as the hem in his freshly pressed trousers. Except for his hair, he could pass for a naval officer.

The captain returned the glance before responding, "Good evening, ladies. Invitations please?"

"Yes, we are that," Pattie said with a laugh. "Jerry asked us to represent him."

"Ah, you're the girls from the agency." The man's demeanor changed as he stepped aside. His voice became less formal and more slurry. "By all means, welcome aboard *Hamilton's Bench*."

Pattie led April up onto the deck. The captain walked around them slowly. Pattie had warned April they'd be getting a lot of eyes burning at them. That was part of the job. "We're like fresh flowers they set around to spice up the decor. Just don't let anybody sniff you if you don't want to be sniffed." April heeded the warning and remained still as the captain continued his inspection. During the same time, April did her own inspection. The wooden deck of the yacht was as polished as the fiberglass hull. The oiled wood handrails presented a pleasing contrast. She knew nothing about boats, but quickly decided this one was impressive.

"Two of Atlantic City's finest," the captain said, breaking her train of thought. "Thank you both for coming."

"Our pleasure," Pattie returned.

He motioned toward the rear of the boat. "The first door is the pilot house. The main salon is the second. You ladies go ahead and make yourselves comfortable. The bar's open and there is plenty of food. Help yourselves. We expect the guests to be arriving shortly."

"May I ask the occasion?" Pattie said.

"Nothing special," the captain said. "Mr. Hamilton is just entertaining a few friends before he heads north for the summer.

"Heads north for the summer?" Pattie inquired.

"Yes, we leave for Martha's Vineyard with the morning tide," the captain explained. "No hidden agenda here tonight except to have a good time."

"I assume Mr. Hamilton is the same as *Hamilton's Bench*?" Pattie inquired.

"Good assumption…"

"Is he aboard?"

Before he could respond, a voice came from inside the pilot house. "Phillip… Phillip… You around here?"

A man of fifty or so stuck his head out the door. Spotting the target of his inquiry, he stepped out. He was taller than the captain, more slender, and dressed in a black tuxedo and red bow tie. His hair, graying around the edges, was cut short and combed back. His skin was as tanned as the captain's, only much smoother.

"Oh, excuse me, ladies. I didn't mean to interrupt." He moved toward the trio.

The captain started to make introductions before realizing he didn't know any names. Pattie could have let him flounder, but knew better. Regardless of what she thought of him, and her first impression wasn't all that positive, she knew never to irritate a customer. "Hello, sir. I'm Pattie, and this is April. We're here representing Jerry."

"Jerry?" the older man said.

"They'll be helping us with the guests this evening," the captain quickly explained.

"Then welcome aboard," he said extending his hand. "I'm George Hamilton."

Pattie shook his hand first before passing it on to April who did the same, only with a lot less enthusiasm. It was not a purposeful shyness, it was just that the man standing before her was not at all who she imagined would own this boat. He was very attractive and fit well into his tux. He immediately conveyed a sense of ease—unlike the captain who came across as aloof and up-nosed.

He took April's hand, squeezed firmly, yet without pain and said. "It's a real pleasure to meet you April… Pattie. Thank you for coming."

"Thank you for having us," Pattie said.

Hamilton nodded. "Please excuse me for interrupting, but we have a problem, Phillip." The yacht owner shifted his attention to the captain. "Louis tells me there's no entertainment for this evening."

Both girls watched as the captain's face turned from tan to red. His eyes darted between the three. Pattie took the cue and grabbed April's hand. "If you excuse us, we need to go on in and get the layout of everything before the others get here. Besides, I need to find… what do you call it?"

Mr. Hamilton managed a smile. "If you're referring to the bathroom, it's called the head… Someone in the salon will gladly show you the way."

In a few steps, they were in the main salon. Again, April had to do a double take at the exquisite decor. Even Pattie paused and let out a soft whistle. "Wreaks of money, doesn't it darling?"

The couches and chairs lining the walls were covered in a variety of white materials. Glass tables in the middle of the floor were decorated with vases of fresh flowers. Inlaid lighting speckled the ceiling. Silver trays of food stood ready for the guests. A bar stood against the back wall. A crew member dressed in a white yachting outfit was there adding the finishing touches to the polished stemware lined up to be filled with the champagne chilling in a row of silver ice buckets. Before April could get a further look, Pattie dragged her to the bar. "Come on, honey, let's get us a little warming up medicine. My bladder can wait."

She nodded to the bartender. "Good evening. I'm Pattie, and this is April. We're the entertainment for the evening."

The bartender gave them a big smile and laughed. "You heard, huh?"

"We were just coming on board when Mr. Hamilton caught up to the captain," Pattie said.

"Did he have his hands around his neck yet?" The bartender laughed. "This is twice in a week he forgot something important like this. Mr. Hamilton, he's a great person to work for. Honest, fair, and more than generous with the crew, but man is he a stickler for perfection. Phillip Rogers is probably one of the best boat handlers in the business, but he loses it once we're docked. Too busy worrying about emptying his prostate, if you get my drift. Anyway, welcome aboard, I'm Louis, your friendly barkeep, and other duties as assigned. What can I get you ladies?"

Sally pointed to one of the bottles that was already open. "Bubbly'll be fine."

"Dom Perignon. Nothing but the best served here." He poured two glasses and sat them atop white linen cocktail napkins.

Pattie handed one glass to April and took the other for herself. "Cheers."

Louis nodded and smiled.

"So, what was the entertainment going to be?" Pattie said, running her fingers along the rim of her glass. It let out a screech indicating the glass was real crystal.

"I'm not sure, but I suspect a piano player."

"Piano?" Pattie said.

"A piano?" April repeated with even more surprise.

Louis pointed between the two girls. "That's what I said."

The two pairs of eyes looked toward the forward part of the salon. Sitting in the far corner was a white baby grand piano. April did a double take as she saw *Steinway* printed in gold letters. She inhaled so hard she started to choke. Louis grabbed her glass so it didn't fall while Pattie pounded her not so gently on the back. "Take it easy there, girlie girl," she instructed.

April coughed and sneezed her way out of a bronchial spasm. She wiped the tears from her eyes. She coughed a couple more times, wiping her nose on a tissue offered by Louis.

"Air's supposed to go down the windpipe, liquid and food down the food pipe," he instructed with a laugh.

"You look like you just saw a long lost friend," Pattie said.

The earlier tears caused by the coughing fit were replaced by another set of liquid droplets. Since arriving in Atlantic City and no longer being on the run, April was able to think about what she had left behind. She missed her mother, which was to be expected. She was surprised, however, how much she missed Danny. She never realized how many voids her stepbrother filled until the second night on the mountain. She wasn't normally a person to get lonely. She was always able to find something to occupy her time, whether it be her schoolwork or her music. However, on that particular night, somewhere deep in the woods, she had nothing to do. She had bedded down for the night. There was no dinner to fix. There was no trailer to clean. There was no schoolwork to finish. There was no piano to play. There was no Danny to bug. It was the first time she could ever remember truly feeling lonely. It was the only time since the night of the dance she actually thought about going home. While she had few close friends in Worthington Valley, she had become comfortable with the people in her immediate surroundings. She never verbalized it to anyone, not even to Danny, but she had grown accustomed to her life in Worthington Valley.

That was all gone, erased by one moment in time—one moment she wished she could erase. Only she couldn't. Her life would never be the same. Things happened. Ticks of the clock passed she would never be able to reverse. Decisions were made she could never undo. The initial decision to run had been Danny's and hers together. The decision to continuing running had been hers alone, and it was a decision she would have to live with, maybe forever.

The big question: how long was *forever*? In mathematics, it meant infinity. What did it mean in life? Were they one and the same? Or were they different? One common ground for both, however, was their reference to the future. There was no looking back. There was no going back. The decision had been made. Worthington Valley was in her past. Her family and friends were in the past. Danny was in her past. She argued to herself that night on the mountain it was in the best interest of everyone. It was the only way she could protect herself. It was the only way she could protect her mother. It was the only way she could protect Danny.

But she missed her music. If she could solve that problem, the rest would be easy. The issue came to the forefront the day before in one of the casinos. There she heard a piano and watched the musician play popular tunes that delighted the crowd. Some songs she recognized; some she didn't. The experience engulfed her in a cloud of sadness. Seeing a piano aboard *Hamilton's Bench*, this one without its master, heightened those earlier feelings. "Sorry," she said, wiping her eyes and accepting a glass of water from Louis.

"Dying aboard *Hamilton's Bench* is frowned upon," Louis said.

"Especially before the guests arrive," Pattie added.

"Speaking of which, looks like some are here." Louis looked down at his watch. "Eight o'clock sharp. Excuse me ladies. I need to get to work." He turned his attention to the champagne bottles.

"Come on, girlie, let's go earn our keep." Pattie headed toward several tuxedoed men.

April followed before realizing she didn't have a clue what she was supposed to do. She watched as Pattie attacked the crowd with a swagger of her hips and a smile on her face. April followed a few steps before veering off to a corner. Her glass in hand, she watched as the room quickly filled with bodies. There were a few women, each dressed in evening gowns. Each gown was different. While there was a variety of ages, April guessed the average to be mid-forties, early fifties, the latter being in the ballpark age of George Hamilton. Hellos and handshakes were exchanged, and the room quickly filled with conversation—conversation coming from a whole lot of people. "Just how big is this boat anyway?" she wondered aloud.

Several servers passed by with trays of exotic foods. She saw chocolate covered strawberries, steamed shrimp, various cheeses and what she later learned was a plate of caviar. Each was offered to her. Afraid of setting off another coughing spell, she declined.

She stared out a window. The lights of the marina combined with the neon lights of the casino foiled any darkness threatening the area. She looked across the water. The sky was already filling with stars. She caught a glimpse of the moon rising above the water in the distance. It was the Atlantic Ocean, something she had never seen until a couple of days before. She never thought much about being around the water. Tonight, however, a warm glow came over her as she pictured herself standing alone on the deck of *Hamilton's Bench*, far out in the ocean where no one could find her. She looked at the sky and saw nothing but stars. She wondered if the sky was as beautiful on water as it was in the mountains.

"Beautiful night, isn't it?"

She turned sharply as the voice intruded on her thoughts. Captain Rogers was standing beside her, a glass of champagne in one hand, a shrimp in another. "Beautiful night, isn't it?" he repeated.

"Yeah… Yes," she stuttered.

"The sunset tonight was especially spectacular," he said. He did not look out the window. Instead, his eyes remained on April. "Sunrise and sunset, the two best times to be on the water."

"I wouldn't know," April said. "I haven't been on the water much. Actually, I've never been on a boat before."

"Really? Well, you picked a good one to start with. This is one of the finest yachts in the country… world for that matter."

"It's beautiful," April said. She felt his gaze continue to burn into her. She reminded herself it was part of the job.

"The rest of the boat is just as luxurious."

"You mean there's more?"

The captain laughed. "Much more." He took a bite of his shrimp. "If we get time later, I'll give you the twenty dollar tour. But first, I've got to mingle a bit and pretend I'm having a good time."

"Why wouldn't you have a good time?" April asked without thinking.

"I would if I had a piano player. The old man threw that on me at the last minute. Now, he expects miracles."

"Miracles do sometimes happen."

The captain cocked his head to the side. "You as naïve as you act?"

April straightened her posture and forced a smile. "Just a simple statement, that's all."

"Mine's a simple question."

Any sense of comfort she was beginning to feel evaporated as he stepped closer. "Don't forget that tour later," he added. He swallowed the rest of the shrimp and licked his lips in a seductive manner. He winked and turned away.

She watched as he disappeared into the crowd. She made her way back to the bar and set her glass down. Louis saw her and said, "Want me to freshen that up?"

"Have any soda?"

The bartender tipped his head to the side. "You feeling okay?"

"Fine. I'd just like a soda, if that's okay?"

"Whatever." He poured her a glass of Diet Coke. "I saw Phillip talking to you. None of my place to interfere, but I'd be leery of him if I were you. Like I said, he's a horn ball ready to explode. Then again, if he's your type…"

"He's not," April quickly stated. "Thanks for the warning."

"Anytime." He tended to a couple of men who walked up with empty glasses before turning his attention back to April. "Don't get me wrong, Phillip's a nice guy. His ego just gets in his way sometimes. All in all, there isn't a better captain to work for… owner, too, for that matter."

"You're not here just for the evening?" April asked, wanting to make conversation.

"When you sign on aboard *Hamilton's Bench*, you immediately become a jack of all trades."

"What about the food and stuff?"

"Best captain, best owner and most importantly, best chef. Cookie was trained in France, although you'd never know it by talking to him."

"How's that?"

"He has the mouth of a sailor, but we love him just the same."

April took a long swallow of her soda while Louis tended to his duties. He was back in front of her a few minutes later. "So, how'd you end up here tonight anyway?"

April pointed across the room to where Pattie was surrounded by a group of men. "I came with her."

"Well, you may have come with her, but you sure aren't anything like her."

"What do you mean by that?"

"Don't get defensive. If anything, it's a compliment."

April hesitated. "Then thank you, I guess."

"You're welcome." He refilled her glass.

"What kind of music does Mr. Hamilton like, anyway?"

"Classical, and he'll ask you if there's any other kind?"

"Really?"

"He likes Beethoven, Mozart… anything classical," Louis explained. "Yes, old Phillip'll be on Mr. Hamilton's shit list for a long time for this one."

"For not having a piano player?"

"Details, sweetheart. You gotta pay attention to details if you're going to work for Mr. Hamilton. Just look at this boat… Ain't a barnacle out of place, is there?"

She glanced around the room. Even the guests were perfect. Feeling a little more comfortable talking to Louis, April straightened up and asked, "What would happen if there was someone here who could fill in for the missing pianist?"

Louis laughed. "These are all businessmen. They support the arts heavily. They may even like the stuff. But their talent is in the board room, not on a keyboard."

"You should never underestimate someone's talent," she teased. She blushed as she realized the implications of what she had just said.

Louis laughed loudly. "Like I said, you're not anything like your friend there."

"Our talents are different, that's all."

He laughed again. "I can guess about her talents, I'm not so sure about yours."

She looked in the direction of the piano. "Like I said, they're different."

Louis looked at her, at the piano and back at her. "I'll be damned. You gonna tell me you can…"

April winked at her newfound friend. Remembering the real reason she was here, she said, "What do you think it would be worth to the captain for a miracle to happen?"

The corners of Louis's mouth rolled upward. "A five spot at least, and if he ain't good for it, I am."

"Five dollars?"

The bartender chuckled. "Five *hundred* dollars."

April's mouth dropped open. "That's a lot of money."

"Chump change for Mr. Hamilton. As for Phillip, I've seen him drop that in a night at the tables. It would be more than worth it to get back in Mr. Hamilton's good graces."

"Beethoven, huh?"

Louis leaned forward. "I'll even throw in an additional hundred just to see the look on the captain's face when the music starts."

She smiled and spoke softly. "His five will be good enough."

55

Phillip Rogers made his way back to the bar for another refill on his champagne. While his head was starting to feel the effects of the bubbly, his gait was still steady. He was getting disgusted in that he had yet to find a catch for the evening. The two girls from the escort service were possibilities, but he had a rule of never paying for sex. It was too demeaning, and while he might be desperate, he wasn't that desperate. The one seemed like she might warm up to him. If she came on to him, there'd be no charge. He'd just have to time the *tour de boat* right. *Hamilton's Bench* had never failed him before. She surely wouldn't tonight. After all, he was the captain of one of the finest yachts in the world. What woman wouldn't want to see his private cabin?

He picked up one of the filled glasses of champagne sitting on the bar. He glanced around, trying to appear nonchalant, but in reality looking to make sure no one was watching. Deciding the coast was clear, except for Louis behind the bar whom he ignored, he downed the liquid in one gulp. He sat the glass down and picked up another. Still feeling Louis's frown, he did slow the rate of ingestion. This time he took two gulps. As he sat this glass down, he caught motion out of the corner of his eye. He saw two new guests making their way toward the bar. Both were women, both looked alone, and both were gorgeous. He had seen the guest list earlier in the day and tried to guess which names belonged to which body. He wiped his mouth on one of the gold inlaid cocktail napkins bearing the yacht's name. He turned their way as the ladies continued their approach. Both were almost close enough for him to utter a greeting when his concentration was interrupted by a noise from across the room. He tried to stay focused, only the sound continued. When he saw the two ladies stop in their tracks and turn away from him, he had no choice but to delay the hunt. Turning his head in the direction of the intrusion, he realized the sound was not really a noise, but rather something pleasant. His facial expression slowly changed from initial disgust, to disbelief, to one expressing joy. The noise… the sounds… the glorious vibrations that were going to get him out of hot water with his boss were coming from the piano.

"Son-of-a-bitch," he muttered. While his vision was 20/20, he still found himself squinting. Like with his hearing a moment ago, his mind did not want to believe what he saw. The pianist was the girl from the agency he planned to give the tour to later. There she sat, all decked out in her blue evening gown. At the same time, he noticed another phenomenon taking place. As the music filled the room, conversations, regardless how important, had slowly diminished.

He listened as the notes flowed, softly and then becoming louder and louder. He recognized the piece as Beethoven's *Moonlight Sonata*. The pace was slow as designed by the composer, yet there was a touch of flare with certain passages that made the notes sound different… better… more beautiful… just like the person sitting at the instrument. Now Rogers was not an expert on music, except for the rock and roll he himself loved, he did know this much, *Hamilton's Bench's* piano had never sounded better. He watched the girl as she sat with her eyes partially closed, her fingers moving effortlessly over the keys. He imaged a halo above her head as she continued serenading the guests. Other fantasies tried to fill his alcohol sautéed mind, but he forced them aside. Even he realized something special was happening.

The piece lasted for several minutes, and when the last note sounded, the quiet in the room continued for a long moment before spontaneous applause broke out. Phillip Rogers watched as the crowd continued clapping way beyond the normal polite length of time. He watched as the girl just sat there, her head bowed, almost as if she were afraid to acknowledge what was happening. He contemplated going over to her and saying something. He was beat to the punch, however, by his boss, who was at her side, his arm draped over her shoulder. He leaned forward and whispered something in her ear. He straightened up and stepped aside. The girl looked up, forced a smile which brought on even more applause. She raised her hands above the keyboard. The room fell silent again as fingers struck keys. He immediately recognized the beginning thrill and following run of *Rhapsody in Blue*. Besides Beethoven, Mr. Hamilton's other favorite composer was Gershwin. Captain Rogers admitted to himself he liked this particular piece. He leaned up against the bar, took another glass of bubbly and looked over at Louis. The bartender had his hands on his chin and was staring straight at the piano. The earlier frown was gone.

Shaking his head up and down while he mentally patted himself on the back, Rogers downed the champagne in a gulp. Yes, just as quickly as he had gotten on Hamilton's shit list, he had jumped off. His head nodding continued.

There was indeed rhapsody in blue.

56

The wooden slats were wet from the early morning dew. The surf, still sleeping from the darkness, slapped easily against the freshly cleaned sand. While the sun itself had yet to rise off the ocean bed, the first rays of light bounced off the low puffy clouds. A seagull swooped low, its feet skimming the tops of the gentle swells. With the blink of an eye, the bird suddenly dove into the water. A pool of froth formed and the seagull emerged an instant later, a small fish dangling from its beak.

April took off her shoes and headed across the beach. She watched the seagull until it disappeared from sight. The sand felt good between her toes. She approached the water's edge cautiously. In spite of her care, an especially eager wave gushed up around her ankles, splashing sand and water between her legs. She had pulled her gown up, but the water still caught the hem. She giggled as the water trickled down her leg, leaving a streak of sand in it's path. She stood still, letting her feet erode further into the sand. Another wave, this one not so powerful, came up around her toes. The water felt warmer than the day before, even with the cool morning air. She could tell the season was changing. She was glad she had gotten out of the mountains when she did. Her food and water requirements would have increased drastically with warmer temperatures. It always amazed April how things in life could change so quickly—much like the weather. One day it was hot, the next you needed a sweater. One day it was sunny, the next day it rained. One day she and her mother were living in an old trailer in rural Alabama, the next day they were living in a mansion in Ohio. One day she was happy with her new life, the next day she was running for her life. One day she was running for her life through the mountains, the next she was walking the beaches of Atlantic City in a long evening gown.

Another wave came up and massaged her legs. Another seagull came into her field of vision. A swift dive beneath the water's surface and breakfast was had. The water subsided.

When she first went aboard *Hamilton's Bench*, she was nervous, unsure of what she was doing, unsure of what was expected. A short time later she saw the piano, and another quick change took place in her life. From the moment she sat down and the first notes drifted from the Steinway, she felt happier and less stressed than she had in a week. She quickly became engrossed in her playing and forgot she was a guest at a party where she was supposed to be working the crowd, as Pattie called it. April even stopped in the middle of *Rhapsody in Blue* and started to jump up when a voice asked her what she was doing.

"I'm sorry Mr. Hamilton, I know I shouldn't be playing this. It just…"

Mr. Hamilton looked at her and broke into a laugh before realizing she was serious in her concerns. He laid a hand on her shoulder and gently pushed her back onto the bench. He leaned forward and whispered in her ear. "I understand what you're saying. Phillip brought you here to mingle with the crowd. But your music is doing that for you."

He took his arm off her shoulder, nodded to add a touch of encouragement and turned to face the crowd who had remained totally silent through the whole ordeal. "Ladies and gentlemen, she has graciously agreed to play more for us this evening." The sudden eruption of applause shocked April to the point she refocused her eyes on the people around the room. They—the well to do of Atlantic City and elsewhere—could all choose to be doing a lot of other things at this particular moment, including talking to their friends or consuming the platters of hors d'oeuvres offered by the host. Instead, they chose to stand there and stare at her. She looked around the room and caught a glimpse of Captain Rogers, who was standing by the bar, a totally spellbound and shocked look on his face. She remembered thinking that he would now be allowed to live. Her scanning continued and she caught Pattie's eye. She too was staring. She raised her fingers and wiggled them as if playing the piano. The motion brought April back to reality. She closed her own eyes, raised her hands above the keyboard and took a deep breath. The music continued.

The party went on into the night. April remembered little except Louis making sure her glass of soda remained filled. Mr. Hamilton left her alone, although she often sensed he was nearby focusing on her instead of paying attention to his guests. She saw Pattie several times over the next several hours, once when her roommate brought her a plate of food and told her she was knocking them deader than a doornail. April wasn't sure just what that meant. She did recognize it was a compliment, however, so she played on.

Later, when the guests were finally starting to bid their farewells, several stopped by and thanked her for helping make the evening so wonderful. Thank goodness for Pattie, who sensed this was a potential danger spot for April. She came over and stood at her side to help intercept any comments other than the thank you's. When the final guest left and the crew started to clean up, Mr. Hamilton reappeared, this time dressed in more casual attire. He asked April if he could speak with her a moment. She looked at Pattie who nodded her approval. The yacht's owner led her away from the others into the pilot house.

Unlike the main salon, which was decorated and designed for impressing and entertaining, the pilot house was designed for working and running the boat. The equipment was state of the art, and there was plenty of it. Everything seemed to have a place and a purpose. The one thing that did stand out, however, was the ship's wheel. Unlike what one might expect on such a luxurious yacht, this one was of the old wooden variety. Even though it was highly polished, one could still see the markings of its age in the wood. April walked right up to the center of the counsel and laid her hands on the wooden spokes. "This is beautiful," she said.

Mr. Hamilton chuckled.

"I'm sorry. Did I say something wrong?"

"No… No," the man insisted. "There's nothing to be sorry for. On the contrary…" He hesitated. "As you might expect, a lot of people have been aboard *Hamilton's Bench*. Many, especially those who know about boats, always ask to see the pilot house. You see, this is the brains of the ship. This is where all the true action takes place. The rest of the stuff, all the fancy decorations and things, is just window dressing. When these people come in here, they marvel at the vast array of electronic gadgets. Then they see the ship's wheel, and they react, if only for a moment. It may sometimes show in their eyes, or a blink, or a short inhaled breath… but there is always a reaction… usually not a positive one. You, on the other hand, ignore all the gadgets and are drawn right for the wheel with an appreciation that matches my own."

"One could argue that it's all the other stuff—gadgets as you call them—that are really out of place," April said. "You could say the same for the piano in the main room back there… the salon is it?"

Mr. Hamilton nodded.

"That seems awfully out of place on a boat," April continued. "Yet, if I may take a guess, it's one of your favorite pieces of furniture."

"That it is," the man said. He watched April a moment. "Please don't take this the wrong way, but you look quite good standing there at the wheel. It's like you belong there."

April laughed. "As long as we're tied up, I guess that's okay."

"She really handles pretty well underway."

"I wouldn't know. I've never been on a boat before."

"Never?"

"Not even a row boat."

Mr. Hamilton laughed. "Well, I hope your first experience was a positive one."

"I didn't get sea sick."

There was laughter before the man's face turned serious. "You play beautifully."

"Thank you. But I haven't practiced in over a week." April bit her lip realizing she had set herself up for a line of questioning she knew she wasn't going to like.

Hamilton continued. "In my line of work, one never asks a question if you don't already know the answer. Instead, it is often best to simply make a statement and let the person's reaction provide the response. With that, I assume you have papers to prove whatever age you claim to be. And I assume they are good enough to pass even the most prudent inspection. After all, we are in Atlantic City, and there isn't much money can't buy around here. That said, I have a proposition for you."

April's spine stiffened.

George Hamilton reached out and touched her arm. "It's not what you think." He let the words register a moment before continuing. "Also in my business, you have to be a very good judge of people. Now, there were a lot of people at the party tonight who pretended to be something they weren't. Yes, they may have all been rich, but money doesn't make the person. One thing even the devil can't buy around here is one's soul. Your body maybe, but not your soul. While I'd be lying if I said anything negative about your appearance—you are very attractive, you know—your soul is from another world. You're not one of them." He motioned to the back of the boat. "And you're definitely not cut from the same mold as your friend… not saying that you're bad or she's bad. You're both just different, in spite of you two trying to dress alike."

April didn't like the idea that she was so easy to see through. Where a few minutes before her comfort level was rising, caution flags now started to take over.

Mr. Hamilton sensed her discomfort. "But that's all I'm going to say to the matter. Besides, what right do I have to pass such judgment on people?"

"It's your boat."

"That's no excuse. You're still a guest."

The flags stopped flapping so wildly.

The yachtsman continued. "I have a lot of skills, some commendable, some questionable. One of my best is judging a person's character. I know a good person when I see them. I also know when a person is out of place from where they really belong." He paused for effect. "I believe I'm looking at one right now."

April felt her face redden.

"One of the ways to be successful in life is to surround yourself with good people, and you fall into that category. So with that, if you ever want a job aboard *Hamilton's Bench*, you just let me know."

April stared at him a long moment. "You're offering me a job?"

Hamilton nodded.

"To do what?"

The man's posture straightened. "This is a big boat. It takes a lot of work to keep her looking nice. Some think it's hard work, but compared to a lot of options it's really not. The pay's two twenty-five a week plus room and board. Every crew member gets their own cabin… not big, but all yours. Once you learn the ropes and are able to earn your keep, people say I'm more than fair with raises and bonuses. After a year's service, I throw in some money toward health benefits if you want."

"But I told you, I've never even been on a boat before, much less know anything about them," April said.

"Boaters I can train. Good people I can't. If you want to learn more than your specific duties, fine. If not, so be it. I have one crew member who's been with me for three years now. Freddie's one of the best wax men in the business, knows absolutely nothing else about boats."

"Is that why the boat's so shiny, because of Freddie?"

Mr. Hamilton laughed. "Some of it has to do with the materials the boat's made of. Mostly though, it's the Freddie touch."

"What would I be doing?"

"Freddie's always asking for an assistant. Also, I would hope to hear you play at any parties I might have."

"I would imagine working on a boat like this would be a dream come true for many."

"Owning one sure has been."

April continued to stare at her host. She didn't know anything about yachts such as *Hamilton's Bench*, nor anything about their owners, nor even why one would buy something so extravagant. She did know from their brief conversation that *Hamilton's Bench*'s owner was more than just an owner. He was a boat lover as well.

"Well," Mr. Hamilton said, looking at his watch. "The sun will be up in a couple more hours. I didn't mean to take up so much of your time. I just wanted to—"

"There hasn't been an ounce of this evening wasted," April said. "And thank you for the offer."

"You'll think about it?"

She nodded.

"No one on board plays the piano, so she's all yours whenever you're off duty. And if you need any music or anything, I have almost anything you could want… in the classics that is."

April cocked her head to the side.

Mr. Hamilton's eyebrows rose. "Did I say something wrong?"

"No… no. I just never heard anyone call a piano a she. Isn't that how you refer to a boat?"

He pondered the point. "I guess I never called it a she before. Then again, never had it… she sounded so beautiful. Mr. Steinway himself would be pleased, I'm sure."

April blushed again.

"Like I said Ms. April, I know a lot." He reached out and took her right hand in his. "You have a talent… a gift." He let her hand go. "Anyway, the job's open to you anytime."

April brought her attention back to the present just in time to avoid a nasty wave that broke on shore. She had left *Hamilton's Bench* a few minutes later and had thought of nothing else since. She hadn't even opened the envelope handed to her by the captain as she and Pattie made their way down the steps to the pier. Pattie's contained three $100 bills. While the money was important, the way she was treated and the feeling she got from Mr. Hamilton was far more significant. It seemed he was offering her everything she needed at the moment. A job, a place to live, money, security, no questions, and...

A piano that was all hers.

But she wasn't sure. There were so many unanswered questions. For one, besides Martha Vineyard, where else did the boat go? Was it big enough to go out in the ocean?

She looked past the breaking waves. Maybe what she needed to get her mind off the past was an adventure in the future. Instead of hiding in the mountains, she'd be hiding at sea. Images of big waves flowed through her mind—very big waves—a different set of trees, a different kind of mountain range. She thought of Danny. What would he say? How would he react? Surely he'd have some advice for her. She contemplated calling him. She just as quickly snafued the temptation. She had cut those ties to that part of her life. She was determined to keep it that way.

As she made her way back to the boardwalk, she decided to ask Pattie. She'd probably have something intelligent to say. She had given her good advice so far. April quickened her pace before remembering Pattie was probably still asleep. She had no reason to get up early. April only knew her a few days, but it was enough to know Pattie was a person who lived one day at a time, all the time. She never spoke of future, of what she wanted to do with her life. She never spoke of other people in her life. She only focused on the next source of dollars.

April looked down at her sand covered feet. One step, one day, at a time.

She looked up and turned her head toward the west. Tall buildings—concrete, steel and glass structures—jetted into the sky. While a gentle breeze had started to develop, the buildings were too strong to sway back and forth. They just stood there, warehouses for mankind's fantasies. She closed her eyes and imagined she was still back in Worthington Valley out in the woods with Danny. What she would give right now...

Her eyes snapped open and she stared back down at her feet. "One step at a time," she said aloud.

Back on the boardwalk, she brushed the sand off her feet and slid them into her shoes. She looked out toward the water again. What was she thinking anyway? How could she even consider such a lame brain idea? She'd be lost aboard a boat such as that... aboard any boat for that matter. The one thing Danny had always preached, "Keep control." In the woods, she had control. In Atlantic City, she at least had some semblance of control, and she could always move on if needed. *Hamilton's Bench*, while tempting, was just that—a temptation. And temptations never worked out.

After all, saying yes to Eddie had been a temptation, hadn't it?

April decided to throw the idea past Pattie, if for no other reason than to make conversation. So that was it. She made her decision. She'd stay in Atlantic City. She stopped at a donut shop and got a bagel and a soda. She handed the clerk a twenty dollar bill and remembered she hadn't opened the envelope from the Captain Rogers. Sitting on a bench, she opened the envelope and quickly closed the packet. There were several—no, many—one hundred dollar bills. She had never had so much money in her possession at one time. She ate quickly and headed for the nearest casino. Pattie had told her to take any big bills into the casino to get changed. They handled that kind of money all the time and wouldn't bat an eye.

The thought of making so much money so easily finalized her decision. Again, she'd stay in Atlantic City.

Or so she thought.

57

The pounding persisted as the young girl hurried up the steps toward the front of the house. Halfway there, the phone started ringing. She ignored the ringing as the knocking on the door was more annoying. She wished later she had done just the opposite.

As she opened the front door, the bright glare served as a reminder that her hangover was still lingering, in spite of a hand full of aspirin, a beer, and a few puffs of marijuana. Shading her face, she let her pupils constrict and slowly lowered her arm. A big bulky man stood before her. Looking like an eclipse of the sun. It took her a second to realize the silhouette was an officer of the law. She heard a growling noise and looked down. She was better able to focus on the big dog standing at the man's side. She contemplated shutting the door and running. She was sober enough to know that would be fruitless. She decided to play it cool. "May I help you?"

"Is Bernie Smith in?"

The girl hesitated. At the same time, the dog's nose fell to the ground and started sniffing excitedly. The two pieces of information were all the sheriff needed. He stepped forward.

"He's busy," the girl replied.

The sheriff was already in the doorway so there was no way for her to close the door. In the distance, the phone continued to ring. She thought the ringing was in the correct code sequence that meant an emergency, but she wasn't sure. She had other more important things to focus on. At least the man was here to see Bernie and not her.

"I need to see him right away," the sheriff persisted. His voice was not very polite and quite stern.

The girl noticed the ringing had stopped.

The dog's head popped up and the animal let out a loud bark. The sheriff moved forward another step. Now he was looking almost straight down at the frightened girl. She thought about asking for a warrant. After all that's what they always did on TV. Instead, she looked to the side to get a view of the porch.

The sheriff said, "Don't worry sweetie pie. I'm alone, and I ain't got no business with you—that is unless Bullet here gets anxious and takes a bite out of your leg." As if on cue, the dog barked again, this time looking right at the girl. The girl moved aside.

The sheriff stepped inside and looked over his shoulder, watching as the girl bolted out the door and down the front steps "Yeah Bullet, this is the right place. Now let's find the bitch."

He stood still and listened. The house was quiet at first. Then he heard what sounded like a voice. He moved toward the rear of the first floor. The voice grew louder. The sheriff found the stairwell to the basement and cautiously stuck his head through the open doorway. As he neared the bottom of the narrow stairway, he heard a man's voice talking excitedly on the phone.

"He's looking for who?" There was a pause. "What-the-fuck does he want with her?" Another pause followed. "What time was he there?" Another pause followed. "Why did you wait so long to—"

Bernie stopped talking when he saw the two figures at the bottom of the steps. One stood on two legs, the other was on four. He hung up the receiver and quickly wondered where he had put his gun. It was in the desk drawer the other day, only he had taken it out the night before to clean it. Did he put it back? As one of his favorite movie characters, Dirty Harry would say at a time like this, did he feel lucky?

He decided not to worry about the gun. Most cops couldn't shoot straight anyway. It was the dog that bothered him. There, he did not feel so confident. He contemplated which stance to take: tough guy or pussy cat. He stared at the man's face. He knew all the cops in Atlantic City, and most of the feds in the area as well. This one he didn't recognize. So he assumed that meant a warrant versus anything else. With that, he decided to be his normal self. "What-the-fuck do you want, and what right do you have barging in here like this? And where's Julia?"

"If you mean the underage girl upstairs, I imagine she's in another state by now, she was running so fast. And I didn't barge in. She invited me in."

"Bullshit."

"Where's April Blackstone?" The sheriff already knew from the disappointed reaction of Bullet that the girl was not in the basement. The possibility always existed she was somewhere else in the house, but Bullet, his hearing still as keen as ever, would alert him if there was any movement upstairs.

"Who?"

Telling himself to play along, the sheriff repeated the name. "April Blackstone."

The man shrugged his shoulders. "Can't say I ever heard of her."

The sheriff rubbed his chin. He had purposely failed to shave so his toughness would stand out. "The lady at the boarding house thought you might say that, and I'd venture to take a guess that was who you were just talking to on the phone just now. I imagine now she's on the way to the hospital to have her leg looked at. Seems a stray dog in the area took a bite out of it."

The sheriff reached down and grabbed the release clip on the dog's collar. "I also suspect Bullet here is still hungry. We ain't had time for breakfast."

"Just who-the-fuck are you?"

"That shouldn't matter none to you, just like my business with April Blackstone is no concern of yours." The sheriff paused and looked around the room. "Quite an impressive operation you have here," he said sarcastically. "Now what sort of a business would a scum ball like you be running out of the basement of an old house with cheap furniture and a pile of telephones?" He hesitated again. "Now I'm going to give you the benefit of the doubt and assume you're on the up and up, and that you turned Blackstone away because she's a minor. However, if you didn't and gave her false papers, then you're in real trouble."

Smith again contemplated his options. There weren't many. He hated to lose the girl. Pattie told him she was a real success and the captain had already called and inquired about future engagements. Girls came and went. His business, however, had to be protected at all costs. Still though, he had his pride to think about. "Let's see the warrant."

The sheriff shrugged his shoulders. "Seems I left it back at the office."

With the realization there was no warrant, and thus no legal reason for the visit, Bernie rose to his feet and leaned forward across the desk "Get the fuck out of here before I throw your fat ass out," he demanded.

For a big man, the sheriff moved quite well. So well, he had a hold of Bernie's wrist before the smaller man even knew what happened. There was the distinct sound of bones cracking, and then there was the pain. Bernie Smith was too surprised to even cry out though.

The sheriff was leaning across the desk as well, his fingers still gripping the now deformed arm. "You want to play tough guy, or do you want to be the wimpy ass no good mother fucker you really are. I know if I blow the whistle on your operation, you'll be back in business in a couple days. Still though, the loss of income for just that short a period of time might be…Well, you do the math." He dropped the arm and it landed on the desk with a thud. The man almost fainted from the pain. If it wasn't for the sensation of sharp teeth gripping his ankle, he surely would have. He stared down at the dog in disbelief.

"Now the choice is up to you, sir. Do I give the command to back off, or attack?"

This time there was little hesitation. "Tell him to back off," the man with the deformed arm pleaded.

And so the sheriff did.

58

Danny saw the money machine up ahead. He stepped out of the way of a jogger and a man pushing a couple in a funny looking cart. He stopped several feet from the machine and circled around the safe mounted on a wooden pedestal. One side was the machine.

The other side held two pay phones. He wasn't sure what he was looking for, but if April had been there, she would have left him a sign of some sort. He pulled his spare bank card from his wallet. He approached the machine and proceeded to make a withdrawal. While the computer was verifying his information, he reached under the ledge and felt around. Except for several pieces of stale gum, there was nothing. He took the money, put it in his pocket and dropped the card on the ground. Reaching down, he looked up under the metal structure. Gum was all he saw. He wiped his hands on his pants and walked away. He had seen a cop patrolling the boardwalk earlier and didn't want to draw any unnecessary attention to himself.

He bought a soda and a soft pretzel at one of the food stands and sat on a bench next to a building. His back to the wall, he had a good view of the boardwalk in both directions. If she had come once for money, surely she'd come again. She had only taken $40, and how long would that last in a place like this? But why hadn't she left him some sort of a sign? Surely she would have known he would be able to trace her when she used the card.

The whole way to Atlantic City, his mind was filled with hope—a thin strand of emotion that helped people through the daily tragedies of life. The hope that he would find April got him through the long trip, through the night, through the fog that seemed to be everywhere between Worthington Valley and Atlantic City. Hope—what everyone in his family had been clinging to so desperately these past few days. Now suddenly, that emotional strand seemed so thin, so weak, so vulnerable. It was being challenged by yet another powerful emotional weapon—doubt.

First one negative thought, then another crossed his mind. Maybe she didn't think he'd be able to be traced her through the card. After all, he hadn't thought of it at first either. Maybe there was no sign because she didn't want to be found. Maybe she had indeed been here two days before, but was now long gone.

If either idea were true, he was wasting his time. He looked at his watch. She had made the withdrawal late in the morning. He'd wait until then. He took a sip of his soda and a bite of the warm pretzel. As the salt burned his lips, the thought that he might fail in his search grew stronger. He forced it away and told himself to think positive. He wasn't ready to accept defeat. He had to find her. He had to help her. After all, it was really all his fault.

59

April stepped through the doors of the casino, pausing to adjust to the light and noise, and to settle her nerves. She walked to a cash window, laid two of the eight hundred dollar bills out on the counter and asked that they be changed into twenties. The man behind the bars did so without a blink of the eye. He also seemed unconcerned how she was dressed for so early in the morning.

Back outside, April headed down the boardwalk towards the hotel, her pace quick, her steps light. Between last night and now, she was starting to feel better about her situation. She let a smile cross her face. She ignored the people walking by, and they ignored her. She looked up ahead and realized she was nearing the money machine. Her smile widened. She wouldn't be needing that anymore. Off to the side, she saw an old woman picking through the trash. She hoped it was Ms. Sally, but knew from the build it wasn't. April was about to continue her journey when she noticed a figure sitting on a bench, slumped over, his face hidden by a baseball cap. His head was turning back and forth much like sprinklers watering a lawn. The head was now coming in her direction. She froze in her tracks, but only for an instant. She turned her back and stepped behind a group of people on bicycles. Several more steps and she was pressed up against the side of the buildings. She told her heart to slow down and forced her breathing under control. Her vision was good, but she still couldn't tell for sure. It certainly looked like Danny. But why was he here? A stupid question, she thought. More importantly, how did he find her? Her eyes surveyed the area and locked on the structure in the middle of the boardwalk—the money machine. He had traced her through the bank card. She scolded herself for being so stupid.

She turned and walked quickly to the first break in the buildings before darting down the side street that ran perpendicular to the boardwalk. She was a block away before she slowed her pace. She told herself to concentrate and think. He had found her, or at least was close. The question still lingered: was it really him? If so, what should she do next? Like the dials on a slot machine, combinations of options churned through her mind. The ideas spun and spun, finally stopping on an image of her roommate. Pattie. She'd get Pattie to come to the boardwalk and approach him while she stood off to the side. Being the gentleman he was, he'd stand. Then April would be able to get a good look at him and know for sure. She'd decide what to do after that.

Her pace quickened again. Her eyes moved from side to side as her paranoia returned. She cursed herself for having become too laid back over the past day. She had let her guard down, and almost paid the price for it. Had she accidently run into Danny? She cursed again, reminding herself that she had to remain in control. In the game fox and hound, the one that remained in control usually won.

Her pace increased even more as she rounded the corner and headed toward her hotel. She slowed when she realized there was a lot of activity in the front for this time of day. Her caution heightened. She told herself not to overdo it. Paranoia could work in your favor.

April assumed all the traffic in the front of the hotel was the expected line of cabs waiting for the next fare to come out the doors. She stopped when she realized the vehicles were not cabs. They were police cars. Her curiosity was high, but her sense of danger overrode the desire to enter the building through the front. Instead, she went past the main entrance, forcing herself to keep a steady pace and keep her eyes in a forward direction. She made her way along the line of police cars and turned left at the corner. At the side entrance, she used her room key to open the door. This let her in midway between the lobby and elevators. She stole a glance around and saw twice as many people in the lobby than she'd expect.

She stopped to gather her thoughts when she felt a tap on her shoulder. She looked around to see Bobby, one of the security guards, standing beside her. It was the same guard who had been there the first day she'd come into the hotel. Pattie told her that Bobby was on their side and that the agency took good care of him on holidays. His fingers gripped into the material of her gown.

"Right this way, Miss," he said. She noticed the tone of his voice had lost its normal pleasantness. His eyes pleaded with her to follow his lead. She nodded and he released his grip.

She followed him past the elevators and through the *employee only* door which lead to the main kitchen. The aroma of fresh breakfast rolls filled her senses. Her stomach instantly protested as they walked by several trays of hot pastries. They went down a narrow hall that led to an exit in the back of the building. As they approached the door, Bobby slowed and then came to a complete stop beneath the emergency exit sign. He turned and faced her.

"What's going on?" April said with anxiety in her voice. "And why is the place crawling with police?"

Bobby looked past April to make sure no one had followed them. "It's Pattie. Someone broke into your room and roughed her up pretty good. She has a black eye, a fat lip and possibly a broken nose. I was just coming on duty when the ambo crew was wheeling her out. She saw me and motioned for me to go outside with her. Once in the ambo, I leaned over to give her a hug and she whispered in my ear and she said to tell you some big fat sheriff did this to her. He was trying to get information out of her about you. She said he had a mean looking dog with him. It was only a hotel housekeeping supervisor making her early morning rounds that kept her from getting it any worse. The sheriff bolted as soon as she passed by their door."

"Is she okay?" April asked in a panicky voice.

"Yeah, don't worry. She's had it worse. She's tough. She'll be okay." The hotel guard looked around nervously. "Anyway, she told me to tell you to high-tail it over to the agency house and tell them what happened. She said they'll take care of you. She also said for you not to worry, she didn't tell the sheriff anything. She didn't tell the police anything either."

April stared at her new found friend in disbelief. A big sheriff with a mean dog… but how? How did he trace her here? She had tried to distance herself from everyone back home, but they found her anyway. Both the sheriff and Danny had traced her to Atlantic City. Danny had succeeded because of her own stupidity. She should have realized the activity would be traceable. The sheriff, on the other hand, posed a different dilemma. How did he find her?

She shook her head to clear her thoughts. There was no time to dwell on what had happened. She had to focus of what to do next. Pattie had said to go to the agency house. While that sounded good, it also smelled of more trouble. If the sheriff had traced her to the hotel, why couldn't he do the same to the other side of town? Besides, the two places were intimately connected. Still not sure what to do in the long run, she did calm down enough to realize she had to get away from the hotel. She reached into her purse and pulled out the envelope of money. She took out two $100 bills. As an afterthought, she took out two more. Handing them to Bobby, she said, "I know I can trust you. Take this and see that Pattie is okay, will ya?"

He hesitated before accepting the money. "Yeah, I'll see she's okay... But what about you?"

"I'll be okay too."

Bobby stepped to the emergency exit door. He pulled a set of keys out and turned off the alarm. He pushed on the panic bar and the door opened without a sound. "See you around?" he questioned.

As April hurried into the daylight, both knew her answer was not affirmative.

60

Bullet pulled at the leash, impatient to move ahead. Never having been far from Worthington Valley, the animal smelled a new scent—the ocean air. The sheriff gave a light tug, causing the choker collar to tighten. In spite of his eagerness to hurry towards the smell, the dog heeded the command and slowed his pace. The sheriff loosened the tension and the German Shepard responded. The sheriff picked up the pace. He guessed correctly the animal was responding to the strange environment. The sheriff had to admit the salty air was pleasant and did attract one towards the east. He glanced over his shoulder to make sure no one was following them. He was sure he had gotten out of the hotel without anyone spotting him. He cursed the cleaning lady, but knew she had not seen his face. He saw no security cameras to cause a problem. He thought that a little strange until he realized this particular hotel had no casino. Convenient for him and anyone else who might be trying to hide from someone or something. So overall, he felt he was in the clear, and could focus on finding the girl. He didn't know whether to believe the girl in the hotel or not when she claimed April had skipped town the day before. She didn't know why or where the bitch might have gone.

He initially planned to go back in his patrol car and head out of town. With the confidence he'd made a clean getaway, he decided to give into the temptation and go up to the boardwalk and have a look around. It would also give him time to think through what he should do now. He started to blow the trip to Atlantic City off as a waste, but realized he at least verified the girl was alive. It also told him she was much more resourceful than anyone back in Worthington Valley thought. She had indeed made it beyond the catchment area... way beyond.

This, however, was a secret he would keep to himself. Let the others think she was hurt, or worse.

He brought his thoughts back on track. If anyone asked what he was doing dressed in his uniform, he had a variety of stories ready. His favorite, he was in town looking for potential convention sites for his department. Hopefully, people would just leave him alone.

He glanced down at the dog and smiled. With Bullet at his side, that would be a good bet.

"Come on boy, let's go give you your first look at the ocean," he directed.

The tension on the leash again tightened.

61

April hurried away from the building, putting as much distance between her and the line of police cars as possible. She didn't slow her pace until she was several blocks away. Her mind raced, searching for answers to the inevitable question: what to do now? While her options were many, one loud voice instructed her to get out of Atlantic City. She thought from Worthington Valley to the east coast would be enough distance. Obviously, it wasn't. Another voice, however, told her that distance didn't matter. The sheriff would always be able to find her. What she needed was help. But who?

At the top of the ramp leading to the boardwalk, she paused to let a line of bicycles pass. She continued to churn with possibilities. She did need help, and there was only one person she could trust.

She just hoped he was still on the same bench.

62

Sitting on the same bench, Danny's chin fell to his chest, causing his head to snap upright and bringing him fully awake. His eyes popped open and were met with the glare of the morning sun. He stood up, one hand rubbing his neck, the other shading his eyes. He glanced at his watch. He had only dozed off for a couple of minutes. Still, it wasn't good. He acknowledged the all-night drive had worn him out. His body was screaming for sleep. But what good would the drive be if he missed April because he had failed to stay awake. He walked a half a block to the north and bought a cup of coffee. He turned and headed south.

By now, the crowd on the boardwalk had thickened. There were bicycles mixed with joggers, mixed with walkers, all being dodged by roller bladders weaving in and out among the crowd. Danny was careful not to get run over or to spill his coffee. He desperately needed the caffeine.

Initially, he failed to notice the man and dog making their way across his path. He was less than twenty feet away when the dog's bark caused him to look up. He almost dumped his coffee as his feet froze to the boards. He couldn't believe what he saw.

But he had no choice.

63

April stretched. The glare from the sunlight and the increased density of the crowd limited her ability to see too far ahead. She saw the pole supporting the money machine first, but could not see the bench that sat up against the storefronts. She sidestepped to her right for a better view. The bench was empty. She felt a sense of disappointment, but didn't panic. She scanned the crowd. Her disappointment started to rise when she noticed a figure ahead of her. She shaded her eyes. It was Danny, she was sure. She was about to call out when she noticed he himself had stopped. There was a break in the crowd that allowed her to follow his line of sight. What she saw caused her knees to go weak. Coming right at her was a dog and a big fat sheriff. Lucky for April, the dog was more interested in the activity around him and the smell of the ocean than a familiar scent that was starting to tease his nostrils.

April had never fainted before, but knew she was very close to it. She spun, took a deep breath and told her body to keep taking in oxygen. One step at a time. One foot in front of the other, she thought. She started to move, quickly picking up her pace. She left the boardwalk at the first ramp, all the while cursing herself for being so stupid twice in one day. Although she didn't want to believe it, the answer to how the sheriff found her had to be connected to Danny.

That thought quickly mixed doubt, and then anger. How could he, she wondered? Her own stepbrother sold her out. The disappointment overpowered all the other emotions. Her eyes filled with tears. Now she had only one option, and that was to put distance between her and the town she had grown to like so quickly.

What would she do? Where would she go? She just knew she had to get further away from Worthington Valley. She looked out towards the ocean.

She stopped in mid-step as an option materialized. She hesitated only an instant before turning toward the main street. She glanced at her watch. Mr. Hamilton said they were planning to leave with the outgoing tide. He figured that to be around 7:30. It was now 7:15. She looked up and down the street for a taxi. "Please God, make the boat still be there," she prayed aloud.

64

Jennifer stared at the computer screen. It stared back. She blinked every so often, trying to focus on the words in front of her. Every so often, the screen blinked back. She tried to concentrate, to think, to create, but to no avail. This was the first time she sat down at the computer in months. Besides being too busy with the restaurant, she had simply lost interest in her writing. Ever since Daniel's death, she had lost her motivation do anything but work. It was her salvation, and she did it with a vengeance. Without an official title, she had taken over managing the staff. This freed up her mother to focus on the kitchen and her father to focus on the business itself. Besides, her parents mentioned they were looking at other options. When asked for specifics, they shrugged it off, saying they were just talking about their dreams. On the other hand, her dreams had come to a sudden halt. She had not been in a relationship since Daniel's death. Her nursing career was *kaput*, at least in Annapolis. Her self-esteem had been blown apart and she almost dipped into a deep depression. She survived by immersing herself in the *Riverboat Inn*.

The restaurant continued to be successful, but there was always room for improvement. She focused on two areas where she felt she could have an immediate and measurable impact. First was inventory control. Because their location was on the water and thus drew a lot of boaters, much of their business, especially in the summer, was weather dependent. Weekend afternoon thunderstorms—predicted or real—could have a significant effect on their business. It was a nightmare trying to forecast the number of meals they'd serve on any particular evening. It wasn't a problem for the bar in that alcohol and the related supplies didn't spoil. However, ninety percent of the items on the menu were prepared fresh daily. The inevitable inventory problem of not running out of something versus minimizing waste was an ongoing issue.

Besides working on the inventory problem, Jennifer looked at the employee compensation package. She developed a plan where a larger percent of the staff's salary was based on performance and the overall success of the business, making potential compensation much higher. However, everyone had to work together to ensure this. At first, her father balked at the payroll rising over ten percent. When she showed him that other costs had decreased and business was actually up in certain areas (desserts for example), he conceded and supported these ideas. He was pleased his daughter was taking a greater interest in the business. That she was succeeding so quickly was an added bonus.

With the passage of time, her depression faded and she regained some of her confidence. While work was tiring, Jennifer was actually enjoying the daily challenges of the food industry. Like in the emergency room, there was always a fire to put out, usually dealing with staff. Balancing the wants and needs of individual staff members with the needs of the business was a constant juggle. In spite of her demise at Annapolis General, Jennifer did have good people skills.

She decided the physical plant was something she needed to discuss with her parents. The place hadn't been remodeled in many years, and she felt it was way past due. Annapolis was becoming a younger and younger town, filling rapidly with the preppie crowd. Baby boomers now had careers with disposable incomes. While the tourist crowd was still a big part of their business, Jennifer knew they'd have to do something to target a younger market for year round out of season patronage. The restaurant business was becoming more and more competitive.

All these thoughts and decisions were for another time. She had gotten her desire to write back, and wanted to focus on that. Yet, writer's block continued to haunt her. It was a wall she was unable to scale. She always seemed to write in spurts anyway—spewing out pages of work for a week or so before losing the flow for a similar period of time. This time however, the down cycle was much longer than ever before.

She pushed away from the desk and fired off a few profanities. Why was she having such trouble with one of the things she loved to do? She pointed at the computer and said, "It's all your fault." Feeling a little better and able to laugh at herself, she went into the small kitchen and grabbed a soda from the fridge. Back in the living room, she plopped down on the couch and pulled the remote control from between the cushions. She flipped through the channels. Her dissatisfaction continued. There were 200 plus channels to choose from and she couldn't find anything to watch. She cursed again and finished her soda. She lay down, covering her head with a pillow. "Writer's block," she thought out loud in disgust. It was more like writer's bomb. After all, that's what she had done over the past months—totally bombed out.

She realized as long as the present stressors in her life stayed front and center, she'd be unable to concentrate on writing. To start, the hospital was still open and still struggling. Little had changed. Sam Robertson remained in charge, although his position with the board of directors was said to be weakening. The nursing shortage continued and the census remained low. The previous negotiations to sell had leaked to the public (not by her) and had broken down as a result. Robertson was desperately looking for a buyer or another hospital for a merger, but the debt was too great to attract any interest. Speculation was that the hospital would close within a year.

If he had only listened!

She rolled to her side and pulled a pillow tighter around her ears. She told herself she needed more time. She accepted the demise of her nursing career at Annapolis General, but had yet to complete the mourning process for Daniel. That, she feared, might never end. She had to find something on which to focus her energies. She was happiest when overwhelmed, working on several projects at the same time. Yet, in spite of her work at the restaurant, there was still a large void in her life. Her inability to write wasn't helping matters either.

She got up and went back to the computer. She moved the cursor to the icon in the lower left corner. With another click of the mouse, she chose the *shut down* option. When the screen told her it was safe to turn off the power, she did so. She knew it would be a long time before she started the computer up again.

"Screw it," she said pushing her chair back from the desk. She rose to her feet, stretched and headed for the shower. While she wasn't expected in the restaurant for another couple of hours, she was anxious to go over the numbers from the night before. They had an exceptionally good Wednesday night, and she wanted to see if her theories were proving true. She smiled as she peeled off her jeans. One of the things she had recently implemented was a financial analysis of the business based on the specific day of the week. Her parents knew the basic patterns. Fridays were always the busiest bar nights. Saturdays were the busiest in the dining room. Monday nights during football season were also good, especially since they put in a couple of big screen TVs in the bar. Beyond that, except for certain holidays, her parents did not track the data on a day to day basis. Their argument, all the predicting was fine and dandy, but the real factor was the weather. It could produce a boom. It could also turn on you. Jennifer's analysis, however, demonstrated a more discernable pattern based on the particular day of the week. The pattern was clearer than Jennifer's parents thought, and their daughter set out to prove it.

The Blackstones knew their daughter was smart, and was an especially good problem solver. She was good with numbers and she was good with people. They just hoped that as she took on more responsibilities at the restaurant, she'd be able to focus more on the future and dwell less on the past.

Jennifer knew this was her parent's plan, and she did not think it a bad one. If anything, immersing herself further in the *Riverboat Inn* would help fill the void in her life. She vowed not to disappoint them. She vowed not to disappoint herself.

65

The town of Rock Hall was well positioned for both its seafood business and the tourist trade. The spacious harbor, close to, yet protected from the Chesapeake Bay, offered good access to the variety of marinas, shops and restaurants lining the inlet. With the proliferation of the boating industry on the Chesapeake, the town had arisen from a quiet seafood port to becoming a Mecca of activity. While many larger ports such as Annapolis and Baltimore took the brunt of the increased boating traffic, smaller ports such as Rock Hall saw significant growth in their tourist trade. The town's people were mixed in their feelings about the increased hustle bustle environment.

Cliff remembered coming to Rock Hall at an early age with his uncle. The official reason was to sell crabs, especially when the prices were better on the Eastern Shore. Unofficially, the trip across the bay meant crab cakes from Ms. Virginia's. For many years, she ran a small eatery in Tolchester, an even smaller town a few miles north of Rock Hall. She moved to Rock Hall several years back, and now worked out of a corner restaurant across from the old ice cream parlor. The crab cakes were the same, however, and in many people's minds, the best around. People came from all over the bay, and even further, to order up one of her delicacies.

The crab cakes were made fresh throughout the day, deep fried in cooking oil, and served on a plain hamburger roll with a slice of fresh tomato. You had your choice of tartar sauce or ketchup. That was all. If you wanted it any other way, it was suggested that you might not know how to properly eat a Maryland crab cake.

Cliff first met Ms. Virginia as a young boy. While Cliff had matured into a young man, Ms. Virginia had not changed. She was the same stately gray haired lady who was always hunched over and whose smile was thin and wide. She wore an old style printed dress, stockings and high top black shoes. It mattered not what the season or what the temperature; the lady always dressed the same. She never complained about the cold, nor about the heat.

Steering through the rock lined breakwater, Cliff imagined he could already smell the crab cakes cooking. His stomach growling from not eating all day, he reluctantly pulled back on the throttle as the nose of the *Mona Lisa* cleared the inside line of rocks. The badly-in-need-of-paint sign reminded those entering the harbor that the speed limit was six knots, and that you were responsible for your wake. Cliff laughed whenever he saw such a marker. The *Mona Lisa* only ran six knots at full speed, and her wake wasn't enough to wiggle the feathers of a sleeping duck.

Cliff had called ahead for a slip at Rock Hall Landing. He checked the chart and steered to the port. Finding his assigned slip, he pulled in bow first, tied up, plugged in the electric cable and connected the water hose. He and Chessie went ashore to make the obligatory doggy walk and to register at the marina office. Cliff was glad he made port when he did. It was only Thursday and the place was already hopping. The dock master predicted all transient slips would be filled by the weekend.

Having been on the boat for the past two weeks, Cliff planned to stay at least until Monday. The forecast called for it to be exceptionally hot the next few days, so he didn't mind the thought of frequent showers without concern over water supply. Besides, he wanted to give himself and Chessie a couple days of good workouts. If things got too busy, he could always move on. While he never minded being around people, he was enjoying the solitude, the privacy afforded by anchoring out. Overall, life was good. Decisions were few and simple—when and what to eat, when and what to work on regarding his art, and where to spend the night. The *Mona Lisa*, knock on wood, continued to perform up to expectations without any major problems (except for a sticky port side winch which he corrected with a liberal amount of oil). She sailed true and was easy to operate and provided an excellent platform for his easel.

Brisk spring breezes gave Cliff ample opportunity to improve his sailing skills. The *Mona Lisa* was very forgiving of small mistakes, so long as the mistake didn't involve challenging her draft. While Cliff had yet to officially run aground, he did wake up one morning sitting on the bottom of a cove. He tried blaming the error on a charting mistake, but his boating knowledge disallowed any such nonsense. The chart was right. He had simply read the numbers wrong. Anyway, after sitting through a tide change, hoping the boat didn't heel over any further, they finally made it off the bottom. He knew his uncle was watching from above and having a good laugh at his expense. But that was okay. He needed to remember his uncle in that manner.

During this time, his portfolio of partials grew. Underway, he could get the basic outline of the drawing down on paper rather quickly. However, while he had several books of partials needing completion, he had very few finished works. He told himself not to worry; there'd be plenty of time for that in the future. If nothing else, he knew his luck with the weather wouldn't hold forever.

After a run with Chessie and a shower to follow, Cliff headed into town. To no one's surprise, Ms. Virginia was working behind the counter, her hands in a bowl of fresh crab meat, picking out the few shells that dared to get into her food. To Cliff's surprise, she recognized him by name and spoke a few minutes about his uncle. She asked Cliff what he was doing and how he was making out. Cliff left out the details, but did explain the basics of what he was trying to accomplish. She wished him luck before turning the conversation back to his uncle. She laughed as she told a story of how his uncle once told a couple from the Midwest that crab cakes came out of a shell just like an oyster. He said that they were seasoned by watermen spreading tons of Old Bay seasoning out across the water and letting it to drift down to the crab cakes which grew on the bottom. Word spread that this same couple was later seen down at the local crab house trying to buy a bushel of crab cakes.

"Your ole uncle could tell a tale with the best of 'em. He had a way of making people believe everything he said. Most people in the business listened when he did say something important. He was a smart man… and a good one, too. I was an old lady and he still taught me a thing or two."

"You ain't old, Ms. Virginia," someone down the counter said.

"Just seasoned real well," another customer chimed in.

Ms. Virginia laughed. "Go on now, you boys behave."

By now, Cliff's order was ready and Ms. Virginia set the paper plate in front of the hungry boy… man… young man. Age was all a perspective.

Cliff dug his teeth into the hot sandwich. Keeping an ear on the conversation around him, he told himself that life was good.

And so it was… for now.

66

A set of chimes rang loudly as Cliff pushed open the door. He paused, allowing his pupils to dilate before taking a quick look around. A smile crossed his face as he saw before him a marina store typical of many he had been in over the years. The theme of the store was simple—not fancy but containing most anything a boater could want. Cliff took the list of needed food and supplies from his pocket, grabbed several carrying baskets from a pile next to the door and began his journey up and down the aisles. As his uncle used to say upon entering such a place, there was crap everywhere. The shelves were filled with everything from bright yellow dockside electrical cords, to replacement parts for heads, to a wide array of navigational equipment, and life jackets of every size and color. Dispersed amongst all this *stuff* were food supplies. It was a boating supply store and a grocery store combined into one. While indeed cluttered and in need of better lighting, the place was clean—symbolic, Cliff figured, of most people's boats. It was certainly representative of the *Mona Lisa*. His smile widened as he noticed boxes of dried prunes stacked next to biodegradable toilet paper. He chose a pack of each.

Two aisles later, he was startled from behind as he tested the freshness of the bread. "May I help you?" a pleasant voice said.

He turned and came face to face with a girl about his age, maybe a year or two older. She sported long brown hair that hung well below her shoulders. Her face was round, smooth and perfectly tanned. She wore a red tee shirt with the words *Tom's Supplies* across the left pocket. She was a few inches shorter than Cliff, and did nothing to improve her vertical status by being barefoot.

"Steady Duke," he told himself, quoting from his favorite book, *The Voyage*. He forced his mind back on the task at hand. "Ah, yes, I need to stock up on a few things." He held up the list to add credibility to his statement.

She took the piece of paper from Cliff's hand and scanned it briefly. "On a boat?"

Cliff nodded.

"We got the best fuel prices around."

"I do need a few gallons of diesel," Cliff said.

She laughed. "Must be a sailboat."

"You don't sell to sailboaters?"

"No, no," she said defensively. "I love sailboats. Just can't move any fuel that way. But you guys usually buy more groceries."

"Because we're cheap and don't eat out a lot?"

She cocked her head to the side, the smile shrinking slowly. "Because you're smart and want to soak every ounce of pleasure from your time on the water."

"Right…. right," Cliff said.

The smile again returned. "Are you always this easy?"

Cliff tried not to blush and shrugged his shoulders. She could have let him stand there and suffer, but she didn't. Handing back his list, she said, "I imagine we have most everything you'd want. If not, let me know and I'll see if I can find it for you."

"Are you always this accommodating?" Cliff asked.

She turned and started to walk away. Looking over her shoulder, she winked. "Depends."

Moving up and down the aisles, Cliff concentrated on gathering the items on the list. Typical of similar stores, there was no rhyme or reason how the place was stocked. As the baskets filled, he caught himself sneaking a look through the breaks in the clutter. Other customers came and went, and the girl was cheerful with each. While the overall atmosphere of the store was dull because of all the stuff piled around and the low lighting, she made up for any lack of ambience with her friendly personality. Several times she caught him looking at her. Each time she smiled and wiggled her eyebrows back at him. Finally, he took the overflowing baskets up to the counter.

Sliding a case of dog food towards the scanner arm, she half asked, half pronounced, "You got a dog on board?"

"Yeah," Cliff said, starting to unload the baskets.

"You look like a Chesapeake retriever kind of a guy."

He chuckled. Was she that good, or was it a lucky guess. He decided it didn't matter. He nodded in the affirmative.

"Best boat dog there is," she proclaimed.

As the baskets were emptied and plastic bags filled, she made small talk, never asking anything specific except the name of his dog and the name of his boat. She never asked him what he did or why he was out on the water. Cliff figured that didn't really matter. If you had a boat and you were out on the water, that was good enough. After all, boating was boating. Why or what you did to afford it was of little consequence.

When the checkout was complete, Cliff had more stuff than he realized. Luckily, there was a dock cart outside. She helped him load the cart, asking, "Anything else you need?"

"Fuel, but there's no rush for that. I just want to top off the tank."

"Let me know."

"Oh, yeah, I need ice." He looked at the stuff piled in the cart. "I'll come up and get that later."

He paid the bill, said good-bye and headed down the dock. He spent the rest of the afternoon reorganizing things and putting the new supplies away. It always amazed Cliff how a short list could grow into a big pile once purchased; and how that pile could grow even larger once loaded aboard a boat.

Emptying a bag, the image of the girl came to mind. "In my dreams," he said aloud to Chessie, who was under foot trying to find which supplies were hers.

67

Satisfied the supplies were secure and wouldn't come crashing onto the floor as soon as the *Mona Lisa* heeled over, Cliff washed down the decks. He made a mental note to add another coat of varnish to the teak trim. It was already showing signs of weathering from the sun and salt. Maybe he'd also add another coat of wax to the gel coat to ensure a lasting shine. The *Mona Lisa* was ten years old. She still looked good, and with a little bit of makeup, looked even better.

Cliff worked up a good sweat, then hosed himself off. The water was cold, but it felt good. Naturally, Chessie wanted to get in on the fun. The two played in the water a few minutes before Chessie decided she'd had enough. She shook the water from her body and went to the bow to get dry. Cliff laughed as she had managed to spray fur laden water over most of the cockpit, meaning another wash down was in order. He contemplated squirting the hose at her, but decided against it. That would only cause the dog to *attack*, and they'd be at it again. Instead, he rinsed everything off, rolled up the hose and reopened the hatches and windows. He grabbed a can of Coke and moved forward to sit with his companion.

He finished the soda, felt the urge to take a nap, but rose to his feet as the pile of unfinished drawings lurked in the back of his mind. He reminded himself that while he was doing what he loved, it was still a job. If he was going to make a career out of this, he had to work hard and long. Just like crabbing with his uncle, there'd be many missed naps.

He chuckled as he backed down the steps into the cabin. "Well, maybe not many missed naps."

After a quick shower, he grabbed an apple and slid into the booth. He pulled a drawing pad from the shelf and opened to the first page. A line of sharp charcoal pencils at his side, he went to work completing the drawing of fishnets he'd passed on his way across the bar that protected the entrance to Rock Hall's harbor. At first, he noticed the sounds outside, especially the footsteps up and down the old rickety pier. He felt a dip in temperature as the sun started its decline. A gentle breeze picked up for a short period, causing Cliff to change into sweat pants and a tee shirt. Another apple, a bottle of water and he was back to work. As time passed, he became less cognizant on the activities outside. He barely remembered Chessie coming into the cabin after a nap.

The first drawing completed and separated from the spiral pad, he carefully trimmed the edges and placed it in a matted frame. He set it aside for later placement in a waterproof case. He turned his attention back to the pad of partials and flipped through several more images of the fish nets he sketched while circling the area earlier in the day. The drawings were a lot rougher and would take time and effort. He was anxious to get more completed works added to his portfolio so he moved on to a drawing of a skipjack headed down the bay. He sharpened his pencils and again focused his energy on the image before him. Time passed quickly. A second partial completed, he was about to choose a third when he was distracted by a knock on the side of the boat. He slid out of the booth and stuck his head up through the galleyway.

Standing on the pier beneath the light post holding a couple bags of dripping ice was the girl from the store. He blinked and stepped up into the cockpit.

"Hi," she said.

"Hi," he managed to say in return.

"Hope I'm not bothering you. You said you needed ice. We closed at eight."

Instinctively, Cliff looked at his arm without a watch. "Is it that late?"

"Eight-thirty now."

"Gee." He stared at her. He noticed she had changed into a long sleeve tee shirt and jeans. Where it had been free flowing earlier, her hair was now pulled into a ponytail. She was still barefooted.

Cliff stepped up onto the gunwale and reached out with both hands. She handed him the ice which he promptly dumped into the ice chest stored in front of the wheel. He looked up at her. Now she was holding out a twelve pack of Bud Light. "Can't have ice without beer, can ya?" she said.

"I thought it was beer without ice?"

She laughed. "Whatever."

He took the twelve-pack and helped her aboard. By now, Chessie had stirred and was up on deck. The girl immediately bent over and started petting the dog. "I knew you were a Chesapeake… and what a beautiful girl you are, too."

The animal responded to the praise by sitting back on her hind legs and allowing the guest to continue rubbing her head. The girl looked back at Cliff. "Again, I hope I'm not bothering you."

"No… not at all. I was just working."

"Working?"

"Yeah, doing some drawings."

"Drawings… you an architect or something?"

"I'm trying to be an artist."

"Oh, yeah, can I see some of your work?"

Cliff shrugged his shoulders. "Why not?" He raised the pack of beer. "Thirsty?"

"Why not?"

He led her down below, handed her a beer and motioned for her to take a seat. She popped the metal tab on the can and looked around the cabin. "I've never been on such a big sailboat before. It's really nice. There's a lot more room than you think."

"Never enough, though," Cliff added.

"That's true on any boat." She took a swallow of her beer and looked down at the drawing pad lying on the table. "May I?"

"Sure."

She pulled the pad toward her and opened the first page. A smile crossed her face as she recognized the fishing nets outside the entrance to Rock Hall. The smile disappeared as she leaned in closer. Cliff could tell immediately she was distressed at the roughness of the drawings. "Is there something wrong?" he asked innocently.

"No… no… these are real good."

Cliff laughed.

"Really, they are."

"Then you're a poor judge of art."

She tilted her head to the side a bit. "Okay, wise guy, what's wrong with them?"

"They're not finished."

She stared back down at the empty page. "Oh, I knew that."

Refraining from orating an expletive referring to cow waste, Cliff laughed again. "I knew you did."

She looked up and smiled. "What's the scoop?"

Cliff explained his method of doing partials while out on the water and completing them at a later time. He went to the aft cabin and pulled out several completed works for her to view, including the finished drawing of the fishing nets. The girl's eyes widened as she looked at the picture. "That's more like it," she said. "It's beautiful… simply beautiful. I especially like the shading effect."

"The sunlight happened to be perfect when I came across the bar, laying down a long shadow past the nets." He pointed to the area he was talking about.

"So this is the *work* you were doing?"

"Yes, I was working on this one." He turned the drawing of the skipjack.

"Wow, that's beautiful too. Is this one complete?"

"Almost."

"What do you do with them when they're finished?"

"Hopefully sell them at an art show in the fall."

"You have your own art show?"

"I wish. I usually display them in places like malls."

"I see." The girl continued flipping back and forth between the various drawings. "People really buy them in places like that?"

"That's the idea," Cliff said.

She motioned to the finished drawing of the Rock Hall nets. "How much for this one?"

The question caught Cliff by surprise. "I haven't priced them yet. That usually depends on what kind of show I'm at."

"How about a one person show on a boat in Rock Hall Harbor?"

Cliff smiled. "Never did a show like that before."

"There's a first time for everything, isn't there?"

Cliff swore she had a flirting look in her eyes. At the same time, she brought up a very good point. His tone turned serious. "You have more experience in retail than I do. What do you think it's worth?"

"Depends on the buyer," she said. "Stuff like this… rather, items that have an intangible value, can be hard to price. There's a fine balance between what someone will pay and what someone wants. Boats are a lot like that. Services provided to boaters fall into that category as well. For example, you paid for this transient slip tonight, right?"

Cliff nodded.

"What's this space in the water really worth… and how much are you willing to pay to be here?"

Cliff smiled. "Tonight, probably a lot. Tomorrow night, once I get resupplied and have a couple good meals, maybe not as much."

"Exactly. Tonight, I may be really fascinated by your work, especially since I am in the presence of the artist. However, no offense, but tomorrow it may not appeal to me as much."

"No offense taken," Cliff reassured. He was beginning to realize that behind her youthfulness, her flirtatious behavior and her sometimes sharp tongue, she was a very bright girl.

She took a deep breath and finished her beer. "Anyway, I better let you get back to work." She tapped the drawing. "You decide on a price and let me know." She started to slide out of the booth.

Having been out of contact with people for a while, he suddenly didn't want her to leave. "You hungry?" he said.

She paused. "I haven't eaten yet."

"Want something?"

"What're you offering." There was that flirting look again.

"Let's see, I got fresh bread today... nice looking tomatoes. I make a mean tuna salad sandwich."

"I bet you do," she mocked.

"I do really!"

"Okay, sounds like an offer a girl can't refuse."

"There's just one condition," Cliff said.

"I knew there'd be a stipulation," she mocked. "What is it?"

"You gotta tell me your name?"

She broke into a smile. "Cheryl... Cheryl Smith."

Cliff nodded. "Pretty name. I'm Cliff... Cliff Davidson." He held out his hand.

She took it without hesitation. "A handsome name."

Cliff slid out of the booth and went to the galley. Luckily, he found the can of tuna without a problem. Cheryl sliced a tomato while Cliff focused on making the tuna salad. He joked about forgetting the recipe. "Mayonnaise and tuna," Cheryl reminded.

As the two worked side by side, Cliff continued to be enthralled by his new acquaintance. While true, his experience with girls was limited, he did have a lot of female friends in school. Never, however, had he met one with such a combination of sharp tongue and charm. It was a trait most attractive to Cliff. She also seemed to be genuinely interested in his work, his dog and his boat. The opposite of America's favorite pastime, three strikes and she was in. With caution flags popping up all around, he refused to let his thoughts return to the past.

On several occasions, Cheryl rubbed up against him. She never balked at the contact. On the contrary, she seemed to keep the contact longer than necessary. He was glad he came to Rock Hall for a respite. The question now, how long would he stay? He grinned to himself.

"Steady Duke," he instructed silently as he slowly folded the mayonnaise and tuna. He added diced onion and a pickle.

With the gourmet dinner plated and new beers opened, they returned to the dinette. After a few bites, Cliff said, "Is the store yours?"

"Mine and... a friend's."

"How long have you had it."

"About two years. It was my uncle's before he died. I sort of inherited it from him."

There was an immediate bond, only Cliff chose not to explain. "You sure have a good supply of stuff."

"Short on art supplies," she laughed. She took a drink of her beer. "Tell me how you came about doing this."

Cliff summarized how he had always dreamed of becoming a full time waterscape artist, and how through some unfortunate circumstances he got the chance. He didn't go deep into details and she didn't ask.

"Do you actually earn a living at this?" she did inquire.

Cliff explained further about displaying at various art shows and festivals around the area. He added, "They can be unpredictable, but for the most part, I've done okay. Most of the times I actually run short of some material."

"Like what?"

"Contrary to what I expected, people want paintings as well as the drawings and photographs. However, paintings take a lot more time, and I haven't tried that on the boat yet. Although, I'm considering giving it a go soon."

"You draw, paint and do photography? Isn't that a little unusual for an artist?"

Another insightful question, Cliff thought. He shrugged his shoulders. "I want to stand out from the others. You may not think so, but the field is very competitive."

"I would think you'd stand out just in the quality of your work."

"Thank you."

"I'm serious," Cheryl insisted. She fell silent as she worked on her sandwich. He could tell from the way she attacked the tuna, she was hungry. He rose once to fetch another round of beers. Starting to slide back into the booth, he had to steady himself as the *Mona Lisa* rocked in response to a passing boat's wake.

"You lost your sea legs already?" she said through a mouthful of food.

"My sea legs are just fine," he insisted, getting back into the booth. He opened two cans and slid one towards her. He took a long swallow of his own. He had to admit, it felt good to have someone to talk to other than Chessie. It also felt strange not worrying about the anchor holding. His eyes rose off the table to find her staring at him. "Something wrong?" he asked instinctively.

"No, I'm just looking."

"At what?"

The smile widened. "At you."

He didn't know whether to laugh or to blush. So he did a little of both.

"And what are *you* looking at?" she asked.

"At you."

She pushed up in her seat slightly. "Like what you see?"

"Yes." Luckily, he caught himself before he said more.

She leaned across the table and grabbed his hand. At the same time, her foot started crawling up his leg. "I was thinking I'd like to get to know you better," she said.

"How much better?"

"Oh, much better." She slid out of the booth and stepped to his side. She leaned over and kissed him gently on the cheek. "Is that better?" she whispered.

"Uh, huh," he responded.

She kissed him on the lips. "And that?"

"Uh, huh," he responded.

She took his hand and guided him to the couch across the way. Once he was seated, she straddled his legs. She kissed him again, this time holding the contact longer and guiding her tongue into his mouth. "Still better?"

He wrapped his arms around her and tried pulling her into him. She resisted his move, arching her back instead and sitting up straight. She reached down and pulled her shirt up over her head. She leaned forward and teased his ear with her tongue.

"I think you'll agree, it's going to get even better," she said.

And so it did.

68

The tongue was wet and cold as it lapped against the side of his face. Memories of the night before filtered through his mind. There had been a lot of wetness then, too. A shiver went through his spine as the images flashed by. He let out a soft moan and readjusted his position. He felt the wetness against his ear again. "Stop it," he mouthed softly. He knew, however, he was lying. He didn't want it to stop at all. More images and he moaned louder. The reply was a loud bark.

Cliff sat up with a start. "Chessie!"

The dog took a step back, startled at his master's roughness. She barked again.

"What are you doing?" Becoming fully awake, Cliff looked around. The fantasies evaporated like a blue crab in seaweed. He dropped his feet to the floor. Reaching out, he rubbed the animal's head. "What time is it anyway?"

Chessie waddled to the bottom of the steps and looked up toward the partially closed hatch.

Cliff's eyes went in the same direction. The day was well past dawn. "That time, huh?" Cliff said. "Give me a second." He stood up, pausing to let his blood circulate. He started to take a step and realized he was weak in the knees. He stood firm, refusing to give in to the urge to collapse back on the bunk. A smile crossed his face. "Sea legs, huh?" Snapshots from the night before again flashed before him.

He dressed and took Chessie out for a walk. She wanted to have a run, too, but much to the dog's chagrin, they took it nice and slow. Back aboard the *Mona Lisa*, Cliff showered and shaved what beard he had. He cleaned up the cabin and washed the few dishes. There was some left over tuna salad in the ice box. Normally, that would have been just fine for breakfast. This morning, however, he decided to go up to the store and to get something fresh. He also forgot to pay Cheryl for the beer and ice. He had other reasons, too.

He entered the store and let his eyes adjust to the dim lighting. He moved toward the cash register but stopped when he heard a voice. He turned and saw a man dressed in camouflage pants and a green tee shirt walking down one of the aisles. He was about the same age as Cheryl, but a couple inches taller. He was lean and very muscular with short cropped blond hair. He saw Cliff and said, "Mornin'. Can I help you?"

Cliff cautiously took another step forward. "Ah, yes. I was looking for Cheryl. I owe her money for some beer yesterday."

"She's in the back going through a delivery. You can settle up with me." He moved toward the cash register. "How much was it.?"

Cliff hesitated. "I don't know the amount. It was a twelve pack of Bud and a couple bags of ice."

The man moved behind the counter. "Let me take a look. She usually sticks IOU's around here somewhere." He started looking through piles of papers.

Cliff scanned the store quickly. Cliff did not like that the man was so casual. Other warning flags started rising. "You work here?" the artist inquired cautiously.

The man laughed. "Cheryl lets me sometimes. But I'm full time National Guard, so that keeps me pretty busy. I'm only here now because two of our trucks broke down. Otherwise, I was headed out for three days of proving to Uncle Sam that I know how to live in a tent."

Just then Cheryl came out from the back room. As she did, she was yelling in a loud voice, "Honey, did you remember to order—" She caught a glimpse of Cliff and her jaw dropped. Cliff was speechless as well. Lucky for everyone, the man now known as *Honey* was still trying to find the IOU. In all the confusion, Cliff was perceptive enough to catch the signal Cheryl was giving him by shaking her head side to side. At first he didn't want to believe what he was sensing or seeing. He wanted to walk out of the store, turn around and come back in. With *Honey's* back still turned, Cliff held up his left fourth finger and wiggled it slightly. He watched as the color drained from Cheryl's face. His face did the same as she nodded in the affirmative.

By the time the man turned around to acknowledge he had failed in his search for the IOU, Cliff was on his way out the door. *Honey* started to say something, but his wife interrupted. "Don't worry about it, babe. He paid for everything yesterday. He just forgot."

But forgetting was not one of the artist's fortes.

69

The *Mona Lisa* pulled gently at her anchor line. A gentle breeze blew across her bow causing the boat to swing side to side. Gentle swells of the bay added to the soothing motion. The sun was only an hour from setting and the temperature was starting to drop as well. The rays of light, broken apart by the metal beams of the north span of the Chesapeake Bay Bridge, sent a geometric pattern of shadows across her decks. As she was anchored a half mile northeast of the main span, the traffic above passed in near silence.

Oblivious to all this, Chessie, awakening from a long afternoon nap, shook out her fur and waddled back to the rear of the boat to see what was going on. She had many keen senses, including the ability to pick up on the physical as well as the emotional state of her master. There seemed to be nothing wrong with him physically, but she knew the something was wrong mentally. Something had happened. When he had come back to the boat, his mood was different. He was generally a pretty level kind of a person. He showed excitement rarely. He displayed anger with the same frequency. Now, however, he was displaying something different—a behavior she had only seen once in the past, when her other master had disappeared. He was sad then. He was sad now.

She was a brave dog and had no fear but one—losing her master. She, too, had been sad when her other master left. Now there was fear the same was happening again. Was he about to disappear? He had said little since they left the town. Instead, he seemed to be focused on a far off place. They had left in a hurry, her master not taking the usual slow lackadaisical pace they had been running at lately. He didn't put up the sails like he usually did when the wind was blowing in her face. Instead, the motor stayed on the whole time. They motored until they came to the big bridges where they stopped. Why there, she didn't know. What had happened, she didn't know. What was going to happen next?

She tried several times to nuzzle up to him. Each time, however, he gave her a token pat on the head and told her to go lie down. Each time, her level of concern rose. This was not like him, and while she possessed an understanding and patient disposition, she was still a dog. Her patience and understanding would only go so far. Her intelligence, however, overrode the inborn instincts to raise a ruckus as a way of getting attention. She stretched, lay down beside her master and waited for the mood to pass.

70

Cliff rubbed the top of Chessie's head all the while staring straight ahead. His eyes were unfocused, his mind oblivious to anything going on around him. It was a state of mind not unpleasant. After all, in order for his eyes to focus, his brain would have to do the same. If that happened, the earlier agony would surely return.

Time, he kept telling himself. Time would fix it again, just like it did when his parents died, just like it did when his uncle died, just like it did with Robin. He reminded himself time was the healer of all wounds, but it was a tough pill to swallow.

He felt an utter sense of disbelief mixed with waves of anger. At times he wanted to cry. Then there were moments he wanted to deny it had ever happened. But the memories were not a dream. He felt so guilty, so used—just like the time with Robin. Twice in his life he had done it. Twice it had been wonderful. Twice he had been burned afterward. Again, it was a tough pill to swallow, but swallow he did. He promised himself that in the future, he'd be more pessimistic, more untrusting. When he was growing up, friends told him he was too soft, too easy, too gullible. He was the proverbial nice guy.

For the most part, he ignored all this. He tended to stay to himself and focus on his art. He only came out of his shell occasionally, and only for brief periods. The past two times he had been burned. No one would get to him again, no matter how hard they tried. He'd continue to harden his shell to strengthen his armor. He'd be better prepared for the next attack on his soul. Two strikes maybe, but definitely not three.

So he'd work harder, longer and focus on nothing but his art until he became void of inspiration.

As Chessie nuzzled her head against his elbow, he reached out and rubbed her head. "Chessie," he said aloud. "A man's best friend. A man's only friend." He looked out toward the north span of the bridge. Tipping his head back, he looked for the painter who had been up there earlier. He was about to write the man off when he spotted him high up on the eastern side of the main channel. He was just a speck in the distance, but he was there. "Afternoon, Mr. Twain," he said softly.

"Good afternoon, Cliff," the painter seemed to reply.

"It's awfully hot for so early in the year," Cliff said.

"You think it's hot down there. You ought to be up here."

"Nice breeze, though."

"None up here."

"You look like you're making progress," Cliff said.

"Maybe, but you're not."

"It's not been a good day for me."

"Something wrong with your equipment?"

"No, personal problems."

Mr. Twain's face twisted into a look of disgust. "Never let personal problems interfere with your work. You're a painter and that comes first."

"But…"

"No buts. They only get in the way of success. Stay focused and you'll do just fine. Let your emotions wander and you're doomed to fail. Like me up here, if I don't focus… SPLASH!"

Cliff didn't know whether to laugh or cringe at the comment. He glanced away as the *Mona Lisa* rolled heavily in response to a large wake. He watched as a container ship passed beneath the bridges in near silence. The decks were empty. There was not a person in sight. If it was night, the ship would pass for a ghost.

Cliff looked into the sky. He lost sight of the painter as the figure disappeared behind a large steel beam. Cliff waited, but the bridge painter didn't return. Chessie's cold nose again pressed against him. "Yeah, girl, I know." He rose to his feet. "No splash for me."

He stood up, stretched and bent forward, he worked a crick out of his back. He looked to his right. The Eastern Shore loomed in the distance. Memories of past few hours seemed so far in the past. He turned his head to the left. The western shore, while farther away, was much more appealing.

Cliff reached down and gave the dog a hard rub. "What say we play cowboy and head west?"

Happy to see a little enthusiasm back in her master's voice, Chessie barked in agreement.

Mid July

71

David Blackstone's office looked more like that of a successful politician's than the office of a busy restaurateur. The room was large, neat and tidy. The furniture was solid oak, dark and highly polished. Organized piles of paper sat across the front of the large desk. The elder's chair, rich black leather, also served as an occasional recliner for short naps. Historically, when he was younger and starting the *Riverboat Inn*, overnight sleep-ins were common. The hard wood flooring was covered with scattered rugs, each depicting a scene from the old steam shipping days. Two Queen Anne chairs stood in front of the desk with a long conference table to the rear. Several other more casual chairs and a couch rounded out the furnishings. The eye catcher in the room was the hundreds of framed pictures lining the four walls. Each photograph was of David Blackstone shaking hands with some other POI (Person of Importance), usually a recognizable celebrity or politician. Often times the photograph was autographed by the POI. The only exception to the wall coverings was a large ship's wheel bolted to the wall behind the desk. The wheel was authentic from an old Mississippi riverboat. It was symbolic of just who was at the restaurant's helm. David Blackstone, however, was quick to point out that while he may indeed be the captain, a higher force prevailed. He'd point to a photograph of his wife hanging beside the ship's wheel. A plaque beneath the photograph read: *Elizabeth Blackstone: cook, chief bottle washer, Admiral.*

No one ever accused David Blackstone of not knowing his place. No one ever accused David Blackstone of not being a good politician, in and out of his family. When queried regarding the why of this decor, Blackstone always downplayed his part and played up the testimony to the *Riverboat Inn* itself. The restaurant's captain liked to boast that people from all walks of life ate aboard the *Riverboat Inn*—the same mix of people who used to board the old riverboats that cruised up and down the Mississippi.

While Jennifer had been in the office thousands of times, she still stopped to look around. There was always something new to see—a new knick-knack sitting on one of the many bookshelves lining the walls beneath the photographs, a new photograph, or something else that a customer brought in. This visit was no different, so it took her a moment to settle into one of the Queen Anne chairs across from her father. He called her that morning, waking her up from a sound sleep and asking her to meet him in the office as soon as possible. This was not an uncommon call and she normally would have taken her time. On this occasion, however, the tone of his voice had a hint of excitement she had not sensed in a while, so she hurried. So much so, her hair was still damp. She ran her fingers through it now as she said, "What's up?"

Just as she spoke, her mother came into the room. She rose to her feet, kissed her mother on the cheek, saying, "You got the call too, huh?"

As always when teased in such a manner, Elizabeth Blackstone (the admiral) immediately took the offensive. "No, I did not get the call. I was asked if I had a minute."

Mr. Blackstone laughed. He rose to his feet and came around to the front of the desk. Standing beside his wife who had taken the other chair, his face turned serious. "Your mother and I realize you've been under a lot of stress these past many months, and we've tried to be as supportive as possible."

"You have, Daddy," Jennifer injected.

"We're glad you feel that way."

Jennifer shrugged her shoulders and added. "Besides, like you always say, shit happens but life moves on." Jennifer ignored the stare she knew was coming from her mother. She winked at her father who had to work hard not to a laugh.

Her father continued. "That said, have you given any thought about trying to work somewhere else as a nurse?"

"Mind you Jennifer, we're just asking. We're not putting any pressure on you," her mother injected.

"No pressure felt," Jennifer reassured. She did notice how smoothly the conversation had become a joint effort of her mother and father, meaning her mother was in on whatever her father was up to. That didn't bother her. It just made the whole thing more interesting. It also put her on guard. She straightened up in her seat and stared across the room. She noticed a new photograph of her father and the Governor. She knew it was recent because her father was wearing the tie she gave him for Father's Day.

She was about to comment on her father and Maryland's Governor being good buds, but her father broke her train of thought. "Nursing is something you can always fall back on," he said.

"You can always fall back on concrete too," Jennifer pointed out.

Her parents laughed. Her father continued. "Anyway, as you know, your mother and I have worked hard to build *the Riverboat Inn* into one of the premiere restaurants in the area. It's taken a little blood, a lot of sweat and even a few tears, but we've been on top the past few years." Jennifer wondered why she was being given a speech which usually indicated something big was about to happen. The elder Blackstone did not make his daughter wait long for an explanation. "It looks like we'll be there again this year as well," her father continued.

"That's wonderful," Jennifer exclaimed, referring to the insinuation that the *Riverboat Inn* would be again voted Annapolis's # 1 restaurant by the local newspaper.

"We're heard through sources," her mother cautioned. "Nothing official's been announced."

"Your sources have never been wrong before," Jennifer said. She knew without being told the source was the editor in chief of the local paper. He and her father were good friends.

"It's all off the record," Mr. Blackstone injected. "So it stays in this room for now."

"I know, I know," Jennifer laughed. "We'll all act surprised when the paper comes out this week… It is this week, isn't it?"

"Supposed to be," her father said.

"*Baltimore Magazine* is also doing a feature article on us next month," her mother boasted.

"Baltimore's Best oyster stew with no close challengers," Jennifer said. "But that's not news. Been that way for years. Still, a feature article…" Jennifer cocked her head to the side. "You bought a big ad, didn't you?" She knew how such articles were decided. One back was never scratched without another.

Mr. Blackstone laughed. "A small one, yes."

"The back inside cover," Mrs. Blackstone corrected.

Jennifer's jaw dropped open. "What's going on?" In the recent past, her parents had always discussed such things with her. Now…

"Your mother and I have made a decision," her father began.

Oh my God, Jennifer thought. It was something she had always feared. Her parents were going to sell the place. They had been talking about retiring for several years. They already had a place picked out in one of the more prestigious golf communities in Myrtle Beach. But why now? Jennifer felt things were going well. Both revenue and profits were up. She had seen no indication from her parents of displeasure in her performance. If anything, it was just the opposite. They said more than once just how pleased they were that she was taking a more active role. They were especially pleased with the work she did with the daily numbers. Her father was more relaxed and her mother was less loud in the kitchen. They had even increased their golf outings to twice a week. But again, why the decision to sell now?

Then the answer hit her.

It was the right time. Sales were up, profits were up and the *Riverboat Inn* was about to be named the number one restaurant in Annapolis for the third year in a row. What better time to unload the place. Cash in while the money was good. While she couldn't blame her parents, she felt a sudden sense of disappointment as the question of her own future passed before her. What was she going to do? And what about their employees?

The heaviness descended further as her father continued. "It's time to expand."

Hearing the words caused the tears to flow. Her sadness intensified. Other emotions started to pour forth when suddenly her eyes widened. She looked at her father. "What did you say?"

A caring smile formed across his face. "I said your mother and I have decided to expand. After all, isn't that what you've been telling us we ought to do for years?"

"Yes, but I thought you said expanding would be too difficult with all the permits needed." Her parents frequently talked about expanding the restaurant into the property they owned in the back. However, because Annapolis was the state's capital, and because the townspeople had a very peculiar attitude about what could and could not be done, business expansions always ran into a lot of red tape—red tape that was thick, sticky and very difficult to cut. "Has something changed?" the youngest Blackstone inquired.

Her mother took over the explanation. "No, nothing has changed. We don't mean expand here. We mean go elsewhere."

"Elsewhere... where?"

"We're looking at buying a place in a little town across the bay," her father said. He allowed a hint of teasing to come forth.

"A small town... which one?"

"Oh, you've probably never heard of it."

By now, Jennifer had fully recovered from her sense of doom, her emotional state having taken a 180 degree turn. "Where?" she demanded in her best, agitated daughter-to-parents voice.

"Ever hear of St. Michaels?"

"Jesus, you're kidding?"

"Jennifer?"

"Sorry, Mom, but damn..."

Her father laughed as the disapproving look on her mother's face deepened.

From the first time she went to St. Michaels as a child, Jennifer fell in love with the place. She and her mother went over for a day trip on one of the local tour boats. They ate at the *Crab Claw*, a restaurant that sat right on the water. Afterwards, they walked up and down Main Street, going in and out of the many shops that lined the road. Most were old homes remodeled into retail sites, thus maintaining the romance of the bayside town. They got lost (or so her mother claimed) trying to find a shortcut back to the water, and ended up going through several side streets where life looked like it had stood still for many years. While the styles varied, all the houses were well maintained. Each had a large front porch, some with swings hanging from the rafters. Her mother said that at night you could walk along the narrow road and hear the chains holding the swings squeaking like crickets in the night. Tall stately oak trees lined the streets, protecting the houses from the sun. Long shadows fell along the irregular sidewalks, making the placement of one foot in front of another an action that required specific attention. They passed an old cemetery with headstones dating from the 18th century.

After an hour or so of aimlessly wandering around the area, they found their way back to the docks. Jennifer's passion for the town remained strong. She and her mother made the trip an annual summer event.

Yes, she loved St. Michaels, and to hear that her parents were now expanding to the town. Her mind began to race. "What about you always saying no one could compete against a place like the *Crab Claw*?" she asked.

"Only if the timing was right," her father added.

"Besides, the *Crab Claw's* only a restaurant," her mother said.

"If my memory serves me correctly, isn't that what we do?" Jennifer quipped.

"In Annapolis, yes," her mother replied.

Jennifer slid to the front of her seat. Her thoughts flowed aloud. "Only a restaurant in Annapolis…meaning there we'd be more?"

"What do you think about a full conference center and marina?"

Jennifer looked over at her mother who was sitting calmly in her chair. From past experience, she realized this whole meeting was a set up to show her what they were planning to do, and to get her support. She didn't bother wondering why they even needed her support. She was sure her father already had what he wanted to say laid out in his mind. While he was a successful restaurateur, Jennifer always thought her father's forte was in sales. Then again, Jennifer always felt that running a restaurant required salesmanship in that you were selling an image to the public and once you made the sale, you had to produce the goods, which in the restaurant business was service, atmosphere and food. No, her father was more than a salesman. He was a politician and a great businessman.

As on cue, David Blackstone straightened his posture, cleared his throat and began speaking. "For many years now, you have said that we ought to do two things. First, we should expand. Second, if we can't do it in Annapolis, we should do it in St. Michaels. I think you've always been serious about the first, but a little tongue in cheek about the second because of your and your mother's love of the town. Your mother and I have always snafued the idea of expansion outside of Annapolis for two reasons. First, we have never had anyone to run the project. Second, as you full well know, in any business the name of the game is location, location, location." He paused briefly. "With that said, while we have indeed kept our ears and eyes open over the years, we have never found a place with the right location. Nor have we come across anyone we felt could handle such a plan. That is, until now."

"Until now," Jennifer queried.

"Two recent events are giving us what we think is an excellent opportunity. First, Old Lady Mitchell died."

"Old Lady Mitchell?"

"The owner of *Mitchell's Marina* – the property across the harbor from the *Crab Claw*."

"Right across from the *Crab Claw*?"

"Location, location, location."

"That's right in their back yard! Anyway, the Mitchell place is just a hole in the wall," Jennifer commented.

"Perception, perception, perception. While the waterfront footage is only the marina, there are close to seventy-five acres behind the place that are undeveloped," Jennifer's father explained.

"Really?"

"Everybody thinks it's a public park. In reality, the place is deeded to Ms. Mitchell. Been in her family for generations."

It didn't take long for Jennifer to realize the brilliance of the concept. What better place to put a new business in St. Michael's than right across from the *Crab Claw*. It was the theory of multiple gas stations on the same corner or department stores opening in the same mall. They could only help each other succeed. On the surface, it looked suicidal. Underneath, however…

Jennifer looked back at her father. "Ms. Mitchell's death was the first event. What's the second?"

Father's and mother's eyes met. The captain yielded to the admiral. "You seem to have put nursing behind you."

The room fell silent as Jennifer digested what she was hearing. "Me?"

"Why not?" her father threw back at her. "You've got a good head on your shoulders, you're smart as a whip, you're excellent with numbers, you have management experience in a chaotic environment, and you can be trusted without hesitation. Besides that, and perhaps most importantly, you know what you don't know."

"Me?" Jennifer repeated. She looked over at her mother for verification. A subtle nod of the head gave Jennifer just that. What a turn of events, she thought. Only a few moments ago, Jennifer thought she was going to get unwanted news about selling the *Riverboat Inn*. She told herself to settle down and regroup her thoughts. This was no time to go to pieces. There was undoubtedly a lot of work to do, and as she had experienced in the past, no time.

Time?

"What's the time frame?" she asked.

"The property goes on the auction block Saturday morning," her mother said. "Unless someone antes up their asking price ahead of time. Your father's been negotiating with the two sisters for over a month. They're close. It's just a matter of nit-picking through a few details."

Weeding through the hundreds of questions swirling through her mind, Jennifer tried to think of something intelligent to say. "What are the barriers to success?"

She watched her father beam. "The planning's the easy part. Now, we've got to sell it to the town council."

"What do you think?"

"Too early to know for sure, but it'll be close."

"Time line there?"

"Naturally, we're pushing for quick decision. But remember this is the Eastern Shore where things go a lot slower."

"Like cold molasses in winter," her mother grumbled.

Mr. Blackstone laughed. "We'll just have to find a way to heat the molasses up."

Mother looked at daughter. "That's your job."

"Mine!" The answer was obvious. In a softer voice, she said, "Do you really think I'm qualified for this, to develop a project from the ground up?"

Her father responded immediately. "You're correct, you will need help. But what your mother and I do feel you're capable of doing is putting together the necessary team to get the job done."

"You're talking about a big project and a lot of money."

"We're not going to let you flounder over there alone," her mother said.

"Ditto to that," her father injected. "We'll be there to support you all the way."

The ex-nurse took a deep breath. "When do I start?"

"We'll go over there tomorrow and take a look around. I also want you to meet some of the players," her father said.

"Players?"

"The town council meeting is tomorrow night," her mother said. "Your father wants to be there so you two can do a little *schmoozing*."

"It's called lobbying, mother," Jennifer insisted.

Her father beamed. "That's my girl."

An idea flashed through Jennifer's mind. Aloud, she said, "Why wait until tomorrow? Let's go over today."

"Whatever for?" her mother inquired.

"I want to see the sunset and sunrise on the property. Weather's not supposed to be so good tomorrow."

The Blackstones absorbed Jennifer's request. It was good to see their daughter showing signs of her old self—a pop in her step, her head held high, a smile on her face. They believed this project could bring Jennifer a new start.

"I assume we'll be continuing toasting the sunset," Jennifer said. She was referring to the daily ritual at the *Riverboat Inn* where all activity came to a halt just as the sun officially set over Annapolis. All patrons and employees were provided a complimentary glass of champagne, and a toast was made. With a clear sky, it was a spectacular view out the windows of the restaurant.   It was a tradition started years before by her parents and had continued every evening since. Some might argue it was an expensive thing to do, costing at least two cases of champagne every night, but the Blackstones believed the publicity and good will were well worth it. The ritual continued even on overcast or rainy days. Even if you couldn't see it, the sun still set every day on the *Riverboat Inn.*

"I see no reason why not," her father answered. "You'll just have to watch the layout of the restaurant to ensure you have the view."

Jennifer tried to picture the layout of the present marina. As she did, another idea cropped up. "What about a name?"

The elder Blackstones hesitated. "To be honest, we haven't decided," Mrs. Blackstone conceded.

"Then it's imperative we have a good view of the sunset," Jennifer said.

"Why imperative," her father inquired.

"If we're going to name the place *Sunset Landing*."

"*Sunset Landing*," both parents mouthed.

"*St. Michaels Sunset Landing*," Jennifer completed.

Jennifer's parents looked at one another. "I like it," the captain said.

"Me too," confirmed the admiral.

"What about the restaurant itself? What are you going to name that?" Mr. Blackstone challenged.

Jennifer contemplated the question, still trying to figure out how she came up with the first name so easily. Having learned from her father the politician, she said, "Let's wait and decide the decor first."

Mr. Blackstone laughed. "I think we got a good one, Elizabeth."

"A good what," Jennifer asked.

"A good project director."

72

Just as expected, Old Man Hooper was sitting on the starboard side of the old skipjack, a large fishing net draped across his lap. His left hand wrapped in twine and a large needle in his right, he slowly and meticulously repaired a large hole in the net. All ten fingers were crooked from arthritis, the skin covering the bones calloused and scarred. They moved slowly without wasted effort and the hole disappeared over time. It had been fifteen years since *Windskater*, his skipjack and the only woman ever in his life, worked the oyster beds of the Chesapeake Bay. It had been two years since she had left her present mooring, the concrete wall in the Annapolis Harbor. Her last trip was over to *Dorman's Boat Yard* to have her bottom painted and a few rotten planks repaired. She, along with her skipper, were now relegated to serving as a tourist attraction for Annapolis's inner harbor. Originally, Old Man Hooper would have nothing to do with retiring and serving as a spectacle for everyone. Nor did he need anyone looking after him. He had been independent all his life. There was no need to change now. He could still work. His fishnet repair business was doing well. Jennifer's mother drove the nail home that sealed the deal.

Jennifer remembered the conversation as the old man sat across from her and her father, nursing a bowl of his favorite food, her mother's oyster stew.

"You won't be a spectacle," her father argued. "You'll represent part of the bay's heritage. Sort of like a living museum."

"Museums are full of old things," the old man snorted.

"The operative word here is living," her father argued. "You ain't old till you're dead, then we definitely won't want you hanging around the docks."

"Why the hell not?"

"You'll smell up the place. Dead people tend to do that, you know."

While she never really understood the humor that often passed between her father and the old man, Jennifer watched Jonathan Hooper manage a smile. Her father continued. "Dockage will be free. You'll have electric too. And you can do whatever you want with your net repair business." There was a pause. "You know we'll do whatever we can do to help with repairs to *Windskater*."

"Don't want no handouts," the old man snapped, the smile disappearing.

"Won't be no handouts," her father snapped back.

"What do I got to do to earn my keep?"

"Promise not to bite the tourists when they walk by."

"Can't promise that."

"Bullshit."

"Bullshit to you." The smile returned, but only for a moment. "I don't know. I gotta think about it some."

Jennifer and her father looked at one another. They knew before the meeting started the battle was going to be tough. Jonathan Hooper had been a proud waterman all his life. He had survived by working hard and bothering no one. He loved his boat and poured every dime he made into her upkeep. The skipjack was still afloat and looked good on the surface, but beneath the waterline was another story. Albert Dorman told them the last time he had her hauled that she'd last another year at the most before she'd need a complete refurbishing.

The Blackstone family never discussed how they were going to pay for the repairs, but they knew they'd find a way. If nothing else, Papa Blackstone would simply get out his check book. Besides the *Windskater* being only one of a handful of skipjacks left in the area, her captain, Jonathan Hooper, was himself a relic worth salvaging. He was like one of the family. And many locals felt the same. He was tough to get to know at first, his stubbornness being an obvious barrier. But for every ounce of stubbornness, there was a pound of kindness and pride in his work. First though, they had to convince him to stay in the inner harbor where he'd have a chance to share the dignity of his life's work, and where they could keep an eye on him and his boat.

The bickering continued, with each pausing now and again to enjoy another spoonful of stew. Father and daughter Blackstone were getting frustrated. They sensed Jonathan Hooper's stubbornness would overshadow common sense.

Suddenly, appearing out of nowhere, Mrs. Blackstone swooped down on the trio. She reached around the old man and grabbed the half-filled bowl of stew right off the table. Holding the bowl out of reach, she said, "Jonathan, I swear on my mother's grave, if you don't come to your senses, you'll never eat another bowl of my 'aryster' stew so long as you shall live." She turned and walked away, leaving the startled man with an empty spoon dangling from his hand.

Jonathan Hooper looked up at Jennifer's father who was just as startled by his wife's action. He struggled not to burst out laughing. Jennifer felt the old man had a similar tickle in his throat. "Guess that kind of ends the debate, don't it?" the old man said.

"Works for me," Jennifer's father said.

And so it was decided, the *Windskater* would dock permanently along the bulkhead of Annapolis's inner harbor. Dockage and electric would be free so long as the old man let the tourists stop and look. He didn't have to talk to them. He just couldn't bark like a wild dog. It was a win-win for everyone.

Jennifer brought her thoughts back to the present. She stood in silence and watched as the hole in the net grew smaller and smaller. Old Man Hooper never looked up, but he knew she was there. A cigarette dangling from his mouth dropped to the deck and was snuffed it out with a foot. Jennifer shook her head and sighed. It would do no good getting on him about the habit; and as the old man said, it would waste a lot of precious oxygen. He insisted that global warming could be eliminated if people stopped fussing at one other. Jennifer took it all in stride. She was forty years his junior but often served as his mother. He pretended to resent her meddling until last winter when her mothering saved his life.

During one of the colder spells, he showed signs of being ill. He caught a cold, a little unusual in itself. Then the cold lingered. Jennifer kept a close eye on him, and felt he was actually starting to get better until one day she heard him barking like a dog, and not at the tourists, either. She went below deck and found him wrapped in blankets and shivering wildly. His eyes were glazed and his skin ashen. She didn't hesitate and called 911. He was too weak to protest. Everyone said he would have died had she not gotten to him when she did. Later, even Jonathan Hooper conceded he was a might beneath the weather.

Surprising to those who didn't know him, but no surprise to those who did, he recovered from the pneumonia quickly and totally. He was out of the hospital in a week. Once discharged, he refused an offer to stay with Jennifer, insisting on returning to the *Windskater*. Someone above was looking out for him, as there were a few days of warm weather upon his return. Jennifer continued her mothering and soon he was back to his normal cantankerous self. He still coughed and smoked, and continued to reject anyone fussing over him.

During this time, he did thank Jennifer for her help, insisting in his subtle round about way, that she had saved his life. She downplayed her actions, instead focusing on the numerous times over the years he had saved her soul. It was he who told her to stick with it when the negotiations at the hospital became tough, saying, "Even if you lose and if time proves you wrong, if you believe, you have to proceed." When she went to see him the day she lost her job, he simply shrugged his shoulders and said, "So time proved you wrong. It was still a journey you had to make. You'll never find happiness otherwise."

Now, on this hot summer day, she stood silently and waited for the people watching to move on. When she was the lone observer, she told herself not to waste her breath, but the mothering instincts won out. "You know, you shouldn't be smoking?" Her voice was a bit harsher than she had intended, although the actual words were reruns of previous conversations.

His finger motion did not stop and he did not look up. "Don't see no one smoking around here. Do you?"

"It's a wonder your feet don't catch on fire with all the cigarettes they stomp out," she retorted.

He leaned forward a bit and looked down at his feet. "Don't see no smoke coming from my feet, either."

Jennifer knew she was wasting her time and she let him know so with a loud *humph*. She followed with, "Permission to come aboard?" When he nodded, she stepped across the gunwale, slowly transferring her weight onto the deck so as not to rock the boat. She walked up to where he was sitting, sat a paper bag down by his feet and said, "Eat it before it get's cold. Mother wants to know if it's okay."

The standing joke—although not really a joke—was that Jonathan Hooper served as the official taster for Mrs. Blackstone's oyster stew. The tradition started a couple years before when he actually offered criticism a couple of times that proved correct. One day he felt it was too salty. An investigation back in the kitchen showed that indeed one of the assistant cooks had measured the salt wrong. Another day he claimed the oysters were too tough. And sure enough, they were from a new supplier and were a different species than normal. So while nothing official was ever said, someone in the Blackstone family made the daily trip to *Windskater* where a sample of the oyster stew and other specials of the day were placed before the *Riverboat Inn's* chief taster.

Few things interrupted the old man's work. The smell of Mrs. Blackstone's homemade oyster stew was one exception. The aroma urged him to pull his hands away from the net and reach for the bag. Jennifer watched as his motions quickened ever so slightly. He pulled the Styrofoam bowl from the bag, took the spoon that was rubber banded to the side, flipped off the lip and raised the cup to his mouth. His hands quivered as the hot liquid touched his lips.

Jennifer smiled. Human beings were funny. They were very good at hiding all sorts of emotions, except one. Maybe it was from her experience at the *Riverboat Inn*, but she could tell when someone was hungry.

Old Man Hooper swirled the liquid around in his mouth as if he was testing a newly opened bottle of wine. He slurped an oyster that happened too close to the edge. He passed the cup back and forth in front of his face to further appreciate the delicate balance of seasonings. Another sip, another oyster, and he took the spoon and began eating in earnest. Jennifer once commented that he was the *Riverboat Inn's* resident critic. He lived by the rule that no comment meant nothing to criticize. His silence told Jennifer all she needed to know. The speed at which he devoured the cup of oyster stew told her he hadn't eaten yet today. He was hungry. Only a little too hungry for her peace of mind. She made a mental note to make sure he had enough food below deck.

Jennifer looked up as she heard voices out on the pier. Several people had gathered to watch the ritual. While never publicized, the local business community knew about Jonathan Hooper's daily tasting. If out and about, they often gathered to watch as the popular figure gave his stamp of approval, or vice versa. Jennifer recognized most of the people in the crowd. She nodded and winked as Mr. Hooper ignored the added attention and continued on with his meal. The people on the dock smiled, waved to Jennifer in silence and headed toward the restaurant, knowing they'd better get there before the pot ran dry. It never did, but Mrs. Blackstone claimed it was always close.

When the bowl was empty, Hooper reached into the bag and pulled out a fresh turkey sandwich wrapped in cellophane and another Styrofoam box containing a piece of homemade apple pie. He picked up the fork and ate the pie first—a routine practice as well. Jennifer asked him about it once and he explained that he always ate his dessert first in case he had a heart attack. He claimed he'd go straight to hell if he died and left the dessert behind. When asked why the stew before the pie, he replied that the only thing worth eating before dessert was a bowl of Mrs. B's oyster stew. He went on to add that coal miners had a different reason for eating their dessert first, but he didn't explain and Jennifer didn't ask. It wouldn't be until months later that she understood what he was talking about.

The crowd moved on and was replaced by a short thin man wearing a dark business suit. Jennifer looked up again as he called her by name. "Afternoon, Jennifer... Mr. Hooper."

"Afternoon, Senator," Jennifer said. Mr. Hooper said nothing. The man was James Meriweather, the state senator from Annapolis. He had become friends with the Blackstones over the years because of his frequent visits to the restaurant and because the Blackstones supported his campaigns.

Having missed the daily tasting, he said, "How'd you find the stew today, Jonathan?"

The old man remained silent.

"I found it a bit salty today myself." As a politician, he was good at stretching the truth.

"Soup's just fine," the old man snapped. "It's your damn republican taste buds that are all screwed up."

The senator laughed loudly. "Well, I've no doubt you're right about that. If you say it's okay, then it's okay." He winked at Jennifer and held out his hands as a way of inquiring about the man's condition. Jennifer nodded in the affirmative. Satisfied his own assessment was correct—that as long as the old man had his bite he'd have his health—the senator bid farewell and continued his journey back up to the capitol building. Jennifer nodded thank you. She knew Meriweather cared about the old man, and usually stopped by at least once a day to check on him, often bringing him supplies or other sundry items. Jennifer also suspected the senator was the old man's source for cigarettes. While the two men might differ on various political issues, the tobacco lobby was not one of them.

Senator Meriweather was no different from a lot of people in town who took a casual stroll along the inner harbor to enjoy the ambiance of the moment, and to check up on the old man. It made Jennifer feel good that so many people cared. She wondered if Hooper himself realized as much. She imagined he did. While Jonathan Hooper pretended to be oblivious to most things around him, in reality, very little got past him.

He proved her correct a few moments later when he said, "What's on your mind?"

Taken back at his perceptiveness, she responded defensively. "What makes you think something's on my mind?"

"You're pacing as if you have ants."

"Pacing? I haven't moved a step since coming aboard."

"I didn't say your body. Your mind—it's jumping all over the place."

Jennifer let out a sigh and looked around. Senator Meriweather was well on his way back up the hill. No one else was standing on the pier so she pulled up an empty crate and sat down.

"Did you eat?" the old man asked.

"I'll eat something later."

He picked up the second half of his sandwich and held it out for her. "Here."

"Na, thanks anyway."

"Eat!" he said sternly.

Jennifer wondered who mothered whom the most. When the hunger pains subsided, she spoke. "We're thinking about expanding the business."

"Around here?"

"No… starting a new place up elsewhere."

"St. Michaels'll be a good location. The Mitchell's place is for sale. Right across from the *Crab Claw*. A good spot, if you ask me."

Jennifer's mouth dropped open. "My father's already talked to you, hasn't he."

"Ain't said a word about it."

"Bullshit."

"But if he did ask me, I'd tell him he'll never get the permits."

"Why's that?" Jennifer said.

"Same reason you can't get the permits to expand your place here—people want the tourist's dollars only they don't want the tourists. Too much noise, too much traffic… stuff like that."

"But it's the tourist traffic that brings in the dollars," Jennifer pointed out.

Hooper took a bite of his sandwich. "Didn't say it made any sense."

"My father doesn't think it'll be a problem."

"Your father is a wise man… most of the time."

Jennifer smiled.

The old man chewed and continued. "But if it does happen, it's going to be your baby, isn't it?"

"What else did my father tell you?" Jennifer demanded.

"That you're smart, too… most of the time."

Jennifer could only laugh. "So you think it's a good spot, huh?"

He shrugged his shoulders. "Ain't my field of expertise. My gut feeling though is yes, if you can get through the bureaucracy. For my money, I think you'd be better off expanding right here."

"But we can't get the permits for here," Jennifer pointed out.

"A fight's a fight, regardless which alley you go in." He continued to chew slowly. "Besides, it may be easier than you think—here that is."

"We've already tried and were turned down."

"That was then. This is now."

Jennifer shrugged her shoulders. She knew it would be useless arguing any further. He was as stubborn as he was smart. For being an old coot who was negative towards any politician who stopped by, the old man was certainly up on what was happening in the local political world.

Wiping his mouth on his bare arm, Hooper looked up at her. His voice softened. "If this does happen, you'll still come visit, won't you?"

Tears welled up in Jennifer's eyes. She wanted to lean down and hung him, but knew he wouldn't like that, least not in public. "Yes, and thank you," she said.

"That senator had better go have his taste buds checked," the old man said. "He wouldn't know good 'aryster' stew if it landed on his head."

"You'll just have to teach him," Jennifer said.

"Fat chance." Finishing his sandwich, he added, "Remember, water will run downhill, only if given a hill down which to run."

Jennifer had heard a lot of quotes from the old man, but never that one. She smiled. "You know, you may pretend otherwise, but you're pretty smart."

"I'm one of the smartest people in Annapolis," he boasted.

Jennifer tilted her to the side. The cockiness was a feature seldom seen. "What makes you say that?"

Old Man Hooper scanned the scene around him. "Show me someone else in this town who doesn't pay slip rent."

She laughed and rose to her feet. She stepped forward and gave him a big hug. "Thanks for being such a good friend."

To her surprise, he didn't resist the affection. "Good only gets in front of the word friend when there's a two way street."

73

April finished rubbing the zinc oxide on her nose, recapped the tube and dropped it on the deck beside the can of varnish. She contemplated putting on more sunscreen, but decided against it. She was as tanned as Freddie. Besides, the lotion did little except make her feel greasy. Her nose, however, always seemed to burn. She bent forward and focused her eye close to the teak railing. She was careful not to get too close as the wood was still sticky from the coat of varnish applied an hour earlier. Seeing no signs of bubbles in the coating, she straightened up and pulled the hair off of her neck. In spite of the early morning hour, she already felt the sweat running down between her shoulder blades. She knew she'd be a lot cooler if she cut her hair. She almost did recently, but she knew her hair was one of the features that made her look good at the piano.

She had adjusted well to her role aboard *Hamilton's Bench*, serving as the designated entertainment whenever Mr. Hamilton hosted one of his many parties. The yacht's owner had received more than one compliment about the fact that he not only had a piano aboard, he had a pianist as well. Although serving as *Hamilton's Bench's* resident pianist remained her primary assignment, her responsibilities and value as a general crew member had increased. She started working with Freddie, which meant a lot of washing and waxing. She proved to be a quick learner at *wood management* as everyone aboard called it. While not the pro Freddie proved to be, she quickly picked up the necessary skills to almost keep up with him, and to get an occasional compliment. He attributed her success to her ability to play the piano, which easily transferred to her slow steady hand with a brush. She argued it was simply something new and different for her, and she liked seeing the results when they were finished. She also liked being outside.

April showed interest in other aspects of the yacht, and in boating in general. While the engine room meant little to her and sparked no particular interest, she became fascinated by the navigational aspect of traveling through open waters. The workday was long and required a good dose of physical stamina. The crew was treated well. They spent most of their downtime playing cards and sleeping. April practiced the piano, or was up on the fly bridge or in the pilot house, asking questions and learning about seamanship and navigation. She proved a quick learner. She especially liked steering the boat, and even though *Hamilton's Bench* was equipped with an autopilot synchronized with GPS, there was ample opportunity to actually handle the wheel. She became quite adept at maintaining a course, and spent the time the autopilot was on learning as much about navigation as possible. She learned that the basic principles of boating applied to all vessels, regardless of their type or size. Navigation was navigation. The rules of the road were the rules of the road. Using the satellite Internet connection in the pilot house, April found a wealth of information on all aspects of boating.

She was like a kid with a new toy. And what a toy! She felt like Cinderella hiding in a big castle. The more she learned, the more she realized *Hamilton's Bench* was far from a simple castle. The yacht was a well-oiled, well-run factory, and what you saw above the surface was only the tip of the iceberg. Below deck was an array of engines, generators, pipes, electrical switches, valves and storage tanks, all of which made little sense to April and caused her a great deal of anxiety at first, especially when she learned she was actually sleeping under water. But once over the initial anxiety, she realized that everything combined together was intended to get the ship where it was going safely, quickly and in great comfort, with *comfort* being the key word aboard the luxury yacht. What amazed April even more was their ability to get from one place to another via satellites hundreds of miles in the sky. And if they lost the electronic navigation ability, they could turn to celestial techniques that depended on planets and stars light-years away.

So the woods behind her house had been replaced by the sea surrounding her new home.

Thunderstorms were replaced by squalls. Mountains became waves—at times quite big ones at that. Deer, snakes and other wildlife became fish, birds and porpoises. She especially liked when the porpoises traveled alongside the boat, darting in front, behind and beneath, as if the fiberglass hull was their toy.

And she had her music.

She did miss her mother; otherwise, she felt few emotions about her past. Even her anger and disappointment towards Danny was slowly fading.

With the days being long and the work expectations high, time passed quickly. She practiced at least four hours a day, even when they were in port. As promised, Mr. Hamilton remained supportive of her needs. He ordered several books she requested, even a couple on music theory. However, once she became proficient with the Internet, she was able to get a lot of information for free. Music theory and history from cyberspace—it was quite fascinating. She once asked Mr. Hamilton just what all she could get off the Internet. He responded that she didn't really want to know. She put herself on a schedule where she spent time practicing the piano and learning about the intricacies of music. While she loved to play, she was fascinated to learn the theory and history of music.

For the first time in a long time, she felt happy and relaxed. She always had a nagging fear she'd be found out someday, but that dwindled with time. She was accepted by the crew, and she was accepted by Mr. Hamilton. No one asked prying questions, and if anyone ever ventured across this line, she was quick to change the subject. The only lie she ever told pertained to her name and age. Everything else, she just didn't tell at all.

With her mind adjusting to her new environment, her body followed suit. While the work was not what one would call back-breaking, it was physical. She always thought she was in pretty good shape from her hiking in the woods with Danny. However, after one week on the boat, every muscle in her body ached. The pain passed though, and she actually started putting on some *meat* (as Freddie called it). She never focused on her appearance before, always believing that one's external looks seldom resembled what was inside. She was never a slob. Her attitude towards the latest trends was simply nonexistent. But as her tan darkened and her body matured, she started to look at herself in a different light—not in a cocky way, but in one that boosted her self-esteem. She especially had good feelings about herself when she performed at one of Mr. Hamilton's parties. He made sure she was properly dressed for the occasions, even buying her a beautiful long black dress for the more formal affairs he often hosted. If she was in therapy, her therapist would say she was making progress, but there was still a long open sea ahead.

She realized the importance of time. It helped her forget about others. Time would help others forget about her. Still, she wondered what was going on in Worthington Valley. Did her family and friends miss her? Was her mother okay? What was Danny doing? What were people at school saying? She had a lot of questions, but no answers.

In spite of her anger toward him, she often contemplated trying to contact Danny to see how everybody was doing. Her instincts, developed from the skill he had taught her in the woods, told her that her trail was cold. Calling him would only freshen the scent. It was a chance she wasn't willing to take. The trail was dead and so was her past.

She focused her attention on the varnished teak. She resisted the temptation to check the level of dryness with her finger. No fingerprints for Freddie to see. *Boat detailing* could not be rushed. Freddie told her more than once that the difference between good and excellent was patience. He compared varnishing to the effort necessary to learn a new piece of music. One could learn to play a new piece quickly, but to play it with excellence took time and patience.

April straightened up and looked across the water. She sucked in a breath of the morning salt air. The humidity already felt close to a hundred percent. Sweat covered her forehead. She made sure it didn't drip on the wood railing. She pulled her shirt out of her shorts, found a dry spot and wiped her brow. They had been in Bermuda for three days, and each day the weather had been the same—hot and very humid. She never perspired so much in her life. But she didn't care. It was the first time in weeks she felt really safe. Captain Rogers told the crew during one of their regular early morning meetings, Mr. Hamilton expected to stay in Bermuda for at least another week before heading down to the Bahamas where they would spend the winter. The Bahamas—a place she never dreamed of visiting; a place hard to imagine; a place with more distance between her and Worthington Valley. She got caught up in the anticipation with the crew, who claimed that, while Bermuda was wonderful, the Bahaman Islands were even better.

While careful not to talk too much, she was glad the crew had taken her under their wings. At least from her perspective, she seemed well liked. She made sure she held up her end of the bargain. She did as she was told, following orders without hesitation, although at times with a lot of questions based on curiosity. They seemed genuinely pleased with her work. She was friendly, but only to a point. Most of the crew behaved the same. She had no doubt there was a lot of unopened baggage aboard the yacht. She told herself to follow Danny's rule of thumb for survival in the woods—one step, one day at a time. And always with an occasional glance over your shoulder.

She heard footsteps and looked behind her. She smiled as she saw Freddie moving in her direction.

"One day at a time," she told herself.

74

Phillip Rogers widened his stance ever so slightly as *Hamilton's Bench* rocked in response to a strong gust of wind. The waves off Nassau's harbor were already over three feet and building. The wind only made the yacht's motion worse. Like most vessels of her size, *Hamilton's Bench* rode the seas well when underway. She didn't, however, like sitting on the hook. They'd been anchored for over an hour awaiting clearance to enter the narrow harbor. The harbor master said the passenger liner scheduled to depart was delayed because all the passengers weren't back aboard. Rogers wanted to know how a few idiotic people could bring a busy port to a screeching halt. He knew better than to piss off the harbor master, especially before they cleared customs. So let him do his job, Rogers told himself. As long as George Hamilton was still asleep, there was no problem anyway. They had plenty of time before the guests for that evening were due aboard.

He signed off the radio and turned his attention to the backside of his favorite crew member. She was standing portside of the wheel, binoculars pressed to her eyes as she stared between the two buoys marking the harbor a half-mile ahead. "See anything?" he asked, knowing the answer before he asked.

"No sir. Nothing's been in or out."

"Not a surprise. When one of the big boys is due to leave, they generally close the whole place down," he explained. "Keep a lookout just in case."

He hoped she didn't ask, "In case of what?" He just wanted her eyes glued to the glasses so he could stay glued to her. The more she became interested in the workings aboard the boat, the more time he spent around her. The more time he spent around her, the more he wanted her. These urges grew stronger the last couple nights when she pulled watch with him on the bridge. He continued to be amazed, and impressed, at the eagerness with which she wanted to learn anything and everything about boats. Most people who signed up for work aboard a yacht were either running away from something, or simply liked being out on the water. Few were interested in anything more than their area of responsibility. April was like no one he had ever encountered during his fifteen years in the business. There was no doubt she was running from someone, especially the way she came running down the pier just as they were casting off from Atlantic City. He saw fear in her eyes at the bottom of the gangplank as she asked if the position was still available. Luckily, Hamilton was up on the bridge and saw her coming. Otherwise, Phillip wouldn't have had any idea what she was talking about. The girl's fear subsided once she was aboard and they were underway. It didn't fully disappear until they were out of the harbor. Then, and only then, did he see her relax. Weeks later, she still kept her distance. She spoke little about herself, and asked few questions of others. This was not all that uncommon to Rogers. She was, however, an eager maritime pupil and he was a more than willing teacher.

The trip from Bermuda to the Bahamas was uneventful, thanks in part to good weather, and in part to the favorable Gulf Stream. The days were hot and muggy; the nights, cool and balmy. Skimpy clothing during the day, especially for the one female crew, and sweat shirts at night to keep out the chill—perfect boating weather for him.

As they prepared to enter port, the dress code changed. April wore the standard work uniform of thigh length khaki shorts, tan polo shirt with the *Hamilton's Bench* logo and boating shoes without socks. Her hair was pulled in a ponytail and partially hidden beneath a tan cap, the yacht's logo across the beak. She had a pair of sunglasses hooked to a chain around her neck. Her arms were raised and holding the binoculars, causing her to look taller than she was. The position also helped accentuate her figure.

She was a looker all right, and Phillip Rogers liked to look. But that was the only thing allowed aboard *Hamilton's Bench*. Mr. Hamilton had a strict rule about cohabitation between crew members. Rogers couldn't really argue with the rule either. He fully understood the issues related to interpersonal relationships amongst staff, especially when they worked so close together, and were at times isolated from the rest of the world.

One of his jobs as captain was to make sure the crew was happy. That he did very well, especially with the lights out. He had broken the rule several times over the years, all in the line of duty, of course. But never aboard *Hamilton's Bench*. He was too afraid of the owner, and besides, none of the rare female crew members interested him all that much. He kept such activities to shore leave, often times with one of the lonely wives of Hamilton's guests from the evening before—all in the line of duty, of course.

That was until April came along. Now his desire was burning. The coals grew hotter as she rejected any attempt he made at advancing their relationship. She showed no interest in him, or anyone else for that matter. She seemed only interested in learning as much as she could about the boat, and in her damn music. Mr. Hamilton kept a close eye on her, so Rogers had to be especially careful not to do or say anything that could be misconstrued. After all, he was the captain of one of the most luxurious yachts in the world. No fling was worth risking that.

So in spite of his fantasies, he told himself to keep his mind on his work and his hormones under control. He looked out again towards the harbor entrance. Still no sign of the cruise ship leaving. He cursed under his breath and reminded himself to keep his mind on his work.

And so he did… for now.

75

Robert Granger surveyed the pile of supplies accumulating on the counter. "Looks like you've been busy," he said.

"So far so good," Cliff replied. "I'm getting a lot of partials completed. But that's easy when you don't have a lot of distractions."

"Distractions like what?" the art store owner inquired.

Cliff hesitated, searching rapidly for a response. "School."

"School… I thought you liked school," Robert said.

"I do… or rather, did," Cliff returned. "It just interfered with my work, that's all."

Starting to check out the supplies, Robert reflected over Cliff's last year in high school. He and Carol had grown close to Cliff, and kept an eye on him whenever the opportunity arose. While Judge Donnelly was his official guardian, they did what they could. The couple knew Cliff's favorite subjects were math and art, and that he'd rather have his nose stuck in a drawing pad than a textbook, although he did graduate a year early. The boy never smiled much, but he had a proud face graduation day. If he was sad because Robert, Carol and Judge Donnelly were the only guests present for him, Cliff never showed it. He was free, and that was all that mattered. He kept reiterating the theme throughout the small celebration later in the evening.

The only sad part of the day was when Cliff's art teacher and mentor came up to him after the ceremonies and presented him with a large, brightly wrapped package. Cliff opened it on the spot. It was a framed poster board. The border was geometrically scrolled in beautifully designed yellows and reds. Centered was calligraphy in script that read: "Always remember, your talent is a gift. Use this gift to help others as well as yourself."

The teacher went on to say, "There is one condition attached to this."

"What's that?" Cliff asked.

"The frame's mine. I'd like it back someday, only not empty."

Robert thought he was going to see Cliff tear up. It was a simple compliment of immense value. Cliff's art teacher, a successful artist himself, was a harsh critic, and did not give out kudos frequently.

"It's a deal," Cliff said as the two shook hands.

Robert brought his attention to the present. He sped up his actions as Cliff added another armload of pads, boxes of charcoal and artist's pencils to the pile. The storeowner wanted to keep the conversation going without seeming to pry. His level of curiosity was heightened by not having seen or spoken to Cliff in several weeks. He said, "I'm glad it's working out for you. I know you were concerned at first."

"I just have to stay focused," Cliff said. "Can't let anything get in my way. Once the routine is broken, the concentration is gone. And once that happens…" He didn't add the word *splash*.

Robert waited for further explanation. He felt there was one. He knew prying was not the way to get it. One of the reasons he and his wife had become close to the young man was that they never meddled in his personal affairs unless asked. Most of Cliff's questions were on a professional level. Cliff was a very warm and caring person, but he didn't easily share his emotions.

"Did you find out anything about new film?" Cliff said.

While not a product they normally stocked in their store, Cliff had asked Robert to look into the possibility of getting film in bulk. "I did."

"And?"

"I asked."

"No deal, huh?"

"Maybe if we buy a whole tractor trailer load."

"That bad, huh?"

Robert nodded.

"Well, thanks for trying."

"No problem. Anything else we can do for you, just let us know."

Cliff almost took the bait, but closed his mouth before any words were able to escape.

Robert hid his disappointment and continued with the work at hand. "How's the *Mona Lisa* doing?"

"A few minor glitches here and there, but no major problems. I haven't run aground and neither Chessie nor I have gone overboard yet."

Robert laughed. "How long you going to be around?"

"Ruby says he'll have the boat back in the water by this afternoon. I'll probably hang around a day or so to make sure everything is okay." Cliff had called Robert the day before from the marina. He'd returned to Ruby's after picking up a vibration in the wheel. He also noticed the bilge pump was running frequently. A look around found a significant leak where the engine shaft goes through the haul of the boat—the stuffing box. Cliff knew this was supposed to leak a little, but this was more than normal. Plus, the bolt to tighten it was frozen. It was a good excuse to return to Middle River and have Ruby check the *Mona Lisa*. Besides, he was running short on art supplies.

Carol came back from getting coffees. Seeing the large pile of supplies waiting to be bagged, she said, "Where in the world are you going to put all this stuff? This is more than you had the first time."

"It's amazing how many nooks and crannies you can find on a boat if you look hard enough," Cliff said.

"But is there room for you and Chessie?" Carol asked.

Cliff laughed. "Barely."

Carol took the plastic lids off the cups so the liquid would start to cool. "I bet one thing you miss is good coffee."

"Na," Cliff insisted. "There's nothing like a cup of bilge water coffee in the morning."

Carol's face wrinkled at the thought.

Cliff continued. "Actually, I've gotten pretty good at coffee and other things in the galley. Neither Chessie or I have lost any weight, so I must be doing something right."

"Maybe Chessie can stand to lose a few pounds, but you surely can't. You get any skinnier, you'll blow overboard."

Cliff patted his stomach. "It's not all muscle there. Sailing can be hard work at times, but mostly it's *diddly squat*. Not as much work as hauling crab pots."

"Anyway, drink up," Carol said, handing him one of the cups. She blew across the top, took a sip and sat the container back down. "Too hot for me."

"Me too," Robert said.

Cliff took two big swallows. "Almost tastes as good as bilge water."

Robert laughed. Then his expression turned serious. "You were saying earlier you had a lot of partials done. How many drawings do you actually have completed?"

"Only a handful," Cliff admitted. "But I plan to change that. I want to build my inventory. Winter'll be here before I know it and I'll be back on the mall circuit."

"Have you thought about where you're going to spend the winter?" Carol asked.

"On the boat."

"No, silly, I don't mean that. Where on the boat?"

"I generally sleep in the main salon, although sometimes…"

"Clifford!"

Robert knew Cliff loved to tease his wife. He did too, only the repercussions for doing so were usually far greater for him. Cliff took another gulp of the coffee. "Don't really know. I've been to a few towns that look promising, but they're all so isolated. I thought about sailing up to the Inner Harbor in Baltimore when I leave here and check it out. I haven't been up there in years."

"It's really built up." Carol explained.

"I hear it's pretty crowded."

"That's an understatement, especially on weekends."

"That can work for or against me," Cliff said.

"Good point," Robert chimed in. He tested his coffee to see if it was cool enough. "Speaking of crowds, you have a schedule for displaying yet?"

"I've got a few offers, but I haven't made any commitments yet," Cliff said.

"Malls are a good place to get started," Robert said, "But they really are a limited market. You have to travel a lot if you're going to get on the circuit. Plus, there's a certain perception with that sort of marketing."

Cliff's immediate instinct was to defend the practice, especially since it served him well so far. A sixth sense, however, told him to think a moment. The Grangers had yet to steer him wrong. "I wonder if Picasso started at the mall?" he said.

"Exactly our point," Carol said. "He may have started there, but he didn't finish there."

"I'm no Picasso," Cliff pointed out.

"Neither was Picasso when he first started," Carol countered.

"But…" Cliff failed to finish the sentence when he realized the above comment was a compliment. He took a sip of his coffee. "What are you suggesting?"

Robert explained. "We have a friend, Ned Adams. He has a store similar to ours in Philly. He has never been satisfied with just one store, and has always talked about starting a chain. He's even used the word franchise recently."

"Franchising art supplies?" Cliff asked to make sure he understood the picture.

"Yes, only he wants to expand. First, he wants to start an art school for those with limited talent."

"Which in turn will expand his market for art supplies," Cliff injected.

"Exactly," Carol said. "The second is he wants to have a gallery at each store and showcase the hidden talent he finds."

Cliff thought over the possibilities. While he didn't have a swollen ego, he did know he was good at what he did. He also knew there were a lot of similar artists out there struggling for a break. Like a lot of ventures in life, success or failure often depended on a planned or chance meeting with someone. How many movie stars were nobodies until discovered by someone already successful? Were artists like him any different?

"I've never sold anything except originals," Cliff pointed out.

"We told him that," Carol said.

"You've already talked to him about me?"

"She more like bragged as if you were her own son," Robert laughed.

"I wanted to make my point," his wife defended.

"That you did," her husband acknowledged.

"What did he say about everything being original?" Cliff asked, beginning to feel some excitement.

Carol smiled. "A simple four letter word… fine."

"Fine?"

"He wants to showcase new artists, not control them."

"Anyway, we don't want to interfere," Robert said. "We just thought it might be a good idea for you to meet him."

"It certainly won't do any harm," Carol pointed out with a stern look.

"I'll have to look at my schedule and see when I can fit him in," Cliff teased.

Carol continued her stare. "He'll be at the Crisfield crab feast a week from Saturday. You be there too."

"Getting bossy," Cliff said. He glanced over at her husband.

Robert nodded. "Yes she is. So just take it and keep your mouth shut. That's a suggestion, not an order."

"Point well taken," Cliff laughed. Thinking about the idea, Cliff added, "Isn't that crab feast mostly politics? I remember my uncle helping supply crabs to it one year. He said it was a huge political gathering, the last big event of the season."

"That it is," Robert said. "Only this year they're trying to do more. They're having a display of local craftsmen and artists."

Cliff felt a sense of disappointment "What's the big difference from a mall show?"

"Location, location, location," Carol said.

"And why is this Ned…"

"Adams," Robert prompted.

"Adams. Why is he going to be there?"

"If he's going to get into the franchise business, he'll need a few contacts to get the right locations. Second, he'll be snooping around for talent."

"Like me!"

"Like you!"

"Cool!" Cliff exclaimed. A moment later, "Not so cool."

"What's the matter?" Carol asked.

"That's not much time."

"You'll just have to do the best you can."

Cliff shrugged his shoulders.

The couple helped Cliff bag up the supplies and load them into the shopping cart. "Please keep in touch," Robert said, holding the door for Cliff.

Cliff assured him he would. Robert was about to go back behind the counter when he noticed two large packages wrapped in brown paper leaning up against the front with notes attached to each. He knelt down and looked at the one on the left. It was from Cliff, asking them to deliver this one to Mr. Boardman. Bruno Boardman was Cliff's art teacher who gave him the empty picture frame at graduation. Robert remembered the inscription and remembered Cliff's promise to fill the frame one day. The package on the right also had a note attached. It read: "To Robert and Carol. Thank you both for all your help and support. I've titled the drawing *The Dance of the Morning Sun*. It's a scene from my first morning aboard the *Mona Lisa*. Thank you both again. Cliff."

"Carol!" Robert called out as he lifted the package up onto the counter. Carol came out from behind the counter. Both hearts started beating rapidly as they ripped open the paper. Neither were disappointed.

76

Two Saturdays later found Crisfield jammed with boats and people. It was so crowded, Cliff and Chessie had difficulty getting in their early morning run, a habit Cliff was trying hard to maintain whenever they were in port. They seemed to spend more time dodging people and excusing themselves than they did running. By the time they got back to the *Mona Lisa*, Cliff was exhausted and Chessie was panting heavily. It evolved into one of the best workouts they had in a long time, but it only gave them thirty minutes before the show officially opened.

There was anticipation and hope among the vendors that the day's activities would prove more beneficial than Friday's. Much to everyone's disappointment, the rain that began early in the morning hung around all day, and didn't move out until nightfall. By then it was too late. Friday was a bust. The organizers claimed Saturday was the big day anyway, when all the politicians piled into town to attend the crab feast. The organizers argued this was the first year they had tried anything different and that it would take time for people to acclimate to the change in schedule. They also claimed lack of control over the weather. Cliff didn't really care. He was able to spend the day completing more partials. By Friday evening, his inventory nearly met his goal.

Aboard the *Mona Lisa*, Cliff fed Chessie and showered. Then with a loaded dock cart, he headed to the vendor tent. After returning the cart to the end of the pier, he headed back up the hill but stopped. Someone the day before suggested he bring his dog along. He had always shied away from that, figuring people might be afraid of Chessie. He also assumed Chessie would be bored. But the person, an iron sculptor several displays down, went on to say that the dog might entice people to stop by. "Believe me," the burly man with multiple tattoos said, "we need any gimmick we can get to compete with the crabs and the politicians."

So Cliff took Chessie up to the tent, figuring he could always take her back if necessary. Chessie didn't seem to mind. She was always very friendly, especially now that she spent long periods of time cooped up aboard the *Mona Lisa*. She thrived on any attention paid to her by strangers. Cliff figured there wasn't a better place for a Chesapeake Bay retriever than at a crab feast in Crisfield.

Saturday found the sky clear, the sun out and a rapidly rising humidity. By noon, it felt like a typical muggy summer day, but in mid-September. It was a true Indian summer on the Chesapeake. Not a breeze was to be had. If it weren't for the half dozen industrial fans spaced around the area, the tent might have been unbearable. Outside the heavy canvas, the conditions weren't much better. Locals swore that the Chesapeake Bay was the only place in the world where the humidity could rise above 100 percent. This weather did nothing to deter the many people who poured into Crisfield. Politicians were there to promote their campaigns. Volunteers were there to work for and support their candidate of choice. Many were there to be seen by others. Few were there simply for the crabs.

Cliff watched from a distance as the red ribbon was officially cut and the mob swarmed into the barricaded area. Some headed right for the tables to scope out a good spot to eat and to be seen. Some simply walked around, soaking in the sights and mystique of the event. There were groups of people dressed in matching, brightly colored tee shirts with handfuls of literature to distribute. At the head of each group was a well-manicured, buffed and polished person known as the candidate.

Cliff continued watching as the crowd seemed to have forgotten there was an art exhibition. A concern that this day was going to go like the one before quickly permeated the vendors as few from the crowd made their way to the tents. Those that did were simply looking for tables in the shade. Cliff joked that they should all feel privileged to be in the midst of such a fine group of people. That caused a laugh. A man next to Cliff displaying a beautiful array of hand carved ducks retorted, "You are so humble, fine young sir. Only I ain't seen the day yet when such a feeling ever paid the mortgage." There was more nervous laughter.

The tent had nearly fallen to silence when a voice at the far end called out, "The Governor's coming! The Governor's coming!"

"Sounds more like a warning than anything else," the duck carver mumbled.

"He's probably looking for a table too," someone else piped in.

A short time later, Maryland's governor and his entourage entered the far end of the tent. Governor Wilson possessed the largest contingency, so the area quickly filled as he slowly made his way past the various exhibits. He was the ultimate politician, so he naturally stopped at each exhibit, taking time to look over the displayed items. He always seemed to have a word or two with the artist. Word got out quickly that the governor was over at the art display so the tent soon became crowded. Cliff didn't think much of it until the man drew closer and Cliff's pulse rose. Chessie, who had been asleep for the better of the morning, rose to her feet, shook out her fur and walked out to the front of the display to see what all the fuss was about.

There she stood when Governor Wilson finally made his way to Cliff's display. The governor looked down, smiled and stooped to a squatting position. "Well, well, now just whose wares are you promoting?"

Sensing the attention, Chessie squatted on her hind legs, barked once and turned her head towards Cliff. Realizing his dog was impeding the way of the state's top leader, Cliff quickly moved out from behind the display and took Chessie by the collar. "Sorry sir, I didn't realize she was awake."

The governor laughed. "That's okay, so long as she's registered to vote." Cliff wasn't sure he got the joke, but everyone else around him laughed. The state's leader continued rubbing Chessie's head, who in turn continued to accept the attention without objection. "Girl?"

"Yes sir."

"Name?"

"Chessie."

The Governor rose to his feet. "Well, Chessie, looks like you've done your job well. And please, that's intended to be a compliment. I have to be careful what I say over here." More laughter followed from the crowd that had gathered around Cliff's display.

The governor leaned forward to get a closer look at Cliff's name badge. "So Cliff, what is your area of expertise?" He broke off eye contact and quickly scanned the display behind the young artist. He started to say something, but stopped as he leaned in closer to one drawing in particular of the Chesapeake Bay Bridge. It was a close up of the south span with the center of focus being a barely discernible figure high up on the east tower. It was the painter Cliff had seen earlier in the summer.

"Look, Jane, there's the painter we saw a couple weeks ago. Remember, we were coming back from Ocean City?"

An attractive young lady who had been standing unnoticed several feet behind Governor Wilson stepped forward. "Yes, sir, I do."

The governor straightened up and looked at the other drawings, photographs and several small paintings on display. He leaned towards Jane who was now at his side and whispered something in her ear. Looking back at Cliff, he said, "You're work is very good. It goes far to capture the true spirit of the Chesapeake. I like that." He reached down and patted Chessie on the head and spoke directly to the dog. "Thanks for making sure I stopped by for a visit." He pointed to the drawing of the bay bridge. "Put that one aside for me, will you? I'll be in touch later." Without waiting for a definite response, he shook Cliff's hand and moved to the next display.

The visit to the tent by the state's chief executive was relatively brief, but the effect lasted the rest of the day. From that point on, the tent was packed. A rumor spread that the governor was especially impressed with an unknown local artist who did scenes of the Chesapeake Bay. That was enough to fill the space around Cliff's display for the next several hours. He sold over two thirds of his total inventory. He also had several offers on the drawing put on hold for the Governor, including one to double the asking price. Cliff held firm, however, politely stating that the drawing was reserved. He did get the interested party's name and address and promised to contact him when a similar drawing was completed in the future. It was a first for Cliff in that he now had a work officially commissioned.

The activity around Cliff was so intense, the duck carver next to him commented during a brief lull that he wouldn't mind if Cliff funneled some of his patrons over to the next booth. While he made the comment in jest, he failed to hide the jealously from his voice. Cliff could have easily offered a piece of advice to increase the attention to his work: "Drop your prices." The young artist wisely kept his thoughts to himself. After all, the value of someone's art was based on many factors, including the value the artist put on each piece. While the decoys were indeed beautiful, they were way overpriced for a function like this, at least in Cliff's mind. He also admitted that he didn't yet have a complete grasp on the whole pricing thing.

Chessie proved to be a big hit, partially because she was a warm and friendly retriever, and also because she had captured the attention of the governor. She stayed by Cliff's side the whole time, politely rising to her feet whenever someone showed her attention. She shook hands on command as Cliff had taught, and she even licked the face of a three year old toddler who insisted on giving the animal a big hug. Cliff heard someone in the crowd comment that the dog was a natural, having already mastered two very important requirements for being a good politician: getting someone's attention and kissing babies. The decoy man did inquire about renting Chessie for a few hours. Cliff laughed the offer away.

"Cliff Davidson, is it?"

Cliff looked toward the voice, his thoughts coming back to the present.

The lady who had been with the Governor earlier was standing in front of the display. Holding out her hand, which Cliff took, she said, "I'm Jane Syzeman. I'm Governor Wilson's Chief Aid. He wanted me settle up with you for the drawing." She handed him an envelope. "That should serve as a down payment. Sorry he didn't pay before, but you see, he can't exactly whip out his wallet here and pay cash. It'll look bad to the other people here."

Cliff thought he understood the logic. "No problem."

The lady glanced around at the near empty display. "From what I can remember, looks like you've done pretty well," she commented.

"We were worried at first, but things picked up after the Governor came through. It was like he took a barbed wire fence down or something."

"He does have that effect on things."

"No one around here's going to complain about that."

"I'm sure he was glad he could help." She bent down to pat Chessie on the head. "What's his name?"

"Her name is Chessie."

"That's right. Sorry, girl."

"She's big for a female," Cliff said.

"Not fat though."

"Not yet anyway. She's been stuck with me aboard the boat all summer and hasn't gotten her normal amount of exercise."

"Aboard your boat?"

Cliff explained briefly how he did his work aboard the *Mona Lisa*.

"That's one reason why you're so good. You actually live what you draw."

"Thank you."

"No, thank you." The chief aid stood still a moment looking over the display. "You know, Governor Wilson doesn't get excited over much these days except polls and bond ratings. But you seemed to have brought out a spark in him. He wants to meet you if possible in Annapolis next week. Is that possible?"

"Meet me?"

The lady laughed. "He wants to talk to you about your work. He also wants to know if you can bring the drawing with you at that time."

Cliff couldn't help but blurt out the next sentence. "The Governor wants to see me?"

"I'll let him explain more when you two meet. Don't worry, it's nothing bad." She reached into her pocket and pulled out a business card. "The number in red is my personal number. Call me and we'll set up a time."

Cliff stared at the card a moment. Looking up, he gave her a very perplexed look.

She returned a big smile. "I guess I shouldn't be toying with a constituent. We're in the middle of a major renovation in the governor's office. He wants a Maryland theme, with a lot of artifacts and things that include work of local artists. We have a few pieces already, mostly gifts from people who've heard about the project. To be quite frank and I trust you'll keep this to yourself, you're the first artist he's actually solicited. He was impressed." She paused and tilted her head to the side. "So was I." Another pause. "See you next week?"

Cliff nodded in the affirmative.

The Governor's Chief Aid turned her attention to Chessie. "Smart dog... very smart." She turned and hurried away.

77

The crab feast was officially over at five. The art festival was scheduled until six in the hopes people would drop by on their way out giving vendors business and spreading out exiting traffic, thus helping with the traffic problem. Downtown Crisfield, with its one main road, was not designed to handle such a large volume of vehicles. By five-thirty, however, most of the vendors were packed and ready to go. The show, at least from what Cliff heard, was a relative success. There was already talk of increasing the display to a second tent next year.

Sliding a box into the back of his van with Cliff's help, the decoy man shook hands and said, "In spite of what it may appear, these shows are a cutthroat business, especially for those of us who depend on it."

Cliff learned earlier that the duck carver was a plumber by trade, but was disabled from a work related back injury. So he was forced to look for another career. While the man always dreamed of one day turning his skill with a block of wood into more than just a hobby, the opportunity came much sooner than expected. Cliff was glad the man had sold a couple of carvings near the end of the show.

"Turnover in this racket is pretty high," the wood carver told Cliff. "A lot of people think they can just take their hobby and turn it into a business. Unfortunately, it doesn't work like that. The show itself is just the tip of the iceberg. You have to put in the time before you ever get here. Then, you have to have a unique quality product. Take me for instance… aren't too many good carvers left around here. I know my prices are high—people have told me that on numerous occasions—but that gives the image of value. I dropped my prices at a show a couple years back. Didn't sell a damn thing. Next week, I went back to my previous pricing schedule and sold five birds—a funny thing, that pricing."

He and Cliff together loaded the last box into the van. Cliff could tell he was in pain and appeared weak on the left side, but he never complained. "A bit of free advice—listen to what others have to tell you, but decide for yourself." He paused and wiped a bare arm across his forehead. "While you're new—least to these parts—you seem to have the knack for what it takes. You seem to rise above all the hoopla. That's a rare beginner's talent. I noticed that you stood back and watched while everyone else bitched and moaned yesterday about how slow things were. You and me, we just took it in stride—maybe a joke here or there, otherwise mouths shut. Makes you stand out, it does." He slammed the door to the van. "Another piece of advice—stick to your game plan. Don't let a lot of outside distractions get in your way. You'll do just fine."

"Thanks for the advice," Cliff said. "Hope to see you again."

"Me, too," the man said. "Only next time I get the dog."

Cliff laughed. "Deal." He shook hands and headed back to the tent. While he had already started packing himself, he'd left a few drawings and photographs set about. With the exception of the drawing put on hold for Governor Wilson, all the larger drawings were gone. So were the paintings. It had been a very good day.

As Cliff started packing the rest of his stuff, a tall man wearing a green polo shirt and tan slacks came up the display. His hair all in place, his face clean-shaven, it was obvious the man had not spent the day sweating over a pile of steamed crabs. Beside him stood a lady about half his height. She was petite with a dark complexion and long black hair pulled back in a ponytail. She wore a near matching outfit. Cliff thought at first they were simply strolling by. When he realized they had indeed stopped, Cliff straightened up. "May I help you?"

"Are we too late?" the man said. His voice was as deep as he was tall.

Cliff glanced around. "Not really, but I don't have much left."

The man leaned forward and examined the several drawings that were sitting on the table. The girl flipped through the pile of unframed photographs. The man reached into his pocket and pulled out his wallet. "How much for everything you have left?"

The question caught the artist off guard. "I'm sorry?"

"How much for everything?" He pointed to a couple of boxes Cliff had already loaded.

"You want it all?"

"Why not?"

"With all due respect, you haven't even seen some of my work. Besides, if you don't mind my asking, what are you going to do with it all?"

"As to your first question, you're wrong there. We've been watching you off and on all day—well, most of the day."

"We did go back to the motel to get cleaned up first," the girl chimed in.

"Yeah," the man added. "She made sure we looked nice for our first visit. You know, first impressions and all that." He laughed at his own humor. He put his wallet away. "Didn't mean to toy with you. Just trying to break the ice."

Suddenly, a light went on. "The man from Philadelphia… Mr. Adams?" Cliff said.

Both smiled. "It's a real pleasure to meet you," the girl said. "We've heard so much about you."

"The Grangers speak very highly of you," the man added. He held out his hand. "I'm Ned Adams. This is Brenda Adams." He didn't explain their connection.

Cliff shook hands with both. "It's a pleasure to meet you." Because of the hectic afternoon, Cliff had forgotten the real reason for the trip to Crisfield. He didn't have time to dwell on his forgetfulness. Something the man said caught his attention. "You said you've been watching me?"

Brenda Adams spoke. "We don't want you to think we were spying on you. We were just in and out of the tent several times."

"Why didn't you say something?"

"You were always busy," Brenda explained.

"And," Ned interrupted, "we were sort of spying. I wanted to see you in action—how you interact with the customers and things like that."

"We heard you were a real hit with Maryland's governor," Brenda said.

"You heard about that?"

Ned laughed. "Remember, this is a political event. Gossip spreads fast."

Cliff looked over his shoulder at the boxes. "Sorry I don't have more to show you. They pretty well cleaned me out today."

"What about that one with the 'Sold' sign across it?" Brenda was pointing to the one of the Bay Bridge.

"Sorry," Cliff said sheepishly. "someone already bought that one."

"And they haven't picked it up yet?"

"I'm delivering it."

Ned laughed. "I guess you're going to tell me it's for the governor."

"Maybe it is," Brenda scolded. "Don't be a smart ass."

"Actually, it is," Cliff said softly.

"He?—"

"There you go," Brenda said.

Anxious to get the conversation back on a more beneficial track, Cliff asked, "How did I do?"

"You were just fine," Ned said.

"More than fine," Brenda corrected. "You were wonderful. Everyone who stopped by your booth left with a smile, whether they made a purchase or not. That's a pretty impressive feature."

"We spent the bulk of the day mulling around the area, taking in the sights and watching what was going on in the tent," Ned continued. "I must say, politics played much more of a role here than I was expecting."

"I thought you were down here to do some of that yourself," Cliff commented.

"We were, but it was quite difficult with all the other stuff going on."

Brenda spoke up. "He's just mad because we didn't have matching tee shirts like everyone else."

"You match now," Cliff pointed out. They both wore red polo shirts and khaki pants.

"A dime too late," Ned said with a laugh.

"I kind of think we stood out because we didn't match," Brenda argued.

"Whatever," Ned conceded. "Anyway, we didn't come here tonight to take a lot of your time. We know you've had a long day, so I'll cut to the chase. I don't know how much the Grangers told you, but we're in the process of opening a chain of gallery and art supply stores in the Philadelphia area, with potential for expansion. While we will probably end up offering the usual array of frames and prints, we also want to showcase new and unknown talent."

"We want you to be one of our first discoveries," Brenda said with enthusiasm.

Cliff refused to allow the enthusiasm to penetrate his persona before making sure he got the next point across. "Everything I do is original. I do no printing or copying. Two drawings or photographs may be close, but they're always the real McCoy."

"Our goal is to serve as the agent for the artist," Ned said. "We may make suggestions and have some control over the pricing if it comes into our store, but the rest is up to you. You show us what you have to offer. We say yes or no to particular pieces, then together we come up with a price. You get sixty percent and I get forty. I also reserve the right to drop any price by twenty percent. This gives me leeway if someone comes in and wants to negotiate. And that'll only happen with big ticket items. If you want to offer originals only, that's up to you." The man paused. "I will tell you this... No, let me *ask* you this. Just keep an open mind on that point as we move forward. I agree, if you sell something as an original, and claim it will never be duplicated, you should stick to that. However, happenings in the future may make you think differently. So, again, just keep an open mind, okay?"

Cliff couldn't argue the point. "Sure."

The man continued. "Two other conditions to the deal; first you have to be available occasionally to make personal appearances. Second, I get first dibs on anything you put up for sale."

"I don't follow you there," Cliff said.

Brenda took over the explanation. "We don't require total exclusivity. In other words, you can still display other places if you like, although we do require a geographic barrier. We just want the right of first refusal."

"So if you don't want it, I can sell it somewhere else."

"Outside a fifty mile radius of any of our stores."

"What if I want to put together a show somewhere and don't want to give you everything you want at that time?"

"If we reach such an impasse, then the same deal will hold as if the works were on display in the store," Brenda said.

"You mean sixty/forty?"

She nodded.

Cliff fell silent a moment. "Can I ask a question?"

"Ask away."

"Justify to me why I should give you forty percent of what my work brings, especially if I'm selling it myself without any problem?"

"Good one," Brenda said. "It all falls under the theoretical concept of agency. An agent adds value to a product or service through image building and marketing. In return, he or she gets a portion of the increased value. In your case, or any artist for that matter, we feel we can get a higher price for your work in one of our stores than you can at a mall show or similar forum. In addition, we feel we can actually help you move more pieces because our arrangement gives you more time to create."

"But the artist being there helps sell the product," Cliff said.

"Sometimes. That's why the requirement for personal appearances," Ned said.

"But it would also be a two or three hour block of time versus the whole day," Brenda added.

"So I wouldn't have to worry about which show to go to and all the issues surrounding that," Cliff said.

"You can if you want, but it's not required."

Cliff mulled over the information he'd heard so far.

As if reading his mind, Brenda added, "Remember, the issue related to you paying us a commission on things you sell yourself only applies to those items we may want that you don't want to give us. If we don't want it, it's not an issue."

"Although to be fair and honest, I suspect the latter will be minimal at first," Ned clarified.

Brenda continued. "In any agent client relationship, there has to be a high level of trust. We are not out to screw you, or take advantage of you in any way. Our number one goal is to help you succeed in the best possible fashion."

Cliff decided the positive potential outweighed any negative issues, and his enthusiasm was sparked. There were caution flags, though. "There has to be a catch somewhere."

"There is," Brenda acknowledged. "Actually there are two. But both have already been laid out on the table. One is the forty percent commission. The other is right of first refusal."

The two watched as Cliff mulled over the idea. "Listen, Cliff," Brenda continued. "We're not here to pressure you into anything. We don't work like that. All we're doing is laying an opportunity out on the table with the attached conditions. The decision is entirely up to you."

"What kind of volume are we talking about? What if I can't keep up with the demand?" Cliff asked.

"The only demand will be that created by the public for your work. We place no conditions on productivity. Doing that to an artist will only dilute the quality, and that's the one thing we definitely don't want to happen," Brenda insisted.

"Although we will expect a certain amount of minimal productivity, say what you're producing now," Ned injected.

"Understandable," Cliff thought aloud. Questions continued spinning like cherries in a slot machine. When the spinning stopped, "How long?"

"How long? You mean the length of the agreement?" Ned asked.

Cliff nodded.

"Another good question," Ned continued. "Twelve months the first go round. It'll be negotiable after that."

Brenda continued. "While no business deal is perfect, we think it's a pretty good package. There really isn't any risk to you."

"Only if I can get the same price for my work as you," Cliff said.

"Don't forget your time," Brenda stressed. "But you don't need to decide tonight. We have papers in the car you can look over. Sleep on it and let us know?"

Cliff smiled. "By tomorrow I want to focus on increasing my inventory. Just tell me where I have to sign."

Ned smiled. "What say we help you clean up here, then all go somewhere and grab a bite."

Cliff suddenly realized he hadn't eaten all day and was starved. He held out his hand. "Sounds like a deal to me."

Not wanting to be left out of whatever was happening, Chessie nosed her way in the middle of the trio as handshakes were exchanged.

"Now I guess it's official," Brenda laughed.

78

Monday morning found the *Mona Lisa* docked alongside the gas pier at St. Michaels Eastwind Marina, the Mitchell's place. Cliff left Crisfield early Sunday morning after a late night with Ned and Brenda Adams. A dinner of crab cakes (and several pitchers of beer for the Adamses), on top of the activities of the previous sixteen hours, left all parties tired yet anxious about the future. Cliff got back to the boat after midnight, worked on drawings until three, but was still up by six the next morning eager to get underway. His plan was to go directly to Annapolis, sailing into the evening if necessary. He figured he had plenty of time for the trip. However, the weather deteriorated with each passing hour. By mid-morning, the waves were well over three feet and the winds were gusting at twenty knots. The weather forecast called for conditions to worsen. Cliff pulled out the chart book to look for a closer port-of-call.

It wasn't fear that drove him into protected water; nor was it his lack of boating experience. The *Mona Lisa* took the heavy seas with little complaint, although she did take more spray over the bow than Cliff would have liked. What really bothered him was the *conditions are expected to worsen* portion of the forecast. His uncle always preached that a good boater was always prepared to handle anything the bay may throw at him; and a smart boater avoided, if possible, having to put those skills to use.

They pulled into the marina Sunday evening. When the office opened in the morning, Cliff could register and get a transient slip for a few days. Since he was here, he planned to spend a couple of days working the town. St. Michaels was already on his list of stops, and he had even considered making it his next destination after Crisfield; that is, until the need to go to Annapolis developed.

He finished washing the boat down just as the dock master made his way down the pier. Seeing a sailboat tied alongside his gas pier caused a scowl on the man's face, but Cliff jumped down onto the pier, introduced himself and explained the situation. And without being asked, he also said he was planning to pay for the night's dockage as well as staying a couple of additional nights. He ended by saying that he also planned to put at least a gallon or two of diesel fuel into the *Mona Lisa's* tank.

The young man's honesty, the ease with which he carried himself and the willingness to pay for the dockage without having to be threatened, quickly endeared him to the dock master. The frown turned to a smile. He held out his hand. "Then I'm Brian Holmes. Friends call me Butch. Welcome to St. Michaels. What you say your last name was again?"

"Davidson. Cliff Davidson."

The man looked at Cliff curiously a moment. Butch was tall and wiry. He looked to be close to fifty, although Cliff knew age was difficult to estimate in people who worked outside most their lives, especially around the salt spray of the bay. He wore a dirty plain white tee shirt, denim coveralls and a pair of stained Docksiders that looked like they should have fallen apart the year before.

"What do I owe you so far?" Cliff said.

The man studied Cliff a moment. "You staying another night?"

"At least two… that is, if you have room."

"No problem there. Just pay for those two. Last night's on the house. We do have an obligation, you know, to help those that come in out of the weather, even damn sailboaters." Butch cocked his head to the side and smiled.

Just then Chessie moseyed up on deck to see what all the conversation was about. Seeing her master, she ducked below the cables and jumped down to the pier. She started toward Cliff who said, "Chessie, say hello to Mr. Butch."

The dog diverted her attention to the man introduced by her master. She hesitated, stuck her nose in the air, sniffed deeply and hurried to the man's side where she circled him excitedly.

"Chessie!" Cliff scolded. "Mind your manners."

Chessie paused in her actions, lifted her head and barked loudly.

The marina manager laughed and reached down to pat the dog on the head. "Now I know why I recognize the name. You're George Davidson's boy, aren't you?"

"He was my uncle, yes." Cliff said.

"And this here is the old man's dog?"

"Well, he's mine now, but yes. This is Chessie."

The tall man paused. "Sorry son, 'bout the accident. Lightning strike, wasn't it?"

Cliff nodded.

"Davidson was a good man. We called him Crabby. He'd catch crabs when no one else could. He used to bring crabs to the *Crab Claw* when they were short." He motioned to the popular restaurant across the harbor. "He'd stop over for fuel and we'd have a chat or two. Loved to talk about his dog and his boy—guess that's you—though I got to tell you, son, Chessie there got more conversation time than you." Both laughed. The man continued. "Nicest fellow you'd ever want to meet." Butch reached into his back pocket and pulled out a dog biscuit. Holding it out for Chessie, he said, "And your dog here just loves my treats. Make 'em myself. All the dogs around here love them." He watched a moment as the animal scarfed the treat from his hand and carried it a few feet away.

Butch continued. "Your uncle used to talk about you being able to draw… That was you, wasn't it?"

Cliff nodded.

"He said you were going to be a great artist one day."

"Trying to be. That's the reason for the sailboat. It makes a good platform to work from. And since I'm in no hurry…"

The man shrugged his shoulders. "Makes sense to me I guess." He looked around to make sure no one else was around. He leaned in towards Cliff. "Just don't tell anyone I said that, okay?"

Cliff laughed. "Sounds like a deal to me." Chessie barked in agreement as she returned to the man's side to investigate the possibility of seconds. The thought of food made Cliff's stomach growl. "I have even a worse idea for you," Cliff said.

The man looked at Cliff with suspicion.

The younger man continued. "How 'bout we get the *Mona Lisa* fueled up here—should take a whole seven or eight gallons—then we'll get her away from the gas pier. After that, I'll whip us up some breakfast. Only condition is you'll have to come aboard to eat it."

Butch broke into a laugh. "Me eat aboard a sailboat?"

"I make a mean omelet."

The laughter grew. "Son-of-a-bitch, blackmailed by a damn rag hauler."

A short time later, the aroma of breakfast filled the *Mona Lisa's* cockpit. Cliff kept the flame on the alcohol stove low in case an unexpected wave came tumbling through the marina. St. Michaels harbor was well protected except from idiot boaters who insisted on plowing through a crowded area putting up a dangerous wake.

Butch arrived just as the coffee finished brewing. He asked permission to come aboard and stepped over the safety cables with ease and without comment. He accepted a cup of coffee—black with two sugars—and made himself comfortable on the portside seat. When a plate filled with a steaming cheese omelet was placed in front of him, he grabbed the salt and said, "You know, a boy like you could ruin a man like me's reputation."

"I won't tell," Cliff said, dumping the next batch of eggs into the skillet. "I'm willing to bet though you've been on a sailboat before."

The man wiped the corner of his mouth and took another bite. "Used to sail every Wednesday night when I was a kid your age. My dad had a 27 Catalina decked out for racing. It was great fun."

"Why'd you stop?"

"When my old man died, I sold the boat. Ain't been out under sail since."

Cliff said nothing, understanding how the man felt. The artist had yet to set foot in a work boat since saying good-bye to *Rose Bud*. He realized they were only a few hundred yards away from where she was resting, and contemplated going over to the Maritime Museum for a visit. However, the desire to avoid painful memories fought against the idea.

They ate in silence a few minutes. Washing the last bite down with the coffee, Butch said, "You know, I was always fond of your uncle. He was a good man. I imagine you'll turn out the same."

Cliff remained silent. He knew that at times like this it was the best option.

"Where you headed from here?" the man asked.

"I've got to go to Annapolis to deliver a drawing."

"A delivery?"

"Yes…" Cliff hesitated, not wanting to sound smug. "Someone bought one in Crisfield and asked if I'd deliver it."

The man put his hand on his chin. "Someone… must have been a VIP not to have taken it with him."

Cliff shrugged. "Only the governor."

The man laughed. "I'll be damned."

"Thank you." Cliff gathered up the dishes and headed below.

"No, thank you. Breakfast was great. It's nice to have someone to eat with once in a while."

"Well, anytime you need an eatin' buddy, you can call me," Cliff said.

A voice from the pier interrupted their conversation. "Is that you, Butch, I see on a sailboat?"

Butch Holmes froze in his seat. He turned his head slowly towards the bright sunlight. Shading his eyes, he said, "Damn. I've been caught red-handed." He squinted some more. "Jennifer?"

Cliff stuck his head through the hatch to see what was going on. He noticed a girl who looked to be in her late twenties standing on the pier looking down at the *Mona Lisa*. She had shoulder length dirty blonde hair pulled back in a ponytail. She wore a red polo type shirt and white shorts. Her feet wore white sandals. A pair of sunglasses rode atop her head.

Seeing Cliff's head come out of the cabin, she said, "How the devil you ever get him on a sailboat?"

Butch answered, "The boy here tricked me. He invited me for breakfast."

"Men," the girl laughed. "Slaves to their stomachs." She readjusted her position so the sun's glare off the polished fiberglass wasn't so bright in her eyes. "I'm Jennifer, by the way."

"Cliff," Cliff said.

"Nice to meet you. So, what did you fix?."

Cliff shrugged as if it wasn't anything special.

"The best omelet you ever tasted," Butch spouted.

"Looks like I missed it."

"Not really," Cliff said without thinking. "I have some eggs left and the skillet's still hot."

"Come on aboard," Butch motioned. "Then I can blame it on you."

"Blame what on me."

"I had to come aboard to save a damsel in distress."

She laughed. "Who saved who?" She looked at Cliff who nodded his approval. She stepped aboard with ease. Sitting down on the starboard seat she said, "So how do you two know one another?"

"Don't," Mr. Butch said. "Until about a half hour ago."

"And you just invited yourself aboard for breakfast?"

"I was kidnaped," the man insisted.

"Fat chance." She turned her attention to Cliff. "Fact is, I'll bet he never turns down a meal, and he stays so skinny."

"So how do you two know each other?" Cliff returned from the galley where he restarted the stove.

"Business," Butch said.

Cliff ducked back below and focused on fixing another skillet of eggs. It wasn't how he had intended on spending the morning. Then again, it wasn't often he had guests aboard the *Mona Lisa*. He had to admit it was quite enjoyable. Besides, the girl—Jennifer—seemed nice enough.

"What brings you to St. Michaels?" Jennifer asked.

"Chased in by foul weather," Cliff answered.

"It was awful windy yesterday," Jennifer conceded.

"Wasn't the wind as much as it was the water. Pretty rough, and it got worse as the day went on. Made working awful hard."

"Work?"

"He claims he's an artist," Butch chimed in. "Although I think he's really a short order cook myself. Won't you be looking for one soon, Jennifer?"

The girl laughed. "Hopefully."

"How's that?" Cliff asked, handing her up a plate filled with eggs. "Coffee?"

"Sure."

Cliff's head disappeared again. Jennifer grinned in approval as the flavor of the eggs caressed her palate.

Butch took it upon himself to answer the earlier question. "She's buying this place."

Cliff watched as his female guest continued to devour the plate of food. She didn't look like the marina owner type. Her hands were too smooth and her face wasn't weathered.

"Actually, my parents are buying the place," Jennifer corrected. "I'm just here to help."

"Goin' a turn it into a big resort too," Butch continued. "Some locals are opposed to it. As for me, I think it's about time. We lose a lot of business because we don't have any place for conventions, even small ones."

"Gonna be that big?" Cliff said, coming out of the cabin with three mugs of coffee.

"We'll see," Jennifer said. "Well intended plans don't always work out the way they're put down on paper."

After taking a long draw on his coffee, Butch continued. "St. Michaels always had a strong tourist draw—by boat and by land. Lately, however, a lot of other places have gotten smart and jumped on the bandwagon. There're some pretty big resorts going up here on the Eastern Shore. Competition's a word used to be reserved for across the bay. Now though, people 'round here are starting to get out their Webster's to look it up."

"You think the solution is building a big resort?" Cliff said to neither one in particular.

"I don't know your definition of big, but resort is the correct word," Jennifer said.

Cliff looked back toward land and tried to imagine the place with a big building sitting in the middle of the property. He could see the advantages, especially being right across from the *Crab Claw*. At the same time, he felt the harbor was picturesque as it was. A hotel would only mar the landscape, or so he thought.

As if reading his mind, Jennifer continued. "St. Michaels has a beautiful harbor. Our plan is to add curb appeal, from land as well as from the water. Right now, all you see is an empty parking lot and an old marina building. What we have designed will blend in much better with the overall surroundings. This side of the harbor could use some upgrading."

Cliff wasn't sure he agreed with the last comment, but he kept his thoughts to himself.

"Anyway," Jennifer continued. "There's a lot more work to be done politically before we even break ground on the project. People resent change, even if it's positive. Someone will oppose it just on principle."

"Has that someone come forth yet?" Cliff asked.

Jennifer chuckled. "If it were only that easy!"

Again, Cliff wisely kept the next question to himself. Instead, he let his thoughts wander to what his uncle might say. While the elder Davidson would undoubtedly oppose the idea on principle, he would also acknowledge that you really couldn't stop progress. Change was inevitable.

Cliff glanced up towards land again. He did so only for a moment as Butch said, "Thanks for breakfast, Cliff. I really need to get back to the office. The phone'll start ringing any minute now for weekend reservations. This Indian summer certainly has been good for business. Let me know if there's anything you need."

"Thanks," Cliff said. He rose and shook hands with the man.

"I'll be up in a few," Jennifer said through a mouth full of eggs. "I want to finish eating and help clean up."

"You don't need to do that," Cliff insisted.

"Well, I do want to finish eating. These are some of the best eggs I've ever had."

"Thank you." Cliff smiled. "It all has to do with being out on the water. When I used to crab with my uncle, we'd make sandwiches on the boat. To this day, I've never had a ham and cheese sandwich that tasted so good."

"You've got to give yourself some credit."

"Some, maybe."

Cliff watched her quickly clean her plate. Wiping her mouth on a paper towel and finishing her coffee, she said, "So what brings you to St. Michaels?"

"On this occasion, the weather."

"That's right, you already said that. Where were you heading"

"Trying to make Annapolis."

"Annapolis!" Cliff noticed the rise of pitch of her voice. "What's there?" she asked.

"It's the state capital for one."

Jennifer laughed. "No silly, I know that. Why were you going there?"

"I was planning on going there a couple weeks ago, only I got diverted because of a boat problem. Then I thought I'd wait till next summer, but now I got an offer the other day I can't refuse."

"Yeah?" Jennifer encouraged.

Cliff hesitated. She seemed genuinely interested so he continued. "The governor bought one of my drawings the other day in Crisfield. He asked me to deliver it. His chief aid also said something about remodeling his offices and wanting to look at local artists."

"Jane Syzeman?" Jennifer suggested.

"Yes, that was her name. You know her?"

"I live in Annapolis and I see her quite frequently. Actually, my parents and the Governor are good friends."

"That's impressive," Cliff said. It was also somewhat eerie.

Chasing the last piece of egg across the plate, Jennifer said, "An artist… you must be good?"

Cliff gave his normal shrug of the shoulders.

"The governor doesn't get impressed by much. So if you caught his eye…" Just then Chessie came strolling out of the cabin. Jennifer turned her attention to the animal. "Well, well, look what we have here." She held out her hand and allowed the dog to smell her scent. When the dog started licking her hand, she reached up and patted her atop the head. "You're beautiful. You smell breakfast, don't you?" Chessie whined on cue.

"She's what really caught the governor's eye." Cliff went on to explain how Chessie sat down right in the governor's path.

Jennifer's laughed. "Don't feel bad. He's a sucker for few things, and dogs are one of them." Chessie laid down at her feet. "Can I see some of your work?" she asked, continuing to rub the dog's fur.

Cliff shrugged his shoulders. "I don't have much left, but you're welcome to see what I've got."

"That'd be great."

Cliff disappeared below and returned with a drawing pad. He exchanged the pad for an empty plate. While he started cleaning up, Jennifer turned her attention to the book. He watched her from inside the cabin, glancing at her frequently for short bursts of time. He tried not to stare, but there was something about her that intrigued him. While she didn't look the part, she was a rich businesswoman (so he thought) coming to St. Michaels to make her mark on the community by building what sounded like a plush waterfront resort.

Her voice interrupted his train of thought. "I'm not an art critic, but you're good."

"Thank you," he said. "I'm trying to make a go of it."

She climbed down the couple steps into the cabin. Setting the book on the table, she said, "What's stopping you?"

He contemplated the question. "I'm new—well new in the professional sense. I've had an interest in art all my life. Maybe *unproven's* a better term."

"Well, we'll just have to change that now, won't we?"

Cliff didn't ask how *we* were going to do that. He didn't have to wonder long.

"I'll put in a good word for you with Jane," Jennifer said, looking at her watch. "Looks like we both have let the time go by without a blink. I imagine you've got plans to work and I've got a meeting with some people in town. Thanks for breakfast. Hopefully, someday I can return the favor."

Cliff was somewhat caught off guard by her sudden departure. Then again, like he thought a few moments before, she was a bigwig and he was just… a good short order cook.

He told himself not to make too much of the conversation. It was a chance meeting, a good breakfast and some fun conversation. "Stay focused," he said aloud.

79

Jennifer stared at the computer screen, a blank look on her face as usual. She shook her head to clear her thoughts, trying to focus on the words—or lack thereof—before her, but it was no use. The creative juices just weren't there. What had once been simple irritation at her inability to enjoy her one hobby had now turned into a high level of frustration. The speed at which this frustration turned to anger also increased. She couldn't blame it on the computer. It booted up without a problem, so she blamed it on writer's block, whatever that meant. She had hoped, with time, she'd forget about the past and be able to concentrate more on her writing, but history was a tough meal to digest.

She chuckled as a new idea came forth. Maybe she should start from scratch… something entirely new… entirely different. Perhaps the story of her own life—a fictional autobiography so to speak. The back cover would contain a photograph of her in a nursing uniform. The narrative below would read: "Jennifer Blackstone—nurse *extraordinaire*, fired from her manager's position at the local community hospital because she cared too much about her patients. The very next day, her one true love in life, Dr. Kildare, dies of a heart attack. At the same time, her parents, who are approaching retirement age, want her to get more involved in the family business, and have assigned her the seemingly impossible task of developing a major project miles away from home. Follow her story as she fights the demons from the past and struggles to move forward with her life. Can she succeed both professionally and emotionally? Does she have the skills and emotional fortitude necessary to continue? What else happens to her along the way?"

Her laughter turned to tears. She had always considered herself a strong, caring person. It helped in emergency medicine. It took patience to deal with the inevitable problems surrounding her relationship with Daniel. It took a wide set of skills to deal with the day to day problems of the restaurant business. It took fortitude when all the above came crashing together like opposing freight trains on the same tracks. It took all that. And she had it. But *had* is past tense. The question: what about the present, and more importantly, the future? She was beginning to have serious doubts.

Her tears turned to anger—a human fight or flight response when faced with a nagging fear. "Screw it!" she muttered. She reached over and hit the power button. She knew when she booted up the next time, she'd have to go through a whole time consuming process because she had shut the system down incorrectly. "Screw that too," she scolded, although she did feel a twinge of guilt for taking her anger out on a machine. After all, Bertha was the least of her problems.

She picked up a thick brown folder lying on the floor. It contained the various papers from the St. Michaels project. She thought medicine was bad with all the paperwork. In some cases, property development was worse. She understood medical jargon. *Legalese* was a whole other language.

At least that part of her life was going well—or so it seemed. Negotiations with the owners were complete and settlement was scheduled for a couple of weeks. The town council, while not yet completely on the bandwagon, had come around once they saw the drawings of the facility and how it would actually enhance the beauty of the harbor area. They also became more supportive once they had their first look at the economic impact statement. The report was developed by their own people and their numbers were even better than the Blackstones'.

There were, however, a couple more roadblocks to overcome, specifically two council members who weren't completely sold on the idea. Their concern, real or perceived, was the environmental impact on the area. What would the increased traffic (water and land), the increased number of people and the increase in noise do to the serenity of the environment? What about pollution? What about wildlife disturbance? They were asking a lot of questions, all of which the Blackstones were ready to answer. There would be an impact, no one argued that. The debate: to what degree would it be negative? Another meeting was planned in a couple of days to discuss the issues—a meeting she would attend with her father. There was a lot of work to do before then. She told herself she should be worrying about that instead of her writing.

She spent the next hour stretched out on the couch going over the figures. She wanted to be sure she could *talk the talk*, as her father liked to say. They were also meeting with their attorney on Monday to put the finishing touches on the financing package given to her for review.

Feeling her eyelids growing heavy, she set the papers down and took a deep breath. The earlier questions regarding her ability to cope flowed like a scrolling screensaver. She told herself she was not going to dwell on the past. She had to look ahead, yet the past kept creeping to the surface.

She lay with her eyes closed for several more minutes. Unable to relax, she jumped to her feet and made her way to the bathroom. She turned the shower to hot taking her time undressing to let the room fill with steam. She looked at herself in the mirror. Reaching down, she squeezed the skin around her navel. There was more to pinch than normal. She turned sideways and looked at her silhouette. She automatically pushed her shoulders back and sucked in her stomach. But the action was too late. She had already seen what she was hoping to avoid. She tried imagining what someone would say about her. Such a description was difficult in that eyes facing outward were usually objective. Eyes focused inward usually were not.

She let go of the skin and waited until her image was blurred by the steam on the mirror. Too much stress and not enough exercise. She didn't add another factor for keeping herself fit—an incentive to look good for someone she cared about. She had always been proud of her body, and while she dressed conservatively, at least compared to the *stuff* she saw coming into the restaurant, she always made sure her clothes accented her body. As Daniel liked to compliment, she could turn a head with the best of them.

She stepped into the shower and turned her back on the stream of water. She grabbed the towel rack and bent forward. The heat dug into her lower spine, forcing the muscles to relax. She took a few deep breaths and straightened up. Turning, she leaned forward and wet her hair. A stream of shampoo ran down her chest. The bubbles, combined with the heat of the water, caused her nipples to rise. An unconscious moan escaped her lips. Her washcloth encased hand touched her breast. Her skin felt soft. Her other hand moved down to her belly button. A finger dug inside her navel, pretending to look for lint. In reality, she always liked her navel teased. It was like the outlet hidden behind a couch—full of electricity, but seldom used. Her hand dropped lower. Like bristly briars protecting the entrance of a cave, curly hairs wrapped around her fingers. Nature's guards were no match, however, for the determined intruder.

She let out a fast breath. Her pulse quickened. Blood was diverted from her brain as the human computer sent an increased supply to other parts of her anatomy. Her finger flexed and entered the first portion of her womanhood. She spread her knees, careful to hold steady. Her breathing quickened in response to the demand for more oxygen. She reached up and pressed her free hand against the wall. Her finger flexed more. She pushed in further. She struggled to focus, trying to think of someone pleasant… of someone hot… of someone she'd like to be with at this very moment.

Faces passed through her consciousness. The guy at the bar the night before who offered to buy her a drink… the man whose wife complained about everything during the entire meal… a guy on the street earlier in the day driving a convertible. He stopped to let her cross the street, not purely to be polite, but to get a better look. She made sure she gave him his money's worth.

The faces continued to spin. A person here… one there… mostly having something to do with the restaurant.

The spinning suddenly stopped. There was a face… a person… he was young… dirty blonde hair, a firm body… a smile that penetrated the hardest defense, and eyes that did the same. Yes, he stared like all the other XY chromosome species on the planet. Only he seemed to stare as much into her mind as her body. It was like he was trying to undress her thoughts. It took time to remember just who he was and where she met him.

Then she remembered. He was the artist in St. Michaels the week before, the boy on the boat, the *very* good looking boy, the ace egg cooker. She had never been attracted to younger men, always preferring someone older, more mature, more established in their life. But this one was different. She struggled to remember his name… Cliff something or other… David… Davidson. Cliff Davidson.

She felt herself break into a sweat. Suddenly the room felt hotter. Her knees started to quiver. Another moan escaped. She pressed harder into the wall as the quivering increased. Time stopped as she remained focused on the boy. He was such a good artist. She wondered if he was good at anything else. She imagined his fingers as the brush and her body the canvas. A wave of embarrassment changed to one of electrical shocks, soft and easy at first, and then increasing in intensity. More lightning. More thunder. And suddenly the big boom.

An instant later she started to cry. Even though she told herself there was no reason for it, a wave of guilt engulfed any sense of pleasure she may have felt. She felt so… so… dirty.

No, not dirty… unfaithful. But unfaithful to whom?

The boy's image disappeared and Daniel's face appeared. He was motioning for her to come to him. There was a tea towel across his shoulder and… and there was moisture on his upper lip. She started to say something, but the image slowly faded into the fog of the shower. "No… no," she called out. But he did not listen. He was gone… again.

The tears increased. Her body, a moment before shaking in pleasure, now shook in despair. She leaned forward, banging a fist gently against the wall. "I'll never be able to make it," she said aloud. "Never."

"You have to," a voice of reason argued.

"I can't."

"You can."

"But…"

"No buts. You've got to get yourself together. Stop feeling so sorry for yourself. There's a great opportunity ahead of you, but you've got to take the first step."

"I can't."

"You can."

"Just leave me alone," she demanded.

The voice did, momentarily.

80

He was sitting at a booth near the back of the room. Jennifer didn't believe it was him, figuring her imagination was playing tricks on her, especially after what had happened in the shower a few hours earlier. She had stayed in the shower several more minutes to regain her composure and to finish washing the parts of her body that had initially been ignored. By the time she was dressed and ready for work, she was re-energized. Her mood had brightened. She'd put thoughts about Daniel in the background. For that matter, she had put all thoughts concerning her past on hold, telling herself she would never make it into the future if she let a storm anchor filled with bad memories weigh her down. It was like her voice of reason said, yes she could. Or would something else come along and knock her off course?

The restaurant was busy as expected for a Friday night, and she dug right in, mainly helping with the hostess chores since one of the new girls had already called out sick—an ongoing problem with the new hires. She didn't know when he came in, nor had she noticed him before now. She watched as Martha, his waitress, approached the booth. She was balancing a bottle of root beer on a small tray. He looked up as she bent over, set a glass down and poured out some of the liquid. While Martha partially blocked her view, Jennifer was able to get a good look. There was no doubt it was him. She headed for the kitchen. Intercepting Martha at the salad stand, she said, "Hey, Martha. How ya' doing?"

Martha was one of the oldest *Riverboat Inn* waitresses, both in age and experience. She also happened to be one of the best. She complained infrequently (except about customers and tips), she was always cheerful and she never called out sick. She had become somewhat of a friend to Jennifer. "Busy as all fuck—otherwise great. How 'bout you?" She was also known for her skill with words.

Jennifer helped Martha make a salad. "You have table two?"

Scooping out a generous portion of croutons, the waitress responded, "Yeah—and yes, I'm sweating him, even if he is young. But I'd do him" Martha was never one to beat around the bush with her vocabulary or her intentions.

"I only asked you if you were waiting on him," Jennifer laughed.

"I know what you were thinking."

"Martha!"

Tomatoes and a slice of onion were added to the salad. "Don't bullshit me, girl," the waitress said.

Jennifer laughed again. "What did he order?"

"Root beer, salad and a bowl of oyster stew to start. Said he'd make up his mind about more later." She set the salad on her tray. Sliding it towards Jennifer, she said, "Do me a favor girl, take this out for me while I go check on the oyster stew. While you're at it, check him out and tell me what you think."

Jennifer wisely complied with the request. As she headed into the dining room, salad in hand, Martha called out, "You're a consultant, remember. A consultant never steals clients from the customer."

"He's too young for you," Jennifer pointed out.

"He's too young for both of us," Martha countered.

Jennifer smiled. "When did age ever matter to either of us?"

"You can look, only I saw him first," Martha said.

Jennifer chose not to correct her friend. She'd fix that point later if necessary. She slid her free hand through her hair, pulled her sweater down on the side and headed toward the table. Circling around to approach him from behind, she leaned over and set the salad in front of him. "We're all out of eggs. Hope this is okay."

The figure looked up with a start. "Jennifer," he said. "What a pleasant surprise."

She was impressed with his memory for names. "Feeling's mutual," she said. "How you doing, Cliff?"

"Fine thanks, but… what are you doing here?"

"I brought you your salad."

"I meant—"

"I know," she interrupted, giving him a gentle smile. "My parents own this place. I'm just helping out tonight."

"Oh."

"I see you made it to Annapolis okay."

"The trip across the bay was just the opposite of St. Michaels. Calm as could be. Had to motor most of the way."

"Where you staying?"

He motioned out the window. "Right there at the city dock... a perfect spot."

Jennifer leaned over and followed the line of his finger. She thought she recognized the sailboat sitting in one of the slips. She also thought she caught a whiff of him. He wasn't wearing any cologne, but he did have a clean smell about him. "Which one is yours?" she asked as an excuse to stay close to him longer. After all, a consultant should collect all the data possible.

"The one with the fenders hanging off the back. They're obstructing the name."

"The *Mona Lisa*, right?"

"You remembered!"

"I remember a lot," Jennifer boasted. She straightened up before she fell into the table and really embarrassed herself. "I'm glad you made it. Martha will be here in a minute with your stew. Anything else you need in the meantime?" She cursed herself for giving him such a set up line. She normally was very good at not letting her guard down in the restaurant.

"Not right now, but thanks," he said.

She stared at him, her customer service smile plastered across her face. He didn't take advantage of her vocal slip. Anyone else would have. There was a constant battle between the hormone driven male customers, especially the Naval Academy midshipmen, and the let's-work-for-a-big-tip waitress staff. The battles, often fun to watch, were often subtle but relentless.

Jennifer made a mental note reinforcing her earlier impression that this one was different. He did not want to do battle. "Did you order yet?" she asked.

"Up to the oyster stew."

"You up for some recommendations?"

"Sure."

"You like fish?"

"Ditto the sure."

Jennifer's smile widened. She liked his sense of humor. "Then I'd go with the stuffed rock fish. Both the crab meat and fish are fresh."

Cliff raised his glass in a toast. "Here's to the stuffed rock fish."

Realizing her time had run out, she said. "I'll check on your stew."

"No hurry. I know you guys are busy."

"Thanks." Jennifer nodded and backed away from the table a few steps before turning and hurrying away.

Luck, faith, coincidence—the term didn't really matter. Just as Jennifer got back to the front, a party of nine came through the door. Naturally, they didn't have reservations. However, while the place was busy, Jennifer told them it would only be a few minutes until she set up a table. As she was doing that, she searched the dining room for someone to take the party. All the wait staff was scurrying around trying to keep up with the tables they already had. Martha, however, saw Jennifer's dilemma and said as she slid over an extra chair. "Let's make a deal." Martha was always making a deal.

"I'm listening," Jennifer said.

"I'll take this one if you help with my other tables. All their orders are in. You just have to serve 'em."

Without thinking of the consequences, Jennifer said, "Deal."

Martha laughed. "You're awful quick on that one."

Jennifer looked at her friend. It took a second for the implications to sink in.

"Remember, Ms. Consultant, I saw him first," Martha said as she walked forward to tell the party of nine their table was ready.

Jennifer cursed herself, and then changed the verbiage to a compliment. For once, she got the better part of the deal. She hurried into the kitchen and saw the bowl of oyster stew sitting under the hot lights with Martha's number stuck beneath the saucer. She grabbed a serving tray, gathered a soup spoon, pack of crackers and balanced the soup carefully. She had waitressed for many years, yet she never fully trusted herself with trays of food. No one-hand-over-the-head-balancing-with-the-wrist technique for her. She used both hands.

She went straight to table two and sat the bowl of oyster stew in front of Cliff. She explained that Martha was busy. Cliff nodded and immediately tore into the soup. She cleared the salad plate and empty root beer bottle, and headed back to get another. When she returned, she said, "How's the stew?"

"Great."

"I'm glad you like it." She hesitated before asking the next question. "Did you have your meeting with the governor yet?"

"No, but I did call Ms. Syzeman. She said she'd get back to me in a couple of days. She said the governor was really busy but would definitely work me in. She claimed he even asked about me earlier in the day."

"I'm sure he did. Nothing much gets by him. I'm anxious to hear how it goes."

"I could use some pointers. I've never met anybody like this before. I don't know the protocol or anything like that."

Jennifer laughed. "He's the Governor of Maryland, not the Queen of England. He's a regular guy like you and me."

"I don't know about that."

"Believe me, he is."

"I could still use some pointers."

"Well, I've got some I guess."

"Then grab a seat," Cliff offered easily.

Jennifer laughed. Maybe her assessment of his hormones was wrong. "Thanks. But I've got a couple other tables to see to."

"Maybe later," Cliff said.

"We'll see if it calms down."

"If not, you know where my boat is. I'm sure I'll be up working late."

Jennifer surprised herself with her response. "That would be nice." She quickly added. "But I'll see what time I get out of here."

"Whatever, if you're interested, I'll be in town a few days," Cliff said. Again, there was no sense of the pressure she was used to.

"Sure," she said immediately. "Let me check on your food."

"Thanks," Cliff said.

Jennifer hurried away, not believing she had that conversation. She didn't usually encourage customers, even if it was someone who interested her. "This was different," she told herself, almost speaking aloud. "He was different." After all, it wasn't everyday one got summoned to the governor's office.

81

April stared out over the bow, waiting impatiently for her eyes to readjust to the darkness. She loved the colors and layout of the instrument panel on the bridge of *Hamilton's Bench*, but the brightness tended to ruin one's night vision. Already on the edge of the helm seat because of her height, she rose to her feet and looked at a crystal clear sky. A few degrees left of their course, the moon, a day from being full, laid down a soft beam of light across the water. The stars were out in droves. She struggled to remember the names of the various constellations Phillip had been teaching her. She found the North Star without a problem, drawing an imaginary path to the top edge of the Big Dipper. She focused on one spot to see if there were any falling stars. She had seen a few before, and had to admit she was frightened by the first one she ever saw. Phillip reassured her she was safe; and once her fear passed, her fascination was free to soar. She had forged a good grasp of astronomy during her time aboard *Hamilton's Bench*, but she was still in awe of the concept that she could see light from an object trillions of miles away. To think there might be life out there on some other planet was both fascinating and scary.

It was also scary that she was totally surrounded by water—very deep, dark, mysterious water. What was out there that she couldn't see? What was out there that could see her? A chill went up her spine as she chuckled softly. Months before, lost up on the mountains, she would have died to have so much water at her feet. Now…

Realizing she had been staring upward for more than the a few seconds, she snapped her eyes to the horizontal position. The sky above shone like lights on a thousand Christmas trees. The horizon, however, was indefinable. She could imagine the intersection of the two. In reality, they blended together without a hint of transition. She turned slowly left to right. She saw nothing indicating any other vessels in the area. The surrounding sea was all hers. She looked down at the compass and made sure the autopilot was doing its job. She contemplated turning it off and steering herself, but she knew any change in noise would awaken Phillip, who was on *stand-by* in the chair next to her. She knew he should really be awake. She also knew his actual depth of sleep was light. The slightest change in noise or wind against his face would bring him instantly to his senses.

As long as he stayed asleep, she didn't have to make small talk, something he seemed more interested in lately. When she first came aboard, he was all business—nice and polite with his conversation remaining focused on what needed to be done. As she showed more and more interest in learning other aspects of boating besides waxing and varnishing, he took her under his wing and began teaching her the ropes. He kept things simple, spoke to her level of understanding and was always willing to answer questions. However, as they spent more and more time together, he tried to make other conversation. He was subtle at first, and April almost missed his prying into her personal life.

When she first came aboard *Hamilton's Bench*, she told herself she'd be safe so long as she kept her mouth shut and stayed focused on her job. Her comfort level grew and she started to relax. She knew better than to raise her hopes too high, or her vision too far ahead. But if she had to do something with her new life, it might as well be something she liked—such as crewing aboard a multimillion dollar yacht. Between practicing the piano and her duties as a crew member, she had little time to dwell on the future. By the end of her day, she was usually exhausted and she simply collapsed in her bunk. That was okay, as sleep came quickly and soundly. Lately however, Phillip was starting to approach uncharted territory—ground she was not willing to have trespassed upon. It made her nervous.

She refocused on the instrument panel and checked the positioning line of the GPS. The autopilot was doing its job. She watched the radar through one revolution. She was about to turn around to scan the horizon from astern when her eyes snapped back to the radar screen. She leaned forward. There was a bleep at 3 o'clock, just on the fifteen mile radius line. She straightened up and looked to her right. Squinting, she saw nothing but what looked like a bunch of stars on the horizon. She looked back at the radar screen and back up at the stars. She stole a glance at the numerical clock in the corner of the GPS screen. She'd wait three minutes and reassess the situation.

The seconds ticked by ever so slowly. The bleep was still present, only now inside the fifteen mile marker. Off to her right, the stars still sat on the horizon. She remembered one of the lessons from Phillip during a night run several weeks before. He told her it was a big ocean, but vastness meant nothing if two objects were on a collision course. Time and distance then became the important factors. The old speed x time = distance was still haunting her. She allowed a smile to form. The circumstances were a lot different now.

The bleep on the radar continued to move toward the center of the screen. Her smile receded as she took a deep breath, turned off the autopilot and turned up the squelch on the radio. She was about to reach over and touch Phillip on the shoulder, but the static from the radio brought him to his feet. "What's the matter?" he demanded with a start.

"You know how you told me if a constellation of stars isn't lifting off the horizon, it isn't a constellation?"

He was already turning in a steady clockwise fashion. "Yes."

"That constellation isn't rising," April said, right arm straight out perpendicular to their course.

Phillip's rotation stopped when his eyesight was in line with April's arm. He looked down at the radar screen and saw the blip. There was still plenty of time. He raised the binoculars draped around his neck to his eyes. "What's your assessment?"

"A Christmas tree heading our way until proven otherwise," April said, forcing her voice to remain calm. A Christmas tree was how Phillip described the lights on a vessel far enough away that the actual vessel wasn't identifiable. The fact that there were multiple lights meant it was something big.

"Plan?" the captain and teacher queried. Continuing to look through the binoculars, he turned in a full circle.

April reviewed the procedure in her mind to make sure she had already started the right sequence. "Identify a potential danger, take control of the wheel, make sure the radio is on and alert the watch commander… that's you."

Rogers smiled. "Very good. Then what."

"Keep the hell out of its way," April said, managing to put an acceptable seaman twang onto her words.

Phillip broke into a loud laugh. "Very good. Want me to take the wheel?"

"That's up to you."

Phillip didn't hesitate. "Then steady as she goes." He glanced at the radar screen.

April did the same and sucked in a deep breath as she saw the bleep was getting closer to them with each sweep of the antenna. "Whatever it is, it's hauling as—" She stopped before the curse word slipped out. Unabashed cursing was one part of being a seaman she had yet to conquer.

"I can't make her out completely, but she does look high in the water," Phillip said, lowering the binoculars.

"What should I do?" April asked, unable to hide a slow developing panic from her voice.

Phillip Rogers grabbed his chest. "Your watch mate just had a heart attack. He's got to go below to see the doctor. The decision is up to you."

While they were many months and hundreds of miles from Worthington Valley, her thoughts returned to her time in the woods with Danny where he used to do the same thing to her. He called them fight or flight decisions—moments in time when one's fortitude was truly tested. How many such decisions had she already made since leaving Worthington Valley? How many had been right? How many had been wrong? She mentally shrugged her shoulders. She guessed she was doing okay so far. But now she was being tested again. She knew Phillip wouldn't let her do anything that endangered *Hamilton's Bench*. She also knew that if she passed the test, there'd be more opportunities in the future. If she failed—

"Failure's not an option," she said under her breath.

"What was that?" Phillip inquired.

"Just talking to the wind," she quoted. She turned the wheel to starboard and aimed right at the mass of lights.

"Talk to me, not the wind," Phillip encouraged.

"I thought you were having a heart attack."

"The doctor gave me a clean bill of health."

"How's your pain?" It wasn't often she toyed with anyone, but she couldn't resist. She glanced at the radar screen. The bleep was approaching the five mile line.

"Okay, smart ass…"

April's voice turned serious. "If I adjust our course and set a new one directly at where the ship is now, we'll pass her well astern. The Christmas tree always has the right of way—even in a swimming pool like the Atlantic."

Phillip Rogers took a look at the radar screen and the compass. He lifted the binoculars and focused on the ship's lights. The silhouette of the tanker was now easily ascertained against the dark background. Satisfied at what he was seeing, he did a full circle sweep. "All clear otherwise," he announced. "See if you can raise her on the radio to let her know our intentions. I bet they haven't even seen us yet. It'll scare the shit out of 'em."

"Why wouldn't they see us?" April asked.

"The number one cause of collisions at sea—they aren't looking!"

The implications sank in quickly, sending a chill up the helmsman's spine. "Too bad we couldn't just wait till we were right alongside and sound the horn," she quipped.

"Good one there," Phillip laughed. "Good decision, too." He dropped the binoculars and sat back down in his chair. "Steady as she goes."

"Steady as she goes, course 048," April replied. She picked up the radio's microphone and pushed in the transmission key. "This is the motor yacht *Hamilton's Bench*, Whiskey Romeo George eighty-two eighty-five. Come in, big daddy."

She imagined the scurrying of activity as people on the bridge jumped up and rushed to their respective positions. There was only a brief pause before the static was cut off by a return response. "This is the tanker *Wanderer*. Come in, *Hamilton's Bench*."

She smiled. She could tell by the voice they had no clue about *Hamilton's Bench's* presence. She looked over at Phillip. Even through the darkness, she caught a similar expression on his face.

She turned and looked at the tanker. Her own smile widened. This time she had made the right decision.

82

It was after eleven before the dining room finally settled down. Jennifer helped Martha and a couple of the other girls with a large party that arrived behind the earlier group of nine. People were in a jovial mood which meant the tables took longer to clear. Once Cliff had his food, Jennifer turned him back to Martha to close him out and get the tip. Jennifer made sure the waitresses always collected the tip. She was there to help, not compete with the staff.

The late evening news was under way by the time Jennifer returned to her apartment. She kicked off her shoes and plopped on the sofa. She tried to relax and divest her mind of the day's events, but she was still pumped. The adrenalin took a while to clear after a busy night. She changed clothes and headed out for a walk.

She thought about going up Main Street to hit one of her favorite watering holes. She hadn't been uptown for a while, and figured tonight was as good a night as any to break the cycle. She crossed the near empty lot and strolled along the waterfront. A band was playing at the outside café across the water. People were mulling around. Some were on boats. Others were just hanging out at the bar. The music was loud rock and roll, and the noise easily carried across the narrow causeway.

She stopped after passing a few slips. The pier light illuminated the boat occupying slip number 5. The letters *MONA LISA* were painted across the stern. Jennifer hesitated. Her mind told her to keep moving. Her body, always the more curious part of her soul, won the argument. She took a few cautious steps along the narrow catwalk that ran between the boats. The curtains were drawn, but the hatches were open and the cabin lights lit. When she reached the widest part of the vessel, she tapped lightly on the hull. She heard movement below deck as the *Mona Lisa* rocked gently. A head popped up through the main hatch.

Cliff looked around and saw Jennifer standing on the pier. "Well, hello there."

"Hope I'm not disturbing you," Jennifer said.

"No, not at all. I'm glad you stopped by." He disappeared back into the cabin and resurfaced through the rear hatchway.

"I just happened to notice your lights were on," she said.

It was a bold-faced lie, but if he didn't buy it, he didn't show it. "I was just working on some drawings." Cliff climbed the rest of the way out the cabin and made his way along the pier-side gunwale. He grabbed the nearby piling and pulled the boat closer to the catwalk. He reached out with his free hand. "Come aboard?"

Below deck, she saw his drawing pads spread out across the table. Several large black cases sat on the couch. He pushed the pads aside and motioned her to take a seat. "Beer?"

"Sure."

He slid into the booth opposite her and twisted off the caps on two bottles of Budweiser. "I know you're not supposed to have glass bottles on a boat, but I splurged today. It's much better, you know."

"Thank you." She liked that he knew the difference between bottled and canned beer. "What are you working on?"

"I'm trying to put some ideas together for a portfolio," Cliff said. "When I talked to Jane Syzeman, she asked if she could make an observation about my work. Naturally I said yes. She said she really liked my work and thought I did a good job of accurately depicting life on the Chesapeake Bay, which is my basic theme. However, she suggested I take that theme and develop sub-themes. She called it *ratcheting down* the ideas. In other words, she suggested doing a whole series of photos, drawings and maybe even a painting or two around one particular part of the bay, either geographically or otherwise. She gave as an example doing a whole portfolio on Chesapeake Bay lighthouses, or a whole series on the Bay Bridge. Another example was a whole series on a specific place. Naturally, she suggested Annapolis."

Jennifer smiled. "Smart girl."

"Anyway," Cliff continued. "I've always tried to be objective when someone gives me advice, especially someone so important, so I came back here and pulled out all the stuff I've been working on. And sure enough, it all fits into *Life on the Chesapeake Bay*, but like Ms. Syzeman said, it's a big bay."

Jennifer thought about the idea. "What's the advantage?"

"I asked her the same thing, and she said there might not be any. On the other hand, a *tighter* portfolio, as she called it, might get more attention. She compared it to politics. The governor has to worry about a lot of things. It's a big state! But when he goes before the public, he usually focuses on one or two specific issues that he feels will get people's attention."

"Makes sense," Jennifer said. "Although, I'm not sure I see the connection between politics and art."

"A politician is an artist. Only instead of using a brush or pencil, he or she uses the spoken word."

"It's still a stretch to me, but like I said, Jane's a very smart lady." She took a swallow of beer. "What have you decided?"

"Probably a compromise. I'll continue to work on a variety of things. At the same time, I'll try emphasizing something, only I can't come up with anything specific that hasn't already been done. Ms. Syzeman mentioned lighthouses, but everybody does those. Birds are another possibility."

Jennifer glanced at the drawings spread across the table. She noticed something peculiar… something missing in his work.

Cliff continued. "Before I do any of that, she wants me to do a painting of the capital building for the governor. They… meaning his staff… want to give it to him for Christmas."

"That's impressive!" Jennifer exclaimed. "What did you tell her?"

"Yes, of course. It's an opportunity I really can't refuse."

"The building is actually quite beautiful," Jennifer said.

"That it is," Cliff agreed. He rose to his feet and fetched more beer. "I've never been commissioned to do anything before. A lot more pressure, it seems. And now I have two pieces to do." He explained about the man who wanted a drawing of the Bay Bridge similar to the one for the governor.

"You don't strike me as someone who worries too much about pressure."

Cliff shrugged his shoulders. "We'll see."

Jennifer picked at the label on the bottle. "Tell me, how does one go about doing such a painting? Do you go out there and set up your easel, or what?"

"You could do it that way. But then you're locked into the location, and you're dependent on the weather. Most artists I know who do commissioning projects work off of photographs."

"And you do photography, right?"

"Actually, I shot a roll earlier today before I went to the restaurant. I wanted to see what angles worked best."

"I never thought about that," Jennifer admitted. "It is a building you can approach from many sides."

"And each side has something special about it, too," Cliff pointed out.

She smiled as she started her second beer of the evening. This was a far cry from her initial plan to stop by one of her favorite watering holes. The idea was to get out and relax, and see some old friends. She missed the camaraderie of her coworkers. The nurse management team, while spread out all over the hospital, was very close. There was always someone's shoulder to lean on, someone with a friendly piece of advice and a much needed pat on the back. However, as her role at the *Riverboat Inn* continued to evolve, she found herself more and more isolated from the staff. Before coming on board full time, she was simply the owner's daughter—someone who the staff could go to for a *behind the scene* chat—code for complaining about something her parents did or did not do. Jennifer often took on the mediator role, and had actually gained a lot of respect from everyone regarding her ability to help put out small fires before they grew into larger ones. As she became more and more the boss, those chats diminished. Calls from her ex-coworkers had dried up as well. Jennifer hoped the visit to Main Street might rekindle some of those friendships.

She nursed her beer. While she might not be rekindling old friendships, she enjoyed the idea of making a new one. She smiled to herself, swallowing a laugh. She told herself to stay focused on the word *friend*. After all, he was at least eight years her junior.

She squinted to get his face in better focus. The cabin was well lit, yet there were still the unavoidable shadows caused by the small interior lights on a boat. He was well built, fit as a rock, yet not grotesquely muscular. His tanned skin seemed to glow. His clean curly blond hair needed a few more swipes with a brush. He had changed clothes and now wore a yellow tee shirt and cutoff jeans. She fought the urge to lean forward to get another whiff of him. She wondered if he still smelled as good. Like Martha said, in spite of his age, he did stir one's emotions. She remembered the earlier shower.

"Everything okay?" he said, breaking her train of thought.

"Sure… sure. Sorry, I was just daydreaming."

He smiled. "Want to share?"

She blushed. "Not really." She cursed herself for letting her guard down. She prepared herself for the next attack.

"Okay."

Her eyes widened. No attack? She left him a wide opening.

"I do that a lot," he said instead.

She pulled one of the drawing pads toward her. Flipping through several pages of various views of the Bay Bridge, she stopped when she came to one in particular. She leaned in closer. "Is that someone up on the bridge?" she asked, turning the page for him to see.

He didn't look down. "He's a bridge painter."

"Really."

"His canvas is just bigger than mine."

She chuckled. "Nooo!"

He laughed with her.

Her face suddenly turned serious. She realized what she had noticed earlier. She flipped through several more drawings, finally saying, "None of your drawings have any people in them."

Cliff shrugged his shoulders. "Got the bridge painter."

"He's so far away." She said. "Is there a reason?"

"Reason for?"

"For not having any human life in your work—or am I wrong?"

"I just don't do human forms." He didn't add that the last portrait he did was of his uncle. "The bridge painter, he's just an extension of the bridge."

Jennifer took a swallow of beer. "That could be your portfolio."

"Huh?" Cliff said.

"You could do a series of pieces depicting the people of the Chesapeake. After all, they are part of the bay's life."

Cliff rose and returned with a bag of pretzels. Taking a handful and crunching down on one, Jennifer let her thoughts regroup. She took a long swallow of the beer. "Let me ask you something, Cliff. If someone wanted to hire you to do a whole series of pieces for them, would you be interested?"

"Depends."

"Depends on what?"

"The circumstances—what they wanted, by when and for what."

"I see."

"I have an agreement with an agent who might have something to say on the matter."

"An agent?"

Cliff briefly explained the Philadelphia deal, then, "Did you have something in mind?"

"Just a very *unthoughtout* thought."

"An *unthoughtout* thought... what does that mean?" Cliff laughed.

"Hell if I know." Jennifer drank the rest of her beer and set the bottle down with a loud clunk. "I've been struggling with what to do as a theme for the place in St. Michaels. I definitely want nautical, but I wasn't sure of anything else, that is until now when I just had a brainstorm," Jennifer said.

"You've lost me."

"What if the theme revolved around the people and faces of the Chesapeake Bay?"

Cliff pondered the idea. "I'm not an interior decorator, but it certainly sounds interesting."

"Not to be a smart ass, but it's more than interesting."

"What would you name the place?"

"The entire complex is going to be called *St. Michaels Sunset Harbor Marina and Resort.* The name of the restaurant is undecided."

"That's a mouthful," Cliff said.

"I agree," Jennifer said. "But we wanted both location and attraction in the name."

"Attraction?"

"That we're both an attraction and a resort. In other words, more than just a marina."

"I see." There was a hard crunch on a pretzel. "Why *Sunset Harbor?*"

Jennifer explained the tradition at the *Riverboat Inn* of toasting the sunset.

"I like that," Cliff said. "Did that happen tonight?"

"You must have just missed it."

"But it was cloudy."

"You don't have to see the sunset to toast it."

Cliff laughed. "I still don't see where I fit in."

"You could supply some of the art work... maybe not all of it, but you'd definitely be a featured artist... or whatever you'd call yourself."

"Artist in residence," Cliff joked. He took a swallow of beer. "Is this the biggest project you've ever developed?"

"You mean the St. Michael's place?"

He nodded.

Jennifer hesitated. "Actually, it's the only one."

"Oh."

"And yes, I'm treading water trying to keep my head above the surface."

"You'd never know that talking to you. I thought—" Cliff stopped.

"Go on, you can say it," Jennifer encouraged.

"I'm having an *unthoughtout* thought of my own," Cliff said. He started to get up to fetch more beer, but Jennifer held up her hand. "I thought you were some big time land developer or something," he added.

Jennifer laughed. "Thanks for the compliment, but honey, I'm just a local girl trying to help her parents retire early." She did not expand on the other reasons related to the project. "I hope you're not disappointed."

"Not at all."

"Anyway," Jennifer continued, "if I can survive as a floundering property developer, than surely you can draw people."

"I don't see the relationship," Cliff said.

"If I can do it, you can do it."

Cliff paused. "The question is where to start? It just doesn't fit into what I've been doing."

Jennifer hesitated. "You could start with me."

"Huh?"

"Do me… draw me."

"Oh."

She pushed a pad towards him. "Go ahead. Try it." Subconsciously, she pushed the hair off her face and pulled her shoulders back.

"You want a portrait of yourself?" he asked.

"Don't make me sound so vain," she directed. She followed with a smile.

"Just asking."

"I'm just asking, too. Besides, there's no one else around to draw at the moment, unless you have someone hidden in the forward cabin."

"Chessie's around here somewhere," Cliff laughed.

Jennifer laughed with him. "I just want to see what you can do, that's all."

Cliff opened the pad to a blank page. Picking up a pencil and checking the point for sharpness, he leaned forward across the table and stared.

"Tell me what you want me to do?" Jennifer said.

"Nothing special… Just relax and be yourself."

Jennifer chuckled. "I haven't figured out what that is lately."

Cliff didn't respond. The model-to-be watched as the portrait-artist-to-be continued staring at her face. It was almost as if she could feel his inspiration, his stare was so intense. His whole demeanor changed. She saw the muscles in his neck tighten as his concentration rose. "A portrait shouldn't just be a snapshot of the person. It should tell a story," he explained.

"Isn't that a little personal?"

"Exactly."

"Then what kind of story?"

"Andrew Wyeth's *Christina's World* depicts a handicapped girl sitting outside on the grass looking up at a house. The snapshot is just that—a girl sitting on the ground. The story, however, depicts the struggle this person—who happened to be a neighbor—had dealing with her handicap. It's a wonderful painting." Cliff looked down. First he drew a large circle. He drew in smaller ovals where her eyes would be. He looked up before tracing in a nose and mouth. His strokes were short and swift, almost vibratory in nature. An outline quickly took shape. He spoke as he worked. "The most famous portrait ever done is full of stories. Whole books have been written about her."

"Who might that be?" Jennifer said, making sure she didn't move.

"A lady named Mona."

"Mona?"

"Mona Lisa."

This time she couldn't help but move as she laughed. "Da Vinci, right?"

Cliff nodded.

"What story is he trying to tell?"

"That's the mystery of the painting. Everyone can tell there's a story, but no one knows for sure what it is. It doesn't really matter. In reality, it's whatever you see when you look at the painting."

"So the story itself is a mystery?"

"That's right. Least, that's what all the critics say."

"What do you say?"

"I say it's a great painting that causes one to really study her. And when someone studies something, they think. And when they think, their imagination kicks into gear, followed by pleasure. To me, that's what art is all about."

Jennifer digested his words. "So you're telling me the Mona Lisa is full of stories... full of mystery."

"Just look at her eyes. You know she's saying something, you just don't know what."

"What about the other *Mona Lisa*. What stories does she hold?"

"The other *Mona Lisa*?"

"This boat."

"Oh..."

She knew she had caught him off guard. She wanted to pretend that was not her intent. She also knew it was a lie. His eyes, just like the famous lady's, were full of mystery.

"I'm not drawing the boat. I'm drawing you. So why don't you tell me your story."

God, he was good, Jennifer thought. She sat back and again brushed a piece of hair from her face.

"No, don't do that," Cliff directed. He reached over and gently placed the hair back across her forehead.

Did his hand linger longer than necessary, Jennifer wondered, or was she wishing? "I guess you want me to start at the beginning," she said.

"Whatever makes you comfortable."

Just what was her comfort level around this person—this new friend? Jennifer had only known him for a short period of time; and for all intents and purposes, knew nothing about him except that he had a boat and was an artist... an exceptional artist.

But was that all? Did she know more than she wanted to admit? His eyes emitted a gentleness she hadn't seen in a long time. His demeanor had a calmness about it. He never seemed rushed, with words or with actions. It wasn't that he was lazy or lacked energy. She imagined he was really the opposite. She guessed he was someone who could stay focused, regardless of what was happening around him. He didn't try to impress anyone— a rarity in the male species. She cautioned herself not to get too comfortable, even though she considered herself an expert at getting past the surface of people quickly.

She told herself to let time answer her questions. "My name is Jennifer Blackstone. I'm 27 years of age. I'm the only child of Elizabeth and David Blackstone. I was born and raised in Annapolis—educated in the area as well. My parents have owned the *Riverboat Inn* for nearly thirty years. I've worked in the business since I was old enough to lift a scrub brush. My parents' dream was for me to take over the place someday. My dream—or at least until lately—was always different."

"A story within a story," Cliff commented. The pencil continued to move.

"Isn't that true with most good stories?" Jennifer asked.

The artist nodded. "What was your dream?"

The model continued. "As I was growing up, I wanted to be a variety of things. First a firefighter, than a policeman, then a lawyer. Anything except feeding people all day. I thought I wanted something different, more challenging, more exciting. I finally decided on nursing. It was everything I imagined, only more."

"A *good* more or *bad* more?"

She paused. "Both." She readjusted her spine to work out a kink. "I found it very challenging. At the same time, it was very scary. In the restaurant business, your worst case scenario is getting an order wrong or dropping a tray of food. In health care, your worst case scenario is that you'll kill somebody. The opportunity to make such a mistake confronts you every day. But you take the good with the bad, prepare in earnest and hope for the best; and tell yourself you're doing a good thing.

"Then it all started to go downhill." She fiddled with her empty beer bottle, wishing now she had accepted the offer for a refill. She was feeling quite comfortable and didn't want the feeling to wear off. "I don't know how much you know about medicine, but healthcare isn't what it used to be. For one, it's become big business. For another, we no longer provide health care. We provide illness care, and at times very little of that. Small hospitals, like the one here in Annapolis where I worked, are struggling to survive."

"And with struggle comes conflict," Cliff said.

"Exactly."

Cliff continued adding marks to the page. The face on the paper, initially a faint oval, was quickly becoming recognizable. Jennifer tried not to look, but was unable to keep her curiosity in check. As her own eyes focused on the page, she gasped.

The sound caused Cliff's eyes to rise. "You okay?"

She stared at the paper and told herself to be cool, and not let too much excitement show. The drawing on the table was marvelous. It really looked like her, and in a very positive fashion. "I'm okay. Sorry."

Cliff said nothing and returned to his work. After several minutes, he said, "So you got caught up in all this conflict?"

"In more ways than one."

"There… another story within a story."

Jennifer chuckled. "If you only knew."

"Only if you want me to."

Her mouth opened and closed. There he went again, being so kind and understanding. She tipped her head to the side. "Are you always this smart?"

Cliff looked up. "I wasn't meaning to be smart," he said apologetically.

"I didn't mean smart as in smart-ass. I meant smart like intelligent. Maybe a better word would be insightful."

"I've been called a lot of things, but never that," Cliff chuckled. "Now keep your eyes up please. And keep on with your story. It's inspiring."

Readjusting her position, she did as she was told. "There really isn't much more to tell. After I left the hospital, I focused all my energy on the restaurant. Then, just a few days before I saw you at the Mitchell marina, my parents dropped the St. Michaels bombshell in my lap. I'm not sure I fully understand their motive for the project. Did they do it to keep me distracted from what had happened at the hospital? Or did they do it as a way of expanding—something I've been suggesting for a long time? Or is there a hidden agenda I don't know about?"

She thought about the last point a moment. It was the first time she had that idea. The more she mulled it over, the more she wondered. Was there a hidden agenda floating around somewhere?

Her mulling was cut short by Cliff. "Why would they want you out of Annapolis?"

He didn't miss a beat, she reaffirmed. "We get a lot of customers from the hospital, and my father is friends with a couple of the board members. While he wasn't anticipating any problems, you never know. St Michaels is a place to escape if need be."

"Not to pry, but have there been any problems?"

"On the contrary, everybody has been very kind. My friends have been concerned about my future and about my state of mind. Those who fall in the other category are glad to be rid of me. So everybody's happy, happy, happy."

"Everybody but you."

"I'm happy."

"Are you really?"

She broke her pose and leaned toward him. With somewhat of a demanding tone, she said, "What makes you think otherwise?"

"I'm an artist. I'm trained to see through things," Cliff said. He wasn't boasting.

She started to get defensive, but stopped short.

"It's okay if you're not happy. Whatever you went through must have been devastating. Many people probably would have simply cracked up. You're here trying to go on with your life. The St. Michaels project is symbolic of a new beginning."

"It's probably more of a defensive reaction than anything else," Jennifer said. She couldn't believe she was telling him all this.

"A good defense can often turn into a good offense."

"In sports maybe, but not in real life."

"Don't underestimate the lessons in sports."

"Don't underestimate the lessons in life," Jennifer corrected, straightening her posture. "I think I've told you enough."

"Let's get less intense," Cliff suggested. "What do you like to do for fun?"

"Nothing lately."

"No hobbies or anything."

"Well, I do like to—" She stopped, reminding herself she was talking too much.

He looked up. "You afraid to say?"

"Why would I be afraid?"

"You don't know me and therefore you can't fully trust me."

"Damn."

"What did I say now?"

"It's not what you said. It's what you didn't say. You didn't press me."

"A story's only good if it comes from the heart and isn't forced—just like a piece of art."

Jennifer glanced down at the table. The drawing looked finished to her, but his pencil strokes continued. "Are you working just to work now?"

"Not if the story continues."

She laughed. "You are good! You seem to be so full of wisdom, and with all due respect, at such a young age."

Cliff laughed. "Maybe I'm older than I look."

"And I'm twenty-two."

"Oh yeah, I thought you were twenty."

Jennifer laughed. "So you do have some bullshit in you."

"I have my moments." Cliff took a long swallow of beer. When it was empty, he held it up, motioning to her. Jennifer nodded. Cliff set down his pencil and went to the galley. "My uncle was the wise one. I guess some of it rubbed off on me."

"What did your uncle do?"

"He was a waterman."

"They are a bright bunch. There's an old man who lives on his skipjack right up the way. He usually says very little, but when he speaks…" The sentence finished itself in silence. Jennifer accepted the beer and took a quick swallow. She put her body back into position. "I like to write," she muttered softly. She could not believe she had just said that to him. Her writing, or lack thereof, was something she had never discussed with anyone, not even Daniel. She didn't have time to dwell on the issue as Cliff jumped right on the point.

"What do you write about?"

"I'm writing a book."

"About medicine?"

"Sort of." She chose not to elaborate.

Cliff focused back on the drawing. "I promise not to tell anyone, so if you feel comfortable, tell me about it."

She did feel comfortable, and without looking away, she started talking.

83

Phillip Rogers stared at the computer screen. He tried focusing on the naked girl before him. His mind, however, was on another figure—one just as beautiful, and one he lusted for just as much. But unlike the girl on the screen, this one was more than a fantasy. She was real. She was there, on the boat with him, probably only a few feet away in her own cabin, sleeping, lying there sensually, much like the girl on the screen.

One of the perks of being captain was the largest cabin in the crew's quarters. A second perk was a computer with unlimited Internet access. He used the Internet for its intended purpose—weather reports, reservations, ordering supplies and communication with other captains. There were other purposes as well.

A smile crossed his face as he clicked on the image to enlarge the photograph. His mind again failed to focus on the figure, his thoughts drifting back to April. Like the blonde on the screen whose legs were spread wide enticing him to come to her, he knew very little about April. Her actions were proper. Her legs were tightly closed. Why was she like that, he wondered. Why was she so standoffish? What secret was she hiding? There was definitely a mystery there. It was the mystery—the unknown—that was most attractive. He had no doubt if he could solve the mystery, everything else would fall into place… or spread apart.

"Bye bye, darling," he said quietly, clicking on the *x* to close the screen. "I have a mystery to solve." He moved the cursor to the mailbox, glanced down at a piece of paper lying on the desk and typed in the new web address. Hitting the enter key, he waited for the connection to complete.

Yes, there were some perks to being captain.

84

George Hamilton started to slam the mobile phone down on the desk, pulling up just before plastic met wood. Reminding himself to maintain control, he allowed his frustrations to come out verbally. "Asshole. When are they going to stop screwing with us and deal straight? We have them by the balls, and they still want to try and squirm away. All they're doing is wasting everyone's time."

He turned and faced his assistant, Adam Strupinsky, who was standing at the ready with a legal pad and pen. The assistant knew a flurry of orders was about to come his way. He was not disappointed.

"Get Arthur Kent on the phone, then I want James Israel. I know James is in Africa on a safari, but find him. Elephant or no elephant, tell him to get his butt back here right away. I want to meet with both of them ASAP."

Adam knew that meant within the week.

Hamilton continued. "If they want to play hardball, then we'll play, but under my rules."

Recognizing there was no more air left in his boss's lungs, therefore no more orders, Adam turned his attention to his pad where he started feverishly making notes. First on the list was the thankless task of finding someone trekking around in the African bush. Adam smiled to himself. James Israel had a satellite cellphone, and the aide just happened to know the number. "You'll be meeting here, sir?"

Hamilton contemplated the idea. He really wasn't ready to leave the islands yet. Even though his work kept busy the past couple months, he was still relaxing. He cursed to himself. "No, let's do it in New York in case we need to go back to the courts."

"I assume you'll be flying to New York."

Hamilton stared at his assistant. "How long have you been working for me, Adam?"

Adam recognized his mistake immediately. "It will be three years in a month, sir."

"Have you learned anything in that time?"

"Yes, sir."

"Care to tell me what that might be?"

Adam wanted to smile as he knew he was being played with. "Not to make assumptions, sir."

"Well, I'll be damned. There's hope for you, yet," Hamilton exclaimed. "Learn anything else?"

"If you can possibly get there by boat, then go by boat."

"Damned again."

Adam let the smile form. "I'll send the Captain in."

"There you go making assumptions again. How do you know I want to see him right now?"

"With all due respect sir, that wasn't an assumption. That was a decision on my part."

Hamilton eyed his assistant and he smiled. As Adam turned to leave, Hamilton said, "Hey, Adam."

The assistant turned.

"Bad assumption—good decision."

"Thanks, boss."

Before George Hamilton could gather his thoughts, Phillip Rogers knocked on the cabin door. He was holding two cups of coffee. He, too, had learned several lessons during his tenure with Hamilton. One was that you never entered the owner's quarters with only one cup of coffee. The captain handed a cup to his boss, saying, "You wanted to see me, sir?"

Hamilton took a sip, nodded thanks with a bob of the head. He set the cup down. That he didn't motion for Rogers to do the same meant the meeting was going to be short. "What's the status of our provisions?" the owner asked.

"Replenishing finished an hour ago," the captain answered.

"Fuel?"

Although she didn't carry full tanks because of weight, *Hamilton's Bench* sported enough fuel capacity to cross the Atlantic. "I can have her capped off without a problem."

Mr. Hamilton stared out the window. "We need to get to New York by..." He took another sip of his coffee and glanced down at the calendar on his desk. "Tell you what. I don't want to seem too anxious. Let them wonder what we're up to. Besides, we may have trouble tracking James down." He looked up. "What say we go into Annapolis first. I have a check I want to drop off to the governor, and I could go for some Maryland seafood as well."

While the check dropping didn't faze him, the thought of steamed crabs did stir the captain's taste buds. Besides, he wasn't all that fond of New York anyway. It was too expensive and the women way too stuck up.

"I haven't seen the weather reports yet this morning," Hamilton said.

One of his responsibilities as captain of *Hamilton's Bench* was to have the yacht ready to go anywhere at any time with short notice. While a quick departure didn't happen all that often, it occurred frequently enough to keep everyone on their toes. "Weather's clear all along the east coast. There's a storm trying to brew east of Bermuda, but we'll be in the Chesapeake way before it materializes, if it even does."

"How's your wrist, by the way?" Hamilton said.

The captain opened and closed his fist. "Pretty sore still."

A disgusted look crossed the owner's face. "I guess I'll have to take her out then."

The captain drew a look of shame. "Sorry, sir, but I guess you'll just have to do that."

The owner winked. "Thank you, Phillip."

The captain chucked. "It's your boat, sir." Many captains would have cringed at the thought of their owners talking the helm in open waters, much less in port. However, George Hamilton was not like other mega-yacht owners. He was hands-on, and that meant taking the wheel at times. Phillip Rogers took it all in stride. What did he really care, it was Hamilton's boat. He'd still have to keep a close eye as they pulled out. In spite of the highest possible steering technology, including state of the art bow thrusters, *Hamilton's Bench* could be troublesome to *wake-up*, as Phillip liked to say when the hull first inched away from the dock.

"That's why I have you here, to see she stays mine... and out of trouble."

The captain laughed. "Today's a good day. Winds are calm."

Phillip correctly sensed the meeting was over. He turned and headed for the door. As he did, Mr. Hamilton said, "By the way, is April up?" He hadn't heard her playing the piano yet this morning.

"She's up on the bow throwing a coat of varnish on the teak."

"Ask her to come in for a second, will you?"

"No problem." The captain left without further interruption, or wondering why the owner wanted to see one of the crew. It was a frequent occurrence, usually to simply make small talk and see how they were doing. For an owner, George Hamilton treated his crew well—too well at times, in Rogers' opinion. Only he didn't have time to worry about that now. While *Hamilton's Bench* was ready to roll, there was still a lot to do before they charged up the diesels. First on the list was to ensure all the crew was back aboard from the previous night.

He closed the door and headed down the hallway. He allowed his mind to wander to April. "Yes, she's up on the bow," he muttered under his breath. She had warded off his advances yet another night. He wasn't sure how much more of her shit he could take. He was hot for her and she knew it. He assumed she felt the same about him. After all, why wouldn't she? So why was she being such a pain? Yes, he couldn't take much more. Then he corrected the *couldn't* to *wouldn't*.

But first, he had a boat to prep.

85

Danny was headed toward the front door when the phone rang. He slowed his pace to see if the housekeeper was going to pick it up. She'd been told to answer the phone, although she still didn't seem to hear it half the time. His father called it selective hearing. He thought of it more as plain ignorance. With the third ring, he changed direction ninety degrees and headed into the living room. "Hello," he said with impatience. He looked at his watch. It was past five o'clock—time for the telemarketing calls to start. He swore if this was one of them, he'd...

"Hello," the voice on the other end said. It was a man's voice. While that didn't rule out a telemarketer, it did lower the odds. "Is June Blackstone there, please?"

The *please* caught Danny off guard. "Who's calling?"

"A friend—" There was a moment's hesitation. "From a long time ago."

"She's not available."

"May I call back later?"

The man was being so nice. Danny knew it was probably a trick, but he took the perceived bait anyway. "No, she won't be around for a few days... maybe more."

"Is she okay?"

The concern in the man's voice seemed genuine. A salesman would never take the time to ask such questions. They'd hang up and move on to the next call. Danny had learned that in one of his business classes. "Who is this?" he said in a more demanding tone.

A period of silence followed. "This is her brother, David Blackstone."

It was Danny's turn to hesitate. He didn't know whether to get angry or laugh. "She doesn't have a brother, asshole." He started to hang up the phone.

"Wait... please... wait."

Danny hesitated.

The man continued. "Is this her son—I mean stepson?"

The fact that the man was able to make the correction raised Danny's interest. The man continued. "This isn't a prank call, and I'm not selling anything. I am her brother, like I said. Although I suspect she never said anything about me. We haven't been close for many years. But I am who I say. I haven't heard from her in a long time, and I'm just calling to see if she and April are okay."

The fact that he knew about April raised the curiosity bar even higher. The fact that he assumed April was still around doubled the height. "They're fine."

"They around?"

"Like I said, June won't be back for a few days."

"Or maybe more?" the man added. "You said that, right?"

Danny was confused. While he always felt there was more to June Blackstone and April than met the eye, he never pried. Just like he never asked a lot of questions about how his stepmother and father actually met. What really bothered him was that April never said anything about this—about having an uncle. She always claimed there were no other relatives. What else was there he didn't know? Maybe there was something that would help him find her. Maybe this man, who claimed to be family, knew something he didn't. "How do I know you're really her brother, and not someone else?" he said cautiously.

"You don't. Especially if she's not there to ask. But again, I'm only calling to check on her and to see if she's okay."

"She's getting better," Danny let slip out.

"Better... has she been sick?"

Danny cursed himself for making such a mistake. At the same time, there was something about the voice, and there was the possibility of information about April. He decided to let the conversation continue. He glanced down at the caller ID box. "Where's 410?" It was a real question, and also a test to see if it scared the caller away.

"Excuse me?"

"410. That's the area code you're calling from."

The man on the other end chuckled. "Oh, 410 is in Maryland. Annapolis to be more specific."

Danny couldn't verify or deny the information.

"I'm calling from a restaurant named the *Riverboat Inn*," the man continued.

"Why you calling from there?"

"My wife and I own it."

"Oh."

"Has June been sick?" the man repeated gently.

"Sort of."

Danny sensed the man was struggling with what to say next. "Is she in a hospital?"

"Sort of."

There was more hesitation. "Well, I'm not going to pry anymore. Like I said, I'm just calling to check up on her. Sorry to bother you. And sorry to surprise you that she has a brother. Please don't blame her for that. She'll probably tell you that she *used* to have a brother."

Danny sensed that the man was about to hang up, but he hadn't found out what he wanted to know yet. "Wait…"

"Yes?"

"She is in the hospital so to speak. She's doing okay, at least from what we've been told."

"I appreciate that. And if you want to tell her I called, fine. If not, that's up to you. You obviously have caller ID, so if you want to give her the number, that would be okay, too."

Danny again sensed the conversation was about to end. "When's the last time you saw her?" he quickly said.

"In person, about seventeen years ago. She was pregnant at the time with April."

"And April?"

"What about her?"

"When was the last time you saw her?"

The man's tone conveyed a shade of sadness. "I've never seen my niece. We have a couple old photos, that's all. We used to exchange pictures at Christmas, but again, I haven't heard from her in several years. I knew she was getting married and now has a stepson. That's you, right?"

"Right," Danny said. He quickly added. "How'd you get this number?"

"June said she was moving to Worthington Valley to a man who owned the factory there, plus the last letter did have a return address. It wasn't too hard after that. I'm just lucky your number isn't unlisted."

To Danny, the explanation made sense and seemed like the truth. But what was the real reason for the call? At the same time, why was he—Danny—protecting his stepmother? After all, she had become a real pain, although Danny really couldn't blame her for falling apart. Only, did she need to go to this extreme—drinking herself to near-death several times? He was surprised his father put up with it, especially as strict as he was with his own son. But his father did, continuing to foot the bill each time she needed to dry out. When she was sober, she was a great stepmom. She was caring, friendly and would do anything he asked. They had even grown kind of close. But once April disappeared, she changed. She wasn't a mean drunk. The more she drank, the more withdrawn she became. Often, she didn't come out of her room for days. Danny felt sorry for her, but didn't understand why she drank so much. She said it was to ease the pain, but when she did drink, she said the pain was still there. It was a vicious cycle since April's disappearance. Drunk, sober, drunk, sober, rehab. This was the third time his father had put her away. His father said it was a disease—one that wasn't easily cured. Matter of fact, there really wasn't a cure, he said, just periods of sobriety. Danny knew a couple kids at school whose parents sent them away to dry out from drugs and booze. However, when they came back, they stayed sober. So what was the big deal?

Danny looked at the date on his watch. If he remembered correctly, Ms. June had about another week in rehab. Then she'd be back to try it all again. Each time she'd lasted a week or so before the cycle started all over. She once told him the only thing that would sober her up for good was for April to return home. Danny wanted that as much as anyone. He wanted it for himself. He wanted it for April. He especially wanted it for Ms. June, who he had become quite fond of her in spite of all her troubles.

An idea crossed Danny's mind. "If you're really her brother, tell me why you think she's in the hospital."

The other end of the line fell silent. Finally, "I may be able to answer that. At the same time, I may be giving away family secrets she doesn't want anyone to know."

"Like what?" Danny demanded, unable to control the curiosity.

"If I answer that, will you answer my question?"

"Which is?"

"Tell me about my sister and niece, and if they're okay."

Danny was negotiating with a man he had never met nor spoken to before, about something that he wasn't really sure he should be discussing. What if this was all a trick for some sinister reason he knew nothing about? But the desire for information about April overrode any sense of protection. "Okay, you talk first."

"What do you want to know?"

"Does April have any brothers or sisters?" What if there was an older sibling who was protecting her.

"No," the man said.

"You sure?"

"We haven't been in touch lately, and we have had our differences over the years, but we've never lied to one another. April is her only child."

Ms. June never said or did anything that led one to believe she was ever lying. That was different than not telling the whole truth. "What secrets were you referring to?" Danny said.

The man hesitated. "She used to drink a lot at times, especially when she was upset. You said she wasn't home and was getting better. You also said she was in a hospital *sort of*. So my guess is she's in rehab somewhere."

"Maybe you're lucky."

"Sometimes a little knowledge increases one's luck," the man said.

Danny hesitated. "She's doing okay. She should be home in another week."

"What about April?" the man said.

"She's away, too."

"She okay?"

"Last we heard, she was." That wasn't a lie.

"When was that?"

He suddenly felt very nervous. If the man knew something about April, he would have told it by now. On the other hand, if he was looking for information for some alternative reason.

Danny looked down at his watch. "Look mister, I gotta go. I'll tell Ms. June you called, okay?"

He hung up the phone without waiting for an answer. He waited to see if the phone rang again. When it didn't, he turned and walked out the door.

It was the first anyone had talked about April in a long time. Even in his own house, the topic had dropped down to an occasional wailing from her mother. Talk around town had dried up as the consensus was that she had perished somewhere in the mountains. Atlantic City was never mentioned. He wanted to believe she'd surface someday, although he was more and more concerned she didn't want to be found. While it hurt to think that way, he certainly understood the strategy. Once you've escaped, stay escaped. Contact with the past would only lead to trouble. Still, he told himself to keep thinking positive.

And so he did.

86

David Blackstone placed the receiver back in its cradle. He stared at the phone before looking up at his wife who was standing at the desk across from him.

"Sounds like you at least spoke to someone this time," Elizabeth Blackstone said. "June's stepson?

"Apparently so," her husband said. "Sounds like June's in rehab, which isn't a surprise. He said she's okay, though." He looked across the room to collect his thoughts. "There's something else—something about April."

"And?"

David Blackstone hesitated. "I don't think he knows where she is."

"Really!"

"Really… or maybe I'm reading too much into it."

"Well, as I see it, you have a couple choices," his wife said. "You can check out the rehab hospitals in the area, although I doubt they'll give you much information. Or you can wait a few days and call again. The boy talked to you once. Maybe he'll talk to you again."

"Maybe."

"At least you're trying, David. That's all you can do. That's all I asked."

Elizabeth Blackstone had been after her husband for over a year to try and make contact with his sister. He had made a couple of calls over the recent months. However, until today, he had no success. "It's a start," she encouraged.

He nodded in acknowledgement. "But something just doesn't feel right."

"What doesn't feel right is you're losing your stubborn streak."

David Blackstone smiled. "Maybe you're right, dear."

But there were other thoughts.

87

George Hamilton watched as Rogers made his way out of the office. Hamilton took a sip of coffee and took a deep breath. His gut was telling him there was a problem brewing with his captain. He had no hard evidence but sensed it had to do with April. In his profession, one's sixth sense was often the true reason for success.

Phillip Rogers was a great captain, one of the best boat handlers in the business. He was good with the crew, willing to teach and was magically fair in his handling of conflicts and disciplinary issues. He also knew how to manage the owner's ego. Luckily, Hamilton's own ego was well encapsulated and allowed to surface only when advantageous to his business dealings. The ship's captain also served as ambassador for Hamilton. Phillip Rogers was great at public relations, and was especially good with the ladies.

At times, too good, Hamilton thought.

Unlike many mega-yacht owners, Hamilton took an active role in the boat's operation. He was all over the ship all the time, and often overheard conversations not meant for his ears. Most of these conversations dealt with petty stuff. A recurring theme dealt with Rogers's inability to control his zipper. To Hamilton, there was a big difference between a loose zipper and one that was uncontrolled. Most crew members lived for the moment, planned not and dreamed only about the next time they'd get laid. Not a bad way to live, if you could get away with it. But with Rogers—

A knock on the door interrupted his thoughts. "Come in," he said, rising to his feet.

April entered the office, closing the door behind her. Hamilton could tell her hair had been patted down with varnish-coated hands. There were streaks of varnish across her face. She wore the uniform shirt of the day and khaki shorts. Her feet were covered in a pair of nearly new boating shoes. He could see why Rogers would be attracted to her. She was, even in such a messy state, an attractive girl. And when transformed into the yacht's resident pianist, she was quite stunning. "Afternoon, April. How you doing?" he said.

She stepped forward. "Fine, sir, thanks."

"Have a seat." He motioned to one of the leather chairs across from the desk.

"Thank you, but I'm pretty sweaty. Besides, I've been varnishing."

Hamilton noticed her shirt had more wet areas than dry. "Varnishing the boat or yourself?"

The young girl blushed. "I have to learn to keep my face above the railing."

Hamilton laughed. "I wouldn't change how you do it. The teak looks great. The whole boat does for that matter."

"Thank you."

Hamilton came around to the front and leaned against the desk. "So, how's everything going for you here?"

April smiled. "Great. I'm having a wonderful time. Everyone's been so nice, and I'm learning a lot. I've even gotten to steer the boat some." Her hand flew to her mouth trying to catch the words before they escaped.

Sensing her panic, Hamilton said, "That's okay. They even let me drive sometimes."

Her smile returned.

"You doing any navigating?"

"I've gone through all the piloting and advanced piloting material," April said. "I know how to chart our position and plot a course. I know the rules of the road and all the buoys. I'm getting GPS down, too."

"Any celestial work?"

"Some, but we can only do that at sea."

"You're right there."

"It's hard."

Hamilton gave her a reassuring nod. "I'm sure you'll do just fine. Anyone that can play the piano like you can surely master a sextant."

"Thank you."

"You had no boating experience before this?" Hamilton continued.

"Not that I recall."

Hamilton laughed. "I think you'd remember if you were ever out on a boat."

"Yeah, guess so—I mean yes, sir."

"Speaking of the piano, do you have everything you need?"

"Yes, sir. And thanks for all the books on music theory. I can get a lot off the Internet, too!"

"Are you getting enough practice time?"

"There's never enough time for that, but it's more than I've had before."

Hamilton resisted the urge to pursue the *before*. "If you need anything, let me know. We'll be leaving here today, so maybe you'll get to drive the boat some more."

"Leaving… Where are we—or rather, may I ask where we're going?"

"You can ask me anything at any time," Hamilton said. He silently wished she'd return the gesture. There was very little he knew about her. Name, rank and serial number—like she was a prisoner, not aboard the boat, but within herself. He was sure there was a lot of unseen baggage aboard *Hamilton's Bench*. He learned a long time ago that not knowing something was often better than knowing. He paused to make sure he had eye contact. "We're heading north to New York City. We're making a stop in Annapolis first. Maryland's governor is up for reelection and he's a good friend. I plan to do a little fundraising for him."

He watched as she struggled, but failed to keep her face from turning pale. One's normal response would be to ask, "Are you okay?" Instead, he said with a fatherly voice, "If there's anything you need, or want to talk about, please don't hesitate. It's my policy not to pry into the personal lives of the crew, so long as it doesn't interfere with their work. All I care about is if we're treating you fairly and you're doing the same for us. But with you, I have to admit, there's a greater interest. And I don't mean anything bad about that either. You have a talent… a gift."

The blood rushed back to April's face as her paleness turned to a blush.

Hamilton continued. "So, if there's ever anything you need."

"Thank you," April said. She straightened her posture. "I'd better be getting my stuff cleaned up. I imagine Mr. Rogers will want to leave right away to take advantage of the outgoing tide."

Hamilton was impressed that she knew the tide schedules. "That'll be fine. Thanks for stopping by."

"Thank you."

Hamilton watched as April left the office. Her steps were short and quick. He guessed her mind was running at the same speed. As he feared, she showed a negative reaction to hearing they were returning stateside. Usually the crew, regardless of where they were, looked forward to returning home. April conveyed an opposite reaction. He wondered why. What was the mystery behind this girl who one night showed up and saved the party, and returned the next day a member of the crew? She molded quickly to life aboard the boat. She was hard working, respectful to a fault and got along with everyone. In return, they responded positively to her. Hamilton never overheard anything negative about *Hamilton's Bench's* resident pianist. She was friendly, yet she never warmed up to anyone. She always kept her distance. The distance was showing no sign of shortening.

Walking back to his chair, Hamilton reminded himself he had become successful by getting to the facts and listening to his instincts. After all, why would she nearly faint when hearing they were heading back to the United States? He debated what to do, deciding for now to do nothing. At the same time, another idea came to mind. Aloud, he said, "Annapolis, Maryland—just a hop, skip and a jump from Baltimore, the home of—"

Just then the boat moved so the sun reflected sharply off the teak railing. He raised a hand over his eyebrows as the light pained his eyes.

"You want to offer an opinion?" Hamilton said with a laugh. An educated man beyond need, he still had a few peculiar beliefs. One was that *Hamilton's Bench*, the one true lady in his life, had a mind of her own. "So you think Baltimore's a good idea, huh?"

The reflection grew brighter.

88

April stared at the ceiling. Her eyes remained unfocused, her attention on the motion of the boat. For the past hour, they had been in a following sea. Long deep swells caught *Hamilton's Bench* by her stern, sweeping her forward and causing her to roll gently from side to side. Equipped with stabilizers, *Hamilton's Bench* rode the waves with a smooth, steady motion as she journeyed on a northwest course towards the mouth of the Chesapeake Bay.

Initially, April found it frightening to lie in her bunk and listen to the sound of the boat cutting through the water. The fear was accentuated when she learned her cabin was actually below the water's surface. She never thought much about death, but it crossed her mind the first few nights aboard *Hamilton's Bench*. She imagined it would be sudden, scary… and very wet. With time, her fears subsided, replaced by a true love of being close to the sea. Usually after a full day, sleep was easy. Tonight, however, sleep was hard coming. The crew was excited about getting back to the states. The trip up the eastern seaboard had been uneventful. The weather remained favorable and the yacht performed flawlessly. There were no guests aboard, so the crew was able to relax and enjoy the trip. Mr. Hamilton originally told them they would only be in Annapolis a couple days, but on the way, he reported they'd be there at least a week. Several of the crew planned to go home a few days, and where home was a long distance away, George Hamilton offered to pay the airfare. There was a big party planned for the Governor of Maryland. April, Louis, the captain and Cookie (the chef) were asked to remain behind. When Phillip Rogers asked about her plans, she shrugged it off saying she didn't mind staying aboard. It would give her more time to practice the piano. Playing underway could be a challenge.

For the first several months aboard *Hamilton's Bench*, April looked little to the future, simply being thankful she had escaped the past. As her skills improved and her comfort level aboard her new home followed, thinking about the past took less and less of her time. She was better able to look ahead. Still, future thinking focused on the next day, the next watch, the next meal, the next time at the piano or the next time for sleep. She fell easily into a moment to moment lifestyle. Time passed quicker when what you looked forward to was not far away.

Future moment to moment thinking also caused the same in reverse. A law of physics says that for every action, there's an equal and opposite reaction. One could speculate that the mind works in a similar fashion. You think backwards only to the same degree you think forward. For April Whiterock, the past stopped at whatever happened yesterday. It helped prevent loneliness, homesickness and the conglomeration of separation issues she and other crew members faced.

April knew *Hamilton's Bench* was a bridge from the past to the future. The length of the bridge or how long it would take to cross were irrelevant. She was happy for the most part. She liked what she was doing as she continued mastering the skills of a crewman, and she had her music. Considering the past, she had few concerns, except for one thing—*Hamilton's Bench's* captain. Phillip Rogers's questions were getting more personal and more intense. She knew the day would come when she'd have to leave *Hamilton's Bench*. She surmised that their statewide destination and Rogers's curiosity might demand a sooner than desired departure. The question was how and when. Mr. Hamilton had been very good to her during her tenure. She had grown fond of him and concluded the feeling was mutual. If she left, she wanted to do it the right way. And there laid the conflict. The right way may not be the best way, especially if the goal was to make a clean break and disappear again.

Listening to the water pound against the hull, April told herself not to make a hasty decision. She liked what she was doing. She was content. She knew she could be worse off. She trusted her instincts and believed she'd know when the time was right.

89

The light breeze felt good coming across the bow of the *Mona Lisa*. Without it, the heat index would be over a hundred. Cliff didn't mind the weather, but the points of his drawing pencils softened in the heat, making detailed work difficult along with the threat of water dripping from his forehead. For the past couple of days, he simply prepared partials, completing them at night when the heat of the day had passed.

He slid around a little and wiggled his toes to get the circulation back. He focused back on the drawing in his lap. The scene depicted a mother duck with five ducklings swimming across the water. They seemed so small in contrast to the boat in the background that cast a long shadow across their path. Was the boat a threat or a haven for food and shelter? The five ducklings swam in a haphazard fashion, oblivious to any danger around them. The mother exhibited a different attitude. Not only did her head motion show concern, her feathers were raised in encouragement for her offspring to hurry along. The scene was rather humorous. Later, when people saw the finished drawing, they always came away with a smile. They'd want to know if the ducklings made it across the water safely. It amazed Cliff how compassionate people of all ages became when seeing a flock of baby ducks in perceived danger.

He worked on the piece until satisfied the details could be added later. He turned to a blank page and looked up as two high performance speedboats made their way out of the narrow inlet. The noise woke Chessie from a sound sleep. She raised her head, saw what disturbed her dreams and lay down without so much as a whimper. Cliff reached over and patted her on the neck. "I know, girl, they're ruining the atmosphere."

Cliff followed the boats as they passed, paying special attention to the bikini clad girls on the foredeck. "Babes on the bow," his uncle would always call out when such a site approached *Rose Bud*. He would then go on to joke that they (the girls) were the most expensive accessories on the boat. Cliff forced a chuckle to block a wave of sadness. "Babes on the bow," he muttered quietly. He pulled his eyes away, wishing his uncle were there to share in the moment.

Adjusting his position, Cliff scanned the harbor. His eyes stopped at the dock directly across from the *Mona Lisa*. The large motor yacht that cast the shadow across the ducklings was side tied at the T head. The breeze was light in the narrow waterway. The current, however, was strong, causing the boat to pull against her mooring lines. The sun reflected off the hull with a painful glare. The bow lay in contrast to the old wooden bulkhead at the end of the pier. It was this contrast that caught Cliff's attention. Pencil in hand, the artist waited patiently until the boat moved enough to remove the glare. While the colors were varied and vibrant, the excessive sunlight turned the colors into a variety of grays. It was these shadows and the contrast in textures Cliff strove to capture.

He worked quickly, laying down three partials in less than an hour. He set the drawings aside and pulled the camera bag towards him. Normally, he would have moved around, shooting the scenes from various angles. However, he was able to remain put as both the *Mona Lisa* and the yacht moved enough to give him a variety of shots. While each particular image was close to the one before it, the shadows cast by the sun gave each a uniqueness he'd only be able to fully appreciate when the film was developed.

Satisfied he had studied the scene to its fullest, he packed the cameras away and rose to his feet. He looked up at the yacht. She had snuck into the harbor sometime during the night. It was one of the most impressive boats he had ever seen. He started to look away when he saw movement up on the bow. He squinted to help fight off the sun. A female figure came into focus. She had a rag and bucket in her hand. Bending over the railing, she started wiping down the wood.

She looked so small, so petite against the backdrop of the yacht. He made the analogy of the painter on the Bay Bridge that had captured his imagination earlier in the summer. Such a small human figure contrasted against such a large inanimate structure. "Babe on the bow," he said softly. He sat back down and was pulling out his camera when he noticed the girl had looked up from her own work. She stared at him, her facial expression almost blank. He grabbed the Nikon with the long range lens and zoomed in on her.

Her sun bleached hair was pulled back in a ponytail. She wore a red polo shirt and khaki shorts. She was petite, pretty and nicely built. Both arms and legs looked well formed and strong. But it was her face that drew his attention the most. She was really quite beautiful.

Cliff told himself to stop looking and start shooting. He adjusted the focus a couple of notches. His index finger reached for the shutter button. He moved slightly to the left to center the shot. He was about to fire the shutter when the girl's expression suddenly changed. She had obviously noticed him. Only instead of a smile and a wave, he saw a look of fear. Startled by her reaction, he hesitated before pushing the button. It was enough time for her to turn away. The opportunity was lost. Cliff watched as she disappeared from view.

Her behavior was peculiar, but he didn't give it much thought. Some people just didn't like their pictures taken. It would have made a good shot, though. After all, Jennifer told him he needed more humans in his portfolio.

Putting his camera away, he nudged Chessie in the side. She stood up and shook out her fur. Cliff looked at Chessie as she waited to go ashore. "I know girl," Cliff said. "I got the best of the two deals 'cause I got you."

A few minutes later the duo were making their way up Main Street towards the Capital Building. The girl on the yacht was a thing of the past.

Or so he thought.

90

April pressed her back against the portside bulkhead. Sweat from her forehead stung her eyes as she wiped her face with the back of her hand. She had been sweating before. The water now rushed from her pores. Hyperventilating, she sucked in a couple deep breaths. She peered around the corner and realized she left the bucket sitting beside the rail. She'd have to go and get it; but for now, the panic in her chest prevented her from moving.

She took in another deep breath, at the same time scolding herself for such a reaction. It was simply a guy taking a picture. What was wrong with that? After all, it wasn't everyday you got to see something like *Hamilton's Bench*. She learned that down in the Bahamas. People, even those with money, were impressed with the yacht—a yacht that made the top ten list every year. She told herself she'd better get used to the photography. It didn't bother her in the Bahamas. There were plenty of tourists who stopped by to take a picture or two. Only this time, there was a difference. The guy on the sailboat had focused the camera directly on her.

Why was he taking *her* picture? More importantly, why had she reacted so strongly? (Little did she know, the guy on the sailboat wasn't the only one taking her picture at that particular moment.) She mulled the question around as she continued to get her breathing under control. She decided the *why* of the picture was a random act on his part, not directed at her personally. As to the *why* of her behavior, she decided she simply overreacted. She told herself numerous times on the trip from the Bahamas that she couldn't act differently once back in the states. Others would notice. She did worry when they had to clear customs coming up the bay, but Mr. Hamilton took care of that by simply radioing into the Coast Guard office in Annapolis. There were no questions. There were no problems.

Again, why had she panicked? It had been over a year and her appearance had changed. She was totally tanned, and she had actually gained a few pounds—not fat, she told herself. She was more muscular, her body having filled out from the physical work. She certainly looked the part of a crewman. She no longer looked like the short skinny girl from—

She cut the thought off and scolded herself for her behavior and for thinking about the past. She reminded herself that the way to raise suspicion was to act suspiciously.

Breaking her train of thought, Mr. Hamilton appeared from the side door of the pilot house. He no doubt had seen the whole thing. April's mind turned on its fight or flight mode. She struggled to come up with an appropriate response to the unavoidable question. A lesson from Danny came to mind: Be proactive, not reactive.

As Mr. Hamilton's mouth opened to ask the question she knew was coming, April said, "That was one of the biggest bees I've ever seen. Did you see it?"

George Hamilton's mouth closed. April let out a slow breath as he spoke. "I was wondering what happened. I was in the pilot house looking at the ship's log when I saw you fly by like a bat out of hell. A big bee, huh?"

"A bee, or something like that. Whatever it was, it wasn't happy to see me."

"Did it get you?"

"No… no."

Hamilton hesitated. "Okay then. Just be careful. We can spray the deck if need be."

"I'll let you know if I see any more."

"You allergic?"

It was April's turn to hesitate. "I don't know. I've never been stung. Where I come fr—" She stopped short. Her face reddened.

The fatherly smile he was able to turn on so quickly crossed Hamilton's face. "You know, April, you can talk to me if you want." He chose not to push the point. He turned and went back into the pilot house.

April again focused on getting the sense of panic under control. They'd been in Annapolis less that a day and she was already feeling pressure. Didn't Danny tell her the sixth sense was the most important?

91

George Hamilton headed back to the pilot house without further comment. His mind swirled with thoughts over what he saw. Something obviously frightened April. Was she really startled by a bee? Her back was to him. When she turned, her expression was fear—more than what he would expect from someone trying to get away from a bug—even a big bug. He was an expert at reading people and knowing when they were telling the truth. He had doubts about her big bee story. He did give her credit for quick thinking, however.

He stared out the forward window. There was a lot he didn't know about April, but as he told her recently, he made it a policy not to interfere in the crew's personal life so long as their personal life didn't interfere with their work. In his eight years of owning *Hamilton's Bench*, he had never wavered in that attitude… until now. There was something about April that bothered him, that challenged his principle of hands-off. His curiosity was high. What was the mystery surrounding April? What had frightened her so? He told himself not to go there, with *there* being defined as sticking his nose where it didn't belong.

Only he had already done that, hadn't he? A couple of his people were looking into her background—nothing too deep—just nudging around to see what they could find. Hamilton called it a gentle investigation. It was okay to turn the stones over. Just don't drop them back too hard. So far, they had found nothing. Her background was a mystery. It was as if she didn't exist until that night in Atlantic City.

Hamilton was staring across the harbor when his cellphone buzzed. He looked at the number and smiled. He picked up the phone and pushed the green button "Afternoon, Governor."

92

The bounty hunter stopped in the middle of the bridge over Black Creek. He propped both elbows atop the concrete wall. He pulled the bill of his hat down to minimize the glare of the sun. He squinted and pulled the camera in tighter against his chest. He supported the body of the camera with one hand, the heavy zoom lens with the other. His waist pivoted slowly from left to right as he scanned the length of the boat. He ignored the impulse to simply stare, reminding himself he had work to do. He did allow himself the thought that maybe… just maybe if he had a couple lucky breaks… someday he could own such a boat.

He chuckled to himself. "It would take more than a couple of breaks."

He found the girl by accident—a common occurrence in his profession as a bounty hunter.

He had taken a rare day off to go fishing on the Chesapeake with a couple of buddies. It was hot, the waters calm and the fish *unhungry*, so he spent the bulk of the time drinking beer and daydreaming about catching the big one. In his profession, big catches meant big rewards. It was after the fourth or fifth beer that he caught movement out of the corner of his eye. He sat up and looked into the sun-glared horizon. A boat came into view. A very big boat. A private yacht. A *beautiful* private yacht. Well over a hundred feet. His daydreaming intensified. "Half that size would do," he mouthed, pulling out a pair of binoculars.

It was while drooling over this magnificent structure that he noticed a figure out on the bow. Closer inspection showed this to be an attractive young girl. She appeared to be working on the teak railing. The binoculars stayed focused longer than normal as both boat and girl added a spot of joy to what so far was proving to be a boring day. He was pleased at what he saw.

That is, until she turned his way and his pleasure turned to shock. It was a face he recognized. She was not someone he knew personally, but rather, a face from his work— one of many burned into his photograph-filled mind. He struggled to pull up the information that had crossed his computer screen more than once over the past year. A picture with a reward attached to it. A rather big reward if he remembered correctly. Also, a reward that had been increasing over time. This meant there was a certain level of desperation to find her, which meant to the trained mind of the bounty hunter, the price was not fixed in stone. After all, all things in life were negotiable.

His shock cleared. The smile returned. A boring day had suddenly turned into one of great potential. The fish, unknowingly, just started biting.

Feigning a need to get out of the heat, the bounty hunter went into the cabin and laid across a bench. He learned from the chattering on the marine radio that the yacht's name was *Hamilton's Bench* and she was headed for Annapolis. While the bounty hunter had planned to spend the night in the arms of a babe he had met at a bar the previous evening, those plans now changed—not uncommon in his profession. He'd be heading towards Maryland's capital as soon as they reached shore.

He smiled again, thinking that you never know what you're going to catch when you went fishing.

He arrived in Annapolis shortly before ten. He parked in a garage near the harbor and walked to the water's edge. *Hamilton's Bench* was not hard to spot as she sat majestically against the harbor's south bulkhead. There was no crew on deck. They had either disappeared inside to get out of the heat, or had gone into town to find some heat.

The bounty hunter spent the next couple hours roaming the pubs and bars in the area, looking and listening for information about the girl. His arrival in Annapolis was delayed because after the fishing trip he stopped by his office where he verified what he thought earlier. Her name was April Blackstone. She was from a town in Ohio named Worthington Valley. She was wanted for questioning in the shooting of the sheriff's son— a sheriff whom he had actually worked with in the past. As he studied the information on his computer screen, three areas of interest were noted. First, the reward for information leading to her had again been raised. Second, there was not an actual warrant out for her arrest. Finally, she had been missing for over a year.

And now he had her.

Disappointing, yet not surprising, he saw no sign of the girl. Nor did he hear anything about her or any other crew members. He contemplated flashing her photograph around, but decided to keep a low profile until he noticed a man in his early to mid-thirties trying desperately to pick up a girl next to him at a bar.

He was hovering over her like a vulture, only she wasn't interested in serving as his dinner for the evening. The man was drunk. The girl was getting agitated. Finally, the girl was able to slip under the man's arm and escape out the door. The man ordered another drink in frustration. Besides being drunk, the man possessed another interesting feature. He was dressed in a captain's uniform, and not the military variety.

The bounty hunter took the girl's seat, ordered a beer for himself and counted patiently to a hundred. As the bounty hunter hoped, the man in the captain's uniform spoke first. The bounty hunter listened with compassion, spoke a few words of support, asked a few questions and slowly drew out the information he wanted.

After a short night, the bounty hunter found himself perched on the bridge over Black Creek. He wished he was on the inside of the boat looking out instead of the outside looking in, which at the moment was unproductive. He couldn't penetrate the tinted windows, even with one of the most powerful zoom lenses on the market,

He took a deep breath and told himself to stop complaining, remembering an assignment the winter before, and how cold he was on that job. He swore he'd never get into that position again. But he did a few weeks later on a similar project because the money was too good.

He looked away, resting his eyes. His face pushed back into the camera. Again, he scanned the boat bow to stern. He was about to look away when he saw movement. He focused the lens. A door opened and a figure stepped out. It was a girl. She was dressed in shorts and a tee shirt. She carried a bucket and a brush. She moved up toward the bow and set the cleaning instruments down. He zoomed in tighter on her face. His heart quickened as her face came into view. There was no doubt, it was her—April Blackstone—alias April Whiterock.

The bounty hunter closed his eyes and concentrated on his hands. He still got excited when he finally spotted his prey. His hands listened, and the jitteriness subsided. His eyes opened, his finger hit the shutter button and several quick shots were taken. The sound of the automatic winding mechanism sang in his ear. He continued until she turned her back to him. He waited patiently for her face to reappear. He remained focused on her body, zooming in on her backside as she bent over. He was about to take a couple shots of her rear when she straightened up. She seemed to look out across the water before suddenly spinning around. This time the angelic look was replaced by a look of fear. Something had startled her. The shutter started clicking again as she moved in his direction. Afraid she might see him, he lowered the camera and turned away. He resisted the urge to look back, telling himself the job was done. The fish was in the boat.

93

The weather had cooled to the low nineties. Better than the above a hundred earlier in the week. A cold front had moved through and it was hoped the change would produce some needed rain, but the weather gurus nixed the thought and recommended people keep doing their rain dances. A breeze swirled around the harbor, although this offered little solace to those outside braving the heat.

Inside the *Riverboat Inn*, the climate was the same as always—a crisp seventy-two degrees. The two oversized compressors on the roof ran constantly, but were keeping up. Monthly checks by the service contractor ensured an adequate supply of coolant. The Blackstones believed the atmosphere on first entry was one of the most important aspects of the entire restaurant. The extra money spent to ensure a constant environment was spent without reservation, although Mr. Blackstone still let out a stream of profanities each month when the electric bill arrived.

Jennifer's apartment above the restaurant was a different story. It was far from the comfort of the restaurant below as the vent to the apartment sat the end of the duct system. Jennifer really didn't care as long as there was some semblance of coolness so she could sleep at night. The heat during the day didn't bother her. She reminded herself that winter was only a few months away and then she'd be complaining about the cold again. She'd take the heat over the cold any day.

She stood, her arms folded across her chest, and gazed across the harbor. It was high noon. On a normal summer day, the whole area would fill with people enjoying their lunch break. Today, even with the drop in temperature, people stayed in. Across the way, the outside bar was busy, but lighter than usual. She knew that would change as the weekend forecast called for the temperature to continue dropping. There were plenty of boats in the anchorage, with a few moving in and out of the harbor. Her eyes dropped down to the city docks below the restaurant. No matter what the weather, they were always full. She spotted the *Mona Lisa*. The boat swayed gently in the breeze, the only exercise the sailboat had in several days.

Jennifer squinted through the glare coming off the glass. She could make out Cliff sitting cross legged on the bow. He had a drawing pad sitting across his knees. Chessie was sprawled out beside him. Cliff's sun-bleached hair moved gently in the breeze. He was wearing his usual nondescript tee shirt and khaki shorts. While she couldn't tell for sure, she suspected he was barefoot. He'd joked the evening before that the only time he wore shoes was when it was required by law.

"The evening before…" she mouthed silently. A shiver went up her spine. She squeezed her arms together. It was the third evening out of four she had stopped by after work. On each occasion, she just happened to be out for a walk. On each occasion, he welcomed her aboard without hesitation. He did a drawing of her each night—a different angle of her physique. On each occasion, her stay lengthened, until the night before, she had barely gotten home before sunrise.

Did each drawing actually take that long to do? She chuckled to herself. Who was she trying to kid? In spite of their age difference, and in spite of everything else going on in her life, she was attracted to him. Did he feel the same about her? If he did, he hadn't shown or said anything yet. He was quiet, soft spoken and wavered little from a steady, cheerful yet polite demeanor, even after a few beers. Most people's personalities, at least from Jennifer's experience, changed with alcohol. However, like a ship at sea, Cliff followed the motto: steady as she goes. It was this uniqueness, this willingness to be different, that attracted her to him. At least he wasn't repulsed by her banging on the side of his boat every night. And in a way, she hoped he didn't feel anything one way or the other. She certainly didn't have the time for such a thing, nor the energy. Still, the possibilities… The fantasies brought a smile to her face.

And that day in the shower…

She stepped back from the window, but was unable to pull her eyes away from the boat. She was kidding herself when she wished he wasn't interested. If anything, she was beginning to feel a sense of disappointment. What was it about him that drew out these responses? There had to be something else. Yes, he was good looking. Then again, she was confronted by that every day in the restaurant. But he wasn't an asshole like most of the guys she knew. He was kind, soft spoken and seemed very caring—one emotional response that did manage to seep out. And perhaps most of all, he possessed a very rare quality—he had excellent listening skills.

So in terms of how she and her fellow nurses usually described men, he was a keeper. She laughed aloud. "Before you keep 'em, you have to catch 'em."

Her laughter turned to a sense of melancholy. She suddenly felt lonely as she fought back the tears. She was over the issues at the hospital, that void was filled by her work at the restaurant. She even felt like she was over Daniel. But the problem—there was no one to replace him. That void had yet to be filled. That void tore at her like the ultimate knife.

She yearned to be held, to be touched, to touch back. She yearned to be kissed, to be fondled, to fondle back. She yearned to—

"Stop it," she scolded.

Her eyes blurred from tears as she struggled to keep focused on the *Mona Lisa.*

"Are you really all that unhappy?" she asked herself. "Or are you just feeling sorry for yourself?" She never afforded anyone the option of self-pity in the ER. It was a destructive force that could eat you alive. It was one of the strongest barriers to the road of recovery, whether the damage was physical, emotional or both. Why was she allowing it to happen to her?

"You're not," she said aloud.

She held her eyes shut for a long blink before wiping away the tears. She had to admit, except for this momentary regression, she was feeling a little better the past few days. The reason came back into focus.

Except for his right hand moving across the drawing pad, Cliff had not budged.

94

The white domed rotunda of the Maryland State House rose high above the tree line. By boat or by land, it was one of the first landmarks seen when approaching Annapolis. Cliff kept his eye on the structure as he made his way up the hill on Main Street. A hundred yards from the harbor, he stopped. He lowered his head to the ground to sharpen the angle from the street level. He crossed the street and repeated the action. It was a great shot with the dome seeming to sit right atop the trees—except for one thing. The leaf filled trees caused the mid-portion of the scene to blend together in a sea of green. Cliff decided it would be a fantastic study in the fall when the trees wore their autumn colors. For now, it was a wash. The artist filed the idea away for later use. It was a common practice. He often saw interesting scenes to either draw or photograph, but the lighting wasn't right or the season was wrong. Cliff stood up and continued his climb. His heart beat faster, his palms moistened. He blamed it on the heat and the leather case he was carrying. He was dressed in long pants and a polo shirt. He even wore socks with his boating shoes. All this was an easy excuse for his reaction, but he knew that was a bunch of bull. The bottom line, he was nervous. After all, it wasn't every day you made a personal delivery to the governor.

Climbing what seemed like a Mt. Everest of steps, Cliff entered the building's vast lobby. He inquired at the information desk how to get to the governor's office. A tall muscular security guard eyed him. The *Do you have an appointment?* question followed. Cliff replied in the affirmative and gave his name. A list was checked, a phone call made, security was cleared and the young artist was on his way up in a private elevator escorted by yet another guard.

Cliff followed the guard down a long hallway filled with people moving in all directions, each seemingly in a hurry and each with a bundle of papers in hand. Cliff compared them to people in a mall during a shopping frenzy, only here political agendas were being bought and sold, not hats and mittens. Cliff knew very little about politics except what he heard on the radio and what his uncle used to tell him. His uncle would go on tirades every time something happened in Annapolis that affected his ability to practice his trade, whether it be a discussion on restricting crabbing or a proposal that relaxed water pollution. Cliff listened to these sermons intently, realizing there were usually two sides to every story—sometimes even three. Cliff did take time before his visit to do a little research. He learned Governor Wilson was a strong supporter of the environment—a fact that would surely please his uncle.

They entered the outer office of the governor's suite. It contained several desks. Behind each sat a secretary-type person either on the phone or working at a computer. The security guard said something to one of the girls who immediately rose to her feet and motioned for Cliff to follow. The artist was led through yet another set of doors into a large office. The room reeked of political power. A large wooden desk sat in the far center of the heavily carpeted floor. The far wall contained a large window overlooking Annapolis in the direction of the harbor. While it was difficult to see the water because of all the foliage on the trees, Cliff had no doubt it was a spectacular view in the fall and winter. It was the view Cliff saw coming up the hill in reverse. On each side of the window was a Maryland and U.S. flag respectively. The other three walls were covered with photographs, each one with the governor and some other famous person or persons. Cliff recognized a few, including the previous President of the United States. Most, however, were foreign to him. He assumed they were all important. They had *that* look.

A sitting area was left of the desk with two facing couches and several chairs. A glass table in the middle held several books about Maryland. Governor Wilson was sitting there talking on the phone when Cliff entered. He held up his hand to indicate he'd be finished in a moment, which he was. A wide smile crossed his face as he rose to his feet. "Mr. Davidson, thanks so much for coming." He walked over and shook Cliff's hand. The boy noticed the firm grip, remembering that his uncle always told him a firm grip meant a sincere hello. A side door opened and Jane Syzeman walked into the room. She, too, smiled brightly and took Cliff's hand. This was not quite the grip of the Governor's, yet strong.

"Can I get you anything, Cliff? Soda? Coffee?" the Governor asked. "It is okay if I call you Cliff?"

Cliff nodded. "Yes sir, and no, thanks, I'm fine."

"How 'bout you Jane?"

"A cold beer and a shot of bourbon."

The governor smiled. "That bad an afternoon, huh?"

"Just the house leadership acting like fools again."

"The slots bill?"

"Yes, sir. They're threatening to hold it up if we don't restrict the locations."

The governor paused. "Well, that is some progress, isn't it?"

"You can look at it that way."

The governor turned his attention to Cliff. "You see son, that's a fine example of looking at a glass of water. Is it half full, or half empty? While I tend to look on the positive side of things, Jane here tends to do the latter."

"That's my job, sir," the chief aide injected.

"That it is, and you do it very well."

Jane turned and looked at Cliff. "I don't know how much you know about Maryland's Governor, Cliff, but he's known for his heart of gold. Some say he's too soft and lets people run all over him. So he surrounds himself with people like me to do his dirty work."

Cliff started to say something, but thought better of it.

The governor noticed this. "Go ahead, son. Say what's on your mind."

"My uncle used to tell me that a heart of gold is much more powerful than a sword of steel."

"Your uncle sounds like he was a very bright man."

"Thank you, sir."

Governor Wilson motioned for them to all be seated. He leaned back in his chair. "Anyway, Where's your dog... Chelsea, wasn't it?"

"Chessie," Cliff politely corrected. "She's on the boat."

"Why?"

The question caught Cliff off guard. Ms. Syzeman came to the rescue. "The invitation said Cliff Davidson, not Cliff Davidson and friend, sir."

The Governor laughed. "Next time you bring the dog, okay?"

Cliff nodded and swallowed hard.

"Again, thanks for coming. Is that the drawing there?" The Governor motioned to the case Cliff held on his lap.

"Yes, sir." Cliff opened the case and pulled out the drawing. It was wrapped in heavy brown paper.

He started to open it when Governor Wilson stopped him. "Please, let me."

Jane Syzeman let out a chuckle. "Don't mind him, Cliff. The Governor likes to open his own presents. He's really a kid at heart."

"Shame on you," Wilson scolded. "You know there aren't many things I get to do in this office that are fun." His took the drawing from Cliff. "Believe it or not, I've been looking forward to this all day."

Cliff was genuinely impressed. He handed the drawing to the state's chief executive and watched as the man attacked the package like a kid at Christmas. The drawing unwrapped, the governor held it upright and stared. In spite of all the activity Cliff knew was going on in the outer office, this room was dead silent. Except of course for Cliff's heart, which was threatening to pound its way out of his chest. Governor Wilson finally laid the drawing on the glass topped table and said, "I must say, Cliff, I'm impressed. You are an amazing young man." He paused. "I should be honest and tell you we did a little background check on you. Please don't get upset. I didn't invoke any special powers. We just reviewed the public records available to any citizen. I did go a step further though and called Judge Donnelly. He and I graduated from law school together. He's a great person. I have to admit while I had my doubts initially, he has turned into a great adjudicator. And as many accolades as I can throw at him as a judge, he throws at you as an artist... and as a person I might add. I'm very sorry about your uncle. I understand he was a good model and mentor."

"Thank you," Cliff said. "My uncle was a good man. Best crabber on the bay."

"That's what the judge said."

All eyes turned to the drawing on the table. Cliff admitted to himself he was taken aback that the governor knew so much about him. It wasn't that the man dug into his personal life. It was that he took the time to do it. Cliff was also surprised the governor knew Judge Donnelly so well.

Looking at the drawing, Cliff said, "I owe Judge Donnelly a lot. It was his willingness to believe in me that gave me my real start."

"He told us the story," Jane Syzeman said. "He's very proud of you, you know?"

Cliff shrugged his shoulders, not knowing what to say.

The governor straightened up. "You up for a couple pieces of friendly advice?"

"Yes, sir."

"Never hire a woman as your chief aide. They'll stop you cold in a debate every time. *He's proud of you, you know?* Now how-the-hell you supposed to answer that one?"

He laughed which told Cliff it was okay to laugh as well. The aide simply stuck her tongue out at her boss. Cliff was surprised at her action, although the governor didn't seem to take any offense. Instead, he looked down at the drawing without further comment. "You still living on a sailboat?"

"Yes, sir."

"What kind?"

"A Hunter... a 33.5 Hunter."

"She have a name?"

"The *Mona Lisa*."

The governor's eyes widened. He looked up. "How fitting."

"She's like a mother. She keeps a close eye on me," Cliff said, chancing some humor.

It worked. The governor laughed. "Didn't know the lady had any children."

"Adopted."

It was the kind of banter the governor enjoyed. He rose to his feet and reached into the pocket of his suit coat. He pulled out an envelope and held it out toward the artist. "This should cover the balance for the drawing," he said.

Cliff stood up as well. Words from his uncle came into focus. "Remember, boy, a well-placed gift can reap great rewards in the future. And even if it doesn't, you'll get a good feeling about it. So be generous with your talent." It echoed his art teacher's advice.

Cliff said aloud, "That won't be necessary, sir."

"He insists," Ms. Syzeman piped in.

"There she goes again," the governor said.

"I insist," Cliff said.

The governor hesitated. "Okay… then thank you."

"My pleasure, sir."

"How 'bout I make a donation in your name to the Chesapeake Bay Foundation?"

"That would be great." Cliff liked the idea. He knew his uncle would be proud.

"Well," Jane Syzeman said. "I'm glad you two have hit it off so well." She looked directly at Cliff. "And don't worry about us. I really do love the old geezer, even though he gets on my nerves at times." She leaned in closer. "He really is a great guy."

"But if you are going to hire a woman," the governor said. "Make sure it's someone like Jane here. She can always find a way to take a bad day and end it on a good note."

Cliff assumed and hoped the governor was referring to this meeting. The artist was struggling for something else to say when a comment from a moment ago resurfaced. "Can I ask you something, sir?"

"Go ahead."

"You mentioned a couple pieces of advice."

The governor looked at his aide. "Doesn't miss a trick. Shows he's paying attention. I like that in a person." Looking back at Cliff, he held the envelope out as a chance for the artist to reconsider. Cliff nodded in the negative. Governor Wilson leaned forward. "Jane here is going to take you to her office in a second. She's going to offer you a contract to supply artwork as part of the capitol building renovation project. I think she'll be more than fair in her offer. My advice is to take it. It'll be good for your career."

Cliff's mouth dropped open.

"I assume that's an affirmative," Governor Wilson said with a smile. His face turned serious. "I'll tell you one thing, young man. I will expect the same quality as this." He pointed to the drawing on the table.

"No problem, sir. No problem at all… and thank you… thank you very much." Cliff started to add something else, but stopped short.

The governor picked up on this. "Go ahead, son. Like I said earlier, you don't need to be afraid to speak up. I was elected by the people of this great state. I work for you. You don't work for me."

Cliff wisely chose not to get into a debate over the issue. He did, however, decide to let his thought come forth. "If you're concerned about quality sir, the *Mona Lisa* is open for inspection anytime… and the root beer's always cold." He turned his attention to Ms. Syzeman. "You'll have to bring your own bourbon."

Governor Wilson and his aide laughed. "I may have to check that out sometime," the governor said. He picked up the drawing and carried it to the south wall where an empty space had been created. He sat it on the floor. "They'll hang it tonight once I leave."

He walked back to Cliff and held out his hand. "Judge Donnelly is a good judge when it comes to the law. He's a good judge of character, too."

95

Jennifer had never seen Cliff so excited, so animated. He had not stopped talking since he came into the restaurant twenty minutes earlier. She sat across from him at a table in the back and listened, all the while keeping an eye on the dining room. The evening was young and things were slow, so she was able to sit and relax. Time with Cliff was always relaxing. He had a smooth story-telling quality to his voice. He tended to mesmerize you with whatever he said, whether it be something simple, or telling a lengthier yarn.

Cliff was talking about his visit to the governor's office, and about the contract they offered him to be one of the principle artists for the State House's redecoration project. While the demand for pieces was great, the exposure was priceless. He had already talked to the Adamses in Philadelphia who assured him there would be no conflict with their Philadelphia deal. On the contrary, they agreed the opportunity was too good to pass up, and in the long run, would benefit all parties. It would certainly set Cliff apart from other artists.

Cliff was also looking for advice. There was lingering doubt if he was making the right decisions, or was he setting himself up for failure. Things were happening so fast, he was concerned about his ability to remain focused. He was also concerned about his vulnerability. He still didn't fully understand the concept of having an agent, or why he needed one.

The listening part, Jennifer could handle without any trouble. Advice, however, was a little tougher. She did offer one idea. "In the business world, never assume someone is the enemy until they show themselves completely." She also offered to run the problem by her father. He might have insight from a different perspective, she argued. Cliff hesitated, reluctant to take up her father's time. Jennifer countered with a second piece of advice. "Never turn down free advice." Cliff smiled and nodded in agreement.

"Was Jane there?" Jennifer asked.

"Ms. Syzeman… she was the one who actually went over the contract with me."

"What'd you think of her?"

"She certainly had a strange relationship with the governor."

"What do you mean by that?"

"Maybe strange is the wrong word. It just wasn't what I'd expect, that's all."

"How so?"

"She was rather informal with him."

Jennifer laughed. "Don't let that bother you. Governor Wilson's one of the most down to earth people you'll ever meet. That's one reason he's so popular."

"He certainly impressed me," Cliff said.

"No kidding." There was a hint of sarcasm in her voice.

Cliff blushed.

Jennifer worked to undo the damage. "That's okay. He's an impressive guy. That he took so much time with you means he was impressed with you."

"He certainly liked my work."

"That he did." Just then, Jennifer noticed a commotion at the front door. A moment later, one of the hostesses hurried to the far corner of the dining room and started barking orders at two bus boys who were taking their time clearing off a large table. Their activity immediately increased in pace. Jennifer rose to her feet. "Excuse me a second, Cliff. I'll be right back."

His back to the room, Cliff was oblivious to activity. Besides, his mind was full of thoughts from earlier in the day.

Thoughts that were suddenly interrupted by a booming voice directly behind him. "You know son, when you invite someone over for a root beer, you should be there to serve it to 'em."

Startled, Cliff looked around. Governor Wilson stood hovering over him. Cliff half rose, half fell to his feet. "Sir."

The governor gave the boy a big smile. "Didn't mean to startle you, Cliff, but I had to come over to say hello."

The two shook hands. Without thinking, Cliff spewed out, "You came by the boat to see me?"

"Did you or did you not invite me over for a root beer?"

Cliff stammered a moment before getting his mouth coordinated with his brain. "Yes sir, I guess I did."

The governor looked at the table and saw that Cliff was alone. "Mind if I join you? You can get me that root beer now."

Cliff was so shocked, he was speechless. He looked around the room for help. Luckily, Jennifer had come back to the table and threw him a life ring. "I told you he was personable. What I didn't tell you was don't invite him over and expect him not to show up. He'll catch you every time. Right, sir?"

"How many times have I caught you, Jennifer?"

Jennifer leaned over and gave the governor a hug. "You know you're welcome here anytime. I'll get my father."

"No rush with that. To be truthful, I didn't come here to see your dad. I came to see Cliff." The governor took a seat across from the still speechless artist. "But first I stopped by Cliff's boat to get that root beer and to see his dog. "

"Chessie was on board," Cliff managed to say.

"That she was, only she couldn't get the icebox opened. She did tell me where you were, however."

Cliff wasn't sure how, but had no doubt the last statement was true. Recovering somewhat, Cliff said, "Actually, I'm all out of root beer. That's why I came up here."

The governor laughed. "You lie just like a good ole politician."

The commotion in the dining room settled down as the staff saw they didn't need to fix a large table for the governor. Except for a state policeman who was standing in the corner, he was alone.

"Is Bobby going to join you?" Jennifer asked, taking two bottles of Heineken, and Cliff's root beer off a tray that had miraculously appeared.

"Once he's satisfied no one in here's going to try and harm me." The Governor held his glass while Jennifer poured. Looking at Cliff, he said, "You talk about a fidgety bunch of people. I certainly appreciate their efforts, but they drive me nuts sometimes."

Jennifer filled Cliff's glass and set the third beside the Governor for Bobby. "You have any preference tonight, sir?"

"You know the answer to that one."

"I'll get right on it," Jennifer said. She started to walk away, and then stopped. "By the way Cliff, the first round's on me. The rest are yours."

Still in awe at what was happening, Cliff raised his glass in response to the governor doing the same. "Here's to the Chesapeake Bay," the governor toasted.

After a long swallow, Cliff leaned into the table and dropped his voice. "Why are you here, sir?"

The governor didn't hesitate. "I told you. I came over to get that root beer, and to see you. I wanted to see the studio where such fine work is created. You do your work there, right?"

"Most of it."

"That's amazing. She's a fine looking boat."

"Anytime you want to go for a…" The artist stopped.

The governor laughed. "Don't offer 'cause I do like to be out on the water."

"It would be my pleasure, sir."

Governor Wilson stared at the artist. "It would be mine as well."

Their conversation was interrupted by Jennifer's return with three steaming bowls of oyster stew. She looked over and nodded her head at Bobby. The plain-clothed policeman took one more look around and headed for the table. He introduced himself to Cliff and sat down next to the governor. "Beautiful dog," he said. "She didn't take too well to me at first, that is until the governor told her I was harmless. Then she wouldn't leave me alone."

"Why was that, I wonder?" Cliff said.

"His wife raises retrievers," the governor explained.

"Oh," Cliff said, "she smelled 'em, huh?"

"No doubt."

The three men focused on the stew for the next couple minutes. A second round of drinks was served. Pushing the bowl away, Bobby said, "Mrs. B. sure knows how to make a stew."

"Best in the state," the governor boasted. "And believe me, I get around."

Cliff smiled at the remark. He still, however, was unable to shake that questioning look.

Bobby saw this and said, "The *gov* and I come here a lot for dinner… least once a week when we're in town. We start with a walk, mingle with the people, drop in on the favorite watering holes of the legislators and then come over here. He did say that we had to stop and see someone's boat, and he was disappointed that you weren't there. But we found you."

The governor picked up the explanation. "You see Cliff, one of the many great things about our state is her people. Maryland is made up of a diverse group of individuals; and amongst this population, a few of these individuals stand out. I believe to govern effectively, you have to understand the wants and needs of the various groups. You also have to get to know those who stand out from the crowd. I think I found one in you." The politician paused for a sip of beer. "One of my biggest jobs as Governor is to tote the benefits of our state, whether it be to tourists, small businesses or big companies. We pay a lot of money to a lot of people trained in public relations to get the message out. We print up a lot of fancy fliers, hang posters everywhere, develop ad campaigns, and I even go on television to tell everyone why they should pick our state over the other forty-nine options, who by the way, are all doing the same. This is what all the experts in the field say we need to do to stay competitive. But I believe just as effective is to recognize people with talent, and give them the tools and support so they can do their thing—which I believe is the best way to promote and get to know Maryland." Another pause. Another sip of beer. "I get great satisfaction out of discovering such people."

"He made me come into his office and see the drawing," Bobby said. "I tried convincing him it was a security risk in his office and I should take it away."

"And hang it on your own wall," Governor Wilson quipped.

"All in the name of security," Bobby laughed.

Governor Wilson smiled. "And what makes it even more special is when the person behind the talent is genuine as well. Now that's a true find."

"What is it about my work that's so special?" Cliff asked curiously. "There are a lot of Maryland artists more famous than me."

"Ah," the governor said. "Never confuse popularity with quality. That's true in music, art and even politics. Some of our most popular state senators are poor legislators. They couldn't debate themselves out of a wet paper bag."

"They're called Republicans," Bobby injected with a smirk.

The governor leaned forward. "A few Democrats fit the mold as well." He emptied his beer "But back to the popular artists, as you call them. Their work doesn't sing. Where was it we first met? Crisfield, right? I saw a lot of talented displays that day, a couple of the artists you're talking about, too. But none sang like yours. None depicted Maryland in the same light. Your ability to put real emotion into a two dimensional drawing is amazing. I wanted to get to know the person behind that talent. So far, I haven't been disappointed. Self-serving maybe, thinking I can find or learn something that will make me a better governor, a better person, but that's exactly what I should be doing. If you benefit some from the attention, so be it. It's a win-win all around."

Cliff realized immediately the benefit of simply having the man come into the restaurant and sit at his table. Talk about a vote of support.

"Let me ask you something, Cliff," The governor said. "You have anything else finished?"

Cliff pondered the question. "Not entirely, but pretty close."

"What is it, if I may ask?"

"A few drawings of the Annapolis harbor."

"Let me ask you this, how long does it take you to do one of those?"

"If you mean in time, it's hard to say. I usually do what I call a partial in the field and add the finishing touches later—at night when it's dark, for example. I find it makes better use of my time."

"Can you finish one in say, three days?"

Cliff shrugged his shoulders. "It really depends on the subject matter, but it's possible."

"Huh." The Governor retreated into deep thought a moment. "There's a boat docked in the harbor—a yacht name *Hamilton's Bench*. You can't miss it—it's the biggest one there. I believe it's docked right across from you. How 'bout a drawing of it against the background of the harbor?"

"A drawing—not a painting?"

The governor's eyebrows rose. "A painting would be even better, but I know you don't have time for that. A drawing would be fine. You see, George Hamilton, the owner of *Hamilton's Bench*, is hosting a fundraiser for me on Friday evening, and I thought a drawing of his boat might be a nice thank you gift."

It was Cliff's turn to raise eyebrows. Correctly reading the expression on the artist's face, the chief executive said, "And yes, Cliff, your work is good enough for George Hamilton. I suspect he'd be most pleased to meet you, too."

Cliff told himself to act cool, although it was difficult with a new opportunity opening up around every corner. He heard his uncle's cautionary voice in his head. "Don't dig a hole you can't get out of." Still, these were opportunities he couldn't afford to turn down. Besides, the thought of maybe getting aboard such a yacht did indeed interest him.

"There's only one condition," the governor continued.

"Yes, sir?"

"You will accept full payment for this one."

Cliff hesitated. He glanced over at Bobby who gave him a reassuring wink. "Yes, sir," the artist repeated.

"Good," the governor said. "So Friday night isn't too far-fetched?"

"I'll do my best," Cliff responded.

"That's all anyone can ask."

96

Because she missed her early morning walk, Chessie's pace was eager. Cliff, usually a slow, meandering walker, had to pay attention to keep up with his companion. Chessie pulled at the leash, giving her master a hint. Cliff did what he could short of breaking into a jog.

The camera around his neck prevented anything else. Besides, it was too hot to run. Cliff told Chessie he'd take her for a run later in the afternoon when the temperature was cooler. He was already sweating and Chessie was panting heavily.

They made their way past the Naval Academy's main gate, along the fence separating the federal property from the town Traffic was heavy, and as always, there were several joggers out. Cliff considered himself to be in good shape and able to tolerate the heat, but he still thought people were nuts who ran in the hottest portion of the day.

The two circled the back side of the State House where Cliff contemplated various angles and viewpoints of the all-white structure. They made their way down the south side of town, arriving at the other side of the harbor. They went through an underground parking garage and came out on the waterfront. A fence separated the public area from the Annapolis Yacht Club's private docks. Several large boats were crammed into the overcrowded space. The club did have a T head now occupied by *Hamilton's Bench*. It took only a quick glance to see that she was beautifully maintained. There wasn't a speck of dirt on her hull, and the waterline looked as if it had just been painted.

Cliff stopped and pulled Chessie to a heel position. His eyes started at the bow and slowly made their way to the stern. Her lines were magnificent. Cliff was impressed. He looked across the waterway towards the city docks. The *Mona Lisa* sat quietly in her berth. She looked so small in comparison. Cliff's uncle told him once that no matter how much, how big or how beautiful a *something* you may have in life, some son-of-a-bitch will always come along with a *something* bigger and prettier. That was especially true with boats. The man concluded with, "Never try keeping up with the Joneses. Stay true to yourself and live within your means. Remember, money can't buy you happiness. Happiness is something you have to earn."

Regardless, *Hamilton's Bench* was beautiful, and the possibility of actually getting aboard was very appealing. Cliff looked to see if the girl was around, but the decks were empty. He stepped back and focused on the surrounding area. He turned toward the city. As with the drawing of the State Capitol, the question was which angle to use. Should the harbor be the background, or the city? His art teacher taught him how to crop a scene so the background was not necessarily real, but more of what the artist wanted it to be. He called this *cheating* realism. In this case, Cliff could easily have the background be both the harbor and the building. No one would know the difference except for those who knew Annapolis.

Cliff laughed. That was a lot of *no ones* to cheat.

He and Chessie walked through the parking garage and headed across the Back Creek bridge. Cliff stopped and looked toward the city. His art teacher had also told him that sometimes you were good and sometimes you were lucky when setting up a scene. In this case, the latter held true.

Hamilton's Bench sat off to the left, her bow majestically pointing toward the middle of the scene. The right side encompassed the inner harbor, including the city dock and the *Mona Lisa*, which now really did look small. At the top middle was the dome of the State

House. Cliff's smile broadened. He couldn't have cheated the scene any better. Yes, today he was lucky.

He led Chessie to the highest point of the bridge and looked into the sun. Not ideal lighting, but he could take a few preliminary shots and take the film to one of those photos-in-an-hour shops. He could lay out the scene that evening and begin working the next day. Giving Chessie a biscuit to chew on, he slid the camera off his shoulder and went to work.

97

A law of nature states that when the sun goes down, the temperature follows. However, nature is not always the most law abiding citizen. Three days later, the sun had been down for over three hours. The temperature had dropped a scant three degrees. If not for a couple of small fans, the inside of the *Mona Lisa* would be unbearable—at least to Jennifer.

Cliff didn't seem to mind. His head bowed over the drawing pad as sweat formed on his forehead. He subconsciously wiped it away before it dripped onto his work. Jennifer watched as he remained focused on the paper. He was working on a large drawing of the yacht docked across the way. It was the drawing the governor commissioned and Cliff had been working feverishly the past two days. Remembering the sketch from the day before, Jennifer could only shake her head in amazement.

Jennifer sipped her beer and cocked her head to the side, trying to see something she'd noticed earlier. Her eyes scanned the paper left to right. She was right. There were no people in the scene. She had seen the series of photographs Cliff had taken, and there were human figures in them. Yet now...

"Still no people?" she said.

Cliff looked and shrugged his shoulders. "Guess not."

"There a reason?"

"I know we've talked about this before, and I've given it some thought," Cliff said.

"And?" Jennifer encouraged.

"Present company excluded, I find most people rather boring and uninteresting from an artist's point of view. People are so afraid to show their emotions—to let someone see them for who they really are. They cover themselves in armor for protection. That makes for a difficult subject matter."

"I don't understand."

"People are always trying to pretend they're somebody they're not."

"Maybe they don't like themselves," Jennifer offered. "It's a self-preserving defense mechanism."

"Then they should change and become somebody they do like. In the meantime, don't hide reality behind fantasy."

"People are not always so open about themselves." Jennifer paused. "Besides, what's so boring with learning about people, good or bad?" Jennifer asked. "I find trying to get to know somebody fun at times. Didn't we talk about a story within a story?"

"Maybe boring isn't the right word," Cliff said. "Maybe disappointing is a better description."

"Disappointing?"

"Yeah. You take the time to get to know someone and you find out they aren't who they really are. What becomes disappointing is their lack of honesty to begin with."

Jennifer thought the idea very profound, guessing Cliff had been hurt in the past.

Cliff continued. "When you look at a piece of art, whether it be a photograph, drawing, painting or otherwise, the first goal of the artist is to generate some sort of a response. Sometimes you go for the shock effect—a lot of modern art is like that. Sometimes you go for the *wow* effect. Ansel Adams, the famed outdoor photographer was big on that. Sometimes you go for tears and sympathy. Sometimes you're just trying to get one's curiosity to rise."

"Give me an example," Jennifer said.

"Okay," Cliff said. "This boat's namesake—the *Mona Lisa*. Scholars have tried for years to understand that composition. Why are her eyes the way they are? What do her hands represent? Why is the look on her face so peculiar? Questions have even been raised about the actual dimensions of the drawing compared to Leonardo da Vinci's birthday. There are a lot of mysteries about the lady. Whole books have been written by people who have devoted a good part of their lives studying this one painting."

"Do we know who she really is?" Jennifer asked.

"The story goes a Florentine merchant commissioned her. She was his third or fourth wife. It took Da Vinci four years to complete the work. Interestingly, he never delivered the painting.

"Why?"

"Yet another mystery behind the *Mona*."

Jennifer paused. "Why is this particular painting so popular, where others of equal quality are not?"

"Good question," Cliff said. "Her popularity started when she was stolen. If I remember my art history correctly, it was 1911. She was found two years later after a Louvre employee was caught, and the mystique of the *Mona Lisa* was born."

"Interesting," Jennifer commented. "But how do we know she's not wearing any emotional armor?"

Cliff went back to work as he spoke. "What we do and do not know isn't important. That only matters to the artist. You can't convey emotion to others unless you're convinced yourself that what you're seeing is true."

"You could still be wrong?"

"An artist's eyes are trained to see reality."

"So Michelangelo could see through whatever armor *Mona Lisa* might have been hiding?"

Cliff didn't correct the obvious blunder. "If there was armor, yes."

"That still doesn't explain why you don't have people in your work."

Cliff looked up. "Because I haven't learned the knack of seeing through the armor."

"I guess one can't be more honest than that." Jennifer pointed to the drawing on the table "What look are you looking for here?"

"The majesty of the yacht itself contrasted against the gentleness of the surrounding scenery," Cliff explained.

"The *wow* look?"

"Exactly."

Jennifer leaned in closer. Readjusting the direction of her finger, she said, "Isn't that the *Mona Lisa* in the background?"

He chuckled. "That's what I call the *anti-wow* look. She looks so small, doesn't she?"

"Yes, but that only adds to the perceived size of the yacht."

"Exactly."

"Wow!"

"Exactly!"

Realizing she'd fallen into the artist's trap, she laughed loudly.

Cliff's hand motion stopped. "There was one person I did see the other day I thought would have made an interesting character study."

"Who was that?"

"Even before the Governor asked me to do this drawing, I was shooting some shots of *Hamilton's Bench* when a girl—a real pretty one—came out on the bow. When she looked over and noticed I was taking her picture, a look of fear crossed her face and she ran away."

"Did you get a picture of her?"

"No. I was so startled by her reaction, I missed the shot. Anyway, it wouldn't have worked with this drawing. But that's one example of a person I would have liked to study."

"Because she was pretty?" Jennifer teased.

"Because of her facial expression. She was hot though… in more ways than one."

A weird sensation electrified Jennifer's spine. Although it lasted only a second, it was strong enough to stop her laughter. She recognized the feeling as jealousy. It had been a long time since she felt such a twinge, having buried it when she started seeing Daniel. She shook her head and focused on Cliff. His hair was clean, but severely in need of a brushing. He wore his standard faded tee shirt and khaki shorts. He was barefoot. His face was windblown and tanned, his skin showing few signs of a beard. His eyes remained focused on the drawing as he leaned forward, his right hand continuing the steady motion of laying marks down on the paper. He was sweating enough that his shirt stuck to his chest. She cautioned self-control as she thought of a male wet tee shirt contest. A side of her wished he'd sweat even more.

She studied his hands. It was here the final bridge was built between human talent and the tools of the trade—a graphic pencil. His fingers were lean and long. All women had their top ten list of what turned them off in a man. Number one her list was dirty fingernails. His were clean and short. Her mind wandered as she fantasized about any other talents his fingers might possess. The thought… the possibilities… caused another wave of electricity to shoot down her spine. Only this time the sensation moved further south in tiny ripples.

"Jesus," she almost said aloud. She was actually getting aroused by him. It was one thing to sweat 'em, it was another when the reaction coaxed other body fluids. She straightened her posture, pressing her spine into the back of the booth. She squeezed her legs together and told herself to behave. After all, she wasn't in the shower.

"After all what?" she thought. Why was she being so hard on herself? After all, he was good looking, he was kind and caring, and although not a career tract in the usual sense of the term, he did have a plan for his future and knew what he wanted to do. What's more, he was doing it! That was more than she could say for herself. So why not enjoy the pleasure she got from spending time with him, from looking at him, from thinking about him. After all…

She realized he was looking up at her. "You okay?" he said softly.

Yes, he was so kind.

"Yeah," she stammered. "I was just thinking about all I have to do tomorrow, that's all."

"If there's anything I can do to help."

There he went again. "Thanks," she said. So kind and caring. She cursed him under her breath.

"By the way," he said, breaking her train of thought… thankfully. "I called Philadelphia today, and we had a nice talk. He was real supportive, and when I told him all the stuff that was happening down here he said I was a fool if I committed everything to him. We adjusted the deal by eliminating the exclusivity clause. He said to give him what I could."

"Sounds like you got the best of both worlds," Jennifer said.

"I still feel an obligation to give him as much as possible. After all, he did give me an opportunity before anyone else."

"Just remember," Jennifer said. "Your first obligation is to yourself. What's best for Cliff Davidson?"

"Sometimes that's a question best answered with hindsight," he remarked.

So kind, so caring and so smart, she thought. "Well, I'd place my bet on you making the right decisions."

He tilted his head to the side. "Thanks."

"Advice is free. Compliments'll cost you a beer."

He smiled. "Fair enough." He laid the graphic pencil aside and slid out of the booth. "What do you think?" he asked, holding the drawing for her to see.

"It's wonderful," she said without hesitation.

"Now, I guess it's two beers."

"Only if you want me to pass out here."

"That would be okay," Cliff said without thinking. "Nothing bad meant by that," he quickly added.

"Nothing bad taken," she said.

He went into the galley and returned with two beers and a bowel of corn chips. "If you want more than this, I can whip something up."

"This'll be fine," she said, taking a beer in one hand and a chip in the other. "So tell me, why do you think the girl on the boat was so startled?"

Cliff crunched on a chip. "I don't know. At first I just thought she didn't want her picture taken. I get that reaction once in a while, although I would never take photographs of anyone that would be recognizable without first getting their permission. But if she didn't want her picture taken, she would have looked annoyed, not frightened."

"I agree."

"Strange."

"How's that?"

"A mystery aboard the yacht *Hamilton's Bench*."

Jennifer laughed. "Don't read more into it than's really there." She paused. "Can I ask you a personal question?"

"Go ahead."

"You've been hurt in the past, haven't you? And I'm not referring to your uncle's death."

"What do you mean?"

"By a girl."

Cliff squirmed in his seat. "Why do you want to know?"

"It'll answer another question I have."

"Which is?"

"A couple minutes ago you I mentioned what's best for Cliff Davidson, and you said that's a question best answered with hindsight. Understanding the power of hindsight is not something you learn in high school. That only comes from the school of hard knocks."

Cliff chuckled in a defensive manner. "I guess I've had a few hard knocks in my life."

"A few?"

He hesitated. "Okay, one… no, two."

Jennifer waited to see if the count upward continued.

Cliff took a sip of beer. "You know, you make decisions in life, sometimes with a lot of thought, sometimes on the spur of the moment. But regardless of how they're made, you have to live with the consequences. You think you know someone, you make a decision accordingly, and then bam, you get kicked in the ass."

"Take this Philadelphia thing for example. As I was trying to understand the contract, I was also trying to figure out what it all meant. I decided that in a lot of ways, he was offering me a ring of protection so I could stay focused on my work and not have to worry a lot about the business end of it."

"Isn't there a fine line between protection and entrapment?" Jennifer asked.

"Exactly. That's why I made the call today. I gave up the protection for fear of the entrapment. Not that I think he had a hidden agenda about that or anything. The risk was just there. The question's going to be, was that the right decision on my part? Regardless, I now have to live with the decision."

"Can you blame yourself if you didn't have all the information to start with?" Jennifer asked.

"Blame? Maybe no. Live with, think about, regret… yes."

Jennifer finished her beer. "With the two times you were hurt, do you regret the decisions that led to that?"

"Yes."

"Why?"

"I should have known better."

"Should you have?"

An uneasiness showed on Cliff's face. "Where you going with this?"

Jennifer smiled. "Trying to see if there's any armor I'm missing. It's just hard to believe you're as genuine as you seem. I've never met anyone like you before. I don't think you realize just how special you really are."

"I think everyone's special in their own way," Cliff said.

Jennifer tipped her head to the side. "You think I'm special?"

Cliff nodded. "To me, you are."

A warmth came over her, along with a few electrical impulses. She held up her empty beer bottle. "Got another?"

"What about you making it home?"

"We'll make that decision when the time comes."

Cliff went to the galley and pulled two more bottles from the icebox. He held one out for her. Instead of grabbing the bottle, she wrapped her fingers around his wrist. "I'm about to make a decision I hope I won't regret." She pulled him down to her and kissed him. She held his wrist loosely so he could pull away if he wanted.

He did not.

98

The sheriff's face was beet red as he breathed heavily into the phone. He stared out across the town square. It was a beautiful summer day, but the heat had chased most people inside. Except for a couple of young mothers out for a stroll with their newborns and a teenager riding his bike, the scene from his office window was pretty much lifeless. The tree limbs hung lower than normal. He knew August could be hot, but this was ridiculous.

He squeezed the phone tighter as he inhaled an enormous breath. He made use of the air as he bellowed into the mouthpiece. "Listen, Goddamn it. I've paid you a lot of money—a lot of fuckin' money. It's all been wired to your account, just like you directed, and I'm sure you've already verified that, or I wouldn't be talking to you now. I've held up my end of the bargain. It's time you do the same. I don't want excuses either. I want results. Time's running out, and I want this wrapped up before the election." He didn't mention the money was running out as well.

He refused to think about other expenses stressing his finances. "Do you hear me? Just find the bitch. Remember, results, not excuses." He turned and threw the cellular phone against the far wall.

Another expense he'd have to take care of.

99

The man pulled the phone away from his ear as the sound of anger resonated through the cellular system. There was a loud crash and the phone went dead. "Son-of-a-bitch," the man said in disbelief. "He not only hung up on me, he threw up on me."

He let the laughter subside and his anger swell. He flipped the phone shut. Stuffing it in his shirt pocket, he said aloud, "You want to threaten me, huh? I'll show you, you bastard." He picked up a fax from his desk that had come in an hour earlier. It was a copy of an invitation to a fundraiser for Maryland's Governor Wilson. It was hosted by one George Hamilton aboard his yacht *Hamilton's Bench*. While the fundraiser was of no interest to the man, the fact that the boat would be in Annapolis at least until Saturday gave him a little extra time—time to let the Sheriff sweat a bit. "I'll give you results, but it'll cost you a lot more than you expected," he muttered.

He looked at the folder on his desk. The photographs of the girl on the boat could prove to be more valuable than originally thought. The sheriff was desperate, and the resolution of desperation costs extra.

He mouthed an additional thought. "And everyone thought bounty hunting was dead!"

100

Jennifer woke early every morning for the past week and went directly to the computer, determined to dissolve her writer's block. Every morning, the results were the same. She'd sit at the computer without inspiration. She was unable to get her creative thinking warmed up. Her mind always wandered, whether it be to the *Riverboat Inn*, to her parents or the St. Michaels project. She was slowly seeing her dream—her fantasy—of becoming a writer fade. While the desire remained strong, the results were not. She always found an excuse. She was too tired. She was too preoccupied with other things in her life. It was too hot in her apartment. It was too cold in her apartment. Was... was... was... all ways of avoiding the fact that she just didn't have what it took to be a writer.

Now there was another excuse: Cliff Davidson. She glanced at her watch. It had only been a few hours since they first kissed. It had been a wonderful kiss, full of passion, full of desire. And there was another... and another.

Then he abruptly stopped. "Are we going too fast?" she said softly.

Cliff took a swallow of beer. "I don't think it's the speed."

She took a sip of his beer. "Then what?"

"It's the conclusion that's bothersome."

Jennifer laughed, the effects of the alcohol loosening up her tongue. "It's called ecstasy."

"After that. I've been burned before. I don't want to be burned again. We're friends. We've established that. I want that friendship to strengthen, to prosper, to grow. I don't want a moment of passion to ruin that."

"You wouldn't give up my friendship to have sex with me?" Jennifer joked.

"The pleasure of ecstasy is momentary. The pleasure of friendship can last a lifetime."

Jennifer started to argue, but stopped. He was right. She needed a friend a whole lot more than she needed sex, she thought. "So, two people can't have an intimate relationship and still be friends?"

"It complicates things."

Jennifer didn't counter with the thought that not having sex could make it more complicated.

"Maybe we can define some expectations," Cliff continued.

Jennifer kissed him lightly on the forehead. "Are you always this insightful?"

"In the past, I've just been stupid."

Another kiss on the forehead. "How about an agreement that sex will only make our friendship stronger?" Jennifer suggested.

"There's still a risk."

"Damn, Cliff. There was a risk the first time I stepped aboard your boat in St. Michaels. There was a risk the first time I came aboard here in Annapolis. I'm taking a risk being here now. We take risks in everything we do. It's who we choose as a partner in risk that's important. Maybe in the past, we've made mistakes. But we learn from our mistakes and move on. We can't change the past. We can only control the present and have an effect on the future."

Cliff arched his back. "Now who's being insightful?"

Jennifer laughed. "That's just the beer talking."

"I think it's the beer allowing you to talk."

"Whatever."

Cliff leaned forward and kissed her gently. "God gave the game of baseball three strikes. I've already used two."

"And you want to be careful with the third."

Cliff grinned. "But I'm still at bat."

Jennifer laughed. They made out for another half hour. She thought she was going to explode before she finally took his hand and pressed it between her legs. The sensation of his fingers—fingers that were so delicate and precise—fueled her desire. She told herself to move slowly. She also told herself she had been doing just that. Several weeks had passed since she first laid eyes on him, since she thought about him in a romantic way, since she fantasized about him while in the shower. She had been taking it slow. Now it was time to change directions.

She was always the aggressor with Daniel. He even liked it when she took total control. He claimed that in his role at the hospital he had to keep up a certain aura. With Jennifer, he could do just the opposite and be passive. Jennifer didn't mind. She was an A type personality in and out of the bedroom.

That all changed with Cliff.

She knew he was young and inexperienced, but as they lay side by side, their bodies pressed tightly together, she knew he was willing and eager. For the next hour, she served as the canvas, he the artist. His caresses, his kisses, his strokes awoke feelings she had not felt in a long time… maybe never before. He was Da Vinci she was his *Mona Lisa*. When he finally entered her, she was so hot, so eager, she exploded almost immediately.

Daniel Baker was always attentive to his patients, but his goal was to get the case over quickly and effectively. Face lifts and boob jobs were all done the same. He made love the same way. He never failed to complete an operation. He never failed to satisfy Jennifer. The results were always predictable both in time and quality. The opposite was true with Cliff. Nothing with him was predictable. They made love for two solid hours, and with each passing moment, there was a new sensation, a new surprise, a new twist. Every moment was an original.

Afterwards, they talked… another new experience for Jennifer. She was the most relaxed she had been in a long time, and after another beer, she mustered up the courage to tell him more about her dream of becoming a writer. She also confided in the difficulties she was experiencing. Cliff's eyes never left her as she lay in his arms. They were stronger than she imagined.

"All artists go through that," Cliff said.

"I'm not an artist. I'm a writer… or a wannabe writer," she corrected.

"They're one and the same," he countered. "Art is expressing one's self, one's emotions. Art takes many forms. Writing is just one form. I express myself through drawing, photography and painting. You express yourself with the written word. All artists have lulls, periods when their creative juices are too thick to flow smoothly."

"Why?"

"My art teacher said it results from putting too much pressure on yourself. Wanting it too much overrides the creative process. That's what I'm afraid is going to happen to me if I'm not careful with the amount of work I take on. That's the reason I pulled out of the Philadelphia deal, or rather changed it to where the pressure isn't as great."

"Some people work well under pressure," Jennifer commented.

"True. However, to work well under pressure, you have to see the endpoint.

"I look at it as the vast array of emotions we have going on inside us all the time. When these emotions get all mixed up, the pressure builds and the creative juices stop. It's one thing to be under pressure to get one thing finished, like the drawing for the governor. It's another for the pressure to continue long term. For me, the moment I let that happen, I'm cooked as an artist."

"I just want to get started," Jennifer said.

"Are you sure you're on the right track?"

"What do you mean?"

"Maybe you're trying to force words onto paper about something that's all wrong for you. Maybe you need to think about another topic."

"But I'm writing a novel!"

"Then start a new one."

"But—"

"Just an idea," Cliff said quickly.

They lay together quietly for several minutes. Consciously or otherwise, people were like a radio—they constantly gave off signals. Jennifer thought her ability to read these signals was a reason for her success as a nurse and as a restaurateur. As time passed, as their heart rates returned to normal, as their lungs demanded less and less oxygen, she sensed a change in Cliff's signal. It was subtle, but he had definitely pulled back emotionally. She chalked that up to his talking about himself, probably more than he had in a long time. She drew her fingers across his wet back and said, "A penny for your thoughts."

He rolled towards her. "I'm all out of change," he said.

She laughed. "I can tell." She reached down and fondled him gently. When he said nothing, she added, "You're avoiding the question."

"Which was?"

"Your thoughts."

There was a long pause. "You asked if I've ever been hurt before, and I told you yes, twice. Both times were after... you know. I know we've talked about this, but the one thing I hope is that the past doesn't repeat itself."

Jennifer pulled his face up to hers. "You can only fall off a mountain if you climb it to begin with."

"And water will run downhill, only if given a hill down which to run," Cliff added.

"Huh?"

"It was one of my uncle's sayings. You've got to put effort into something before you can expect anything in return. If you're lazy and pour water on level ground, it'll lay there and do nothing. But, if you put in the energy and climb the hill, the water will give you energy in return as it runs down the hill."

"Kind-a-like my father saying there ain't nothing free in life," Jennifer said.

"Yeah," Cliff said. "What's the cost of tonight?"

"Depends on how high we've climbed the mountain," Jennifer replied.

"How high did we climb?"

"I don't know. What do you think?"

There was a pause. "Water, mountains... all symbolisms for emotions within ourselves we don't fully understand," Cliff said. "But there's one saying that's probably the most realistic."

"And that is?"

"Time—time will tell."

Jennifer laughed. "What do we do in the meantime?"

Cliff kissed her softly. "I'm still at bat."

101

Sheriff Richmond hovered over the fax machine, one hand on each side of the box. His facial expression warned that if the box failed to give him the correct information, he'd snatch the machine from the table and smash it against the wall. There were still broken parts on the floor from the last time something didn't give him what he wanted. Why was it, he wondered, when something came across the fax unsolicited, such as ads for more fax paper, the speed was fine? When it was something important, it arrived like a stream of molasses. He took a deep breath and told himself to be patient. He had waited this long. A couple more minutes wouldn't matter.

He watched the fax come out face down. He closed his eyes, said a brief and rare prayer, cursed the bitch and turned the paper over. The photograph was fuzzy, but the close up view made identification easy. He held the paper away from him, and then pulled it closer and his hands started to shake.

Her hair was shorter, and it looked lighter, although it was difficult to tell in a black and white faxed photograph. In general, she looked older, which he expected. However, there was no doubt, it was her.

"Bitch," he said aloud. He willed his hand to stop shaking. "I've got you now."

He focused on the rest of the image. The photograph had been cropped clean, showing only her face. The background was entirely white. He started to curse, but stopped short. Why waste the effort? The man was good, there was no doubt about that.

Richmond picked up the new cellphone lying on the desk. He took a quiet breath, telling himself to stay calm. He knew what was about to happen, and he needed to remain in control.

"You got it?" the bounty hunter said.

"I got it."

"Well?"

"It's a good image, but I'm not sure. Where'd you say you took this?"

The bounty hunter chuckled. "Nice try, Sheriff, but I didn't say where. And you and I both know it's her."

"Perhaps," the sheriff said, refusing to concede the point. There was long pause as the sheriff contemplated his options. He knew realistically, he had few. The only question was going to be the price. The last time he had talked to the man, he had been very abrupt, demanding results. Now he had those results. This time he took the softer approach. "Where do we go from here?"

"That's much better Sheriff. Or are you going soft on me?"

With the wisdom of experience, the sheriff bit his lip.

The bounty hunter continued. "Your tone is acknowledging that I'm in the driver's seat. So what say we stop beating around the bush, huh? I'm sure you're a fine upstanding officer of the law, and that you do your homework when investigating a case. Well, I do the same, and I've found a couple additional pieces of information on this one. I know who she is and why you want her. And, one thing I know that you don't…" The bounty hunter paused. "I know where she is. And that's the key to this whole thing, isn't it?"

The sheriff continued to use what training skills he could muster. He imagined himself negotiating with a terrorist. Calm, steady and caring were key. He was unable to totally hide a sense of panic. He really had a limited amount of funds. Deciding to lighten the tone, the sheriff said, "I'm glad you didn't beat around the bush."

"Very good, sheriff. Very good. Humor. Keep the subject calm by injecting humor. Keep things light. You forgot, I'm the one who taught the seminar, remember? And I'd still be teaching if I hadn't taken early retirement."

The sheriff said nothing.

The bounty hunter continued. "I suspect the cat's got your tongue. I also suspect you're afraid to say anything for fear I'll pick up the panic that's setting in. I know you're not a rich man and you have limited funds. I also know you have access to other moneys right now as well. Aren't you running for reelection?"

Another pause.

"What say we double the original price and we'll call it a deal?"

The sheriff cursed under his breath. That was a lot of money. But in reality, he had expected worse. "I'll need a couple days to get that kind of money together."

"Ah…" The voice hesitated. The tone softened and became less threatening. "I'm not sure you have a couple days, sheriff."

"You know I'm good for the money."

The bounty hunter laughed. "You know, sheriff, you ought to consider retiring and coming to work for me. The hours suck, but the pay's better. You're good. I'll give you credit for that. And…" There was a calculated hesitation. "Like with the girl, April Blackstone, I also know a lot about you. I know your name. I know where you live. I know what you're doing, and why. I also know you're running for reelection. So putting this all together, I know a lot about you—a lot that'll ruin you, if not even land you some jail time—not for what you're doing, but for how you're funding it so to speak, so I know your credit is good." The tone of his voice hardened. "You've got seventy-two hours from the time I give you the information to transfer the money to my account. If not, I make a few additional phone calls not in our original deal. You understand me?"

"Yes."

"Tell me when you want the information, and I'll start the clock."

"Seventy-two hours?"

"Not a minute more."

"Can I ask if she's in the United States?"

"I'll give you that. She's in the country… for now."

The sheriff hesitated, but only for a moment. "Now. I'll take the information now."

102

Jennifer smiled as she thought about heading west to Main Street and the center of town. Instead, she headed directly across the parking lot towards the waterfront.

"Why do you even pretend?" she said aloud. Her pace quickened as her urges grew more intense. It had only been a few hours since she had been with Cliff. She told herself she needed to put some time between them. Not that she regretted anything. On the contrary, all had been wonderful. So much so, she doubted the truth of her emotions. She cautioned herself to keep control—not always her strong suit. She considered their agreement. Their friendship was the most valuable part of their relationship. Caution, she thought. Only, caution with a smile.

Her mind wandered as her feet moved forward. Were things finally starting to fall in place for her? She was happier than she had been in a long time. She was stressed by the St. Michaels project, but happier nevertheless. Was she finally on the rebound? She hoped the St. Michaels project would fill the voids in her life. Her nursing career was kaput, at least in Annapolis. Her writing career was going nowhere. And her love life…

Her smile widened. Cliff certainly filled that void.

Maybe things were looking up.

"Maybe."

Caution flags fluttered around her. What was it this time? She and Cliff were going to be okay. But there was something still bothering her. She realized it was the St. Michaels project. There was something about it she couldn't put her finger on.

She came to a stop in front of Old Man Hooper's boat. A good omen, she thought. Someone to talk to. Someone to listen. Someone she could count on for sound advice. She looked across the gunwale. She expected to see Mr. Hooper sitting in his usual spot below the wooden mast, his head bent down, his hands slowly and steadily working on a net draped across his lap. But the old beer crate he called a chair was empty. She walked the length of the boat. The vessel had no portholes, so she could not see in; and while both the forward and amidships hatches were open, she heard nothing from below. She glanced at her watch. It was after 9:00. She expected him to be up and working. What started as a good idea had quickly turned to a bad omen. There was no one to talk to. A queasiness filled her stomach. She swallowed hard to erase the bitter taste. She told herself to get a grip. "Caution," she mouthed. She turned away from the skipjack. What to do now? Main Street was to the right. *Caution to the wind* lay to the left.

She struggled with her feelings—feelings that led to the question of what to do. As she saw it, the choices were simple: Main Street or the *Mona Lisa*. Even with the short passage of time, her body yearned for the second. She was in conflict. Would seeing Cliff so soon help, or would it make matters worse?

A gust of wind struck her cheek causing her to lean to the right, toward Main Street. She turned in that direction. She needed to give Cliff some space. They both needed time to digest what happened the past couple days. Time was a good healer. And like Cliff said, time will tell.

Jennifer caught a glimpse of the yacht docked across the waterway. The boat's arrival was all the talk, at least among those interested in such waterfront activities. It looked huge up against the other vessels tied at the yacht club. It was one of the largest private yachts she had ever seen up close. And one of the most beautiful. She wondered what it looked like on the inside. She could only imagine. She also wondered who owned such a boat? And why?

Her queasiness was replaced by hunger pains. She decided to stop at the market and pick up a couple of Maria's sausage and biscuit sandwiches. That should help her stomach, and her mind.

Exiting the market with the greasy taste of sausage in her mouth and a much clearer head, she headed down the south side of the harbor. Approaching the gates of the yacht club, she stopped and stared at the boat. Her thoughts returned to her earlier questions of who and why. Luxury was one thing, but this…

She cocked her head to the side, shading her eyes against the glare of the early morning sun. The boat was big all right. She laughed again, mouthing quietly, "Maybe they need a crew member and I'll sign on."

She punched in the numbers on the keypad and passed through the heavy gate. Her eyes remained focused on the boat as she made her way out the main pier. Stopping halfway, she failed to notice something behind her. There was a coldness against the back of her leg. She snapped around. Chessie was sitting on her hind legs, her tongue hanging from her mouth. Seeing that she had gotten Jennifer's attention, the dog barked.

"Chessie!" Jennifer said, patting the animal on the head. "What are you doing here?"

"She could ask you the same thing?"

Jennifer looked up to see Cliff coming down the pier, the dog's leash rolled in his hand.

"Cliff, what are—" She stopped in mid-sentence.

Responding to the unfinished question, Cliff said, "I came for one last look at the boat. I'm pretty much done with the drawing. I just want to make sure the details are right. Anyway, what are you doing here?"

"I had an urge for a sausage biscuit and I thought while I was halfway, I'd come over and get a closer look at what everyone's talking about."

"They are, are they?"

"It's the buzz of the bar."

"It's not all that impressive." Cliff teased.

"She's big, even by Annapolis standards," Jennifer countered.

"Who's the owner, do you know?"

"According to my father, a man named George Hamilton."

"What's he do?"

"My dad didn't tell me that, but he's a close friend of the governor's, so I bet he's a lawyer type."

Cliff laughed. "I doubt that. Lawyers don't have this good of taste."

"Anti-lawyer, are we?" She didn't add he was in the wrong town to be carrying such an attitude.

"Handed down from my uncle, I guess." Cliff stared at the yacht. "He always blamed lawyers for the demise of the bay. He said the bigwigs in Annapolis, most of whom are lawyers, pushed through legislation a few years back that allowed for the dredging of the bay. According to my uncle, this may have saved the Port of Baltimore, but it damaged the fishing and crabbing. Now that's his opinion, of course."

"Do you think dredging the bay was bad?" Jennifer asked, curious on which side of the environmental lobby Cliff stood. The same lobby was the biggest barrier her family was facing with the St Michaels project, or so she thought.

"Depends which side of the fence you're on," Cliff answered.

"You're talking like a politician yourself."

Cliff continued. "If you're an environmentalist, anything you do to change what God created is bad. If you're a businessman, progress is inevitable and change is needed for the betterment of society."

"Betterment seems to be the key word," Jennifer pointed out.

"Therein lies the debate."

Jennifer paused. "You still haven't answered the question."

"Which is?"

"Which side of the fence are you on?"

Cliff stepped forward and kissed her on the cheek. "Whichever side you're on."

"You're full of shit," Jennifer said, blushing.

"Nice to see you, too."

Jennifer felt her body go limp as the kiss penetrated her skin. Her mind wandered to earlier emotions. She threw her arms around Cliff's neck and planted a return kiss on his lips. "Nice to see you, too."

The greeting complete, Cliff redirected his attention back towards the yacht. The mass of wood-trimmed fiberglass loomed over them. A series of heavy lines ran from her deck down to the cleats on the pier. The docks of Annapolis Yacht Club were the floating variety, so there was no problem dealing with the tide. *Hamilton's Bench* was tied tightly against the series of fenders that had been deployed along the side. The significant discrepancy between the height of the boat and that of the pier raised the question: was the boat tied to the pier, or the pier tied to the boat?

Cliff started his gaze forward and methodically moved his eyes along the profile. He wanted to make sure he had incorporated all the correct details into the drawing. Satisfied he had missed nothing, he turned his attention back to Jennifer who stood at his side petting Chessie. "Isn't this a private club?"

"My father's been a member for years."

"He have a boat?"

"Used to. He sold it a few years back. Same old story with most people—a lot of desire, but no time."

"I'm lucky there," Cliff said.

"Yes, you are," Jennifer acknowledged. "But you've got to give yourself credit for planning it that way."

"Someone still gave me the opportunity."

"The opportunity's called talent," Jennifer argued.

"It's more than that," Cliff said. "Just like the guy who owns this. He may have taken advantage of a situation to become this successful, but the opportunity had to be there in the first place."

"Whatever." A thought crossed Jennifer's mind. "By the way, how did you get in here?"

"I asked."

"You asked?"

Cliff chuckled. "I told the guy at the office what I was doing. Told 'em he could call the governor's office if he wanted to verify it. He looked down at Chessie who gave him one of those *my master's an honest kind of a guy* looks, and he let us in. Said he'd be keeping a close eye on us with the video cameras and all that." Cliff finished with a wink.

It took Jennifer a second to realize what Cliff was alluding to. The dockhand had watched their actions on cameras. Her mind tried to think who might be on duty this morning. Regardless, it would definitely cost her a few drinks at the bar. A smile crossed her face. It was worth it.

Her thoughts were interrupted as the dock started to rattle beneath their feet. Both turned to see the yacht club's electric golf cart heading their way. Cliff stepped to the edge of the pier and pulled a tight rein on Chessie's collar. Jennifer moved beside them. They saw that Bobby, the governor's bodyguard, was driving the cart, with Governor Wilson sitting in the passenger's seat. In the rear was a man about the governor's age. All were dressed in suits, although it took only a quick glance to know the suit in the rear was much more finely tailored.

The cart slowed on its approach. The governor recognized the trio and held up his hand for Bobby to stop. "Morning, Jennifer. Morning Cliff." He stretched his neck forward so he could look down at Chessie. "Hey, girl."

Chessie rose to all fours and wagged her tail.

"Morning Governor... Bobby," Jennifer said.

Bobby nodded and smiled.

"Didn't know you two knew one another so well," the Governor said. Jennifer couldn't tell whether he had a smirk or a smile on his face.

Cliff jumped in to save her. "Morning, sir. Jennifer is showing me the sights."

"Well, you have a most beautiful person to show you a most beautiful town." The governor looked over his shoulder. "George, these are friends of mine. Jennifer Blackstone—her parents own the *Riverboat Inn* I was telling you about. Chessie here is one of the finest Chesapeake Bay retrievers you'll ever meet. And believe me, if she wants to meet you, she will."

The dog barked on cue.

Pointing towards Cliff, the Governor continued. "And this is Cliff Davidson. I'd tell you about him, but that would ruin the surprise. Jennifer and Cliff, this is George Hamilton, the owner of this illustrious yacht." The governor pointed down the pier.

"Please to meet you," Cliff and Jennifer said in unison.

"Surprise!" Hamilton said, ignoring the people standing to the side. He leaned forward. "What surprise?"

"You'll just have to wait till Friday."

"Now, Governor, you know I don't like surprises."

The governor ignored the protest. "I'll wager you'll like this one."

The man in the rear shrugged his shoulders. He looked at Cliff and Jennifer. "He always has to be in control. Anyway, nice meeting you." He nodded to Cliff and Jennifer then smiled at the dog. His gaze returned to Jennifer. "The governor says your mother makes the best oyster stew around."

"Many people think so," Jennifer replied, a little embarrassed at the governor having stopped to talk to them. There were times when she liked being recognized by the highest officer in the state. There were times when she didn't.

"I'd like to try it sometime," the yacht owner said.

"I'm sure we can arrange that."

"Thank you," he said with a genuine tone. Their eyes met briefly. Hamilton turned his attention to Cliff. "And Cliff, I'll just have to wait for the surprise. Regardless, your retriever is beautiful... as is your other companion." He caught Jennifer's eye again and nodded politely.

Chessie barked again. Jennifer blushed.

Cliff motioned towards the yacht. "Your Chesapeake Bay retriever's beautiful, too."

Hamilton tipped his head to the side. "Thank you," he said with a chuckle.

"Mine's named Chessie," Cliff said.

Mr. Hamilton laughed. "Mine's named *Hamilton's Bench*." He saw the inquisitive look on Cliff's face. "It's a long story."

Cliff nodded. "Maybe we can get to that story another time."

"Maybe we can do it over a bowl of oyster stew," Hamilton suggested

"Sounds like a plan to me," Cliff said.

Everyone laughed. The governor turned around. "Okay, Bobby, onward ho, please. We have a lot to do before Friday evening."

Everyone waved and the cart moved on toward the end of the pier.

Turning to Jennifer, Cliff said, "Friday night's the big fundraiser. You going?"

"Two thousand bucks a pop's a little pricey for me. He knows I love him and all that, and I'll support him to the end. Still…"

"Your parents going?"

"Naturally. They said they'd buy my ticket if I wanted, but I declined. Besides, I don't have a thing to wear."

Cliff laughed. "You certainly look good in that."

"In what?"

"In nothing."

Jennifer blushed again. "Clifford, that's so unlike you."

"Sorry, just a momentary lapse in manners."

She slid her arm inside his. "Just so it doesn't happen again, that is until we're alone." She kissed him on the cheek. So much for caution to the wind. Her eyes remained unfocused however, as her thoughts returned to the night before. Cliff's kisses lingered. A chill went up her spine. She told herself to behave. She told herself to keep control. She told herself not to read more into it than what it was. After all, both had been hurt in the past. Neither wanted to experience that again. And they had an agreement. Jennifer watched as the three men reached the top of the gangplank. A figure came out the side door to meet them. Parts of her body were willing her to get back to her fantasy. The images were broken, however, by Cliff's voice.

"That's her!" he said excitedly. "That's the girl who I spooked the other day. Remember, I told you about her?"

Jennifer was about to speak when the figure turned and faced their direction. Jennifer's mouth was opened, only no words came forth. She could only stare. The girl, oblivious to the two people on the pier, greeted the new arrivals and motioned them toward the rear of the boat. While Jennifer only had an instant to look at her face, there was no doubt in her mind. She knew the girl!

But who was she?

Jennifer wracked her brain trying to remember. An array of faces flashed through her memory. Some faces with names, others anonymous. Some faces from the distant past, others from more recent times. Her mind churned like a spinning hard drive searching for a piece of lost data. "I know her," she stammered.

"Know who?"

"The girl… that girl."

The two watched as the group disappeared through a door near the rear of the yacht.

103

As the sun approached its peak, the temperature jumped three degrees. The earlier breeze had subsided, raising the heat index even more. Used to the controlled environment where air conditioning was taken for granted, Jennifer initially had trouble adjusting to the heat aboard the *Mona Lisa*. Yet, as her visits increased, so did her tolerance of the environment. She didn't know whether her body had become accustomed to the heat, or if she learned the skill Cliff had suggested during one of her early visits—to simply ignore it—a difficult task when self-bathing in sweat. In any case, it was again hot and stuffy inside the cabin. The fans did little except circulate the misery. She ignored it, or at least tried, as she put the finishing touches on a plate of bite-sized tuna sandwiches. She actually left the restaurant with ham and cheese sandwiches only to return for tuna fish when she remembered Cliff's vegetarianism. She poured two bowls of oyster stew and made her way on deck.

Cliff looked up from his drawing pad. "Need a hand?"

"Not as long as the boat doesn't rock," Jennifer answered.

"There's always motion in here," Cliff said. Regardless of how calm the water appeared, ego alley sported a strong current. Cliff set the drawing pad aside and unfolded the cockpit table. Seeing the steam coming from the bowls of stew, he quipped, "Nothing like hot soup to take the chill off your bones."

"Don't complain," Jennifer directed. "You have no idea how hard it is to get oysters this time of year, especially ones that'll meet the Oyster Queen's standards. I think I heard her say these came from somewhere down south." She was referring to the reputation her mother had for demanding nothing but the best from all the *Riverboat Inn's* suppliers. Over the years, both she and her father learned not to question the Oyster Queen. Her father demanded high quality service from the staff. Mrs. Blackstone demanded the same quality in the kitchen. Although Jennifer did think that her mother went a bit overboard at times. She sent a whole case of lettuce back once because there were a few wilted leaves. Jennifer never argued. The *Riverboat Inn's* reputation was of quality food and quality service at a fair price. Her mother preached that a restaurant's reputation was only maintained if the owners were the toughest critics.

"Oysters are out of season," Cliff said. "The last time I looked, August doesn't have a letter R in it."

"Maybe out of season every other place in the world," Jennifer said. "Not at the *Riverboat Inn*. There's always an R in riverboat. It could be a hundred and twenty degrees out and people would still come in wanting to know if the oyster stew was ready. Notice I said *is it ready*. No one ever asks if we have it. That's assumed."

"Not a bad problem to have," Cliff commented, grabbing a bowl. He took a couple spoonfuls. "I know of two people who aren't going to complain."

"You and who else?"

"Mr. Hooper."

"Don't worry. He already had his oyster fix for the day."

"You take him his meals every day?" Cliff asked.

"If not, he wouldn't eat."

"He has you wrapped," Cliff said. Jennifer gave him a nasty look. Cliff quickly continued. "Don't mean nothing bad. If anything, I'm a might jealous."

Jennifer's glare turned to a smile. Mimicking a southern accent, she retorted. "Well, honey bunch, I do declare, I think you've been treated pretty well lately, if I do say so myself." She flicked her eyelashes at him.

Cliff blushed and turned his attention to the food. Jennifer watched as his eyes lit up in response to the various flavors of the stew. He chased an oyster around the bowl with his spoon, caught it and then devoured it with two chews. A look of pleasure crossed his face. Jennifer recognized it as the same unknowing expression when they kissed the night before.

She looked away as her heart had suddenly started to race. Just as suddenly, the temperature seemed to rise even more. She took a couple deep breaths and wiped her brow with the back of her hand. She felt more sweat form on the back of her neck. A few droplets started down her neck, under her collar and down her back. She knew she couldn't blame this just on the weather.

She continued watching him eat. Working in both the hospital and the restaurant allowed her to meet a lot of men. Most were assholes. Those who weren't were either happily married, about to be married, gay or devout priests. She was sure there were a few other categories she hadn't covered—with *few* being the operative word. Exceptions to the rule were rare. She had known only two men in her life who she couldn't categorize. Daniel Baker was one; Cliff Davidson was the other. Cliff was different in so many ways. He was kind and considerate—a true gentleman. His sense of humor was just enough, and he lacked the normal satire common with most young people these days. While most men she knew, and many women, were emotionally superficial, Cliff was genuine. There was a depth to his personality she had yet to scratch.

She loved watching people. She loved to meet someone and try to figure out just what made him or her tick. If she couldn't get an immediate answer, she made up something. With Cliff, except for his love of the water and art, she had only hints of who he was. He didn't talk in details about his past, although he did tell her briefly about his uncle's death and the subsequent events. Nor did he talk about his dreams, except to say that he wanted to survive solely as an artist. Jennifer surmised there was much more to the young man than simply a struggling artist. Something else—some other mystery—was buried inside his soul. She let her eyes rove down his body. Not bad in that category either, she thought.

Physically, he looked his age. He claimed he was nineteen, and she had no reason to believe he was lying. She guessed he was much smarter than he acted. He spoke as if he were well read; although, except for an old copy of Chapman's *Piloting and Seamanship*, she had yet to see any reading materials aboard the boat, good or bad. She continued to explore. She still got electrical shocks thinking about him lying next to her. The voltage increased as she extended the thought. She closed her eyes and imagined that Cliff

Davidson was the best lover she had ever experienced. Maybe initially not the most knowledgeable about a woman's body, but he was a quick learner; and once educated, was relentless in his pursuit of giving her pleasure. His own pleasure only came when he was sure she'd been satisfied. To her, it was the ultimate sign of a gentleman.

He was the perfect man, the perfect friend, the perfect lover.

So why was she feeling so shitty about the whole thing, and why had she come down here to tell him they needed to back off some. Things were getting too intense too quickly. She strongly believed that whirlwind romances did not breed long term relationships. Relationships only lasted if both parties worked at controlling the velocity of the emotions that drove such feelings and passion. She just hoped he understood it the way she did. She knew what she was going to say. She knew how she was going to approach the subject. The only thing left to decide was the timing.

"Then why not now?" she thought.

And so she did.

104

It didn't surprise Jennifer that the bar was packed three deep and the dining room was only half full. She expected a slow dinner crowd. Those not going to the fundraiser would be mulling around the harbor, hoping to get a glance of someone important. Or better yet, have that important person get a glance of them. The activity in and around Annapolis functioned much like Washington, DC, only on a smaller scale. Egos however, were just as big. It was here, as in state capitals all across the nation, that tomorrow's national leaders were primped and prepared. While nothing specific had surfaced, Maryland's governor had already been mentioned in national terms. The rumors were vehemently denied, however, as the governor and his staff kept the focus on the upcoming election. Governor Wilson had been around long enough to know you never took anything in politics for granted. Politics was a fickle business, and the tide could turn in a heartbeat. His numbers in the polls were good. He had every intention of keeping them that way.

Jennifer never played the political game. She had no desire for political power, satisfied with letting others bask in the spotlight. Besides, she didn't need to fight to get into Annapolis's inner circle. Thanks to her parents, and their generous support of the governor and other prominent politicians over the years, she was already there. She knew most of the *in people* in town. Many of them used the *Riverboat Inn* as their base camp for after-hours meetings. She had to admit it was fun having the governor know her by name, and for him to stop and speak. He had known her since she was an infant and had been friends with her parents even longer. She was content to sit back and watch others struggle for the perceived power.

Tonight was being heralded as one of the biggest events since the inauguration three years earlier. The whole town was buzzing with talk of who'd be there and who wouldn't. There was even a rumor that the Vice President might make an unexpected appearance, although Jennifer had kept an eye out across the way all day and had yet to see any increased activity around the yacht by anyone wearing dark glasses and talking into their sleeves. Nothing surprised her, however, and an appearance by someone of his caliber would only add to the governor's war chest. Jennifer looked up and down the bar. The fundraiser was still a good sixty minutes away, but about a third of the patrons were decked out for the event, eager for an early start to the evening.

Satisfied everything was under control, Jennifer ducked into the office. Her father hung up the phone as she entered the room. "How's everything going, kiddo?" He asked. He looked especially handsome dressed in his best black tux. The joke amongst the Blackstones was that her father had three tuxes—one for special occasions, one for extra special accessions, and one for extra extra special events. The reality dealt not with the event's formality, but rather with the circumference of his waistline on the night the tux was needed.

"Everything's fine," Jennifer said, planting a kiss on his cheek. "Slow in the dining room, but we planned for that. That little boat over there's drawing all the attention."

David Blackstone laughed. "I'll let the governor know."

"You do that."

Her father's head leaned to the side. Jennifer turned and saw her mother enter the room. She was dressed in a long silver evening gown, cut low in the back with a high collar. While the years of long hours and hard work in the restaurant had taken their toll, Elizabeth Blackstone still dressed nicely. Her daughter said as much as she kissed her on the cheek. David Blackstone rose to his feet and did the same. Looking down at her feet, he said, "Nice shoes."

Jennifer's mother laughed. "You've been watching *The American President* again, haven't you." It was her husband's favorite movie.

"What makes you think that?"

She ignored the question, turning her attention to her daughter. "You sure you don't want to come along?"

"Only if I can bring a dozen or so of my closest friends," Jennifer joked.

"We'll see if the Governor will let us fix you a plate to go."

"I'm sure he'll go for that," Jennifer laughed.

Mr. Blackstone's face turned serious. "For you, I'm sure he would. After all, you are one of his favorite people. He tells me that all the time."

Jennifer changed the subject. "How you two getting there?"

"We each have new shoes," Mr. Blackstone pointed out. "Good time to break them in."

"Or break an ankle," Mrs. Blackstone injected, flexing her ankles to test their strength. Otherwise, she didn't protest. She was looking forward to the walk—something she and her husband used to do a lot in their earlier days.

"Then you'd better get going," Jennifer instructed.

"We are in a few," Mr. Blackstone said.

"Anything you need?" her mother asked.

Jennifer started to say no, and then laughed. "Yeah, fix me up with the owner of the boat."

"If anyone gets fixed up, it'll be me," her mother quipped.

Jennifer kissed her parents good-bye and started to leave the office. "By the way, don't forget to keep an eye out for the girl I was telling you about."

"You still haven't figured out who she is?" her mother said.

"Not a clue."

"I'll keep an eye out," her mother promised. "And I'm sure your father's eyes will be wide open as well."

"I'll only have eyes for you," the man insisted.

"Watching James Bond, too," Elizabeth Blackstone said.

"You two have a good time, and both of you behave." Jennifer smiled. "Understand, young lady?" she added. Oh, if she had a dollar for every time her parents said that to her!

The two elders said in unison, "Don't you have work to do?"

Jennifer turned and left the office.

105

Phillip Rogers sat at the far corner of the bar where he could monitor the activity of the staff, and monitor the crowd to ensure their needs were met. It also gave the crowd a good view of him. A tall handsome man in a starched white uniform perched atop a stool was easy to spot. He straightened his posture to make sure. He had been mingling with the guests earlier, and as expected, the party was proving to be pretty lame. The crowd was more interested in who else was there, who they could be seen with, and talking to the governor. Almost unnoticed was the lavish spread *Hamilton's Bench* was offering. He knew, however, people's attention would eventually turn to the food. People were polite and made many positive comments about the boat's elegance, but no women had yet inquired about him personally. It was disappointing and irritating to the handsome captain. He'd been looking forward to coming back to the United States—for a change of food and beverage, and for the women. The first two items had been amply cared for since arriving in Annapolis. The third, however, was still unfulfilled.

The sound of applause broke his train of thought. He turned in the direction of the piano where April sat smiling like she always did, appearing to be almost embarrassed at the attention paid to her by the crowd. She was dressed in a long ivory gown that Mr. Hamilton had bought her for the night's occasion. Her freshly cut hair was piled in a bun atop her head. Her make up was applied just enough to accent her eyes and lips. She was by far the most beautiful person in the room. When the applause subsided, April's eyes returned to the keyboard. As she started the next piece and the crowd returned to their previous conversations.

Phillip kept his eyes fixed on the figure at the piano. For the most part, her eyes remained closed, opening for only brief periods to glance down at the keys. The melody flowed forth. He recognized the piece as one of Mozart's—he forgot the exact one, but he'd heard her working on it recently. He was never into classical music, but the more time he spent around April, the more it grew on him. She had a way of hypnotizing the listener. While the crowd carried on their we're-at-a-political-fundraiser-and-have-to-act-out important business, they often paused as the music volume rose briefly. Many of the guests made a point of stopping at the piano during one of April's infrequent pauses for a comment or two. Phillip had to admit, she was magical with the piano. He overheard Mr. Hamilton brag on more than one occasion about April being the most important feature of his parties. Mr. Hamilton was careful to keep his comments out of earshot of Cookie, the yacht's executive chef.

Phillip watched and enjoyed the ambience April created. He reminded himself he had yet to score. A glance at his watch told him time was running out. He ordered another drink, guzzled it down and made a decision. To himself, he said, "Captain my man, you have scored tonight. Only she doesn't know it yet." He continued staring at the pianist. "Yes sir, tonight will be the night." He ordered yet another drink. The bartender supplied by a private catering company made it a double.

106

"More champagne, dear?" David Blackstone said, holding a glass out for his wife.

"I haven't finished the first one," she said, showing him the one she was holding.

"Then drink up," her husband encouraged.

"You know what happens when I drink champagne," she said.

"You get real giddy. Then you get real sexy. Then—"

"David, behave please. I think you've already had too much yourself."

"I am behaving… for now."

Elizabeth Blackstone gave her husband one of her infamous looks—although she didn't make it too severe. She knew they both needed this evening out, and was actually pleased to see her husband relaxed and enjoying himself. It didn't happen often of late. She emptied her glass then took the one he was holding for her. "Isn't there a Chinese proverb that talks about taking responsibility for that which you create?"

Her husband smiled widely and slid his now free hand around her waist. They were outside on the aft deck of *Hamilton's Bench* looking east toward the Severn River. They stood side by side and looked across the water. It brought back memories of their early days together when long slow walks in the evening along the Annapolis waterway were common. Sometimes evenings were replaced by late nights. Hand in hand, they'd whisper sweet nothings to one another and talk about their life, their dreams, and their want of a family. Now that those wishes had come true and their lives had become so hectic, sweet nothings were often forgotten.

The harbor was filled with boats seeking shelter for the night with glowing anchor lights too numerous to count. It was a beautiful moonlit sky. The stars were out in force, on the ground and in the sky. It was as if the whole universe had turned out for the fundraiser.

"Proverb or not, sounds fine with me," David Blackstone said. "Besides, no one's paying us a bit of attention. All eyes are in there on the governor. Why I bet we could…"

She slid from his grasp. "Another proverb says that good things come to those who wait."

He had a comeback for that, but wisely held his tongue.

His wife reached back and took his hand. "Come on, let's go back inside. I heard music earlier. I want to see who they got to play tonight." As the *Riverboat Inn* frequently had live music on the weekends, Elizabeth Blackstone was familiar with all the local bands. She wanted to see who got the lucky gig tonight. All bands liked this sort of work. It paid well and had good exposure with people who had the power to make decisions about music in the future.

It took a full five minutes to make their way from the aft deck around the starboard side to the door leading into the main salon. Again, they found the room full of people. It wasn't quite elbow to elbow, but it was close enough. They recognized many people they knew, supporters of the governor, as well as those present to champion their own political futures. In a brief conversation with the governor when they first arrived, the state's chief executive told them, "For the price of a ticket, they can do whatever they want when they get here." Political fundraisers, even at the statewide levels, tended to draw friend and foe.

The Blackstones made their way across the main salon towards the music. Earlier, Elizabeth Blackstone thought she had heard a whole band, but it was only a piano. The more she listened, the more she realized the pianist was more accomplished than anyone she knew. There were a few locals who could handle classical requests, but this musician was more than handling a few requests. "Imported for the occasion," she whispered loudly into her husband's ear.

While *Hamilton's Bench* was indeed a mega-yacht, she was still a boat, and the ceilings were low. The noise level was high and the temperature was rising. The crowd was upbeat and starting to show the effects of free flowing champagne. The Blackstones were pleased. It would be a memorable and successful evening for the governor.

They continued to inch through the crowd, stopping frequently to speak to acquaintances. The journey across the room was slowed by David Blackstone accepting a taste of various appetizers. So many servers with so many trays! Elizabeth Blackstone had little doubt the crowd could be cut in half if the catering staff were reduced. She was about to say something to that effect when she was distracted by a voice from behind. She turned in time to see her husband shaking hands with Samuel Robertson.

The man turned his attention to her. "Evening, Elizabeth. I must say, you look radiant tonight."

"Thank you," she said politely. She did not return the compliment.

"Lovely party," Robertson said.

"It is, isn't it?"

"Wilson should add a good hunk of change to his war chest after tonight."

"That's the purpose." David Blackstone said pointedly. The handshake was over.

Robertson shrugged his shoulders. "I guess so, but he doesn't need it, least not for this election."

Knowing the man was looking for information about the governor's intentions for the future, David Blackstone said nothing. It was well known that David Blackstone had been offered a prominent position in the state government three years earlier. He respectfully declined, claiming he'd be more valuable on the outside. Rumor had it, David Blackstone was one of Governor Wilson's most trusted advisors. While he never denied the rumor, he never admitted to it either. *Keep em' guessing* was his motto. Just like now with Samuel Robertson. Finally he said, "A good politician knows you can never have enough money in the bank."

"But this?" Robertson swept his arm around the room.

"Good financial planning is a key to success of any organization," Blackstone said. The tone in his voice was harsh. He ignored the pressure being put on his arm by his spouse.

"A lesson hard for some to understand," Robertson said, not willing to back down.

Elizabeth squeezed harder. "Especially if one isn't privy to the true goals and objectives of the organization," her husband continued.

Sam Robertson's eyes widened. "David, I know you're—"

"He's not anything," Elizabeth Blackstone injected sharply. "Now David dear, why don't we get moving along. I want to get a closer look at the piano."

Both men forced a smile. "Nice to see you both," Robertson said.

David Blackstone's manners returned. "Nice to see you."

Distance found its way between the couple and the administrator. "He was and still is one son-of-a-bitch," David Blackstone said.

"You used to think of him quite differently," Elizabeth reminded her husband. "Especially when you needed a golf partner."

"That was before…"

"You've always been critical of how he ran the hospital, with or without Jennifer. So why are you getting all railed up now?" the wife asked. "It's been almost two years. Nothing has changed."

"Because."

"That's not a good enough reason."

"You know perfectly well why."

"Because he fired your daughter." She took a sip of her champagne. "I still think it was the best thing for her."

Her husband stared at her. They had never really talked about the actual incident, focusing conversations instead on their daughter's well-being and her future. As owners of one of the most popular restaurant in the area, and wanting to keep it that way, they were careful what they said about anything controversial in public. That habit easily rolled over into their private life. During the surprise 25th anniversary party Jennifer had thrown them a few years earlier, David Blackstone was asked the secret to their success. He answered quickly and vehemently. "Never, ever argue with your wife!" The comment received a large round of applause and a room full of laughter. But today, the thirty year husband of Elizabeth Blackstone was not in a joking mood.

Elizabeth Blackstone was about to say something to help settle her husband down when a voice from behind interrupted her efforts. "David… Fancy running into you here." Elizabeth turned toward the voice. A short stocky balding man was holding his hand out towards her husband. What little hair he had was wind-blown and he appeared short of breath. He seemed anxious to get to them. Elizabeth suspected their meeting was not by chance.

Her husband did the introductions. "Elizabeth, this is Douglas Myers. He's the President of the City Council in St. Michaels. Douglas, Elizabeth Blackstone, my wife."

Elizabeth smiled and took the extended hand. She had heard her husband and daughter talk about the man numerous times when the topic of the St. Michaels project arose. He certainly didn't look like she imagined, nor did he have the look of a politician. She felt a successful politician had to be able to dress nicely. You had to wear a suit well. Douglas Myers not only looked bad in his tuxedo, he looked uncomfortable. But like her husband always said, they were a different breed on the Eastern Shore. He also didn't look the part of a multi-million dollar land owner. Rumor was he owned land that nearly encircled the town of St. Michaels.

He spoke before Elizabeth could think further. "Again, David, I'm glad I ran into you tonight."

"I hope so you could give us some good news," David Blackstone said. They were expecting word on the council vote any day. Myers had insisted there would be no problem getting the unanimous vote required by the town council for any project of this magnitude. He claimed the new environmental impact numbers looked good.

The smile on the politician's face faded slightly. Both Blackstones picked up the subtle change. Elizabeth squeezed her husband's arm to let him know she was still there at his side for support… and control. The politician continued. "Unfortunately, a couple of the council members still have concerns."

"Concerns about what?" David asked sternly.

"That same old thing, the environment."

"What about the impact study? You said yourself, the numbers look good."

"The numbers do look good, I agree. But…"

"Still concerns?"

"I'm sorry, David. As you know, a project of this magnitude requires full support of the council. And in spite of our best efforts, you don't have it." Elizabeth Blackstone squeezed her husband's arm tighter. The short balding man in the funny looking tuxedo continued. "Again, I'm sorry. The Mitchell property would have been a nice property for you to purchase. You would have liked the people in St. Michaels. We're really a good bunch."

Elizabeth Blackstone often came off as a down-to-earth, simple housewife, which indeed she was. However, under that layer of personality, she was a tough intelligent woman. She spoke before her husband could respond. "Well, Mr. Meyer, I'm sure you are correct regarding your statement just now. I've been to St. Michaels numerous times. Everyone there has always been lovely. You're also correct about the Mitchell property. It is a good buy. That's why we're going to go ahead with the purchase."

As Elizabeth predicted, any remaining smile on the councilman's face disappeared. He turned pale. She continued. "Anyway, it was awfully nice meeting you, Councilman. If you'll excuse us, it seems my champagne glass is empty. Come on dear; let's go fill 'er up. After all, this is supposed to be a celebration, isn't it?" She led her husband away, leaving Councilman Meyers stuck in his tracks and even more uncomfortable in his tuxedo.

David Blackstone wisely chose not to resist his lovely wife. That would have been a mental error, as well as a physical mistake. She now had a strong grip on his arm. When they were well out of ear shot, he did manage to say, "You going to tell me what that was all about? You do understand the property is worthless without the building permits?"

"I understand," the wife said.

"So…"

At the bar, Elizabeth Blackstone exchanged the empty glasses for two full ones. Handing one to her husband, she said, "Your friend there is full of shit."

David Blackstone choked on the bubbling liquid in his mouth. His wife seldom spoke negatively about anyone. She cursed even less. The two together warned him her comments had little do with her alcohol level. "So…" he repeated, drawing the word out.

"He's the barrier to the permits, no one else." Elizabeth took a sip of her champagne. "Then again, others may be involved, but he's the leader."

"Why would he do that?"

"So he can buy the property for himself."

"He had the chance. He didn't do it."

"That's right. He waited for someone else to go in, do all the dirty work, spend all the money on environmental studies and then take over for himself. He has a free ride with little expense except the cost of the property, which is now probably a lot less with our expected pull out. You did it all for him."

"Are you suggesting we were set up?"

"That may not have been his original plan, but, once the opportunity presented itself… Well, he is a politician."

"That's why I married you dear." David Blackstone knew his wife was smart. He figured it would take her a little longer to see through the ruse he suspected from the beginning.

His wife made the appropriate correction. "No dear, you married me because we fell in love. You let me be your business partner because once in a while I am smart. Maybe smarter than you think."

"Well," the husband said. "You're smart a lot of times. I just don't always realize it."

"Now that's the wisest thing you said tonight." Elizabeth was about to add an additional comment when another voice interfered in their conversation.

"David, Elizabeth, good to see you. Thanks so much for coming." Jane Syzeman gave each a kiss on the cheek. "You both look great."

Elizabeth eyed the governor's aide. She failed to hide a smile. "There's only one person I've seen here tonight I'd worry about with my husband, and darn if she isn't standing right in front of me." Her smile widened. "Jane, you look gorgeous, dear."

Which she did in a long, red, floor-length evening gown. While Elizabeth Blackstone wasn't up on the latest fashion, she did know the aide's dress didn't come off the rack at Macy's.

"Thank you Mrs. B. You look stunning as well."

Mr. B. let out a cough. Jane chuckled. "And you look quite handsome yourself, Mr. B." She took a sip of her champagne and scanned the crowd to make sure everything was okay with her boss who was nearby and surrounded by well-wishers. "How's everything going? I saw you talking to Councilman Meyers," she said.

David hesitated.

"He's full of shit," his wife said.

Her husband choked on his champagne.

Jane Syzeman smiled. "He is that," she agreed.

"Thank you," Elizabeth said.

"Anyway," the governor's aide continued. This time her eyes remained focused on the Blackstones. "Word is that you're moving your operation to the Eastern Shore."

"That's not quite true," David Blackstone said. "You know that, too."

"The word on the street doesn't always coincide with the truth—especially in this town," the governor's aide said.

"I don't know how that rumor got started," Elizabeth Blackstone said.

Both Blackstones noticed a twinkle in Jane's eyes. They had known her for years and watched her career grow from a volunteer in Wilson's first campaign for the House of Delegates, to his run for the Senate, to the Governor's mansion a few years later. She was smart, good looking and loyal to a fault. They had become friends through her frequent visits to the *Riverboat Inn*, usually in tow with some delegate or senator she was trying to whip into shape. Sometimes she was brought by a lobbyist trying to whip her into shape. Those who knew her well knew the whip never took the whipping. She was liked by everyone who met her. David Blackstone commented more than once that Jane would be the perfect match for their son, at which time Elizabeth would remind him they didn't have a son. David would shrug his shoulders and mutter, "Details, details."

Yes, Jane Syzeman was smart, good looking and loyal. She also had the knack to subtly tease. Sometimes it was a good tease. Sometimes it wasn't.

"Jane," Elizabeth Blackstone said sternly.

"Word is some people around here are upset about the possibility of you moving away."

"Jane!"

"Word is you had trouble before getting the necessary permits to expand here in Annapolis."

"You know that's true," David Blackstone said.

"Word is if you reapply, things might be different this time."

"Word is?"

Scanning the crowd, Jane said, "Sometimes the word on the street is right on."

The Blackstones looked at one another and then back at Jane. David spoke. "What's the word on the street say about the project in St. Michaels?"

"That it's still a go."

"Really!"

"And that Douglas Meyers is full of shit," the aide said. Both Blackstones laughed. "But I wouldn't wait too long before reapplying for the permits. The word may change quickly."

"We may do just that."

Jane emptied her glass and started to turn away. "Jane," David Blackstone said. The governor's aide looked back their way. "Thank you."

"Don't thank me," the aide said.

"Bullshit," said Elizabeth Blackstone.

The twinkle in the eye returned as the aide made her way towards her boss.

"Well," David Blackstone said, "that was an interesting five minutes." He didn't tell his wife things were going exactly as he had hoped. The sound of applause broke his train of thought. The piano music was starting again.

"Come on," his wife said. "I want to see who that is. We can talk about all this later." Still holding her husband's arm, she led him to the musical source.

David followed willingly as his wife guided him across the room where they were able to get a good view of the piano. To her surprise, the musician looked awfully young. She was very pretty too, at least from the back. Even without a look at her face, Elizabeth knew it was no one from the area. The Blackstones stood side by side listening to the girl play. Neither was into classical music, but they were able to appreciate the quality of what they were hearing. The piece ended to a round of enthusiastic applause. The girl rose to her feet, turned and faced the crowd, and nodded politely. As her face turned in their direction, Elizabeth set her now empty glass on a passing tray and applauded louder. She turned to her husband to make a comment about the crowd's enthusiasm.

Her own expression of joy was short lived as she read the look on her husband's face. It was not one of joy, but one of surprise.

107

Jennifer plopped down on the overstuffed couch against the far wall. The small metal side vents made a hissing sound as the air released from the cushions. She waited for the noise to subside before grabbing the wooden handle on the side and pulling the footrest into the reclined position. With a sound similar to the cushions, she let out a long breath. "Did you guys give out tickets for free drinks? I think the whole boat came over here afterwards."

Her mother and father were both behind the desk, her mother sitting, her father looking over his wife's shoulder. Her mother looked up. "Don't worry, your father was toying with an idea of how to get them to come back here."

"Well, whatever you did, it worked," Jennifer said. "We were packed till last call."

"Everything go alright?" her father asked.

"Luckily, Mike and Mark were at the bar playing customer and relaxing," Jennifer said referring to two of their part-time bartenders. While they were not related, they were referred to as the M and M twins. They didn't look alike either. They just worked together all the time. The name came from a couple of the young female patrons at the bar who claimed they never melted in your hand, nor in your mouth.

Jennifer felt a blush thinking such thoughts standing in front of her parents. Thankfully, her father got her back on track. "Relaxing and looking for women," he corrected.

"They struck out because I put 'em to work."

"They agreed to work?" her father said, surprised. Mike and Mark were two of their best bartenders, but both were adamant about when they worked and when they didn't.

"They saw the tips flowing as smoothly as the booze and wanted in on the action. Besides, I sort of blackmailed them," Jennifer admitted.

"What did you do?" her mother demanded with a smile. One of her daughter's best traits was her ability to talk people into working when they were off. The food industry in general had a high rate of turnover and no shows, so there was always a scampering for help, especially when there was an unexpected influx of customers.

"I couldn't get their credit card to clear… they were over their limits… so I told them I was going to cut them off."

"That's unusual isn't it?" her mother asked. Both young men were good customers, and often had receipts totaling several hundred dollars a month.

Mr. Blackstone laughed. "Especially considering they both have American Express cards, which have no credit limit on them."

Mrs. Blackstone's eyes narrowed as she stared down her daughter. "Jennifer!"

"It's called creative management," their daughter argued. "When you're desperate, you take desperate measures."

"Lying to a customer?"

Jennifer laughed. "Actually, it was Mark himself who called the cards in. It was he who came up with the story." Of the two men, Mark was far more money hungry.

"Don't worry," David Blackstone directed. "I'm sure both were well rewarded for their efforts."

"Just so happened, I lost their drink tab."

Mr. Blackstone smiled his approval. If you were going to give something away, let it be booze. High value to the customer. Low cost to the restaurant. "Creative management," he said aloud.

"They did well in tips. Plus, I threw mine in the kitty," Jennifer said, referring to her share of the tips from the couple hours she worked the bar. "Anyway, it all worked out, and everybody went home happy."

"I saw Mike and Mark walking around the harbor when we came back a little while ago," Mr. Blackstone said. "They each had their arms around some young thing, so maybe they didn't miss out on anything tonight."

"David!" his wife scolded. "Such discussion."

"Yeah, Dad. Such language. And in front of your daughter no less."

They each were treated to an evil look.

"Anyway," Jennifer said. "How was the party? From what we heard it was hot and packed."

"Hot and packed," her father repeated in agreement.

"It was very nice," her mother said.

"Did you meet the owner?"

"Mr. Hamilton… he was very nice," her father said.

"Quite charming, actually," her mother added.

"Yes, I know," Jennifer said.

Elizabeth Blackstone's eyes narrowed. "When did you meet him?"

"The other day. He was with the governor. Remember, I told you I saw Governor Wilson at the yacht club."

"You didn't say anything about Mr. Hamilton."

"Well, sorry, sorry, sorry," Jennifer teased.

"Trying to keep him all to yourself," her mother protested.

"I wish!"

"Now you two behave," David Blackstone directed. "He wasn't all that good looking."

"From the mouth of the man who thinks Richard Geer is ugly," his wife said.

"Anyway, so the party was good?" Jennifer said, trying to get the conversation back on track.

"I'd say it was a most successful fundraiser," her father said.

Her mother added, "Best one we've ever been to."

"It was worth it. The food was great." The usual combination of humor and sarcasm when speaking about food eaten elsewhere was noticeably missing from David Blackstone's voice.

"Your father tried at least two of everything," his wife said.

David Blackstone patted his abdomen. "First time I ever went to a fundraiser and came away without hunger pains.

"What about the boat itself?" Jennifer asked.

"A floating mansion," Her father replied. "Not as ornate as you might think. Very tastefully done if you ask me."

"I agree," her mother added. "It was decorated quite nicely, at least from what we could see. It was so crowded."

There was a pause during which time Jennifer's father adjusted his position. There was also a glance towards his wife—a look not meant for their daughter to witness, but seen by her anyway. Jennifer had seen the look before. Something bad was about to happen. "So let's have it," she said in anticipation.

"Have what?" her father returned, realizing the look to his wife had been intercepted.

"The bad news."

"What bad news?"

"Daddy!"

Her mother broke in. "You're right, Jennifer. There's good and bad news."

Jennifer hesitated. "Bad news first, please." She learned a long time ago not to try and anticipate what was to come. She waited… impatiently.

"The St. Michaels project is dead," her mother said.

Jennifer failed to keep a stunned look off her face. "But—"

"As you know, we needed unanimous support from the town council," her father explained. "We thought we had it. We learned tonight we didn't."

"What happened?" Both disappointment and anger were intermingled in her voice.

"It's a long story that your father can tell you another time. In short, someone tried to screw us, only we screwed them back."

"Your mother screwed them back," David Blackstone corrected.

Elizabeth Blackstone smiled.

Again, Jennifer knew not to press for details. They would come in due time. "What's the good news?" Sarcasm now dominated her tone.

Her father answered this one. "The St. Michaels project has now become the Annapolis renovation project."

Jennifer laughed. "You're joking?"

The question was not denied.

"You're not joking!"

"Word has it our application to expand the *Riverboat Inn* will be accepted this time."

"Damn. Anything else happen tonight I should know about?" Jennifer said, not knowing what to feel at this moment.

Another pause. Another glance between husband and wife. "Actually there was," her father said.

Jennifer was about to inquire further when she noticed her mother turning a page from a book on the desk. She rose to her feet and walked to the desk. "What're you two looking at anyway?"

"Family photographs," her mother said without looking up.

Jennifer laughed loudly. "It's after two in the morning, you both have been to a huge fundraiser, had a good time, ate and drank more than you're willing to admit, and now you're looking at family photos. I swear, I really don't..." Jennifer stared as the answer to the question that had been eluding her the past several days suddenly appeared. "The girl. You saw her?" She looked down at several pictures that were laid out across the top. She picked up the largest print. "My cousin, April. She's my cousin April, isn't she?"

Jennifer stared closely at the photo. It was from years before—one of those Christmas photo post cards. Her aunt and cousin were standing beneath a large oak tree. A field of corn could be seen in the background. There was an old trailer off to the left. Each wore what looked more like Easter dresses versus clothes for the Christmas Holiday. They stood side by side. Her aunt was a tall woman. She was thin and rather pretty, although her facial features looked washed out. She had long brown hair that was pulled off her face. She was well built, and the flowery dress she wore did nothing to hide her figure. If anything, Jennifer thought the dress a little much. April stood beside her mother. She was shorter by at least a foot. Her hair, also brown and long, had been curled and hung over her shoulders. She stood with her hands crossed in front of her. Her mother was smiling, but the girl simply stared at the camera. She was thin and petite, her figure not yet developed. She was still pretty, and with a little effort and a little maturity, would be knock-em-dead gorgeous. While the photograph was old, the resemblance between her cousin and the girl on the boat was...

"Is it all just a coincidence?" Jennifer wondered aloud.

Her father straightened up. "That's a question your mother and I've been mulling over since we got back."

"There are people in the world who do look alike," Elizabeth pointed out.

"What about the circumstances surrounding all this?" Jennifer questioned again. "There has to be more to it than that."

"Doesn't have to be," Elizabeth said.

"All we have are coincidences so far," Jennifer's father added.

Jennifer looked down at the photographs. It had been several years since she'd seen the pictures, or any family photos for that matter. She had never met her aunt or her cousin, and the topic wasn't often discussed in the Blackstone household. Jennifer always knew there was a story, but never pursued it. Her mother told her more than once the whole thing was a sore subject with her father. Undeniably, Jennifer had her moments of curiosity, about the story and her extended family. However, she also learned early in life that when her parents wanted her to know something, they'd tell her. A strategy of persistent pestering would simply prove pointless.

Her father stepped to the side and perched on the corner of the desk. He motioned to the photo on top. "This was the last photograph she sent."

Jennifer looked up. She could tell her father was in pain. He was usually very good at masking his emotions, but tonight his guard was down.

"Anyway, there is the time factor," her father continued. "And I couldn't be sure anyway, especially since I've never seen my niece. But the girl on the boat sure looked like her."

"What was she doing, anyway?" Jennifer asked. "The girl on the boat, that is."

"Playing the piano."

"She was the entertainment," her mother added.

"She was quite good, too," her father said. "I'd even venture more than good."

"I agree," her mother said.

"Does April play the piano?"

"Your aunt mentioned one time many years ago about teaching her how to play on an old upright piano they had," Jennifer's mother said.

"We did have an old upright," David Blackstone acknowledged.

"This girl was good," his wife reiterated. "Very good."

"Too good to be taught on an old upright?" David Blackstone queried.

"Even if she had access to a piano when your sister married, she's still so young to have come that far so quickly. What is she now, sixteen or seventeen?"

"Eighteen, I think."

"Unless she's a prodigy," Jennifer suggested.

Her father pondered the point. "That's possible I guess. Blackstones have always been known as quick learners."

Jennifer chuckled. "Too bad some of that musical talent hasn't rubbed off on me."

Her mother's face wrinkled. "Don't be so hard on yourself," she directed. "Your father can't sing worth a damn either."

Father and daughter's eyes met. Both realized the profanity was spoken without realization. An silent message passed from father to daughter that Elizabeth Blackstone had indeed partaken in a few glasses of bubbly. Both knew, however, not to broach the subject. Instead, David Blackstone said, "We're also known for our stubbornness." He regretted the comment immediately.

"Demonstrated by your father tonight," Elizabeth Blackstone said.

"How's that?" Jennifer asked.

"I ran into an old friend."

Wanting to get back on the subject of April, Jennifer let the comment slide, although the look in her father's eyes told her just who he was referring to. "Sometimes quick learning and stubbornness coexist," she said. She tilted her head to the side. "So, I recognized April from seeing this photograph?"

"She really hasn't changed as far as her facial features are concerned," Elizabeth Blackstone said. "You used to look at these all the time. Remember?"

"Then what's the problem?" Jennifer said. "Why don't we just go over there and introduce ourselves. Or did you guys already do that?"

"No, we didn't say anything to her. I told your father he should, but he didn't want to in case he was wrong."

David Blackstone looked up and stared across the room. "More like in case I was right," he admitted. "Your mother has been bugging me for years to contact my sister and make up."

"Make up?" Jennifer said surprised.

"It's a long story that I'll get to in a moment. Let me go here first," her father said. "I have called a couple times over the last year or so. The first two times the phone was answered by someone who claimed to be the housekeeper. She simply said Ms. June, as she called her, wasn't available. I didn't press the point, nor did I leave a message. The third time a young boy answered and said he was her stepson. He almost hung up on me at first, but I was able to talk to him before he got too suspicious." Jennifer's father conveyed the story of the recent phone conversation.

"When was the last phone call?" Jennifer asked when her father was finished.

"Last week."

"That's freaky."

"To say the least."

"If the girl is April, how in the world did she end up aboard *Hamilton's Bench*?" Jennifer said.

"That's a good question," her father acknowledged.

"An even better question is why?" her mother offered.

"You're still not sure if it was her?" Jennifer said.

David Blackstone spun the photograph around. "Not really, but if it's not, then they're twins. Besides, I reacted immediately when I saw her. I doubt I would have done that if the pianist was simply a look-alike."

Jennifer turned toward her mother. "What do you think, Mother?"

"I can certainly see the resemblance."

"Did she recognize either of you?"

Her mother responded. "I questioned your father about that. She did look in our direction, that's for sure. Did she actually see us? We don't know. She certainly didn't act like she recognized us."

"Yet, she spooked so easily the other day when Cliff tried to take her picture." Jennifer explained what she was talking about.

"Also remember," David Blackstone said. "We've never met her. We have sent photographs at Christmas, but heaven only knows if my sister even showed them to April."

"We're family," Jennifer protested.

"Only on paper," Her mother said. "In reality, your father and sister have been miles apart for years."

"Why?" Jennifer asked.

David Blackstone looked across the room. "Your grandfather died when we were just kids—killed in an accident at the paper mill where he worked. Your grandmother, God rest her soul, worked two jobs so we could stay together as a family. She was determined to make a good life for us, which she did, at least for me. Your aunt, on the other hand, never got over Dad's death, and never really appreciated what Mom was doing for us. First she became rebellious. Then her grades in school started to drop. About the same time, she started hanging out with the wrong crowd... or at least a crowd that wasn't up to our mother's standards. Within six months, she dropped out of school. This was a big blow to Mother, because she promised our father at his funeral that if she did nothing else, she'd see that we were educated. Neither of my parents completed high school—not because they didn't want to, but because of World War II. Anyway, your aunt became pregnant soon after and ran away with this boyfriend of hers. We tried to talk her into staying at home, but she kept right on going. Mother didn't handle all this and became very depressed."

"How did grandma die?" Jennifer asked, realizing it was yet another question to which she never knew the answer.

Her father let out a long sigh. "She ran off the road late one night coming home from work. The coroner said she fell asleep at the wheel."

While his tone was neutral, Jennifer knew there was both grief and resentment interwoven in the comment. "You think something else happened?"

Her mother continued the story. "It doesn't really matter. The results were the same."

"What happened with Aunt June and her boyfriend?"

"Times were tough and they had little money. Any extra, he spent on booze."

"Was he violent?" Jennifer queried.

Her father's eyes answered the question.

"Was April ever hurt?"

"From what we knew, no. My sister took the beatings for both of them."

"Why didn't she leave? She ran away once. Why not again?"

"She eventually did. She and April hid for several years on a farm in Alabama. That's where this photo was taken," David Blackstone said, looking down at the desk. "We offered to help—"

"With all due respect, your father's offer of help always carried with it a good dose of guilt," Elizabeth Blackstone injected.

"Over grandma's death," Jennifer said factually.

Her father continued. "One thing my father instilled in us from an early age was a sense of pride. No matter what we had or didn't have, we were always proud of who we were. He used to say that when all else fails, pride coupled with a good dose of determination, will get you through the toughest times."

"So Grandma failed eventually, not because Aunt June got into trouble, or even ran away, but because..." Jennifer stopped, unsure where her thoughts were heading.

"She lost her ability to feel proud," her father said. "Remember, back in those days, children were raised to respect and obey. We didn't have all the freedom you kids have today. We weren't perfect, and if someone got into trouble, you faced up to it, took your licking and went on with your life."

"So the issue wasn't that Aunt June got into trouble?"

"Or even ran away," David Blackstone continued. "It was when she really needed help, she refused it. That's what really broke my mother's heart."

Elizabeth Blackstone reached over and put her hand on her husband's shoulder. "Your father has tried to make contact on numerous occasions. We sent letters and cards at all the holidays. We've never heard back, until about six years ago when we got a short note and a couple of pictures. More time passed, then there was a letter that June got married and moved to Ohio. For the first time ever, there was a return address on the envelope. That's how your father got the number to call."

David Blackstone agreed. "From what I gathered, it's a real nice community, too. If nothing else, I assumed she's at least doing okay."

"What made you decide to call when you did?" Jennifer asked.

"It had been awhile since we'd heard from her, and your mother is always after me to try and make amends. If we've argued about anything in our life, it's been over my sister."

"Not your sister, but your stubbornness," Elizabeth Blackstone corrected.

"Whatever."

"Why don't we go over to the boat in the morning and ask Mr. Hamilton her name. If it's Blackstone, then we have a match. We can play dumb and say we're simply trying to find out who the pianist is so we can see about her playing for us here in the restaurant."

"He may not know her name," her mother said.

"He should be able to at least head us in the right direction."

David Blackstone looked at the clock on the far wall. It was well past two. "He did mention something about wanting to try some of your mother's oyster stew. We'll take over some around lunchtime. Sound like a plan?"

The two women in the room nodded their approval.

108

April lay in her bunk, hands folded behind her head, staring at the ceiling. She was physically exhausted. She had worked hard all day helping get the boat ready for the party. She played the entire evening with only a couple of short breaks. Even her fingers were sore. She was emotionally exhausted as well. Too much worrying, she told herself. The party kept her distracted, but the earlier concerns still loomed in the back of her mind. She wondered if she was overreacting, but she knew she had to be cautious. Still, they were in Annapolis, not Atlantic City. Except for that one time she caught the guy on the sailboat trying to take her picture, she had seen nothing to indicate a problem. As for the photographer, she decided that was just someone taking a picture. She told herself that with tonight being such a success, she should relax and enjoy the moment.

"I feel loved," Maryland's Governor said in his remarks to the crowd at the end of the evening. He made these comments standing beside her at the piano. A generous round of applause followed. He recognized and thanked Mr. Hamilton, the crew and everyone else who helped put on the fundraiser. He then presented Mr. Hamilton with a wrapped package. As Mr. Hamilton opened the package, the governor said, "This is the surprise we were talking about the other day." Mr. Hamilton opened the package to find a large drawing of *Hamilton's Bench*. April swore she had never seen her boss so excited. She had to admit, the drawing was impressive. The attention to detail was phenomenal. A close look showed the drawing had been completed while they were in Annapolis.

Before April could think any more about the drawing, the governor asked the crowd to give her a special round of applause. He said he had heard many pianists in the past, but never one so beautiful "In her playing and in her looks." She looked over at Mr. Hamilton for help. He was smiling and applauding right along with everyone else. With the governor's prodding, and a nod of approval from Mr. Hamilton, she rose and took a bow. It was by far the largest applause she had ever received.

It was a full hour before the last guests left and they were able to get everything clean. All the while, April continued thinking about the evening and how good she felt about what had happened. She never allowed herself to think about the quality of her playing. Tonight, she realized she was good. Maybe all the accolades she'd received over the years were more than just talk. She possessed a streak of stubbornness that helped her learn difficult pieces of music. But until tonight, she lacked true confidence. Tonight's applause broke through the barrier of self-doubt.

She reminded herself she still needed to be cautious. Danny always told her the best way to survive was to focus on what was going on around you, not inside you. The skills learned from her brother worked regardless of the type of wilderness. She knew that time was the deciding factor. As Danny always said, nothing did more to cool a trail than the tick of the clock.

Time… Maybe it was time to think about the future, to think about more than the next day. Maybe it was time to move on with her life as April Whiterock—move out of this wilderness and into the next.

As a sailor, she took one day at a time. Tonight, she realized she was more than just a sailor. She was more than just a crew member. She was a musician… a pianist… and evidently a pretty good one. So what should she do? What were her options? She saw a very short list. One thing she knew, she'd never go back to Worthington Valley. The past was the past. Only salmon could swim against the current. And she was no fish.

Like life in general, April never looked far ahead with her music. She played. She practiced. She improved. Where was this going? She hadn't a clue. But tonight, for the first time, she decided she wanted it to go somewhere. While she loved working aboard *Hamilton's Bench*, she realized tonight she loved the piano even more. She wondered if she could play music and maintain her false identity. There were millions of musicians in the world. Just like there were a lot of sailors. If she could blend in in one profession, why couldn't she in another? After all, she had papers stating she was April Whiterock. She had a social security card to go with it. What else would she need?

The idea increased the adrenaline in her bloodstream. Her earlier fatigue evaporated. She felt a surge of energy. She was tired, but… She threw her legs over the edge of her bunk and jumped to her feet. Earlier she had changed out of her gown and into a pair of shorts and tee shirt. She looked in the mirror and made sure her hair was straight. Pushing a strand from her face, she slipped on a pair of boat shoes and opened the door to her cabin.

Her heart skipped a beat as she nearly crashed into a figure standing at her door. The ship's captain seemed to be as startled as she. Phillip regained his composure a lot faster than April and said, "Evening, gorgeous. I was just stopping by to see if you were still up."

His eyes were glassy and she could smell the alcohol on his breath. She forced a smile and asked, "Why are you still up?"

"I was working on payroll."

Phillip seemed a bit too intoxicated to be messing around with payroll. April didn't ask whether he was sure the numbers were correct. "I was just going for a walk," she said. She immediately wished she hadn't told him that.

"I'll go with you. Could use some fresh air myself."

April cursed herself for being so stupid. A walk with Phillip Rogers was the last thing she wanted, but like a dutiful crew member, she followed him down the corridor. He took his time, making sure he held onto the rails as he walked. The boat was dead still, but watching him, one would have thought they were in heavy seas. On the upper aft deck, he stopped, leaned up against the rail and looked up at the sky. "Moon'll be full in a couple days," he said correctly. "Jupiter will be out by then."

It was Saturn, but April didn't correct him. She took a deep breath of night air. It was still hot and muggy. She leaned against the rail and felt the dampness on the freshly varnished teak. She made a mental note to wipe the rails down in the morning. She was sure they were full of fingerprints. She leaned over and looked at the water. With help from the moonlight, she could see her reflection. There was no breeze, so the surface was mirror-like. She leaned out further, hoping to get a clearer view of herself. Ever since coming aboard *Hamilton's Bench*, she liked looking at her reflection in the water. She smiled as her reflection smiled back.

She considered the reflection her guardian angel, there to watch over her. April wasn't especially religious, but she did believe in God. She remembered saying bedtime prayers when she was young and going to church. The services themselves were boring. The material and message flew right over her head. But the music… it was the anticipation of the next song that kept her awake and alert. Their church was small, but it had an old pipe organ, donated, according to her mother, by some woman in the community right before she died—donated so there would be music at her funeral.

The organist had a knack for bringing out the best in the instrument, and while everyone else sang, April listened, mesmerized by the various sounds and how they combined together to provide a beautiful melody. It was these experiences that first drove April to the piano they had in their living room. It was the same piano she had in the trailer, and it was the only one she had even played prior to Worthington Valley. So yes, April believed in God. She also believed a couple of other things about this spirit. First, he was good at music. Second, he was looking out for her.

April continued staring at the reflection in the water. She was about to mouth thank you, when the vision suddenly disappeared. She turned and found herself face to face with Phillip. She wrinkled her nose as her stomach objected to the smell of alcohol on his breath. "Phillip!" she said in protest.

"Yes, beautiful, that's me." He grabbed the rail on each side of her. "That was a fine party we had earlier. And you… you played beautifully. I must say, I never heard anything like it." He leaned in closer. "I don't know how much money the governor raised, but I bet it was a bundle. It was a great celebration. Now what say you and I celebrate ourselves? Ever since you've come aboard, I've had my eye on you. Not only have you met all the expectations as a crew member, you've proven to be a very quick learner. On top of that, you're beautiful. I think you and I'd make quite a couple, don't you?" His arms came off the rail and wrapped around her waist. His voice turned into a hiss. "Besides, I know some things about you nobody else does, April.. whatever your last name is… Blackstone, isn't it?"

She had felt the sensation before. It seemed like so long ago. It was panic. Her nausea increased. Her heart pounded against her chest and she broke out into a sweat.

Why? her mind screamed. Why was this happening again? And how did he find out who she was?

Phillip pressed against her and pulled her into him. He tried to kiss her, but she turned away. She was able to get her hands between them and pushed hard. In anticipation of this however, Philip had already tightened his grip. Both panic and anger increased their intensity. He tried kissing her again. She turned her head the other way, their cheeks brushing together in the process. Her stomach continued to churn as the stench of his breath filled her nostrils. "Get off of me," she hissed, "or I'll scream."

His fingers released their grip and he took a step back. She tried to step away, but he managed to reach out at her and grab her arm. "What's the matter, babe?"

"Just—just go away."

"Now, that's not going to happen tonight, is it, April… April Blackstone?"

It was at that moment April knew her time aboard *Hamilton's Bench* was over. Tears filled her eyes as a sense of sadness developed. She knew this day was coming. It was in the cards. There had been too many signs, too many comments, too many gestures. She had seen them, but she was still surprised at the timing. Then again, why should she be surprised at anything? She'd been there before. First at the stream with the boys. Then in the car with Eddie. Then the truck driver. Now on a boat. Each time she bailed out as if jumping from a plane. As if the action had been ingrained in her soul, she spun around to bail out yet again.

She didn't remember the actual fall. She did remember hitting the water. The pain against her skin was nothing like the pain in her heart.

109

Dr. Jimmy Stanford heard the EMS alarm go off. He tried ignoring it, but the noise persisted. He rose to his feet and headed to the call box. Tons of modern day equipment stuffed in every corner of the emergency room, communication with the paramedics was still through an old antiquated gray box. He picked up the receiver. "Annapolis General."

There was the usual run of static before a voice came on line. He recognized the voice as belonging to ambulance 25, which just happened to have one of the prettiest paramedics in the business. His mind was immediately distracted by thoughts of seeing her. At least something good would happen during this God-awful night. It was after three am, and things were supposed to slow down by them. However, two heart attacks had kept him busy (and awake) since the start of his shift five hours before. The paramedic's voice brought his focus back to the newest crisis.

"Morning, Annapolis. This is medic 25. We're bringing you a twenty year old white female who was pulled out of the harbor after she jumped from a boat in what appears to be a suicide attempt. No medical problems. We're unclear about alcohol or drug use, although she denies all this. She is agitated and wants to leave, so we're having difficulty getting info from her. She has been EP'd by the police. How do you copy?"

Jimmy Stanford smiled. He loved it when they went through half of the consult and then stopped to see if you were hearing them okay. Sometime in the future, he planned to say he heard nothing, and make the person go through the whole report again. Not tonight, however. He was too tired to listen to the whole thing again. Plus the paramedic was too cute to get her mad. Besides, as long as the patient was EP'd (the filing of an emergency petition indicated the patient could be held against her will), he had to do little except to clear her medically. The behavioral health people would do the rest. "Go ahead medic 25," he responded.

"Thank you, Annapolis. There are no apparent injuries. Vital signs are stable. BP is 128/78. Pulse is 70 and regular. Respirations are 18. We didn't get a temperature, but she was only in the water a few minutes so I doubt she's hypothermic. Besides that, it's summer."

Stanford smiled. She had a sense of humor. He liked that.

There was more static as the paramedic continued. "We have her on two liters of nasal O2 but no IV. Like I said earlier, she is agitated, but the police are with us and have threatened to shackle her if she doesn't calm down."

The emergency room doctor wondered what the patient thought of that.

The paramedic continued. "She did calm down somewhat, so we're requesting no intervention at this time. Our ETA to you is... We're pulling up to your back door as I speak."

"Thanks for the warning," the doctor said.

"You're welcome."

Dr. Stanford hung up the phone and headed toward the rear of the ER. The paramedic and her driver wheeled the stretcher around the corner a moment later. Andy, one of Annapolis's night shift police officers, brought up the rear. The patient, a young woman who looked her stated age—maybe younger—was lying with one hand folded across her chest. The other was cuffed to the railing of the stretcher. Her head was hung low and her eyes remained closed. Her hair was wet and tangled. Stanford still got a knot in his stomach whenever a young person was brought in following a suicide attempt. He did an elective rotation in psychiatry and even considered specializing in that field before finally deciding on emergency medicine. Not enough blood and guts in psychiatry for his taste. Had he gone into psychiatry, however, he would have specialized in adolescents.

Memories of his older sister came into focus. He remembered the phone call late at night, his parents waking him up seemingly only a few moments after he dozed off. He remembered the panic in her mother's voice as she told him to get up and get dressed. He was told there was an accident, and it involved his sister. All other questions were rebuffed as he was shooed into his coat and out the door. In the emergency room a short time later, he found out it was not an accident.

Stanford followed the stretcher into the trauma room. "Hey guys, went fishing tonight, huh?" It was sick humor, but it kept him sane and his mind prepped for the more serious side of the business.

"Didn't have to," the cute paramedic said. "The boat's captain pulled her out."

"Got a name?"

"April Whiterock," the police officer said.

"Where's she live?"

"Aboard the boat she jumped from." Officer Andy's hands spread wide. "A big mother, too. I bet it was at least half a football field... maybe more."

"A crew member?"

"That's what we've been told."

The doctor turned his attention to the patient. "I'm Dr. Stanford," he said. "Why don't you open your eyes and look at me."

The patient's eyes opened slowly and said, "She's 112 feet... about a third of a football field, if my memory serves me correctly."

"That's better," the doctor said in a calming voice. "And you're right. It is about a third of a football field. You like football?"

The patient's mouth opened and closed just as quickly.

The doctor's voice remained calm. "Okay then, why don't you tell me what happened?"

"I slipped and I fell over the rail," she said tartly.

"The officer here said you jumped."

"He wasn't there."

Stanford looked at Officer Andy.

The policeman spoke. "The boat's captain said he tried to talk to her and tried to stop her. She went over anyway."

"How high was she?"

"They said it was the upper deck."

The doctor did the math in his head. He said nothing, instead looked back at the patient. "That must have been a half a football field high, huh?"

The patient failed to prevent a short lived grin. In the same crisp voice, she said, "Now that we've established that no one around here 'cept you and me knows anything about lengths or heights of boats, can I go?"

"You've been brought in by the police on what's called an emergency petition," Dr. Stanford said. "That means we have to evaluate you. That'll include some blood work, and we'll need a urine specimen. Once we get you registered and all that, I'll be back to talk to you."

"I'm okay," the patient snapped. "I just want to leave."

The ER doc picked up the sense of fear in her voice. It was subtle, but it was definitely there. He guessed her reaction wasn't from having to stay, or even having to go through an examination, if you could call it that. (One of the attending physicians during his ER residency said that if you took more than three blinks of an eye with a psych patient, you were taking too long.) No, she feared someone would find out something about her she didn't want anyone to know. That usually came down to several things: she was pregnant, her toxicology screen would be positive, she was using a fake name or a combination of the above. "Well, I'm afraid you can't do that just yet."

"Am I under arrest?"

"Not exactly. Like I said, you've been brought in under an emergency petition, which means we have to evaluate you for potential risk to yourself and to others."

"You can't keep me here against my will!"

"Oh, but we can." The doctor leaned forward. He switched from the calming voice to his more forceful tone. "And we will. So I suggest you cooperate and let us do what we have to do. The sooner you do that, the sooner we'll be able to make a determination about your condition."

April had sat upright on the stretcher during this time. The handcuffed wrist impeded any further movement. She flopped back down and closed her eyes.

Jimmy Stanford turned and walked away. He smelled something, and it wasn't a suicide attempt. The upper deck of a boat wasn't all that high. Even if she were jumping onto solid ground, odds are she couldn't kill herself, unless she landed right on her head. No, there was more to this story than met the eye. He'd wait until they had more privacy, then he'd delve more into the situation. He headed across the room to check on his two heart attack patients. His mind changing gears, he cursed softly. Why weren't they upstairs yet in the CCU?

He mumbled a few more expletives.

110

George Hamilton held the receiver tightly against his ear. The lines across his face were taut, showing the intensiveness of his concentration. "I see," he said. Following a pause, he repeated the phrase. His eyebrows raised ever so slightly. "Is all that really necessary?" he asked.

Finally, the facial tension expression eased. "You're name again?" Another pause. "Okay, thank you Dr. Stanford. Like I said before, you do whatever you need to do. I'll take care of any expense." He sat the cellular phone down on the desk and stared into space. His pupils contracted and his focus returned, landing on the figure sitting across from him. Captain Rogers, normally a self-assured confident man, sat slouched in the chair. He usually had no trouble making the eye contact he was now avoiding. He tried to hide his discomfort, only Hamilton, well trained in the art of human observation, recognized all the signs. His captain was more nervous than upset. Hamilton knew Phillip had been drinking heavily, even after he cleaned himself up, combed his hair and put on a fresh uniform. The owner also knew alcohol doesn't disappear from one's system at will, and you really couldn't hide its effects. In this case, it made the man sitting across from him even more pathetic.

"What did the doctor say? Is she okay?" Phillip said.

Mr. Hamilton's eyes continued to stare directly at the man. He leaned forward as he spoke. "I'm going to ask you one time, and one time only. I know what you said to the police earlier, and I know what you said to the crew. Now, I want you to tell me what the hell really happened—and I want the truth. Understood?"

Hamilton Bench's captain knew answering the last question was pointless. What he didn't know was the answer to the real issue: What did Hamilton know and not know? Rogers knew his boss was slick and probably knew more than he was saying. What did the doctor say? Was it good? Or was it bad? Phillips was cautious as he swallowed hard and wished he hadn't drunk so much. Then again, he had planned to be sleeping it off right now—with a young crew member at his side.

He readjusted his position. "Like I said earlier, I didn't get to talk to April much during the party, but afterward while we were cleaning up, I had a chance to see how she was doing. She seemed real happy… more so than usual. She even had a glass of champagne in her hand. She doesn't drink… least not that I've ever seen… so I guess the booze went to her head. Anyhow, I told her she should be careful. She laughed and asked me to get her another, sort of on the side you know. I figured what the hell, she deserved it after the way she played. So I did.

"Anyway, we finished cleaning up and she said she was going to her cabin. I had a few things to finish up, and then I went forward to make sure she was okay. I rapped on the door lightly in case she was asleep. She answered the door right away. I asked her if she was okay and she insisted she was. She came out of the cabin, almost falling in the process. She said she wanted to get some fresh air. I thought that was a pretty good idea. I offered to go with her, but she insisted she was okay. I didn't press the point, said good night. I had some payroll stuff to catch up on, so I was up for a while. I was about to turn in when I realized I hadn't heard her come back. I was concerned so I went out to look for her. I found her on the aft deck, staring into the water. As I approached her, she turned towards me. She had a strange look in her eyes... real glassy... like she was looking straight through me. I took a step towards her, but she became agitated and told me to leave her alone. I backed off and tried to reason with her, but she would have none of it. I guess the champagne was really doing a number on her. I was getting concerned so I stepped forward and grabbed her arm real quick. But she was a lot stronger than I thought and managed to pull away."

Phillip paused and looked away. "And then she jumped."

He looked back and met the stare he knew was pointed in his direction. "There wasn't time to stop her."

"What did you do then?" Hamilton said in a totally emotionless tone.

Phillip ignored the lack of sympathy. "Like I told the police, I grabbed a life ring and jumped in after her. I knew she could swim, but with the champagne and all that..."

Hamilton sat quietly a moment. Finally, "Okay, Phillip. Thanks. That'll be all for now. Hang around in case the police want to ask you any questions."

The captain rose to his feet. "Is she going to be okay?" He forced empathy in his voice.

"They're not sure yet. She's in pretty bad shape." George Hamilton could lie with the best of them.

"It's a shame," the captain said. "She was a good crew member. I really hate to lose her."

Hamilton maintained eye contact. He knew his next few words would tell the true tale. "Well, Phillip, you won't be losing her. I cancelled my meeting in New York so we'll be staying in Annapolis a few more days. You can tell the crew that, and go ahead and extend their shore leave."

The captain's eyes widened and his jaw dropped. To his credit, he managed to recover quickly.

But not quick enough. Hamilton had seen what he wanted.

"That's very generous of you, sir." Phillip managed to utter.

"Thank you," the yacht owner said.

Phillip nodded. He rose to his feet and headed for the door.

"Phillip."

The captain stopped dead in his tracks. He glanced over his shoulder without turning his body. "Sir?"

"Ask Louis to come in please."

The captain exhaled a long breath. "Yes sir, right away." He hurried from the cabin.

111

George Hamilton stared at the door and shook his head side to side. He always viewed information—both words and numbers—with an open mind and a high level of cynicism. He learned through experience that failure to do so often led to false conclusions and disastrous outcomes. He learned to be quick yet cautious as information was digested. As he first listened to the doctor and then to Phillip, he practiced the same style of disciplined thinking. Unfortunately, the words from Dr. Stanford didn't add up to the words from Phillip Rogers. And the numbers Dr. Stanford relayed didn't add up to those Rogers wanted him to believe. Phillip Rogers claimed April had been drinking and was acting intoxicated. Dr. Stanford claimed he saw no signs of alcohol intoxication. Matter of fact, her alcohol level was zero. Neither numbers nor words coincided. All this led to a series of problems Hamilton now had to deal with.

First and foremost, good captains were awfully hard to find.

112

Louis entered Hamilton's office a minute later. It was obvious he had also been up all night. Earlier, he was dressed more like a naval officer in full ceremonial regalia. Now, he wore khaki shorts and a polo shirt. The crew member was unshaven and his hair had simply been pushed back with his hands. Normally, he would have stood patiently and waited for his boss to address him first. This morning was different. He hardly gave George Hamilton a chance to look up before saying, "Have you heard anything, sir? Is she alright?"

Hamilton gave his most trustworthy crew member a reassuring smile. "She's going to be fine."

Louis let out a long breath. It was obvious he was also holding back his emotions. "That's great news, sir. And thank you."

"No problem, Louis. I know you very fond of her."

"That I am, sir… in all the correct ways."

"I know that, too. I wasn't referring to anything else."

Relieved to hear that April was okay, Louis realized he looked a mess. He started to offer an apology and explanation.

Hamilton held up his hand. "Yes, I know you look a mess. And yes, I know why. Don't worry about it."

"Thank you, sir." There was a pause. "So what did you want me to see you about?"

"Let me ask you a question. Did you see April drinking any champagne last night?"

Louis couldn't resist laughing. "Sorry. No sir, I did not. But that's not a surprise. I've never seen her drink any alcohol. Even that first night in Atlantic City, she didn't drink anything. I was bartending, remember?"

"That's what I thought."

"Was she drunk last night?"

"On the contrary, her alcohol level was zero."

"I could have told them that."

"So could I." Hamilton paused. As he had with Phillip Rogers, he maintained eye contact. "I need you to help me with something."

Louis didn't hesitate. "You know that's a given, sir. What's up?"

"I need you to help me look for a new captain."

Louis's mouth opened and closed quickly. He was unable to hide a smile.

Hamilton returned the expression. "This is between you and me for now, okay?"

Louis's posture straightened up. "I'll get right on the problem, sir." He headed across the room. At the door, he turned. "You sure she's going to be okay?"

"She's going to be just fine."

Louis nodded and left the room.

Hamilton stared at the door as it closed. All his suspicions were just confirmed. "Son-of-a-bitch," he muttered.

113

Sheriff Richmond instinctively pulled the pillow over his head to block out the noise. But the ringing persisted and the sheriff cursed in his state of half-sleep. It took three additional rings for him to realize the sound was the telephone on his bedside table. A moment later the receiver replaced the pillow.

"Yeah," he said with a lack of politeness. He glanced at the clock. Seeing it was only 5 am, the scowl on his face intensified. "This had better be important," he added.

"And a good morning to you too, Sheriff," the voice on the other end spouted. "You got the money, I hope?"

It took the Sheriff a moment to recognize the voice. "I got it." He glanced at the clock again. "But why the hell you calling me at this hour?"

"There's been a development," the bounty hunter said.

"I'm listening," the sheriff said, rolling to a sitting position.

"I don't have all the details, but something happened to your little girlfriend last night. Seems she ended up in the water somehow. She was taken to a local hospital where she's been ever since. And so far, that's all I'm able to find out."

"Did she get hurt?"

"Like I just said, I'm not sure. They're not giving out any information. They won't even verify she's in the hospital."

"That's strange," the sheriff said. Not verifying someone was or wasn't in the hospital could only mean one of two things. Either she was under police protection—a rarity—or she was on the psychiatry ward where the rules for releasing information were much stricter. Aloud, he said, "Well, if you want your money, you'd better keep an eye on her."

"You threatening me again, Sheriff?"

"Just taking care of business."

"See that you do, you hear?"

The sheriff didn't respond, hanging up the receiver without further response. He looked at the clock again, let out a loud moan and stood up. His desire for additional sleep was quickly eradicated by remembering that his hunt was nearly over. He already planned to leave for Maryland later in the morning. Yelling for Bullet to get up, the sheriff shuffled off toward the bathroom. Looking in the mirror and rubbing the stubble on his face, he smiled. Yes, the hunt was almost over.

114

Normally, George Hamilton did not accept incoming calls unless they were returned calls, calls from a VIP such as Maryland's governor, or dealing with emergent issues such as what was going on with April. He detested talking on the telephone, even though it was often a major part of his day. He prized his free time and had refined the art of time management into a personal masterpiece. A big part of this technique was to control who he talked to and when. Unless prescheduled, all calls were screened by Adam if he was aboard, or by the officer of watch. That's how the call from Dr. Stanford came in. That's how the call was returned a short time later.

This morning, Hamilton had gone to the galley to get a cup of coffee. It had been a short night and he didn't wait for the caffeine to be delivered. Louis was already starting to organize the activities of the day. The phone rang for the second time in just a few hours. Early morning calls to *Hamilton's Bench* were not uncommon so he didn't pay it much attention. Louis picked it up on the third ring. Hamilton's attention did sprout when he heard the words "Piano player?"

Hamilton rolled his hands out as if to say, "Who is it?"

Louis put his hand over the mouthpiece and spoke softly, "A Mr. David Blackstone. Says he met you last night at the party. Says he's the owner of the *Riverboat Inn*—that's the restaurant across the way. He's calling asking about the piano player."

Hamilton gave Louis the *what about* look. Louis shrugged his shoulders.

Vaguely remembering the man—a good friend of the governor's—Hamilton motioned that he'd take the call. Back in his office, he punched the flashing light on his desk. "Good morning, Mr. Blackstone. I do hope you're not calling to complain about anything last night."

There was laughter on the other end. "If you can complain about perfection, then I guess I have one," the man said.

"That kind of complaint I can deal with," Hamilton responded.

A few more pleasantries were exchanged. "So what can I do for you this morning?" Hamilton listened a few moments as the question was answered. The conversation ended with, "How soon can you get here?" A pause followed. "I look forward to seeing you then."

115

David Blackstone shook the man's hand. He remembered the firm grip from the night before. He liked that in a person. "Thank you for seeing us on such short notice."

"My pleasure," George Hamilton said, not yet knowing if that was the truth or not.

David Blackstone continued. "This is my daughter, Jennifer."

Hamilton cocked his head to the side. "A pleasure to meet you—again—if my memory serves me correctly." He knew that to be the case in that he never forgot a face.

"Yes sir, we met the other day out on the dock. You were with the governor."

"That's right," the yacht owner said. "You were with the gentleman who did the drawing." He motioned to the drawing that was leaning up against the wall. "I've seen hundreds of photographs of *Hamilton's Bench*, but never a drawing or painting. I must admit, I was quite moved and quite impressed with the work. Mr. Davidson is a talented young artist." He stared at the drawing a moment. Looking back at his guests, he continued. "Anyway, at our meeting on the pier, wasn't there something also promised about oyster stew?"

Jennifer smiled. "Yes, there was. We'll just have to see what we can do about that."

A pure gentleman in his thoughts and actions, Hamilton scolded himself for silently wishing she'd make the delivery herself. There was something about this woman that intrigued him. He remembered a similar feeling the other day on the pier. Reminding himself there was a more pressing matter at hand, he dismissed the feelings. "Please sit down," he said. Jennifer and her father each took one of the chairs sitting in front of the desk. "May I get you coffee or something?" the host offered. Both guests declined. "Before we begin, may I ask you a question?" Hamilton said.

"Please do," David Blackstone replied, leaning back in the chair and noticing the richness of the leather.

"How'd you get my phone number?"

David Blackstone smiled. "I called you directly through the shore line on the pier. I've been a member of Annapolis Yacht Club for years, and most of us know the private numbers that run out the docks."

Hamilton laughed. "Ask a simple question and get a simple answer." He paused. His expression turned serious. "So, you want to know about the piano player?"

"Yes." David Blackstone hesitated.

Jennifer spoke next. "Unfortunately, I wasn't able to attend last night's gala—someone had to mind the store—but my parents both came back talking up a storm about the affair. They were especially impressed with the entertainment. So much so, we wanted to find out who she was, and to see if she might be interested in playing at the restaurant sometime."

"I see," Hamilton said. It was a comment designed to stall for time. An expert at seeing behind the words, he decided that while this woman was not necessarily lying, she wasn't coming forth with the whole truth either. Curious to her real agenda, he said, "I can tell you she's not available. She's actually one of my crew."

"Oh," Jennifer said. She wasn't sure where to go from here.

Her father spoke up. "As I mentioned on the phone, there's another reason we're interested in the girl." He pulled a couple photographs from his pocket and slid them across the desk. As George Hamilton studied the pictures, the restaurateur continued. "We're pretty sure she's my niece. While I've never met her, and haven't talked to her mother in years, the resemblance is too good to pass up."

"These photographs are old?" Hamilton pointed out

"That they are," Jennifer's father acknowledged.

"Her name is April Blackstone," Jennifer injected. She and the yacht owner's eyes met. "We have reason to believe she's run away from home." She paused. "She may also be a minor."

"I acknowledge the resemblance is remarkable," Hamilton said. "But I can assure you, all my crew have appropriate papers. We travel out of the country, so they have to have their papers in order."

"I've always heard that if one is determined, one can get fake IDs," Jennifer said.

Hamilton smiled. "I assure you, I examined April's papers myself, and everything was in order."

"April?" David Blackstone injected.

Realizing he had let her name slip, George Hamilton sat back in the chair. "Yes, her name happens to be April, too. But that's a very common name these days."

"And her last name?" Jennifer pressed.

As if to settle the matter, George Hamilton said with confidence, "Whiterock."

Jennifer's eyes widened at the same time the similarity clicked into place for the man sitting across from her.

Not wanting to cause any more friction, David Blackstone spoke up. "Mr. Hamilton, I assure you, our intentions are nothing but good. All we want to know is if she's okay. We're not here to cause trouble. It's just that, like Jennifer said, we have reason to believe she's run away from home."

"How old would she be?" Hamilton asked.

"Seventeen… eighteen at the most."

"There's a big difference between the two ages—from the legal point of view that is."

Jennifer forced her voice to remain calm. "Again, we're not here to cause any trouble."

George Hamilton hesitated. He continued looking at the photographs before him. Three things were required in his profession. First, he had to be able to piece data together quickly and accurately. In this case, he had little doubt the person in the photograph and April Whiterock were one and the same. The conclusion was supported by the same first and similarity of the last names. While her papers appeared genuine, they could still be fake. And while she looked and acted her stated age of twenty, he had no doubt she could also be younger. Kids these days were much more mature, both in physical appearance and in mannerisms. If she had been on the run, she'd mature even faster. The second requirement was that he be able to make accurate decisions based on the information placed before him. Sometimes there was time to study, analyze and study some more. On other occasions, time was short and decisions needed to be made quickly, as in this case. The third requirement was that he be a superb judge of character. He always considered that one of his strong points, until the Phillip Rogers issue rocked his confidence. However, he was sure the two people sitting in front of him were above board in their interest in April.

He looked up. "April came to us in Atlantic City about a year and a half ago. She was working a party I was having for a few associates."

"Working?" Jennifer piped in.

Smart girl, Hamilton thought. Even if they were family liked they claimed, they didn't need to know all the details. "We do most of our own food preparation on board, but we do hire servers on occasion." Jennifer seemed satisfied with the explanation. "Anyway, luck had it the piano player we hired failed to show up. So we were in a bind for entertainment. Next thing I knew, April was sitting at the piano."

Hamilton remembered the moment as clearly as if it were yesterday. His first impression had been very positive. During the eighteen or so months April had been with him, she had never once done or said anything to challenge that feeling. If anything, his feelings about her had only strengthened. She was not only a wonderful young lady, she was an exceptional musician.

"Anyway, as you heard last night, she's superb. When the party was over, I offered her a position aboard the boat. She declined at first, but came back the next day just as we were pulling out."

"Why'd she change her mind?" Jennifer asked.

"I didn't ask," the yacht owner admitted. "Anyway, she's been with us ever since. She's hard working, has taken a keen interest in learning about the boat and about navigation, and she plays at all our parties. In short, she was a real find."

"Has she said anything or talked at all about her past?" David Blackstone inquired.

"I have to admit, we sometimes get crew whose true motivations are suspect. However, as long as they have good papers—which again, April does—and as long as they are hardworking and follow orders, I don't really get into their personal lives. We do have some family men aboard, but for the most part, we get young people looking to find themselves or who want to travel. I assumed April was a lost soul looking for her calling in life."

"She never said anything about her family?"

"No. But I can tell you this, when she came aboard, she knew nothing about boating. She was as green as they get."

"That could help explain the one conflict in all this," the elder Blackstone said.

Hamilton's look asked the obvious question.

"My aunt and cousin were poor and lived in a trailer for most their lives. They did have a piano, but we doubt there was any money for music lessons. My aunt did marry a couple years ago and moved to Ohio. This was evidently a much better situation. But even if she started piano lessons then, it takes a long time to master a musical instrument. Your April is far beyond what we'd expect our April to be."

"I've watched April practice," Hamilton said. "She's very disciplined and very determined. I've supported her as much as I can with music and books about music. She's also been able to get a lot of information from the Internet, so she's had ample opportunity to progress. And..." he paused. "She's a very fast learner." Another pause. "She's also very very talented."

"So I heard," Jennifer said looking at her father who nodded in agreement.

"Anyway," George Hamilton said. "As to your reason for being here, I can tell you April Whiterock—Blackstone—or whoever, is fine." He hesitated. "That is, until last night when she had a little mishap after the party."

"Mishap!" both guests said at once.

"Seems she fell overboard."

"Overboard!"

"Overboard." Hamilton's shoulders lowered a bit. Tension crossed his face. "To be honest, I'm not quite sure what happened. She did end up in the water, we do know that. However, why is still a mystery. She claimed she simply fell in. My captain claimed she jumped."

"A suicide attempt?" Jennifer said.

"That's what the hospital is saying."

Jennifer couldn't avoid a chuckle. Both men looked at her for an explanation. "Jumping from what... fifteen feet at the most into the water doesn't usually classify as a suicide attempt... a gesture maybe, but not an attempt."

Jennifer's father explained the justification for her comments. "Jennifer's a nurse and used to work in the emergency room at the hospital here in town. She's seen her share of similar cases."

The ex-emergency room nurse continued. "Do you know any other details, or at least any that you're willing to share?"

Hamilton hesitated, contemplating what he should and should not tell. Deciding it was best to get the cards out on the table early, he said, "I really don't have anything to hide. I don't have all the details yet as I haven't spoken to April, but after the party, seems one of my crew members was intoxicated and may have gotten a little frisky with her. I've been assured by all parties that nothing happened, but still..."

"Crew member—what crew member?" Jennifer said.

"The captain… the same person who jumped in after her and pulled her out."

"I'm not sure I understand," Jennifer said. "Why did he have to jump in after her?"

"According to him, he wasn't sure whether she intended to swim or not," Hamilton explained.

"But she's okay now?" Mr. Blackstone said.

"Physically, yes. They're still doing the psychological evaluation, or whatever it is they do." Anticipating what was coming next, George Hamilton added, "As far as the captain is concerned, he's the ex-captain."

There was a pause as all parties collected their thoughts.

Hamilton spoke next. "Since you used to work there, Jennifer, do you know what will happen next? How long will she be there and when can I see her?"

"I imagine she was taken to the hospital on what's called an emergency petition, probably filed by the police," Jennifer said. "That means she's been committed involuntarily—against her will so to speak. So they can keep her for a couple of days at least."

"Against her will—on what grounds?"

"A danger to herself. Hospitals are very cautious about letting suicidal patients out… gestures or the real thing. It's as much a legal issue as a clinical one. As far as seeing her, I don't know what visiting hours are on that unit, but I'm sure you can see her during that time."

David Blackstone spoke up next. "I'm not trying to pry, but what are your intentions regarding April?"

"If you mean am I going to wait here until she gets out of the hospital and see that she gets whatever care she needs, the answer is yes." He allowed a thin smile to cross his face. "Besides, I can't go anywhere anyhow."

"Why's that?" Jennifer asked, taking the baited statement.

"*Hamilton's Bench* is without a captain."

"That's very commendable of you," the elder Blackstone said.

"Thank you, but I do care about my crew, especially someone like April. People like her don't come along very often."

"I'm not sure what you mean by that," Jennifer said. Her tone continued to give off a sense of distrust.

"She's a special person in a lot of ways. As someone who's very fond of the arts, especially music, I've seen a lot of musicians in my time. While I'm sure she's a little rough around the edges, she's one of the best talents I've ever come across."

"She that good?"

Mr. Hamilton looked at Jennifer's father, who quickly said, "Don't look at me. I can judge a good cut of beef, but that's about all."

Mr. Hamilton laughed. "Yes, Jennifer, she's that good."

"Wow."

Her father rose to his feet. "Anyway, we appreciate your time and please keep us informed."

Hamilton rose as well. "I sure will. How about if I call you later today after I try and see her?"

"That would be wonderful," David Blackstone said.

"Maybe I'll also stop over at the restaurant later and try some of that oyster stew first hand."

"That'd be better yet," Jennifer said.

George Hamilton looked at Jennifer. "Will you be there?"

The girl met his stare. "Depends… I might be studying."

"Oh, what are you studying?" It was his turn to grab at the bait.

"I'm thinking about sitting for my captain's license."

While Jennifer's father laughed, Mr. Hamilton tilted his head to the side. A slight smile crossed his face. "That would be fine."

116

"Want something to eat?" Cliff offered, leading Jennifer below deck. He was especially tired this morning since he was up late working the night before. One smile erased his fatigue.

"Na," she said following him down the steps. "Did I wake you?"

"I just got back from taking Chessie for a walk. I was getting ready to fix some breakfast. I promised her eggs this morning." He was glad he had turned the fans on as it was already proving to be a muggy day.

"You feed her eggs?"

"Once in a while. She'd eat 'em every day if I let her. Sure you don't want something?"

Jennifer hesitated. "Okay. If you're cooking for the dog, then why not me, too."

Cliff tilted his head to the side. "You seem in a foul mood this morning."

"What makes you think that?"

"There's a sharpness in your voice I've never noticed before. You sick or something?"

"I'm okay I guess."

"*I guess* means you're not." Cliff didn't pursue the point, instead he turned his attention to fixing a skillet of scrambled cheese eggs over English muffins. He had to chase Chessie away several times during the process as she kept getting under foot. In a few minutes, three plates were served—two were placed on the table and one on the floor. Cliff watched with a smile as his boat guest and animal companion attacked the food with vengeance. "You know, I can make more if need be."

Chessie ignored the comment. Jennifer did, however, look up. "Guess I was hungry after all." She took a sip of the coffee.

"They okay?" Cliff asked.

"You make the best."

"No need to exaggerate. An okay is fine."

"I'm not exaggerating," Jennifer said flatly. She wiped her mouth on a paper towel.

"That's because they're cooked on the water for one, and you're hungry for another. Just like that time in St. Michaels," Cliff said.

"Maybe so, but the chef has something to do with it."

Cliff smiled. "Flattery will get you everywhere." He attended to his own plate before the food got cold, watching Jennifer as he ate. She sat quietly, chewing slowly now that the initial hunger pains had been satisfied. Her hair, freshly combed, hung down to her shoulders. Her face was smooth and she had just the right amount of make up to bring out her near perfect complexion. She wore a red polo shirt and white slacks. She had a pair of sandals on her feet. Usually though, she wore a wide smile and cheerful disposition. Today, her shoulders were slumped forward and she had worry lines beneath her eyes.

Clearing the dishes, Cliff said, "Want to talk about it?"

"Talk about what?"

"Whatever's bothering you."

"There's no need for me to burden you with my problems."

"Maybe there's no need. On the other hand, maybe there is."

Jennifer looked him in the eye. "You know…" She hesitated. "Where've you been all my life?"

Cliff laughed to hide a blush. "Developing into the fine outstanding gentleman I am today."

Jennifer tried not to, but failed to hold back a laugh. "You might want to add *conceited* to the description,"

"Whatever."

Jennifer paused. She reached down and patted Chessie on top the head as the dog rubbed her cold nose against an exposed foot. "The day hasn't started out all that great, and it's only what… 9:30?"

Cliff slid back into the booth and leaned forward to let her know she had his undivided attention.

Jennifer sat back, let out a sigh and continued. "The project in St. Michaels has taken a turn."

"For the worse?"

"Worse than worse. It's finished, at least for the foreseeable future. On the flip side, however, we may now be able to get the necessary permits to expand right here in Annapolis—something we've been wanting to do for a long time."

"Why haven't you?"

"Like I said, couldn't get the permits."

"Because?"

"Supposedly, environmental concerns."

"What's changed now?" Cliff asked.

"My parents think the threat of us going to St. Michaels loosened up some support here at home."

"Loss of business?"

"We pay an awful lot of taxes, plus have a huge impact on the local economy."

"I'm sure you do," Cliff commented.

"Anyway," Jennifer continued, "I guess it's a good thing, staying here that is. Only, now it seems we have to start all over."

"What else is bothering you?"

"One of the hostesses called out. So I have to work tonight. And the day's just begun, so heaven only knows what other staffing problems we'll have."

"You're always complaining about staffing."

"Yes, and it's getting worse. The work ethic of people today is terrible. They take no responsibility for their jobs. It's always me, me, me. Never a consideration for the employer. Scares the crap out of me thinking about hiring a bunch of new staff once we expand."

"Not all people are like that," Cliff protested.

She looked him in the eye. "Except for that rare person who comes around once in a lifetime…" She stopped a moment. "I was really hoping I didn't have to work tonight."

"Why?" Cliff said without thinking.

Jennifer tipped her head to the side and gave him a smile. "I had other plans."

"What time do you get off?"

"If I'm lucky and only have to play hostess, probably around 11:00, 11:30. If I have to close, then…"

"I'll be here working."

Jennifer smiled. "Really?"

"Really."

The smile widened. It had been a long time since she remembered anyone making her feel so good. She was already starting to regret the *pulling back* of their relationship. The smile suddenly disappeared. "Also, remember the girl on the yacht from the other day, the one I thought I knew?"

"The same one I spooked?" Cliff said.

"My parents saw her last night and my Dad recognized her. He figured out she's a cousin I've never met. I've only seen pictures. That's why I recognized her but couldn't put my finger on who she was." She spent the next several minutes explaining further.

"So did… what's his name… Mr. Hamilton verify it was her?"

"Not exactly. But he didn't deny it either."

"Why did she run away?"

"A multi-dollar question."

"Is she still in the hospital?"

"For now. My fear is that they'll release her and she'll disappear again."

"Wouldn't she go back to the boat?"

"Maybe not. Especially if she thinks the captain is still aboard."

Cliff shrugged his shoulders. "Why don't you go and visit her?"

"I thought of that, but I don't really want to go near the place. Plus, I don't want to spook her."

"She doesn't even know who you are."

"Still…"

"What about your mother or father?"

"My father's afraid the idea of seeing long lost relatives at a time like this would be too much for her. The last thing you want to do to someone who's already struggling with a lot of issues is to give them more stuff to deal with."

"I can see that," Cliff acknowledged. He paused. "Want me to go see her? It's somewhat of a compromise."

Jennifer's mouth opened to decline the offer. It closed just as quickly. "You could go as a representative of the family, only with no strings attached. If she wants to see us, fine. If not, then no harm done."

"I'll say I'm there to make sure she's okay and if she needs anything, to let us know. Maybe I can take the photographs to prove who I am."

"That's a good idea."

Cliff hesitated as another thought crossed his mind. "What if she doesn't want to see anyone in the first place? Does she have that option?"

Jennifer contemplated the point. "If she's a minor, not really. If's she's an adult—that's over eighteen—then she can ask that visitors be restricted. I imagine that's how she's registered because according to Mr. Hamilton, she has papers."

"Papers?"

"Federal law requires that you verify that anyone you hire is a U.S. citizen or a legal immigrant. Plus, Hamilton would want to make sure he wasn't hiring any minors, especially since he travels out of the country."

"Isn't that what he did?"

"Not intentionally."

"Oh."

Jennifer returned to the previous topic. "Now, the hospital staff can restrict visitors in the interest of the patient, but they don't like to do that a lot unless it's absolutely necessary. In reality, they try and get families involved as much as possible."

"She doesn't have any family other than you all, least not here."

"No one at the hospital knows the connection. She doesn't even know she has family here. Anyway, at the very least, I want to make contact with her in case she needs help."

"When do you want this to happen?"

Jennifer wrapped her arms across her chest. "Something tells me it needs to be as soon as possible."

"My uncle told me to never argue with a woman's intuition."

"Then don't."

And so he didn't.

117

Sheriff Richmond shook his head in amazement as yet another car pulled from the middle lane right across in front of him—no blinker and less than a car's length of space. He cursed under his breath, hit the brakes and reached down for the blue bubble resting on the passenger's seat. He had already dropped the driver's window and was ready to put the magnetized apparatus on the roof when he reminded himself he was not on that sort of mission today. It didn't matter that he was out of his jurisdiction. He thought about pulling the driver over and reading him the riot act. After all, he was in uniform and the driver probably wouldn't know any better. Again, he reminded himself the purpose of this trip. Besides, an inkling in his bones said he shouldn't be wasting time. The sooner he got to Annapolis, the better. It was just an instinct—developed from years of experience. It took two things to be a good detective: patience and instinct. He smiled, crediting himself with having practiced both in this case. Soon he would be rewarded for his efforts. He said additional choice words, put the window back up and put more space between him and the son-of-a-bitch in front.

He thought about the uniform issue again. He debated whether or not to wear it, but finally decided to do so. It made him stand out in a crowd—along with his size. It also often got him into places with few questions—such as a hospital. If confronted by someone in authority, he always had a story. In this case, he was following up a lead on a murder case back home. Naturally, he'd use a name other than April's. That would at least justify his probing around.

He slowed to let a car merge between him and the car in front. That would also help with his anger. Then he accelerated back up to sixty-five—the posted speed. Cars continued to pass him with regularity. He shook his head in disgust. In Worthington Valley, the posted speed meant the speed limit. The closer he got to the east coast, the more it meant the lowest speed you could possibly travel without getting rear-ended.

He told himself to quit worrying about the traffic and get his mind back on task. He glanced at the envelope laying on the passenger seat. It contained the receipt for the transfer of funds from his bank account to the bounty hunter's. He outwardly complained and criticized the practice of paying for information. He also knew it was a necessary cost of doing business. The sheriff had to admit the man was good. The bounty hunter had succeeded where no one else had. He found the girl. So Sheriff Richmond paid the fee without argument. That decision was the easy one. More difficult was what to do with the girl once he got to her.

Sheriff Richmond smiled. In reality, that decision was easy, too.

A green interstate sign came into view announcing they were seventy-five miles from Annapolis—still plenty of time to think. He glanced in the rear view mirror. The storm that was chasing him ever since he left the Ohio valley area was still back there, although no closer than before. He shook his head again. He couldn't imagine how people would drive in the rain around here.

118

The first thing April noticed was the smell. She lay in her bed, arm across her head, eyes closed. She slowly came out of a restless sleep as the pungent odor agitated her further. It wasn't necessarily all that unpleasant, yet it wasn't a fragrance any Hollywood superstar would rush to endorse. It was just strange, yet something April thought she recognized.

Her eyes blinked opened, her arm moved and she found herself staring at a bare white ceiling. She blinked several times to clear her vision. She wiggled her fingers and then her toes. Slowly at first, then with a sudden shock, her alertness returned. She sat up. A wave of nausea filled her throat. She swallowed, willing herself not to vomit. She took in several deep breaths and looked around. The room was small, about fifteen feet by ten. One door stood off to the left. Another was at the foot of her bed. She correctly assumed the first door led into the bathroom. There was a wooden desk and chair across from her. A single florescent light fixture was buried in the ceiling. The bed was small, and set close to the floor. The linen was clean, but torn in several places, and the pillow should have been retired many moons ago. There was one small window that let in natural light, although much of the outside world was filtered by the heavy screens covering the glass. Again, the overriding stimulant was the smell. She rose to her feet and stretched. As her mind further cleared, the odor became more recognizable. It was the same disinfectant her mother used in the trailer—cheap and effective, her mother used to say.

April walked to the door. It was unlocked. She turned the handle. The door opened outward. She peered into the hallway. White walls, white tiled floors, fluorescent lights and the ever present smell of disinfectant. Someone at the far end of the hall was passing out food trays. In spite of her nausea, she knew she needed to eat. She felt weak from the night before and knew she needed to get her strength back quickly. Still dizzy, she went into the bathroom. There was a small towel, washcloth and cake of soap sitting on the sink. She looked at herself in the mirror, or rather a piece of shiny metal bolted to the wall. She looked awful, but then again, it wasn't the first time. She realized her clothes were gone and she was dressed in a paper top and pants. Her feet were bare. The nausea returned.

Additional pieces of time from the night before came at her like a tidal wave. She was in the water. She remembered it was much warmer than she might have thought. Before she could get her bearings, there was a splash nearby. She spun in the near-darkness and recognized Phillip Rogers swimming toward her. As soon as he was within reach, he started grabbing at her. He was also yelling that she was going to be okay. She told him to get away. He didn't listen and kept coming towards her. She tried to swim away, but he was too fast. He grabbed her by the back of the hair and told her to quit struggling. Again, she told him to leave her alone. Again, he ignored her protests. He told her to cooperate or else. *Or else what?* she remembered wondering. Before she could come up with an acceptable answer, she felt his hand move to the top of her head. Then adding to her already surprised state, he pushed her beneath the surface. She tried to fight him off, but he was too strong. She thought of Danny. What would he tell her to do? Surely he'd have an answer. He'd taught her many survival techniques, in life and in the wilderness. But never had they discussed what to do in the water.

Her mind started to go hazy as the oxygen in her bloodstream dropped rapidly. In her daze, she remembered actually chuckling a bit, letting out bubbles of precious air. She told herself not to panic. She laughed again. Why should she listen to herself? No one else was. She felt the urge to cry and then wondered whether that was even possible under water. Her mind started losing focus. Do whales cry, she questioned? How about fish, especially when they saw members of their family gobbled up by larger species of the food chain? Do they shed tears? Is this what her life had come down to, simply part of nature's food chain? Craving air, she instinctively opened her mouth. As water rushed into her lungs, she passed out.

When she awoke, a large mask was being pressed against her face. This time, instead of starving for oxygen, someone was forcing large volumes of air into her lungs by squeezing a funny looking rubber bag. Her cough reflex fired, and she spit up a large volume of water. Her head was forced to the side as the liquid spewed from her mouth. She coughed several times as more water cleared her lungs. A glance around told her she was in the back of an ambulance. A sudden jolt told her the vehicle was moving. She thought she heard a siren in the near distance.

A voice startled her. "She's coming around. Check a blood pressure, will ya?"

April felt a squeezing pressure in her left arm and her pulse bounding against the blood pressure cuff. By the time they pulled into the emergency room parking lot, she was fully awake. As she was wheeled through the doors, she remembered feeling like a lone piece of bread being attacked by a flock of hungry birds. First there was a doctor who seemed nice enough, until he started asking questions she was not interested in answering. Others in white coats pounced on her as if they were angry she had disturbed their peaceful night.

She told herself not to panic. She was alive. She tried to remain focused, but too much was happening too quickly, and she was still feeling the effects of having breathed water versus air. She told herself to remain calm, to keep her wits about her and to keep her mouth shut. She told herself this was going to be quick and easy. A few more minutes and she'd be on her way.

A sixth sense also told her to remain cooperative which she managed to accomplish with some effort. The handcuffs holding her arm to the bed were removed. A needle was jabbed in her arm. She nearly fainted, not from the pain, but from the sight of her own blood pouring from her body. She was told to pee in a cup or else. Another sense told her not to inquire about the alternative *or else*.

More time passed. The clock on the far wall showed an hour had gone by. She waited and wondered. Her confidence quickly eroded in spite of her best efforts to remain positive. Another forty-five minutes, and then a short petite lady came into April's room. She said she was from behavioral health and was one of the counselors. Her voice was soft and gentle. She asked how April was feeling and if she needed anything. April was thirsty but decided to remain mute. Surprisingly, a Styrofoam cup of water appeared a moment later. April took it with a nod, knowing Danny would have advised her to drink. He always preached that when lost in the woods, water was number one. And while it was a strange type of wilderness, the girl had no doubt the place was wild. She swallowed several long gulps. The counselor, who said her name was Stacy, started asking questions. Did she have any major illnesses? Any surgeries? Were her immunizations up to date? How much did she drink? Smoke? Do drugs? Then the questions started focusing on the past and her family. Where was she from? Where were her mother and father? How old was she? Through it all, April was stoic. She continued to say nothing.

That is, until the counselor asked why she jumped.

"I didn't jump," April said without hesitation. She cursed herself for speaking without thinking. At the same time, she knew that was the one issue she needed to address. "I slipped."

"That's not what we were told," Stacy said.

April realized debating the issue would be pointless. At the same time, she sensed she was losing control. Danny always preached to keep control of your environment. If unable to do so, stay alert and keep an eye out for the next opportunity.

That's where she was now—waiting for an opportunity. "I slipped," she repeated.

Finished in the bathroom, April returned to her bed to sit and wait. She was hearing some activity outside her room. She was unsure of the precise time, but based on the light outside and the presumed food tray in the hallway, she reckoned it was around noon. She didn't know what was going to happen to her. She had little doubt she'd find out soon enough.

119

Jennifer picked up the phone. She put it back down an instant later. She repeated the action. On the third try, her hand simply rested atop the plastic device. The call was to see if she could get any additional information on April. Jennifer knew she shouldn't as she reminded herself of the regulations regarding patient confidentiality. Yet, there were too many unanswered questions to let it go. Did she and her parents have the right to know? Therein lay the debate. She decided until someone told her otherwise, the answer was yes. However, making the call could create a whole host of other problems—wounds from the past would be reopened. Did she want to do that? Did she want to go down that road? Did she—

She cut the string of questions short. It didn't matter what she wanted. What mattered was April. What was in her best interest? But what if Jennifer made the call? What if she opened the wounds only to discover April was really April Whiterock as the girl claimed?

"Stop it!" Jennifer said aloud. She picked up the phone and made the call. It was answered on the fourth ring. The voice on the other end had obviously been asleep.

Jennifer glanced at her watch. It was a few minutes past 1:00 pm. She made sure she had pleasantness in her voice. "Hey, Sarah, did I wake you?"

"Who the hell is this?" the voice known as Sarah responded.

"Jennifer… Jennifer Blackstone. Your old buddy, remember?"

The voice perked up slightly. "Jennifer, you bitch. How the hell are you?"

"I'm fine, and you?"

There was an attempt at a laugh interrupted by a sneeze followed by a cough. "I was wonderful until a few seconds ago when the phone rang. I was having a spectacular dream."

"About sex, I bet."

"How'd you know?"

"That's all you ever dream about," Jennifer reminded. Sarah Covington had been one of Jennifer's best nurses and best friends. She was very opinionated, outspoken, crude at times and even downright obnoxious if you got on her wrong side. Yet, there wasn't another nurse Jennifer would rather have at the bedside in a true emergency. Sarah was one of the best in the business, and she and everyone around her knew it. That was the only reason she could get away with her behavior, which was never directed at any of her patients or their families. She received more positive mail than anyone in the department. Jennifer had nominated her for nurse of the month on several occasions, only the well-deserved girl never won as she always managed to piss someone off right in the middle of the selection process.

"Sorry if I woke you. I thought you'd be up by now," Jennifer said.

"What time is it?"

"A little past one."

"One o'clock on a Saturday afternoon and you expect me to be up?"

"Sorry," Jennifer said, trying hard to sound sincere.

The semi-cheeriness of the voice changed to a more cautious tone. "Anyway, you know all that. So this isn't just a *let's get reacquainted* call, is it?"

"We used to be best friends," Jennifer said as a reminder.

"Used to be was a long time ago."

"You still angry?" Of everyone left behind, Sarah took Jennifer's leaving the hardest.

"Aren't you?"

Jennifer hesitated. She sensed the memories she feared were about to be exhumed. "I've tried to move on."

"And so you have. But we're still stuck in this rat's hole." Jennifer knew that was a lie. Sarah could go anywhere she wanted.

"How are things going?" Jennifer asked.

"No different than before. No staff, no supplies, no morale. We're mostly agency now. There's only a few of the old gang left." Her voice faded away.

Jennifer started to ask why Sarah was still there, only she already knew the answer. The girl thrived on chaos, and in spite of the bitching and moaning, was probably loving every minute of it. Besides, like Jennifer, she was a true Annapolitan, having been born and raised in the town. She lived only a few blocks from the hospital and walked to work every day.

"Did you work last night?" Jennifer asked. She hoped the answer was positive; otherwise the call was for naught.

"This is my weekend."

"Did you happen to take care of a girl by the name of April Blackstone... I mean Whiterock?"

Hesitation followed as Sarah's voice dropped in volume and became more serious. "Why do you wanna to know?"

Jennifer hesitated as well. Deciding the truth was probably the best track to take, she said, "What I'm about to tell you is the truth, not some cockamamie story I've made up. Okay?"

Sarah remained silent.

"I think she's a long lost cousin who's run away from home. But we're not sure as no one in my family has ever met her before. But there are just too many coincidences not to be suspicious. Even the name she's using, Whiterock, is close. And then there's an old photograph that sort of seals the case, or at least the suspicions about who she is."

"You know I'm not supposed to talk about cases. You yourself used to harp on patient confidentiality and all that crap."

"I know, and I don't want you to tell me anything you're not comfortable with. I'm mainly concerned that she's okay."

There was a long pause. Jennifer thought she heard footsteps and Sarah's breath increase slightly. There was a rustle, then the sound of running water. "You in the bathroom?" Jennifer asked.

"I got to take a pee. Don't most people in the morning?"

"Not while you're on the phone."

"You ain't got one of those camera phones, do you?"

Jennifer laughed. "No, and even if I did, I certainly wouldn't want to be watching you right now."

"You ain't gonna see anything you ain't seen before."

"That's not the point," Jennifer protested.

"Fuck you. First you go and wake a girl up at this ungodly hour, and now you're telling me I can't take a leak. And I thought you were my friend."

Jennifer laughed loudly. Sarah's total unabashed attitude was one of her best features. There was never a question where one stood with the girl.

There was the sound of the toilet flushing, and then Sarah said, "I'm finished."

"I'm certainly glad you didn't have someone in bed with you this morning."

"How do you know I don't?"

"Because you're too much of a bitch when you get off work to take anyone home."

Her old friend didn't dispute the accusation. One of the downsides of emergency medicine, at least for the single women, was that the stress was hard to leave at work, and thus personal relationships outside the workplace were especially difficult—at least relationships that meant anything. There were always enough horny doctors floating around to get laid if that's all you wanted. The problem—the doctors wanted to get laid and then go home to their wives. The nurses wanted to get laid and become wives.

Jennifer thought back to her time with David Baker. She remembered making a promise to herself the first day she worked as a nurse that she would never get involved with anyone where she worked. But she had broken that rule rather quickly, having caught David Baker's eye within several months of her arrival at Annapolis General.

Sarah's voice brought Jennifer's attention back to the present. "EMS brought her in around 2:30. They pulled her out of the harbor after she nearly drowned. It was called an apparent suicide attempt, but I'm not so sure about that myself."

"Why's that?" Jennifer asked.

"For one, she jumped from the deck of a boat, a big boat, but just the same, the distance wasn't all that great. For another, she told us she slipped and fell overboard. She's a crew member on some big-ass yacht downtown. It was the boat's captain who pulled her out of the drink. Anyway, they slapped a cert on her and now she's up on the psych unit."

"So they did certify her?"

"She definitely wasn't going to sign herself in. She wouldn't even sign the admission papers. How do you know her again?"

"We think she's a cousin, but we're not sure," Jennifer repeated. "If she is, we also think she's run away from home."

"Sounds like a lot of speculation."

"Call it intuition," Jennifer said.

"In that case, it must be true." Those words were not spoken with any hint of sarcasm. Both nurses respected one another, not only as highly skilled clinicians, but also as individuals who knew how to read people and situations

"Thanks," Jennifer said.

"This isn't your normal *I'm upset about my parents so I'll show them* kind of a case," Sarah said.

"What makes you say that?" Jennifer inquired.

"Stacy, who was on call for behavior health, said the girl wouldn't answer any questions. She basically gave no information… except…"

"Except what?"

There was a pause. "She kept claiming she didn't jump."

"What is so strange about that? Most suicide attempts want to claim it was an accident once they realize they didn't succeed," Jennifer pointed out.

"Agreed," Sarah said. "Only it wasn't what she said, it was how she said it."

"Meaning?"

"Stacy thinks she may be telling the truth."

"What do you think?"

"The pieces just don't fit for a suicide attempt."

"I agree."

"Anyway, what are you going to do?" Sarah added.

"I'm not sure yet. I don't want to interfere. At the same time, I want to make sure she's okay."

"Well, if she's locked up on the psych floor, she'll be okay."

"Good point."

"I'll be back there this evening," Sarah said. "I'll see if I can find out anything else important and call you tomorrow."

"I'd appreciate that."

There was a pause. "You know, we all miss you girl."

"Let's not go there, okay?"

"Bitch."

"Fuck you!"

There was laughter on both ends of the line as the connection was terminated.

Jennifer hung up the phone. She again went into deep thought. She wasn't convinced Sarah would be able to get a whole lot of information, even if she tried. And then if she did, it would not be until tonight, or even later. Jennifer's instincts again kicked in. For unclear reasons, she sensed a hint of urgency. Someone needed to go see April, and the sooner the better. Cliff had offered to do so. Jenifer hoped the offer was still valid.

120

April followed the nurse down the same hallway as earlier when she took a shower. She was led to a waiting room where several tables were set up surrounded by folding chairs. Two tall narrow windows let light in through barred glass. There were a couple old paintings of flowers on the walls and several framed papers listing the various rules of the unit. She noticed one that was titled: *Patient Rights*. She made a mental note to check that one out later. For now though, she was anxious to see who had come to visit. She said a silent prayer for it to be Mr. Hamilton, and that he had come to get her out of this place.

Since she woke up, she had taken a shower, changed back to her regular clothes which had been laundered, met the staff, sat in on a group session where everyone except her talked about their problems, and spent the rest of the afternoon lying in bed trying to think of how she was going to escape. She hadn't quite figured it out yet, except she knew it had to happen quickly. She knew they were bound to figure out who she was, which would lead to a whole host of other problems. From what she had seen so far, the place was locked down like a prison. Doors at both ends of the hallway were locked, accessible only through keys carried by staff members. And every window she had seen so far was also barred or covered in a heavy mesh screen type of material. It was easy to conclude that escape wouldn't be via physical actions, but by using her mind. Danny always said that survival was more a thinking man's game than anything.

Her newfound excitement, however, was quickly replaced by disappointment. Except for one boy sitting alone at a far table, the area was empty.

"I'll leave you two alone," the nurse said. "Just let me know if you need anything."

April remained in her tracks as the nurse headed back towards the nurse's station. The boy rose to his feet and smiled at the nurse. "Thank you," he said. He waited until the nurse was out of sight before taking a couple steps towards April. "Please don't be afraid. I'm not here to hurt you."

Closer examination made April realize the boy was actually older than he looked. He was April's age, if not a few years more. "Who are you?" she demanded, remembering to keep her voice low. She thought he looked vaguely familiar. "Are you from the boat? Where's Mr. Hamilton?"

"No, I'm not from the boat, at least the one you're talking about. And I don't know where Mr. Hamilton is." The boy motioned to April to move into the room further so they could have more privacy. "My name is Cliff Davidson, and I'm a friend of your cousin's."

"Cousin... I don't have any cousin. You must have the wrong person." She turned and started to leave.

"That may be true. Then again, it may not be... April."

April stopped and turned back around. "Good guess."

"How about April Whiterock? Does that narrow it down some?"

"So you know my last name. Big deal."

Cliff made sure he had eye contact. "Is that really your name?"

It was an ever-so-slight reaction, but she did flinch. "What else would it be?"

Cliff hesitated, wanting to make sure his timing was right. He glanced around the room. They were still alone. "Does Blackstone ring a bell?"

The girl turned pale. She had not heard that word spoken in a long time. While she had always feared her past would catch up to her one day, she was still taken aback by the boy's response. She sat back down across from him. "I didn't touch the gun," she said softly, tears welling up in the corners of her eyes.

"I don't know anything about that," Cliff said. "Who got shot?"

Realizing she may have spoken too early, she recovered and said, "What do you want?"

"To make sure you're okay."

"Who wants to know?"

"Like I said, your cousin... and your aunt and uncle."

"I don't have any aunts and uncles."

"That you know about."

"My mother was an only child."

"That's what she told you."

"Why would she lie?"

"That's something you need to ask her," Cliff said.

April started to speak, but didn't have anything productive to say. She was very uncomfortable, and angry with herself for having opened her mouth so soon. But she made an assumption that if he knew who she was, then he knew everything. Danny always said that in the woods, assumptions were okay, but you had better think them through first. She had failed to do that. She waited silently.

Cliff continued. "I know you're confused, especially after ending up in here. But please believe me, we have nothing except your best interest at stake." April started to speak, but Cliff held up his hand. "Let me explain first. Then if you want to talk, fine. If not, that's okay." He watched as her shoulders slumped and she sat back in her chair. While somewhat unkempt at the moment in that her hair was simply pulled back in a ponytail uncombed, and her clothes were wrinkled, she still looked pretty. Her cheekbones were long and smooth, her smile, he imagined, was wide. Her eyes, however, were the most prominent part of her facial features. It was if she were boring right through him, trying to read his mind or anticipate his next move. And while he was not a mind reader, he saw a deep mysterious glow. He couldn't tell much about the rest of her body because of her clothes, but he remembered from the time on the boat that she was quite petite and quite pretty. He refused to allow his imagination to continue. He was again drawn back to her eyes.

He met her stare as he continued. "Let's assume you are April Blackstone, and not April Whiterock. If that is the case, you have family here in Annapolis. Your mother had one brother, David Blackstone. Your mother left home when she was young and ran away with her boyfriend. She was pregnant at the time with you. Your mother and father did eventually get married, but it didn't last. Evidently there were physical as well as emotional problems. Your mother never kept in close contact with your uncle, but there was enough correspondence to know the basics." Cliff paused. Her expression had not changed. "Anyway, your mother ran away one night, taking you with her. You both hid out for several years somewhere in Alabama. You lived in a trailer or something like that. During this time, your mother met another man, married him and moved to Ohio where your situation improved, or so it seemed from a couple letters and pictures your mother sent. That's how the Blackstones came to recognize you."

"How did they find me here?"

Cliff remained silent on the fact that she just acknowledged who she was. Instead, "You remember someone taking your picture a few days ago while you were out on the bow of *Hamilton's Bench*? You're a crew member aboard there, right?"

"Go on."

"You didn't seem to like that and ran away. Well, that person was me. I'm an artist and am staying on a sailboat right across the harbor. I just happened to be taking photographs for a drawing I'd been asked to do." He ignored that he was stretching the truth.

"A drawing?"

"Yeah, I did one of the boat you're on."

"*Hamilton's Bench?*"

Cliff nodded.

"Did someone happen to give that to Mr. Hamilton recently?"

"If you mean the governor, yes."

"You did that?"

"I guess."

"It was…" April realized she was starting to talk too much, even though she had been very impressed by the drawing. She returned to her state of silence.

"Anyway," Cliff continued, "I've also become friendly with the Blackstones. They own the *Riverboat Inn*, the restaurant across the way. Jennifer, their daughter and presumably your cousin, and I were walking down the pier one morning looking at the boat when we ran into the governor and Mr. Hamilton. The governor is also close friends with the Blackstones. You were there to greet them when they went aboard. Jennifer saw you and recognized you as someone she knew. Only she couldn't remember from where. She told her parents about it, and they kept an eye out for anyone they recognized the night of the fundraiser. Mr. Blackstone saw you playing the piano.

"Mr. Blackstone always felt bad about not being in closer contact with your mother. A few months ago, he started trying to call her. He didn't have a lot of success until one day recently when a boy answered the phone."

"What was the boy's name?"

Cliff struggled to remember whether Mr. Blackstone had mentioned the name. His meeting with Jennifer and her father had been brief and hurried. He was simply asked to go visit the girl and see what he could find out—specifically if she was April Blackstone. "Donald… David… No, that's Mr. Blackstone's first name… Dudley… Danny… Danny Worthington. You lived in a place called Worthington Valley and your stepfather owns the factory there."

"How old is my cousin?"

"Twenty-eight or so. She's their only child. And from what I've been told, your mother and uncle were the only children of your grandmother's."

April's mind filled with questions about her heritage, a natural tendency upon hearing that her immediate family was not what she thought. She also wondered what other mysteries existed. First and foremost, was she an only child? With a strong force trying to distract her, she put these questions in the back of her mind. She told herself to stay focused. "Why are you here and not my cousin or uncle?"

Cliff could not help but chuckle at the question. "That's a story in itself we can talk about another time. But basically, the Blackstones didn't want to scare you."

"So you came to check me out."

"If the circumstances were reversed, wouldn't you?"

April didn't respond immediately. "If I was April Blackstone, maybe." Her stare hardened. "But I'm not." She rose to her feet.

Cliff remained in his seat. He correctly chose not to cross examine her any further, or to remind her that she had practically admitted to her identity twice. Instead, "Like I said earlier, I'm here representing the Blackstones. While I acknowledge they have questions and concerns, their first priority is to make sure you're okay."

"I'm okay. This whole thing has been a big misunderstanding anyway. I'll be out of here as soon as I see the doctor. So thank them for me, and tell them I hope they find their lost cousin soon."

Cliff stood up. "You know where my boat is. I'll be here a couple more days at least. If there is anything you need, don't hesitate to stop by. And if you want to meet the Blackstones, I'm sure they'd be happy to see you… regardless of who you really are."

"My name is April Whiterock," she said with conviction. She turned and walked away.

121

April lay completely still as she stared at the ceiling. She forced air in and out of her lungs in a controlled fashion to keep her respirations smooth and slow. She could do nothing about her racing heart except to let it calm down on its own. The last thing she need was to panic. What she needed was to think.

She started at the beginning and rehashed the conversation that had just taken place with her one and only visitor, a guy named Cliff Davidson. Who was he? He claimed to be a friend of the Blackstones. Who were the Blackstones? He claimed they were relatives she didn't even know about. April's first task was to decide whether he was telling the truth. His story certainly made sense, and he knew enough about her past to add credence to his authenticity. But why hadn't her mother ever told her about these people?

She frowned. As April grew older, she realized there were many details missing about her past. She knew little about her father, only what she could remember as a young girl. He had always been nice to April, but angry and mean at times towards her mother. April's mother—while always warm, caring and at times a bit overprotective—seemed to be carrying an untold burden on her shoulders. She was often on edge, as if looking over her shoulder. April always assumed that was because of her father. She learned today there may have been others. But these others, at least from what this Cliff person told her, didn't seem to be bad people. They just wanted to make sure she was okay.

A gene unique to humans called *I-have-a-family-I-didn't-know-I-had* kicked in and overshadowed her thinking. Deciding Cliff Davidson was on the up and up, her curiosity rose. Just who were her aunt and uncle? How old were they? Was her uncle younger or older than her mother? What did they look like? She struggled to remember the fundraiser. While less than twenty-four hours had passed, it seemed an eternity. She tried remembering the many faces she had seen that night. She had met so many people. Cliff said that her aunt and uncle were there, and they had seen her. Surely, she had seen them. But no one looked familiar and no one had raised any questions as if they knew her. She knew the mental exercise was useless. She changed her focus to her cousin, a newly learned fact that raised her interest even further.

While she had never spoken about it, she often missed not having a brother or sister. She was born a loner and had lived most her life that way. True, she made friends in school, both in Alabama and in Ohio, but no one ever satisfied her desire to have a true sibling. She remembered being jealous of the three brothers on the farm. They were always together and always had someone to play with. She remembered wishing their father would adopt her so she could become part of their family… that is, until the day down at the stream. She remembered when she first met Danny. He was so distant and seemed to be in a different world most of the time. He was very into sports and the outdoors. But as they grew more comfortable with one another, he began to show an interest in her music, and she in his outdoor activities. Her wish for someone to play with came true. While there was a *step* between the two of them, she now had a brother… and a friend. As they grew closer, the *step* was often forgotten in their conversations. While she could talk to Danny at a level closer than anyone else, she was still cautious in what she said. He was the only true friend she had in Worthington Valley, and she wanted to ensure he maintained that title. She had heard from other girls in school that boys could be quite fickle and react with a short fuse in a heartbeat. So their relationship continued to grow, and then in an instant, with one jump from a motel window, it was over.

She was able to make friends aboard the boat, but for many reasons, including her constant fear of being discovered, she never let anyone really get to know her. It was difficult at times, but it was the way it had to be. She suspected others were in a similar situation—hiding their true identity or running away from something in their past. She realized she acted just like her mother, always looking over her shoulder for that unknown intruder. Now she discovered there were others—an aunt, an uncle and a cousin.

Who was she… her cousin that is? What did she look like? What was she like? Had April met her before? She struggled to remember who she had seen since being in Annapolis. She did remember that day on the boat when she was spooked by Cliff across the way taking her picture. Cliff said her cousin saw her on the pier. April raced through faces that had crossed her path recently. She stopped the exercise, knowing the search would be futile. April's thoughts turned to her mother. What else hadn't she told April? What was the big deal? Why did everything in her mother's life have to be cloaked in mystery?

April frowned. "Like mother, like daughter," she mouthed. Her mind focused on Danny. He was the one person who seemed to not have anything to hide. What would he say to her now? She thought a moment, and came to a conclusion. Everything in life occurs for a reason. It may be hard to find the answer, but it's there somewhere. Never stop looking, and you'll be okay. Even in the worst of times, never stop looking.

She sat up in bed to clear her mind. "Thank you, Danny, wherever you are," she said aloud. "Thank you." Continuing to speak aloud, "Well, April, before you can look for anything, you first have to get out of this hell hole." She told herself to make that her primary objective. For now, her newfound family would have to wait.

122

David Blackstone stared silently at the photographs laid out in front of him. His head moved ever so slightly as his eyes shifted from one to the next. "Are you sure we're not barking up the wrong tree?" he finally said.

Recognizing the self-doubt arising from her father, Jennifer leaned forward on the couch and looked over at Cliff, who was standing at the side of Jennifer's father. "What do you think, Cliff?" she said.

Cliff spoke with more confidence than her father was demonstrating. "I'm not an expert, but if that's not the spitting image of the girl I just visited, then it's her twin."

"You sure about that?" Jennifer's father queried.

"About the picture being a replica of the girl, yes," Cliff said. "I'd bet a pretty good wad she's a Blackstone and not a Whiterock. Like I said, she as much as admitted it in the middle of our conversation."

"You did get some emotional response from her?"

"She was pretty good at covering her feelings, but she reacted when I started telling her about having relatives she didn't know about."

Jennifer looked over at her father. "What do we do now?"

David Blackstone gathered the photographs and put them in a side drawer. "I think we need to stay on track as to why we're meddling in this in the first place. We wanted to make sure she's okay, and she appears to be that."

"As long as she's in the hospital," Jennifer pointed out.

"How long will that be?"

"They can keep her a couple of days before they have to hold an administrative hearing. With hospitals focusing so much on length of stay, it usually doesn't go that far anymore."

"Meaning?" Cliff inquired.

"She'll probably be discharged on Monday morning. That's when they usually empty out the unit."

"What if she was really trying to hurt herself?" Cliff asked.

"That was Friday night. By Monday, she'll be cured and ready for outpatient treatment."

"Quick, isn't it?" Jennifer's father commented.

"Compared to the past, yes, but well within today's standard of care. Anyway, I imagine I'll hear from Sarah later tonight. This is just the sort of thing she likes to get her nose into."

"This is *some thing*," Cliff remarked.

"She'll be there until at least tomorrow?" David Blackstone asked.

"Yes. About the only way you can get out any quicker is if you come in on your own, claim you're suicidal and then deny it the next morning, claiming you only came in to get detoxed. And then the addicts who do that know not to pull that stunt on a weekend." This time anticipating Cliff's question, she added, "Detox centers usually don't take admissions on the weekend."

"You think drugs played a role?" Cliff asked.

"Having seen April play the piano and having talked to Mr. Hamilton, I think that's highly unlikely," the elder Blackstone said.

"What about Aunt June?" Jennifer said.

"What about her?"

"She's your sister… and April's mother. She has a right to know about her daughter."

David Blackstone gave his own daughter a hard stare.

Unfazed, Jennifer continued. "If things were reversed, wouldn't you want to know about me?"

A long sigh followed. "Let's see if we can verify her identity first. Then I'll make the call. Last thing I want to do is set off false alarms."

"Fair enough," Jennifer said. She rose to her feet. "I guess we'll just wait to hear from Mr. Hamilton and Sarah."

Her father stood up. "My old bones just tell me there's more to this than meets the eye."

"Your old bones are just reacting to the rain we're going to get in a little while," Jennifer said. "They're already strong storm warnings posted for this afternoon."

"Regardless. Anything else?"

Cliff, who started to move toward the door, stopped. "Yes, there is," he said with a hint of excitement in his voice. The other two looked at him. "I just remembered something else she said early on in the conversation. She said in quite a definitive manner, 'I never touched the gun.'"

123

A knock on the door followed by the sound of squeaky hinges awoke April from a sound sleep. She sat up quickly, disoriented at first, and then rapidly regained her memory. The nurse who had seen her earlier came into the room.

"I looked in on you earlier, but you were out cold. Did you have a nice nap?" she said with a cheerful voice.

April sucked in a couple deep breaths and rubbed her eyes. "What time is it?" she asked, throwing her legs over the side of the bed. Something told her she slept longer than she intended.

The nurse pointed toward the window. "You'd never know it by looking out the window, dark as it is, but a big storm is about ready to hit. It's only 7 o'clock."

"At night?"

The nurse laughed. "Yes, sweetie. You took a nap. You didn't sleep all night." April's stomach let out a big growl. The nurse laughed again. "I saved your dinner tray."

"When am I leaving?"

The nurse's facial expression lost some of its pleasantness. "That'll be up to the doctor."

"What about up to me?"

"The doctor will be here in a little while. You can talk about that with him. In the meantime, go ahead and freshen up. I have a couple things to do first because we're short staffed as usual. No one seems to want to work here anymore." She let out a frustrating sigh. "Anyway, when I'm done, I'll show you around the unit. You haven't had the grand tour yet. And if you'd like, I'll take you down to the recreation room. There are all kinds of activities and games down there. We have a pool table and air hockey, too. Sometimes we even have a piano if they're not using it for something else in the hospital. In the meantime, I'll have them heat up your dinner so it'll be ready when we get done. Go ahead and get dressed. I'll be at the nurse's station."

April did as she was told, brushing her teeth with a small toothbrush provided and fixing her hair the best she could without a brush. It did feel good to have her teeth cleaned. When she came out of the bathroom, a food tray was sitting on her bed. She lifted the lid. The smell of the reheated mystery meat filled her nostrils. Her stomach recoiled in protest, threatening to send her back into the bathroom. She swallowed hard and sat down on the bed. She knew she had to eat. She tried convincing herself she had eaten worse out in the woods. She opened the plastic pack of silverware. She was about to take a bite of applesauce that accompanied the main course when a wave of paranoia washed over her. She dropped the spoon. As hungry as she was, the desire to get out of the hospital was far greater. What if they had drugged her food?

She put the cover back over the plate. She had done the same at lunch.

As promised, the nurse gave her the tour a short time later. She pointed out several areas of interest, including the visiting area where April had seen her only visitor, the two seclusion rooms where unruly patients were kept, and the showers, which April utilized earlier in the day. With mild fanfare, the door at the far end of the hallway was opened with a key from a set the nurse carried with her. The door was checked to make sure it locked when closed. April followed the nurse down a flight of steps. Another locked door was opened and they entered a large room filled with furniture, a pool table and air hockey table. There were various other games and activities scattered about the room as well.

"Officially, this is called the activities room," her nurse said. "It's where we do our activity therapy. I'm sure Dr. Collins will order that for you, so you'll be back here tomorrow sometime."

April didn't debate where she planned to be tomorrow.

"Anyway," the nurse continued, "take a look around if you like. We're quite proud of all this. Most of the stuff is here because of the staff. The hospital won't give us crap, so we've had various fundraisers to raise money so we can make it nice for you all. Activity therapy is an important part of treatment for depression."

April didn't debate the diagnosis of depression either. Instead, she migrated across the room to where a spinet piano stood against the wall. The cover had been pulled over the keys, and April pushed it back. Instead of a bench, there was a metal folding chair. She sat down. Her hands dropped into her lap. She fought back tears as memories of what she was doing twenty-four hours previously filled her mind. She contemplated raising her hands over the keys. She battled the urge.

Her focus was disrupted by the nurse who was now standing behind her. "You play?"

April hesitated. "I used to," she replied. There was definitive sadness in her voice.

"Music's good therapy." The nurse reached around her and struck a couple keys. The instrument was out of tune, although the lady didn't seem to notice. April correctly guessed no one who heard the piano lately noticed either. The nurse continued. "This was donated by the auxiliary several years ago. They got it at an auction. We used to have music therapy available for the patients, until our new fearless leader brought out the budget ax."

"That's nice," April managed to say.

"That it was cut from the budget?"

"No, the piano—that the piano was donated." April said. She rose from the chair and studied the room. It was large and rectangular. The furniture lining the walls consisted of a hodgepodge of chairs and old sofas. The pool and air hockey tables were placed side by side in the middle of the room. Fluorescent lights were buried in the ceiling. April noticed they were covered with the same metal screening material as the windows in her room. There were a couple of windows covered as well. A few prints and other nondescript art hung on the walls. The door they had come through stood at one end of the room. Another door, with the panic bars chained closed, stood at the other. A red lettered emergency exit sign hung above this one. April glanced out the window. While it was indeed dark, a couple bolts of lightning gave her enough light to tell they were on the ground floor looking right out at onto a parking lot. She thought she saw water in the distance. Since she couldn't see the water from her room, she figured they were on the other side of the building.

While the nurse let her be, April knew she was watching her every move. She forced her facial expression to remain neutral, not wanting to show any emotion for fear of triggering the wrong response from her caretaker. Her mind raced as instincts told her this room offered the best chance for escape.

But how?

April walked slowly around the room. She stopped at the pool table, her hand rubbing across the green felt material. She scanned the room, looking for anything that would indicate a way out. While part of her felt that she'd be free as soon as she saw the doctor, another part warned it might not happen. She decided she'd better not put off until later what she could do now. The question of how repeated itself.

The windows were barred and the door was chained. She eliminated the possibility of actually getting her hands on the nurse's keys. April wasn't a violent person, and even if such an attempt were made, she had no doubt she would be overpowered, drugged and strapped down, thus delaying her departure. So there had to be another way.

April sensed the visit to this area was about over. But that would never do. She needed more time to think. Turning from the pool table, she walked over to the piano. "May I play?" she asked, remembering to sound innocent and polite.

"If you'd like." The expression on the nurse's face told April the lady was pleased the girl had taken an interest in something in the room.

April sat down and warmed up with a few scales. The exercises also gave her a chance to get the feel of the keys. The touch was much firmer than she was accustomed to aboard *Hamilton's Bench*. As her fingers loosened and she adapted to the feel of the keys, she relaxed, closed her eyes and began playing Beethoven's Moonlight Sonata. The nurse moved away to give the pianist space. April sensed her caretaker was impressed.

So April had bought some time. Only what was she going to do with the newfound resource? She had hoped Mr. Hamilton would come and rescue her. When that didn't happen, she realized she was on her own. She also realized the time was now or never.

There was a bright flash of lightning followed instantly by a loud clap of thunder. April knew by the short time difference between the light and noise that the storm was right on top of them. She continued to play, making sure she appeared focused on her music. The storm intensified. She could hear the water driving against the windows as more lightning lit up the sky. The lights in the room flickered. They were out but an instant before the hospital generators kicked in and the lights came back. However, the break in circuitry set off the alarm system upstairs.

"Oh my," the nurse said. April stopped playing and saw the nurse reach into her pocket. She pulled out the wad of keys she'd used to gain entrance into the recreation room. "I have all the keys to the unit. The alarms can't be turned off without them. Come on, we'll have to go back upstairs."

April felt panic well up in her throat. She took a deep breath, told herself to remain calm and think. "Can't I stay here?"

"No, you need to come with me."

"Why can't I stay here?" April didn't intend for her voice to sound so threatening.

"Now, April dear, let's not have any trouble. We need to go back upstairs, and now."

April forced her voice to change direction. "I don't want any trouble. I just want to play the piano a few more minutes. I haven't played in a long time, and I miss it. Please!"

The nurse hesitated. She was in a dilemma, and she knew it. Pushing the issue with April might get the girl upset and then there could be real problems. Letting her stay here alone was against the rules. Yet as happens so many times in the field of medicine, the nurse had to choose between two options, neither of which were the perfect choice. "Okay, you can stay, but I'll be right back. Please don't do anything stupid. There won't be time, okay?"

"I just want to play the piano."

"I'll be right back," the nurse repeated as she hurriedly left the room.

April listened, and sure enough, the door was relocked. There was still no way out. She looked around the room, once, and then again. Each time she saw no solution. She asked herself what Danny would do in a situation such as this? What would he tell her if he was there? She waited, but he didn't answer. Out of frustration, she buried her head in her hands and let her elbows hit the piano keys. The noise of the musical instrument was in unison with yet another clap of thunder. She sat up with a start and found herself staring at the one exit door leading to the outside. She jumped to her feet and ran to the door. The chain was looped through the panic bar and locked with a padlock. She examined the chain more carefully. It wasn't a heavy gauge. She guessed the door probably shouldn't be chained locked in the first place. After all, it was an emergency exit.

She examined the chain again. She pulled at the links, more out of frustration than anything. She started to push open the door, but stopped, realizing that might set off yet another alarm. She examined the chain more carefully. It was looped through the panic bar and then once around a thin U shaped bolt that had been screwed into the door frame. She pulled at the bolt. Even though it didn't budge, she surmised it couldn't be well secured. She tapped the painted door frame. It was made of wood. She turned her attention back to the room. What was there she could use to break through this contraption? Her eyes fell on the pool sticks. That was short lived as she realized they'd simply break. She continued her search. Her eyes fell back to the piano. There was no part of that she could use. Her glance started to move away, and then returned suddenly. Her eyes dropped to the dolly on which the piano sat. There was no part, but what about the instrument as a whole.

She hesitated as a plan formed in her mind. Could she really do that to the piano? She told herself it was her only hope. Time had run out. It was now or never. Music had saved her before. Music would save her again. She was sure the Music Gods would forgive her. She knew she needed to hurry before the nurse reappeared. The alarms she heard earlier had now stopped.

She ran up to the piano and leaned against the far end. There was a resistance, almost as if the heavy instrument knew its fate. Then with an increased push, the wheels started turning. April guided the piano to the middle of the floor and lined it up end to end with the emergency exit door. Aloud she said, "You're only going to get one chance, so you'd better make it a good one."

And so she did.

124

The nurse was not only relatively new to the nursing profession—less than six months— she had only worked in adolescent psychiatry for two months. She was confident, though, in her ability to deal with the patients whose care she was responsible for. Besides liking to work with young people, she liked the dress code—casual civilian attire. She didn't even have to worry about wearing a name badge, even though hospital regulations called for it. If she had one on now, you would have known her name was Kathy Anderson.

Nurse Anderson fell into a trap not uncommon with new graduates. They were scared at first, but usually by the end of their orientation, their confidence was dangerously high. One of the responsibilities of the more experienced nurse charged with orientating a new graduate was to help them develop a balance between caution and confidence. The number one message was that you could never let your guard down, especially on a psychiatric unit.

Kathy Anderson's orientation to the adolescent psych unit at Annapolis General Hospital had gone without a hitch. Her end-of-orientation evaluation gave her high marks for the compassion and firmness she had with the young patients on the unit. The conclusion of the nurse evaluator was that Kathy Anderson was a fine catch for the hospital, especially in these times of severe nursing shortage.

The above mentioned evaluation had just been reviewed with Nurse Anderson that very morning, and she was quite high on herself. She easily fell into the role of an overconfident neophyte. She knew to watch what she said and how she acted in front of her colleagues, but internally she beamed like a thousand suns. She always felt she would make a good nurse. She did well in nursing school. She did well on her clinicals. She placed in the 90th percentile on her nursing boards, and had just aced her orientation at Annapolis General. She would be off in less than an hour, and she planned to go out with her boyfriend and celebrate.

She was just starting to think about her outfit for the evening when she heard another alarm go off in the distance. She turned around in disgust. She had just reset all the alarms on the unit. What was going on? She headed back down the hall. Abreast of the nurse's station, she realized the alarm wasn't coming from their floor. But where was it?

The answer struck her like the bolt of lightning that flashed at the same instant. Her face paled. Her knees threatened to buckle. Kathy Anderson had done well in nursing so far for many reasons. First and foremost, she was very smart. It didn't take her long to realize the implications of the alarm she was now hearing.

She regained her composure and raced down the hallway, yelling for the unit clerk to call security. How the hell had she gotten out, she wondered? What had she used? Anderson's hands were shaking so it took extra seconds to get the first door open. She bolted down the stairs, almost slipping in the process. She quickly unlocked the door at the bottom. She took two steps into the recreation room before stopping dead in her tracks. Her fears suddenly came to fruition. The door leading to the outside was now open, the chain torn from the wall, all thanks to the piano that sat half-in half-out of the doorway.

She told herself not to panic, but she did anyway, fainting a moment later.

125

Bullet could sleep through most anything if he put his mind to it, anything except thunder. Like many animal species, nature's applause was not pleasant to his ears. After the third time being jarred from a sound sleep, the old dog moved to the front passenger's seat, his head moving side to side as the rain pelted the car windows from all directions. He sensed by his master's behavior that the trip was near its end. He blinked as the lightning widened his pupils and ignored the thunder that followed. While he could not sleep through it, he certainly wasn't afraid of it. He had spent many hours at his master's side tracking through such messy weather.

Realizing the dog's attention was piquing, the sheriff reached over and patted the animal atop the head. "If you're thinking we're almost there, boy, you're right. The hospital's about two blocks away."

The sheriff squinted through the rain covered windshield, struggling to see the street signs. While visibility on the actual road wasn't all that bad, you could hardly see anything off to the side. Stopped at a traffic light, the sheriff glanced down at the map in his lap. Two blocks looked about right.

The sheriff reached over and again patted the dog on the head. The sheriff's spirits were higher than they'd been in many months. His patience and persistence had finally paid off. Soon the prize would be his. Exactly what he was going to do with his trophy, he had yet to decide. He knew, however, it would be satisfying for him and not for her.

He let his mind wander back over the past months. So much time, so much patience, so many leads—all failures—until now. As for the frustration, he was able to keep that bottled inside his soul. His many years in law enforcement helped him develop a level of confidence few others were able to appreciate. The list of cases he investigated showed few failures. Patience, time and money distributed in just the right fashion almost always paid off. He had proven the worn out adage that *crime doesn't pay* time and again, and he was just about to add another feather to his cap—the biggest and prettiest of them all.

He focused on the aspect of time. The inexperienced law enforcement officer would have dismissed the many months between crime and capture as all negative—a burden that interfered with bringing the case to a close. He, however, saw it in a different light. First, the suspect—the girl in this case—would have her guard down. The factor of surprise would definitely be on his side. Second, the passage of time also lowered the expectation and hopes of others that she would ever be found. Most Worthington Valley citizens bought into the idea that the girl had died up on the mountain somewhere and the mountain had sucked her up whole. It was a good theory in that it kept everyone's attention close to home. Little energy was devoted to other options. The sheriff knew, however, that in criminal investigations, the obvious wasn't always the right choice.

The sheriff smiled. You had to think outside the box.

While not impossible, it was extremely difficult to simply vanish without a trace. If you were trained in such tactics, maybe. If you had the government, power and money behind you, maybe. But for a young inexperienced teenager to simply disappear—not likely, unless she was dead—dead in a ravine somewhere.

There were many theories as to how it happened. The most prevalent was that she had gotten hurt, and then was eaten by one of the many wild animals that roamed the mountains around Worthington Valley. There were reported packs of wild dogs still around and people occasionally spotted a bobcat or puma. There were definite and confirmed sightings of black bear!

It was just a matter of time before some hunter came across a pile of bones that would prove to be hers. Little did the citizens of Worthington Valley realize just how true their theories would eventually prove to be; only the bones had yet to be put in their place. Sheriff Richmond smiled to himself. He had done a good job deceiving the townspeople, helping wherever possible to fuel the fires. Now it was just a matter of finishing the job.

He made a left turn at the next block and slowed to a crawl so as not to miss the hospital's entrance. He saw the sign before he saw the actual driveway. He made the turn and came to an abrupt halt. The path was blocked by several police cars, all with their lights on, and all with officers milling around cloaked in heavy rain gear. The one closest to him walked over to his car. The sheriff rolled down his window. When the policeman saw the driver was also in uniform, he smiled.

"Evening." The policeman leaned in to get a closer look at the insignia on the uniform. "Sheriff."

"Evening, officer," the sheriff replied. He forced a smile even though a sinking feeling was starting to develop. In the field of law enforcement, that didn't happen by chance. There was a definite reason the police were outside the hospital. He hoped it wasn't connected to April.

"What seems to be the problem?" he inquired.

"No problem, just searching for a patient who seems to have gotten lost."

"Lost?"

The policeman smiled and looked around to ensure no one was nearby to overhear their conversation. He leaned in further, oblivious to the rain dripping from his wide brim hat. "Seems they let one get away from the psych unit—a young girl."

"Was she a crazy one?" the sheriff inquired, keeping his tone light.

"Not crazy, but possibly suicidal. They had to pull her from the harbor last night when she jumped from a boat. Now, we got to go find her… in all this rain. I'm sure she's around here somewhere. She couldn't have gotten far in this weather."

The sheriff raised his hand to block the police officer from seeing the blood rushing to his face. He took a deep breath before daring to speak again. "How long ago did it happen?"

"We got the call about fifteen minutes ago. It couldn't have been too long before that."

The sheriff did a few quick calculations in his head regarding how far someone could run in that time period. He also reminded himself the girl had eluded him in the past, so he knew time was of the essence. "If you need any help, let me know," he offered.

"If you see a wet girl running around who looks like she's lost, grab her." The two law enforcement officers laughed.

The sheriff bid the policeman good day and rolled up the window. He backed out of the entrance and searched for a place to park. There was a parking lot across the street, but he didn't want to be anywhere he might be noticed, especially if a quick exit was warranted. He drove down the street a block and saw a couple of spots on the other side of the road. Just as he was about to make a U turn, Bullet's ears shot back, his head pushed forward, and he started barking wildly. "God damn son-of-a-bitch. You got her scent already? Good boy," the sheriff said. The dog's keen sense of smell never ceased to amaze him.

He pushed open the door to let the dog out. The sheriff knew the animal would take a moment to get a true bead on the scent—plenty of time for him to park.

Pulling the keys from the ignition, the sheriff started to head toward the dog without his rain gear. He stopped and returned to the trunk for the equipment. He remembered the policeman outside the hospital was wearing yellow. His was luckily the same color—a sure way to blend in with the search party. He just hoped he found her first. His confidence rose as he realized this unexpected turn of events might work in his favor. It certainly solved the problem of how he was going to get her out of the hospital. And as for him finding her first, he had two other aces in the hole. He knew what she looked like and Bullet knew what she smelled like.

Appropriately dressed for the hunt, he whistled for his dog. Bullet came pounding around the corner of a house, his ears still pointed, ignoring the rain that had already soaked his coat. There was no sign of fatigue or old age in the animal now. The dog heeled directly in front of the sheriff. The sheriff knelt down and wrapped an arm around the dog's neck. "Go get her, boy." He gave the dog a smack on the hind quarter, and the animal was off. The sheriff followed.

126

April pressed against the building and looked around to get her bearings. Visibility was severely reduced as the storm still hovered overhead. The wind was blowing a steady twenty knots with gusts doubling that at times. The rain, thick and heavy, soaked her in a matter of seconds. She cursed herself for not having spent some time walking around the town. It might have proven beneficial now as she struggled to figure out where she was. But even if she knew, she still had no clue where to go. One thing was certain, she had to get away from the hospital and the alarm which was announcing her unexpected departure. A lightning bolt lit up the sky, giving her some sense of her surroundings. There was water directly in front of her with houses to the left and right. As long as she remained near the hospital, there was nowhere to hide. She struggled to get a glimpse of the water again. However, the light had faded and she was engulfed in near darkness. She headed toward the right as she thought the houses in that direction looked to have more shrubbery. She crouched low and ran, dropping to the ground each time there was a lightning bolt.

The first house had lights on, so she gave it a wide berth. The second house was dark and the driveway empty. She crept up along the side. She made her way around to the front and hid beneath a tall line of bushes. The street was empty. She looked back in the direction of the hospital. She could see what looked like the main entrance. It was quiet for now. She had little doubt that would be short lived. She contemplated heading down the street versus moving along the backside of the houses. She needed to put distance between herself and the hospital. At the same time, she needed to look as inconspicuous as possible, although she realized that would be difficult in the pouring rain. Her instincts told her to get closer to the water. This was supported a moment later by a police car heading toward her at a high rate of speed, lights flashing, siren blaring. She stayed pressed against the bushes. The car passed without slowing until it came to the hospital entrance. It turned into the driveway. She didn't have time to mourn that fact as yet another patrol car came from the same direction and followed the first car. So much for a quiet hospital entrance, she thought.

She made her way to the back of the house. There was a deck facing the water. She crawled under a small overhang to try and get some protection from the storm which showed no signs of abating. She was now totally soaked and was even beginning to shiver slightly. She wished for the storm to continue, however. She knew that would be good cover. Wiping the water from her eyes, she looked around, using the lightning as her guide. She knew she didn't have much time. She also knew she had to somehow get her bearings. She saw a bridge in the distance. She thought it looked familiar. She remembered a bridge near the marina. Was it the same one? But going back to *Hamilton's Bench* was out of the question—that would be one of the first places they'd look. She crouched under the deck, weighing the options over in her mind. She kept telling herself she had to get moving, but the rain and lack of visibility made that difficult.

Finally, there was a slight reduction in the storm's intensity and she was able to move from beneath the deck. She ran across several more yards, inching her way closer to the water. There was a gazebo four or five houses down, and she ducked inside. Pushing the hair off her face, she stared in the direction of the bridge. She waited until lightning lit up the sky. Now, she was sure it was the same bridge. She contemplated what to do, and decided to wait to see if the storm was going to let up. While she was not afraid, she was not a fool either. The storm was still directly overhead and the lightning it was generating was fierce. She had no desire, as Danny called it, to become barbecued supper for the angels. Several minutes passed without any sign of relief. She was now shivering even harder and was starting to think about the need to get out of the weather all together. The only question was where? She heard several more sirens go down the street. She knew time was definitely against her.

What she did not know was the accuracy of that determination.

127

Bullet ran in a couple of large circles to loosen up his joints. He knew he only had a few moments before his master would call him back. Ducking at the sound of thunder, he took off across the sidewalk to search for a place to relieve himself. He sniffed around one bush, but found it had been used earlier by another animal. He crossed the driveway to another. He was about to choose this as the spot when his keen sense of smell rose a notch. He circled the bush counterclockwise, repeating the action in the opposite direction. To his surprise, the scent they'd been looking for was there. And it was fresh. Ignoring the pressure in his bladder, he pressed his nose hard to the ground and circled the area. He found the direction of the scent and took off. He ran around to the back of a house. He slowed as the trail passed beneath a deck. It took him only a moment to distinguish between the scent of a rabbit and the one he wanted. Chasing a rabbit would be fun, but he knew that's not why he was here. He picked up the scent again and was about to head in that direction when he heard the familiar whistle of his master. He paused briefly, torn between the urge to continue the hunt versus the discipline to obey his master. Remembering a sharp stick applied to his hindquarters as a pup, he turned and headed toward the whistle. He hurried, instincts again reminding him the trail was weakened with each drop of rain.

The sheriff was waiting for him. The dog heeled, his tail moved back in forth in rapid fashion. He barked loudly. He turned and came to a point in the direction of the scent. The sheriff saw the eagerness of the animal. He patted the dog atop the head. "Go get her, boy." A friendly smack on the butt reinforced the command.

The dog didn't need to be told twice. Bullet headed back around the house with renewed vigor. First though, he relieved himself at the previously selected bush.

In spite of the rain, he picked up the trail without difficulty. Nose to the ground, he headed across the yard. The scent strengthened, telling him he was close. He paused and lapped a drink of water from a puddle. He raised his head and looked back over his shoulder. He barked twice. He was about to bury his nose in the ground when he saw movement ahead. He came to a dead stop. His ears pointed back. His head rose high. There was a wooden structure and someone was in it.

He remained motionless. His bark, however, had alerted her. She was now staring directly at him, a look of surprise on her face. Bullet remained perfectly still, wishing his master to hurry before the prey got away. As he had been caught off guard, he was not in a perfect point, but he knew the message would be clear. The girl continued to stare at him.

Then to Bullet's surprise, the girl took off. She went out the back side of the structure and headed across the yard. He sprang forward with renewed energy, and with the feeling that whatever he did, he couldn't let her get away. They had been looking so long. The dog knew there was water close by. He had picked up that scent even before he left the car. Only, he didn't know just how close. He was again surprised when he realized the water's edge was only a few feet in front of the girl. She stopped at the edge, looked down and turned to face the animal. Bullet slowed so as not to lose control. He had her cornered now. He approached a few more feet, went into a point and waited for his master. He looked over his shoulder and barked loudly. When he looked back, the girl was gone.

Bullet ran up to the water's edge. He saw her surface a few feet from the bulkhead. She looked back at him once, then disappeared below the water's surface. While his sense of smell had not faltered over the years, the keenness of his vision had diminished. He also lacked experience dealing with anyone in the water. His years of training, however, overrode the anger and confusion he was now feeling. He came to a perfect point and started barking wildly.

128

The sheriff heard the barking through the fury of the storm. He quickened his pace, although the noise of the storm made it difficult to tell exactly which direction to head. He finally made it around the correct house. A bolt of lightning flashed and he saw Bullet up ahead. From working with Bullet for years, the sheriff knew that meant the dog had found his prey. Yet there was something wrong. It took a moment to realize the animal wasn't supposed to be barking while on point. The sheriff hurried his pace, ignoring the shortness of breath rapidly developing. They were close, and he knew it. She was out there somewhere—somewhere nearby. He sucked in another breath and broke into a trot.

Because he was not blessed with a keen sense of smell, his olfactory system had not warned him of the water nearby. He was quite surprised when he finally made it to the dog. He stopped, put his hands on his knees and sucked in several liters of air. He unzipped the rain coat, figuring he was as wet on the inside from sweat as on the outside. He reached down and laid a hand atop the dog's neck to let him know he could come off point. The dog responded by taking off and running up and down the bulkhead, continuing to sniff at the water several feet below.

The sheriff didn't have to ask what had happened. The question was how long ago had it been since she was here? How far of a head start did she have? He looked into the driving rain, ignoring the water pounding at his face. He waited for lightning to increase his visibility. When it did, he scanned the water surface quickly. The water was rough from the fierce winds, so he really couldn't see much there. He did, however, manage to see they were in a small cove off the main body of water. The far side was less than a hundred feet away. The next question was how to get over there. He waited again for the sky to lighten up. When it did, he looked in both directions. To his right, there was water as far as he could see. It was the same to his left, only in that direction he also saw a bridge.

He turned and headed back across the yard, hollering for Bullet to follow. She was so close, yet still so far away.

"Bitch!" he said loudly.

Bullet barked as if to repeat the surname.

129

The shock wasn't from the roughness of the water, or from the fact that the temperature was much warmer than the night before. It was from the terrible taste. April didn't remember that. She spit out a mouthful as she surfaced and sucked in a much needed breath. She treaded water, using her hands to move in a slow circle. She caught a glimpse of the shore from where she had come, having swam underwater as far as possible. She wasn't nearly as far away as she had hoped, her underwater strokes inefficient because of the panic they carried with them. She caught a glimpse of the dog on the water's edge, its nose buried into the ground, its tail straight up in the air. She tried telling herself it was all her imagination, but she knew otherwise. The dog had been real. She also knew that with the dog came the sheriff. The question of how he had found her raced through her mind, but she told herself now was not the time for reflection on the bad luck she seemed to be having of late. She turned in a circle one more time and saw the bridge she noticed earlier through a flash of lightning. She decided anyone looking for her would assume she'd simply swim to the other side of the cove. She imagined a line of police officers staring down at her as she neared the shore. In front would be the nurse from the hospital, the sheriff and the dog. Again, she told herself there was no time to dwell on these issues. Time was more precious than ever. But where should she go? Which way should she head? She looked in the direction of the bridge. She took a deep breath, ignored the foul taste in her mouth and dove back under the water. This time she made sure her strokes were efficient.

Surfacing twenty or so yards later, she realized the bridge was further away than estimated—a common error when swimming in strange waters. She looked back, saw that darkness had engulfed her, and decided to stay on the surface. The wind was strong enough to mask any commotion she might make. Taking another deep breath, she swam steadily. The distance slowly closed. She stopped under the bridge to catch her breath. Feeling like she was just starting to loosen up, she decided to continue out the harbor toward *Hamilton's Bench*. She wasn't sure what she was going to do when she got there, but would decide that at the time. Staying in the middle of the channel, she continued eastward. The frequency of her stops increased as the distance between her and the boat shrank. She turned to the right and swam to the piers that were now abeam of her. She reminded herself not to grab hold of the pilings as they were covered in sharp barnacles. She came to a boat with a swim platform and she rested there. She kept attuned to anything going on around her above and beyond the storm raging overhead. Using the line of pilings as a guide, she moved in the direction of *Hamilton's Bench*.

She soon found herself beside the main pier leading toward *Hamilton's Bench*. The boat had been her home for the past eighteen months. She dismissed earlier thoughts and decided that was her safest destination. Besides, she was starting to tire and her legs were threatening to cramp.

Suddenly, she heard the pounding of feet coming down the pier. She slid behind a piling and sank low in the water. Two sets of steps passed in a great hurry. She swam to the edge of the pier and pulled herself up. As if on cue, a flash of lightning lit up the sky. She watched as two police officers in yellow rain slickers headed up the gang plank of what used to be her home.

She dropped down into the water and pushed away from the pier. The heaviness of her heart threatened to pull her below the surface. The yacht had been her last hope, and now that was gone. For the first time in many months she had no idea what to do. She had nowhere to go, no one to turn to, no place to hide. As a writer of spy novels might describe it, her cover was blown and her safe house destroyed. She was again totally on her own—back to where she had started the first night in the woods after the shooting.

Realizing the crew aboard *Hamilton's Bench* might guess she'd head in their direction, she made her way back to the boat whose swim platform she had rested on earlier. This time she didn't stop and swam across the narrow inlet to where a line of boats were docked. Hiding between the hulls, she treaded water and tried to figure out what to do next. She cursed Danny for not being there to help her, and then realized he had no experience in a situation like this. He was a mountain man. She wasn't sure if he even knew how to swim. One thing she did know, she had to get away, and get away fast. She also knew she had to get out of the water. Her fatigue level was rising rapidly. She contemplated stealing one of the boats, but decided against that. For one, that wasn't in her nature. For another, she doubted whether she'd get very far. She had acquired a fair set of sailing skills while aboard *Hamilton's Bench*, but she didn't know the Chesapeake Bay.

She was about to move out when she suddenly sensed something above her. She heard a soft bark. Her heart literally skipped a beat in response. They found her again! But how? She froze, hoping the dog would lose interest and go away. She slowed her motion, but quickly sank below the surface. She grabbed at the side of the boat. The slippery hull refused to offer a handhold. She turned slowly in the water so she could face the sound above her. She saw the reflection of the animal as it peered down at her. She remained as still as possible, hoping—praying—it would go away. Time seemed to stop as she sank lower and lower. She leaned back to keep her mouth above the surface. Her legs were now screaming in pain as the lactic acid build up threatened to block further movement. She knew if she cramped up, she'd be doomed. Her mind raced for a solution, but her thinking was no longer clear. A chill flowed through her body. She raised a hand out of the water. It was shaking. She realized her whole body was shivering. Her mind continued to struggle for solutions. Time passed ever so slowly… or was it really passing quickly? She didn't know. Instincts told her it was time to panic, but she was too tired to even do that.

Her left calf cramped first, followed an instant later by her right. She struggled to keep her legs kicking, to keep treading water. Her legs would no longer move. She gasped for a breath of air, only to find her mouth was only half out of the water. She choked, sucking the wonderful tasting water into her lungs. She slid her hand against the side of the boat. There was nothing to grab hold of. The storm was howling overhead, only it now seemed as if was so far in the distance.

She suddenly knew a lot of things. And they all had to do with who and what she missed. She missed her home. She missed her mother. She missed Danny. She missed the people on *Hamilton's Bench*. She missed the piano. She thought she had gotten away. These past eighteen months had been wonderful—full of new experiences, new adventures. She was just starting to feel comfortable and to gain confidence in herself and the people around her. And then they came back to the states. She knew that was a mistake. Her senses told her so. But she ignored them, instead going along with whatever Mr. Hamilton wanted. And now…

And now, it was almost over. She knew what was happening to her. She didn't know how. But she knew. She told herself besides panicking, she should also be frightened. After all, she was about to…

She heard a splash in the water. Her legs might be cramping, but her arms could still move. She vowed it was her time. She vowed not to go without a fight. The vicious dog would never get her. He would never return her to the sheriff. She would take the dog with her. Yes, that's what she would do. She'd show the sheriff—that terrible man who chased her all over the place—that terrible man whose son had caused her so much grief. She spit out a mouthful of water. "I didn't shoot him," she shouted. She reached out to defend herself as the animal swam towards her.

In doing so, she sank below the water's surface, her body now acting like a brick. She had to get the dog. She had to get back up to the surface. She had to show the sheriff. She willed her legs to move, but they were cramped to the point of paralysis. She pulled upward with her arms, but nothing happened. Why wasn't she rising? Was this the end?

She willed her mind to stay awake. It was a battle she was quickly losing. She reached upward, trying to feel the water's surface. If she could only get something to grab onto. Then she felt something solid… something furry.

She grabbed a handful of fur. She tightened her grip and pulled. "I didn't shoot him," she screamed in her mind. "I never touched the gun."

And then things went blank.

130

Even living the life of luxury aboard his yacht, George Hamilton was still a workaholic. He put in long days, and just as often, long nights. He enjoyed his work, but he did not like it when work and pleasure intertwined, which had been the case on this particular day. So much was happening on so many different fronts, from having to find a new captain, to his New York office clamoring for decisions, to needing to visit April—he was being pulled in many different directions. As one who demanded total control over his time, this chaos exhausted him. He had stayed focused, however. He took care of the issues in New York and put out the word that one of the world's greatest yachts was looking for a new captain. Now he could devote what was left of the day to what was prime on his mind—April.

He had met many people over the years. Some he remembered, some he did not. Some intrigued him, some didn't warrant a shrug of his shoulders. He had few true friends, and they were mostly related to business. He had no family to speak of. One younger brother, an alcoholic in Florida, hadn't spoken to him in years and never returned calls or letters. He was sure his brother was still alive because alcoholics don't die easily. They simply embalm themselves with alcohol. Both his parents had died when he was in college, and except for a few cousins strung out across the country, there was no one. His only family were those aboard the yacht.

He worked at maintaining an informal atmosphere aboard *Hamilton's Bench*, but there was still a distance between himself and the crew. There was that invisible line drawn in the sand that no one was willing to cross. The only thing that really mattered to them was how high should they jump when someone barked and when would they get their next shore leave. The only *bonding* that occurred aboard *Hamilton's Bench* was when something needed gluing back together.

Then April came aboard. From the moment he heard her play that night in Atlantic City, he knew she was someone special. She had a talent he had never experienced in such a young person. Was he overreacting, or was she a prodigy? He'd bet on the latter. But like a raw diamond, it was difficult to forecast the quality before it was cut and polished. But regardless of how bright a diamond she might turn out to be one day, she already glittered in the sunlight. A wave of guilt for not having gone to visit her sooner tried to work its way through his armor.

He'd be at the hospital now except for the storm churning outside. He went up to the bridge earlier and looked at the latest weather plot which showed a large line of thunderstorms tracking across Annapolis. He estimated another hour before they cleared—plenty of time for him to catch a power nap and a shower before heading to the hospital. He looked out the port windows and watched as the wind tore through the boats moored in the marina. There was a sense of horizontal motion, but the boats were too big to be bothered much by the wind. Besides, the buildings surrounding the yacht club offered a certain amount of protection from the elements. *Hamilton's Bench* was well secured to the floating pier. Lines had been checked and additional fenders deployed before the storm hit. In that he no longer had a captain, he supervised the crew himself in making sure all was ready as they watched the storm roll in off the bay. In the harbor, all was secured and protected. He had no doubt things were vastly different out on the bay. Even boats as large as *Hamilton's Bench* would feel nature's fury then.

He returned to his cabin, undressed and laid across his queen size bed. He didn't realize just how exhausted he was. Work had been near nonstop since arriving in Annapolis. His schedule was crammed full before they ever docked. The unfortunate events that occurred since then only added to the stress. So a forty minute nap would be good. He set his mental clock and pulled a pillow out from beneath the bedspread and rolled onto his left side. He was asleep in less than sixty seconds. Sixty seconds after that there was a loud knock at the door.

He awoke with a start and sat up immediately. That someone was knocking on the door of his private cabin could only mean one thing—something was wrong. Pulling on the robe draped across the foot of the bed, he made his way toward the door. He'd see who was there before getting fully dressed. He had no doubt the problem was related to the storm. He also had no doubt the reason he was being bothered was because there was no captain. He liked being a hands on owner, but there where advantages to having a captain, such as having uninterrupted naps. He cursed Phillip Rogers under his breath.

"Come in," he announced, pushing his hands through his hair.

Louis came through the door immediately. "Sorry to bother you, sir. But, I thought you'd want to know. April's escaped from the hospital."

"Escaped?"

"That's what the police officers said."

"What police officers?" Hamilton demanded.

"The ones that are in the salon now."

Hamilton started to say something when he realized further conversation would be fruitless. "Thank you, Louis. Please tell them I'll be there in a minute."

131

The lights flickered for the fourth time since the storm started. This time they stayed off for at least an entire second. As she had with each occurrence, Jennifer froze in her tracks, held her breath and waited. A second was a long time when the electricity went out, especially for a business such as the *Riverboat Inn*. While the restaurant had a generator, the lights going out would still cause all sorts of problems. The dining room would do fine. They carried a large supply of candles for such emergencies. The bar would sell more liquor as people became even more festive. The kitchen, on the other hand, would turn to chaos. The routine of the prep line, where people worked with fire and sharp knives, would be altered due to lighting changes, especially during a busy time. And they were busy, even by Saturday evening standards. The dining room was packed and there were people crammed into the foyer and bar waiting for a table. The last she checked, the wait was over ninety minutes. The fact that people were willing to wait such a long time amazed her. The fact that they were willing to wait at the *Riverboat Inn* pleased her. The one thing she detested in life was to wait in line, especially when she was waiting to spend her hard earned money. Even during the holidays when the nearby malls were crowded, it was something she was rarely willing to do.

The lights did come back on just before the generators kicked in. She let out a long breath and gave a thank you to whoever above was on watch. She hurried across the dining room to where one of the new bus boys was struggling to clear a table. This was his first night, and while the restaurant had established guidelines for orienting new employees, because of the evening's unexpected volume, he'd been thrown to the wolves. She'd been keeping an eye on him and so far, he was doing okay. Except now, he was falling into one of the common traps of new help. As his confidence grew, so did the pile of dishes on his tray. It was a disaster in the making. She hurried over to him and thirty seconds later, the problem was solved. She made sure she threw in a positive comment about how well he was doing. She also made sure she thanked him for his effort so far. Finally, there was her smile—the special one saved for special occasions such as this. It was the one that really meant nothing, yet could be interpreted by the receiver in a multitude of ways. She watched his reaction, saw what she wanted and spun around. Her eyes scanned the dining room for the next fire requiring her attention. She saw one of the hostesses motioning that she had a phone call. Jennifer wondered who would be calling her at such a time, and right in the middle of a thunderstorm. She concluded it was one of their regulars looking to get seated quickly. It happened all the time. Their regulars walked in, saw the wait, and would go outside and call on their cellphone, asking for a quick reservation. Depending who the regular was determined the response. However, at the moment there just weren't any tables to be had. Added to the problem, because of the storm outside, people already seated were in no hurry to leave. Jennifer cursed the invention of the cellphone.

She took the portable phone from the hostess, walked around to the coat room where it was a few decibels quieter and covered her free ear with a hand. "This is Jennifer. Can I help you?"

"Jennifer, good evening. George Hamilton here. Thanks for taking my call." It was seldom anyone thanked her for taking a call. The man continued. "Sorry to bother you, especially at work. I'm sure you're busy, but I think you'll agree this is important."

"Who is this?" Jennifer shouted above the noise.

"Hamilton... George Hamilton... *Hamilton's Bench*... remember?" His voice rose in volume as he heard the noise in the background.

"Oh, Mr. Hamilton. Sure I remember." She stepped back around the corner and scanned the dining room. No doubt he'd want a table right away, and most probably would bring a contingency with him. And yes, while not a regular, he would fall into the VIP category, a very big VIP. But as her mother liked to say, you can't squeeze blood out of a turnip. At the moment, there was just no room at the inn. Maybe she could stall him a half hour or so, and then maybe something would open up. She knew she was only kidding herself. It would take at least an hour after the storm stopped to bring things back to the normal.

The voice on the other end continued. "Good. And no, I'm not calling to ask for a table. I imagine you're packed, especially with this storm."

"An understatement," she acknowledged. A weight lifted off her shoulders as she continued to scan the crowd.

There was a brief pause. She pressed the phone into her ear tighter to make sure she was able to hear. He continued. "I'm afraid I have some bad news to tell you... nothing too drastic, but I do think you'll want to know." Another pause ensued. "It seems your cousin, or probable cousin, April, left the hospital unexpectedly."

"Unexpectedly? You mean she was discharged?"

"No, she left on her own."

"How in the hel—heck did she do that? She was on a locked psych unit."

"It seems she escaped."

"Escaped… you mean eloped from the unit."

"I think that's the word the police used."

"When?"

"About thirty minutes ago."

"Right in the middle of the storm?"

"Seems that way."

"There certainly are a lot of *seems* here," Jennifer pointed out, trying not to sound too negative.

"I understand," Hamilton said, not reacting to her tone of voice. "But I'm only getting information second hand."

"May I ask from whom?" Jennifer was curious who he had talked to at the hospital.

"The police just left here."

"Why are they involved?" she said, surprised at first. "Oh never mind. The hospital has an eloped involuntary patient, so naturally they'd be involved. They need to find her before something bad happens."

"I understand that's exactly what they're doing."

"Seems that way."

In spite of all that was going on at the time, Hamilton couldn't stifle a laugh. "I'm just telling you what I know."

"Sorry, I don't mean to be so sarcastic, but that hospital and I have a history, and it isn't all positive."

"I'm sorry to hear that."

"Nothing to worry about." She paused. "They have something big to worry about, however, don't they?"

"You mean the public relations of having a patient simply walk out?"

"More than public relations. If anything happens to her…" She chose not to finish the sentence. "More than public relations," she repeated. "Patients aren't supposed to walk out of a locked down psychiatric unit," Jennifer explained.

"My understanding is she didn't simply walk out. She actually mounted an escape." Hamilton said.

"Mounted an escape?"

Hamilton continued. "She apparently used a piano to force open an emergency exit."

"Didn't anyone try and stop her? After all, that isn't something someone can do in a heartbeat."

"I asked the same question, but the police didn't have an answer."

Jennifer paused again. "Besides, I thought the psych unit was on the second floor?" She didn't remember the recreation room on the first floor below.

"The plot thickens," George Hamilton said. "Anyway, the police wanted me to keep an eye out for her. They think she may try and come back here. They asked about relatives and things like that. I told them I didn't know of any."

"Thank you," Jennifer said. The last thing she needed was for the police coming around asking a lot of questions, even though she knew everyone on the force. The *Riverboat Inn* was a favorite of the officers during their off duty hours. "I'll keep an eye out and let you know if she turns up or if I hear anything." Jennifer paused. "Do you think she's okay?"

"I hope so," Hamilton said.

"Me, too," Jennifer acknowledged. They bid each other farewell and broke off the connection. Jennifer returned the phone to its cradle. She thought about going out and joining in the search herself, but a look around the dining room nixed that idea. They were busier than ever. She glanced outside and saw the storm was starting to taper off. The lightning and thunder had stopped, and the rain was now about half of what it was earlier. She again thought about going out to look for April, or at least make contact with one of the cops she knew to see what was going on first hand. Then she had another idea. Finding the hostess working the front, she said, "Listen, I gotta run outside for a quick second. I'll be right back."

"Take your time. I'm sure things will be just as crazy when you get back."

Jennifer laughed. She felt guilty about leaving the restaurant at such a time, but she knew she'd only be gone a few minutes—the same amount of time it took staff members to sneak around the back for a quick smoke. Besides, in spite of what she wanted to believe, once the evening started rolling, there was really little she could do except put out a fire here and there.

She made her way to the kitchen and told her mother she was taking a short break without offering an explanation. She went out the back door, grabbing an umbrella on the way. She headed around the building towards the waterfront. The storm had calmed from just a few minutes before. The wind was dropping rapidly and the rain was falling vertically. Before she was halfway to the city dock, the rain stopped entirely. She chuckled as she folded up the umbrella. Chesapeake Bay storms—they started and stopped with a flick of a switch. She looked up toward the sky. The clouds were already allowing a few rays of evening sunlight to break through. "Thanks," she said softly.

As the parking lot was flat, puddles of water stood ready to capture an unexpecting foot. She kept her head down to make sure her feet didn't become one such prize. She made her way to where the *Mona Lisa* was berthed and stepped up onto the wooden pier. She looked up and stopped in her tracks. She leaned forward and saw the slip number nailed into the piling. She was at the right place, only the slip was empty.

The *Mona Lisa* was gone!

132

Cliff scanned the horizon left to right in a slow steady fashion. His night vision had taken full effect and visibility was excellent. The next three buoys leading him out the Severn River were already in line. The water, still churned up from the storm, was showing signs of calming nicely. The wind had dropped to ten knots. With the southerly movement of a couple of straggling clouds, the sky would soon be totally clear.

He pointed the bow of the *Mona Lisa* into the wind another couple degrees and tightened the jib so the sail rode just off the spreaders. He checked to make sure the boom was amidships and looked down at the compass. They were headed on a course of 136 degrees—a course that would lead them down and across the bay. While he had no specific destination in mind, he wanted to put as much distance between his back and Annapolis as possible. He had yet to figure out why he felt that way, but instinct told him he was doing the right thing. He usually fired up the iron jenny (the engine) when the hull speed dropped below four knots. There was no need for that tonight. They were making good time under sail. He had checked on his passenger a few minutes earlier and she was still fast asleep, in much the same position she had passed out in soon after they cleared the Annapolis Harbor.

He had some surprising things happen to him in his life—some tragic, and some pretty nice. Finding the girl in the water alongside the *Mona Lisa*, in the middle of a raging storm and nearly drowned, had to be the strangest. Talk about the crossing of paths in life. First he saw the girl on the bow of the big yacht. Later he learned she was probably the long lost cousin of Jennifer. He visited her in the hospital. Now she showed up nearly drowned alongside his boat in the midst of a storm. He wondered if there was a message… an omen somewhere. One thing for certain, there were an awful lot of caution flags flapping around him. Just what the hell was he doing packing up and leaving Annapolis the way he did anyway? He had ignored the flags in the past and paid the price. Was he about to get burned again? A part of him said that this time was different. This time he was doing something for someone else. His high school art teacher, Mr. Boardman, told him to use his talents for something good. Cliff didn't think this was quite what Mr. Boardman had in mind, but it was still something good… wasn't it? Good or bad, sometimes you just had to take a chance. Sometimes you just had to follow your instincts, like now.

Only *now* almost didn't happen. If Chessie hadn't awoken from a sound sleep and immediately sensed something was wrong outside, and hadn't insisted she be let out of the cabin, Cliff may have found the girl floating the next morning face down. The image of that possibility was difficult to shake. As it was, Cliff thought she was already dead when he finally got her aboard. Once out of the cabin, it took Chessie only a moment to realize someone was in the water and in need of help. She leaped over the rail without hesitation. She managed to pull April to the surface and drag her to the back of the boat where Cliff was waiting to see what had caused his companion to go over the side without waiting for permission. Chessie was a very obedient animal and would never do such a thing without good reason. It didn't take long for Cliff to realize the dog's actions were well merited. He climbed down the swim ladder and pulled the girl up into the cockpit. Luckily he was strong and she was small. He thought he was going to have to begin CPR, which he learned in high school as easy credits in gym. However, as he rolled her onto her side and was about to pound on her back, she vomited a large volume of water, gasped for a couple of breaths and came to. She immediately started to thrash around, trying to get to her feet. He held her down by the shoulders and told her she was okay and that he wasn't going to harm her. It was only when she rolled over onto her back and looked up at him at the same time a bolt of lightning lit up the sky that he realized who she was. He quickly told her who he was and about Chessie's rescue. She accepted the explanation without question, instead focusing her attention on the need to get up. She tried to do so, but was too weak. In a calm voice through the roar of the storm, Cliff talked to her, reassuring the frightened girl she would be okay. She kept repeating, however, that she needed to go. He pressed her about needing to go where. She refused to be more specific. It amazed him how quickly her senses had cleared. One moment she was near death. The next she was awake, alert, agitated and anxious to move on. Cliff wasn't so sure that would be the main focus of his attention if he were in her shoes.

Cliff was finally able convince her to go below and get out of the storm. He again reassured her she was safe and that nothing would happen to her. Below deck, he offered her a couple of blankets, a towel and some oversized clothes. He figured her shivering was winning out over other desires. As her body temperature rose, her mental state cleared and she became even more adamant about getting away. She wouldn't say why; she just said she needed to get out of Annapolis. The thought of physically stopping her never crossed his mind. He was not that kind of person. But a sixth sense told him that she was in real trouble. After all, why else would she have ended up in the water during a storm? Instincts also warned him about getting into something he'd regret. There was more than one storm rolling around the area—more flags flapping in the breeze.

His thoughts returned to the other night with Jennifer. He didn't listen to the warnings then. Why should he now? His feelings toward Jennifer had grown very strong very quickly. The more he was with her, the more time he wanted. He often caught himself staring blankly at his drawing pad, daydreaming about her—her smile, her touch, her body. He initially told himself the feelings were a normal reaction, just like in the past. Only this time, he was better prepared. Jennifer told him she thought things were progressing too rapidly. They made an agreement to remain friends. True, he was sad. He was disappointed. He felt déjà vu. Then again, so what? His personality was much harder than it had been in the past. He liked Jennifer—he liked her a lot. And they were terrific together. But…

There was always a *but*!

A smile crossed his face as he remembered a one-time lecture from his uncle. "Be careful when a woman gets a grip on you." His uncle didn't define what he meant by *grip*. "Because once she does, she won't let go. A woman's like booze. She's addicting in the worst way. You get some, and then you want more. You get more and that still ain't enough. The cycle repeats itself till she drives you plum crazy. Then she'll let you go suddenly, and there won't be any more. Then you'll go even crazier." Cliff used to chuckle when thinking about that lecture. Not anymore. Father Time had proven the lesson true more than once in his life. He had no doubt it was about to do the same again. He told himself, however, it would be different with Jennifer. They had an agreement.

"Our friendship is the most important thing," Jennifer said.

Cliff remembered the day beneath the Bay Bridge watching the painter hanging high above, and the words he'd muttered as the man finally disappeared from view. "Be careful, my friend."

His thoughts turned to a short time ago when they were still in Annapolis. Like the storm raging outside, the question loomed overhead: what should he do now? He had looked out the cabin window toward the east and saw the rain was still coming down hard. While he really couldn't see much because of the darkness, he sensed the storm was trying to abate. And while he didn't relish the thought of going back outside and getting soaked again, an idea came to mind.

"I'll make you a deal," he said. "I'll take you away from here, if that's what you really want. But on one condition." He sensed her tense up. "Nothing bad," he quickly added.

"I'm listening," she said, pulling a blanket tighter around her neck.

"You have to tell me what's going on. If you don't want me to tell anyone, that's fine, but you've got to tell me the truth."

She stared off in the distance. They both heard the sound of a police siren. Her eyes widened. "We can leave now—in the storm?" she asked.

"It'll be good cover. Besides, I think it's starting to pass over anyway," Cliff added.

She nodded and said, "What can I do to help?"

Cliff started to accept the offer, and then realized that could be a mistake. "Nothing. You stay below, out of sight. Chessie here'll protect you."

So with flags—caution and real—flapping wildly in the breeze, Cliff prepared to get underway.

He was glad he had. The girl was still on board. She was sleeping below, no apparent ill effects from her experience in the water. He felt good about what he had done. He had never saved anyone's life before, and the thought of that simple yet astonishing feat was spellbinding. He did not know whether he should feel frightened, exuberant, relieved or what. He also knew it was good to get away from Annapolis. He even wondered if finding the girl in the water was another sign. His uncle always said that things happened for a reason. Sometimes the reasons were not all that clear, yet they were there nonetheless. He never intended to spend so much time in one place anyway. Sure, he'd miss the hustle-bustle of the city, the laughter along the city pier, the noise in the restaurant. He remembered past cookouts at *Loafer's Glory*—the laughter, the noise, the food, the fun, his uncle being king of the world for a day. These were all things of the past.

Annapolis… Jennifer… parts of these were as well.

They were just friends, he reminded himself. Time would tell if that were indeed true. Time would tell if finding April was a fluke or something more. Was April his bridge from the past to the future? "Patience," he muttered aloud.

He looked up at the night sky. The storm had passed. The sky was clear. No falling stars. No images of Mark Twain to advise him. He turned in a full circle. It was turning into a beautiful night. He chuckled aloud. Chesapeake Bay weather—it could turn in a heartbeat.

So could a lot of other things in life, he added.

133

Jennifer had been listening to the three men for more than fifteen minutes. The man sitting to Jennifer's left, an administrator from Annapolis General Hospital, had an ever increasing look of fright, while the man sitting across from her, George Hamilton, was turning redder and redder. The man sitting catty-corner to her, the Annapolis police chief, for the most part just sat and listened. He tried, but failed, to hide an occasional smile. The four were sitting at a back table of the *Riverboat Inn*. As the restaurant was closed, it didn't matter that the conversation was quite loud at times as George Hamilton fired one question after another while the hospital administrator desperately tried to provide answers.

Hamilton wiped his mouth carefully after a sip of coffee before continuing. "So what you're really telling me is you don't know how April was able to escape from what is supposed to be a locked down psychiatric unit."

The administrator had introduced himself as Robert Madison. He was obviously new to the job, and just as obviously didn't know Jennifer's history with the hospital. Otherwise, he would have never agreed to meet at the *Riverboat Inn* to brief April's boss and her on the events from the night before. Everyone except him was dressed in casual attire. He was outfitted in what was probably one of his best suits. Jennifer had no doubt he was the administrator on call, and that was why he had drawn the short straw. Notifying family members that a patient had escaped from the psychiatric unit was not one of a hospital administrator's favorite tasks. And in spite of Madison trying to spin it otherwise, neither Hamilton nor Jennifer would concede April was anything but a very distraught suicidal patient to whom the hospital had failed to properly provide medical care. Jennifer was unimpressed at Madison's ability to handle the line of questioning from George Hamilton. She would have expected more from one of Annapolis General's finest. She was not surprised, however, that in spite of the seriousness of the incident and the potential implications for the hospital, the administrator still maintained a high air of arrogance.

Jennifer was impressed at Hamilton's ability to do the questioning in such an organized and effective manner. It was the first time Jennifer really let her curiosity rise as to just what the man with the big boat did for a living. Maybe after they were finished here, she'd get up the courage to ask.

Robert Madison addressed the latest question shot his way. "We know how she escaped. Like we've been over, she pushed a piano through a locked door. The question we're still working on is why she was able to do this in the first place."

"Obviously, some policy was broken," Hamilton suggested.

"Obviously," the administrator agreed a bit too quickly.

"Can I quote you on that?" Hamilton said. It was a question Hamilton had already asked on several occasions, all to which the administrator could only answer with a nod of the head. Jennifer recognized the new administrator was digging a deeper and deeper hole. The real question was not how deep the hole would eventually get, but what Hamilton intended to do once it was finished.

"Go over with me again what the nurse said. I was getting the coffee when you discussed that," Jennifer directed.

Glad to get away from the Hamilton attack, Madison turned his attention to Jennifer. He looked at her before speaking. If she didn't know any better, Jennifer would have sworn he was using the time to eye her up. Then she scolded herself for being so naïve. That's exactly what he was doing.

He is really stupid, she thought silently. She contemplated breaking off the eye contact and showing her displeasure at his behavior. She decided instead to use it to her advantage. She let a soft smile cross her face. Her eyelids rose ever so slightly. "What did she say?"

The young, stupid, horny administrator smiled as well. "Her story is that she was showing Ms. Whiterock around the recreation room when the lights went out and the fire alarms went off. As the nurse in charge, she had all the keys to the unit and had to go upstairs and turn off the alarms."

"Why didn't she take April with her?"

"She couldn't answer that."

"What do you mean couldn't?"

"Well…" He let his smile widen to try and deflect the conversation from where it was going. "One of the problems we're having is with this particular nurse. Right after the incident happened, she was so distraught, we thought we were going to have to give her a sedative. We left her alone on the unit to get her wits about her while we focused on making sure the search was organized. When we finally got back to her, she had left and gone home. She hasn't returned any phone calls."

Both George Hamilton and the Chief of Police chuckled at the same time. The administrator was forced to break eye contact with Jennifer to stare at the other two. "You find humor in that, gentlemen?"

The police chief came to their defense. "Can't keep your patients or staff under control, huh?" It was well known that the police chief had a great disdain for the hospital for their frequent 911 calls for police assistance. He had been overheard more than once complaining that Annapolis General's security force was not only understaffed, they were also under trained. And when Annapolis's Chief of Police spoke, people listened. He not only had a deep draw to his voice, he could be quite voluminous if necessary. During his tenure, he had made many friends, not through playing the political game, but by keeping the crime down in the city. Under his direction, Annapolis was one of the safest places to live in the state. When his men were pulled off the streets to do what he felt was a private sector job, he never found humor.

"Have you learned yet that most businesses, health care included, get into trouble not because of big issues, but because they lack attention to details?" Hamilton continued without giving the young man a chance to respond. "So no, there's no humor in this, just a sense of poor control." Hamilton added after a short pause. "I wonder what your quality assurance department will have to say about all this. You do have a quality assurance department, don't you?"

"If you're referring to our performance improvement department, yes we do."

"Well, I suspect you have a few performances to improve upon, don't you?"

"They also have quite a busy risk management department," Jennifer piped in. She ignored the sudden look from the hospital administrator.

"Risk management—is that the area that deals with malpractice suits and things of that nature?" Mr. Hamilton asked, looking directly at Madison.

The young man nodded.

"I can tell you this, if you don't find April Whiterock soon, and unharmed, you're going to need to hire more staff."

"Are you threatening me?" The young man continued to play the tough role, his arrogance unyielding.

Hamilton leaned back in his chair. "Why, no, sir, that's not what I'm doing at all. For you see, the definition of a threat is to claim that you are going to do something harmful, physically or otherwise, to someone or something. A threat implies an action sometime in the future, with future being the key word." That said, Hamilton reached into his pocket and took out a cellphone. He pressed a couple buttons and pressed it to his ear. A moment later, "Yes, operator, good morning to you as well. May I have the emergency hotline number to the State Health Department?" He paused before adding, "Thank you, and you have a nice day too." He slid the compact phone back into his pocket. Glaring at the administrator, he said, "I'm going to finish my coffee and my conversation here with these fine folks. Then I'm going to take a leisurely walk back to my boat. If when I get back aboard, you aren't there with some definitive information about April's whereabouts I will be calling the number I just obtained and be filing a formal citizen's complaint against your hospital. I'm sure you're well aware what happens when someone files a health department complaint against a hospital." He took a quick sip of his coffee. "And then, I'm going to call the Joint Commission hotline as well." Another sip of coffee followed. "Now, Mr. Hot-shot-hospital-administrator, what I just said is not a threat. It's a fact!"

The man to whom the above tirade was directed had by now turned bright red. Jennifer guessed he finally realized he had underestimated his opponent. He rose to his feet and turned to walk away.

As he did so, the Chief of Police spoke up, "By the way, when you go back and call Sam Robertson—I assume that's who you'll be calling—be sure and tell him all the details of this conversation, including where you met and who was here. And make sure you emphasize that both Jennifer Blackstone and myself were present."

A quizzical look came over the man's face as he exited the room.

The three remaining at the table waited until the man was on his way out the door. The police chief looked at George Hamilton. "If I do say so myself, we certainly put a fright in that young man."

Hamilton wasn't yet in the mood for jokes. The administrator had obviously infuriated him with his arrogance. He turned his attention to Jennifer. "Are they all like that?"

"The CEO is worse."

"I'm sure I'll be meeting him soon, Hamilton said. "I wouldn't be surprised if he doesn't come a calling this very afternoon."

Jennifer wanted to ask him what he meant by that, but was distracted by the police chief who said, "I didn't even know the State Health Department had an emergency hotline."

"I don't know that either," Hamilton said.

The chief cocked his head to the side.

Hamilton picked up the cellphone he'd laid on the table. He raised his voice an octave or two. "At the tone, the time will be…" He allowed a smile cross his face, but only for an instant. He continued. "Now why don't you tell Jennifer and me what you know."

The police chief straightened his posture. "We know the exact time she got out because we ran the security tapes on the alarms. Like they always do, and because they're so God damn short staffed, they contacted us immediately. My first officer arrived three minutes later. He was at the busted exit door in less than two minutes after that. He did a quick sweep of the area before calling for back up. Remember, there was a terrible storm going on at the time, so I think my men did a good job getting there when they did."

"It was too late to find April" Hamilton said.

"I don't think arriving a minute after the incident would have helped. She wanted to get away, and she did."

"That's exactly the point," Hamilton reassured. "There wasn't anything your men could have done, except if they happened to be standing at the door when she came through."

"Anyone willing to smash a piano through a chained door has a determination tough to do battle with."

"The door was chained?" Jennifer broke in.

"That it was. Pulled it right out of the frame."

"It was an emergency exit, right?"

"Yes."

"Is that noted in your report, Chief?" Hamilton asked.

"It is."

"We'll deal with that another time," Hamilton added. "For now, I want to focus on finding April."

The police chief continued. "Unless she's holed up in some vacant house—and we have very few of those in town—she's out of the city limits."

"I'd venture to guess that with her history, she's far out of town by now," George Hamilton said.

"Her history?" Jennifer inquired.

"That's what I was starting to get to when our friend here showed up," Hamilton said, referring to the earlier arrival of the hospital administrator. "The Chief and I were comparing notes."

Hamilton looked at Chief Smith who took over the conversation. "We don't have all the pieces put together yet, but it appears Ms. April Blackstone, alias April Whiterock, has been on the run for almost two years. She's wanted in the shooting of a teenage boy in a small town in Ohio called Worthington Valley. The boy just happened to be the star quarterback on the high school football team. He also happened to be the son of Worthington Valley's sheriff."

Jennifer Blackstone turned pale.

Annapolis's Police Chief held up a hand. "Don't worry Jennifer. While true, all law enforcement officers do stick together and help one another whenever possible, we still have to maintain our objectivity and do our jobs. In this case, there are too many questions unanswered to pass any kind of judgment just yet."

"What kind of questions?" Jennifer said, allowing a hint of curiosity and impatience to project forth.

The police chief continued. "For one, like I said, she's wanted 'for the shooting of,' but there have been no warrants issued by the town or the state. For another, we're all a close bunch, especially the chiefs of various cities and towns. While I can't recall ever meeting anyone from Worthington Valley, I would have expected to hear about it if a chief's son was murdered. Hell, stories a lot less drastic than that make the news every night. Surely it would have shown up somewhere. We ran a search for the past two years and found nothing—not a word. I have our people right now searching to see if Worthington Valley's newspaper has a web site to see if we can get information from back issues."

"Maybe Worthington Valley doesn't want you to know anything," Hamilton offered.

Jennifer's eyes widened. "What makes you say that?"

"He may be right," the chief supported. "Usually when one police department calls another, there's an unwritten code to cooperate as much as legally possible, and sometimes even beyond that. However, when I called, I got vague answers to my questions, and when I asked to speak to the sheriff himself, I was told he was unavailable. When I asked when he might be available, I continued to get the runaround. It was almost as if the deputy I was talking to didn't know where the hell his boss was. I will tell you this, my men always know where I am and how to get in touch with me—twenty-four seven."

The chief sat his coffee mug back on the table. "I changed directions a bit with the conversation and was able to get some personal information from the deputy. His last name is Richmond. He's been the sheriff there for over twenty-five years."

"Almost as long as you," Jennifer quipped.

"But much older," the Annapolis Chief retorted. The two friends exchanged smiles. "It was almost like the deputy I was talking to was afraid. But I still got a sense he wanted to talk, even though he didn't."

"What do we do?" Jennifer asked.

"There's an old saying in police work. You can't investigate a crime away from the crime scene."

"Then someone will just have to go out to Worthington Valley and find out what's going on," Jennifer announced.

The two men laughed.

"What's so funny about that?" Jennifer demanded.

George Hamilton's face turned serious. "Everyone's so tight-lipped now. Showing up and asking a lot of questions might make it worse."

"Besides," Chief Smith said. "I can't up and send someone out there. For one, all we're doing so far is looking for a patient who eloped from the hospital. And from what I've been able to ascertain, Worthington Valley is the last place she'll go. For another, the murder investigation isn't ours to investigate. That's Sheriff Richmond's ball game. If he wants help, he needs to ask for it. Otherwise…"

"What if something bad happens to April?" Jennifer pressed.

"I certainly hope that isn't the case," Chief Smith said. "But as I'm sure you're aware, we only have so many resources we can throw at the problem."

"Besides that," Hamilton injected. "I'm not sure I want the Chief to find her, at least not yet."

Jennifer's eyes snapped towards the yacht owner.

He continued. "To start, he'd be obligated to return her back to the hospital. And then, because of the information he knows and because he is an exceptionally ethical law enforcement officer, he'd be obligated to put a call out to Worthington Valley telling them he had her."

Jennifer cocked her head to the side. "You don't think she's a danger to herself—i.e. suicidal?"

"She's not a murderer, either."

The chief's eyes lit up with curiosity. "A very interesting, and I would think, risky position for someone like you to take, Mr. Hamilton."

Hamilton explained without being asked. "She's not suicidal because she didn't jump into the water Friday night to try and kill herself. On the contrary, she was trying to protect herself."

"From what?"

"My asshole of a captain… or ex-captain."

"He was trying to…" Jennifer couldn't quite get the word out.

"No, I don't think he'd go that far, but he'd certainly push the edge of the envelope. April was very shy and naïve in a lot of ways, and in spite of the way I first met her, I don't think she was very experienced in certain social aspects."

"What do you mean by that?" Jennifer said, almost demanded.

Hamilton took a sip of his coffee. "Like I told you before, she was hired to help entertain the guests."

"To play the piano?"

"Not initially. That actually came as a surprise. The pianist who was hired never showed up. The next thing I knew she was at the piano. She's one of the best pianists I've ever heard—a little green around the edges, but an excellent talent."

"What do you mean, help entertain the guests?" Jennifer asked.

Hamilton hesitated. "The male to female ratio at this particular gathering was very unbalanced."

Jennifer's eyes lit up in anger. "You mean you hired her as a—"

"No, I did not!" Hamilton snapped back. "She was simply hired to come to the party and mingle."

"With the word mingle being very loosely defined," Jennifer snapped back.

"Jennifer," Chief Smith said in a soothing voice. "It's not an uncommon practice for such a thing to happen; and it doesn't always end in the fashion you're thinking. And, it's perfectly legal."

"Not always, but sometimes it does."

Hamilton stared at Jennifer until he got her undivided attention. "She was not what you're suggesting, Jennifer. She was too naïve."

"How can you be so sure of that?" Jennifer's opinion of the man sitting across from her was dwindling rapidly.

"I earn a good part of my living because I'm an excellent judge of character. Now, I'm not saying April wouldn't have headed down that road if she stayed in Atlantic City. I also think that's one of the reasons she came aboard *Hamilton's Bench* the next day… to avoid what she saw if she stayed. I think that same character trait came forth the other night with my ex-captain. He wanted to go down a certain path. She didn't. So, she escaped again."

"This time by jumping overboard," Jennifer said.

"Probably her only way out," Chief Smith suggested.

Jennifer paused. "Could there have been a similar situation with the shooting of the sheriff's son?"

Annapolis's Chief eyes sparkled. George Hamilton allowed a thin smile to form.

"How do we find out?" Jennifer was feeling very exasperated.

"We have to find April," Hamilton reminded.

"I've got every available man on that one," Chief Smith said. "Just in case she's still around."

"She's not," Jennifer said.

"What makes you say that?" Hamilton asked.

Jennifer hesitated. "You said it yourself, based on her history." She hesitated again. "Besides, I think I may know where she is, or at least who she's with."

"Care to explain?" the chief said.

"It's just a hunch."

Hamilton interrupted. "It may be best for Jennifer to keep her thoughts to herself. After all, it is just a hunch."

The chief, having quickly developed a deep respect for the man sitting across from him, contemplated the idea. "I can't act on information I don't have."

"Exactly."

The chief took a sip of coffee. "Let me ask you this, Jennifer. Is it your hunch that April is still in Annapolis?"

Jennifer nodded negative.

"Is she safe?"

"I think so," Jennifer said.

"How confident are you about your hunch?"

Jennifer shrugged her shoulders.

"Let me ask it this way. Are you confident enough I can call off the search?"

This time Jennifer's nod was positive.

134

"You don't seem yourself today," Old Man Hooper said, carefully taking the lid of the Styrofoam container. He raised the container to his nose and let a rare smile cross his face. The aroma of oyster stew filled his nostrils.

Jennifer handed him a napkin. "I've got a lot on my mind."

"You've always got a lot on your mind."

"It's usually not all mixed up like it's been lately."

"Anything to do with your friend down the way?"

She failed to hide a look of surprise. "Who?"

"Who!" the old man mimicked. "You know who. That young artist several slips down."

"Oh him. His name's Cliff Davidson."

"I know his name."

"What about him?"

"You've been spending a lot of time with him."

"Mr. Hooper!"

"Don't mean no harm." He took several bites of the stew. "He's a fine young man. Hell-of-an artist, too."

"He is that."

"He don't say a whole lot."

Jennifer laughed. "Funny thing, he says the same thing about you."

"That I'm a hell-of-an artist?"

"No, silly, that you're quiet."

"Am I?"

"Sometimes."

"Nothing wrong with a little peace and quiet."

"No there's not. Regardless, we're just friends."

He gave her the look of an experienced person who didn't believe what the less experienced person was saying.

"He left last night," Jennifer said.

"During the storm," the old man said.

"I imagine after," Jennifer corrected.

"No, he left during the storm… seemed to be in a big hurry, too."

"How do you know all this?"

"I watched him take off."

Jennifer tried, but couldn't resist the next question. "Was he alone?"

Old Man Hooper paused his chewing. "Couldn't really see. Just saw the boat go out. Revved the engine up pretty good because of all the wind and that." He watched a disappointed look come across Jennifer's face. "Was he supposed to be alone?"

Jennifer fiddled with a sandwich wrapped in foil. The old man returned to his stew. He knew she'd explain when she was ready.

"I'm not sure what he was doing," Jennifer said. She let out a long sigh which told the old man an avalanche of information was coming. He settled back to listen. Jennifer continued. "We did have some words earlier in the week. Not bad, but he was upset."

"You dumped him?"

"No, I didn't dump him. I told you, we weren't like that."

"Maybe in your mind."

Jennifer started to say something then stopped. Cliff never said anything about his feelings toward her. Except for talking about his meeting with the governor, he never expressed much emotion about anything. "Whatever. I didn't think it was so bad he'd go taking off in the middle of a storm. If that were the case, why didn't he leave earlier?"

"Why didn't he?"

"I don't know. But I don't think he left during the storm simply because he was pissed at me. I think something else was going on." She bit a piece of sandwich. "I told you about my cousin, or at least who we think is my cousin, didn't I?"

"One of the crew on that big ugly yacht over there?"

"You think the boat's ugly?"

"If I had that kind of money, I certainly wouldn't buy a Tupperware boat." Tupperware is what Old Man Hooper called boats made of fiberglass.

"I think she's beautiful."

"Whatever boats your float."

Jennifer laughed at the old man's ability to twist words so easily. "Anyway, we were talking about the girl, not the boat. I told you about the other night when she allegedly jumped into the water. They took her to the hospital and locked her up in the psych ward. Well, she escaped yesterday and has yet to be found."

"When'd she escape?"

"During the storm."

"Same time your boyfriend left."

"He's not my boyfriend, and yes, about the same time."

"You think there's a connection?"

"Maybe."

Old Man Hooper scraped the plastic spoon across the bottom of the Styrofoam cup to ensure he got all the residual juice. "A moment ago, you used the word alleged in front of the word jumped."

"I think she jumped alright, but for a different reason than initially thought."

"I can think of only one reason to jump off a perfectly good boat, even if it is Tupperware, and that's to go for a swim."

"That's because you're a man. If you were a woman crew member aboard a boat with a captain who had trouble keeping his hormones in check, you might think of another reason."

"To get away from a man."

"Eye of the bull."

The old man smiled at her attempt to mimic him. "Nice try."

"At least you're giving me credit for trying. Never did that before."

The oyster stew finished, the old man attacked the ham sandwich. With half a mouthful, he said, "You still haven't shown me any good reason for you to be so down in the dumps... other than the fact that you probably dumped one of the nicest boyfriends you ever had."

"How can you say something like that? You've never met any of the guys I've been out with."

"You have talked about them."

"Sometimes."

"I did say *probably* dumped. Besides that, I'm an old man. I can say anything I want and blame in on senility."

"Senile, my ass."

"Let's watch our sailor tongue, young lady," Mr. Hooper ordered half-heartedly.

Jennifer stuck her tongue out at him.

The old man ate in silence as Jennifer filled him in on what she knew about April and the murder of the sheriff's son.

"How do you know it was murder?"

"We don't really."

"You're making assumptions, and that can lead you down the wrong trail." It was a piece of advice he had given her before in life. The ham sandwich a thing of the past, Mr. Hooper continued, "So regardless, the quandary is what should you do?"

"Sort of."

"Yes or no?"

"Okay, yes."

"What do you think?"

Jennifer had already spent a lot of time pondering the same question. "If she's not my cousin, then I really shouldn't be messing in her business. If she is, I feel a certain obligation."

"What's the difference?"

"Between what?"

"Family versus not family."

"There's a…" Recognizing where he was headed with his question, she stopped. "She's not old and senile like you. If we all didn't mess in your business, you'd probably be…" She stopped again.

"You're right, I'd probably be dead. But because you cared, you got involved. And while I'll never admit it to anyone but you, I am very appreciative of everything you did and do for me."

"Well, hark the herald angels sing. There is hope."

"Don't get carried away."

Jennifer continued. "So you think that regardless of who she really is, I should get involved?"

"Sounds like before you answer that question, you need to get more information."

"But to do that, I have to get involved."

"Every gain is married to a venture."

"I was just about to say that," Jennifer said.

"Shit from a bull."

Jennifer laughed.

The old man's expression turned serious. "I've said this to you before, don't—"

"Don't start something I'm not going to finish," Jennifer interrupted. "Don't worry, I won't."

"You make sure of that."

135

Jennifer glanced in the side view mirror and clicked on the left turn blinker. Making sure the left lane was clear, she pressed down on the gas pedal and passed a slower moving truck. The passing gear of her six-cylinder Honda Accord kicked in and she cleared the truck in short order. Back in the right hand lane, she set her cruise control at sixty-eight.

The weather was clear, the sun just reaching its highest peak. She adjusted the rear view mirror slightly and wiggled her butt to get a more comfortable position. Traffic on the Pennsylvania Turnpike was light, just as she had hoped. She had a long way yet to drive, and a lot of thinking still to do.

Although an understandable tendency, she refused to second guess her decision to head to Ohio. It really wasn't a difficult decision. Chief Smith said you had to be at the scene of the crime to investigate the crime, and since neither he nor George Hamilton was available, she took it upon herself to make the trip. She ignored the problem of what she was going to do once she got there. She tried putting herself in Chief Smith's shoes, but quickly realized that was a fruitless task. He was way too experienced for her to emulate. He had a keen mind and could see through the densest fog of useless information. Jennifer was sure there was a lot of that floating around. She took a sip of bottled water and set about digesting what she knew.

Surprisingly, the first image that came to mind was George Hamilton. What role did he play in all this, and what were his true motives? Jennifer wanted to be angry at him for hiring April to *mingle* at his party. She also realized that was probably a saving grace for April. Hamilton seemed genuinely concerned for her well-being. It was interesting that he didn't press her for details concerning April's actual whereabouts. He was satisfied that she was safe. He agreed with Jennifer that they needed to first find out what happened in Worthington Valley before they could formulate any sort of plan. All he reiterated was that April remained safe until they found out more. Jennifer told herself this wasn't all that surprising. In spite of his apparent enormous wealth and success, he seemed down to earth. He was polished, polite and very smart. He was also quite handsome adding to his overall persona.

Jennifer chuckled aloud. "Go ahead and admit it, he was a looker all right. And the person behind the looks wasn't all that bad, either." She cautioned herself not to make a hasty conclusion. After all, her opinion had already flipped-flopped a couple of times. She laughed as her mind started to undress him. "Stop it!" she said aloud. "Stop it," she repeated. "First you rob the cradle. Now you're robbing the nursing home." She knew she was exaggerating on both accounts, but she didn't care. She was angry with herself for having pulled back from Cliff, although she knew it was for the best. They had talked about it a couple days before and Cliff seemed to understand. When they met with her parents after Cliff's meeting with April, he seemed fine as well. Both agreed their friendship was more important than anything. But now there was that *void* again in her life. Was she now rebounding with images of George Hamilton?

"Rebounding in fantasyland only," she muttered. "Although, he would be a nice catch."

She scolded herself again. She was never one to try and *catch* a man. She had never pursued anyone in her life. Her relationships just happened... just like her and Cliff.

She refocused. For now she'd give George Hamilton the benefit of the doubt. Her thoughts turned to April. There was little doubt April Whiterock was really April Blackstone, the cousin Jennifer never met. Their lives were now intertwined—whether they wanted it that way or not. Jennifer always had questions about that part of her family, but the number of questions had suddenly doubled. First and foremost, where was April and was she okay? Jennifer continued to harbor a sense that she knew the answers to both, which were with Cliff and yes. However, this was only a sense, an idea, a feeling. She would feel much better once the intuition was verified. But Cliff didn't have a cellphone. So how was she to get in touch with him, and would he even talk to her? After all…

She refused to let her thoughts go there.

She turned her attention to Sheriff Richmond. What she knew about him had been gathered by Chief Smith. Richmond had been Worthington Valley's sheriff for many years—a career politician and law enforcement officer. Jennifer guessed he carried a pretty big stick around town. He was a widower, and now his only son was dead. That was a recipe for a very angry man. Jennifer thought Sheriff Richmond would have pulled out all stops in his search for April. Yet, that wasn't true. Sure, there was an initial search, but that was called off after only five days, and then the search had been restricted to the mountains around Worthington Valley. The perimeter, Chief Smith thought, had been rather small. The official conclusion was that she had succumbed to the elements on the mountain, but her body had never been recovered. However, to this day, there had been no signs of her. Chief Smith thought this strange as well. After all, she was loose on the mountain dressed in a prom dress. Another peculiar matter Chief Smith uncovered was the lack of an arrest warrant for the murder. She was only wanted for questioning. Even if they thought the girl was dead, you still issue the warrant just in case. Good police work demands you cover all bases. In this case, bases were left empty. Another piece of interesting information, while it was indeed a big event for the town of Worthington Valley, news coverage outside the region was nonexistent. The question here: how did they keep such a story under wraps? And perhaps more importantly: why?

A lot of questions with few answers, Jennifer thought. A sixth sense told her something wasn't right… something was missing. The focus continued to come back on Sheriff Richmond. April was supposedly dead up on the mountains behind Worthington Valley, yet Sheriff Richmond was apparently in Annapolis currently looking for her. Chief Smith said someone had stopped to talk to one of his deputies just after April escaped. The man was dressed in a law enforcement uniform and drove an unmarked car. The man didn't introduce himself, and the Annapolis officer didn't ask, although he did notice the tags on the car were from Ohio. There really wasn't anyone else it could have been.

A twinge of fear rolled up Jennifer's spine. She never met the man, but already knew he was too spooky for her.

Her thoughts turned to Danny Worthington. Her father's conversations with him only added to the mystery. Why was he and everyone else so vague and unwilling to talk about the whole thing. It was as if they were trying to cover something up.

After the meeting with the obnoxious hospital administrator, Jennifer talked to her father. He was concerned for April's safety, but agreed with George Hamilton that it might be best for the girl to stay away, at least for the time being. "It's obvious she needs help," he said. "It's just as obvious we can't offer her a whole lot until we know more." Jennifer and her father debated what to do next. Neither was able to come up with a feasible solution.

Her father asked about Cliff's whereabouts. Jennifer told him Cliff had left Saturday night—apparently right in the middle of the storm. Her father thought that was something Cliff would never do, unless for a very good reason. He didn't press the point. He had grown fond of Cliff in a very short time. Jennifer failed to mention they had become more than just friends, or that their friendship had become strained. That conversation was for another time.

"Too many loose ends flopping around," her father had said. "Like a whole pile of unmatched socks."

Jennifer passed another truck and brought her thoughts back to the present. She had to decide what to do once she got to Worthington Valley. She glanced at the clock. She had at least six hours to formulate a plan.

136

Danny grabbed the phone by the second ring. He cursed under his breath as the new Alicia Keys video was about to premier on MTV. He wasn't all that fond of her music—a little too jazzy for his taste—but she was something to look at. He definitely needed something to look at. After all, that's all he had been doing lately—looking, looking, looking. At times, he wasn't even interested in that. He'd been on an occasional date. Only the desire was gone, his ability to charm tarnished. His mind just wasn't into it. He was not over the break up with Sally, loss of Eddie or the loss of his other best friend, April. He was hurt and angry that April hadn't contacted him. He never raised the topic of her being alive with anyone, not even his family. He felt guilty about this, but didn't want to raise false hopes. Until he had definitive confirmation, let everyone continue to think April was dead, her remains undiscovered up on the mountain.

He believed, however, that somehow, someway, she'd made it to Atlantic City where the trail ended. He had returned to the boardwalk three times over the next several months. Each time he waited, watched and searched the area. He never heard from her, nor had she used the bank card again. He often wondered if the card had somehow been stolen, the perpetrator lucky with the password. He decided that was unlikely as the amount withdrawn was low. He even wondered if the bank made a mistake—a flicker in the computer system, but they confirmed its use with the password correct.

So where was she? Why hadn't she contacted him? He needed something—something to prove she was indeed alive and well. It had been many months since the dance. He had passed the stage of desperation. He had resolved that she simply disappeared from the face of the earth and would resurface only when she was ready.

If she was ever ready.

He pushed the mute button on the remote and hit the answer button on the portable phone. "Hello," he growled, making sure the person on the other end knew he was unhappy about the intrusion.

There was a brief pause. "Hello, may I speak to Danny Worthington?"

Danny glanced at the clock above the television. Five-thirty—right on time for the damn telemarketing calls to begin. "Who's calling?" he snapped.

"This is a courtesy call for Danny Worthington."

"Well, he ain't interested."

He started to reach for the off button when the voice spoke louder. "I'm not selling anything… honest."

The pleading in her voice caught his attention. "Then who's calling?"

"Is this Danny?"

"Yeah, this is me."

"Are you on a portable phone?"

"Maybe."

"If you are, walk to the window and look out."

"What the fu—"

"Please!"

Deciding this was a trick by one of his friends to cheer him up, he complied. He guessed he was about to be mooned. Pushing the curtains aside from the bay window, he said, "Now what?"

"Do you see a green Honda Accord near the end of the driveway?"

Danny saw the vehicle and acknowledged as much. At the same time his mind raced to remember who owned such a vehicle.

"I'll meet you at the back entrance of the football field at nine tonight sharp… and please, come alone."

"Which football field?" he tested. His mind continued to short through his database of friends. The list grew shorter by the day.

"Is there more than one field?"

"What's this about?" Danny demanded. Any of his friends would have known the answer.

There was a moment's hesitation. "April—it's about April. She's alive and well."

Danny felt the blood rush from his head. He put an arm on the couch for support. He shook his head to make sure he wasn't dreaming. He dreamed of April often. Regardless of the beginning, it always ended in the nightmarish evening of the dance. Convinced he was awake, he looked around to make sure no one else was in the room. He sucked in a couple deep breaths. "Yes, there's only one football field."

The line went dead. He watched in disbelief as the Honda pulled away.

137

If she still smoked, she would have been on her fourth or fifth cigarette. It was a habit she had quit cold turkey the day she left Annapolis General Hospital. She had been perfect since then without any slips off the wagon. She took a deep breath as if searching for the calming effect of the tar and nicotine. It was no use. Her hands were shaking so badly, she probably couldn't hold a cigarette if she had one.

She had been second guessing herself for the past four hours—ever since making the call to Danny. Yes, it was the right thing to do; and yes, she was crazy for doing it. But there were too many things that could go wrong. So many *what if's*, she didn't know where to begin. What if Danny never showed up? What if he called the police and she was arrested for some trumped up charge? What if Danny did show up but didn't believe her?

What if? What if? What if?

One hand grabbed the other as she told herself to calm down. She crossed her legs as they were also starting to shake. She always dreamed of writing a mystery novel, of creating strong interesting characters that got wrapped up in a situation way over their heads. She never dreamed of living one in real life.

She was parked behind the south bleachers, hidden in their shadows. She could see the only road leading to the field. Hopefully, anyone coming down the road would not be able to see her. It was now completely dark, the sun having taken longer than she had hoped to set on this particular night. The night was cool. The sky was clear, the moon thankfully absent. While the lack of moonlight made it difficult for her to see anything coming her way, she knew just the opposite was true as well. She glanced at her watch. It was too dark to see. She contemplated turning on the inside map light, only to be dissuaded by the fear of giving herself away. She told herself to be patient. She had confidence Danny would show up. The tone of his voice told her he wanted to know what she knew. Curiosity was a difficult urge to resist. No, she decided, she'd just wait in the dark. The last time she'd checked her watch it was eight-thirty. It shouldn't be too much longer now.

She kept telling herself that. But as more time passed, her fear converted to worry. Her earlier confidence started to erode. Where was Danny? Why hadn't he come? Didn't he care about his sister? The more she thought about it, the stronger her doubts. What was she thinking? She was a nurse and restaurant hostess. What business did she have playing detective? Sure, it might give her leads for a good story. It might also lead to her demise.

At a near panic, she started to turn on the engine. Just as she was about to turn the key, she heard something behind the car. She froze. Fear swirled along her spine. Now, she knew she'd been an idiot. But as so often happens to one's inner soul, when fear is at its peak, the desire to succeed strengthens as well. Her hand was on the key, but it would not turn. She knew if she left now, any window of opportunity would close. She waited, her heart threatening to thump out of her chest.

She heard the noise again, this time closer to the rear of the car. Someone was creeping up along the passenger's side. Grenades of anxiety continued to explode. She talked to herself in silence. "Didn't someone once say that the greatest fear of all was fear itself?

And didn't someone else say that if you conquered your fears, you could conquer the world?" Well, she wasn't after the world. Her goals were much smaller.

The passenger door opened and a figure dressed in dark clothing slid in. Jennifer saw her life pass before her eyes. She thought she'd been afraid before!

"Where's April?" a voice demanded.

She recognized the voice as Danny's. A dam of relief burst. He had come. "She's not here."

"Where is she?" His voice broke, telling her he was as nervous as she.

"Not here!"

"Where is she?"

Back in control of her wits, Jennifer said, "Are you alone?"

"Yes."

"Where can we go to talk?"

"Not here, if that's what you're thinking."

"I'm not thinking. I'm asking." She braved a glance to her right. "You are Danny, aren't you?" The figure sitting next to her was dressed in a long black turtleneck shirt and dark pants. She couldn't see much, but she sensed he was as nervous as she.

"You're in trouble if I'm not," he replied.

"True," she conceded. She knew they were both uncomfortable. She also knew they had to develop at least some level of trust if they were going to get anywhere in the next few minutes. "I believe you," she said.

He looked at her. "Are you sure?"

Jennifer wasn't sure if the question was directed at her or towards himself. His eyes were wide, and in spite of trying to convey otherwise, she could see his face quivering. "April is alive. I saw her a couple days ago," she said.

"Where did you see her?"

Jennifer hesitated. "I'm not ready to divulge that yet."

"Are you related to that man who called me recently? He claimed to be April's uncle."

"Did you tell anyone about those calls?"

"No! Besides, no one would believe me anyway. They all think she's dead."

Something about the comment made her think. "Everyone?"

"Everyone except me."

Information she knew about the case rattled through her mind. Aloud, she muttered, "Then why was he in Annapolis looking for her?"

"Who?" Danny snapped.

"Is your sheriff a big fat man?"

Danny's eyes snapped back ahead. "Let's get out of here."

She turned on the engine and started to do the same with the headlights.

"No lights!" he instructed. "Just drive straight ahead. I'll tell you which way to go." Except for Danny telling her *a little to the left* or *a little to the right*, they drove slow and in silence. When she heard the sound of gravel crunching beneath tires, he told her to make a hard left. At the same time he told her to go ahead and turn on her lights. Even with the headlights, the road was hard to see as there were no markings down the middle or on the shoulders. A short time later, Danny told her to make a turn. They came out on a main road. Jennifer recognized it as the one running in front of the school. "Where are we going?" she asked.

"Away from here." A long minute passed before he spoke again. "Tell me something about April that only someone who knew her real well would know."

"I don't know," Jennifer pointed out. "I've never met her and have only seen her once. " She paused. "She's a terrific pianist."

"That's no big secret," Danny said. "Whole school knows that."

"Her mother has a drinking problem," Jennifer threw out.

"Whole town knows that," Danny said. "Besides, that's an understatement."

"I'm sorry to hear that."

"Not a big surprise. When your only daughter does what she did and then disappears, never to be seen again, what do you expect?"

"So she's gotten worse… your mother… I mean your stepmother."

"Like I said, an understatement."

"Before your mother married your father, she and April lived in a trailer near an old farmhouse somewhere in Alabama." Jennifer reached into her purse and pulled out a plain white envelope. "I'm April's cousin."

Danny took the envelope and found the overhead map light. He slowly flipped through the pictures. "I've never seen any of these," he said. "April claimed they threw all their old pictures away when they moved. I guess she was lying."

"No," Jennifer corrected. "These came to us in Christmas cards years ago. We haven't heard from my aunt in several years."

"Maybe now you can guess why."

Jennifer didn't respond. She could feel Danny staring at her. He was obviously trying to make his mind up about whether to believe her or not. She decided to help his decision process along. "Listen, you're not sure whether you can trust me any more than I can trust you. But somewhere along the line, we have to get our minds together. Like I've said, April is alive, but I still think she's in danger."

"From what?" Danny asked.

She stole a glance in his direction. "A big fat sheriff."

She made another turn at his direction. The road began to wind gently up the side of the mountain. She saw lights in the distance and below. She glanced in the rearview mirror as she had done numerous times since leaving the school.

What a crazy conflict of emotions. She chuckled, swallowing hard so the sound wouldn't escape her throat. Why couldn't she write a story as good as the one she was presently living? An especially sharp curve caused her to change the focus back to her driving.

There was another sharp curve and Danny directed her to turn onto a side road to the right. They came to an opening that looked over the valley below. "Is that the town?" Jennifer asked.

"Worthington Valley at her finest." Danny lit up a cigarette and offered one to Jennifer. While her mouth watered and her hands shook, she declined.

Danny took a long drag and blew the smoke out the open window. "Tell me what you know."

"You sure it's okay to talk here?"

"No one comes here anymore."

Jennifer reached down beside the car door and let her seat recline a few notches. "To make sure we have our background information correct, my father, David Blackstone, had a sister, June Blackstone, who became pregnant at an early age with April and ran away with the baby's father, much against the advice of the family. The father was a real loser and soon my aunt was forced to leave him. She and April ended up in Alabama where they rented an old trailer from a farmer. According to what we know, April's mother got a job in a nearby town and while things weren't the best, they were able to get by. We didn't hear much more until we got a letter saying that she and April had moved to Worthington Valley, and she was getting married. She said her new husband—your father—was very good to her, and April and everyone seemed happy. We got a letter the first or second Christmas, and that's been it."

"Did she say anything about the man she married being rich?"

"No, just that she and April lived in a beautiful home and had a wonderful family. I even think those were her exact words."

"That's just like her," Danny said.

"You want to explain?"

"At first, when my father brought the two of them home, I assumed the worst."

"Gold digging?"

"Is that what you call it?"

"Close enough."

"Anyway, to straighten out your facts, April's mother worked as a cocktail waitress in a gambling hall in some two bit town in Mississippi. My father told me the name, but I can't remember it. He was down there one weekend on business when he met her. For whatever reason, he was attracted to her and she, to him. A couple trips later, he asked her out for a drink. I guess the rest is history." Danny flicked the cigarette out the window. "It was obvious that she and my father were good for one another. She was also very good to me—in the right kind of way, too. She never tried to replace my mother, but always said she was there for me if I needed her. She said I could talk to her about my mother if I wanted. No one ever said that to me before, not even my father. And that's the way she acted. I have to admit, I've became quite fond of her in spite of her troubles. April was harder to get to know. She was very shy and initially seemed afraid. But once she settled in, we became very close."

"So you think the whole marriage thing was for real, and not just a convenient set up?" Jennifer asked.

Another cigarette was lit. Jennifer noticed the lighter was not shaking as much. "I think it was a little of both," Danny answered. "And things were going along just fine until the nightmare."

"The nightmare?"

His eyes bore into hers. "You tell me what you know."

Jennifer continued. "April was on her way to a dance with someone—the sheriff's son. Only they never made it. Something happened and she supposedly shot him."

"What happened after that?"

"She disappeared."

Danny took a long drag of his cigarette. "Actually, she escaped."

"Off the mountain, right?"

"Sort of."

Jennifer sensed there was more to the story than Danny wanted to reveal. She told herself to be patient. "The details are sketchy, but that's what I know."

"Anything else?"

"Somehow, she ended up in Atlantic City where she went to work for—"

"So she was in Atlantic City!" Danny interrupted.

"Yes. How did you know that?"

Danny threw the cigarette out the window. A hint of excitement entered his voice. "When she left, I gave her my bank card. She only used it one time, in Atlantic City. That's the last contact I had with her. I even went there several times looking for her. I bet I was so close."

"Maybe she didn't want to be found," Jennifer offered.

"Regardless. How did she manage to completely disappear from the face of the earth?"

Jennifer decided that to gain his confidence, she would have to tell him something he didn't already know. "By going to sea."

"Huh?"

"She went to work as a crew member aboard a large yacht, and has been there ever since. She's been all over the east coast, Bermuda and the Bahamas."

"So you're telling me everyone around here thinks she's dead—everyone except me—and she's actually living the life of luxury?"

"I don't know if the work is all that luxurious. It's pretty hard."

"Good for her." Danny smiled. It was his first smile. He couldn't hold back a chuckle either. "Everybody thinks her body is rotting away up in these mountains, and she's sunbathing on a beach in the tropics." The smile disappeared. "That doesn't explain how you found her."

Jennifer hesitated. "I'm getting to that." She still sensed Danny had his doubts about her story. She looked around to ensure they were still alone. She reminded herself she had already been snuck up on once that night. "The owner of the yacht is a good friend of

Maryland's Governor and came to Annapolis to do some fundraising. The boat docked right across from my parents' restaurant. I was over there one day looking around when I saw this girl on the deck. She didn't see me, but I recognized her. It was one of those times when you see someone, but can't put your finger on who they are. I knew I knew her, yet it was a day or so later before I put the face to a name. You see, I'd only seen the photographs I showed you earlier.

"Anyway, as it turned out, my parents went to a fundraiser aboard the boat the next evening and April was there. My father agreed it might be the cousin I never met. During this time, my father talked to you. We also met with the yacht owner. He was supportive and told us what he knew which wasn't much. He met April in Atlantic City and that's where she joined the crew." Jennifer paused. "During their time in Annapolis, she ended up in a hospital."

"I thought you said she was okay!"

"She is. She was put in a psych unit for allegedly trying to hurt herself by jumping overboard. But I think she was trying to get away from an overzealous person."

"Meaning a man?"

"That's my guess."

"Meaning a man who wanted something she didn't."

"That's my guess," Jennifer repeated.

"Jesus Christ, it happened again."

"What are you talking about?"

"That's what I think happened when she shot Eddie."

"You mean he was trying to…"

Danny hesitated. Jennifer could tell he was mulling over what she had told him as well as how much to tell her.

"Danny," she said gently, "April's okay for now, with *for now* being the operative word… or words. And while I think I know who she's with, I don't know exactly where she is. But that's okay for now. I am concerned however, that this may not last for long."

Danny turned back to her. "Go on."

"We think your sheriff's in the area looking for her," Jennifer said.

"But he says she's—"

"It doesn't matter what he says," Jennifer interrupted. "It's what he's doing. We have strong reason to believe he was at the hospital about the same time April escaped."

"She escaped?"

"Yeah. She busted through a door with a piano."

"Then what happened?"

"We're not sure, but I suspect she left with someone on a boat."

"On the boat she was working on?"

"No, a sailboat."

"Where is she now?"

"I think she's roaming around the Chesapeake Bay."

Danny stared off in the distance. "You know, the first time I was in Atlantic City, I thought I saw the sheriff on the boardwalk, but I blew it off as paranoia. I wonder if…"

"We have to assume he knows she's alive," Jennifer said. She reached out and touched him on the shoulder. "Danny, we have to trust one another."

Danny turned toward her. "What was she doing on a boat, anyway? She's never been on a boat before."

"Playing the piano… and quite well from what my parents and the yacht owner said. Turns out, that's why the owner hired her. I guess she had other duties, but her main responsibility was the piano."

"The boat has a piano on board?"

"Yes."

"Big-ass boat."

"Big-ass boat," Jennifer concurred.

Danny looked away. "It was the night of our spring dance. April went with my best friend, Eddie Richmond. He's an okay guy once you get to know him. All the chicks drooled over him. He was a real player."

"And April was not?"

"Correct."

"Why would you let April go out with Eddie, and why would Eddie want to go out with her?"

Danny hesitated. Jennifer sensed the answer was a painful one. "The challenge of it, I guess."

"The challenge of what?"

Danny sat in silence. The answer hit Jennifer like a load of bricks. She wanted to ream him a new one, but she kept her mouth shut. No doubt, he was feeling enough guilt over the whole matter. He didn't need a stranger coming into town adding more to the pile. Besides, she needed him on her side. She reminded herself of the trust factor she had just preached.

The story still lacked details, but Jennifer felt she had some of the holes filled in and some of the questions answered. April Whiterock was indeed April Blackstone, the cousin Jennifer had never met. April had been on the run for almost two years because she shot the sheriff's son on a date—a date that turned into every girl's nightmare. As they had been doing all along, another question popped up. "The gun… where did April get the gun?"

"It was Eddie's. He carried it under his seat for protection."

"Protection from what?"

"Mainly bears."

"Bears?"

"There are bears in this area, and once in a while, they'll come up to the cars. A shot in the air usually frightens them away."

Jennifer looked through the front window nervously. Then her eyes snapped back to Danny. "Are you—"

"No," Danny said. "I just honk the horn."

Jennifer decided to believe him and went back to her thoughts. Now, April was on the run again for the same reason, a man who didn't know how to keep his hands to himself. Jennifer couldn't begin to imagine what it would be like to be in April's shoes, to be on the run, to always be looking over your shoulder, to be separated from family and friends, wondering what was around the next bend in her life. Horrifying was probably a good choice to describe the experience… like being chased by a bear.

Anyway, good or bad, the story was unfolding. Loose ends were slowly coming together. But there was still a huge gap in one part of the whole thing. She let her thoughts come out aloud. "Why would the whole town think April is dead, yet your sheriff thinks she's alive? Why wouldn't he tell them as much so they could help in the search?"

Danny contemplated the question a moment. "He obviously doesn't want anyone to know what he knows."

"Have you talked to him about that?"

"I haven't spoken a word to him since the night of the shooting."

"Not one word?"

"Not one word."

"Why?"

"He's been very strange since the shooting. I know firsthand losing a family member can change your life brutally. I lost my mother when I was five. Maybe losing a child is worse."

"You never know exactly how someone is going to react in the face of tragedy," Jennifer offered.

"True, but his is way off base."

A sixth sense told Jennifer this might be the first time Danny talked about the ordeal. The boy continued. "For one, Sheriff Richmond was always very outgoing and friendly. He knew everybody and everybody knew him. He won reelection time after time simply because there was never anyone to run against him. They were all in his camp. Since that night, however, he's just the opposite. He's become totally withdrawn. He speaks very little, and while he is doing his job, the spark is no longer there. His passion for life has totally disappeared. It was tough on him and Eddie when Eddie's mother died, but they got through it. This time it's different. He also disappears without telling anyone where he's going. And when he returns, they say he's angrier than ever. Rumor has it, his deputies are actually afraid of him."

Two quick questions came to mind. Jennifer asked the most pressing first. "Tell me what you mean, the sheriff disappears."

Danny responded immediately. "According to the talk on the street, he would do just that. One minute he'd be in the office working, the next he'd be gone. Sometimes he calls in. Sometimes he doesn't."

"What does he say when he calls in?"

"Nothing except that he'll be gone for a couple of days."

"A couple of days?"

"He's never gone for more than two or three days at a time."

Jennifer started to ask a second question when a follow up to the first popped up. "Danny, you said you haven't spoken to the sheriff since the shooting."

"That's right."

"Where do you get your information from?"

"What do you mean?"

"How do you know all this stuff you're telling me?"

"CB."

"Huh?"

"CB—citizen's band radio."

"Like in the old days?"

Jennifer caught a look of disgust cross Danny's face. "CB's are still very big in some areas of the country, including Worthington Valley. Everybody has cellphones, but the service isn't always dependable. Besides, talking on the CB is free."

"And everyone else can hear your conversation."

"Worthington Valley's a tight-knit town. One reason is because everybody knows everything."

Jennifer doubted that, but did not vocalize her concern. She focused on her second question. "Didn't the town provide the sheriff support during this time?"

"He wouldn't let 'em."

"What do you mean?"

"We had a memorial service a couple days after it happened, but that was all. There was no funeral, no viewing, no nothing."

"That's a little strange, don't you think?"

"More than a little. Hell, I don't even know where my best friend is buried."

"Was he taken to the hospital first?"

"Yes, but later that night the sheriff took him away, claiming he was going to take him to a special place up north."

"Hasn't anyone asked?"

"No one dares."

"Did the sheriff attend the memorial service?"

"No, he was too busy looking for April. They thought she was still alive then."

"What did you do?"

"I was looking for her, too, only no one knew it."

Jennifer collected her thoughts. "From what little I've been able to gather, April sounds like this shy little withdrawn girl. I wouldn't think it should be too hard to find her in the woods."

"That's what you would think," Danny said. "But, she was about as skilled as you could get. She knew all the survival techniques as well as the tricks to evade anyone who might be after her." He briefly explained the game of fox and hound.

"So you like the outdoors?"

"I spend as much time up in these mountains as possible."

"May I ask why?"

"Up here it's just you and nature," Danny explained. "Peaceful, yet challenging. If you can survive the world here, you can survive down there. April had a pretty hard time at first when she came here. She was backwards, had a terrible accent, and looked like she just came off the farm, which in reality she had. But there was something about her that people just took to, and soon everyone just let her be herself."

"Why was that?"

"The kids at my school aren't any different than anyplace else. There are good ones, bad ones, geeks and jocks. Some like to party. Some like to study. But regardless of which category you fall into, everyone likes music. Several months after April got here, we had our annual talent show. While some of the Broadway wannabes took it seriously, most of us used it to have a good time. April had been bugging me to take her into the mountains. She was as curious about that as she was about her new subjects in school. So I made her a deal."

"The talent show for a trip to the mountains," Jennifer inserted.

"Geeks and jocks were all standing together applauding wildly."

"What did she play?"

"Two things by that guy Beethoven. One was real slow and moody, the other was very upbeat and fast. She knocked them dead that day. It was also the day Eddie Richmond added her to his list."

"His list?" Jennifer said. Danny didn't have to explain. She got the message as soon as she uttered the words. Again, she thought about tearing into the boy. She again reminded herself she needed him on her side. "That explains her ability to survive out in the mountains."

"She needed to be hardened both physically and mentally," Danny said.

"You worked on both?"

"She was smart—a quick learner."

"And you were a great teacher." Jennifer failed to keep the sarcasm from her voice.

Danny's head snapped in her direction. "Listen, Ms. Blackstone."

"Jennifer's okay."

"Jennifer, then. I know I'm as much to blame as anybody. I got her into this mess. I also helped get her out."

"How so?" Jennifer said, struggling to control her anger.

Danny explained how he found her after the shooting and how she escaped from the motel. "The problem is," he said, "I taught her so well, even I couldn't catch up with her."

"Why do you think she ran the way she did? Why not just turn herself in and tell the authorities what happened?"

"She probably figured no one would believe her, and she was probably too scared."

"Would anyone believe her?"

"Sheriff Richmond holds a lot of power in this town. Whatever he said happened would be what happened."

"Regardless of the truth?"

Danny hesitated. "I wonder whether April even knows the truth. It happened so fast."

"What do you think happened?"

Danny hesitated. "Knowing Eddie, he was probably trying to get cozy, and April was resisting. We'd all had a couple beers—except April of course, so Eddie was probably being more stubborn than ever." The expression on his face showed his pain. "Anyway, for whatever idiotic reason, Eddie must have pulled his gun out from beneath the seat. There was a struggle and the gun went off."

"Did she ever touch the gun?"

Danny paused. "She did say once she never touched the gun. But what difference does that make?"

It was Jennifer's turn to pause. "It may not make a difference. Then again, it may." She hesitated again. "Was the official investigation ever released to the public?"

"I don't even know if there was one."

"There had to be. Weren't the police called?"

"I called them."

"You! Where were you when all this happened?"

"Sally and I—my date—had stepped out of the car."

Jennifer didn't ask the why behind that maneuver, telling herself to stay on track. "So there had to be a report. I imagine a full-blown investigation was done."

"If it was, nothing was ever released."

"No one ever asked?"

"No one thought to."

"Do you have a local newspaper?"

"Yes, the Worthington Independent Daily."

"What did they have to say?"

"They covered the shooting big time. They also know my father's factory gives a lot of jobs to the people who buy those papers, so while they did report the event, they kept their editorial comments to themselves."

"So it's not truly an independent paper?"

"I'm taking journalism in school now, and one of the things we've talked about is how to get your opinion across without pissing off your advertisers."

"What did it say about there being no funeral?"

Danny thought back. "I remember an article about the memorial service. There was nothing written about the lack of anything else."

"You sure about that?"

"I read the paper every day."

"Isn't that unusual for someone your age?"

"Not if you're thinking about becoming a journalist yourself."

"So you want to be a writer?" Jennifer asked.

"Thinking about it," Danny said.

Jennifer continued. "Then as a journalist, don't you think it odd—the lack of coverage about the lack of a funeral that is?"

"Maybe." Danny paused. "Where're you going with all this?"

"I'm not sure," Jennifer admitted. "There are still too many unanswered questions for my taste. I have a feeling there's more to it than meets the eye."

"Care to explain?"

"The bottom line, does April need to be on the run? And if the answer to that is no, what can we do so she can stop?"

"No one ever said she needed to be on the run to begin with."

"Your instincts said just the opposite; and in fact, you helped her get away."

"But not for this long."

"What has changed from the night of the shooting to now to make you think differently?"

Danny started to argue, and then stopped. "Nothing."

"Well, it's time to change that nothing to something."

"How do we do that?"

"I haven't got that far yet."

They sat in silence, each mulling over the information they had just received. Danny focused on the news that April was alive and well. Jennifer focused on the loose ends she so desperately wanted to tie off.

"When can I see her?" Danny said, pulling Jennifer away from her train of thought.

"As soon as she gives me the okay." Jennifer didn't explain further.

"Her mother will be glad to hear this. My dad will, too. Everyone has forgotten about him in this whole mess, but he's taken it hard as well. He and Sheriff Richmond used to be very close."

Jennifer started to plead for him not to say anything, but she knew that would be a waste of words. It would also be very cruel to keep such information away from the family. As a nurse, she had always been a strong believer that patients and their families had the right to know as much as possible about the patient's condition—even if the news was bad. But in this case, the news was good.

"Please, make sure you emphasize the importance of not telling anyone else. I don't want the lid to blow off this until we know more."

"What more is there to know?"

"I suspect the bomb is about to get even bigger. It's just a hunch, though. I can't explain it any further, but when I put it together, you'll be the first to know."

Having matured above his age, Danny knew not to argue. "Where do we go from here?"

"We need to get more information."

"What kind?"

Jennifer thought a moment. "What are you doing in your journalism class right now?"

Danny shrugged. "Besides learning how to write like a journalist, we're studying the investigative part of the business."

"Perfect," Jennifer said. "I have an assignment for you. Only this time it's for real." She explained over the next few minutes.

"What are you going to be doing?" Danny said when she was finished.

"I'm going to gander around and see what I can dig up."

"What do you mean by gander?"

"I'm not sure, but I'll let you know."

"You'll let me know?"

Jennifer stared him in the eye. "Have you learned anything about trusting your sources in journalism?"

"Sort of."

"Well, we are each other's source—the only sources we have. Like I said earlier, we've got to trust one another."

Danny broke off the eye contact. "I just hope she's okay."

"She is and she will be."

"What makes you think she's on a sailboat now?" Danny asked.

"Good question," Jennifer said. "A short time after she left the hospital, right in the middle of a storm, a friend of mine left the harbor in his sailboat. He knew about April and had actually visited her in the hospital. We did it that way for several reasons I'll go into later, but I suspect April found her way to Cliff's boat and he took her away. That would be the only possible explanation I could think of as to why he would leave in the middle of such a storm."

"Do you think she knew Sheriff Richmond was in the area?" Danny asked.

"Another good question... but something tells me she did."

"So she's still in danger?"

"Possible," Jennifer acknowledged.

"Maybe I should hold off telling my folks about this, at least till we know more."

"I think that's a good idea," Jennifer supported. "At the same time, I understand if you want to tell them something."

"I'll see."

Jennifer sat upright and grabbed the keys in the ignition. "Before all that though, I want to go to where it all started."

"What all started?"

"To where the shooting actually occurred."

Danny hesitated. Then he slowly leaned over and poked his finger into Jennifer's side. "Bang!"

Jennifer turned pale.

Danny sat back upright. "You said you wanted to go somewhere where we wouldn't be disturbed. Like I said, no one comes up here anymore… except me."

Jennifer looked over at Danny. She saw tears running down his face. She had no doubt they were a mixture of emotions. Yes, she decided, she was doing the right thing. At the same time, something told here there was a big piece of the puzzle missing. There was something going on they did not realize. There was another gun ready to go *bang*.

138

The day started with a nine hour drive from Annapolis, Maryland to Worthington Valley, Ohio. The day ended with an intense meeting with Danny Worthington. As might be expected, the gauge on Jennifer's energy tank was reading empty. Her mind, however, was not showing any signs of fatigue. To use a commonly heard phrase heard amongst the staff at the *Riverboat Inn*, she was *wired*. She sped up to make it through the next traffic light. She had always heard you could judge the size of a town by the number of traffic lights and fast food franchises. While Worthington Valley had its share of each, the town itself seemed to be mainly Main Street and a few side roads. Danny did mention that the bulk of the community consisted of residential developments surrounding the actual town itself. Since dropping Danny off back at the high school, she'd been riding around, trying to get a sense of what the town was all about. Worthington Valley had its high spots and low spots, although Jennifer did not run across any areas she'd classified as impoverished.

One thing was clear, Worthington Valley existed for one reason and one reason only—Worthington Industries. The plant, which sat on several hundred acres to the north, made a variety of parts for the auto industry. By far one of the larger auto part companies in America, it had also been one of the industry's most profitable. There had been little labor trouble over the years. Attempts at unionizing continued to be successfully warded off, the last challenge coming the year before. Layoffs had been few, with sales on the rise for the third year in a row. Management's philosophy was you worked your employees hard and paid them well. Worthington Industries's employees had little to complain about. Overall, they were content and very protective of what they had. Jennifer sensed that was the main reason the town's people hadn't asked more enticing questions about the whole affair with April and the sheriff. They wanted to protect the company president and the town's sheriff. Self-centered survival topped their list of priorities. Jennifer doubted whether other towns would have let the story fade away so quickly and with so many questions unanswered. It certainly would have never played that way in Annapolis.

Jennifer again sped up to get through a light. Not that she minded stopping at stoplights, she just had a sense of paranoia around her she couldn't seem to shake. What she really wanted to do was drive to the center of the town and scream at the top of her lungs that April was alive. Then she wouldn't be burdened with such a secret. But she and Danny decided to keep quiet about what they knew. There were too many unanswered questions, and they wanted to address these without a lot of interference. Too many questions. Too many mysteries. Too many mysteries within mysteries. She felt like a detective investigating the *big* crime. She knew she was in over her head. She told herself Chief Smith should be out here instead of her. He would know what to do, where to go, what questions to ask and how to get answers. Then again, wasn't she doing okay so far? Wasn't she on the right track?

She had to chuckle. She might be on the right track, but where was the train? She reminded herself why she was doing this. Family—even those you never met—created a strong bond.

She cleared her mind and began reviewing what she knew. April agreed to go to the spring dance with Eddie Richmond, Danny's best friend and the son of the town's sheriff. They went as a double date, with Eddie driving. However, before ever getting to the dance, they stopped at a place called *Point-To-Point Lookout*. Danny admitted everyone except April was drinking, but he insisted they only split one six pack. When Eddie started putting the moves on April, she resisted. Eddie became more aggressive and pulled out a pistol. A struggle ensued. The gun went off. The police report said Eddie was shot at point blank range. April claimed she never touched the gun.

Danny heard the gunshot and raced back to the car where he found Eddie slumped across the seat and called 911. The police and ambulance arrived a short time later. April was nowhere to be found. While Danny insisted Eddie was still alive when they put him in the ambulance, the boy reportedly died at the hospital later that night. He was buried at an undisclosed location in northern Ohio. Upon returning to Worthington Valley, the sheriff remained very withdrawn and distraught. The mourning was understandable. What had everyone baffled was his refusal to talk about the incident nor give details about Eddie's funeral. All he ever said was that Eddie was gone. He did continue overseeing the search for April, but called it off after a week. He, as did the town in general, officially concluded that April had perished somewhere up in the mountains. After all, all she had on was a long dress, and she certainly wasn't savvy enough to survive in the mountains alone. Danny knew both of those points to be false. Her dress was exchanged for a set of outdoor clothing. Danny was also aware that his stepsister knew much more about surviving in the wild than anyone would have expected. Over the next several days, April somehow made it to Atlantic City.

Several things continued to be bothersome. Why was the sheriff so secretive about his son's funeral? And why was the search called off so quickly? Also, how did Sheriff Richmond find April in Annapolis eighteen months later? And how did April get wrapped up in an escort service? Exactly what she did or how long she was doing this, Jennifer wasn't sure, but from the time frame she was able to put together with the information provided by George Hamilton and Danny, Jennifer concluded April was probably only in

Atlantic City a few days. Jennifer doubted if her cousin could have gotten into too much trouble. During this time, the thought-to-be-dead fugitive was able to change identities. And while Worthington Valley (minus Danny and the sheriff) wrote her off as being dead in the mountains, April was out of the country living on a multimillion dollar yacht.

"A long way from an old dirty farm trailer," Jennifer mumbled aloud. Silently, she added, "A long way from true happiness, too."

Her thoughts returned to the beginning of the story. Again, why did the sheriff act so strangely about the funeral arrangements of his son? She made a note to ask Danny more details about the death of the sheriff's wife and the sheriff's subsequent behavior. Suddenly, the other loose end clarified itself—something Chief Smith said during their meeting at the *Riverboat Inn*. A warrant had been issued for April, but it said she was only wanted for questioning "in the shooting of" Eddie Richmond? While April's story contradicted the events pieced together by the police, this was a murder case. Wasn't it? Jennifer didn't know much about the business of law enforcement, but she did know the system nationwide was overrun with criminals and undermanned with staff. As such, a warrant for a murder suspect, especially when the victim was the son of a police officer, would get much more attention than someone wanted just for questioning.

Jennifer shook her head side to side. There were definite pieces of the puzzle still missing. She suspected one big piece with other smaller ones. If she could find the big one, a lot of the other pieces would undoubtedly fall into place.

As she drove around, she started looking for a place to spend the night. She was glad she had packed an overnight bag. First, however, she was hungry. She hadn't eaten since she left Annapolis. She came to an intersection and saw a McDonald's a block away. The letters below the golden arches announced the drive thru was open twenty-four hours. When the light turned green, she pulled ahead, urged on by her hunger pains. Her continued paranoia, however, reminded her that the last thing she needed was to get a speeding ticket. She turned on her blinker and was about to turn into the McDonald's when yet another sign caught her attention. It was a blue background with a big white H imprinted in the middle.

Suddenly, an idea came to mind. Was the missing puzzle piece right under her nose?

She forgot McDonald's and turned into the hospital parking lot.

139

Chessie sensed the movement before her master. The dog's head rose off the deck, her eyes opened, her ears rolled back. A short moan came from deep in her throat. Cliff heard the activity below deck a second later. Then a head popped up through the hatchway. The girl's hand blocked the sun from her eyes. She scanned the scene behind the boat. Her eyes dropped to Chessie, who was now on her feet, tail wagging, anticipating some attention from a newfound friend. A thin smile crossed the girl's face. She reached out and patted the dog atop the head. She looked at Cliff who was sitting with his back against the port side and his feet up on the opposite seat. A drawing pad lay open on his lap.

"Good morning… or rather good afternoon," Cliff said, dropping his feet to the deck.

April stepped into the cockpit. "Good afternoon. What time is it?"

Cliff looked up at the sun. "I reckon about two or three. There's a clock above the chart station if you want to know for sure."

The girl shook her head. "Where are we?"

"Wharton's Creek."

"Where's that?"

"Across the bay and up north about twenty-five miles from Annapolis."

She turned in a full circle. "Seems so isolated."

"It's Monday. It's busier on the weekends." He watched as her expression turned worried. "Don't worry, you're safe here. No one knows you're with me, and no one knows where I am."

"For now," April added.

Cliff ignored the comment. "Hope you were comfortable up forward. I know it's not what you're used to."

"It's fine, thanks." She didn't add that crew's quarters aren't necessarily proportional to the size of the boat. She continued to look around. They were surrounded on three sides by woods. Off to the right was an opening that led to the bay. They were anchored about a hundred feet off the south shore. "No one lives around here?"

"Not that I'm aware of."

She scanned the shoreline. "How long have we been here?"

"Once the storm let up Saturday evening, I headed across the bay and then went north. It actually turned out to be a beautiful night. We had a ten knot breeze so we made good time. We got in here around daybreak Sunday morning."

"I remember hearing the anchor chain go out."

"Sorry. Couldn't do much about that."

"Don't worry about it." She didn't add that her cabin on *Hamilton's Bench* was all the way forward as well and those chains were much louder.

She sat down on the bench opposite Cliff. "How long we staying here?

"That's up to you."

"Me?"

"Depends on what you want to do."

April's shoulders slumped down. Cliff thought for a moment she might start crying. April regained her composure, however, and leaned forward. Reaching down, she rubbed Chessie briskly atop the head. "Thanks, girl, for keeping me warm last night," she said. Saturday's storm had pulled a cool front into the region. While the daytime temperatures were in the eighties, the nighttime lows were in the sixties.

Cliff wanted to tell the girl Chessie had done more than keep her warm. The dog had also saved her life. Cliff wasn't sure April remembered exactly what happened in Annapolis. He figured that conversation was for another time.

"She's really taking a liking to you," Cliff said, which was true in that the dog had barely left the girl's side since the night of the storm. Except to use the head, April had remained holed up in the V berth. Cliff had checked on her frequently, and each time she was sleeping. On one occasion he stood in the doorway just looking at her, wondering what was going through her mind; wondering what she had really been through; wondering why she had run after the shooting.

Another topic for later discussion.

The shirt and pants he had given her to wear hung loosely on her body. She had pulled her hair back in a ponytail, allowing him to see her face more clearly. It didn't take a cosmetologist to see she had way too many lines for her age. She had a deep tan which only accentuated the markings. Her arms and legs were just as dark. Her body was petite, but her muscles were well developed—not overly so—just enough to show she was a hard worker. Cliff imagined it took a lot of elbow grease to keep *Hamilton's Bench* sparkling. Heaven knows, he tried to keep the *Mona Lisa* looking sharp. It was a never ending task.

In spite of the lines and the deep tan, April was still pretty, and Cliff imagined that if she ever smiled from true happiness, her smile would radiate. He was never one to meddle in someone's psyche, until now when he felt a driving curiosity to delve deep into the girl's soul. He had heard so much about her. His had painted a mental picture of this April Blackstone alias April Whiterock. Cliff imagined she had a hard core exterior. And while she had proven her ability to survive whatever came her way, Cliff believed underneath that armor was a very frail personality. He based that on her reaction the first time he saw her on the bow of *Hamilton's Bench*. She was too afraid too quickly. This impression was reinforced by the visit at the hospital a few days later. While trying to portray a hard exterior, she was unable to hide her vulnerability.

As an artist, Cliff had developed a keen eye for reading a scene. He wondered if this skill were transferable to living subjects. A twinge of doubt crossed his mind. After all, Jennifer pointed out he had no humans in his works. So maybe he wasn't as good as he thought. Maybe he had April all wrong. Maybe she was just one tough son-of-a-bitch… that being said in a complimentary fashion of course. Maybe he was jumping to conclusions, wishing to see something that wasn't really there as justification for doing what he was doing—harboring a fugitive. Or maybe he was just looking for a reason to leave Annapolis. He pondered all this before deciding it was probably a combination of everything. Still, he wondered what was going on in April's brain. If only he could read minds!

April continued to survey her surroundings. Her eyes darted back and forth, stopping for short bursts before moving on to something else. Her expression showed not necessarily fear, but a high level of caution. The only thing that seemed to give her any sense of security was Chessie at her side. She made sure the dog stayed there by continuing to rub her head.

"Hungry?" Cliff said.

The look in her eyes responded with an immediate affirmation. Verbally, she hesitated. "Sure."

"What do you want?"

"We have choices?"

Cliff laughed. "You're right there. Pickens are getting slim. I was planning to stock up over the weekend, but a sudden departure put a crick in those plans."

"Sorry."

"Don't be sorry. I said supplies are getting thin. We still have enough for a day or so before we have to live on Oodles of Noodles. I think there are a couple of eggs left in the ice box and I have some pancake mix. How's that sound?"

"Breakfast in the afternoon?"

"I eat breakfast food all the time. It's easy, hot and filling."

A thin smile crossed her face. "That's fine," she said.

Cliff went below to fix the food. He actually found three eggs, so he made an omelet to go with the pancakes. He made a mental note to check the propane bottles, having planned to refill those in Annapolis as well. Waiting for the last pancake to develop surface bubbles, he glanced up through the hatch. April remained sitting, her head continuing to turn slowly side to side. Both hands were on Chessie's body, as if looking for an extra level of security. Cliff returned a few minutes later with three plates of food and two cans of Coke. Her hunger overrode her sense of caution as she accepted the food with a nod and dug in without hesitation. Her eyes widened as the flavors of the omelet awakened her taste buds.

"This is good," she said with her mouth full. A piece of egg flew out and landed on Chessie's back. She turned red as she hurriedly retrieved the particle. "Sorry," she said.

She ate in silence, finishing her plate well before Cliff. But not before Chessie.

She sat patiently, knees closed, empty plate on her lap. Cliff looked up, realizing she was waiting for him. Shoving the last piece of pancake into his mouth, he set his plate on the deck for Chessie. "So what'd you think?"

"About?"

"Breakfast in the middle of the day."

"It was fine… real fine."

"Good."

April hesitated. "What are you going to do now?"

"The dishes."

"That's not what I meant." April smiled briefly.

"Whatever you want," Cliff said seriously.

"What are the options?"

Cliff paused, wanting to ensure he responded with the correct words. Even before that, he had to decide just how he felt about having someone on board for an extended period of time. Sure, Jennifer's visits were always welcome, but she always went home… eventually. She had never interfered with his ability to work. That had all changed over the past couple of days. April was on board all the time. And with that came a whole new bag of issues.

Deciding he wasn't sure how he felt, he said, "I guess there are several. First, we could stay here for a couple more days. If we skip showers and bathe in the creek—it's pretty clean—and watch what we eat, we can last comfortably. I don't know how much propane is left, but that's not a big deal unless it gets cold, which I don't see happening anytime soon. Second, we can resupply and then continue what I've been doing all summer, which is cruising around the bay. And I guess finally, if you want to go somewhere in particular, I'll take you there."

"Where would I want to go?"

Cliff shrugged his shoulders. "April, I don't know what this is all about. Sure, I know some of the basics, but as far as details…" His voice trailed off.

"What do you know?" April said, staring down at the deck.

Cliff hesitated. "You really want to talk about this. I know we made a deal and all that. But…"

April looked up. "Why not? A deal's a deal. Besides, you have a right to know what you're getting yourself into. All I care is that what you know is correct."

"Fair enough," Cliff said. "I'll tell what I know. You tell me if it's correct."

"I'm listening."

Cliff continued. "While you go by the name of April Whiterock, your real name is April Blackstone. You're the cousin of Jennifer Blackstone, a friend of mine in Annapolis. Evidently Jennifer knew she had an aunt and a cousin, although she had never met either one of you. There have been a few Christmas cards and a few photographs over the years. Otherwise, there has been no correspondence between your mother and her brother— Jennifer's father, David Blackstone, for a long time. I gather from your reaction at the hospital the other day that you never knew about this side of your family." Cliff paused. "How am I doing so far?"

"You're a hell of a storyteller," she said sarcastically.

Cliff failed to keep the surprised look from his face. Her mannerism had reverted to when he met her in the hospital. "Listen," he said with more inflection than intended. "If you are not April Blackstone, then I'm just wasting your time and mine. If your name is really Whiterock, then I'll drop you off on shore somewhere or take you wherever you want to go. I really don't have the time to be fooling around here."

The edge in her voice softened. "What do you have to do?"

"I'm an artist, and I'm way behind in my work."

She looked away. Her tone softened even more. "I'm sorry."

Cliff's tone did the same. "It's not all your fault. I have a propensity to procrastinate with the best of them."

She looked back at him. "A deal's a deal, right?"

"I like to think so."

"Then continue with your story. You won't be wasting your time."

Cliff realized this was probably the first time in months she acknowledged her true identity. He nodded. "You and your mother ended up in a place called Worthington Valley. Your mother got remarried if I remember what Jennifer said. Anyway, something happened and you were involved in the shooting of the sheriff's son. You ran and ended up in Atlantic City and got a job aboard *Hamilton's Bench*. You've been on the run ever since. Fortunately or unfortunately, when the boat came to Annapolis, someone recognized you—Jennifer, your cousin, to be specific. Her parents were actually at the fundraiser the other night and saw you playing the piano. They verified Jennifer's suspicions about you. Jennifer and her father actually met with the owner of the yacht the next day..."

"They met with Mr. Hamilton?"

"That's what they told me."

"What did he say?"

"I was getting to that." Cliff forced a small grin.

April was unable to hold back a similar expression. "Sorry."

"He knew you only as April Whiterock and said you came on board in Atlantic City with all the appropriate papers. He never knew you as anyone else, although he did admit to the resemblance in the pictures. All he was worried about was that you were okay."

"Why didn't he come to the hospital?"

"Jennifer said he planned to visit on the evening you ended up in the water. I presume you left the hospital before he got there." Cliff paused. "Anyway, let me finish what I know. Then you can go back and correct me if you want."

She remained silent.

"Sometime after the fundraiser, something happened and you ended up in the water and were taken to the local hospital. That's where I came to see you."

"Why you?"

"Two reasons. First, Jennifer, your cousin, used to work at the hospital and wasn't comfortable going back there. Second, I'm not family, and thus maybe would not be seen by you as such a threat—although that obviously didn't work."

Faint grins were again exchanged.

"Anyway, you left the hospital and ended up in the water in the middle of a bad thunderstorm. That's where I found you, or rather Chessie did. And here we are."

"Thank you," April said.

Cliff shrugged again.

"Are you always so nonchalant after you save someone's life?"

"Can't say I've ever been in that position before."

"Well, thank you again."

"You're welcome. How do you feel by the way?"

"Weak, otherwise okay I guess."

"Want something else to eat?"

April looked down at her empty plate. "Maybe later. I don't want to press it."

"Let me know."

"So, what are we going to do now?"

"Again, that's up to you," Cliff said.

April stared out across the water. "It's really beautiful here."

"The Chesapeake Bay is full of areas like this."

"I can imagine." The girl's stare continued. She turned and looked at Cliff. "My name is April... April Blackstone." She failed to hold back the tears. "It's been a long time since I said that."

"I couldn't even begin to imagine," Cliff said.

"Since we did make a deal, anything else you want to know?"

"Who were you so afraid of in Annapolis?" Cliff asked.

"The sheriff."

"How did he find you?"

"I don't know. But if he found me once, he'll find me again. You don't know the man. He's very persistent."

"I gather." Cliff paused. "Why'd you do it?"

"I didn't," she said sternly, snapping her eyes at him. "He had the gun in his hand and somehow it went off."

"I didn't mean that," Cliff said apologetically. "Why did you run? Maybe not when it first happened; that I can understand. But to keep on going for so long. Don't you miss...?" Realizing he was about to ask a dumb question, he stopped.

"I've asked myself that a thousand times," April said. "And I keep coming up with the same answer. As soon as the gun went off, I knew my life in Worthington Valley was over. I had screwed it up for everybody, so I figured it would be best if I just left."

"You didn't do anything wrong," Cliff pointed out.

"You don't know Worthington Valley. It's a wonderful place to live as long as the waters are calm. Interfere in their lifestyle, throw a wrench in their daily activities, and watch out."

"You're not the one who threw the wrench."

"You may believe me..." She looked off to the shoreline again.

"How do you know what they believe? You've never given them a chance," Cliff said. "You know, people aren't always what they appear. Sometimes they surprise you."

"Tell me about it."

"Sometimes the truth smacks you in the face like a brick shot from a cannon. Other times you have to take a chance," Cliff said.

"The people of Worthington Valley believe what they're told to believe," April rebutted. "And the teller of the tale is the sheriff. Besides my stepfather, he's probably the most influential man in town."

"What about your stepfather? Wouldn't he believe you?"

"He might, but there isn't anything he can do about it."

"Why?"

"He needs the sheriff too much."

"What's that have to do with believing you?"

Her eyes seemed to bore into him. "Why are we talking about this?"

Cliff started to remind her of their deal, but the last thing he wanted was to get into an argument. "I'm just trying to understand, that's all."

"You don't need to understand. I'm just a stranger to you… someone who happened to swim by on a stormy night. You don't even care about—"

So much for what he didn't want to do, he thought right before he cut her off. "If I didn't care about you, you wouldn't be here right now," he snapped.

Their eyes locked together for a long moment. He forced his anger to turn to compassion. "And the fact that you haven't jumped ship again tells me you care about yourself as well."

She looked away. Tears flowed freely. "I don't know where to go. He always seems to find me. I don't know who to trust anymore."

"You can trust me, can't you?"

"Not really."

Cliff understood completely. Trust wasn't something you gave out lightly. It was something that had to be earned. And then often times it still comes back and bites you in the ass. He knew about that alright, having learned the hard way. "Maybe someday I can find a way for you to trust me," he said.

"I doubt that," April said with determination.

Cliff wisely chose not to argue the point. "Anyway, we're back to where we started. What do you want to do?"

"What do you think?"

Cliff realized her asking him was a first step. "I think we should sit tight until I get ahold of Jennifer and find out what's going on. I'm sure she knows I've left Annapolis. I'm also sure she knows you've disappeared again. If she puts the two together, she'll know you're with me."

"You can't verify that," April said. Determination had quickly converted to panic.

"Why?"

"Because he'll know where I am and somehow track me down."

"By my making a call to Jennifer?"

"How did he find me in Annapolis?"

Cliff couldn't answer that.

April continued. "I don't know how, I just know he's very good at what he does."

"Chasing you all over the place?"

"At solving crimes."

"But you haven't done anything wrong," Cliff reminded.

"The truth doesn't have much bearing in this case. Again, people will believe what he wants them to believe."

"Does he have that strong a hold on the community?"

"You can't imagine."

"We'll just have to find a way to change that."

"Wishful thinking."

Cliff cocked his head to the side. "Have you given up all hope?"

"My past is my past. I can't change it. I can't do anything about it. And I can't go back."

Cliff wanted to tell her she was right on the first point only, but chose to keep the thought to himself. "Well, I need to check in with Jennifer and let her know I'm okay, and that I'm not mad at her or anything."

"Would she have a reason to think that?"

"Probably."

"Please don't say anything about me."

"You've got to trust me on this one. I'm not going to tell her where we are, just that we're okay."

"Every time I've ever trusted anyone…"

"I understand."

She stared at him. "How can you?"

"Someday I'll explain," Cliff said. He rose to his feet and headed to the galleyway.

"What are you going to do?"

"I'm going to make the call. I don't have a cellphone, so I'll use the marine radio."

Her foot shot out across the cockpit and blocked the way. After a long stare across the water, she brought her eyes back to his. "When I was about eight or nine, the boys who lived on the farm where we stayed convinced me to go down to the stream with them. I didn't know anything about trust back then, so I went. Well, their intentions were more than cooling off on a hot summer day. I got away, but it really shook me up."

"I guess so," Cliff said spontaneously.

April continued. "Next I trusted my stepbrother who convinced me to go out with Eddie Richmond. That whole thing ended in a bust. And I'm sure there's the question of how I got to Atlantic City. Well, there was this truck driver who saw me walking along the road one night. He stopped and offered me a ride. I trusted him until he wanted payment for the ride. Again I managed to get away. Again, it was close. Back to my stepbrother, somehow he traced me to Atlantic City—I think it was because I used the bank card he gave me—which was okay except he brought the sheriff with him. Then I trusted the people on the boat. That went along okay until the captain started getting a little too friendly."

"Is that how you ended up in the water?"

"I had nowhere else to go."

"How do you know the sheriff found you in Annapolis?"

"His dog found me hiding after I left the hospital."

"His dog?"

"His sidekick is an old German Shepard. I forgot his name—something to do with guns. Mean as can be, too." She glanced down at Chessie. "Anyway, that's it. That's why I can't trust anyone."

"Until someone proves to you otherwise."

"Don't hold your breath," she said. Her tone again changed intensity. She kept her leg in place. "No calls about me, please."

"Okay, not till you tell me. But don't make it too long. I do need to check in."

She reached over and grabbed his plate. "Thanks for lunch… or breakfast. Why don't I clean up while you get back to work?" She glanced up at the clouds. "You don't have much time before we get a storm anyway."

Cliff looked skyward. While the weather forecast hadn't said anything about thunderstorms, he had to agree with his guest, the sky to the south was changing, and not for the better. "I take it you did more than play the piano."

"Weather I knew before that. Danny taught me all about cloud patterns. He taught me a lot about surviving in the wild." She paused. "That's why I don't understand how come he turned on me."

"You're assuming that."

"I saw him with the sheriff in Atlantic City."

"Maybe there's another explanation," Cliff said.

"Are you always this optimistic?"

"Whatever."

"Whatever," April repeated. "But you're right. I did do more than play the piano. I took in everything I could about boats."

"There's a big difference between *Hamilton's Bench* and the *Mona Lisa*," Cliff pointed out.

"The Mona Lisa?"

"The name of this boat."

April glanced over at the drawing materials. "Very fitting." She looked at Cliff. "The principles of piloting and seamanship are the same. Navigation is navigation."

"But this is a sailboat."

"No!" she mocked.

Cliff didn't know whether to be angry or laugh. Hearing a clap of thunder in the distance, he chose neither. "You go clean up if you want, but be careful with the water. We're running low, I'm sure. I'll check the anchor and put one off the stern… that's the back of the boat."

A thin smile crossed her face acknowledging the duly earned sarcasm. He watched her disappear below deck, and then started gathering up his drawing equipment. There was something about her that intrigued him. He didn't know what it was, but it was definitely there. He had met a lot of people in his life, but never one so strong, and yet so fragile. So superficial looking on the outside, yet so deep on the inside. Never one so beautiful, yet so angry. He had never met anyone like April before. She was a real mystery, a real *Mona Lisa*.

He just needed to find a way to convince her to trust him.

And so he would.

140

April lay in a semi-fetal position, her back pressed against the starboard bulkhead. Her head rested on a small pillow, her hands folded underneath. She listened as the water slapped against the hull. She could tell by the sound that a breeze was starting to develop. She thought back to the many hours spent in a similar position aboard *Hamilton's Bench*. Her favorite time was when the yacht was underway. The vibrations of the hull massaged the muscles in her back. The sensation was always welcome after a hard day with Freddie. Even though she never participated in formal sports, she had always been in pretty good shape. From an early age, she carried a heavy load of physical chores around the trailer. Even though she was considered puny by many, she was strong for her size. She did fill out during her time in Worthington Valley, both as she matured and from the improved diet. In addition, her time out in the woods with Danny helped. Danny taught her that upper body strength was as important as leg strength when hiking in the woods. The physical conditioning continued aboard *Hamilton's Bench*. Regardless of the weather, there was always something to do, something to clean, something to polish. The crew used to say that if you really wanted to appreciate the size of *Hamilton's Bench*, wash her down bow to stern. April worked hard. She worked long. She often went beyond her assigned duties. She was there to help others if necessary. It went a long way to ensure the crew accepted her, which they did with few reservations. If nothing else, they were happy to have a female crew member. They all agreed April put the *class* back into the classy yacht. Extra work was also a way to pass the time. She basically kept to herself, didn't interfere in others' business and expected them to do the same. She was cordial. She was polite. She was friendly, yet she kept her distance. Through all this, her body continued to strengthen. However, her back was always tired at the end of a long day.

So nature's massage was always welcome. Just like the massages her father used to give. Maybe that was why she liked to lie against the bulkhead. Not only was there a gentle massage, there were gentle memories… of her father… of her mother… of…

She cut her thoughts short as her eyes welled with tears. She had left *Hamilton's Bench* and would never be able to return. She knew her stay aboard the *Mona Lisa* wouldn't last long either. She had no doubt somehow, some way, the sheriff would find her, even if she could trust this Cliff person. She did feel safe for the moment. Maybe it was because they were anchored in such a secluded area. Maybe it was because Chessie, Cliff's dog, had stayed at her side nearly the whole time. Maybe it was because…

"Stop second guessing yourself," she said aloud. Danny always said that was a dangerous thing to do if you were lost in the woods. Well, there weren't a lot of trees around, but she was still lost, and she was still in trouble.

She pressed harder into the side of the bulkhead, wishing for the breeze to increase so she'd get a better massage. She knew that wouldn't happen, acknowledging that they were lucky to have any breeze at all. She looked up through the open hatch. The earlier predicted storm had yet to evolve, having teased them for the past several hours. She still bet it was coming though, and when it did, that's when she'd make her escape. She told herself until then she needed to get some rest. She was still exhausted from being in the water Saturday night. She knew she was about to exhaust herself again.

Earlier, while Cliff was up on deck, she had snooped around the cabin looking for a chart to see exactly where they were. She found nothing, however, figuring his local knowledge was far superior to anything found on a chart. But what did he do when the weather went bad? She had heard the Chesapeake Bay could get socked in with fog easily. He had to have a chart book stashed somewhere. She just couldn't find it. While it would be nice to know where she was regarding land, it really wasn't going to change her decision about leaving.

And she knew the sooner the better. Cliff was a nice enough guy, but so was Eddie Richmond.

Neither could be trusted.

141

The first clap of thunder stirred her. The second woke her even more. This third caused April to sit up with a start. She bent her neck back and looked toward the hatch that was now closed. At first, all she saw was darkness. Then a bright flash lit up the sky. Instinctively, she leaned away from the Plexiglas. There was less than a two second pause before another round of thunder and lightning. She listened carefully to the sounds outside. The wind was picking up velocity. Water was slapping against the hull with increasing vigor. Now was a good time for a massage as the hull vibrated in response to the weather outside. Now was also the time for her to make her escape.

She rose to her feet and stretched. The door to her cabin was closed and Chessie was nowhere to be seen. She pressed her ear against the teak. She heard nothing except the noise of the storm. She doubted Cliff was outside, most likely having already taken the necessary precautions. She figured he was either working on his art or asleep. She hoped for the latter.

She changed into her own clothes, even though they were still damp. A chill ran through her body as the cold material pressed against her skin. She listened against the cabin door one more time. She turned and reached for the handle that opened the hatch. She knew she'd have to be quick because even with the storm, both Chessie and Cliff would recognize that someone was topside. Unlike *Hamilton's Bench* where it took a strong wind and heavy seas to rock the boat, motion anywhere aboard the *Mona Lisa* would be felt throughout.

She paused one more time to make sure this was really what she wanted. She quickly acknowledged she had a choice, but while she enjoyed Cliff's company and was most appreciative of everything he had done for her, he couldn't be trusted... just like Danny. No, she had to go.

She put pressure against the hatch to check its tightness and to see if there was going to be any noise. Additional pressure was applied and the handle turned. She was about to pop the Plexiglas off its rubber seal when she heard a noise behind her. The door to the cabin opened and a figure slid in. The brightness of the lightning had ruined her night vision so she could only see him silhouetted against the background.

"Going somewhere?" Cliff said, the usual pleasantness missing from his voice.

She thought quickly. "I was just checking to make sure the hatch was secure. I thought I felt some water dripping in."

"The hatch is tight and without leaks. I check it on a regular basis."

"You can never be too sure."

Cliff's eyes moved up and down her body. "You're leaving?"

Her night vision starting to return, she saw he was dressed only in a pair of shorts. His hairless chest allowed his well-formed body to show off without obstruction. One hand hung over the top of the door jamb causing that biceps to bulge even more. She shook her head slightly to bring her mind back into focus. "I was just checking the hatch."

"After putting your clothes back on?"

"They're pretty dry."

"Why are you leaving?" he said, this time with a demanding tone to his voice.

"I told you—"

"Bullshit!"

Her mouth opened and closed without a word. A moment ago her mind had wandered into the how-nice-Cliff-was mode. Now her mind was sending out caution flags. She looked up at the hand which was still on the hatch handle.

How quick am I, she wondered.

As if reading her mind, Cliff replied, "There's a lock down on the outside to make sure the hatch stays shut in rough water. I put that in place earlier when I set the second anchor."

"Why?" April said with a perplexed tone.

"Because I thought you might try and get away when the storm hit."

"Are you going to stop me?"

Cliff stared at her hard. It was a familiar expression April had witnessed before. Her heart skipped a beat. Additional warning flags rose to the top of her panic pole.

"You're in quite a precarious position here, don't you think?" Cliff said.

"Maybe."

"You're locked in a cabin with a person you barely know aboard a boat anchored out in the middle of nowhere with a raging storm whirling around outside. No one knows you're here. No one knows I'm here. When I'm done with you, I could simply take your body back to the Severn River and dump you overboard. They'll think you drifted out of the harbor with the tide. I'm sure they're still looking, so it won't take too long to find you. In the meantime, I'll… well I'll be cruising on down the bay."

April swallowed hard. She had been in similar positions in the past. She had always managed to escape unharmed. Her senses told her this time would be different. She forced the panic aside and her mind kicked into a fight mode. However, before she could begin forming a plan, Cliff was on her. He grabbed her arms and pushed her backwards. His knees pressed into hers as they hung off the bunk. His arms with the rest of his weight held her down. He pressed his legs inside of hers and forced her legs apart.

She told herself to stay in the fight mode, but this time it was just too much. She knew she was doomed. She knew she was going to lose. She knew she was…

The storm outside continued to beat against the boat. The water had been kicked up in an irregular pattern so the boat was moving on all three axes. And the noise… the noise was deafening.

With his weight increasing against her body, Cliff leaned forward, his mouth stopping close to ear. She could hear his breathing. It was heavy, and it was hard. He spoke softly. "I'll let you go if you want, but first…" He let out an evil laugh. A clap of thunder drowned out the noise coming from his throat. His mouth came even closer. "But first, I'm going to prove you can trust me."

And so he did.

142

Jennifer carried her nursing license in her wallet ever since it had come in the mail. Early in her career, she had a recurring dream about driving up to the scene of what appeared to be a serious accident involving a tractor trailer. She jumped out of her car and pushed her way through the crowd, all the while waving her RN license overhead announcing for everyone to stand back as she was a nurse. They did as she commanded, and when Jennifer moved forward, she came upon a pile of dead pigs. The accident had simply been a tractor trailer that flipped over. The driver was unharmed. Its cargo was obvious. Jennifer returned to her car still hearing the laughter behind her. She always woke up with a start, the laughter still ringing in her ears. The dream didn't derail her, however. She was a nurse and would always be able to prove it.

Like the night before when she sacrificed McDonald's, instead turning into the parking lot of Worthington Valley General Hospital. She parked, found the emergency room and inquired about nursing opportunities. As she had hoped, in spite of the upscale nature of the community, the hospital was still in desperate need of nurses. She had read time and again in the many throw-away journals that no area of the country was impervious to the nursing shortage raking the health care industry.

While the ER waiting area didn't appear to be crowded, the staff still seemed frazzled. Jennifer chuckled to herself, asking silently when she had not seen an ER staff that wasn't. So when Jennifer, a stranger to town, walked into the ER inquiring about a job, smiles came to the faces of the staff. More than one person told her to grab a chart and dig right in. Luckily, the nurse manager was still there arranging beds for the patients who had been boarding in the ER all day. She was able to pull away a few minutes and took Jennifer back to her office for an immediate interview. A few questions were asked, but the bulk of the discussion was more of a recruitment pitch versus a job interview. By the end of the conversation, Jennifer was offered a position. The nurse manager would have liked to follow the lead of her staff and let Jennifer start right away, but hospital rules required Jennifer to fill out the necessary paperwork and pass the pee test (mandatory drug testing). That, along with reference checks, could be done the next day. So at 11:00 pm the following evening, Jennifer reported to work.

The new girl on the block got a whole hour of orientation. The nurse manager was impressed with how much Jennifer knew. She even mentioned during their short time together that Jennifer was already looking like management material, which Jennifer quickly *snafued*, saying politely that she had already been there and done that. She also failed to tell her new boss that she didn't plan to be around very long. Jennifer had already set the groundwork for a quick and unexpected departure by mentioning that while she was glad to be away from the east coast, she was worried about her grandmother who claimed she was going to have a stroke any day.

So here she was—a stethoscope around her neck, a name badge pinned to her new scrub top and a broken nail after only three hours into her shift. She brushed a strand of hair off her face and considered redoing her ponytail. She decided against it, wanting to make the most of her thirty minute lunch break. Contrary to most nursing units where the definition of lunch was often a Twinkie stuffed into your mouth on your way to the next patient's room, at Worthington Valley, you got thirty minutes for lunch and were expected to take it.

Jennifer dried her hands and exited the bathroom, making her way down the short hall to the ER staff lounge. The hospital was old, the original building constructed near the end of WW II. There were hit or miss attempts at modernization, mostly miss. It was clean, however, and all the equipment worked. When you're sick, nothing else really matters. The staff lounge was no different, the decor coming straight from the *hodge-podge* school of design. A long folding table sat in the middle of the room. It was surrounded by a number of chairs, each in a different style. Couches and other discarded office seating lined the walls. In the far corner sat a desk holding a computer. Jennifer had been told this was linked to the hospital-wide system so even when you were on break, you could keep an eye on what was happening in the ER. The computer gave you access to learning tools and other resource sites. The system was also connected directly to medical records—her only real area of interest. She learned about the computer during the job interview the night before. The direct connection was an unspoken prerequisite for her accepting the job.

Jennifer sat in front of the computer and unwrapped an Italian cold-cut sub. She turned her ID badge over to where she had written her ID number and password. She figured she only had one shot at what she was about to do, correctly assuming the information system would monitor her actions. She had an alibi prepared in case someone walked in on her. She would claim she was simply surfing around the system to get used to the hospital's electronic medical records. She knew what she was doing was unethical. Then again, she challenged anyone to claim what had happened to April was ethical either.

She went through the tutorial to give credence to her alibi. She next moved among the patients in the emergency room, looking at labs and other pieces of data. A few of the present ER patients' histories and physicals were already posted, a credit to the speed of the system. She then went into the main patient data bank and typed in a few random names. It never ceased to amaze her just how many people were named Smith in the world, and just how many of these Smiths had already made at least one visit to Worthington Valley Hospital. She played with a few other letter combinations just to see what came up.

Then she typed in the letters R I C H.

There were three Richfords and five Richmonds who came up on the screen. She scrolled down until she came to Edward Richmond. She highlighted the name and hit the enter key. As the hard drive spun to collect the data, she wondered if Eddie's record had been sequestered as a security file. She kept her fingers crossed and watched the screen closely. After a few seconds, the first page of the medical record opened onto the screen. She glanced over her shoulder to ensure she was still alone. Then she clicked the acknowledgment box verifying that she had the authority to enter this record.

The first couple of pages were demographic data, insurance information and a consent for treatment. She noticed the signature lines were all blank. Next were the nurses' notes. She made a note to come back to these later. She wanted to first find the admission history and physical. Finding what she wanted, she quickly read through the information.

> *This is a 17 year old white male (son of Sheriff Richmond) who was shot at point blank range by what is believed to be a 38 caliber pistol. The incident occurred on the way to the spring dance. A call was made to 911 and EMS arrived approximately 10 minutes after the shooting. Initially, the patient was awake but poorly responsive. BP was 90 systolic. Pulse was 145. Respirations were 24 and labored. Skin was cool and clammy. Two large IV's were started, and after consultation with this physician, EMS started normal saline solution boluses. The patient arrived here about 30 minutes after the incident.*

Past medical history was unobtainable at the time, but several staff in the ER at the time knew him and claimed he had no major illnesses. Allergies: Unknown.

On physical exam, he was a well-developed, well-nourished white male who was in acute distress. He was semi-conscious. Blood pressure on admission was 75 systolic. Pulse was 165. Skin was clammy. Pupils were equal and reactive. Neck was immobilized prior to cervical x-ray clearance. Mouth was clear. Lungs showed breath sounds bilaterally. Heart was tachy. Abdomen was soft. Bowel sounds were increased. There was an entry wound in the right lower flank area. No exit wound was seen. Rectal exam showed no gross blood. Neurological exam was inconclusive as patient was uncooperative in moving extremities. Glasgow of 12. (Neurological alertness.) Distal pulses weak but present.

Plan:

1) Monitor, labs and EKG, typed and crossed for four units packed cells.
2) IV boluses continued with normal saline solution.
3) Stat chest x-ray and CAT scan of the abdomen.
4) OR notified.

As with most emergency room charts, the documentation stopped before the story really ended. To Jennifer's disappointment, there were no additional addendums by the ER physician, nor did she find a note by a surgeon or any other consultant.

"So what the hell happened?" she said aloud. She flipped through the chart to find the death certificate. Sometimes it would give a wealth of information. However, it too was missing.

"Something doesn't smell right," she said, again aloud.

She went through the chart again, only this time paid closer attention to the nurses' notes. When all else fails, read those words. If anyone is anal about documentation, it's the nursing profession, Jennifer thought. She just hoped that held true in this case.

And it was. As she read the last line on page six, the blood drained from her face.

143

April was finally getting the massage she had wished for earlier. Lying on the opposite side of the boat's tack, she had no trouble staying wedged between the foam mattress and the bulkhead. The storm had subsided, leaving behind a five degree drop in temperature and ten knot increase in the winds. The water had calmed so seas were running two to three feet. The wind was from the southeast, so as they left Wharton's Creek and headed down the bay, the *Mona Lisa* heeled even further and the water pounded the hull even harder. The vibrations felt good against her legs and back. She could tell by the sounds overhead that Cliff was pointing the boat as high into the wind as possible, causing the large Genoa sail to luff occasionally. She heard the wenches and pulleys squeak as he made the necessary adjustments in response to the subtle changes in wind conditions. She pressed her back into the bulkhead to maximize the efficiency of the vibrations and closed her eyes.

But sleep would not come. She was still too angry. At the same time she felt a sense of relief. It was the first time in a long time she felt a true sense of trust. She hesitated as the word fully formed in her mind. It was not an easy task as the word created such bad memories. It had been missing so long from her psyche. It had been washed out to sea in Atlantic City when she saw Danny with Sheriff Richmond. While she did develop a certain comfort level aboard *Hamilton's Bench*, trust was not really a factor. That she had to jump over the rail to get away from Phillip Rogers angered and surprised her, but she never trusted him to begin with.

Things were different now.

April always felt trust had a weird way of deserting her, such as seeing Danny and the sheriff together on the boardwalk. It definitely had a weird way of returning. But it had. She felt more comfortable around Cliff than she had felt around anyone for a long time. And in spite of the fact that she thought him sick in the mind, she kind of liked him. She had never felt that way about anyone before. She was confused in that she was still angry for what he did to her. She was also happy.

Cliff had taken her by surprise just as she was preparing to leave in the middle of the storm. His whole demeanor was different, the tone in his voice harsh. And the look in his eyes—it was the look she had seen before… the boys at the stream, the truck driver, Phillip Rogers… It was a look she feared.

Suddenly, she found herself staring at the look again, only this time Cliff had her pinned down. Like he said, there was no escape. There was nowhere to run. There was nowhere to jump. There was no one to hear her call for help. He had planned his attack perfectly. What better place than in the small cabin of a boat anchored in the middle of an isolated creek in the middle of a thundering storm? She quickly realized there was no way out. She quickly realized she was finally caught. Anger for having been so stupid was replaced by sudden fear—fear of what was about to happen. She had survived before, but this time her nine lives as a cat had run out. He was on top of her before she realized it. It was then she knew she was doomed. She was finally going to get what all the girls in school talked about, what all the girls claimed they wanted, what she so very much feared. She was finally going to get—

Then just as suddenly, Cliff's attitude changed. The fire left his eyes. His shoulders relaxed. He let go the grip of her wrists. He whispered in her ear. "You may have never been able to trust anyone in the past, April. But I hope I've shown you can trust me. If you want to leave, then go. It you want to stay, you're welcome to do just that. I'll help you any way I can."

With that, he rolled off her, climbed out of the bunk and left the cabin.

She sobbed softly. She tried to clear her mind, telling herself to rest and let some time pass. Let some water pass beneath the hull, as Cliff said. He also reminded her that she could do nothing about what had already happened. She could only control the future. It was a message she had heard before… from Danny. Eighteen months before, it had all been intuition. She ran to get away. Two days before when she escaped from the hospital, the instinct was the same—get out with no thoughts of where to go. Now, the flight commands were being challenged by an urge to do the opposite. She didn't want to run anymore.

The tears continued. While it sounded good in conversation, it was all a bunch of crap. The trust issue may have been resolved for now. The control issue had not. She had no more control of her future than the man in the moon. Sure, she could run again, but where would she go? What would she do? The sheriff and his dog always seemed to find her. It was only a matter of time. The sobbing increased as tears started flowing down her cheeks. Chessie, who had been curled up on the floor, lifted her head and rested it on the bunk beside her. A wet sloppy tongue lashed out and wiped away a tear. The coarseness of her tongue tickled and the girl's sobbing quickly changed to laughter. She reached over and gave the dog a pat atop the head. "Thank you," she said. She closed her eyes and dozed off.

It must have been a sound sleep because when she awoke, she felt more rested than she had in several days. She looked up through the hatch. It was pitch black outside. While they were still on a starboard tack, the conditions had changed. She propped herself up on an elbow and listened. The wind had increased. The waves were pounding the hull with anger. The boat leaned hard to port, rolling her against the bulkhead. At the same time, she heard the sails overhead luff then make a loud snap as they sought to recapture the air lost the moment before. She felt the boat right itself, and she was once again lying on the bunk instead of the bulkhead. She heard footsteps on the deck overhead. She figured Cliff was forward taking down the Genoa. The boat righted itself, coming to a level position. There were more snapping sounds as the sails continued to object to what was happening. The bow turned further into the wind and rolled to starboard. She heard the boom snap to the other side as they did an uncontrolled jibe. April quickly realized what was happening. The *Mona Lisa* had been caught in an unexpected wind shift, and her captain was caught up on deck. April dropped to the floor and headed back through the cabin.

By the time she got to the cockpit, the boat had totally changed course and was now on a port tack. Because he had turned the spreader lights on, she could see Cliff clearly. He was struggling to pull in the sail, but the wind had refilled it partway, wrapping the material around the starboard spreader. April took a quick look about and grabbed the wheel. She untied a line that had lashed it in place and turned the boat back into the wind, which was now blowing at least twenty-five knots. The boat heeled as nature struggled to push the *Mona Lisa* farther to starboard. There was a moment's pause and then nature's physics took over and the *Mona Lisa* headed back up into the wind. April kept the wheel hard over until the wind was directly on their nose. The boat righted itself and came to a near stop.

Cliff looked back and saw her at the wheel. He realized he only had a few seconds to regain control of the sails before the wind found a way to once again create havoc. He got the Genoa unwrapped and down on deck without further delay. He rolled it up quickly and shoved it through the forward hatch. As he closed the cover, April turned the wheel to port and the boat slowly fell off the wind. The mainsail refilled and soon they were back on course.

Cliff returned to the cockpit and watched as April adjusted course to take the luff out of the main.

"Where'd you learn to handle a boat like that?" he said.

"We spent the winter in the islands," April said. "We sailed every day."

"You had a sailboat on board?"

"Mr. Hamilton usually chartered."

"Just for you all to play around?"

"He always went with us. He's not your typical big boat yachtsman. He is very hands on, and can handle a boat with the best of them, regardless of the size." April paused as she had to concentrate on the wheel. "He also loved to sail, and was very good at that, too. He was a good teacher and taught any of the crew who wanted to learn. Most spent their leave in the towns chasing women and seeing how much rum they could consume at one time. A couple of us always went with him. Sometimes we'd even anchor out for the night. He said he loved the peace and quiet it brought."

"Sounds like a special kind of person."

"He is, and in all the right ways too. He's the ultimate gentleman."

"Is he married?"

"No. Never been, least that any of us know about."

"Us?"

"The rest of the crew." She put her foot up on the port seat as the boat heeled over in response to another gust of wind. "You have a small jib?"

"The roller furling's a one-fifty," Cliff said.

"If you want to put a reef in the main we can put that up. The Genoa's way too big for this much wind." She didn't add it was the wrong sail all together. "That'll let us stay on course better."

"I wasn't on any particular course. I was just heading down the bay," Cliff admitted. "Just trying to keep the boat steady so as not to disturb you. Didn't do a very good job there, did I?"

April allowed herself a short laugh. "No, you didn't. But you tried, so thank you."

Cliff nodded.

April hesitated. "I guess I owe you thanks for a whole lot more."

"Just trying to help."

"You certainly have a weird way of doing that," April commented. Her voice was sharp. She managed, however, to keep her anger in check.

"In art, it's called the shock effect."

She started with a rebuttal only to realize there was no need. He wasn't disagreeing with her. Her thoughts returned to a few hours earlier. It was the first time in her life she had been unable to escape. He could have had his way with her, and there was absolutely nothing she could do about it. Just like he said, he could have dumped her body overboard and no one would have ever suspected a thing. After all, she was missing. No one would have been surprised if her body had washed up on shore somewhere.

But he didn't take advantage of her. He didn't do what others had tried in the past. He was the only one who could have succeeded, yet he chose not to. It was weird all right. At the same time, in spite of the wind, there was a calmness around her. In spite of almost losing control of the boat, she felt safe. It was odd, feeling this way aboard a small boat with someone she barely knew. The feeling was there nonetheless. Cliff was different from anyone she had ever met. He was calm. He was gentle. He was genuine. He was able to see through all the fog that surrounds one's life. He certainly was able to see past her outer shell, and he did that in no time flat.

Why was that, she asked herself quietly. Why had he been able to strike notes in her soul when no one else could. What was it about him? Sure, physically, he wasn't bad looking. In fact, she imagined he would clean up real nice—although she wondered if she didn't like the rugged look better. It was the emotional side of him that was the most attracting. He was so cerebral. His art showed it. His behavior showed it... most of the time.

Her mind continued to wonder into the unknown. Questions... images... more questions. She wasn't one to daydream, but she was daydreaming now, in the middle of the night. It created a pleasant feeling, a warmth, a tingling. Her thoughts returned to long ago—to a motel—to a time in the shower with—

"Stop it!" she scolded softly. The dream vanished.

She focused back on steering the boat while Cliff adjusted the sails like she suggested. Soon they were on a gentle port tack, heeled over about fifteen degrees, the wind whistling through the space between the jib and mainsail, which had now been lowered to its first reef. She held onto the wheel with both hands although she really only needed a finger against one of the sprockets to keep the boat on course. The *Mona Lisa* was trimmed perfectly. She looked up at the sky. It was a perfect night. A few stars shone through the thin cloud cover that trailed the earlier front. She guessed that in another hour or so the sky would be cloud-free, allowing all the late summer stars to shine. She found the big dipper. Of all the constellations, it was her favorite—maybe because it was the first one she was able to identify on a regular basis—maybe it was because Danny always said it only rained when the big dipper filled with water—maybe it was because...

Maybe it was just because. Like a lot of things in life, it just was. Not all things had or deserved an explanation. It was the same answer she had decided upon when she found herself wondering why this had all happened to her in the first place. She didn't often feel sorry for herself. She just wanted to know why it happened to her.

It was just because.

She told herself to stay focused on what was going on around her and not worry about things she couldn't. She told herself she had to trust Cliff, and it was okay to feel good about him as long as she kept her emotions in check. She told herself to stay alert and remain cautious, but to enjoy the moment because the next beat of her heart might bring yet another unexpected painful twist in her journey. She told herself to take it one step— one gust of wind—at a time.

And so she did.

144

Sheriff Richmond waited, impatiently of course, until the static cleared so he could once again hear the voice on the other end. He never liked cellphones, in spite of their convenience. There was too much static, too many interruptions and too many delays getting connected. He also wondered about the security of the calls. While ninety percent of the time he didn't care if someone overheard his conversation, there were times when he wanted privacy.

This was one of those times.

"So, what've you got for me?" he said.

"Nothing. They've stopped their official search and have simply put her on their missing persons list," the bounty hunter said.

The sheriff already knew that. "What about dredging the harbor?"

"No one saw her go in the harbor, remember. Matter of fact, no one saw her at al... officially that is."

"Nothing's turned up in the water?" the sheriff said impatiently.

"If it did, you wouldn't need to hear that from me. That'd be all over the local news."

The sheriff knew that.

There was a long pause. Finally, the bounty hunter said, "What do you want me to do?"

"Find her."

"What if she is floating around the bay?"

"She's alive. Believe me, she's too much of a bitch to just drown." He pushed the end button on the cellphone and the line went dead. He stared out the window a long time, focusing on nothing at first, and then watched a man and two children exit their car and head into the McDonald's across the street from where he was parked. The children were two boys, His face turned red. His heart filled with rage.

He spoke softly but with anger in his voice. "You son-of-a-bitch, you got two sons. I ain't got..." He stopped in mid-sentence. "That ain't fuckin' fair."

He watched until the trio entered the fast food restaurant. He laid his head back on the headrest and ran his fingers through his hair. He closed his eyes and gritted his teeth. He told himself to calm down. He had to stay in control. Now was not the time to panic. He found he was having more and more difficulty controlling his emotions. He'd always had a short fuse. He admitted that. Lately, it was as if he had no fuse at all. He knew it should bother him. He knew he was too emotionally involved. He knew all the things he was supposed to know about how he was feeling and behaving. Only he didn't care. The only thing that mattered was finding the girl. That had taken over his life, and would continue until she paid for what she did to his boy.

The father and two sons exited the McDonald's. Each boy carried a Happy Meal bag. Big smiles crossed their faces. The father, smiling also, carried a tray of sodas. What a happy looking family.

"Bastards," the sheriff muttered.

145

Danny threw his duffle bag into the back seat, climbed into the passenger side and closed the door. Before he could demand to know what was going on, the car snapped ahead, causing his head to bang against the headrest.

"Better buckle up. This is liable to be a wild ride," Jennifer said.

"Damn," he said, doing as he was told. "Why the big rush?"

"I want to make sure no one sees us," Jennifer said, leaning forward to better see in the early morning light. While sunrise was officially forty-five minutes away, a faint beam of yellow light was beginning to show above the trees at the east end of the football field. "Did you tell your father you might be gone overnight?"

"Yeah, I told him I was sneaking off with a woman twice my age."

"I'm not twice your age," she snarled.

He could feel her stare, even with her looking straight ahead. "I told him I was going up in the mountains and might be gone a day or so."

"He lets you do that?"

"He knows it's my way of escaping," Danny said. "Besides, I've been doing it for years."

"Alone?"

"Sometimes alone, sometimes with…"

"With April?" Jennifer suggested.

"Yes, with April. She was the only one who ever really understood."

"Understood?"

"The beauty and power of it all."

Jennifer pondered the idea. "Maybe I can understand the concept of beauty, being out with nature and all that stuff, but where's the power?"

"Of being able to survive alone without help from anyone. That's how this country was founded, you know, by people like that."

"They were exploring, not escaping."

"Historians claim they were actually doing both," Danny said. "Exploring the new world and escaping from the old."

Jennifer wanted to ask him from what he was escaping. Instead, she filed the question for another time. She turned onto the road in front of the school, pressed down on the accelerator and headed up the mountain. She kept a close eye on the rear view mirror to make sure they weren't being followed. Ever since the first night in the nurses' lounge, she'd become paranoid about her visit to Worthington Valley. While some questions had indeed been answered, new ones had developed. Her stomach turned in knots as she sensed many of these loose ends were about to be tied together. First though, they had what she estimated to be a five hour drive—time that was needed to bring Danny up to date.

"You going to tell me what's going on?" Danny said. "Is April okay?"

"This isn't about April."

"You haven't talked to her yet?"

"No," Jennifer said.

"Then what the f—" He caught himself. "What are you talking about then?"

There was more pleading in his voice than demand. Jennifer couldn't imagine the toll this whole thing must be taking on Danny. Even with her anger, she felt compassion for the young man. It was obvious he cared deeply for April. It was also obvious he carried a deep layer of guilt.

"You sure you want to know?" She slowed as they approached *Point-To-Point Lookout*—the place where it all started.

"Why wouldn't I?"

Jennifer pulled into the overlook. "Sometimes knowing is harder to swallow that not knowing."

Danny said nothing. Jennifer waited until they came to a stop and pulled the gearshift into park. She wanted to watch the boy's expression. Meeting his eye contact, she repeated, "This isn't about April. It's about…" She watched him closely. "It's about Eddie." Her voice softened. "He's alive."

Danny's mouth dropped open. There was a long pause. "Bullshit," he finally uttered.

It was the exact response Jennifer hoped for. It told her he didn't know. His eyes hadn't flickered and the sides of his mouth didn't twitch. She put the car in gear, made a clean three point turn and headed up the mountain. A sign warned of deer crossing ahead. She wondered if there was anything else of interest in the woods. She focused on the road and kept a sharp eye out for animals. There were additional sharp curves, then the road straightened. They reached the top of the mountain and started down the opposite side. Housing developments could be seen off in the distance as the Worthington lights illuminated the area. The air was cooler, so she put up her window a bit. There was also a better sense of security with the window partially closed.

Danny said, "How do you know?"

"I know."

"How?"

"I talked to him last evening."

"Bullshit." Again, the expected response. "Why are you playing me like this?"

"I'm not playing you, Danny. I'm telling you the truth. Eddie is alive. I understand if you don't want to believe me." She paused. "I'll be able to prove it soon."

"How?"

"We're going to go see him."

"Eddie?"

Jennifer nodded.

Danny started to project the same profanity as before, only this time he cut it short. Jennifer had warned it was going to be a rocky road.

"After I dropped you off the other night," Jennifer explained. "I was riding around trying to piece together all the information we discussed. On the surface, the whole thing looks pretty straight forward. Boy and girl go on date. Boy gets fresh. Girl shoots boy. Girl runs away. Boy dies that night in the hospital. Girl dies up in the mountains a few days later—a major tragedy for any town, regardless of its size. Only, it doesn't seem to work that way around here. There was no funeral. The search for the girl was called off after only a few days. A warrant was issued, but only for the *questioning of,* not for the *murder of.* Your sheriff's gone off the deep end, which according to you, is unexpected, even under the circumstances. The girl shows up in Annapolis almost two years later aboard a multimillion dollar yacht. Now, I don't profess to be an expert in things like this, nor do I pretend to know what you and your family have gone through, but I do know this, there are more questions than answers." She paused. "It's not your typical small town murder case, that's for sure."

"You still haven't explained about Eddie," Danny demanded.

"I'm getting to that." Jennifer took a deep breath. "Like I said, I rode around the other night trying to figure out what to do. A lot of things just didn't add up. Anyway, I happened to pass the hospital when an idea popped up. You took me to the scene of the crime, the overlook. I knew we wouldn't get any answers there. But what about where Eddie was taken after he was shot, the emergency room. There would be records about that. On a hunch, I stopped in. As I expected, they were short on nurses, and I was hired on the spot."

"You're a nurse?"

Jennifer nodded. "I've worked there the last two nights."

"Here in town?"

She nodded again.

"What does that have to do with Eddie?"

"Your hospital's entire medical record is computerized."

"So?"

"Working there gives me access to that system."

"So?"

"Including Eddie Richmond's medical record on the night he was shot."

"S—" Danny cut the word off.

Jennifer glanced over and saw by his expression he was starting to believe her. She continued. "He was in pretty bad shape when he first came into the emergency room. His blood pressure was low and he was in shock. The staff jumped on him right away though and had him stabilized pretty quickly. Then they did a bunch of studies—x-rays, CAT scans, blood work… stuff like that. To make a long story short, the bullet went in his right side and missed all the vital organs in his abdomen."

"Where did it come out?"

"It didn't."

"Then where was it?"

"Up against his spinal column."

There was a long pause. "Don't tell me he's paralyzed."

Jennifer made sure her voice conveyed compassion. "Only from the waist down." She glanced over and saw the color draining from his face. Anger, denial and the demand for information had been replaced by confusion and disbelief. What a mixed bag of emotions, Jennifer thought.

She continued. "He was transferred early that morning to a hospital in northern Pennsylvania that specializes in these types of injuries. He's been there ever since."

"He's not dead?" Danny said.

"No, Danny. He's not."

"He's been at this hospital since the shooting?"

"He was at the main hospital at first, and then they transferred him to their rehabilitation center."

Danny paused. "How come he never called? How come no one ever said anything? People at the hospital had to know?"

"I'm sure they did. But there's a thing in medicine called patient confidentiality."

"I would have thought someone would have leaked something."

Jennifer recognized Danny's journalistic gears kicking in. She was glad for that because there were still many more questions to answer. "I agree," she said. "Except…"

"Go ahead," Danny encouraged. He was slowly regaining some of his composure. Jennifer sensed some of the anger returning as well. She just hoped this time it would be directed in a more appropriate direction.

"There was a note in the medical record specifically addressing that. It stated that Eddie's father—the sheriff—gave specific instructions that there was to be no discussion about his son's condition. There was even a comment made that he threatened to sue the hell out of everyone and anyone who talked."

"Why would he do that?" Danny thought aloud.

"I was hoping you could answer that one," Jennifer responded.

Danny stared out the window. "You actually talked to Eddie?"

"Briefly, before I went in to work last night. He actually sounded pretty good and said he was eager to see you today."

"That's where we're going?" Danny repeated.

Jennifer nodded.

"Why hasn't he called anyone?" Danny repeated.

"That's another question that needs answering."

"I bet his father had something to do with that, too," Danny said.

Jennifer drove in silence.

At the bottom of the mountain, they merged onto a four lane highway. Setting the cruise control, Jennifer rolled her neck around to ease the tension.

"How'd you know I'd get in the car with you without knowing where we were going?" Danny asked. Jennifer had simply called him the night before and told him to be at the far end of the football field just like before. No other details were provided.

"An educated guess."

"Based on?"

"You gave yourself away when you told me you were studying journalism."

"Huh?"

"Journalists—writers—tend to be curious people. I suspect you have a lot of that in you."

"What makes you say that?"

"I'm sure you spend time in the woods for the reasons you mentioned. I also suspect you like it because there's always something new to see—something new to discover—the fulfilling of curiosity."

"Doesn't curiosity kill the cat?" Danny asked sarcastically.

"Curiosity can also answer a lot of questions."

Danny stared out the side window. Jennifer could tell he continued struggling with his composure. Again, a mixed bag of emotions. A couple pretty big bombshells had been dropped in his lap the past few of days. First learning that April was safe, and then finding out his best friend was alive. It was a lot for a young man to digest. It was a lot for anyone to digest. She had seen similar struggles in the emergency room when family members received bad news about loved ones. It was the same look of disbelief combined with despair. It was the same look of not knowing what to say. It was the same look of not knowing which way to go, what to do next.

The composure was finally controlled (at least for the moment) and Danny turned back to her. "Why did you come out here?"

"The same reason I guess. I found out the other day I have a family I've never met and one of them was in trouble."

"Curiosity?" Danny suggested.

"Something like that."

"You're not a journalist."

Before she could catch herself, "No, but I am a writer."

"In what way?"

Jennifer hesitated. She had never discussed her writing with anyone except Cliff. He had encouraged her one night aboard the *Mona Lisa* to talk about her hobbies. When she did, he was very supportive of her efforts. When she rejected his request to read some of her work, he responded with understanding, saying that an artist had to be ready the first time their work was put on display. "Maybe another time," she had said. She repeated the same statement now.

Danny started to argue before deciding otherwise. Jennifer was glad.

The highway ran straight as far as one could see. Plowed fields on either side were rich in corn and other crops whose appearance Jennifer didn't recognize. She didn't realize Ohio had so much farmland. She laughed to herself. She was definitely out of her element now.

More fields passed before Danny broke the silence. "Fill me in on the rest of what you know."

Jennifer checked the rearview mirror and put her window down before responding. "Evidently they were able to stabilize Eddie pretty quickly. And like most non-trauma center hospitals, their focus then became what-the-hell to do with him. Been there myself and can imagine what they were going through. Gunshot wounds in any hospital cause havoc." She paused as an eighteen wheeler whizzed by. She glanced down at her speedometer. She was doing seventy. He must have been doing at least ninety. She shook her head. Bad motor vehicle accidents caused havoc, too.

"I'm speculating here, but evidently, someone knew about a hospital in upstate Pennsylvania that specializes in paraplegics. A call was made, a bed was found and he was transferred a few hours later like I said."

"How?"

"Helicopter."

"Wouldn't anyone have noticed that? We don't have a lot of air traffic around here."

"I thought about that. But with the search going on for April, there was probably already activity in the air."

"My Dad said the sheriff came out to the waiting room sometime before six a.m." Danny said. "That's when he told everyone Eddie was gone."

"He didn't lie," Jennifer mocked.

"Yeah," Danny agreed. Jennifer glanced over and could see her passenger was again in deep thought. She was curious to see what he came up with next. He didn't disappoint her. "Why the cover up?"

"That's one of my top questions."

"Okay," Danny conceded. "But why didn't someone in the hospital say something?"

"Big question number two. Except again, there was the threat of retribution by the sheriff."

"But after all this time?"

"That's why it's on the unanswered question list."

Another truck, this one a tandem, passed just as fast as the last one. "What's question number three?" Danny asked.

"Why did April run?"

Danny repositioned his shoulder strap. "Because I told her to. But I didn't mean forever." He repeated some of what he said during their first meeting. "When we first heard the shot, it took a moment to register what happened. By the time I got to the car, Eddie was slumped over in the seat and April was gone. I assume she simply panicked when she couldn't find me right away. Anyway, Sally, my girlfriend, or rather ex-girlfriend, and I stayed with Eddie until the ambulance arrived. A patrol car took us to the hospital. We talked to the deputies there, telling them what we knew. I learned April hadn't been found. There wasn't anything we could do at the hospital, so I took Sally back to her place and I went home to change. I knew they were in the woods looking for April. I also knew they wouldn't find her unless she wanted them to."

"How did you know that?" Jennifer interrupted.

"I trained her." He paused. "Anyway, I built a tree house several years before on the mountainside behind our house. That's on the other side from the high school. I went up there and sure enough, April was there." He continued the story of how he helped her the next couple of days. He didn't go into details of the motel, but did say the last time he ever saw her was when she snuck away in the dark. "They had an all-out manhunt for her, only they were looking in too small an area. They never figured she could get very far. By the time they expanded the search zone, it was too late. She was gone."

"Gone where?" Jennifer asked.

"I don't know how she got there, but she ended up in Atlantic City."

"So, you did help her get away?"

"In the beginning. Only, my idea was for her to stay away long enough for us to decide what to do," Danny responded.

"How were you going to do that?"

"I didn't know at the time, but I definitely didn't intend for her to leave the area."

Jennifer knew it wouldn't do any good to push him further. It wouldn't answer any more questions.

"What did you learn at the newspaper?" she asked instead. Her assignment to Danny two days before was to go to the local paper and see what he could find out about the sheriff.

Danny started talking immediately. "I met with a man named Robert Madison, one of the writers who cover local issues for the paper. His son, Alex, plays on the varsity football team, so Mr. Madison knows me. That's how I got in to see him. I told him I was working on some extra credit work for my journalism class—just like you suggested. We talked a long time about journalism, how it's progressed, what it's going to be in the future, what's good about it and what's bad. He gave me a lot of good pointers, too, like if I was really interested, I should start now. Little did he know that's exactly what I was doing. Anyway, I was able to get the conversation turned in the direction of just how a newspaper covers a particular story. His eyebrows rose when I asked the question and I thought he may have caught onto me, but he just kept on talking. He said that in the ideal world, you covered everything, and you covered it objectively. However, newspapers are businesses, and therefore have to play politics at times. He also admitted that while journalists liked to claim they were neutral, in reality they were some of the most opinionated people in the political arena. Mix the two together, and you sometimes have very biased coverage."

Danny paused. "I knew I was getting close to the edge, but I continued anyway. Trying to sound as nonchalant as possible, I said at the end of his lecture, '*like your newspaper's coverage of the shooting?*'"

"Well, you would have thought a bomb exploded. His whole demeanor changed. It was quite impressive, really. He recovered quickly and stared at me for a long moment. I kept eye contact, even though I was getting really nervous. Finally, he looked up at his clock and suddenly remembered he had an appointment. He rose to his feet and escorted me from his office. He told me he thought I'd make a fine journalist and that if I ever needed a reference, to let him know. Realizing I had crossed some undefined line, I took my leave with a '*thank you for your time*'. As I left his office, he did put his hand on my shoulder and leaned in close to my ear. He said: '*Remember, son, if you bite the hand that feeds you, you'd better be prepared for the consequences.*'"

Danny lit a cigarette.

Jennifer stared straight ahead, again fighting the urge to accept a smoke.

Danny blew a puff of smoke out the window. "So Eddie's alive, huh?"

"Yes, Danny, he is."

"I wonder how many people know that."

"A good question… a very good question."

Another tractor trailer passed them at a high rate of speed.

146

His chin rested on his chest. His eyes were closed. His face was thin and washed out, the skin around the orbits wrinkled and wasted. He looked pale. His hair was long and tied in a ponytail. He wore a yellow tee shirt, faded and full of holes. Danny recognized the shirt as being one of Eddie's favorites. He wore jeans, white socks and clean, white tennis shoes. The fact that he had socks on was another striking feature. Eddie hated wearing socks, even in the winter. He'd even been known to play football sockless. Because of the bagginess of his clothes, it was hard to tell what the rest of his body looked like. Danny suspected it was much like his face—wasted and thin. One thing Danny did notice, Eddie's arms were well developed. Both sets of biceps and triceps were way out of proportion to the rest of his body. When the realization of why sank in, Danny turned pale. He felt nauseated. It was an unusual feeling for him. Then again, this was an unusual situation—one that was causing him an array of emotions.

Eddie was sitting in a wheelchair beneath one of the many patio umbrellas spread out around the garden. The area was spacious and picturesque. Smooth surfaced pathways wound their way through various beds of summer flowers. Danny recognized several types of roses and what he thought were magnolias, but those were all the flower names he knew. Before the shooting, his stepmom spent a great deal of time decorating the outside of their house, but since then…

Danny glanced at several patients, some in wheelchairs, some kneeling on the ground, their wheelchairs or crutches nearby. Each was working in or around one of the many beds. As there was only one person to each flower bed, he correctly assumed they had their assigned areas. The sun was high; the sky, cloud free. And it was hot. No one seemed to mind, however, as they focused on their tasks. A pair of dirty gloves on the table indicated Eddie had either completed his chores or was taking a break.

Danny stood in silence. It was almost too much seeing his friend this way. Again he filled with a flurry of emotions. All the ones he had been working through these past months came at him like a line of warriors. He fought the urge to vomit. He fought the urge to turn and run. He cursed Jennifer for bringing him here. At the same time, he knew this meeting was inevitable. Ever so slowly, he regained control. He scanned the garden again. A moment ago, all he saw were a bunch of handicapped people working on their respective pieces of ground. This time he noticed something else as well—they were all young people. He saw no one that looked over forty.

Another wave of nausea filled his throat. He coughed in response to the bitter taste that filled his mouth. Eddie heard this, causing his head to bob. His eyes opened and he blinked in response to the bright sun. He turned his head slightly in the direction of the sound. The two friends stared at one another.

Eddie broke into a wide smile. "Hey Danny, where the hell you been?"

147

The first hour of the ride home was without conversation. Jennifer knew Danny had a lot of information to digest, a lot of emotions to work through. To think your best friend was dead for almost two years only to find out otherwise had to be difficult even for the strongest of personalities. While Danny tried portraying his strongest self, Jennifer suspected he had areas of weakness like everyone else. She suspected from what he said about April and his interactions with his stepmother, he was a very kindhearted person. He was unique in that he liked to spend so much time on the mountain—the mountain where the whole saga began. Jennifer wanted to ask if the amount of time he spent in the area had changed since the shooting. She wanted to ask what he did and didn't know about Eddie's and his father's relationship. She wasn't convinced Danny was being a hundred percent forthcoming in what he knew. While one big piece of the puzzle had been found, another showed up missing. She continued telling herself to give him the benefit of the doubt. She told herself to let more time pass and see what happened.

So the quiet in the car was okay with Jennifer. She had her own thoughts to organize. As had been the case from the beginning, every time she got an answer to one question, five more popped up. The mystery surrounding Eddie's funeral had been solved. There simply had never been one. But how did Sheriff Richmond pull this off, and why? How was the deception kept a secret for so long? There were other questions. One big one kept resurfacing.

She was mulling over the thought when Danny spoke. "He kept thanking me for all the flowers and cards."

"That's nice," Jennifer responded.

She could feel the immediate stare that followed. She took her foot off the accelerator and met his look. "You didn't send any cards or flowers. You thought he was dead."

"Exactly."

Jennifer looked back at the road ahead. The question from a moment before took on an even stronger meaning. Her thoughts formed an idea. "Reach in my purse in the back and hand me my cell. I have a couple calls to make."

Danny handed her the phone without comment.

148

Danny called from the car telling his father he was on his way home and needed to see him right away. Danny pretended to be in a bad cell as an excuse to cut the call short. The last thing he wanted was for the conversation to occur over the phone. Besides, Jennifer insisted it was important to watch facial expressions.

On the other end, Samuel Worthington looked at the receiver as it went dead and shrugged his shoulders. Another example of teen-parent communication—short, to the point, with minimal information. Sam Worthington admitted he and his son were not as close as he might have liked. It was difficult running a company in a struggling economy while raising a son. As a widower, he found the task even more burdensome. He'd been devastated when his first wife died. But he had a young son and a thriving business, so he had little time for mourning. Closure was quick and simple. She was gone. He had to move on. Eleven years later when he met and married June Blackstone, some of the pressures were gone. He now had someone to help. She filled a void in his life. However, the torch had been passed back to him that dreadful night of the dance. His new bride had a breakdown the morning after when the police found no trace of April. She had yet to fully recover. Sure, there were moments of hope, but each time she came home, she was only able to last a few days before she started drinking. Once that happened, the downhill spiral restarted. Both Sam Worthington and his wife knew the only thing that would really help was either April's return or some other closure. Sam Worthington didn't believe that was likely to happen anytime in the near future.

During these months he tried his best to play supportive husband, company CEO and father to a son who was now even more isolated. Danny seemed to be doing okay, at least as well as could be expected considering everything he'd been through. Sam Worthington just wished he had more time with his son. So when Danny called and said he needed to meet with him right away, Sam Worthington was waiting.

He was surprised when his son walked through the front door and introduced Jennifer. Danny purposely left off her last name. Sam Worthington looked just like his son, only older. He was an inch taller, but otherwise had the same basic build. His hair was neatly trimmed and combed, in contrast to Danny's. He wore a red polo shirt with Worthington Valley Country Club embroidered across the left chest.

After introductions, which included inquisitive glances from father to son, the trio headed into an ultra-modern living room. The walls were covered with an array of paintings, many of which Jennifer guessed were originals. She thought of Cliff and wondered what he would say about such a display. Scanning the rest of the room, her eyes locked onto the grand piano sitting in the far corner. The cover had been pulled over the keys. Like the first few flakes of a winter's snow, a thin layer of dust covered the top of the brightly polished instrument. Jennifer wondered when it had last been played. Danny took a seat in one of the high backed chairs. She sat next to him in another. Mr. Worthington remained standing on the opposite side of a large glass coffee table framed in wrought iron steel.

"What's this all about?" the elder Worthington said, with only a hint of pleasantness in his voice. "I thought you were supposed to be up in the mountains hiking?"

Danny looked at Jennifer for support. She gave it with a nod. He stared back at his father. Even to a boy as big as Danny, the man could be intimating. Danny swallowed hard. "Eddie's alive."

Samuel Worthington tried, but failed to keep his facial expression stoic. Both the corner of his mouth and his right eyelid quivered ever so slightly. His face reddened a shade or two before he regained his composure. "What makes you say a thing like that?"

"We just came from visiting him," Danny said.

"Visiting him… where?" The steel man tried hard to act surprised.

"At the Northern Pennsylvania Rehabilitation Center." Danny glanced over at Jennifer to make sure she got the name right. She nodded and gave him a supportive smile. He was obviously not comfortable confronting his father like this.

Danny looked back at his father. "But that's not news to you, is it?" He was trying to control his anger, an ongoing task since he and Jennifer learned via Jennifer's phone calls that his father had been bankrolling the cost of Eddie's medical care. Paying for the care wasn't the issue. Lying about it was.

The redness in the man's face changed to a washed out paleness. He ran his hand over the top of his head, messing up the perfectly manicured haircut in the process. Danny's father looked away. Jennifer could tell the man was debating which road to take—the road of *let's keep on pretending I don't know a damn thing*, or the truth. Unfortunately, both were fraught with curves and potholes. "No, Danny, it's not." There was an uncomfortable pause. "Son—"

"Don't *son* me. Why'd you lie to me?" Danny's thoughts flashed back to the many times over these months when he sensed there was something his father wasn't telling him. The boy always figured it had something to do with his stepmother. Now he knew the truth.

His father's face remained flushed. It was obvious he was about to scold his son for talking to him in such a manner. He decided now was not the time. There was a short sigh. "I had no choice."

"Really," Danny said with sarcasm.

"Yes, really." There was a determination in the man's tone.

The answer surprised the younger Worthington. Having no choice meant having no control, and lack of control was not something he ever saw in his father. Jennifer watched as the two Worthingtons stared each other down. His father undoubtedly thought he could no longer trust his son, and Danny certainly felt the same towards his father. There was a moment of sadness regarding the realization, but the moment was brief. Other matters took precedence.

Mr. Worthington continued staring directly at his son. The look of anger had softened somewhat. "Can I speak freely?" he said nodding his head in the direction of Jennifer. He broke eye contact at the same time.

Danny's head bobbed in the affirmative.

Samuel Worthington turned his attention to Jennifer. He debated the level at which he could trust this person he'd just met, and knew nothing about. While his trust in his son had been severely damaged, he also knew it was most likely an isolated incident caused by unusual circumstances. The man questioned how he would have felt in the same situation. The answer further softened his anger towards the boy. The father knew his ability to be trusted had been damaged. He realized he had no choice but to throw caution to the wind. "Sheriff Richmond and I have been friends for many years. We've been through good times together as well as bad times. I guess the worst was when we each lost a wife. Because of our positions in town, we've worked on a lot of community projects together. I've also been one of his biggest supporters for his reelection campaigns. In turn, he's always been a big supporter of Worthington Steel."

"What do you mean by that?" Jennifer interrupted.

Sam Worthington hesitated.

Danny spoke up. "Worthington Industries has one of the best safety records in the industry, but it's still a factory. Any factory that has moving parts is bound to have an occasional accident. We're no different, although again, our numbers are quite low compared to others."

"What's the problem?" Jennifer asked.

Mr. Worthington decided he'd better pick up the explanation. "The accidents themselves aren't the issue. It's how they're reported that can be a problem."

"OSHA," Jennifer said, beginning to get the picture. The federal Office of Safety and Health Administration focuses on safety issues in the workplace. It's considered very good at doing just that. It could also be a real viper for any business caught in its grasp. "Sheriff Richmond helped you fudge the reports."

"No fudging went on. The reports were completed as required."

"Peanut butter, chocolate, with or without nuts, it's still fudge," Jennifer commented. She thought a moment as to why this would be so important. "Your insurance premiums are based on your accident record, right?"

The elder Worthington nodded.

"Fewer accidents reported means lower premiums."

"You're a very smart lady. By the way, I didn't catch your last name."

"Blackstone. Jennifer Blackstone."

It only took a second for the name to register. "Blackstone—June's maiden name."

Jennifer nodded. "Your wife is my aunt."

"Your aunt!"

"She and my father are brother and sister."

"She never said anything about having a brother," Samuel Worthington said harshly. This time the surprised look was genuine.

"They've been estranged for many years."

Samuel Worthington cocked his head to the side inquisitively. Before Jennifer could continue, Danny spoke up. "April's alive and well, too, or did you also know that?"

The man's head straightened back up. "How do you know?"

Danny looked at Jennifer who answered the question. "I saw her just a few days ago."

"Where?"

Jennifer hesitated.

"Where?" the man repeated.

"She's okay," Danny injected. "That's all you need to know for now."

Danny's father started to argue, but stopped short. He looked away. "I had my suspicions, yes. But I was never sure. Sheriff Richmond would never—" The man stopped. A defeated look came across his face. "Where is she now?"

Jennifer hesitated. She wasn't yet convinced that the trust factor worked in both directions. "She's safe."

"For now?" Samuel Worthington added.

"Why do you say that, Dad?" Danny said. His earlier anger had changed to concern.

The expression of defeat continued. "I don't know for sure, but I suspect the sheriff knows where she is. He's been gone a couple days now and no one has heard from him."

"Eddie's alive. We know now the whole thing was an accident. Eddie told us so himself. Didn't he tell his old man that?" Danny asked.

The elder Worthington sat back in his seat and let out a long sigh. "Regardless of what really happened that night, the sheriff's blaming April for Eddie's condition. And I suspect that even though he knows the boy is alive, in many ways he considers him dead."

Danny looked back and forth confused between the other two occupants of the room. Jennifer picked up the explanation. "Eddie no longer fits the image his father created for him. In other words, if he can't be the star in football, then he can't be anything. It sounds strange, I know, but it's a form of denial. Parents put their kids on such high pedestals these days that when they fall off, the landing is very traumatic—sometimes more so for the parents than for the child himself. Sometimes, as I suspect happened with the sheriff, there's complete denial of the child's existence."

"But the Sheriff visits Eddie on a regular basis. Eddie did say that," Danny pointed out.

"In his mind, the sheriff probably thinks he's visiting Eddie's grave," Jennifer said.

"That's why he lied about Eddie's death?" Danny said. "He didn't think he was lying at all."

"Exactly."

"Jesus."

Jennifer turned her attention to the father. "You've been bankrolling Eddie's medical bills, haven't you?"

She watched him start to deny it before realizing she already knew the answer. "I felt it was the least I could do, even if it was an accident."

"But that's not why you really did it, is it?" Jennifer pressed.

"My father is a very giving man," Danny said in defense of the elder Worthington.

Jennifer was glad to see Danny demonstrate some loyalty towards his father. She pressed onward. "There's more to it, isn't there?"

Samuel Worthington stared at Jennifer a long moment. "Like I said, you're a very smart lady. Do you have that figured out?"

"If I do, will you admit it?" Jennifer challenged.

"What happens if you don't?" Samuel Worthington fired back.

"This isn't a game, Mr. Worthington. We're talking about the life of your daughter... or rather, stepdaughter."

"Daughter's fine."

"Whatever. I think it's time to stop screwing around."

Samuel Worthington slammed his fist down on the arm of the chair. "It's not that simple, damn it."

Jennifer didn't blink. "It is if you want it to be."

Danny rose to his feet. "What the hell are you two talking about?"

Danny's father and Jennifer were locked eye to eye. The father spoke first. "Go ahead; let's see if your theory is right."

Jennifer continued looking at the man across from her. With each passing moment her disdain for him rose. With each passing moment, she also felt sorrier for him. She knew the walls around him were about to crumble. But that's what it was going to take if April had any hope of returning to a normal life. "Blackmail." Her eyes continued to burn into the steel man. "Sheriff Richmond is blackmailing you, isn't he—about accident reports involving your company? I suspect he's found a way to blackmail other people as well. That's how he's been able to keep others from talking."

The elder Worthington tried to keep his shoulders square, but the weight they'd been carrying for the past many months finally became too much. They dropped, as did his head.

A lot of questions just found answers.

149

George Hamilton picked up the phone on the second ring and waited for the caller to identify himself. After a return greeting he said, "So, what have you got?" He paused. "I see." He looked over at Jennifer who was sitting across from him. "I'm going to put you on the speaker, okay?" He set the receiver down and pressed a button on the console beside it. "Go ahead, tell us what you know."

A male voice came forth. "No one's seen him around town, although there was an unconfirmed report of someone fitting his description near a McDonald's yesterday. But they didn't get a good look, nor did they catch the license plate or the kind of vehicle he was in. So I'd consider that real soft. I did make a few calls out to Worthington Valley and he hasn't been there for several days. I talked to a deputy who seemed real nervous, and at first didn't want to give any information. He finally agreed to talk and said he hadn't seen hide nor hair of the sheriff in over three days. When pressed further, he said that wasn't unusual in that the sheriff had been disappearing for days at a time ever since his son was killed."

"Any ideas of where he went?" Hamilton asked.

"The deputy claimed the sheriff never said one way or the other," the man on the other end said. "He'd just up and disappear. They assume he's still in mourning, and when he has a bad time of it, he stays home or takes a drive. The deputy said the same thing happened years before when the sheriff's wife died. He was totally okay some days, and others he just stayed home. They'd check up on him and all that, but he'd say he was okay and needed some time alone. That only lasted a month or so, and then he snapped out of it and was back to his old self."

"Anything else?" Hamilton asked.

They could hear the sound of pages being flipped as notes were being checked. "No, not really... wait a second. At the very end of the conversation, the deputy did say he hoped the sheriff was okay wherever he was."

"Meaning?"

"I can only assume they checked on him at home and found he wasn't there."

"Good assumption," Hamilton said.

"Anything else you need, sir?"

"Yes, I need you to check up on a hospital out in Pennsylvania—the Northern Pennsylvania Rehabilitation Center." Hamilton looked at Jennifer to make sure he had the name right. She nodded.

"What's out there?" the voice said.

"That's where Eddie is."

"You mean that's where he's buried?"

"In a metaphoric sort of way, yes. In reality, Eddie Richmond's very much alive."

There was a pause. "You're shitting me?"

George Hamilton put both hands on the desk and leaned into the speaker. "There's a beautiful young lady sitting across from me who just left him there yesterday."

Another pause. "The plot thickens."

"Well, your job is not to allow it to get too thick."

"I hear you, sir. I hear you."

The line went dead.

Hamilton turned his back and stared out the window. When he finally spun around, he had a worried look on his face.

"You think the sheriff's still in the area, don't you?" Jennifer said.

"Don't know that I'd stake my whole life on it, but I would bet a good many years on the fact."

"What do you think he's going to do if he finds her?"

"If he has gone off the deep end like it sounds, then we have to assume the worst. If, on the other hand, he's simply a pissed off law enforcement officer determined to catch his prey, then maybe it's not so bad." Hamilton took a sip of the coffee perched on his desk. "The real question then becomes, how deep a dive did he make?"

"What do you think?"

"I don't have enough information yet to form an opinion."

"Yet?" Jennifer questioned.

"Yet," Hamilton repeated.

Jennifer gave him one of one of those *don't stop there, tell me more, stupid* looks.

Hamilton complied. "I have some people working up a profile on Sheriff Richmond." He glanced at his watch. "I'm expecting a call at any time."

"What are you looking for in particular?"

Hamilton leaned back in his chair. "Like we already discussed, why did he lie about his son's death?"

"Any ideas of your own?" Jennifer asked.

Hamilton looked at her hard. "Your tone leads me to believe you have some thoughts on the matter."

Jennifer took a deep breath and let it out slowly. "Sheriff Richmond lost his wife at an early age. It was tough on him, but he survived. Life goes on, and so did his, probably because he had a son to raise. Then all of the sudden, without any warning, his son was taken from him."

"He was shot and paralyzed. He wasn't killed," Hamilton injected.

"In the sheriff's eyes, it was probably worse," Jennifer argued. "From what Danny Worthington told me, the sheriff worshiped his son, and was especially proud of him because of his football skills. I think Danny said Eddie was also a star lacrosse player. Eddie's father is, or was, the classic sports dad—encouraging and pushing… encouraging and pushing… encouraging and pushing. Besides wanting his son to do well, he was probably living out his fantasies through his son. That's not an uncommon thing, you know."

"How do you know so much about all this?"

"Emergency rooms are full of psychiatric patients, especially teenagers. Adolescent psych beds are the hardest to find. Yet most of the time, what the kids need are parents to get their own acts together."

"I should have talked to you before I ordered the profile," Hamilton said.

"So you agree with me?"

"I think you're on the right track.

"Thank you," Jennifer said.

"No, thank you."

Jennifer stared at him. It was obvious he was deeply concerned about April. It was just as obvious he had mobilized a lot of resources to help her. Not so obvious was how. She was about to ask when Hamilton interrupted her.

"Until we locate the sheriff and find out what's really going on, I am worried about April's safety," he said.

"Then we have to get Cliff to bring April back here."

"Assuming that's where she is," Hamilton pointed out.

"There aren't a lot of other explanations," Jennifer said.

Hamilton didn't debate the point. Instead he said, "She may not want to come back."

"Maybe, maybe not," Jennifer said. "She'll stay where she feels the safest, although I question her ability to make good decisions about that."

Hamilton turned away. "That's all we need are two unstable personalities playing cat and mouse with one another."

"What are we going to do?"

George Hamilton looked back at Jennifer. "For now, you and I are going to do nothing. What my people need to do is find the sheriff."

"How can you expect them to do that?"

"I can expect them to do that because that's what I pay them for."

Jennifer hesitated. "Can I ask you a personal question?"

Hamilton sat up straighter. "I never deny anyone the opportunity to ask a question."

Jennifer hesitated. Her curiosity about this had been building for a long time, and now the opportunity was right in front of her. "What do you do?"

"I'm not sure I understand."

She waved her hands around the room. "What do you do? What kind of work do you do?"

He tilted back his head and laughed. "What you really mean is how can I afford all this so called luxury?"

"I don't think there's too much *so called* attached to it," Jennifer quipped.

"It's all relative, my dear. It's all relative."

"You're avoiding the question."

"Then I'll answer your question if I can ask you one of my own."

Not giving it a second thought, Jennifer shrugged her shoulders. "Sure, why not?"

Hamilton looked at her; a gentle smile crossed his face. "Will you have dinner with me tonight?"

Because of her experience in the emergency room coupled with that in the restaurant, Jennifer was used to sudden unexpected advances from members of the opposite sex. There had even been an advance from a woman once. George Hamilton, however, caught her completely off guard. That was unusual for her.

As if reading her mind, Hamilton said, "I'm just asking you to dinner, that's all. If you want to accept, that would be great. If you want to decline, no hard feelings."

"Why me?" Jennifer blurted without thinking.

Hamilton chuckled. "That's personal question number two."

"Sorry," Jennifer said, embarrassed at her response. She told herself not to be so stupid. Like he said, it was just dinner. She told herself not to be so impolite. Besides, she added, there must be hundreds of women who would die to be in her shoes this very moment. But that argument didn't work either. She never competed for a man.

She was about to consider a third argument when Hamilton broke in. "How about if I answer question number two over dessert?"

His subtle persistence impressed her, telling her he was indeed sincere. "What time?" she asked.

"7:30 okay?"

Jennifer looked down at her watch. It was a little past one and she still had a lot to do today. One good thing, she was off tonight. She rose to her feet. "7:30 is fine." She turned and started to walk away. Turning to face him again, she said, "In the meantime, what do we do about April, just sit around and wait?"

Hamilton nodded in the affirmative.

150

"She's okay, I'm sure," Cliff said for the third time. There was the expected pause. "We're in Cape Charles. We left Annapolis in the storm, went over to Wharton's Creek for a couple days, and then headed down the bay. We got in sometime last night. We're going to provision up and then we'll see." He listened to Jennifer on the other end. "Yes, I'm keeping an eye on her. That's exactly what I've been doing for the past few days. But you know Jen, there's only so much I can…" Another pause followed as he was obviously interrupted. "Yes, I know all that." Following another pause, "Your guess is as good as mine how she'll take the news, although I imagine whatever she does, she'll at least be somewhat relieved. She'd have to be, don't you think?" He listened to Jennifer's response.

"Yes, I'll stay in touch, I promise. I'll call soon." Another pause followed. "Yes, I'm okay." Cliff listened. "Yes, I understand… I'm sure." Cliff listened some more. "No, I'm not mad," he said. "Yes, I'll be gentle when I tell her. I don't know if she'll believe me, but I'll be gentle." A pause. "I miss you too… Yes, we're still friends… Yes, I remember our agreement." Another pause. "Listen, I gotta go. I want to get back out on the water. I'll talk to you soon." He hung up the receiver.

He stood staring at the phone. It was the strangest conversation he ever had. Jennifer told him Eddie Richmond was alive. The whole funeral thing two years before had been a hoax. However, Eddie Richmond's father was still looking for April, and evidently a lot of people were looking for him. Cliff shook his head side to side as he stepped away from the payphone. Eddie being alive was a possibility no one had considered. It was also something that seemed to make Jennifer very nervous—not that the boy was alive, but that his father was still looking for April. Then again, April knew that, didn't she?

What Cliff needed to worry about was making sure April was safe until the sheriff was found. Cliff also needed to think about how to tell April. She was in a very fragile state and anything out of the ordinary might set her off. He didn't want to think about what she might do when she heard the news. He also didn't allow himself to think about the last part of the conversation with Jennifer. He didn't realize how much he missed her. The hurt from a few days ago had subsided. In its place was a yearning—a desire to go back several days to the time before they had *the talk*. Sure, he understood. Sure, deep down he knew it was for the best. Sure, he knew—

"Stop it!" he scolded. He was hurt, just like before. Only this time, being a seasoned veteran, he was handling it better. Besides, this time he had a worthy distraction.

Jennifer left. April arrived. There was something intriguing about the sudden switch. He couldn't put his finger on it, but it was there nonetheless. Time, he told himself. There was always a need for time. Only he didn't have that commodity. If anything, time was of the essence. There was this sheriff thing lurking over them.

If only Jennifer were there to help. She would know what to say, and more importantly how to say it. But she wasn't. Never again would—

He cut the thought off. Jennifer wasn't there, so he'd have to deal with April on his own.

He made his way inside the grocery store, grabbed a cart and started going up and down the aisles. He planned on stocking up enough to stay out a week or more. Whatever happened next, he'd feel more secure on the water.

He picked up his pace as the cart quickly filled. He made a mental note to make sure the marina had filled the propane tanks as requested. They'd fueled up on the way in. The water tanks were loaded at the same time. He grabbed a couple cases of bottled water, just in case. Before heading back to the boat, he had one other place to go, if such a place existed in this town. He contemplated skipping it, then decided to at least try. He knew it would make April happier.

Exiting the store, he looked around. A chill went up his spine. Was he really feeling a sixth sense, or was he just being paranoid? He quickened his pace. The urge to get back on the water persisted.

Time kept ticking in his head.

151

April felt the boat move without any noticeable sounds of footsteps. Startled, she snapped her head around. She saw Cliff stepping onto the port gunwale and let out a sigh of relief. His arms were loaded with groceries. She saw a dock cart on the finger pier piled high with more. He transferred his weight from the nonmoving pier to the moving deck of the boat with ease. Waiting for the boat to level off, he stepped down into the cockpit. She put the small brush down she'd been using to apply varnish to the teak and wiped her hands on a paper towel. Rising to her feet, she headed aft.

"What are you doing?" Cliff asked, looking around nervously.

"I wanted to put another coat of varnish on the teak before we left."

"Why are you out of the cabin?"

"It's hard to do outside teak from inside the cabin," she replied. "Besides, I took your advice."

"Which was?"

"To be a little less paranoid."

"I said less paranoid. I didn't say anything about taking stupid chances," Cliff snapped.

His tone both upset and angered April. "I'm sorry if what you think I'm doing is stupid."

Cliff's mouth opened and closed without a sound. He handed her a couple bags. "None of these are heavy," he said much more softly.

April chose to let him off the hook for his remark. Besides, while she didn't know him that well, she knew something had changed from when he left the boat until now. Her own level of concern rose.

Letting go of the bags slowly to make sure April could handle the weight, Cliff said, "I got another load to bring down from up at the dock house. I'll be back in a few. If you can start stowing the stuff away, I'd appreciate it. We'll take off as soon as I get back."

"No problem," April said, taking the bags from Cliff. She handled their weight without difficulty. Cliff's sense of urgency persisted. "Is something wrong?" she asked.

"No, not at all. I'm just anxious to get out on the water."

"Yesterday, you couldn't wait to get into port. Now, you can't wait to get out?"

"That's the life of a sailor."

His avoidance of the question caused her additional concern. She knew he was planning to call her cousin while at the store. After further discussion the day before, April finally gave her okay for Cliff to make the call. April suspected his change in behavior had something to do with that conversation. So if Cliff was anxious, then she should be, too.

She contemplated doing just the opposite. She could be up and gone before he ever got back. It would resolve any issues for Cliff, and it would once again put her in a position to make her own decisions. While the thought was tempting, for the first time in a long time, she resisted the urge to run. She reminded herself she was already in a position to make her own decisions. No one was holding her hostage. She could leave anytime she wanted.

Couldn't she?

While it had only been a few days, she had grown very comfortable aboard the *Mona Lisa*. She had adjusted easily to the routine of sailing the bay. She loved to sail and Cliff was more than happy to let her handle the boat as much as she wanted while he used the time to catch up on his work. Since his portfolio was way behind schedule, he spent the time either sitting in the cockpit or propped up against the mast, a drawing pad always open on his lap. Occasionally, he'd take out his camera and shoot some photographs. Once they were anchored for the night in some secluded cove, he'd go below to fix dinner and she'd spend the remaining light waxing the fiberglass and doing the teak. The boat was not dirty, but the fiberglass had faded and the teak had turned the expected ugly gray. By the third day, the boat looked almost new. The decks were shiny and the teak glistened for the first time in months. Cliff kept insisting she didn't have to do all this. However, each time she asked for something like another brush or polishing cloth, he was quick to fetch it for her.

The *Mona Lisa* certainly couldn't compare to *Hamilton's Bench* as far as size and amenities. Then again—as Chessie pressed her cold nose against April's bare leg encouraging her to empty the bags quicker and find the treats Cliff surely bought— *Hamilton's Bench* didn't have a Chessie.

As if on cue, April found the box of dog biscuits. Chessie knew this by the sound they made and increased her nudging. Her tail hit the floor so hard it made a thud.

April laughed. "Take it easy, girl. You're going to knock a hole in the bottom of the boat. You know Cliff wouldn't be too happy about that. Besides, didn't he feed you this morning?" She knew that was an unfair question the moment she spoke. The first thing Cliff did each morning was check the boat to make sure everything was intact. Second, he fed Chessie. Then, and only then, did anyone else on board get any attention. April had joked the morning before, saying, "I certainly hope if you had a wife, you wouldn't feed your dog before her."

To which Cliff responded, "I would never have a wife who didn't understand that's exactly the way it has to happen. A wife, a husband, or most other humans for that matter can fend for themselves. A dog doesn't have that option."

His frankness and wisdom surprised her. It also showed a high level of discipline, which she figured would be expected considering his chosen career and how he pursued it. There was no pressure from anyone to do anything. Only, instead of falling into a lazy man's trap, Cliff was very motivated. So yes, life aboard the *Mona Lisa* was tolerable. It had also become fun—something she hadn't truly experienced in a long time.

The next bag of groceries contained nothing but boxes of macaroni and cheese followed by a bag of those little sip-it cartons of milk. A smile crossed her face. She would have to work on the cuisine, but for now, she focused her attention on finding places for the rest of the supplies.

This time she was not startled when the boat rocked in response to Cliff's return. She straightened up as his head popped through the galleyway. "I'm back," he said, much more cheerful this time.

"No shit," she wanted to say. It was a favorite expression of Freddie whenever she said something stupid. But she kept her sarcasm in tow. Besides, she wasn't very skillful in the use of profanity and was sure it would come out all wrong. Instead, "I've got most everything put away. If you bring any more groceries, they'll have to stay outside somewhere. I think I've found every nook and cranny in this boat."

Looking at the empty galley counter, Cliff responded, "I've no doubt about that. Thanks."

"No problem. I just hope I've put things where you can find them."

"If not, you'll have to do galley duty."

April laughed. "They let me in the galley aboard *Hamilton's Bench*, but only so long as I kept my hands folded in front of me." She paused. "I did cook some back home before we moved to Worthington Valley. Wasn't much, though." She let the thought trail off.

Cliff smiled and said, "No great expectations here. I keep things pretty simple."

"No complaints so far," April said. She had actually been quite impressed at Cliff's skill in the galley. Like he said, meals were usually simple, but they always tasted good.

He broke her train of thought. "Anyway, I'm going to need your help getting something down through the hatch. It's kind of heavy." His head disappeared and reappeared a moment later. He slid a long flat narrow box across the threshold of the hatchway. "Grab an end and walk back. I'll bring it down the steps.

A minute later, the long box was lying across the dinette table. "What in the world is this?" April said. "I hope you don't expect me to find a place to store this, too."

Cliff laughed. "Actually, I do. It's yours."

"Mine!"

"A present from me… for all the work you've done on the boat."

"I was just trying to help and earn my keep."

"You do," Cliff said. "Go ahead and open it."

There was a long piece of industrial tape holding the edges of the box together. April peeled up the end with a fingernail and pulled the strip off. She pried apart the cardboard and looked inside. Her eyes widened and filled with tears.

"It's not a grand piano, but it's the best I can do," Cliff said. He helped her pull an electronic keyboard out of the box. She hurriedly pulled the bubble wrap off the instrument. Cliff went back up on deck, returning with yet another bag. "I got you some music. I didn't know what kind you like, so I got a variety."

The bag contained several books of songs and classical pieces. On the bottom was a blank book of music staffs. "What's this for?" April said, holding it up.

"In case you want to write a song of your own," Cliff said.

April laughed through the tears that were still running down her cheeks. "There's a big difference between playing music and writing it," she said.

Cliff shrugged his shoulders. "You never know if you don't try."

April looked at the array of music books spread out across the table. Then she stared back down at the keyboard. "I don't know what to say."

Cliff shrugged his shoulders. "Don't need to say anything."

The tears increased in intensity. Cliff stepped toward her and placed his arm on her shoulder. "It's okay. It's only a piano," Cliff said.

She looked up at him as she wiped the tears away. "It's much more than that, and you know it."

Cliff smiled. "I guess you're right."

She stepped toward him and put her arms around his neck. Their bodies pressed together as she gave him a hug. "Thank you."

"You're welcome." He wrapped his arms around her as well. He felt her pull him tighter. He responded and she did the same. There was a long pause before he felt the pressure release. She stepped back and wiped her eyes. "I'd better get this stowed away somewhere. You want to get going, remember?"

He took a step back as well. "Good idea."

"Where are we going?" April asked, a sense of worry returning to her voice.

"We'll see which way the wind's blowing once we get out in the bay," Cliff said.

"Sounds like a plan to me," April said.

And so it was.

152

The bounty hunter stared out the window. His head didn't move, his eyes darted back and forth. To the untrained observer, he appeared to be sleeping. To those who understood his methodology, he was very much alert. He'd been sitting in the parking lot across from the grocery store, waiting for the boy to finish shopping. The kid fit the description, but the man wanted to make sure. The last thing he wanted was to go on some wild goose chase. He was one of the best because he was careful, didn't take chances, and in spite of the demands of many of his clients—the sheriff in particular—he had patience. Bounty hunters, even when the west was wild, were patient men who stalked their prey, never giving up, always knowing that the rewards went to those who were persistent. His work also required a certain amount of luck—as proven by that day out on the bay when he first spotted the girl.

Finding the boy was lucky, too. Snooping around the docks in Annapolis the day before the girl's *departure* from the hospital, he noticed the boy out on the bow of his boat sitting crossed legged and working on a drawing pad. The man also noticed the boat, more specifically, the boat's name, the *Mona Lisa*. He thought it quite fitting. He always had a fascination with boat names, even growing up as a young boy. His father, a bounty hunter himself, had boats named *Hunter I*, *Hunter II*, and *Hunter III*. He already had the name of his boat picked out, *Hunter on the Bounty*—also an appropriate name, he thought.

As luck would have it, the bounty hunter was in Annapolis the same time as the sheriff, and was actually sitting in the hospital parking lot listening to the police radio when the call came across that the girl had escaped. Naturally, his interest piqued at this unfortunate news. In spite of the storm, he started driving around the area, just in case he got lucky. He never found the girl, but he did notice a short time later that the sailboat from the day before was gone. He remembered it had been there before the storm. He thought it odd that a boat like that would leave in such weather. However, the more he thought about it, the more he began to wonder if there was a connection. Had his luck held true?

Information on the scanner told him the girl was long gone. But where? Again, the missing sailboat came into question.

Information about the *Mona Lisa*, the boy's identity (including picture), and credit card information were all obtainable through Internet sources. The boy's travels were easily traceable via credit card purchases. The boat and crew had arrived in Cape Charles the day before, documented by a fuel purchase charged to the boy's one and only credit card. The bounty hunter was down there that night. He sat in his car the next morning with a powerful pair of binoculars when the boy came out of the cabin to walk his dog. A short time later, a girl's head popped out of the cabin as well. She looked right his way. The bounty hunter had no doubt it was his prey.

Patience, persistence and luck had once again paid off.

153

The cellphone rang twice before the sheriff recognized the sound. He had fallen asleep across the bed fully clothed. He had driven all night, reaching his home in Worthington Valley in the early morning hours. He sat up and ran his hand through his hair. He pulled the phone off his belt and flipped open the receiver. "Yeah," he barked.

"Didn't mean to wake you, Sheriff."

Hearing the voice on the other end, the sheriff sat up straighter. "What've you got?"

"Good morning to you, too," the man said.

"Just answer the Goddamn question." The sheriff glanced at his watch. It was almost ten o'clock. A whole three hours of sleep. That used to be enough. Lately, however, short nights were taking their toll. He stood up to stretch before having to do battle with the son-of-a-bitch on the other end of the line.

"She's alive and well," the man said.

"Who you talking about?" the sheriff said as a way of stalling for time. He walked out to the kitchen and turned on the coffee pot.

There was laughter on the other end of the line. "Let me see now, how many people am I tracking for you?"

"Don't be a smart ass."

"Then don't ask stupid ass questions."

The sheriff's adrenaline picked up. The fact that he was giving the sheriff back that which he got meant the man had something important. "Okay. Just tell me…tell me what you've got."

"Like I said, she's alive."

"We assumed that," the sheriff snapped.

"It was an assumption. Now it's a fact."

In spite of the tone in the man's voice, the sheriff liked what he was hearing. "How do you know?"

"Because I'm standing here looking at her this very moment."

The sheriff knew the bounty hunter gave him a hard time. He also knew the man never lied. "Where are you?"

"Cape Charles."

"Where the hell is that?"

"The southernmost part of the Eastern Shore."

The sheriff tried to remember the map of the region he had studied recently. "You mean all the way down the Chesapeake Bay?"

"Yepper."

The sheriff knew he should have stayed in Annapolis another day. He also knew people around Worthington Valley were starting to question his dedication. He even heard rumors people were questioning his mental status. The sheriff knew that would never do, especially with the upcoming elections. He had campaigned very little throughout the years. He didn't have the time to go through all that rigmarole now. He planned to be out and about in the community and he'd have all that bullshit erased.

He had to give the townspeople credit. They were fully supportive of what he had been through, no doubt about that. They said nothing when he took the initial leave of absence and then another one a year after that. Each time they welcomed him back with open arms. Each time they were anxious to get their lives back to normal. The citizens of Worthington Valley were very dependent on their sheriff.

One more day in Annapolis would not have hurt.

He decided to shower quickly, make an appearance at the office, spend an hour or so making the rounds through town, and then head back toward Maryland.

"You sure it's her?" he asked.

"Call me when you get here." the bounty hunter answered. The line went dead before the sheriff could answer.

154

Cliff stepped into the cockpit from the cabin carrying a bowl of pretzels in one hand and two cans of beer in the other. He sat down on the seat opposite April and offered her the snacks, which she took. He did the same with one of the beers. She shook her head no. "Want something else to drink?" he asked.

"No, thanks; I'm fine with water." She motioned to the plastic bottle in the corner.

Cliff set one of the cans aside and snapped the metal tab on the other.

April cocked her head to the side. "You twenty-one?"

Cliff smiled. "Close enough."

"Well, I guess you look it," April said, crunching slowly on a pretzel.

"Sometimes I do," Cliff said. "Sometimes I don't think it matters… so long as all you're buying is a little beer."

April didn't pursue the point any further. She took another handful of pretzels and passed them back to Cliff. "It's a beautiful night," she said, glancing skyward. It was now totally dark and the first stars of the night were starting to wake up. She found the Big Dipper and followed the base of the pot to the North Star. That night it was the brightest star in the sky. She tried to remember which planet would be up later, Saturn or Venus. She moved her head slowly from left to right. She didn't see anything that looked like either one. The southerly breeze they'd had all day was still strong enough to keep the mosquitos and other bloodthirsty insects at bay.

When they left Cape Charles, they sailed through the Chesapeake Bay Bridge Tunnel and out several miles. Cliff wanted to say the *Mona Lisa* had actually been in the ocean, and thus could officially be called an oceangoing yacht. Not sure why this was all that important, April chalked it up to another example of the male ego run amuck—another call of the wild for mankind. Having learned enough about boats to know the *Mona Lisa* was safe to make such a journey, she went along without objection. Besides, it was a beautiful day. The sky was cloudless and the temperature remained in the mid-eighties. The water was choppy right at the mouth of the bay, but once they cleared land, the ocean flattened out considerably. They sailed around for a couple of hours before Cliff announced he didn't want to press his luck with Mother Nature. Both she and Cliff knew how quickly the weather could change. Back in the Chesapeake Bay, they headed toward the western shore. Not familiar with that part of the bay, Cliff pulled out a chart book from under a seat cushion and looked for a secluded cove to anchor for the night. Remembering her search for such a book a few days before, April smiled. Evidently, she hadn't found all the hiding places aboard the *Mona Lisa*.

It had been a great day for sailing. The winds stayed around fifteen knots, dying down only as the sun dropped from the western sky. Unlike previous days, when they kept the sails loose to keep the *Mona Lisa* on a more even keel so Cliff could work, they sailed hard all day. There were very few times when either the starboard or port rail wasn't in or near the water. Naturally, Cliff didn't get any work done. He didn't complain, saying he was taking the day off to enjoy the ride. By the time they anchored for the night, both were exhausted.

Dinner consisted of macaroni and cheese combined with a can of tuna. April was not surprised at just how good it tasted. She remembered similar types of meals when they anchored out with the crew of *Hamilton's Bench*. While the food was usually more glamorous, the concept was the same—simple yet tasty.

All in all, April felt happy. Except for the trick he played on her in the forward cabin that one day, Cliff was the perfect host. April wasn't sure why he was helping her, but she knew she needed to be appreciative, so she was.

April hadn't given her music much thought since leaving *Hamilton's Bench*. She assumed her music was on hold. Cliff changed that with the electronic piano. She was ecstatic. She played while Cliff fixed dinner. It felt good. She didn't know how much Cliff knew about music, but he got her the perfect instrument. It was a full keyboard and it had very few of the so called bells and whistles so many of the modern electronic keyboards contained. While it did have a different sound and feel, it was better than nothing.

April took a break for dinner, and then at Cliff's insistence, played while he cleaned up the dishes. After making sure Chessie got to shore and back, Cliff sat down and worked on his art. Both worked well into the evening. April stopped once and asked about the power drain on the batteries. (Cliff had an AC / DC adapter already on the boat.) Cliff explained that the electrical drain was minimal. She went back to her music without further comment.

Music was her way of escaping reality. It helped pass the time. It helped her forget. It gave her hope. Only presently, she found herself struggling somewhat. Maybe it was because she was rusty and her fingers failed to cooperate. Maybe it was because she missed the people aboard *Hamilton's Bench*. Maybe it was because of the things that had already happened aboard the *Mona Lisa*—good and bad. Maybe it was because of the mixed feelings she had being around Cliff in the first place.

April watched him work as she played. His fingers like hers, moved effortlessly across the artist's medium. A page with a few rough outlines soon turned into a beautiful drawing. He built a piece of art like she imagined Beethoven building a sonata—simple at first and then more complex with time. As she watched him, her sadness further subsided. Her playing improved. Soon, she was making beautiful sounds. He was making beautiful scenes.

April played until midnight. Her fingers tired, her body hot, she shut off the instrument, grabbed a bottle of water and went up on deck. Cliff and Chessie followed a few minutes later. Chessie laid her cold nose on April's knee. A soft whine earned the dog a piece of pretzel. Two chomps of the jaw, and the treat was gone. April gave her another and the action was repeated. "She likes the salt," April said.

"That she does," Cliff agreed. "Actually, I watch her diet pretty closely, especially when we're anchored. With the heat and everything, you also have to make sure she gets enough fluids, and like you said, salt." Cliff reached down and rubbed Chessie on the side. "You're getting old too, girl. Aren't you? The vet says you'll need to start a daily vitamin soon." Cliff looked up at April. "This is one dog that likes to eat everything and anything, so long as it doesn't have to do with medicine. Getting her to take that is a battle worth watching."

"Can't you mix it with her food?" April said.

"I try, but she knows when something's in her food."

"Smart dog," April said, patting the animal on the head. She focused her attention on the animal. "And he calls you old, too."

On cue, Chessie barked. Then she turned her head in the direction of her master and gave a soft growl. April laughed. "You go, girl. You tell him."

Cliff smiled. He reached over and took a pretzel for himself followed by a swallow of beer. He ran his hands through his hair and arched his back. He looked hard at April a moment. "I've got something to tell you. I've been playing around all day with how to do it, and I ain't figured it out yet. So I thought I'd simply come out and tell you, and we can take it from there."

April sat up straight. She hadn't totally forgotten about the incident with Cliff during the storm, but when he came back from the store with the piano and with the excitement of the sail, she'd put all the negative stuff out of mind. Only here it was again, and all the earlier anxiety returned. She prepared herself for the worst.

Cliff struggled to get the words right. "It's kind of, sort of, one of those good news bad news things."

April forced her face to remain expressionless. "Why not start with the bad news."

"I talked to Jennifer today while I was in town."

"You told me you were going to do that," April said.

"I told her you were with me and that you were alright."

"So?"

"She said to tell you hello and that she was looking forward to meeting you." April started to protest, but Cliff held up his hand as he continued. "She also said to tell you that meeting will occur when and where you decide." He took a sip of beer. "She asked me to emphasize that."

"Fair enough," April said. "So you told her I was her cousin?"

"I think that's a foregone conclusion, don't you?"

"Fair enough," April repeated.

Cliff continued. "This man… what's his name? Sheriff…"

"Richmond," April offered.

"Yeah, Sheriff Richmond," Cliff agreed. "They think he's still in the area looking for you."

The blank look continued.

"You don't seem surprised," Cliff commented.

April turned her head. "He's been looking for me for almost two years. Don't forget, he was in Annapolis. So I'm not surprised, just…" She stopped.

"Afraid," Cliff suggested.

April shrugged her shoulders. "Maybe. Is that why you wanted to leave so quickly today?"

"It made me kind of nervous."

"Do you know why he's looking for me?" April asked.

"I know about the sheriff's son, yes."

"I killed him… Well, I didn't actually kill him. The gun went off by accident. But I'm the one they're blaming for his death."

Before Cliff could say anything, April continued. "If the sheriff is the bad news, what's the good news?"

Cliff took another swallow of beer. He could tell April was struggling to present a confident and calm front. He suspected, however, that her emotions on the inside were just the opposite. His mind flashed back to times in his own past—hearing that his parents were killed in a car accident—hearing that his uncle had been struck by lightning—hearing Robin's voice in her living room—seeing Cheryl in the store with her husband. Life was full of calm oceans with a few tsunamis thrown in for good measure. Cliff suspected April also had her share of big wave knockdowns—so many emotions in such a short period of time. Yet, you had to get past these feelings if the larger instinct was to survive. He wondered if that's what kept April going all this time. The urge to keep one's head above water was a powerful instinct. The question now, would what he was about to say knock her off again or help her stay afloat? He swallowed to make sure his mouth was moist. "You never killed anybody."

April stopped in mid motion as she was about to bite down on a piece of pretzel. "I beg your pardon."

"You never killed anybody," Cliff repeated. "Eddie Richmond's alive," he quickly added.

April turned pale. After a disbelieving stare, she spoke. "You're a real bastard, you know that?"

Cliff was somewhat taken aback at both her tone and her choice of words. This wasn't the response he was anticipating. Not knowing what else to say at that particular moment, he stammered, "You want to explain that?"

She retorted quickly and loudly. "Me explain! You have a sick sense of humor. First you jump on me like you're going to… going to…" She couldn't get the words out. "Anyway, you know what I mean. And now you go and tell me something like this."

Moonlight reflecting off her face, Cliff could see the tears forming. He felt a wave of guilt for not handling the whole thing better. Then he realized he hadn't done anything wrong. Her response probably would have been the same regardless of how or when he told her. He spoke softly and with compassion. "As for that… that incident, I guess we can call it, I told you before, I needed to find a way to show you could trust me. And I did. It may have been bold. It may have been weird. It may have been strange, but it worked."

"Until now," April snapped, sobbing harder.

He stared hard into her eyes. "April, nothing's changed. The trust is still there. You just have to open it up."

She started to snap at him again. Her mouth opened, and then closed without a sound. She kept eye contact for a long moment. The realization set in that maybe nothing had changed. Maybe the trust had not been broken. Maybe he was telling the truth.

When she finally looked away, Cliff took a deep breath. "You talk about weird," he started. "What I'm about to tell you is one of the strangest things I've ever heard. But

April…" He reached across and put his hand on the side of her cheek. He applied a gentle pressure so her head turned towards him. "What I'm about to tell you is the truth. Listen to the whole thing first, and then if you don't want to believe me, fine." She wiped her eyes and nodded. Cliff continued. "I know it's hard to hear. I know it's unbelievable—even for me, an outsider to this whole thing." He wiped away a tear with his left thumb. "I'll give you the short version of what I know so we can get through it all as quickly as possible. We can fill in the blanks later. Okay?"

She nodded again.

"Like I said, Eddie Richmond is very much alive. How do we know? Jennifer—your cousin—went out to Worthington Valley and met with your brother, Danny. Somehow, by snooping around the hospital's medical records, Jennifer discovered Eddie had been transferred to a hospital in northern Pennsylvania early in the morning after he'd been shot. He's been there ever since."

Cliff drained his beer. "April, he's paralyzed and confined to a wheelchair." He forced his voice to be more upbeat. "But, he's alive and doing well. He even asked about you. He said to tell you that he's okay and when he sees you—which he hopes is soon—he wants to tell you just how sorry he is."

"He's sorry! I'm the one—"

Cliff's fingers spread out across her lips. "First off, you've done nothing wrong, April. Second, I'm just the messenger here. Jennifer did say that Eddie seemed relieved to hear you were okay. He also wants you to know that he accepts full responsibility for everything."

"He said that?"

Cliff nodded. "The sheriff evidently pulled the wool over everybody's eyes."

April looked away as she realized she'd been running all these months for nothing… absolutely nothing. And now, with the sheriff hot on her trail, it was too late to turn back.

Her body started to shake as the sobs returned.

155

In many people's opinion, Beethoven's *Moonlight Sonata* was the most beautiful piece of music ever written. April agreed, although there were other lesser known works of Beethoven she liked as well. Regardless, she often used the sonata as a warm-up piece. Like most of Beethoven's piano works, she knew it by heart. She closed her eyes and willed her fingers to do their thing. Her fingers moved across they keys effortlessly, as her mind wandered. She fantasized walking with Beethoven in the moonlight, side by side, close yet not too close, his hand resting on her elbow as she led him along the pathway of a beautiful garden. They could not see the flowers because of the darkness, but their scent, mixed with the dew of the night, filled the visitors' nostrils. The teacher and the pupil; the genius and the genius wannabe. She wished she could journey back into time when the grand master was alive. She wished she could be a student of his. Oh, how she'd love to play for him. How she'd love to hear him tell her what to do to make her play even better. She had few expectations from life, and even fewer dreams. One, however, was to study with someone like Beethoven.

The boat rocked gently, causing her to tilt to the left. The keyboard moved with her and she continued to play as the boat righted itself once again. She squeezed her eyes tighter. The notes flowed forth like a magical stream of gold. She continued imagining she was with the blind composer as she struggled to maintain a perfect performance. She so much wanted to please him.

To the untrained ear, her play was perfect. To the trained ear, it was excellent, but not perfect. To the pianist herself, she felt rusty. While her fingers worked, they didn't move in the fashion she wanted. In disgust, she stopped halfway through the sonata. She told herself not to get into a negative train of thought. She knew being overly self-critical was dangerous. Still, it hadn't been that long since she played.

Music was much like a sport. To excel, it took four basic factors. First, you needed talent. It had taken her awhile, but April finally accepted that she was a talented musician. Secondly, music took practice. Swimmers swim laps. Runners run. Golfers spend time on the driving range. Musicians practice their particular instrument(s). April had no problem practicing. In fact, she thrived on it—in their old trailer and in her home in Worthington Valley, she played three to four hours a day. Aboard *Hamilton's Bench*, she averaged even more, some days putting in as many as eight hours.

The third requirement was guidance. Famous coaches became famous for many reasons, foremost because they were good teachers. Musicians required good coaching as well. In April's case, that wasn't possible. She did have a piano teacher in Worthington Valley, but the woman was really no match for what April could do herself. She realized it too, so most lessons consisted of April playing and the teacher simply listening, offering insight where possible, such as advising April not to be overly self-critical.

Over the years, April developed a skill few were able to acquire. She could self-teach. She was able to look at a music book, hear in her mind what the composer was saying, and then transfer that to real sound. She had perfect pitch, and had acquired the discipline to be objective in her criticism. That she had never been exposed to formal training was of little consequence in her progression thus far. She taught herself the skills needed to reach a higher level of play. Similar to the lessons taught by Danny in the woods, it took patience and persistence. Danny's credo was simple: be self-sufficient or die. Alone in the woods, that was a metaphor easily transferred into reality. With her music, she self-taught or she made no progress. Her life and her music went hand in hand. She had little doubt her ability to survive these past months directly correlated with lessons learned through her music. Again, self-sufficient or die. She acknowledged the concept of self-sufficiency was diluted somewhat while aboard *Hamilton's Bench* in that she had a near unlimited source of information, both via the Internet and in books Mr. Hamilton bought her. Aboard *Hamilton's Bench*, she not only studied and played music, she studied the people and history behind the music. That she had progressed this far without a real life Beethoven at her side was a testament to her determination.

To April, it was just the hill down which she was heading.

The fourth requirement was opportunity. To play golf, you had to have a golf course. Runners had to have a place to run. Musicians had to have instruments to play. April had been lucky, even in her early years, that there was always a piano available. Even when they were still with her father, the piano was the most prized possession for two out of three members of the family. That possession came with them to the farm in Alabama. A piano was the only thing April's mother asked for when she agreed to marry Sam Worthington. It became a wedding gift for April. April later learned her mother even offered to forgo an engagement ring.

Growing up, April dreamed of playing in the great venues of the world. Carnegie Hall was a favorite fantasy. She never dreamed of playing aboard a mega-yacht. But she did. Aboard *Hamilton's Bench*, she never dreamed she'd be playing an electronic keyboard aboard a thirty some foot sailboat. But she was. And while the venues were different, the music was the same.

The Beethoven sonata continued. While not perfect, it was improving. April reminded herself to minimize the criticism. After all, she hadn't played in a few days, her hands were sore from all the hard sailing, and she was using an electronic keyboard. The sound was surprisingly authentic, but the touch was much softer. She finished with a flourish, took a couple deep breaths and started the piece again.

Her thoughts reverted to the night before. It had taken her a while to fully comprehend what Cliff told her. Eddie Richmond wasn't dead. He was very much alive. She hadn't killed anyone! He was paralyzed but doing fine. She didn't understand how you could be fine if you were stuck in a wheelchair, but her thoughts moved on.

If Eddie was alive, why was Eddie's father still after her? Why hadn't Eddie told him what happened? Part of her was glad the boy was alive. Part of her was angry. While the past two years had been difficult, they had not been all that complicated. Once she got over missing her family and adjusted to the loneliness, life was simple. There were actually few decisions to make; and when they came up, she made them without hesitation, such as the two nights she ended up in the water. They had been rather simple decisions— jump or deal with Phillip Rogers's alcohol-driven libido. Jump or deal with Sheriff Richmond's dog.

But that simplicity became complicated when she learned Eddie Richmond was alive. Since the night of the dance, she had been running to escape. It was a simple decision. Now, it suddenly became confusing. From what was she escaping? Why had she been running all these months? What should she do next? And Eddie was looking forward to seeing her? That seemed awfully strange in itself. She wasn't sure the feeling was mutual, although she had to admit there was a certain level of curiosity. She didn't know whether to be relieved, sad or angry.

Until Cliff told her about Eddie, she was actually beginning to feel happy again. Life was simple, and while she was still officially on the run, there was something about being aboard the *Mona Lisa*. Life aboard *Hamilton's Bench* was relatively easy once she got used to the routine, but there was always an air of stress. It wasn't necessarily all that bad. It was there nonetheless. Phillip Rogers was a good captain, or at least she thought so in the beginning. But he never seemed satisfied with how the boat looked in spite of the fact there was seldom a speck of dirt anywhere. There was always something more to do; and while he never raised his voice, you knew when he was displeased, which was often. In the same breath, he took the time to help, to teach the crew, especially the *newbies* like herself.

Plus, you never knew what Mr. Hamilton was going to do next, or whether he was even going to be on board. It was not uncommon for Mr. Hamilton to disappear for several weeks at a time. He always grumbled when he had to leave and always seemed overly delighted upon returning. When he was on board, parties in one form or the other were common. As April always supplied the entertainment, she was well positioned to see what was going on. Mr. Hamilton was certainly friendly towards his female guests, yet she never saw him make any hint of an advance, although there was never a lack of women trying to attract him.

The rule of thumb aboard the yacht was simple. All questions about boating were fair. All questions about the boat itself were fair. But there were no questions about the boat's owner. Yet, there was enough scuttlebutt floating around that April was able to piece together a pretty clear picture of the man. He was in his early fifties. He was kind and very caring about all those around him. He loved the arts, especially opera. April had even learned to play a few pieces for him. He had no known family and had never been married. It was assumed he had no children. Half his life was his boat. The other half was his work.

Compared with *Hamilton's Bench*, life aboard the *Mona Lisa* was much different. There was no pressure to do anything. While she did polish up the boat a bit, Cliff never asked her to do anything other than handle the helm so he could work, and she certainly didn't mind that. She loved to feel the power of the wind and water working in unison as nature moved the boat forward. She remembered the first time Mr. Hamilton explained the physics of sailing to her. She always thought the wind simply blew the boat in the direction you wanted to go. In reality, it was much more complicated than that. At times the boat was actually being sucked forward.

Their biggest task each day aboard the *Mona Lisa* was to make sure the anchor was set for the night; or if they were in a marina, to ensure the fenders were properly set. Cleaning of the exterior was minimized when anchored to conserve water. The inside was straightened as they went along. April was surprised at how neat and tidy Cliff kept the boat. Everything had its place and everything was in place each morning before they set sail.

She realized she knew nothing about Cliff. He did tell her his last name was Davidson and that he was an artist which was obvious. He was a very good one, too. He said his goal was to earn enough money selling his work to be self-sufficient aboard the *Mona Lisa*.

Cliff was pleasant enough and went to great lengths to make sure she was comfortable and had the things she needed, which in reality were very few. He certainly didn't seem bothered by having a guest aboard, and on more than one occasion commented it was nice having the company. And except on that one occasion when he acted like a fool and jumped on her, he was very careful to respect her privacy. She concluded that overall, he was an okay guy.

She quickly reminded herself of other people who had passed through her life that seemed okay at first. From the three boys on the farm, to Eddie Richmond who was just brought back from the dead, to the truck driver who carried her to Atlantic City, to Phillip Rogers—there was always a catch. There was always a debt to be paid. Nothing was ever free. Like she learned in physics, for each and every action, there was an equal and opposite reaction. With Cliff, it was a matter of time before she found just what that opposite reaction would be.

She tried convincing herself he was different and not like the others. After all, he already had his chance to *collect* on his debt; only he didn't, claiming instead it was his way of proving he could be trusted. Still, it was a hard pill to swallow.

She finished the sonata, flexed her fingers and took a deep breath. She flipped through the music books Cliff bought. She opened a collection of Chopin and turned to one of her favorite dances. She had played it before, but it had been awhile. It quickly came back to her. She evolved into her thinking mode before the end of the first page. Her mind wandered as it often did when she played. As long as she was relaxed she could play and think at the same time. It was when she felt tense she had trouble with her concentration. At that moment, she felt very relaxed.

She focused on her feelings toward Cliff. Maybe she had no other choice but to trust him. She wanted to, that was for sure. But could she afford such a step? Then again, could she afford not to? She decided that as long as she had other options, she'd let time answer that one. She had spent one evening while Cliff took a nap carefully studying the charts of the Chesapeake Bay he had pulled out from beneath the cushions. If the time came when she needed to move on, she'd at least have a general idea where to start. So for the moment, she'd hang tight.

She refocused on her playing as the next few measures were more difficult and less familiar. She stopped a couple times, repeating the notes to make sure she had them right. Satisfied, she moved on with her thoughts.

What else could it be with Cliff? Why was she having such a difficult time with this? She'd only know him for a couple days. Cliff was a nice guy and more. Actually, he was one of the nicest she'd ever met. He was, or at least seemed to be, genuine. He reminded her of her stepbrother, Danny. He was the same way—very caring, compassionate and likable—once you got to know him. But there was more with Cliff. She felt something else, something she had never experienced before. Maybe it was because he had saved her life. Maybe it was because he went beyond saving her life to helping her get away from Annapolis in the middle of a raging storm. Maybe it was because he was still helping her. She refused to wonder why. That was his issue. She wanted to stay focused on her side of the coin. Why was she feeling this way? She had never really been attracted to anyone in the past. She had never allowed herself to even get to a point where this might happen. It was unexplored territory, an area she had always avoided. Danny taught her to stay out of the densest part of the forest. He said you could get caught in a maze of underbrush and have a difficult time getting out. As she matured and developed into a young lady, she buried any feelings that came along with the change in her body. Her mother preached that men were only out for one thing. No matter what they said, their minds were controlled by other parts of their bodies. No matter what they said, the end point of their attention was always the same. She almost let out a giggle as the time in the shower with Danny came into focus.

So far her mother's wisdom was proving true.

She knew one thing; she had never felt this way before. Just looking at Cliff made her toes tingle. Sure, she got excited when she played the piano especially well and her audience responded in kind. Yet, there was a different feeling—similar, yet different. Just looking at him…

Her fingers stumbled as she missed a note. The music stopped. Who was she trying to kid anyway? She had felt that way in the past. The feelings that time in the shower with Danny and then later lying in bed together were real. It was one of those occurrences in life you shoved in a box, put on a back shelf in the attic and left there—only to be reopened on very rare occasions.

"You're losing concentration," she scolded.

She started at the beginning and tried to pay more attention, but her sense of relaxation dwindled quickly. Thoughts raced through her mind faster than her fingers crossed the keys. Things were there she had not thought of in a long time. Boxes were being opened that should have remained closed. She used to wonder what it would be like to be held, to be touched, to be liked by a boy. Her mother warned her to stay away from situations that could lead to problems. She never explained what the problems might be. She just said to avoid them. Growing up, April kept to herself, made few friends and avoided all contact whenever possible with the male species, except for the day at the stream with the brothers. When she met Danny, things started to change. Learning about survival in the woods taught her about survival in life. Learning how to get along with nature taught her how to get along with people. She was still very shy, but with time, her willingness to be friendly grew along with her curiosity. What would it be like to have someone care for you? What would it be like to have someone look after you? What would it be like to return the favor? Unlike boys, whose minds were controlled by the volcano in their groins, she thought of the soft romantic elements of a relationship.

Wondering about the physical aspect of a relationship occasionally occurred, but April quickly dismissed these thoughts. She did respond silently to the affection displayed towards her mother by her stepfather when they first came to Worthington Valley. She was happy for her mother, and deep down longed for a similar experience. Deep down is where those thoughts remained, hidden behind years of warnings from her mother, hidden behind memories of the tough times when her father was still in the picture, hidden behind fears of one day finding herself in a similar situation. She had always been able to control these emotions with the simple argument that she would never do anything to jeopardize what she and her mother had in Worthington Valley.

Until the night of the dance.

In an instant, her world turned inside out, her future was rewritten. All dreams evaporated. All thoughts about tomorrow vanished. She was forced to survive minute by minute, day by day. Even during the toughest times in Alabama, she didn't have immediate concerns. She did her chores; she did her homework; she practiced the piano, and life ticked on. Her basic needs had always been met. They might have been old, but she always had clothes to wear. They might have been simple, but there were always at least one meal a day. She might have been hungry at times, but she never starved.

Day by day. That's how they lived then. That's how it was now. There was little time to think of anything, especially boys.

That is, until she woke up one night and found herself aboard the *Mona Lisa*. Cliff *topsy-turvied* everything all over again. And the longer she was aboard, the stronger these feelings became. Her mind wandered away from the music as instinct took over control of her fingers. She tried to concentrate, to stay on task. She wanted to stay objective in her decision making. There was no time for mud in her water. There was no time to look at old boxes in the attic.

She finally decided that, regardless how she felt about Cliff, she had to move on—maybe not right away, but soon. That much was clear. Details of where she would go could be worked out later. In the meantime, she told herself to enjoy what time she had left. Sit tight for the moment. Move on when her instincts dictated it.

She flexed her shoulders and rolled her neck to ease the stiffness. A couple of deep breaths and her mind slowed. "Relax and enjoy," she told herself. It was another lesson her music teacher at Worthington Valley had taught her.

She opened one of the other books of music Cliff bought her. Beethoven never sounded better.

156

Cliff's uncle often described life like a football game. You banged away play after play, gaining only a few yards at a time. And then BOOM—a big gain, maybe even a touchdown. Life for Cliff followed that pattern, only there had been a few fumbles along the way. You'd think he'd learn to hang onto the ball better, but he didn't. He did, however, learn a strong lesson: fumbles weren't always your fault. But they were fumbles just the same.

Yes, life was like a football game. His art career had been edging along with a couple of big successes along the way. Recently though, Cliff started to wonder in which direction he was heading. April had been on board several days now. The first few hours had been instinctive and reactionary. Now settled into a routine, he had a better chance to reflect on the unfolding events. He wasn't upset. He wasn't angry. If anything, he was happy for the company. Besides, April was a real help with the boat. She was as good a sailor as he. She knew seamanship and she knew her way around a boat in general. And while he would have thought she'd be much more of an emotional wreck, she seemed to be taking everything in stride. She did get upset when he told her about Eddie, but she seemed to get over that quickly. She looked a little rough around the edges because of the clothes she was forced to wear—his at first and a few things he picked up for her in Cape Charles, but she was really quite attractive. He could tell by the way she handled the sails she was physically fit—a lot stronger than one might expect. Through it all, she maintained a pleasant attitude, never asking for anything and always helpful. As far as the piano, Cliff thought she was going to jump out of her skin when she opened the box. While he had never really been exposed to classical music, he learned to appreciate what she played. He wasn't a judge of music, but he knew that she was good.

So why was he having so much difficulty with her being on board? Why did he feel uncomfortable with the whole thing? Why did he feel like his football game was now running in circles? Was it because she was a woman? He decided that was a no. Was it because she was on the run? No again. Was it because she was related to Jennifer? Nope. Was it because she was as good or even a better sailor than he? He chuckled aloud. He wasn't known for being vain.

Cliff listened as the music filtered up on deck. It was a beautiful night. The moon was two days short of full. The sky, cloudy most of the day, was now clear. Stars shined with an intensity he had not seen in a while. It didn't hurt that they were anchored in a secluded cove miles away from the nearest town. The hatches were open and the sound traveled from different directions, giving a sense of stereo.

Cliff shook his head in awe. She was good, he told himself... very good.

So why was he uncomfortable? Did he feel threatened by her? Did he think she was a better musician than he was an artist? That was absurd, he told himself. He never felt threatened by anyone. It wasn't a lack of competition; it was that his competitor was always himself. Whatever he did, he strove to be better—a message from his uncle. "Don't worry about what others are doing. Just worry about yourself." A similar message came from the wood carver in Crisfield.

Cliff listened to April play as he checked the anchor. Satisfied, he made his way aft and ducked into the galleyway. He stepped down into the cabin, stopping with one foot on the top rung. She continued to play without pause. The cabin lights were on, casting a shadow across her face. Her eyes were closed. Her fingers, also in partial darkness, moved across the keys like lightning bugs in the night. Cliff focused on the music. He didn't recognize the piece. He noticed the music book on the stand read Beethoven. Again, her eyes were shut. He decided she was either a quick learner or already knew the piece by heart.

Cliff shook his head side to side. She was amazing. Emotionally, she should be so fragile, but in reality, she was the opposite. Physically, she was petite, yet she had a physical strength beyond her size. At first glance, she looked plain Jane-ish. A closer study showed she was quite beautiful. Cliff certainly understood the saying that looks can be deceiving, although he doubted few who first met her would guess she was such an accomplished pianist. Then again, people might say the same about him. Still, she was different. She was so young to have gone through so much already, and apparently the saga was continuing. He wanted to feel sorry for her, but he knew that would be wasted energy. She didn't need it. She wouldn't want it. Besides—

His thoughts stopped as a wave of anxiety flowed over him. Why? As the music continued, the answer became clear. His anxiety had nothing to do with April. It was all about himself. For the first time in many moons, buried emotions were coming alive. These feelings had nothing to do with him being a nineteen year old boy alone on a boat with a beautiful girl. It was much more than that.

But more of what? What was so intriguing about her that caused him to sit and stare, that caused his mind to wander into areas he tried to avoid and bubbled his emotions to the surface like lava from a volcano?

He turned and looked out the galleyway. "Evening, Mr. Twain, any ideas?" he mouthed quietly. He continued staring at the stars. A few twinkled. A few remained steady in their brightness. He was just about to look away when something caught the corner of his eye. A shooting star was in the northern sky. It looked to be heading right at the moon, and in fact curved towards the night sky's brightest object. He stared wide eyed as it disappeared into the moon's silhouette.

His uncle used to say, "Every shooting star carries a message, like an airplane dragging a banner." The key was to figure out just what the message read. Cliff knew a shooting star was a meteor burning in earth's atmosphere, but he couldn't help wondering what would happen if the meteor actually hit the moon. Suddenly, the answer was clear.

He was moonstruck, and in a way never before experienced.

Sure, he had similar feelings in the past, but this time was different. These were stronger, deeper, more intense. He sensed butterflies fluttering in his stomach. He almost laughed as he realized he was once again threatening to get in over his head. He knew he shouldn't go there. He knew he should stay focused on his art. He knew a lot of things. But...

There was always the *but*.

He watched the sky another minute. The shooting star was gone. It had done its deed. It had delivered its message as it took its last breath before dying in the earth's atmosphere.

"Thank you, Mr. Twain," Cliff mouthed, as a burden seemed to drift away. He'd always felt guilty about so many things in his life. He felt guilty when his parents died. He felt guilty when his uncle was struck by lightning. He felt guilty after he was with Robin, and with Cheryl. He told himself he shouldn't feel guilty about something out of his control. It wasn't his fault his parents were killed in a car accident, nor was it really his fault Uncle George was struck by lightning. He didn't know Robin had a boyfriend and he definitely didn't know Cheryl was married. But now his shooting star of guilt disappeared across the universe and crashed into the moon. The reason he was having trouble adjusting to April being aboard was that he no longer had a wall of guilt to hide behind. He was a free man. And it was the fear of this freedom that bothered him the most.

He looked into the cabin and realized the music had stopped. April was staring at him. "Is something wrong?" she asked.

"No, why?" he said defensively.

"For the longest time you were just staring at me, and then you looked away as if something distracted you."

"You knew I was here?" he said, surprised.

"Maybe not at first," she said, to be polite.

"I was looking at the night sky," Cliff explained.

"Oh yeah, and what did you see?"

"I saw a shooting star."

"What did it say?"

"Huh?"

April laughed. "Mr. Hamilton said that a shooting star was always attached to a story."

Cliff cocked his head to the side. "And in what language was this story told?"

April laughed. "In the language of imagination."

"Oh."

"Where did your star go?

"It crashed into the moon."

April laughed again. "Ouch."

"Anyway, sounds great," Cliff said, motioning to the keyboard. The language of imagination, Cliff repeated silently.

"Thanks." She started to turn the instrument off.

"No, No. You're fine. Go ahead and play some more."

"I'm done for the night," she said, opening and closing her fingers until her knuckles cracked.

Cliff made the rest of the way into the cabin. He sat on the couch across from the table. With the shooting star, a lot of questions suddenly found answers. However, just as suddenly, there were new questions. "Can I ask you something?" he said.

"You're the captain."

"That's not why I'm asking." Cliff paused. "What are you going to do with your music?"

"Do with it?"

"Like, what are your plans for the future?"

She returned a defensive laugh. "I never thought much about it," she said.

"Really!" He was genuinely surprised.

"I play for enjoyment."

"It was more than that on *Hamilton's Bench*, wasn't it?"

April looked toward the night sky. "I don't think a whole lot about the future with anything."

Cliff watched her face as she fought back a tear. Without knowing it, she had answered his question. She was simply living day by day. How could he expect her to make plans when she didn't even know what the next day was going to bring.

She said, this time very softly, "Sometimes I dream of playing Carnegie Hall."

"In New York?"

"No, in Denver."

She was quick, Cliff thought. He told himself to let his irritation slide. "So you want to be a concert pianist?"

She shrugged her shoulders.

"If that's what you decide to do, I'm sure you'll make a hell-of-a good one," Cliff said. His enthusiasm had returned.

Her eyes snapped back to his. "If that's what I decide! What kind of a thing is that to say?"

Again taken aback by her response, Cliff leaned back in his seat and tried to figure out what he said that was so bad. Luckily, it didn't take him long. "I see your point," he said. "I didn't earlier… sorry."

The anger on her face quickly evaporated. "You understand?" she said with genuine surprise.

"You believe you have very little to say about your life right now. And…" He hesitated. "I can't disagree with you either. But we can do something about it."

"We!"

Cliff laughed. "You are one sharp cookie, aren't you? Then again, you wouldn't have survived if you weren't." He paused. "Okay, *you* can do something about it. But I'll help if you want and then it will be a *we*."

Her mouth opened and closed without a sound.

157

Jennifer stared at the blank computer screen, her hands poised above the keyboard. She closed her eyes and scrunched up her forehead, trying to get the words to flow. As it had been for the last week, there was no inspiration. She did well the first few days after returning from Worthington Valley, but her ability to write was again gridlocked. It was something that never ceased to amaze her. How could she write so much one day, and her mind be so constipated the next? She used to blame it on the many things going on in her life, rationalizing that the more stress, the greater the chance of writer's block. Only that never seemed to pan out completely. There had been times in her life when she was so stressed, the only thing she could do was write. Other times, the opposite was true. She wasn't sure what was happening this time.

In many ways, life in Annapolis was great. Things were going well at the *Riverboat Inn*. They were having one of their best summers ever. Talk of the St. Michaels project set off a nervousness in Annapolis about the Blackstones possibly moving to the Eastern Shore. Previously impossible-to-obtain permits were now being approved at an astonishing rate. The architect was already working on the design plans for expanding the restaurant into an entire resort and bankers were lining up to offer financial support. The local newspaper called the *Riverboat Inn* expansion project the biggest thing to hit Annapolis in a long time. If all went as planned, it would be one of the biggest resorts for miles around. The only thing lacking was its own marina, but the area marina owners assured David Blackstone of their cooperation. Jennifer's father told her that the St Michaels project, while appearing to be a bust, was actually on hold itself. They went ahead and purchased the marina and surrounding property and leased it back to the present management staff to operate. David Blackstone had no doubt that once the St. Michaels town council saw what was happening in Annapolis, their minds would change. Regardless of what one might say in the open, there was an underlying current of competition between the two sides of the Chesapeake Bay. That was fine with David Blackstone. He was confident both areas would benefit from what he had planned. It took Jennifer a while to realize that her father had this two resort idea planned from the beginning. David Blackstone was not only a dreamer, he dreamed big. So for him, one of the two projects wasn't enough. He wanted both. From the grumbling they heard coming out of St. Michaels, it was only a matter of time. There were already rumors that the loss of the St. Michaels project combined with the startup of the *Riverboat Inn* expansion in Annapolis was causing the town council problems. Seems the people of St. Michaels weren't as opposed to the project as a few council members led others to believe. The word *conspiracy* was surfacing, not against the Blackstones, but against those who blocked them from coming into town and helping improve the tourist trade. There was already speculation that a couple councilmen, including George Myers, would be opposed in the next election, something they seldom worried about.

Also in Annapolis, Jennifer's personal life had taken an unexpected turn for the better. She had seen George Hamilton every day since their first dinner meeting. She wasn't sure where their relationship was going, nor did she have any expectations. He was good company and a true gentleman. Often, their time together was simply a stroll around town. He loved to walk and visit the areas overlooked by most of the tourists—like the old homes tucked away in the back streets of the historic town. He especially liked the back alleys where homeowners hid meticulously maintained gardens. He was wise in many ways, a sound knowledge in historical architecture was a forte. He was well versed in other areas of the arts as well. He especially liked music, explaining his strong fondness for April.

For a man so well-traveled, it surprised Jennifer that he even knew that Annapolis had its own symphony orchestra. The musicians were all volunteers, local men and women who loved to play but weren't accomplished enough to perform with a more renowned orchestra or had other careers that took precedence. On one occasion Hamilton escorted Jennifer to an evening performance on the Naval Academy grounds. Jennifer sheepishly admitted she had never heard the orchestra before. She *unsheepishly* admitted she was very impressed with what she heard. She even recognized a couple of the members as regulars at the *Riverboat Inn*. From their behavior at the bar during happy hour, she would have never guessed they were classical musicians.

And why should Jennifer have been surprised when she and Hamilton sat with the governor and his wife? Jennifer was fine with the whole thing until she realized the local media was covering the event. The possibilities regarding this were worrisome in that she never looked to be in the spotlight. Being in such a position would create a lot of questions—questions she wasn't interested in answering. She told her parents that she went out with George Hamilton a couple of times, emphasizing the companionship and discussions about April, and downplaying other parts of their relationship. Her mother did raise her eyebrows—a response, Jennifer was sure, to their age difference and nothing else. Otherwise her parents made no comments. Jennifer anticipated that would change when her picture appeared in the local paper the next morning.

She simply enjoyed the company of the man and the depth of his personality. He was from the old school, a true gentleman, polite and quick to ensure she was comfortable. He held the door for her. He held her chair in the restaurant. Most of all, he was willing to listen when she talked, regardless what else happened to be on his mind at the time. She never had a man do that before. Sure, Cliff and she talked a lot, but Cliff usually worked while he listened. Hamilton, on the other hand, looked at her the entire time. His eyes focused on her. It made her uncomfortable at first, but she soon adjusted to the attention, and looked forward to it. Yet, unlike other men who stared to undress, Hamilton's gaze sought to get into her soul. He never argued with her responses nor questioned her judgment—the only exception being the first time they had dinner aboard *Hamilton's Bench*, she asked for a glass of white wine when clearly the entrée called for red. And then, his response was simply a set of raised eyebrows followed by the appearance a short time later of a bottle of Chardonnay—a very good one at that. He chose a Maryland burgundy. She chose to remain silent about previous wine drinkers in her life.

Their conversation generally focused on one of three areas, politics, the arts and April—April being the usual start and finish of their encounter. Jennifer would update Hamilton on what she knew about April, which was usually the same—she was with Cliff and doing well. Hamilton would tell what he knew about the search for the sheriff—nothing new to report. He still hadn't shown up at his office, so the assumption was always that he was still in Maryland. Jennifer argued that as long as April was with Cliff and out on the water, she was safe. George Hamilton, on the other hand, assumed nothing, countering that a man like Sheriff Richmond should never be underestimated. Retaining the role of the gentleman, he'd say his piece and nothing more. The two did agree they couldn't do anything about April one way or the other. Both believed if they tried to get her to come back to Annapolis before she was ready, she'd simply run away again, and both knew she was very good at that. The consensus was to let her be as long as Cliff felt comfortable with the situation. Hamilton focused on finding the sheriff. He said more than once, for such a big man in such a small state, the sheriff was certainly hard to spot.

George Hamilton held up his end of the agreement over their first dinner together. He gave her a personal overview. He was fifty-two, younger than Jennifer expected. He was born and raised in New York City, Manhattan specifically, where he developed his love and appreciation for the finer things in life. Both his parents were dead. He had an alcoholic brother who he hadn't seen or talked to in several years. There were a couple far off cousins he'd lost contact with years ago. So like Jennifer (until April came along), he was without any extended family. All his college studies were at Harvard. He had never been married and had no children. There were a couple of serious relationships in his earlier years, but for the past ten or so, he'd been devoted to his work and to *Hamilton's Bench*. He also told her about his professional life, and why *Hamilton's Bench* was so named, something few outside his profession knew.

At the end of their first dinner, Jennifer was impressed. At the end of their second evening together, she was doubly so. There were many factors about the man she admired and found endearing. He was undoubtedly the richest man she had even met, and had the most to show for it. Yet his attitude toward it all was somewhat nonchalant.

Jennifer let the excitement build over these days. She figured it was partially Hamilton's attention towards her, and partially a diversion to keep her mind off April. Not knowing anything new about April was driving her batty. She reminded herself to be cautious. She fought off a fatalistic attitude that things were too good to be true and a bomb was lurking somewhere. Happily ever after endings only occurred in fairy tales, and her life was no Disney movie. She never knew where he got his information, but Old Man Hooper even warned her to be careful. He made the comment that she had gone from one extreme to the other in only a couple of days, to which she replied he was being silly. To which he offered that he was only making an objective observation. She listened; she understood and filed the advice away. Still, she was having fun; and for now, that was enough. She just wondered when the bomb would explode.

One thing that did bother her was Hamilton's seeming lack of physical attraction to her. There was always a kiss good night, but it was always polite and on the cheek. It was like he was playing the role of her uncle or something. In spite of that, the more she was around the man the more she was attracted to him. Daniel Baker had been several years her senior, but she never imagined herself with anyone George Hamilton's age. But she asked herself: why not? Did age really matter that much? She used to think it did, scoffing at the reports in the Hollywood newspapers about young starlets running off with older rich men. And what was the name of that young bimbo a few years ago who married the old man and inherited millions when he died? It made headlines for months. Jennifer couldn't think of her name.

"Stop it!" she scolded herself aloud. "God…" Hers and Hamilton's relationship wasn't anything like that.

She paused, continuing to stare at the blank computer screen. The part of her brain that dealt with creative writing remained fast asleep, unlike the part of her mind thinking about George Hamilton.

She shrugged her shoulders and continued talking aloud. "You have two choices, girl. You can wait and see, or you can ask."

She chuckled. She was never known for her patience.

A light flickered on in another part of her brain. The answer to one of her earlier questions floated to the surface. "Anna Nicole Smith," she mouthed. That was the name of the woman who married the millionaire. A second light flickered in the back of her mind. She blinked and focused on the screen. Suddenly her fingers started moving. Words began pouring forth onto the computer screen. Her smile widened. Sometimes you just have to be patient, she told herself.

And so she was.

158

Sheriff Richmond pulled the curtain back enough to see across the street. The patrol car that had been there the last thirty minutes finally left. He breathed a sigh of relief and opened the curtain wider to dare a glance up and down the street. Nothing else looked suspicious, although he knew that something didn't have to look suspicious to be suspicious. He closed the curtain and made his way across the darkened room. He flipped on the light by the bed and grabbed the remote attached to the bedside table by a thin cable. Turning on the television, he was just in time for the evening news.

The first story was about a murder, the second, about a fire. Nothing was mentioned about himself or the girl. He wasn't sure if that was good or bad. No bodies had been found floating in the waters of the Chesapeake Bay. Did this support the information from the bounty hunter that the girl was alive? Did no news mean good news? Or did it simply not spark the interest of the local news editor? He doubted bodies found would be ignored.

It had been three days since he heard from the bounty hunter and five since the last sighting of the girl in Cape Charles. That wasn't unusual nor unexpected, but it was still annoying as hell. Where was the bitch and why hadn't the bounty hunter found her? After all this time, all this energy and all this money, she had disappeared again. The bounty hunter claimed she was on a sailboat with a boy, but it was unsubstantiated. A good guess, a good assumption maybe, but not a fact. The only thing for certain, she was still on the loose. They were close, but they'd been close before. Only this time his instinct gave a different message. This time the fox would be caught... and soon.

He glanced at the plastic encased alarm clock sitting on the bedside table. It was also bolted down. It was past five o'clock, too late to call into the office. His deputies were loyal and hardworking, but only to a point. When it was time to go home, or to the local watering hole, no one had better be in the doorway. The sheriff cursed under his breath. He knew he was close to crossing the line of neglecting his duties. But why should he give a shit? Soon as he took care of the girl, he'd get back to work and patch things up.

In the meantime, maybe it was better if he didn't call in. That way no one knew where he was. Cellular phones could be traced. He told himself not to get paranoid. He had gone to great lengths to remain incognito. He bought some regular clothes and changed his hair color. He even wore a pair of cheap glasses. Much to the animal's dismay, he was keeping Bullet hidden, and he had parked his car in a garage on the Eastern Shore and was now driving a rented Taurus. He couldn't do much about his size, although he certainly saw enough huskies running around the streets of Maryland. Overall, he thought he did a pretty good job of losing his identity. So yes, not calling in was the right decision.

Now all he had to do was find the girl.

He contemplated calling the bounty hunter. He knew that would be a waste of time. He'd know something when there was something to know. The man loved to tease clients with information as a way of stalling for time until something definitive arose. Then he didn't waste any time.

The sheriff cursed under his breath again. "Where the hell is she?" he said. He looked at the television which continued to spew out the news—all of which had nothing to do with the part of his life that mattered at the moment.

He turned the TV off, grabbed his glasses from the bed and headed toward the bathroom to get Bullet. It was time for their afternoon walk.

"I'll have you soon, bitch," he snarled.

And so he would.

159

The bounty hunter moved his hands across the paper to get the wrinkles out of the chart. His briefcase held one corner, a coffee cup, another. He had taped the bottom two corners directly to the desk. He stared at the outline of the Chesapeake Bay. He found Cape Charles, and then across the bay to the cove they had been in the night before—or rather, the reported cove. He had not gotten over there in time to confirm the report. His eyes moved slowly up and down the waterway. Where would they have gone? He scanned the chart in detail. Years of experience taught him to take his time. Details were often overlooked in a rush. While his boating experience was limited to fishing on a lake with his father when he was a young boy and an occasional charter boat trip, the bounty hunter was an experienced pilot, both in fixed wings and helicopters. He learned to fly the latter in the marines. Surviving two tours of duty in Vietnam made him a very good pilot. It also made him a very good hunter. He knew how to read a chart.

Spread out beside the chart was a series of weather maps from the last few days. Earlier in the week—the day the boat left Cape Charles—the bay winds were out of the southwest. It made sense if they sailed across the bay to the western shore. The past couple of days, however, the winds had shifted and were now coming from the north. The best sailing would be up the bay. The bounty hunter ran his finger along the main shipping channel which also headed almost due north—about 150 miles to the top. A pretty good bet, he concluded. *Guesstimating* the boat made six knots, six nautical miles per hour, they were probably already at their next destination—their next hiding hole. The question was where?

He surveyed the numerous rivers on the western shore of the upper bay. There were several good places to hide, but each was in close proximity to the sprawling suburbs of Baltimore. The Eastern Shore was much more desolate and inviting. There were more options, more rivers from which to choose. He focused on the two furthest north—the Northeast and the Sassafras Rivers. While they were both several miles long and had many coves in which to hide, they were relatively close together as the crow flies. Inspection by boat would take time. Inspection by air, however, was a different story.

He picked up the daily weather maps and studied them a bit more closely. Thunderstorms were a real possibility. Flying through them wasn't a problem—he had been in worse in Nam. Visibility was the main concern. It was still his best bet. He glanced at his watch. It was a little after 4:00 p.m. He could be packed and on the road in fifteen minutes. That would put him up there just around sunset, maybe sooner if he pushed it. He might even be able to get in a flight before it was too dark.

The thought of once again being in the air excited him. He rolled up the chart and gathered the rest of the papers. He would make the calls looking for a chopper once he was in the car.

He thought about letting the sheriff know his plan, but quickly nixed the idea, as the sheriff had not been too congenial during their last conversation.

"Screw him," the bounty hunter said. He could wait.

160

April grabbed the stainless steel handhold forward of the wheel as the boat heeled even more in response to a gust of wind. It was not the first time in the past hour the starboard rail dipped below the water. It didn't bother April that the boat was already hard over on her side. The rail in the water just made it more difficult to maintain course. Cliff had the sails set tight to make maximum hull speed, but April wasn't complaining. The storm crossing the bay from the west was rapidly catching up to them. She guessed they had about fifteen minutes at the most. Cliff said he wanted to make it to the Sassafras, but that was several miles away. She ignored thinking about the consequences of what was going to happen once the storm hit.

She glanced off to the right as the *Mona Lisa* came back to her normal fifteen degree heel. That they were less than a half mile off shore made her nervous. She saw a beach ahead and a man playing fetch with his dog in the water. She looked at the compass. She was holding steady on the course Cliff had given her, although she wished she could turn a few degrees to port. That was impossible as they were already tight into the wind. She also had to make sure they didn't fall off to the right as that would bring them even closer to shore.

Another gust of wind hit the boat and the starboard rail again dipped into the water. She struggled to hold the boat on course. Cliff came back into the cockpit after getting the mainsail ready to reef.

"How you doing?" he asked, a cheerful note to his voice. He seemed oblivious to the dark clouds attacking from the west.

"Oh, just peachy," April snapped, continuing to struggle against the forces trying to push the boat toward shore.

"Feel like you're flying?"

"With one wing in the water."

Cliff half-stepped, half-slid to the downside of the cockpit. Propping his foot against the gunwale, he unwound the jib sheet from the wench and let the line out a couple inches. The tension against the sails softened and the rail rose out of the water.

"Thank you," April said.

"No problem."

April pointed toward the shoreline. "Aren't we awfully close to shore? The depth finder is reading plenty of water, but…"

"Believe it or not, we're right on the edge of the shipping channel," Cliff said. "It runs close to shore along here."

"Ships get this close?"

"When you're standing on the beach over there, you swear you can hit 'em with a rock when they go by."

"What is that beach?"

"Part of Tolchester…. one of the many little towns along the Eastern Shore that survives because of the fishing and crabbing trade."

"There a place to dock?" April inquired.

"A small harbor and marina." Cliff looked toward the oncoming storm. "You and I are probably thinking the same thing."

"Then what are we waiting for?"

Cliff pointed toward the south end of the beach. "The entrance is narrow and protected on both sides by rock jetties. It's still a half mile away. It would be good to get out of the storm, but I suspect just about the time we hit the harbor, the storm'll hit us."

"Can't we turn on the motor?"

"We're already at maximum hull speed."

April looked at the instruments lined across the top of the cabin entrance. "Yeah, I guess we are." She again looked over at the beach. This was where local knowledge played a big role. She hoped local knowledge also meant a good understanding of the weather. She'd been sailing in some strong winds in the Bahamas, but they had always been on sunny days. She had never been in a storm aboard a sailboat underway. She didn't want to add that to her résumé today. "What's the plan?"

"We can get the jib in anytime with the roller furling, and I've already got the main ready to reef." Cliff let the jib sheet out another inch. "What do you think?"

"About what?"

"What do you want to do?"

April looked at the storm and then at the harbor entrance that was now in full view. They were definitely big rocks. "You're the captain," she said.

Cliff laughed. "A lame excuse." A pleading look came across April's face. Cliff continued. "I want to be sure you'll be okay if we ride out the storm."

"It'll be my first."

"There's a first time for everything," Cliff said.

April didn't reply.

Cliff continued. "Let's go ahead and reef the main. Then I'll go dig out the foul weather gear and we can get dressed. By then it'll be time to bring in the jib."

While Cliff made his way forward, April's attention was diverted to another gust of wind. Even with the jib sheet loosened, the starboard rail once again dipped below the surface. The *Mona Lisa* struggled, but came back much easier this time. The gust was the strongest yet. April wondered if they had time to do everything Cliff had outlined.

She rose to her toes so she could see above the canvas dodger protecting the hatch. Cliff had already put on an inflatable life vest and was hooked into one of the two safety lines running along the gunwales. She watched as he worked. He had one arm wrapped over the boom, the other untying the halyard attached to the mainsail. Surefooted, he worked effortlessly, a pleasant expression on his face. He seemed unfazed by the *Mona Lisa* bobbing back and forth beneath his feet. It was simply a part of his day.

April propped her right foot up against the starboard seat in hopes of getting more leverage on the ship's wheel. Mr. Hamilton taught her that the various forces pushing against a boat were tremendous, but a skilled sailor used those forces to his advantage. It required the balancing of the wind, boat direction and set of the sails. She smiled at Cliff's comment a moment ago. Yes, she did feel like she was flying. Yes, there were a lot of forces pushing against the boat. And yes…

She let out a soft laugh. No, she was not using these forces to her advantage. She was simply hanging on for dear life. The boat was basically steering itself.

She kept her eyes on Cliff as he prepared to drop the main halyard. On his signal, she brought the *Mona Lisa* directly into the wind, causing both sails to luff. As the mainsail dropped part way down the mast, Cliff made his way to the back of the boom where he hooked the metal ring sewn into the luff of the sail over the hook on the boom. He brought the main halyard with him, so as soon as the ring was in place, he pulled the mainsail taught. Securing the line, he nodded to April who brought the *Mona Lisa* back off the wind to her previous course. The mainsail quickly filled with air. The jib followed a moment later, snapping like a gigantic towel directed at someone's behind. Cliff turned his attention to the down ties he had prepared and lashed the bottom of the mainsail to the boom. Satisfied with the reefed sail, he hopped back into the cockpit. He unhooked the sheet to the jib and began rolling in the sail.

"Fall off the wind a hair," he said. April did, thus taking the pressure off the sail and making it easier and faster to get the jib rolled up. He again nodded and April again brought the boat back on course.

The storm was now only a stone's throw away. Giving a hurried look, Cliff disappeared below deck. When he returned, donned in a full set of rain gear, he took the wheel and said, "I laid out some foul weather gear for you on the couch. It may be a little big, but it'll work. Just remember to put your safety harness on the outside."

When it was her turn to go below, she didn't hesitate. By the time she returned to the cockpit, the boat was dancing the jitterbug. April had been in rough water sailing with Mr. Hamilton, but never anything this choppy. Ocean waves were certainly a lot different than those on the bay. They were now sailing under the reefed main only. Even with that, the *Mona Lisa* was heeled over with the starboard rail inches out of the water. She had the hatch half shut when there was a commotion from below. Chessie, not quite as surefooted as Cliff, climbed up on deck. She took a look around and curled up on the starboard seat.

"She doesn't like it below deck when it's too rough," Cliff explained.

"Does anyone?"

"Makes it tough to scramble eggs on a griddle, that's all."

"Makes it tough to do a lot of things," April said, pulling the collar of her raincoat tighter around her neck. April finished securing the hatch. The sky behind them darkened. Bolts of lightning flashed giving the appearance of strobe lights. Loud claps of thunder roared overhead. "What's the plan?" April asked.

"Steady as she goes, I guess. I'd like to tack and head more into the storm—make the ride a little easier—but I don't want to get out into the shipping channel."

"Sounds like a good idea to me," April said.

"Wanna steer?"

April started to say no, but hesitated. Maybe this wasn't going to be so bad after all. Then again, maybe if her attention was diverted, she wouldn't realize how bad it really was. "Sure." She made her way to the back of the cockpit and stood beside Cliff.

"Make sure you hook up to the boat," Cliff said, motioning to the safety line attached to her life vest.

Hooking onto the portside jack line, she took the wheel from Cliff.

Cliff let go and moved to the side. A gust of wind pushed the boat over. The bow turned off the wind as well. April struggled to hold control of the wheel, but the forces of nature were too much. "I'm a little afraid here," she shouted above the wind.

Cliff moved to April's side. "Don't fight her too much. Wait for the gust to pass. She'll come back on course on her own. It may not look like it, but we've got plenty of water to our starboard."

April stole a glance in that direction. She hadn't realized they were now even closer to shore. She estimated less than a hundred yards. The gust passed, the boat righted herself, and they were back on course.

"Thanks," April said.

Cliff laughed. "No problem."

"Why are you laughing at me?" April demanded. "I'm not as strong as you, sorry. Besides, the winds are a lot different here, and I'm not used to them."

"I'm not laughing at that. Don't worry, there're times when I'm alone I could use a little help as well."

"Then what's so funny?"

"What you said about being afraid."

"Well, I am."

"Okay, but what's the worst that could happen?"

"We could end up in the water in the middle of a bad storm."

"Yeah…"

Wiping away the rain that was now pelting her face, she said, "What's your point?"

"At least this time you have a life jacket on."

"You're sick," April said, but she smiled. "What about the boat if we both fall overboard?"

"The *Mona Lisa* has what's called a windward helm. If you let go of the wheel, the boat'll swing directly into the wind, and come to a near-dead stop. That's a safety design so that if you do happen to fall overboard, you'd be able to get back without a whole lot of trouble."

"Otherwise the boat would keep sailing away?"

"Exactly. But don't forget you're hooked into the boat anyway. So if you do fall overboard, you're not going to go anywhere."

They stood side by side, April with two hands on the wheel, Cliff with one hand on the wheel and the other on the handhold. It was raining harder now. Lightning was flashing on a regular basis. Claps of thunder followed directly behind one another, rolling across the sky like waves in the ocean. The water around the boat had churned up to a four foot chop. Whitecaps pounded the hull, trying to knock her off course. But the *Mona Lisa* held steady.

Chessie seemed unconcerned. Except for an occasional bucket of rain that was blown under the dodger where she had curled into a ball, she was unaffected by the storm. Her head lying on an outstretched paw, she watched her master and newfound friend.

The whole scene was strange to April. A major storm whirled around them. The *Mona Lisa* rolled, bobbed and bounced in response and the cable stays holding the mast whistled in protest of being stretched so tight. She had been afraid earlier, but with Cliff's calm demeanor and him at her side, she felt a sudden sense of security. Her anxiety level dropped. In spite of the turmoil surrounding them, she also felt a sense of calm. She realized he was standing next to her—*right* next to her. Instinct told her to put some space between them. He was too close!

Only she stayed put, her feet firmly glued to the deck.

She wanted to look at him, but she was afraid. Of what she would see? Or of what she would not see? Of what she would feel? Or of what she wouldn't feel?

It was strange, a feel-good strange.

There was a warmth in her stomach she hadn't felt in a long time. She tried remembering when. A gust of wind struck the mainsail, and her attention was diverted. A sheet of rain pelted her face. She felt the droplets trickling down her neck. Water pelting her face—water running down her neck. Suddenly, her knees felt weak as her thoughts returned to the time in the motel with Danny. How did she feel then? How did she feel now? She wasn't sure.

Danny used to say that when something happened to you, if it didn't make your toes tingle, it was best to put it behind you, otherwise, the past might distract you from what was happening up ahead. When you were out in the wilderness, that could prove dangerous.

Out in the wilderness… she'd been in that environment for almost two years. She had survived because she followed Danny's advice. She never looked back. She concentrated on what was ahead, taking things one step at a time.

However, her mind would only allow her to do that for so long. Memories of the past still bubbled to the surface. Sometimes these came forth with a good reason. Other times they were triggered by something totally unrelated—like being caught out in a storm on a sailboat—like water trickling down her neck—like a warm feeling in her stomach.

She told herself not to go there—not to open boxes in the attic that had been sealed for so long. Her subconscious wouldn't listen. On one hand, there was the night with Eddie in the car. Two nights later there was the thing with Danny in the shower. Such contrasting events, such contrasting feelings. How could things have been going so well and then suddenly turned so bad? How could she have been so stupid? To think Eddie would be any different with her than with any of the other girls he dated. Stupid, stupid, stupid!

Regardless of the reasons, regardless of the answers to the many questions, it had happened, and she was still paying the price. Two years later, she was on a sailboat in the middle of a storm, standing next to a guy she barely knew. Danny's advice was to look ahead, not behind. He jokingly added the only exception was if you were being chased by a big bear, then you'd better know it was coming.

April wiped the water from her eyes and brought her concentration back to the present. She rose to her toes to get a better look over the dodger. It was raining so hard, visibility was almost nil. The wind was blowing well over thirty knots with gusts even higher. She didn't dare look at the air speed indicator. She didn't want to know. She just held onto the wheel with all her strength.

She suddenly noticed something out of the corner of the left eye. Her head snapped in that direction. A big black wall was moving right beside them. "Cliff!" she screamed, her eyes fixed on the container ship passing by.

"I see it, sweetie," he said. His voice was so calm. "Don't worry, it's in the channel and we're not."

"But it's right there." She pointed as if Cliff couldn't see the mass of steel threatening to block what little light was left in the sky.

"I see it. We're both running the same course."

April wasn't convinced. The ship was too close. On a clear day she'd be able to count the barnacles on her side.

"We're going to get her wake, but we'll be okay."

"Okay! We're about to be run over by a ship, and all you can say is that we'll be okay?" Her voice was near hysteria.

His voice remained calm. "I saw it on radar when I was down below. I knew it was coming."

"And you didn't tell me!"

"I didn't want to frighten you. Besides…"

"Besides what?" she snapped. Her hysteria switched to anger.

"I wanted to see how close you were paying attention to what was going on around you."

"You were testing me?"

"You said this was the first storm you were ever in."

"You—"

He took one arm off the wheel and placed it around her waist, pulling her close to him. "You have to keep a lookout in all directions."

She started to speak, but couldn't. In all directions, she thought. You have to watch out for the bear behind you. Her anger eroded quickly as his words dug deep into her soul.

Cliff interrupted her train of thought. "Let's fall off and take this wake on the stern." He turned the wheel and the *Mona Lisa* veered to starboard. The boat took the wake well and soon they were back on course. "That wasn't so bad, was it?" Cliff said.

April didn't reply. His words continued to drill through her. They had almost just been eaten by a bear, and she hadn't seen it—just like times in the past. What other bears were lurking in the woods? She looked at Cliff. Her knees buckled.

Cliff sensed the weakness in her legs as the arm around her waist tightened. His grasp was firm yet gentle. She felt his fingers grab the slippery material of her rain gear. "You okay?"

She snapped back to attention and forced her knees to lock into place. "Yeah," she responded weakly. "I lost my sea legs a moment."

He started to let his hand drop. She reached up and covered it with her own. "That's okay," she said, her voice regaining its strength. "It feels good." His arm remained around her waist.

The beach faded from view as Tolchester passed to starboard. While they hadn't really changed course, it did seem they were further away from the shore. This made April more comfortable. She readjusted her feet and pushed her life vest up to take some of the weight off her shoulders. She checked the lifeline to make sure she was still hooked into the boat. Yes, she decided, it felt good. She felt safe. If she did go overboard, it wouldn't be too bad. Like Cliff said, she still had her life jacket on.

Only she didn't want to go overboard. She didn't want to leave Cliff's side. She didn't want the storm to end. She liked being in the shower with him. Her mind began to think of things, things that had been off limits the past couple of years. Like flowers responding to much needed rain, her imagination blossomed. A day or so before, she might have snafued these thoughts. Today, in the rain, in the shower with Cliff, she let her mind go. Her toes began to tingle.

This time she anticipated that her knees might buckle.

161

"What's the word?" Hamilton said, handing Jennifer a glass of white wine.

She took it, nodded her head in appreciation and set it on a coaster atop the table. They were sitting on the back deck off his office. It was one of three such decks aboard the boat. "Cliff called me yesterday morning and told me they were leaving the Patuxent River. He said where they were going would be based on the wind. Forecasts called for it to be out of north so he guessed they'd be heading up the bay. He said something about the Sassafras River, but would let me know once they got closer."

Hamilton sat across from his guest and looked over the harbor. It was a spectacular view. The sun was setting in the west. There was a stiff five to ten knot breeze that took some of the heat out of the air. The sky was clear except for a few high cumulus clouds.

That was directly behind the boat. He turned and looked over his shoulder. "A storm's coming up the bay. I hope they're where they want to be by now."

"I'm sure they are," Jennifer said. "Cliff strikes me as a very conservative sailor."

"April's become quite a sailor herself," Hamilton said, taking a swallow of the scotch he was holding. "To my knowledge, though, she's never been in a storm. Your Chesapeake Bay has quite a reputation for sudden squalls."

"That it does." Jennifer took a sip of her wine. "But I'm sure they'll be okay. In some ways, maybe they're safer on the water."

"That may be the case, but it's no longer acceptable to me."

Jennifer hesitated. Up until now, she had been careful not to confront Hamilton about anything. She had no specific reason for this except a desire not to ruin anything. She chose her words and her vocal tone carefully. "What's the alternative?"

The man hesitated as he took another sip of his drink. "Go get her. That way we'll know she's safe."

Intentionally or not, he left himself open for a strong rebuke as this present mess started aboard *Hamilton's Bench*. Jennifer kept her mouth shut, however, figuring the man sitting across from her wouldn't let the same thing happen twice. Jennifer acknowledged that she'd feel more comfortable with April back in Annapolis. The question would be April's reaction to all this.

"Then let's do it," she said.

"Do what?" Hamilton said, setting down his glass.

"Let's go get her."

Hamilton laughed. "Just like that, huh?"

"Why not?"

The man hesitated. "When's Cliff supposed to call in next?"

"When they get to Georgetown... that's at the head of the Sassafras."

"We'll go then."

Jennifer was somewhat surprised that he was taking her suggestion. "How?"

"Well, they're out on the water, so we'll need a boat."

"No kidding!" Jennifer returned the tease. Her expression turned serious. "Can *Hamilton's Bench* get up the Sassafras?"

"Actually, the Sassafras is quite deep. Besides, I have a thirteen foot Boston Whaler we can use once we get closer."

"What if she refuses to come with us?"

"Well, between then and now, you'll have to come up with a plan to address that."

"Me!"

"Yes, I have to focus on getting the boat ready."

Jennifer laughed. "You're playing with me."

Hamilton smiled. "No, I'm just trying to throw some responsibility onto you."

"Same thing, isn't it?"

Hamilton shrugged his shoulders.

"At least you're honest," Jennifer said.

His face turned serious. "That's one thing you'll never have to worry about with me, I'm honest to the core."

"Unusual in your profession, isn't it?"

His smile returned. "Now who's playing with who?"

"Is it who or whom?"

Hamilton laughed. Jennifer was glad. She had broken a barrier she had previously been unwilling to challenge. He was able to be teased. She stared at him as his attention was diverted by a loud clap of thunder in the distance. She felt her heart pick up its pace. Her toes curled up. The thunder may have been in the distance, but the bolt of lightning was running through her body. She considered herself a cautious person, but she didn't wait too long or mince words when she wanted to know something. "Can I ask a question?" she said.

She had his attention. Their eyes met. He looked at her deeply. To block the blush she felt across her face, Jennifer put her hand up and brushed back a strand of hair.

"Don't do that," he said. The tone of his voice was more asking than directing.

"Do what?"

"Push your hair back."

"Why not?"

"I like it when the wind blows through your hair."

"You do?"

Hamilton nodded.

"Why?"

"It symbolizes your imperfection."

Jennifer's eyes widened as a frown crossed her face. She had heard that before. Before she could decide to be angry or laugh, Hamilton continued. "That's what I like about you. You don't pretend to be perfect." Hamilton paused. "You are who you are. You don't hide behind some fictional character."

She laughed, both as a defense mechanism and at what struck her as funny. "Who else would I try to be?"

Hamilton leaned back in his chair. "You have no clue."

"Fill me in." She watched him debate how to respond.

He took a sip of his drink. "You're a rarity as a woman, Jennifer… and again, that's a compliment. You're the first person who's come on this boat in a long time who hasn't tried to impress me into believing they're somebody they're not."

"Why would anyone do that?"

His hand swung in a circular motion. "People feel they have to rise to the level of all this because they're insecure with who they really are. You see, people who come on board *Hamilton's Bench* usually have one of two reactions: they're either overwhelmed with the size and immediately start thinking about the cost, or they look at her for the beautiful boat she is."

"*Hamilton's Bench* spews power and wealth," Jennifer said without thinking.

"Power and wealth is only in the mind of the beholder," the yacht's owner said.

Jennifer warned herself to be careful; she was stepping on thin ice. "Well, power may be a perceived asset, but the wealth side of the coin is pretty obvious to anyone who knows anything about boats. Now, I don't hold it for or against you, but this baby cost a whole lot of money to buy, and a whole lot of money to keep up. And that doesn't include the cost of your wine cellar." She picked up her glass and swirled the liquid around. She smelt the aroma and then took a sip.

Hamilton smiled as he spoke. "If you define wealth as zeroes on the left side of the decimal point, then fine. But to me, wealth is so much more. I acknowledge there have been times when I've used *Hamilton's Bench* like the President uses the Oval Office, to pressure, to intimidate, to get what I want. But that's because whoever my opponent may be at that particular moment is too stupid to see that the Oval Office is just another office in the White House or that *Hamilton's Bench* is just another boat in the water."

"Power is more than perception," Jennifer argued. She made sure her tone remained pleasant. "After all, the President of the United States has a lot of bullets backing up what he says, and I'm sure you have ammunition behind you when you talk."

"What kind of ammunition do you think I have?" Hamilton challenged.

"Knowledge," Jennifer said without hesitation but quickly added, "For the record, when I first came aboard *Hamilton's Bench*, I was overwhelmed with her size, and I was somewhat intimidated. And yes, I did immediately think about the cost. That's a natural reaction. But I also got past that and saw her for what she is… one of the most beautiful yachts in the world."

"She makes the top-ten list every year," Hamilton boasted.

"Now, you're starting to sound like one of *those* people."

The man laughed.

Jennifer continued. "But I would guess that's more pride coming out than a need for power."

The smile disappeared. "You do understand, don't you?"

Thin ice crossed her mind. "I try."

He started to say something else, but stopped. "Forgive me for getting you off the track. You wanted to ask me something."

Jennifer regrouped her thoughts. "That's okay."

"No, it's not. I got you off track, and I'm sorry. Please go ahead."

She hesitated. "Where are we going?"

"Going, as in after April?"

Jennifer frowned. "No."

"Then…?"

"We… where are *we* going?"

"As in you and I?"

Jennifer nodded.

"Where do you want to go?"

"I asked you first."

"That's no fair," he argued.

"Why not?"

"Because I own the boat." A smile quickly formed.

She laughed. "And a beautiful boat it is. But remember, I'm no longer intimidated."

Her expression turned serious. "Now, answer the question, please…"

She expected him to look away, but he didn't. His eye contact only intensified.

"I don't know." he said matter-of-factly.

"Fair enough."

"It's the truth."

"Nothing but the truth," Jennifer quipped nervously.

Hamilton's smile widened. "I can offer an explanation regardless of the indecisiveness."

"I'm all ears."

Hamilton looked away. "Thanks to a lot of things, mostly self-imposed pressure, I've focused on nothing in life except succeeding at whatever I was doing. I focused especially on my education. I couldn't get enough. The more information I absorbed, the more I wanted. It started in high school and was like that my whole time at Harvard."

Jennifer waved an arm in a semicircle. "The effort has certainly paid off."

"Yes, but at what price?"

"I don't understand."

Hamilton continued. "I'm not complaining, mind you, but I have no life other than my work."

"You seem so relaxed. I'm sure you work hard when you work, but you play hard, too. You told me that yourself."

He shrugged his shoulders. "I do play hard, but that's to fulfill the life I don't have."

"Life, meaning?"

Hamilton hesitated. Jennifer could see he was deciding whether to continue or not. She saw the same thing in the emergency room. Patients would start to tell their stories and then stop halfway through. Customers at the restaurant would do the same. Only at the *Riverboat Inn*, a couple of drinks usually loosened the tongues. "If you'd rather not talk about it," the ex-nurse, part-time bartender said.

"Oh no," Hamilton said. "It's not that. I'm just not quite sure how to say it."

"How about in English? That's the only language I know."

The man laughed. "I bet you're an awfully good nurse."

She sat back in her seat. "Why do you say that?" she said defensively.

"You know how to talk to people."

"You're obviously very good at that, too."

"There's a difference—you talk *to* people. I talk *at* them."

Jennifer gave him an encouraging smile. "Well, whether you're talking at me or to me, please continue?"

He took a sip of his drink. "I've met a lot of people in my life. I know a lot of people and I even have a pretty good pile of friends."

"Bigger than your pile of enemies?"

"Don't toy with me, young lady."

Jennifer smiled. She was glad he could take a tease.

Hamilton continued. "What I've never been able to find is a companion."

"You mean like a girlfriend." She immediately cursed herself for the last sentence.

"Even more than that," he said unabated. "Maybe a better word is soul mate. I've had girlfriends—the relationships never last very long. And please don't think I'm acting cocky or bragging in any way, but I'm sure I could call any number of women I know and they'd be down here in a heartbeat. Only, they wouldn't come to be with me. They'd come to be with what I symbolize."

"Gold diggers," Jennifer said.

"That's one term."

"If you think that's what I am, you're wrong."

Hamilton held up both hands. "No, Jennifer; you're different."

Jennifer hesitated. "How can you be so sure?"

Hamilton started to argue, and then realized Jennifer had him. "We all make mistakes. Boat captains just aren't one of my areas of expertise."

"There's always a surprise at the end of the rainbow, and it's not always good."

Hamilton pondered the point. "That's true, I guess."

"Tends to make you very cautious and conservative."

"True again."

"I've never been one to complain about being cautious."

"Conservative?"

Now who was teasing whom, Jennifer wondered. She gave him a smirk. "Depends on who I'm with."

He returned the look. "How about if we come to an agreement?"

Jennifer told herself to keep an open mind as caution flags were raised. "Go ahead."

"One step at a time."

Jennifer paused. "With no sidestepping."

"No sidestepping."

"Always open and always the truth."

Hamilton smiled. "Nothing but."

They laughed together.

The storm approached Annapolis at a rapid pace. While the rain was only minutes away, the wind announced what was to come in a most impolite fashion. They rose to their feet, grabbed their glasses, and hurried inside. Hamilton took a quick glance around to make sure there wasn't anything left that could blow away. Then he closed the sliding door and curtains. The office was now almost completely dark. He turned and stumbled into Jennifer, almost spilling his drink down the front of her. "Sorry," he said. Then he laughed.

"What's so funny?" Jennifer demanded.

"I don't think pouring my drink all over you is what either of us meant by the next step."

Jennifer emptied her glass and set it on the desk behind her. Hamilton did the same. Their arms encircled each other's necks. He stepped toward her. Any escape for Jennifer was blocked by the desk pressing against her backside. But escaping wasn't her intention.

Their lips met. They took the first step towards the next step. They were about to take another when there was a knock at the door. Both were caught off guard and stopped cold in their tracks. With much disappointment, Jennifer pushed Hamilton gently away. "I thought there wasn't anyone else on board."

"I thought so, too. I gave the crew the night off. Maybe someone came back early."

"Do they have to check in?" Her sarcasm was used to hide her disappointment. It had been such a wonderful moment. It had been such a wonderful kiss. She was sure what was about to come next would be the same.

Hamilton laughed. "No, no one has to check in." He reached across her and turned on the desk light. His fingers hesitated, caressing her shoulder. He pulled away and headed for the door. Jennifer walked over and opened the curtains. The storm descended on the area.

Hamilton opened the door to face Louis.

"Sorry to bother you, sir," the aide said. "But there are a couple people outside asking for Ms. Blackstone."

Jennifer looked over her shoulder, nodded at Louis and made eye contact with Hamilton. "The only people who know I'm here are my folks."

"It's not them. Two people I've never seen before."

Jennifer walked to the shore side window and looked down onto the pier. "Oh my God," she said.

"Who is it?" Hamilton said, moving toward her. She stepped aside so he could see for himself.

One visitor was obvious. Hamilton was unclear about the other. Jennifer quickly explained.

162

The line of thunderstorms carried away any chance of improvement in the heat and humidity. With the sun setting over the region, it was as muggy as earlier in the day. For all intents and purposes, the storm made matters worse. That wasn't unusual around the Chesapeake Bay. Just when you thought it couldn't get any stickier, a storm came along and proved you wrong.

The bounty hunter didn't complain. He'd made good time with and without the rain. And with the post-storm sky clear and calm, he would indeed have time to make a preliminary flight over the region, which he was about to do. He reached to his right and pushed the throttle forward. The noise overhead increased both in intensity and pitch. When the tachometer read a steady 3000, he pulled back on the stick cradled between his legs. The helicopter hesitated as gravity struggled to keep its grasp. The powerful twin motors won the battle as man and steel lifted off without further interruption. He rose to an altitude of twenty feet then turned the machine toward the west. He pulled back on the stick and the helicopter continued to climb. Satisfied he was clear of anything below, he nudged the machine forward. The bird continued to rise as it headed directly into the setting sun.

He figured he had about an hour before official sunset and another thirty minutes before it would be too dark to see anything below—more than enough time to do a preliminary look-see. And why not he figured, he might even get lucky and find what he was looking for. In his business, luck often played a major role.

163

Cliff found the landmarks he had made note of earlier on opposite shores and waited for the *Mona Lisa* to drift until they were directly abeam of one another on each side of the boat. When the two marks and the boat were lined up, he secured the anchor line to the bow cleat. Satisfied the anchor was set, he checked the lines running into the roller furling. They didn't use the jib in the storm, but the lines took a pounding against the cable stays. He saw no signs of chaffing and moved back to the boom to check the various lines and halyards in that area.

At the height of the storm, wind gusts rose over forty knots and wave heights approached five feet. Not surprising, the *Mona Lisa* held up well. The rigging was intact, the bilge was dry and he saw no signs of leaky hatches or windows. All in all, he was happy.

In addition, the strong wind helped them make good time up the bay. He wasn't as far up the Sassafras as he would have liked, but there were several coves right off the mouth of the river that would give them shelter for the night. He planned to move to a more secluded spot in the morning, but first he wanted to go upriver to Georgetown for supplies and to refill the water tanks. This would allow them a good shower. He certainly felt hot and sticky from the day's sail and from being in foul weather gear for over an hour. He imagined April felt the same.

Satisfied all was shipshape on deck, he looked over at the north shore and whistled for Chessie who had gone to the small beach to take care of business and to explore the area. Cliff hoped she didn't come back with any unwanted dinner such as a bird or squirrel. He put his fingers up to his mouth and whistled loudly.

The loud shriek caught Chessie's attention. The dog hesitated as she was indeed on the scent of something, most likely a rabbit. But she obeyed, splashed into the water and swam toward the boat. Cliff thought about jumping in to take a swim with her, but decided against it. Maybe later when it was dark. Maybe he could get April to go, too.

He was about to yell out to Chessie to hurry it along when his attention was diverted by a loud noise that came over the trees. A few seconds later a helicopter came into view. It flew right at the *Mona Lisa* and seemed to stop and hover a few feet from the stern. In actuality, it was more than a few feet, but it was close enough Cliff could feel the wash from the prop as the blades spun rapidly in the evening air. Cliff didn't know much about helicopters, but it looked like one of those traffic and weather choppers the news stations used. He put his hand over his eyes to block the wind and to try and see who was in the pilot's seat. Blocking the wind was doable, however, his vision was limited by the fact that the helicopter came at them directly from the sun. As Cliff knew nothing about military strategy, an approach directly from the sun meant nothing to him. He just wondered why a chopper was flying around this time of day, and why would they be interested in him? If he was paranoid, the answer would be obvious, but Cliff wasn't the type. He decided it was one of the search and rescue helicopters from the Department of Natural Resources and they were simply checking things out after the storm. Or maybe they were looking for someone who had put out a distress call. In any case, he waved to let the pilot know he was okay. Through the glare of the sun he thought he saw a return motion of the hand and then the helicopter spun on its axis and headed back over the trees.

Cliff turned his attention to Chessie who by now had made it to the swim ladder. He watched as the dog carefully positioned her hind feet on the one rung beneath the water and then pushed upward, sort of propelling herself onto the small swim platform molded into the stern of the boat. While she didn't get any style points, her methodology worked. From the swim platform, she was able to clamber into the cockpit without difficulty. Cliff laughed each time he watched her do this. It was something she learned on her own. Amazing, he thought.

He glanced over the trees. The helicopter was gone, the silence in the cove, restored. Their surroundings were now broken only by the birds settling down for the night and the crickets warming their hind legs. A few lightning bugs were already wandering around the boat, and while they didn't add any actual sound to the symphony of nature, their flashes of yellow-orange served to show that nature's changing of the guard was an intricate embroidery of sight and sound. Cliff stood and gazed at his surroundings. Sunset was his favorite time of day. Doing what he was doing now was his favorite thing to do. It was as if all actions throughout the day were simply to bring nature to this point. It was also symbolic for him as an artist in that his work outside the boat was finished until the next morning when the cycle would begin again.

He reached down and gave Chessie a hard rub, ignoring the fact that the animal was soaking wet. Chessie seemed to sense the power of the moment. Both watched as the sun dropped rapidly behind the trees. Just as the top of the circle disappeared from view, a conductor's baton fell and music drifted from the cabin.

Nature's changing of the guard was complete. An artist's worst enemy was darkness, and that was now rapidly encompassing the *Mona Lisa*. Cliff turned and headed toward the hatch. It was time to turn his attention to other matters, such as food and seeing about getting cleaned up. A swim sounded more and more appealing. He felt so sticky.

As he entered the cabin, he glanced in the direction from which the helicopter had come. He told himself not to turn paranoid. No one knew where they were. And besides, why would anyone look for them from a helicopter? It wasn't as if he was going to be able to outrun them or anything. "Focus on what you're going to fix for dinner," he told himself.

And so he did.

164

The sheriff started to throw the cellular phone across the bed, pulling up at the last second so it wouldn't hit the mattress and bounce into the wall. He said a few choice words as he stared at the small piece of plastic. It slid beneath the pillow, in an attempt to hide from further punishment. The sheriff couldn't believe no one could find Eddie. He called the hospital twice in the past hour and no one knew where he was. It was speculated Eddie was on a driving lesson, but the sheriff knew that was a bunch of bullshit. That service, like everything else at the damn place, cost extra, and he had yet to approve the expenditure. Where was his son? He made a point to call every Thursday at the same time—6:00 p.m. This was the first time Eddie had not been available. The boy was usually waiting for the call. This was also the first time he couldn't be found. The sheriff wasn't surprised, however. The last time he was there for a visit, the boy had told him all about becoming more and more mobile in the wheelchair. His upper body strength had improved to where his stamina was good for an entire day. He was much more comfortable in the wheelchair and spent more and more time out of his room, and for that matter, out of the building. His mental state also improved. He even smiled and cracked a couple jokes—something he hadn't done since he was shot. Initially, his physical rehabilitation had been hindered by his mind. For the first three months, he was in denial of the whole thing, refusing to cooperate with any of his care, and at times even refusing to eat. Then anger and rage took over, followed by a period of depression. The doctors told the sheriff the boy had to conquer the emotional part of the disability before anything could be done about the physical handicaps. The sheriff didn't let these people know that he had his own conquering to do. When asked by the staff how he was doing, the sheriff always blew the question off, claiming he was fine and wanted all energies focused on getting his boy better. The difficulty for the hospital staff was getting the sheriff to understand the definition of the word *better*. The sheriff's expectations were out of line with reality, and that in turn hindered Eddie's own acceptance of his condition.

The sheriff didn't want to hear any of this. All he wanted to know was when his son would walk again. The doctors initially said it was too early to tell just how much damage had been done. Now, they were saying they didn't know if the damage would ever reverse itself. At first, the sheriff listened to all the talk, all the raised hopes, all the *maybes* that were tossed about. He went to the meetings, went to the counseling sessions and went to the seminars. Then he got wise. Every time he went to one of their bullshit meetings, it cost more money, and more time away from his job. And it did nothing to help his boy walk again. So he stopped going. He maintained his weekly phone call and visited at least once a month. It was hard though. It was like Eddie was dead and had come back from hell. And now the damn hospital didn't even know where he was.

"Bitch," he muttered beneath his breath. She did this to him. She was responsible. She would soon pay. The question was when?

The answer came a moment later when the cellphone started buzzing. He threw the pillow off the bed and grabbed the phone. They better know where he is, he thought.

Flipping down the phone's mouthpiece, he said, "Richmond here."

"I found her," the voice on the other end said.

The voice was familiar, but it wasn't someone from the hospital. And they said *her*, not *him*. It took the sheriff a moment to realize who was calling. His anger was set aside and his mental state immediately improved. Being a seasoned professional and having developed enough cynicism for his whole department, he replied without giving away his emotions. "You said that the other day."

"Yes I did, and I was right, but you were too slow," the bounty hunter said. He was referring to the fact that by the time the sheriff got his fat ass to Cape Charles, the boat was gone.

The sheriff started to snap back, but bit his lip instead. The last thing he wanted was to get the bounty hunter all pissed off. Then the price would go up again. At least for the moment, he had no extra funds to play around with, especially if he wanted to see about Eddie getting some driving lessons. "Maybe I was," he said.

An obvious sigh of disappointment came from the bounty hunter. He was looking forward to a good verbal fight with the sheriff, especially when the bounty hunter held all the aces. He contemplated toying with the man, then decided against it. He was already paid in advance, and while most people who knew him had serious doubts, he did have some scruples about him. Besides, he was starting to get tired of this case; or rather, more honestly, the whole thing was starting to make him nervous. Sure, he was helping a law enforcement officer look for a murder suspect, but there wasn't even an arrest warrant out for her. He was a bounty hunter and made no bones about it. He took the good with the bad. While the reputation of people in his business was often questioned, he always did one thing correctly—he never broke the law. He'd go right up to the line as most did, but he never crossed it. He sensed now that he was very close to this line. Yes, it was time to move on. "They're anchored in a creek right off the mouth of the Sassafras River." Knowing the Sheriff was totally lost in this neck of the country, he added, "That's all the way up the bay on the Eastern Shore."

"How the hell they get up there?" the sheriff demanded.

It was the bounty hunter's turn to bite his lip. "Winds have been good the past couple days. Plus, there've been storms in the area that may have given them an extra push up the bay."

"How'd you find them?" The sheriff was always curious how these kinds of people succeeded when he could not.

"Pigeons," the bounty hunter said.

Knowing he would not get a straight answer, the sheriff asked instead. "What's your plan?"

"I'm going fishing at the crack of dawn tomorrow. I heard they're biting good right at the mouth of the Sassafras."

"What if they move up river?"

"I'll suspect they'll do just that, but I'll be positioned where I can see them if they do." He paused. "How soon can you get up here?"

An instinct having evolved into the human psyche, the sheriff looked at his watch. "I don't know. How far away are you?"

"I don't know. Where the hell are you?" the bounty hunter said, trying to tone down the sarcasm in his voice.

The sheriff realized the man's response was appropriate. "Just south of Annapolis."

There was a pause on the other end of the line. "Then you're probably about three hours away."

"I'll be there in four. Just tell me where to meet you."

"There's an old bed and breakfast just as you cross the Sassafras coming into Georgetown. It's right above a big marina that rents boats. I'll book an extra room for you."

"I'll be there," the sheriff said.

"See you then."

The sheriff hesitated. "You sure they're going to stay put for the tonight?"

"Nothing's guaranteed in life, but I'd wager a hefty bet on it. I checked the charts and found the cove where they're anchored. It's pretty secluded, protected on both sides by sandbars protruding out towards the middle. Also, there're no buoys or other aids to navigation, so going anywhere without daylight would be risky."

"I see," the sheriff said.

As there was no need for further conversation, the line went dead.

165

To Cliff's surprise, the temperature dropped a good ten degrees as darkness engulfed the area. A hint of a breeze arrived which kept the mosquitos at bay. He finished the dinner dishes, being careful with the water. But just as he rinsed the last plate, a hiss of air came out the line. He quickly turned the water off.

April, who had been practicing the piano, heard the noise. "Is that air?"

"Afraid so."

"In the water line?

His statement was repeated.

"So much for a shower tonight."

Cliff nodded and laughed. "I have a couple gallons of bottled water hidden for emergencies. We can use that tonight and to make coffee in the morning."

"I don't need much," April said.

"We'll be fine."

"What about Chessie."

"One bottle's for her, the other is ours."

April laughed. "You certainly are a dog's best friend."

"Anyway," Cliff said, putting the plate away. "Did you like the vegetarian stew?"

"It was good."

"It was homemade, you know."

"Out of a can?"

"Good place to store it."

"Right."

"A lot of people think it's weird to eat hot food in the summer, but I've always found a good meal, hot or cold, will make the weather a lot more tolerable."

"We always ate well aboard *Hamilton's Bench*," April said. "But meals tasted even better when we were sailing around the islands."

"Best food I ever ate was when I was crabbing with my uncle," Cliff responded.

He pulled the lid off the counter and put the dishes securely in their place. "Anyway, since there's not going to be a shower, I'm going to go for a dip. Wanna come?"

"You mean swimming?"

"I have an old pair of gym shorts and a shirt you can wear."

April hesitated. "That's okay."

"Or go in your clothes. That way you can do your laundry at the same time," Cliff teased.

April rolled her eyes at him. "I'll think about it. You go ahead."

He hung up the dishtowels to dry and went forward to change. A few moments later he was over the side. Just as his head popped out of the water, he heard a splash beside him. Chessie came very close to landing right on top of him. Cliff laughed loudly. "Well, girl, you're certainly not worried about what you're wearing, are you?"

The dog barked once and then paddled toward shore. Cliff swam around the boat a couple times and then went forward and took hold of the anchor line. The earlier breeze was threatening to fade away. Cliff suspected it would be gone by midnight. Another hot sticky night, he thought. Least he'd be cooled off a little.

He looked skyward. A few stars were out, but nature had yet to turn on the bulk of the nightlights. That would happen in another hour or so. Being in a very secluded area with nothing around them on shore, the sky would be like a thousand candles. There was no moon. Saturn would be out later. He could already see the Big Dipper come into view in the northern sky. The North Star was already bright. There were a few high residual clouds. Otherwise the sky was clear. He knew that could change rapidly. He had listened to the NOAA weather channel earlier for the forecast. There was a high probability of thunderstorms again tomorrow. He planned to get into Georgetown early to resupply. He had scanned the charts and found another secluded cove for tomorrow night. He also wanted to call Jennifer to see what was going on from her end. He thought about doing that now over the marine radio, but decided to wait until morning and use a landline. Less chance of their conversation being overheard, he argued.

His thoughts were broken by the sound of Chessie on the beach scurrying around. He wanted to yell at her not to go bringing back any fresh game. He decided not to break the ambiance of the night. He let go of the anchor line and dove underwater. He ran a hand along the bottom of the *Mona Lisa*. Except for a thin layer of slime, the bottom was clean. No barnacles so far. He came to the surface on the starboard side and swam forward to the anchor line. He was again ready to call out for Chessie when he sensed something in the water behind him. He turned and saw April swimming towards him.

"Where were you?" April said, reaching up and grabbing the anchor line for herself. "I swam all the way around the boat."

"I was just checking the bottom for barnacles."

"You should tell someone you're going to do that."

Cliff started to respond, but stopped short. In a way, it was nice she worried about him. Instead, he said, "What made you decide to come in?"

"You know you shouldn't swim alone, especially at night."

Cliff laughed. "So you're my swim buddy, huh?"

"Whatever."

"I'm glad you changed your mind." He squinted to try and get a better look at her. The only thing out of the water was her head. "What'd you find to wear?"

"You don't need to worry about that."

"You ain't naked, are you?"

"Don't be ridiculous."

"Well, I am."

"You are!"

Cliff laughed again. "No, I have a bathing suit on."

"You'd better."

They hung on the anchor line together, each dwelling on their own thoughts. Cliff could hear Chessie rummaging around on the beach. He wanted to call her back. At the same time, he didn't want to bring his swim to an end. He felt April's foot against his leg as they both tread water gently.

"Sorry," she said. She moved down the anchor line.

"That's okay," Cliff said softly. "You know, I don't bite."

There was a moment's hesitation. "Do I know?"

It was Cliff's turn to hesitate. "Sometimes it's good to have someone to lean on."

"I'm doing fine on my own," April insisted.

"Are you really?"

She paused. "I thought I was doing okay with all this... until you told me about Eddie. Don't get me wrong, I'm glad he's alive, but..." She looked away. "It's been hard. I miss my family and I miss my friends, what few I had. And now it's surfaced again."

"For what's it worth, I'll be your friend," Cliff said.

"I thought you already were."

Cliff chuckled. "Was, am and always will be."

She looked back at him. "Thank you."

"You're welcome."

"Why is that, Cliff?" April asked.

"Why is what?"

"Why are you my friend? Why are you doing all this for me? Besides being dangerous, you may be in big trouble."

Cliff ran a free hand through his hair. "I know in a lot of ways comparing you to me is like comparing apples to oranges. However, we do have a lot in common. I've been in your shoes before… twice, actually. I know what it's like to be going along just fine in your life and then suddenly have the rug yanked out from under you."

"How would you know that?" April said with a hint of tartness.

"My parents were both killed in a car accident when I was young. After that, I went to live with my uncle. He was killed by lightning two years ago. I've basically been on my own, ever since."

"I'm sorry," April said.

"Maybe I don't understand completely, yet maybe I understand some." Cliff could see her nod in the darkness. "We've both been alone, for what, two years now? Maybe it's time for a different sport," he said.

"Like what?" April inquired.

Cliff wiped a drop of water from his eye. "Your music, for one."

"Music's not a sport," April said smartly.

Cliff paused. "It's okay to go on the defensive if you want. I understand. But it's still not what you would have chosen in your life."

"Do we ever get to choose?" April suggested.

"Good question. Sometimes no. Then again, sometimes we at least have some input," Cliff replied.

April tried to keep on the defensive, but failed. Cliff was right. She had been on the run for two years now, and when it seemed like things had settled down, *Hamilton's Bench* pulled into Annapolis and all hell broke loose again. Now, here she was hiding aboard a sailboat anchored in a secluded cove somewhere in the northern part of the Chesapeake Bay with a guy she hardly knew. Was she hanging on an emotional thread? She looked up at the anchor line around which both her hands were wrapped. A little symbolism there, she thought. She looked over at Cliff, the boy she hardly knew. Their stories were like apples and oranges. Yet, like he said, they did have something in common. However, that was all for naught. She couldn't worry about him, or anybody else for that matter. She had to focus on her own situation. What to do about her own predicament and the sheriff? Cliff was being so nice. He seemed to genuinely care. At times she even sensed he liked her. At times she sensed the feeling was mutual. What should she do? She knew she needed to keep moving. She knew that probably meant away from Cliff as well, but she felt safe with him. And she felt—

She cut the thought off. She had no time for such things. "Do not get wrapped up in the emotion of the moment," Danny always preached. "Enjoy the experience of being out in the wild, but stay alert, and stay objective."

She almost laughed aloud, thinking that two out of three wasn't all that bad. Or was it? What would Danny say? What would he think? She laughed again. Especially what would he say if he saw her now? She suddenly felt homesick—very homesick. It was something that had tried to enter her psyche before, but she was always able to ward it off. The past was the past. Now was now. The future was the future. But it wasn't working this time. Her heart felt heavy. She missed Danny. She missed her mother. She even felt a yearning to see her stepfather and her friends in school. She especially missed her piano. While the electronic keyboard was wonderful, it didn't have the same feel as a real piano, and it didn't give her the same sense of comfort and security as when she was at home, or even aboard *Hamilton's Bench*. She felt her eyes begin to swell. She fought back the tears, but failed to control a sob.

Cliff heard this and said, "You okay?"

"I'll be alright."

"Sure?"

"Yes… No. No, I'm not okay." The sobbing increased. "I'm *freakin'* not okay. Okay?"

"Then what are you?" Cliff said gently.

She hesitated. "I'm lonely… very lonely. I'm tired of running. I miss my family. I miss my friends. I'm tired of looking over my shoulder every second of every day. I'm tired of being somebody I'm not. I'm tired of living like this for something I didn't do. I just want it all to end." She started crying harder.

Cliff moved toward her. He reached out and put his arm on her shoulder. "Come here," he said gently. She didn't resist as he pulled her into him. She let go of the anchor line and wrapped her hands around his neck. He held on with one hand and treaded water harder. She buried her head in his neck. Her tears felt warm as they ran off her cheek. "Loneliness is one of the toughest emotions we have to fight," he said softly. "Once it gets a hold, it's hard to break loose."

"You seem so smart. How do you deal with it?"

Cliff couldn't tell whether she was being sarcastic, really looking for help, or a little of both. He gave her the benefit of the doubt. "First thing you do is acknowledge it. Then you tell yourself there're worse things in life than being alone. Then you find something to occupy your time. For me, it's my art. For you, it may be your music. My uncle always said the sun's going to come up in the morning either way. The only question is whether you look at it with a good pair of eyes or a bad pair, whether you look at it with a smile or a frown. It's up to you. Regardless of what's going on in our lives, we make the decision how we're going to face the sun each day. It's hard. It takes practice. It takes determination. But it works."

"For some people," April said.

"Don't cut yourself short," Cliff directed. "You're a lot stronger and a lot wiser than you think. Very few people could have gone through what you've been through, and survived like you've survived. I'm sure times have been tough, but you've managed to wake up each day with a least some semblance of a smile."

"How can you be so sure of that?" April demanded.

Cliff answered. "You wouldn't be here if you didn't."

April started to argue, but stopped. He was right again. Life had been hard, emotionally and physically, but she had hardened right along with it. Like Danny said, you do what you have to do to survive. So maybe she was doing better than she thought. Yes, she wished her situation was different, but at this particular moment, she really shouldn't complain. Things could be a lot worse. She could be hanging on an anchor line alone, not with her arms around Cliff's neck—a guy who she was really starting to like. In spite of telling herself she needed to stay focused on herself, she had trouble avoiding these feelings. They had only been curiosities in the past, heightened maybe by some of the things she did with Danny. This time they were real—real feelings, real people, real time. Not a fantasy—a reality.

She hugged him harder and pressed her body into his. She kissed him lightly on the side of the neck. "Thank you," she said.

"You're welcome."

166

The room was small, the tables, close together. Luckily, there were only two other occupied tables, both in the far corner. The dining room of the bed and breakfast was decorated ornately, the walls covered with dark red wallpaper and a mishmash of paintings depicting the French countryside. The ceiling was high and a large chandelier hung in the middle. The dirty glass fixture was way oversized for the room. Since it was unlit, the only light came from the windows that overlooked the harbor and marina some thirty feet below. The lack of a crowd and the lack of light suited the bounty hunter just fine. Their waitress, the same lady who checked him in the day before, was a pest at first. She did eventually get the message that he and the man sitting across from him wanted to be left alone.

Taking the last bite of his scrambled eggs, the bounty hunter leaned forward and stared at the man across from him. While their paths had crossed several times in the past, it had been years since he saw the sheriff face to face. The man looked much older than the bounty hunter would have guessed. He had always been heavy, but there had been a certain sense of fitness about him. That was gone. Now, he was simply fat. Dark semicircles outlined his sunken eyes. He had obviously shaved in the car because there were several areas sporting more than a day's worth of whiskers. His shoulders hung low, his head remained bowed as he drank his third cup of coffee. He had yet to touch the plate of food before him.

The bounty hunter gave the sheriff the benefit of doubt for looking so bad. He had been driving all night after he got lost, realizing this only when he somehow ended up at the entrance to the Delaware Turnpike. He had arrived at the bed and breakfast only thirty minutes earlier. The bounty hunter gave the sheriff credit for the lack of sleep, but he knew it was more than that. The toll of the past two years was catching up to the man. It had been a long, grueling chase dealing with this girl. The bounty hunter couldn't imagine what it would be like to lose a son. He didn't have any children of his own, and that was one of the reasons. He just couldn't fathom losing a child.

The bounty hunter finished chewing, forced any empathy he might be feeling back into its cave, and said, "Like I said, I don't think us getting a late start today is a problem. We know where they were twelve hours ago. Even if we don't know exactly where they are now, they can't be far. If need be, I'll just go up in the chopper again and find them."

"How much is that going to cost me?" the sheriff said, draining his coffee cup.

The bounty hunter looked out the window. It was a gorgeous day. It was going to be hot, but the heat didn't bother him. Everybody complained about the heat around here. They obviously had never been in Vietnam in the middle of the summer in the middle of a fire fight. That was hot!

The marina below was starting to come to life. People were pushing carts up and down the piers as boats were readied for the day's excursion on the water. He could already see boats heading out the river. There were a couple boats heading for the fuel dock. While he loved to fish, he didn't get that much out of being out on the water for anything else. He never really saw the point. He'd much rather be flying above it all. Why be on it when you could be above it? The view and the ride were much better. He emptied his coffee cup, saying, "If I can get the same bird as I did yesterday, we'll chalk it up to a day of fun."

The sheriff's eyes lifted. Did he actually hear the bounty hunter right? Was he giving him something free of charge? That was a first. "You don't think we're going to need to do that?"

The bounty hunter continued his stare out the window. "No. The girl's right out there somewhere. I can smell her."

The sheriff smiled. He had no doubt as to the truth of the statement. He had had similar experiences in the past when tracking a suspect. You just knew when you were close. He sat up and took in a deep breath. He sensed nothing out of the ordinary. Then again, his senses, sixth and otherwise, were too tired to be of any assistance at the moment. He told himself maybe if he ate. He dug into his plate of food.

The bounty hunter continued. "What I plan to do today is to show you where they were last night. If they moved, we'll find them. And then my job'll be over. I'll leave the rest to you."

That was exactly how the sheriff wanted it. Once the girl was in his view, he'd do the rest. Just what that entailed, he had yet to decide. Finishing his food, the sheriff let his thoughts wander to Eddie. He had called the hospital again late last night. This time they really gave him the runaround. They cut him off twice before he finally got someone to tell him his son was in bed asleep. He wasn't convinced the person on the other end was telling the truth because he refused to wake Eddie to take the call. There wasn't a damn thing the sheriff could do about it now, but the first chance he got, he'd be out there reaming some asses. Eddie's care was expensive and he'd determine when he talked to his son.

He refocused on the matter at hand. He took another deep breath. Yes, maybe there was a hint of the bitch in the air. As the coffee began to kick in and his blood sugar rose in response to the food, his confidence began to build. With that, the gates of experience opened and he did indeed get a sense they were near. If his sixth sense was correct, they were even closer than they actually thought. His heart started to race. His palms became sweaty.

He focused his eyes on the bounty hunter and started to say something when he realized the man was staring right past him. The look on his face told him whatever it was that captured his attention was big. The sheriff turned and looked over his shoulder. He scanned the scene before him. There was a lot of activity going on in the marina and surrounding waters. However, something did catch his eye. It was a sailboat pulling into the gas dock. There was a young boy at the wheel. He had curly brown hair and was dressed in shorts without a top. There was a dog out on the bow of the boat. Standing beside the dog was another figure.

The sheriff leaned forward almost pressing his face into the glass, and squinted. He wasn't sure at first, but the more he looked, the more his heart raced. He turned and looked at the bounty hunter. The man had a big grin on his face. The sheriff turned his palms up and hunched his shoulders, asking the obvious question.

Wearing a big smile, the bounty hunter said, "How's that for laying her right in your lap?"

167

Cliff bent his neck so he could see under the boom. At the same time he pushed down on the gear shift bringing the engine into neutral. He turned the wheel to the left so the angle into the pier wasn't as sharp. There was virtually no wind so docking shouldn't be a problem—except there were a lot of people watching. Murphy's Law of boating warned he'd better be careful. He often wondered why you could dock a boat so well when there was no one around yet have so much trouble under the same exact conditions when people were watching.

He called to April to throw the dock boy the looped end of the line. The young dockhand caught the line with ease and placed the loop over the cleat on the pier. April then pulled the bow into the pier. Cliff put the boat into reverse, turned the wheel hard to starboard and the boat settled right up against the pilings with hardly a sound.

April looked back at the captain, smiled and nodded. "Nice landing."

"Thanks," Cliff said, tossing the dockhand the line for the stern.

"Need a spring line?" the boy asked.

"We should be okay."

The boy nodded. "Diesel or gas?" he said.

"Diesel," Cliff answered. He looked to make sure April was okay. He wasn't worried about her ability to handle the lines. She had already proven herself there. He was worried about her being exposed on the bow. He just didn't feel comfortable with her being so visible. It was one thing when they were out on the water where people never really got a good look, but to be so conspicuous at a fuel dock… He had a sense this was a bad idea and motioned for Chessie to stay forward and keep an eye on her.

He was distracted by the dock boy handing him the nozzle from the fuel pump. "Doors and hatches all closed?" the boy said.

"That's a Roger," Cliff replied.

The fueling and resupply stop took about an hour total. The whole time, Cliff told himself to stay alert. He tried to make April remain on board with Chessie while he went to the small grocery store across the street from the marina, but she protested and followed him. In spite of his concern, their stop in Georgetown occurred without incident. Cliff still sensed someone was watching. He sensed April was jittery as well.

Cliff felt much better once they were underway. They ran with the motor as there was no wind. He kept a sharp eye behind him and saw nothing out of the ordinary. There were a lot of boats coming and going from the area. He was glad April remained below stashing the supplies. They were headed due west and the sky in that direction was as clear as could be. To the south, however, high ominous clouds were already starting to form. The NOAA weather station warned of early afternoon storms as a cold front moved into the area. Cliff chuckled. A cold front in the summer meant the temperature might not break ninety. The threat of a storm, however, didn't bother him. He already had a cove picked out for the night and they'd be there by mid-morning. Then, because they had filled up the water tanks, he was going to take a nice shower.

The river bent to the left and the marina disappeared from view. Once past the six knot speed markers, the power boats that had been following him kicked their throttles forward and whipped past them. He yelled to April that they were going to be getting a lot of wake for a few minutes. She yelled thanks and kept up her work. He looked back one more time. Except for a few powerboats further behind and two sailboats running in tandem with him, all was clear. He sat down and let out a long breath. He was feeling much better about the situation.

He leaned back against the chrome railing, relaxed and enjoyed the ride out the river. The Sassafras was one of the more picturesque rivers on the bay. In this particular area, the south shoreline was covered with large modern looking houses, each with a different style. Each had a long pier as the water was shallow along the shore. Each property had a least one boat docked near the end. The north shore was not yet developed. It was a mixture of woods between farm fields. Cliff knew it was only a matter of time before developers got to that as well. Waterfront property was too valuable to simply farm. When the price was right, the farmers would sell.

Cliff glanced at the instruments sitting atop the hatchway. Boat speed was holding steady at 6.2 knots. Wind speed held steady at two. The day quickly proved it was going to be hot. There was little breeze and in spite of the cloud cover that continued to grow, the sun's intensity treated them like eggs in a hot skillet. Both April and Cliff were well tanned, yet both felt the effects of the heat on their exposed skin.

Except for an occasional powerboat that went buzzing by, once they got away from the marina, traffic was light. Cliff kept a sharp eye out. He saw nothing suspicious. Seeing the buoy he'd been looking for, he steered to the right and curved the boat into the middle of the cove's entrance where he planned to anchor for the night. Like the one they had just left, there were a couple of sharp bends before the actual cove opened into a gigantic pond. It was like skating into the middle of a mirror. He pulled the throttle to neutral. The depth finder showed plenty of water under the keel. Low tide wouldn't be a problem.

He put the engine in reverse a few seconds to make sure the boat came to a complete stop. Then he went forward to drop the anchor. He started to return to the helm, but saw April standing at the wheel. One hand was already perched above the gearshift. He nodded and the boat eased backwards. Satisfied he had enough line in the water, he cleated the end off and motioned for April to bring the engine to neutral. The anchor held firm. He wasn't surprised. It was a muddy bottom, and there was nobody watching.

Chessie was already on the gunwale waiting for her master's okay to plunge over the side. She failed to hide her impatience. Cliff laughed and motioned her to go ahead. He stepped back to avoid the spray. He laughed harder. Chessie had done a perfect belly flop.

April killed the engine and went below to finish putting away the supplies. Cliff spent the next few minutes checking the lines and rigging. His uncle would have a fit if he had to mess with all the ropes and lines required on a sailboat. He was a big believer in keeping things simple. "Fewer things to break, fewer things to repair," he often said. He just as often added, "Not a bad way to live your life either." While the sailboat was more complicated from the equipment point of view, Cliff's life itself was relatively simple. He ate, he worked, he slept.

That is, until April came along, and then things became somewhat blurred. Initially, he left her alone and she stayed pretty much to herself. He worked on his art. She helped with the boat and played the piano. The past few days, however, he found they were doing more and more tasks together, like anchoring the moment before.

He recognized early on that she was special. His opinion didn't change with time. She was beautiful, she was smart, she was strong in body and in mind; and she was one hell-of-a pianist. Before April, Cliff never paid much attention to any kind of music. Now, he was paying a lot of attention. It was almost surreal to be on a boat in the middle of the Chesapeake Bay and be serenaded by live classical music. It was certainly a clash of images. Boating was done outdoors, surrounded by the peace and tranquility of nature.

Classical music was performed indoors, in a majestic concert hall surrounded by walls specifically designed to accentuate the sound coming from the stage. The *Mona Lisa* certainly wasn't any famous concert hall, and her cabin certainly wasn't designed to accentuate any sound. Yet, the music coming out of the electronic keyboard was phenomenal. Cliff had never heard anything more beautiful. He told himself he had never seen anything more beautiful either. The sight of April sitting at the table, perched over the instrument, eyes usually closed, oblivious to anything going on around her, was one of the most pleasant images he had ever experienced. Physically, she was beautiful, even after a hard day's sailing matted her hair and dried streaks of sweat ran down her face. She radiated an inner beauty he had seldom witnessed.

The night before, Cliff did a few preliminary drawings of her at the keyboard. He thought about a few photographs as well, but decided the noise of the camera's shutter would break the mood. While they were still preliminary drawings, he was impressed with the results. He especially liked the mood created by the dim lighting coming from behind her left shoulder. The light cast very beautiful and curvy shadows across the entire scene. The fact that she was playing Beethoven's *Moonlight Sonata* only added to the serenity of the moment.

He struggled at first with capturing the dimension of sound. How does one put the mood created by sound down onto an art pad for people to see? He realized the answer when he noticed there was no music on the music stand. He studied the image a few moments, and then did something rare for him which was to add something extra to the scene. In this case it was a music book with the name *Moonlight Sonata* at the top and *Beethoven* at the bottom.

Her closed eyes and the music captured the mood he was searching for. Even though far from being completed, the three partials were impressive.

They were of a person! Jennifer would be pleased.

Cliff seldom worried about whether someone liked his work. You either liked it or you didn't. You either bought it or you didn't. The couple of times that did concern him were when he was doing a painting as a final exam in high school, and the piece he did for the Governor. He was anxious, however, to see how April would react to these three pieces once they were finished. He planned to start working on them as soon as the *Mona Lisa* was squared away and Chessie was back on board… and he had his shower.

Fortunately, or unfortunately, those plans suddenly changed. April came on deck dressed in the same set of his old clothes she had on the night before. "You ready?" she said.

"Ready for what?" he asked. She was beautiful even dressed in poorly fitting clothes.

"To go for a dip."

He started to explain his plan for the morning, but looking at her, he decided the partials could wait. "Give me a minute to change."

"I'll be counting."

They were in the water a minute later. Chessie, on shore doing heaven knows what, heard them and quickly joined the fun. Cliff chased the dog around the boat several times, playing what he called doggy tag. April joined in the game and together, the two humans were able to outsmart the dog on several occasions. But the dog never seemed to tire of the fun, while Cliff and April had to rest often by hanging onto the anchor line.

An hour passed before they decided it was time to switch activities. Cliff made sure Chessie got up into the boat first. He had one foot on the ladder when suddenly April screamed behind him. He turned and saw a panicked look on her face. In spite of her tan, she was as pale as a ghost. "Something just bit me," she said.

"Where?"

"On the leg."

Cliff slid back into the water and swam toward her. He saw a large white glob of material behind her, floating away in the gentle current. He scanned the area quickly. It was the only one he saw. "It was just a sea nettle."

"A sea nettle. What's that?"

He reached out to her shoulder and gently pulled her toward him and away from the animal. "It's a jellyfish that stings."

"Why didn't you tell me they were in the water?"

"I didn't know. Usually they don't get this far up the bay. But I guess the heat and lack of rain…"

"Well, they hurt like hell." She was trembling so hard ripples of water moved away from her body in a circular fashion.

"Come on, let' get out and I'll take a look."

April grabbed hold of Cliff's arm and pressed into him. Her legs wrapped around his waist as if seeking additional protection from the sea monster. Cliff reached out and grabbed the first rung of the ladder before she pulled them both under. He spun around so he was between April and the sea nettle, just in case the current brought it back their way. April's panic mode faded as she found her composure. She didn't release the death grip around his neck until she felt the ladder pressing into her back. She looked up to see Chessie's head bending down toward her. The dog's curiosity was aroused with all the commotion. April turned and ascended the ladder in a flash.

In the cabin, Cliff examined the ugly welt that ran from her inner mid-thigh down across the top of her knee. The area was getting redder by the moment. "You really react to these, don't you?"

"I wouldn't know. I've never been bitten before."

"Stung," Cliff corrected gently. "They sting. They don't bite."

"Whatever," she said, leaning forward and examining the wound for herself.

"They do hurt," Cliff acknowledged.

"Tell me about it. What do you do? It looks like it's getting worse."

Cliff went into the galley and returned with a towel full of ice cubes and a can of seasoning.

"What's that?" April said pressing the ice on to the affected area.

"Meat tenderizer."

"What are you going to do with that? You don't even eat meat!"

He opened the lid, slid the ice aside and sprinkled the powder over the wound. He spread it around making sure the whole area was covered. Then he replaced the ice. "It's what everybody on the bay uses—something to do with the papaya enzyme in the product."

April sat still a moment to see if the weird remedy worked. The pain slowly began to subside. "Thanks," she said.

"No problem. I should have thought to look for them before we went in, but I didn't expect to find them this far north. They were pretty plentiful when we were down the bay."

"What do they look like?"

"White circular globs with trailing tentacles. They don't actually attack you. Rather, you sort of come into contact with them."

"You ever been bitten, I mean stung?"

"Lots of times, but they don't bother me."

"How come?"

"Lucky, I guess."

"I sure could have used some of that luck today."

"You'll be okay. It's just a local reaction."

"It hurts."

"Keep that ice on it for a while, then go take a cool shower. That'll help."

"Okay." April sat back to wait for the pain to subside.

"In the meantime, I think I'll rinse off," Cliff said.

"Save me some water," April commanded.

Cliff laughed. "Will do."

He kept his bathing suit on so he wouldn't have to worry about privacy when he was finished. He adjusted the water a few degrees as the water in the hot water tank, heated by the engine, was at its maximum. Besides, he wanted to make sure he saved some for April. He grabbed the shampoo, dumped a glob on top of his head, and was about to lather his hair when there was a tapping on the bulkhead. He opened the teak door. April was standing there, still dressed in his tee shirt and shorts. He looked at her a bit befuddled. "What's the matter?"

"My leg hurts," she said.

What does a young man say when confronted with a beautiful girl standing at his door, and not just any door but the door to the shower? "It's tight quarters," he managed. He moved to the side so she could get in. It was indeed a tight fit, but he was able to get the door closed. He sat down on the seat that covered the toilet. "Let me see your leg," he directed.

She reached down and pulled the leg of her shorts up so he could get a better view. He forced his eyes to stay on the sting mark, which was already showing signs of improvement. "It looks better."

"Stinging's gone, but it still hurts."

He slowly brought the water nozzle around and let the tepid water run over her thigh. The meat tenderizer that had caked over the area washed down her leg. He reached out and brushed a few remaining specks away. He took his time, allowing his hand to rest beside the inflamed area. The redness and swelling were already subsiding. In spite of the deep tan, her skin was soft and smooth.

"What do you have on top of your head?" she asked, putting her finger into the glob of shampoo.

"I was just getting ready to wash my hair," he explained.

She reached down and took the water nozzle from him. Wetting his hair, she began to work in the shampoo. He bent his head forward to keep the soap out of his eyes. He told himself to hold in the moan that was forming in his throat. Her fingers felt good. He always liked having his hair shampooed right before a haircut, but this felt so much better, so much different.

She leaned over him to make sure she got the soap out of the back. She let the water run down his neck, her fingers rubbing the muscles as the warmth of the water increased the blood flow to the area. He started to sit up and his head bumped into her chest. "Sorry," he said.

"Like you said, tight quarters."

He stood up. They were face to face. Their bodies touched at all the important places. He took the water from her and ran it atop her head. "Your turn."

She wrapped her arms around his back and pulled him to her. "Okay." He felt her kiss his shoulder as he lathered up her hair. "You taste salty," she said.

"I haven't washed the river off yet."

"Salty, but good." She kissed him again.

Not knowing what else to do, he gently shampooed her hair. That felt good to him as well. She hugged him tighter. He turned the water off and dropped the hose. Their bodies pressed together. She looked up at him. She smiled. He returned the same. While this was not uncharted territory for him, it was certainly the first time he'd been with someone he really cared about, someone he was attracted to more than physically. He didn't want to do anything to chase her away. He remembered how the other times had turned out. A streak of fear coupled with a sense of paranoia ran through him. Was something bad going to happen this time, too?

"Can I say something?" she asked softly.

"Sure."

She pushed away from him ever so slightly. "I'm not sure where this is going to go, but I don't think it's going to go as far as you may want, but I do like being with you a lot."

"It certainly isn't going to go anywhere we both don't want. I don't want you to get hurt, April. I don't want to get hurt either. And even more important, I don't want to do anything to break the thread of trust that's starting to develop between us."

"Thank you," she said. She looked away. "I've never been with anyone before." She realized that officially she had just lied. To correct herself, she repeated. "I've never been with anyone like you before."

"Fate has a funny way of working, doesn't it?"

"Sure does."

Their eyes met again. "I do think I want to kiss you," Cliff said.

She smiled to give her approval. She pressed into him. He felt her begin to tremble as their lips met.

And then Chessie started barking frantically.

168

The sheriff pulled the throttle of the seventeen foot Boston Whaler to neutral and let the rail nudge against the swim platform of the sailboat. He reached out and grabbed the ladder that was unfolded in the water. He made sure he didn't lean over too far. The boat had already rocked enough coming out the river. He never liked boating to begin with, especially since he never learned to swim. The ride out the river would not go down as one of his favorite experiences, even though the trip, by most standards, had been totally benign. Still, a big man in a small boat was not a thing to take lightly. He glanced back at Bullet. The dog had initially jumped aboard full of vigor and excitement. He now lay curled up in the stern, unable to stand, and having already vomited twice. The sheriff didn't know dogs could get seasick, and the smell of the vomit didn't help the queasiness in his own stomach.

He decided to leave his longtime partner be and cautiously stepped onto the swim platform. He let out a long slow breath. Step one was accomplished without ending in the water. He looked into the boat only to be confronted with a new problem. A large dog jumped out of the cabin. Much more surefooted than either the sheriff or his own dog, the animal came to a halt several feet away. She bared her teeth, let out a low growl and then started barking wildly. The sheriff knew it was useless to look for support from Bullet. He was too sick to do more than raise his head and whimper.

The lawman hesitated. The dog was an unexpected obstacle. He contemplated shooting the animal. He had already drawn his service revolver. He quickly decided against that. The dog was only barking, but holding his ground. A few seconds later, a boy's head popped from the cabin. Before he could say anything, the sheriff took the offensive. Pointing his gun directly at the dog, he said, "You'd better call your dog off boy, or he'll be fish bait."

The boy looked stunned as he stared at the sheriff and the gun. "Who are you, and what do you want?"

"No need to worry about who I am, and it ain't you I want. So, if you do as you're told, you won't get hurt. Understand?"

The boy nodded, hesitating a moment before calling to the dog. The animal failed to heed at first. It took two additional stern calls before the dog backed off.

"You have him trained well, son," the sheriff said, climbing the rest of the way into the boat.

"What do you want?" the boy repeated.

"Where's the girl?"

"What girl?"

The sheriff's face reddened. He waved the gun in a circular motion. "Don't give me no shit, boy. Like I said, this ain't about you."

"Well, there's no one else here."

The sheriff stepped forward and slammed the barrel of the gun hard into the boy's stomach. The lad doubled over in pain. The dog lunged forward, but the boy was able to grab him by the collar in time.

There was motion behind the boy and a voice called out. "Leave him alone." April's head came up through the hatch and she bent over to tend to the boy. She looked up at the sheriff. "It's me you want, not him."

"That's what I was trying to tell him," the sheriff said. He motioned for her to come out of the cabin as well. She was wet, her hair pulled back in a makeshift ponytail. She was tan, taller and much more mature looking, but she still had the same innocent face. The sheriff's knees almost buckled from the excitement. He had waited so long for this moment. So many sleepless hours thinking about his son… thinking about her. It had been hard when his wife died, but he got over it. However, he'd never get over what this girl did to his boy. He stared at her hard. He had often wondered what he was going to do once this moment arrived. He always told himself he'd decide that at the time.

That time had come.

He contemplated the problem as the boy regained his composure. The earlier look of fear had left the boy's eyes. In its place was a look of anger. The sheriff had seen the look many times. It was exactly the look he wanted. Keep them angry, and they can't think straight. Keep them angry and they can do nothing but make stupid decisions, easy to defend against.

"You got me. Let him go," April said.

"I'm not going anywhere," Cliff said.

The sheriff laughed. "Such loyalty. Stupid, yet loyal." He waved the gun around to increase the drama. "But he's right. No one's going anywhere." He took a quick look around. They were still alone in the cove. He knew that probably wouldn't last for long. There were too many boats headed out the river. "On the other hand, now that I think about it, we're all going to go."

"Where?" April demanded.

"Let's just say for a little ride." The sheriff stole a glance over his shoulder. Bullet was still lying in the back of the boat, his eyes half open, his breathing hard. The man's stare returned forward. "Here's the plan. You do exactly as you're told, no one will get hurt. If not, then…" A big grin crossed his face and he waved the gun in a wide circle. "But you got to listen carefully."

And so they did.

169

The pain in Cliff's abdomen was subsiding. The nausea, however, persisted. He fought the urge to vomit, knowing that once he started, it would be hard to stop. He also fought the urge to lunge out at the man standing before him, knowing the odds of success were slim to none. He had been around guns all his life. His uncle liked to duck hunt and had a shotgun, and a .22 caliber rifle he used for target practice. Cliff had shot both several times. Guns just weren't something that interested him, especially now with one pointed his way.

When Cliff first stuck his head out of the cabin and saw the man on the back of his boat, he thought he was simply a fisherman who had either stopped to say hello or was in need of help. It only took a second glance for him to realize he was wrong. He had never met the man, but Cliff knew who he was immediately. He had been wondering how the sheriff found them as he focused on getting Chessie under control.

Taking a slow deep breath, he forced himself into an upright position. Having continued to hold Chessie by the collar, he twisted her around and pushed her hindquarters so she had no choice but to go back into the cabin. Making sure the dog stayed below, he turned back toward the sheriff. "We'll do what you tell us to do, only please be careful with that gun. If you put a hole in the boat, no one will be going anywhere."

The sheriff let out a sick run of laughter. "It ain't the boat I'll be putting the hole in. Now let's get moving."

"Where we going?"

"I'll let you know once we get there."

"Well, sir, I need to know which direction to head once we're underway. We going north? South? East? West?"

The sheriff hesitated, a quizzical look forming as he didn't have a clue which way to head. Realizing he might be giving himself away, the sheriff recovered quickly and pointed over his shoulder. "I want to go out that way."

No kidding, Cliff thought to himself. He kept his feelings quiet. He also told himself that regardless of how he was feeling inside, physically and emotionally, he had to show a sense of calm. "Then which way?"

This time the sheriff was better prepared. "Out the river. I want to go out to the bay."

"Which bay?" Cliff tested.

The quizzical look returned, this time only for an instant. "Don't be a smartass," the sheriff sneered.

"I just wanted to make sure you didn't mean the Delaware Bay. It's not that far from here."

"No, the Chesapeake Bay will do just fine."

It was obvious the man didn't know where to go, nor where he was to begin with. Cliff wasn't sure if this was good or bad, but did log it in the back of his mind for future reference. He was determined to come up with a plan before the sheriff did. If only the man didn't have his gun out.

"Please be careful with that gun," Cliff said, forcing his voice to remain neutral.

"You just do what you're told and I'll be careful."

It was obvious this was a man accustomed to getting in the last word. So talking his way out of this was probably out of the question. Cliff had no choice except to do what he was told. The gun was the deciding factor. Keeping an eye on the weapon, Cliff said, "April, why don't you go forward and prepare to hoist the anchor. I'll get the sails ready."

April gave him a curious look of her own. Cliff felt her stare and knew she was about to ask whether or not they were going to turn on the engine. "The breeze is coming from the south so we shouldn't have any problem getting out of here. Once we're out in the river, we'll be fine."

"Doesn't this boat have an engine?" the sheriff said.

Cliff weighed his response carefully. Should he tell the truth, or should he really give the sheriff a test? Figuring even if he got caught in a lie, nothing was going to happen until they got out in open water, "Yes, but it's only for docking and undocking at a pier," he said. "It's not powerful enough for anything else."

The sheriff held up his free hand. "There ain't any wind, is there?"

As if on cue, a gentle breeze floated across the cove. Cliff responded, "There's not much in here, but once we get out into the river, they'll be more." He glanced over the sheriff's shoulders. The earlier clouds were reproducing rapidly. Cliff didn't tell the sheriff what he hoped to find once in the bay. For that matter, he wasn't sure what he was going to when they got there.

"The girl stays back here with me," the sheriff said.

"Fine," Cliff said. "She can handle the wheel. I'll get the anchor and set the sails."

A few minutes later they were under sail, if that's what you want to call it. There was only a two or three knot breeze in the cove, but at least they were moving. It didn't help that they were towing the runabout with a seasick dog. Cliff didn't mind, however. It kept the sheriff's dog at bay.

As they exited the cove, the sheriff took a position on the starboard ledge. One hand held onto the pistol which he now had lowered and hidden at his side, the other held onto one of the lines coming off the boom. Cliff retook the wheel, claiming it would be tricky getting through the mouth of the cove. The truth was he wanted to keep himself between April and the sheriff. He contemplated running the boat aground. He decided, however, until he had a better feel for the sheriff's intentions, he'd best play it safe. Besides that, he had a hunch that once they were out in the bay, the tide would change.

They were headed just off the wind so Cliff had everything set tight, including the mainsail, which was directly amidships. April sat on the port side seat while Cliff stood beside the wheel. He kept one eye on what was going on around him and the other on the sheriff. He told himself that he would cooperate so long as the sheriff did the same. However, any move toward April...

Cliff didn't know what he would do. He just knew he'd do it.

The sheriff was unable to hide his on-the-water discomfort. Every time the *Mona Lisa* rocked in response to a small wave or boat wake, he acted like he was going to fall overboard, grabbing onto the line tighter and tighter each time. The man was dressed in a short-sleeve tan shirt and long khaki pants. Cliff wasn't sure where the gun was kept except if he had a holster buried in his waistband somewhere. The man was well over three hundred pounds, plenty of room to hide a weapon. Cliff tried to read his expression, but that proved difficult as it changed every few moments. He went from a look of anger, to smiling broadly, to a neutral expression, to fear when the boat rocked. The only thing Cliff concluded was that the man was plum crazy... and very dangerous.

Cliff glanced over his shoulder to make sure April was okay. He had given her the eye indicating that she should be as quiet as possible. She was the reason for the sheriff being here and they didn't want to do anything to further fuel the angry part of his mental state. She sat with her arms wrapped around her knees which were drawn up to her chest. She stared out across the water, a blank expression on her face. Surprising to Cliff, she didn't look afraid. If anything, she conveyed a sense of acceptance that whatever was going to happen would happen. Perhaps so, but Cliff was determined that he was going to decide just what that would be.

They followed the Sassafras towards the bay. The breeze picked up with each passing mile. Cliff was thankful for the additional wind. He hoped it didn't get so strong as to cause the sheriff alarm, at least till they got to open water. He also watched the gathering clouds. NOAA predicted late afternoon thunderstorms. Cliff guessed a better prediction would be sooner than that. The task now was to come up with a plan. He had no experience in situations such as this. He did know not to get the sheriff any more agitated. Cliff told himself to be patient. He told himself to sit back and act calm. He needed to do that for the sheriff, for April and himself.

Steady as she goes, he said silently.

170

Since her father was a longtime member of Annapolis Yacht Club, Jennifer had been aboard several large yachts in her life, but none as large as *Hamilton's Bench,* and never one underway. The boat cut through the water with little effort and little noise. Considering they were approaching twenty five knots, the boat's maximum speed, the ride was much smoother than expected.

George Hamilton was at the helm, his crew standing close by in case he needed anything. He didn't. Even more surprising to Jennifer than *Hamilton Bench's* ride, her owner turned out to be a licensed captain. Besides being qualified on paper to handle a boat the size of *Hamilton's Bench*, he also demonstrated his ability as well. In that he was focused on getting out of the Annapolis Harbor, down the Severn River and out on the bay as quickly as possible, Jennifer put aside the question of *what else did she not know about him?* For now, she'd simply enjoy the ride.

She also continued to worry about April.

She didn't know why, she just had a feeling things were going to get messy. It was just a feeling, a woman's intuition.

Everyone met over dinner the night before and decided it would now be best to get April back to *Hamilton's Bench* until they found the sheriff. Additional phone calls out to Worthington Valley only added to the feeling that April was in danger. No one had heard from the sheriff in over a week. Hamilton did talk to a Willard Cluster who claimed to be the Deputy Sheriff. And while the man was willing to listen to questions, his answers remained vague. The tone in his voice, however, gave Hamilton as much information as anything. In short, the deputy sheriff had no clue where his boss was, and seemed more than a little concerned.

They also learned that April was only wanted for questioning in the shooting of Eddie Richmond. A warrant hadn't even been issued. Hamilton thought that odd, as did Jennifer. When you considered that the sheriff covered up the fact that his son was alive and all the bizarre things surrounding that, George Hamilton could only come to one conclusion. Sheriff Richmond wasn't out to enforce the law. He was out for revenge. And that made him a very dangerous man.

Thus, the urgency to get April safely back aboard *Hamilton's Bench*.

The whole thing was too strange, Jennifer decided. She hoped that once they found April, a lot of these questions would find answers. She told herself to be patient. They were moving as fast as possible, but it was hard. The more she thought about it, the more worried she became. George Hamilton didn't help any either. He hid his emotions well. He had a very good poker face. However, he wasn't hiding anything now. He was worried, and it showed on his face and in his voice.

The other guests on board were worried as well.

171

The wind continued to pick up as they turned at the mouth of the Sassafras River and headed south down the bay. Winds were steady from the southeast at fourteen knots. Wave height had risen to two feet, and the water in general was choppy. Clouds continued to roll in from the southwest. The bay was agitated, warning those playing on its surface that danger loomed ahead. Cliff figured the thunderstorm had already formed and would be upon them in an hour or less. He had that much time to come up with a plan, because it would be during the storm that he'd make his move—whatever that might be. He was determined he wasn't going to let this go on much longer. He and April were both in danger, and he knew it. He figured their only hope was to keep the sheriff in a sense of perceived danger as well. Cliff also knew their situation wasn't going to improve with time, and that this precious commodity was running out fast.

The sheriff continued facing towards the stern. He spent most of the time holding on, fighting the motion of the boat and staring at April. It wasn't a pleasant stare either. Cliff wanted to ask him what he planned to do and where he planned to take them. But that would be a moot point. Again, Cliff decided, one way or another, the party would be over soon.

There were certain things, however, Cliff had to do to get the boat ready for the storm. For that, he would have to communicate with the sheriff. He chose his words carefully, and made sure he maintained a nonchalant tone of voice. "Looks like we're in for some heavy weather."

The sheriff's eyes met his. "What do you mean by that?" the man demanded.

Cliff pointed ahead and to the right of the boat. "Storm's a brewing."

The sheriff looked in the direction Cliff was pointing. The man obviously didn't like what he saw, almost falling off his perch in response to the dark clouds looming ahead. "What do we do?" He failed to hide the concern in his voice.

"You tell me. You're running the show."

"Don't be a smartass, boy," the sheriff snapped.

Cliff forced his voice to remain calm. "I'm not trying to be, sir. You just haven't told me where we're going."

The sheriff hesitated. "Where are we now?"

Cliff pointed to the left. "We're running just off the channel. That's Wharton's Creek over there."

"Can we go in there and ride out the storm?"

"Too shallow. We'd be aground before we ever got through the cut." It was a calculated lie.

The sheriff leaned to the side and took a long look. He pointed with the hand holding the gun. "Looks like a sailboat in there already."

Cliff looked harder. There was indeed a sailboat anchored just inside the opening to the creek. He cursed himself for being caught in a lie.

"I told you not to play with me, boy." The man pointed the gun right at Cliff. His finger was definitely on the trigger.

April stood up and moved toward the sheriff. "I told you to leave him alone."

"And I told you to sit down and shut up, little girl."

April stared the man down. "You shoot him, and I swear to God you're going to have to shoot me, too. And then you'll die as well."

The sheriff let out a nervous laugh. "Just how do you figure that?"

Her look didn't change. "You don't know the first thing about boats, and with that storm coming, I figure you'll last a whole five minutes, if that."

"What makes you think I don't know anything about boats? I got out to you, didn't I?"

To Cliff's surprise, April let out a laugh. "Well, anyone who knew anything about boating would know that Wharton's Creek is very shallow, and only boats with shallow drafts can get through the inlet."

"Then how 'bout that sailboat?" the sheriff demanded.

She laughed again. "He's obviously got a retractable keel."

Cliff wanted to warn her not to be so sarcastic. Instead, he kept his eyes on the sheriff. The man gave them both a quizzical look, questioning in his mind, first just what they were talking about, and second, whether to believe them or not. Keeping with the theme that he would always get in the last word, he said, "That's okay. I want to stay out here anyway."

It was the answer Cliff was looking for. "Then we've got to make preparations for the storm."

"Like what?" the sheriff said, this time not quite as demanding.

"Life jackets, for one."

The sheriff's face turned pale. He had the look of having watched too many Titanic movies. To ensure the sheriff remained calm, Cliff quickly added, "Just a precaution."

The sheriff hesitated before nodding his okay.

Cliff turned to April. "Take the wheel, will you. I'll go below and get the gear."

When Cliff's back was turned to the sheriff, he was able to catch her eye a moment. He gave her a reassuring glance that everything was going to be all right. Her return look showed she obviously wanted to know more details, but Cliff looked away. He didn't want her to know that said details had yet to be worked out.

Below deck, Cliff dug out a life jacket for the sheriff. It would be a tight fit, but it would have to do. For he and April, he grabbed two inflatable life vests. He got safety harnesses for everybody as well. He wanted to turn on the weather station and see just how bad this line of thunderstorms was going to be. However, he wanted to minimize the time the sheriff and April were up on deck alone. He checked on Chessie who was curled up on the couch, her head lying across her front paws. She knew there was something going on out of the ordinary. She also knew that when her master was ready for her, he'd call. Cliff gave her a quick pat on the head and reassured her everything was going to be okay. In truth, he was getting more nervous by the minute. He was about to exit the cabin when, as an afterthought, he turned around, leaned over and whispered something into Chessie's ear. A little louder, he said, "You understand, girl?"

Chessie whined that she did.

"We obviously can't outgun him so we'll have to outthink him," Cliff said softly.

Chessie whined again.

Cliff turned and headed through the cabin when he stopped. "Maybe we're not outgunned," he muttered. He opened a locker beneath the electrical panel and pulled out an orange cylinder container. He twisted off the top, reached in and took out a flare gun. He put a shell in the chamber, stuffed the weapon in his pocket and put the container away. He then hurried back on deck.

Predictably, the life jacket was a tight fit on the sheriff, but it worked. At least it looked like it would. Once fitted with her life vest, April went back to her designated seat and Cliff took over the wheel. The storm was now less than five miles away and moving rapidly in their direction. Cliff made a sweep of the area, knowing visibility was going to get bad quickly. The winds had shifted from the southeast to the southwest, but he was still able to hold the course he wanted along the edge of the channel. Waves were now over three feet and the wind meter registered gusts over twenty knots. From the height of the clouds preceding the thunderstorm, Cliff reckoned it was going to be a doozy—just like the day before. He didn't know whether that was good or bad.

He glanced back at the boat they were still towing. The dog hadn't budged since they left the Sassafras. If he wasn't so worried about everything else going on, Cliff would have chuckled. He'd never seen a seasick dog before. He took a close look at the sheriff whose expression was changing more and more to one of concern. His color was also paling. Cliff began to wonder if he was going to follow in the footsteps of his dog.

As a test to that idea, Cliff said, "Want something to eat before this storm hits?"

The sheriff looked at him. The man's eyes were indeed getting glassy. "You sure there isn't anywhere we can go to get out of this?"

"Not really." As an afterthought whose purpose was to keep the sheriff up high, and thus more exposed to the elements and roll of the boat, Cliff added, "You just stay put up there and hold on real tight."

"We're starting to rock awful hard," the sheriff said.

Cliff shrugged his shoulders as if to contradict the man. He scanned the horizon again. He saw the faint outline of a small ship in the distance heading in their direction, otherwise he saw no other boat traffic. He had already pulled the jib in halfway and was contemplating reefing the main, but decided to wait. He wanted to keep the ride as rough as possible. With the main all the way up, their degree of heel was extreme and the pitching up and down way more than was necessary. It was the effect he wanted. The sheriff had tucked the pistol into his life jacket and was holding onto the mast with both hands.

Cliff kept a close eye on the sheriff. It was obvious the man was struggling but failing to maintain his composure. If he got sick, he'd be more predictable. Cliff figured it was only a matter of time.

But the sheriff was no dummy. While he may never have experienced the feeling before, he did know what was coming. He also knew when that happened, he'd lose control of the situation. As if getting a second wind, he suddenly sat up and pulled the gun from his vest. "Where are we now?" he demanded. His voice needed to be loud to carry over the wind that was singing through the rigging.

Cliff didn't like the sudden change of tone. He also didn't like that the gun had once again come into play. The boy looked to his left. Pointing in that direction, he shouted, "We're just passing Wharton's Creek. Tolchester's up ahead."

"Can we go in there?" the sheriff inquired, pointing in that general direction.

"Under normal circumstances, yes," Cliff explained. "It's too rough now, though. There are rocks on both sides of the inlet—sharp rocks that would love to get their fingers on a boat's hull." He paused a moment for effect. "We'll have to ride it out here."

"We seem to be awfully close to shore," the sheriff pointed out. He looked around nervously.

"We are," Cliff acknowledged. "The channel runs real close to shore right here."

Sheriff Richmond hesitated. "What's that have to do with us?" His ignorance of the water was again presenting itself quite clearly.

That was fine with Cliff. It was exactly what he was hoping for. He wasn't sure what he was going to do with the information. He knew that a dumb sheriff was better than a smart one. He forced his voice to remain educational versus sarcastic. "Ships run in the channel where the water is deeper. We have to stay out of their way."

"Are there any out here we need to worry about?" His anxiousness was obviously increasing.

Cliff looked past the sheriff's shoulder. The ship up ahead was looming closer. He saw now that it was actually a large private yacht. "Not that I'm aware of."

The man's response did not surprise Cliff. "You sure?" His level of nervousness was starting to worry the boy. With care, the sheriff slid down off the upper deck. Cliff wasn't sure what was going to happen. A sinking feeling in his stomach told him it wasn't going to be good. He had to do something and do it fast. He looked back at April who was feeling the same sudden apprehension. She was starting to rise to her feet. Figuring he only had a moment to act, making sure he kept himself between her and the sheriff, Cliff turned and faced her. He stared into her eyes. For the first time since the sheriff had come on board, she showed genuine fear.

At that moment, the storm crashed down upon them with a fury surprising even to those accustomed to Chesapeake Bay weather. The *Mona Lisa* immediately responded by heeling far to port. The rail dug into the water and stayed there. Cliff looked at the sheriff who had been thrown against the edge of the seat. Instinctively, Cliff ducked as the gun was waving wildly in the air overhead. Realizing it was now or never, and hoping the sheriff would react in a predictable manner, Cliff did just the opposite of what most would have done. He steered tighter into the wind. The boat heeled even further. He knew the *Mona Lisa's* hull was structurally sound and could take more of a beating than her passengers. The question: how strong was her rigging?

"Hold on, everybody," Cliff shouted, making sure there was a sense of panic in his voice. He turned and faced April again. "I need you to get up on the other seat." He leaned forward and unclipped her safety harness. Pretending to struggle with the clip fastening her to the boat, he put his mouth close to her ear. "The Tolchester beach we went by the other day is less than two hundred feet to the port. The wind's pretty strong, but the waves are moving in that direction."

April looked at him, a quizzical expression mixed with fear.

He continued. "Just wait on the beach for me. I'll be back to get you and Chessie shortly." He paused. "Trust me."

April's eyes widened as she comprehended what he was saying. She didn't say anything though. She was already too afraid.

With April free of the safety line, Cliff turned back around. The sheriff was regaining his posture, although he was basically lying on his back looking up at the sky. And the gun was still pointed in their direction.

Cliff let the *Mona Lisa* fall off the wind. The boat righted a few degrees. Then he gave out a shout and pointed forward. "Look out for that wave," he warned.

The sheriff looked in that direction. In the same instant, Cliff brought the bow hard into the wind. The *Mona Lisa* again objected to the stress by dipping her rail back into the water. This time their degree of heel was worse than before. The sheriff fell back as he continued trying to see what Cliff was pointing to. While the man was facing forward, Cliff turned around and grabbed April by the shoulder. "Trust me," he repeated. He then pushed her over the rail. An even greater surprise came across April's face as she headed toward the water. She let out a scream.

Cliff snapped back around so he was facing forward when the sheriff looked back in their direction. His head cocked to the side. "What the hell happened?" the sheriff shouted. He pointed where April was floundering in the water.

Cliff snapped his head in the same direction. "Oh my God," he said. "Man overboard." There was a brief pause. "Chessie," he screamed.

The dog came out of the cabin in a lunge. Cliff pointed back to where April's head could barely be seen and said, "Go get her girl."

The dog didn't need to be told twice. She was over the rail in a heartbeat.

Cliff grabbed the line that controlled the traveler, the track that the boom moved back and forth on. He started to pull it and said, "We got to turn around." He let the *Mona Lisa* fall off the wind and she again came to a near upright position. He started to turn the wheel.

The sheriff sat upright. A bit of color returned to his face. He steadied the gun directly at Cliff. "No," he said, a sneer to his voice.

"What do you mean *no*?" Cliff demanded. In reality, it was the exact answer he was hoping for. The sheriff was taking the bait.

"What part of N O don't you understand, boy?"

Cliff looked back over his shoulder. "But she'll drown. Chessie will, too."

"The dog'll do fine, I'm sure. The girl on the other hand… what a shame."

Cliff looked back at the sheriff. "But—" he protested.

The sheriff waved him off with the gun. "You know, son, you could be in a lot of trouble, harboring a fugitive and all that."

"I haven't done anything wrong. I don't know what you're talking about."

"Don't bullshit me, boy," the sheriff barked. "Courts frown upon those who hide criminals, especially murderers. You could get up to five years—maybe more."

Three things immediately crossed Cliff's mind. First, the sheriff didn't know they knew Eddie was alive. Second, the more he kept the sheriff talking, the more distance between them and April. The sheriff failed to realize it, but Cliff had regained control of the boat, and she was now sailing smoothly… or as smoothly as one could under the conditions. They were making five knots just with the mainsail. Time meant distance, and that was a good thing. The third thing was that his uncle used to tell him never let the enemy know they are. In his uncle's case, he was talking about negotiating prices for crabs, not negotiating for someone's life. "What are you going to do with me?" Cliff asked, pretending to worry about his own fate.

"Depends on you."

As the storm swarmed around them, Cliff raced through a variety of scenarios about what he should do next. So far, he didn't have any good ones. Visibility worsened as the rain was now nearly horizontal. The yacht he had seen earlier was now well within view. The sight of the boat made him silently wish Jennifer was there to help him. She'd be much better at figuring out what to do. "What choices do I have?" he asked aloud.

"Well, you could be stupid and tell your story about what happened here today one way. Or you could be smart and tell it another way."

"Being smart'll keep me out of trouble?"

"You're showing signs of brilliance already."

"And you think my dog'll be okay?"

The sheriff looked at the Boston Whaler still in tow. "Ole' Bullet there's a land dog. He doesn't even like to walk through puddles of water unless he has to. I should have known he wouldn't do well out here. Your dog, on the other hand, is made for the water. He'd probably rather be in than out, wouldn't he?"

Cliff faked a smile. "Yeah."

The boy watched as the tension eased in the sheriff's face. While not put away, the gun was at least lowered.

"So, where do you want to go?" Cliff asked.

The sheriff contemplated the question. "How soon can we turn around?"

"Anytime you want. We'll just have a following sea, that's all."

"Then let's head back to where we came from."

"What about the girl?"

"No one knows anything except you and me. They'll find her body. Questions'll be asked, only there won't be any answers."

Cliff looked off into the distance as if he was mulling over the possibilities. In reality, he was stalling for time. The *Mona Lisa* bounced hard in the rough seas as the storm continued its fury. The yacht was now less than a mile away, and closing fast. With this, a plan came to mind. Cliff hoped his guess and his aim were right. "Sounds like a plan to me," he said.

"Smart boy," the sheriff said. "Real smart."

Cliff flipped the traveler line off the self-locking cleat. Holding it tightly, he said, "Can you do me a favor?"

The sheriff hesitated. "Depends."

"I need you to get back up where you were sitting before. As we come about I'll need you to unloosen one of the lines running through those cleats." Cliff pointed to a series of lines near where the man had been sitting earlier. "When I tell you, release the red one. It'll be safer for us to turn that way."

The sheriff hesitated again. Deciding he had nothing to lose, he made his way back to his perch by the boom. He grabbed the same line as before and continued holding the gun in the other. It was exactly what Cliff wanted. He let out the mainsail so the boat came upright a few degrees. The sheriff seemed to relax. He also seemed to be happier. Then again, why not? His goal had been accomplished without a lot of trouble. It amazed Cliff that he could be so callous about someone's life, especially since he had a son of his own. And he was also a sheriff, which meant he was supposed to care about people. Cliff didn't let his mind wander to April and Chessie. He told himself they'd be okay. They were probably already up on shore.

He steered closer to the edge of the channel, watching the depth gauge with a careful eye. He didn't want the yacht to think he was getting into the channel. The last thing he wanted was for the vessel to start blasting its horn.

Wiping the rain from his eyes, he glanced in that direction. If he didn't know better, he would have sworn the boat was *Hamilton's Bench*. But that wasn't possible. He had spoken to Jennifer recently and she didn't say anything about George Hamilton leaving Annapolis.

Deciding his eyes were playing wishful tricks on him, Cliff looked away and refocused on the task at hand. He reviewed his situation. While it might look bleak, he was, at least for the moment, in control. His mind worked quickly. He knew he'd have one chance and one chance only.

As it often did in situations like this, time suddenly stopped. The yacht seemed to come to a crawl as the last few yards took forever to close. Finally, the two boats started to pass. The sheriff saw the shadow and reacted as expected. He sat upright and let out a loud curse. "What the fuck are you doing, boy?"

"Nothing to worry about, sir. We're not anywhere near the channel. I'm waiting for her to pass before we turn."

The sheriff's mouth dropped open, his eyes wide and fixed on the huge mass bearing down on them. Cliff knew he was wondering if they were actually going to collide.

Just as the ship passed to the stern, Cliff yelled. "Now!"

The sheriff's eyes snapped back at him. "Now what?"

"I want to turn now. Loosen that line—the red one." Cliff started to turn the wheel.

Startled for the second time in such a short period, but wanting to make sure he did his part, the sheriff let go of the boom and reached toward the red line. He grabbed it and pulled.

"You got to pull hard," Cliff directed. "Hurry!"

The sheriff leaned over and prepared to give the line a tougher pull. Cliff turned the boat away from the oncoming wake of the ship.

"Pull harder," Cliff directed.

In any species of animal, the instinct to survive was stronger than the instinct to be in control. The sheriff got tangled in survival and slid the gun into his pocket so both hands were free for the task assigned him. He pulled, yet the line would not give. He gave it another tug and then turned back to Cliff for help. "I can't—"

His mouth dropped opened and stayed open. For the first time in his law enforcement career, he found himself staring down the barrel of a gun... in this case a flare gun—but a gun nonetheless. He started to curse, but caught himself. His years of training took over as he told himself to remain calm. "What do you think you're doing, boy?"

"Game's over, sheriff."

The sheriff's jaw dropped wider. He, however, maintained his calm expression. "Now why don't you just put that gun down before someone gets hurt."

"Seems you didn't hear me the first time, sheriff. Game's over." Cliff pulled the hammer back on the flare gun. "Now it's my turn to tell you not to do anything stupid. Understand?"

"You're making a big mistake, son," the sheriff said, trying to maintain his cool.

"Oh, am I? I think it's you who's been making the mistake these past two years."

"What makes you say that?" The sheriff was obviously starting to lose control.

"Eddie's alive. You know it, and we know it."

Control was lost. Anger won out over the years of training. "I'm going to tell you one more time, boy, put that gun down." As he spoke, he reached into his pocket for his revolver.

Deciding it would be best if he did as he was told, Cliff did indeed put the gun down. But not before first pulling the trigger.

The flare struck the sheriff directly in the mid chest. There was a loud scream as a large ball of fire attacked the life vest. The sheriff's final mistake of the whole ordeal was to let go of the line with both hands so he could focus on the fire engulfing him.

"Like I said, game's over," Cliff said.

Cliff let out the line controlling the boom. The boom and sail swung away from the sheriff. He watched the yacht's wake closely, and just at the right moment, he swung the wheel hard to starboard. The *Mona Lisa* took the wake full broad side. The boat rolled hard, causing the sheriff to slide towards the rail. Realizing he was about to fall, he reached out to catch himself. But it was too late. The boom came crashing back across the traveler, catching him in the side of his head. Three hundred pounds of burning sheriff went flying over the side of the *Mona Lisa*.

"Man overboard," Cliff said under his breath.

172

George Hamilton had been watching the sailboat on radar even before it became visible with the naked eye. Of all the water in the bay and no one else around, this fool had to head right for *Hamilton's Bench*. It did appear the boat was staying outside the channel, so if Hamilton steered on the inside, they should be okay. He'd feel better if there was more room between the two boats. A near collision course was okay in calm waters, but in weather like this…

Hamilton's Bench drove through the wind, rain and waves with few complaints. Because they were moving fast, they actually cut through the water more efficiently, and thus had less rocking versus if they were moving slower. The storm was intensifying, however, and if visibility shortened any further, Hamilton would have to cut back on their speed, especially with the sailboat up ahead.

He stared through the pelting rain and was soon able to pick out the sailboat's mast as it bobbed up and down. At first he thought it was his imagination in that the boat had her mainsail all the way up. As they grew closer, he realized his imagination was indeed reality. "What an idiot," he said to no one in particular.

"What's wrong?" Jennifer said from the chair behind him. Her notion of how much *Hamilton's Bench* was rocking was a bit more than the captain's.

"There's a sailboat out here that still has its mainsail fully deployed."

Holding onto the side of the chair, Jennifer ventured from the safety of her seat. "Where?"

Hamilton pointed off to their right. "You can just see the sail through the rain."

"Why would they do that?"

"They're stupid," Hamilton said.

"Maybe they had trouble getting it down," Jennifer offered.

Hamilton shrugged his shoulders. "They'll be lucky if the mast doesn't snap off."

Jennifer watched as the distance between the two boats shortened rapidly. She moved off to the right to get a better view over the bow of the yacht that kept climbing into the air. She held on with both hands and stood on her toes. That only lasted a second however, as *Hamilton's Bench* fell off a wave, causing the bow to smack the water with a loud thud. So much for a smooth ride, she thought. Aloud, "It's getting rougher."

"We're going to have to back down some."

He reached over and grabbed the throttles. Just as he did, Jennifer let out a yell. "That's Cliff… that's the *Mona Lisa*."

Hamilton strained his eyes to get a better look. "You sure?"

"I'd recognize her anywhere."

Hamilton looked harder. "Can you pick out anyone?"

Jennifer tried, but was unable to see past the sail that obstructed the boat's cockpit. Hamilton had the same problem.

"What do you think we should do?" Jennifer asked.

"You say Cliff's a good sailor?" Hamilton inquired.

"He's not the best sailor in the world, but he is safe."

"So, he wouldn't have his sail up in a storm like this unless there was a reason?"

Jennifer contemplated the question. "I guess," she agreed.

Hamilton let go of the throttles and picked up the binoculars from a nearby ledge. Leaning both elbows on the ship's wheel, he brought them into focus. "Does Cliff have a dingy or a small boat?"

"Not that I know of."

"Well, he does now. And there appears to be a dog in the back as well."

"He does have a dog."

"Yes, I've seen her. She's a beautiful Chesapeake Bay retriever." As an afterthought, "Why would he have her in the other boat?" Hamilton steadied himself tighter against the dash as the boat rocked in response to an especially large wave.

"He doesn't have a dingy," Jennifer said. Her face started to pale. Their eyes met.

Jennifer's eyes snapped back in the direction of the *Mona Lisa*. "What are we going to do?"

"I'm not going to do anything different until we pass her and can get a look into the cockpit." He first glanced at the compass to make sure he was holding his own course, then at the radar screen to make sure the sailboat was doing the same. Something just didn't feel right as his instincts supported his decision to maintain speed.

And then they saw what looked like the flash of a gun.

173

April sat on the beach, her arms wrapped around Chessie. Her teeth chattered slightly, but the warmth of the dog slowly took effect. It wasn't that she was all that cold, nor was she all that tired. The water was rough like Cliff said, and the waves basically pushed them into shore with little effort on their part. Her life jacket inflated as it was designed to do upon impact with the water. If anything, it hindered more than it helped. She was such a strong swimmer and the distance was so short, it wouldn't have mattered one way or the other. But she was emotionally exhausted from the whole ordeal. She'd been in a lot of tight binds over the past couple years, yet she had never really feared for her life. Even that night in the car with Eddie, she never thought about actual death. Today she did. Few people stare down the barrel of a gun held by an angry man without it leaving an impact. It certainly did with her.

Why had Cliff insisted in getting involved? This was between her and the sheriff. Cliff was just an innocent bystander who happened to be at the wrong place at the wrong time.

Then he went even further and pushed her overboard. When she first realized what he was going to do, she didn't believe it, and she wondered why.

Now that she had time to collect her thoughts, she understood.

He was protecting her. At the risk to his own life, he pushed her over the side so he would then be the center of focus for the sheriff. A smart move for her... very dangerous for him. As for the why...

She cut the thought off. She told herself he couldn't feel that way. After all, they had only known each other for a few days. How could such emotions develop so quickly?

She started to argue with herself when she realized there was this thing called *the shoe on the other foot*. They had only been together for a few days, yet she had strong feelings for him—feelings she had never experienced before, not even with Danny. She wondered what would have happened had the sheriff not interrupted them a short time ago. Could she really trust Cliff that much? Could she really trust herself? What would have happened in the shower?

"Nothing," she said aloud. "Nothing!"

She rose to her feet, telling herself that being pushed overboard was an omen—a sign that it was time for her to move on... again. She brushed the sand from her backside, wrapped her hands across her chest, took one last look out at the *Mona Lisa*, which was barely visible through the storm, and did just that.

She moved on.

174

The sheriff's recollection of the events that followed was sketchy. He had a tremendous headache from where the boom hit him in the head; and when he went over the side, he twisted his right knee on the safety rail that ran along the side of the boat. When he hit the water, the line that tied him to the boat got caught around his arm so he felt like he broke his wrist, and because he was tethered to the boat, his whole body smashed into the hull. He remembered seeing the side of the boat coming toward him as the safety line took hold and kept him from floating away. He tried to brace himself, even dropping his gun in the process, but it was no use. The wind cleared his lungs as fiberglass met fat. On top of that, he was no longer able to control the spinning of his head and stomach so sometime while he was being dragged alongside the boat, he vomited. When he was finally able to clear his head, he realized his face was burning. The smell of burning flesh filled his nostrils. He remembered he had been on fire and that he somehow was knocked overboard. All memory after that had been washed away as another gigantic wave slammed him against the side of the boat.

When he came to, he was being pulled from the water onto the deck of a large yacht. A flash from what seemed like a distant past told him it was the same boat they had passed right before he went over the side. He thought of Bullet and looked back. The runabout was already being tied to the stern of the yacht. Bullet was in the same position as before.

The sheriff tried to clear his mind. Years of training combined with honed instincts reminded him to quickly assess the situation. He knew he had lost control, at least for the moment. He remembered having been shot. He remembered being on fire. He remembered hitting the water. He could still smell the burnt flesh. He could still feel pain. He tried to ignore this as he fought to regain control. He scanned the faces leaning over him. The boy from the sailboat—the boy who shot him—stood to his left. Next to him was a pretty young thing, maybe in her late twenties. While the boy had a noncommittal expression, she wore a look of anger. Next to her was an older, quite distinguished gentleman. He was leaning over the furthest. As such, he was the sheriff's closest target. But not yet, the sheriff told himself. He had not yet finished his assessment. He blinked twice to try and clear the stinging salt from his eyes. His gaze moved to the right. There was another boy... someone he recognized. He blinked again. It looked like Danny... It was Danny Worthington. How...

His attention was diverted by yet another figure. This one was sitting in a wheelchair... a boy... a boy about Danny's age. The sheriff focused on the face. His heart skipped a beat. "Eddie," the sheriff slurred.

The face in the wheelchair turned away.

All hope of control was lost.

175

The bounty hunter took a sip of coffee and unfolded the newspaper that had been left on his desk by his secretary. He cringed as he read the headlines and the story that followed. *The Baltimore Sun* had picked up the story the moment it hit the police radios, and never let go. It had been three days and they still carried it front page. The sheriff was in federal custody, charged with a variety of crimes including aggravated assault, use of a deadly weapon and kidnaping. There was even talk of charging him with maritime crimes dealing with piracy. Once the girl's body was found, he'd be charged with first degree murder as well. Details were sketchy about what actually happened aboard the sailboat during the storm. One thing was certain, the sailboat left the Sassafras River with three people aboard, and when the coast guard arrived on the scene only two were accounted for, and neither was a female. There was a rumor that the girl made it to shore, but this was never verified by the local authorities. The bounty hunter suspected she was alive. After all, she was one of the most resilient suspects he had ever chased.

The bulk of the story focused on how the sheriff had pulled the wool over everybody's eyes these last two years, with everyone thinking his son was dead, when in reality the boy was hidden away at a rehabilitation hospital in northern Pennsylvania. The boy's whereabouts were also unclear in that like the girl had disappeared from the boat, he had disappeared from the hospital. Because they were still digging to get the actual facts, the bulk of the story focused on the deception portion displayed by the sheriff.

The bounty hunter skimmed the rest of the article quickly looking for any flag raising clues. Seeing none, he let out a sigh. There was nothing mentioned so far that would implicate him in the mess. Besides, even if there was, he had done nothing illegal, or so he tried telling himself. He responded to a posted reward, he found the party in question, and then collected the reward—all perfectly legal.

Wasn't it?

He put the main section of the paper aside and turned to the sports section. He searched out the box scores to see how he made out from his bets the night before. His luck had been running good lately. He just hoped it held a little longer.

He was about finished tallying up his winnings when there was a knock at his door. He looked at the clock partially hidden on his crowded desk. It was a little after nine. He didn't have any appointments until after lunch. He was about to get up and answer the door when it swung open and a tall distinguished looking man walked in. He was neatly dressed in khaki pants and a red polo shirt. His hair was speckled with gray and combed straight back over his head.

The man walked over to the desk and held out his hand. "Sorry to barge in like this, but my time as well as yours is very valuable, and neither of us have a whole lot of it to waste."

Normally the bounty hunter would have reacted negatively to someone barging into his office that way. He wasn't one to be pushed around. But the bounty hunter told himself to set his anger aside and remain calm. Besides, the man intrigued him.

The bounty hunter rose to his feet in case the man had more in mind than just a friendly conversation. Extending his right hand, he said, "What can I do you for this fine morning, Mr.?..."

The man in the polo shirt shook hands without hesitation. His grip was firm, almost too firm. "Hamilton… George Hamilton."

"Please, have a seat," the bounty hunter motioned.

"Thank you, but I won't be staying long."

"Then let's hear what you have to say." The bounty hunter also remained on his feet.

Hamilton glanced down at the newspaper sitting on the desk. "Those newspaper people, when they get a story they really run with it, don't they?"

The bounty hunter hesitated. The reference was too close for comfort. Telling himself to remain cool, he shrugged his shoulders. "If you say so."

"A man's career can be totally wiped out by what shows up in a newspaper. A career can be saved, too, by what doesn't," Hamilton said.

"And your point is?"

"My sources tell me you're very good at what you do… one of the best in the business. They also tell me you've been able to keep your nose clean. It'd be a shame for all that to change so suddenly, now wouldn't it?"

Whether it was the right choice or not, the bounty hunter instinctively took a defensive posture. "I don't have a clue what you're talking about."

George Hamilton reached down and flipped open the newspaper. The front page glared at both of them. "Your name hasn't shown up in the paper yet."

"Why should it?" The bounty hunter's defensiveness continued.

"Seems the sheriff had help in finding the girl. Now he's not talking, at least not yet, but you and I both know who that person is."

"You can't prove anything."

"Maybe I can't, but I bet the state's attorney's office would like to know about your breakfast with the sheriff the morning the girl disappeared. I also bet they'd like to know about the boat you rented for the sheriff… the one that took him out to the sailboat. And who might have been driving that boat when it first left the dock? Seems no one has thought about how the sheriff actually got out to the sailboat that morning, much less how he found it to begin with. I suspect a helicopter was involved in the search, too. Wouldn't you say that was a good guess?" Hamilton paused. "Taking someone to the scene of a crime makes one an accessory to the crime, don't you agree?"

"I never took anyone to the scene of anything."

"You at least provided the transportation. Same thing in my book."

"It will never hold up in court."

"Quite frankly, I hope it doesn't hold up in criminal court. I'd like nothing better than to see you get off all charges."

"Why do you say that?"

"Then your name can be added to the two million dollar civil suit that's being filed on April's behalf." There was another pause. "And as the sheriff himself is pretty much broke, that leaves the bulk of the payment up to you."

The bounty hunter made a nervous chuckle. "What makes you think I have any money?"

George Hamilton pulled a piece of paper from his side pocket and laid it on the desk. The bounty hunter looked down at the number written on the page. Hamilton continued. "That's the balance in your checking account as of eight p.m. last night. That doesn't include your stock holdings, but I can have those with a simple phone call."

The bounty hunter turned pale and filled with anger at the same time. "How the hell…?"

George Hamilton held up his hand. "Again, sir, time is wasting, and you have a lot of work to do."

While wanting to lay the man out with a line of profanities, the bounty hunter took the advice. One of the things he learned throughout his years both as a gambler and hunter was never to get emotionally involved in your work. Emotions running amuck only hindered one's ability to think straight and make rational decisions. He also learned when to cut his losses. Calming himself, he said sarcastically, "You obviously didn't come here to tell me the balance in my checking account. Nor did you come here to tell me I might be named in a lawsuit. What is it you want?"

George Hamilton smiled. "Find her."

"Her… as in?"

The smile disappeared. "Don't play stupid with me. You've got twenty-four hours to get April back to Annapolis."

The bounty hunter started to object before realizing it would be for naught. He had been right. She was alive. "To Annapolis, huh?"

"Safe and unharmed," the man said.

"And then I'm off the hook?"

"Off my hook. You'll still have to answer to the authorities, but I reckon that with a good lawyer you can talk yourself out of that one, especially if you cooperate and help with the prosecution of the sheriff."

"That would be—"

"That would be very smart on your part," Hamilton interrupted.

The bounty hunter remained silent.

Hamilton added. "And by the way, if I find her before you, the deal's off. So I suggest you get to work."

George Hamilton turned and left the office.

176

As she had caught herself doing so many times these past few days, Jennifer simply stared at the blank computer screen. Her desire to spend quality time writing had increased lately. Her ability to do so had failed to keep pace. She wasn't sure why she was having such difficulty. When she was writing, she was happy and the stressors in her life seemed to take a back seat. She always felt writing was good therapy. In the past, the more she was stressed, the better she was able to write. The more she wrote, the better she felt. The past few months, however, the stressors certainly were there, only her writer's block wasn't cooperating by moving aside. It was a phase she had been through before. It was a phase she would certainly visit again.

She still wondered why it kept cropping up.

She smiled to herself. She knew why. Stress was one thing. Chaos was another. First, Cliff came to town. Things heated up. Things cooled down. While it seemed like they were going to remain friends, their short time together certainly created a roller coaster ride of thrills. She shivered at the thought as parts of her body missed him… missed his touch, his artist's hands, his artist's lips…

She cut the thought short and smiled as a twinge of jealously pumped through her veins. Since everyone returned to Annapolis, Cliff's focus was on April—which was okay in that it allowed Jennifer to keep her to focus on other matters such as the renovation project and George Hamilton. It was a big relief to know April was okay. She found her way back to Annapolis a couple of days after the storm with Chessie at her side. She was safe and unharmed.

Jennifer's thoughts turned to Eddie Richmond. He showed up with Danny Worthington at *Hamilton's Bench* one afternoon unannounced... right before a bad storm... right before she and George Hamilton... Anyway, it turned out Eddie had also been kept in the dark about a lot of things during his time in rehab. He was not allowed visitors. He was not allowed phone calls. This certainly wasn't the normal policy at the hospital, but the sheriff carried a lot of weight (in more ways than one). Between threats and hundred dollar bills that were frequently handed out, Eddie was kept isolated from the outside world. As for the sheriff, he was found dangling from a lifeline alongside the *Mona Lisa* with burns on his chest and face, a fractured wrist and a twisted knee. He was in federal custody, locked up without bail.

So yes, life had been chaotic. And it only got worse as Jennifer herself came up with the bright idea of having the official groundbreaking ceremony for the *Riverboat Inn's* expansion over the Labor Day weekend with a huge party to follow. Both her parents thought it was a wonderful idea and immediately assigned the task of organizing the event to their daughter. Jennifer could have kicked herself for coming up with such a suggestion. She also realized the value of such an event. She dove into the project with both feet. She still tried to take a few minutes each day to put some words on paper, but the results were the same—she simply sat and stared. She was beginning to wonder if she shouldn't throw everything away and start all over. The only question: start over with what? She had no ideas in the back of her mind for a second book. The idea of emergency room stories had been her only focus for years. There was nothing else.

She pulled away from the screen and stared out the window. Many people argued over which time of day was more beautiful in Annapolis: sunrise or sunset. The town was situated on the water in such a way that the sun came up over the United States Naval Academy campus spreading rays of light out across the waterfront and town. It was a spectacular view when the sky was clear. A similar event occurred from the opposite direction each day some twelve hours later, only this time the sun set behind the capitol building, which on a clear day could be seen from the Annapolis Harbor. Both could be seen in spectacular fashion from the windows of the *Riverboat Inn's* dining room. The view was even better one story higher from the pilothouse of the *Riverboat Inn*—her apartment.

She was already up when the sun rose on this particular day, although she actually missed the official event, engrossed instead in making sure the early morning deliveries arrived on time and were correct. Since officially announcing the renovation project the week before, which coincided a few days after the story broke about April and the capture of Sheriff Richmond, business had been booming. They'd been booked every night. Whether they were curiosity seekers or people who simply wanted to be part of the in crowd, people came from all over. As this was all free publicity for the renovation project, it was imperative the *Riverboat Inn's* high standards be maintained—yet an additional burden to worry over.

Sitting at her desk, which was becoming more of an office than a place for her to write, Jennifer stared across the harbor. It was indeed a magnificent view. The sky was clear, the winds just strong enough to put a few ripples in the water. The anchorage in the middle of Spa Creek was filled and there were still boats coming in from the Severn that would need a place to moor for the night. She heard earlier that all the marinas were sold out and the city docks had been filled for the past three days. She was glad Cliff had gotten back in time, otherwise he'd be one of the ones fighting for a spot in the middle of the Annapolis Harbor.

If the weather held, it would be a beautiful sunset—the exact time for the beginning of the celebration. They decided to switch the original idea and have the party first and the actual ground breaking celebration Labor Day morning. She decided to turn off the computer and simply enjoy the sights before her.

It had been a hectic two weeks since *Hamilton's Bench* returned to Annapolis.

Jennifer knew even prior to this, she had been neglecting her basic responsibilities with the restaurant, instead spending her energy worrying about April. At the same time, as her father said, she wouldn't be much good until her cousin was found anyway. While they never said a lot about it, Jennifer knew her mother and father were just as worried. Her father had even called his sister himself to let her know April was alive and well, and had talked to her several times since. Danny said that his stepmother promised to stop drinking the moment she learned April was alive. She had been holding true to that since talking to her brother for the first time in years. They didn't tell her that April had reached the Tolchester beach safely, as evidenced by footprints and life jacket. They didn't tell her that there had been a couple of more days of panic as April had evidently run off again with Chessie presumably in tow. It was during this time George Hamilton made a visit to the bounty hunter who took to the task of finding April with gusto. At the same time, Hamilton himself threw all his resources behind the search. Because the story had now broken and the sheriff was in custody, law enforcement was involved in the search. However, it wasn't until Cliff called late one night and told Jennifer he needed to see her right away that she knew for sure April was alive and well. When she got to the *Mona Lisa*, April was sitting in the cabin, sipping on a cup of hot tea. Seems she decided she was tired of running and made her own way back to Annapolis. The official reason given by April was that Chessie refused to leave her side, so she decided to bring the dog home to her owner. The two cousins spent the next hour hugging, crying and simply talking about family. Then they got down to business as to what they should do next. A call was made to *Hamilton's Bench* and George Hamilton arrived at the *Mona Lisa* a short time later. Needless to say, he was ecstatic as well. He also couldn't stop laughing in that he kept talking about all the people who were out there looking for April, and she simply pranced back into town. Anyway, another call was made and the official search was called off.

Then the discussion began of what to do with April. She cut the debate short by stating that things would be done on her terms. For now, she didn't want to talk to anyone (meaning the press). She didn't want to see anyone, including her family, although she did talk to her mother and Danny. She definitely didn't want a big fuss made about her return.

That would all happen when she was good and ready. She simply wanted to go back out on the water a few days with Cliff and get her thoughts together.

Which is what they did—of course with frequent phone calls to check on her condition. Jennifer made Cliff get a cellphone before they left. The two spent the time basically doing what they did before—cruising around the bay. Cliff worked during the day while April sailed the boat. At night April practiced the piano while Cliff completed partials. But now they no longer looked over their shoulders every minute and they made more frequent stops at area marinas for supplies and water. They had returned to Annapolis two days before. It was amazing to everyone just how resilient April seemed to be. Cliff said she had an armor plate thicker than most tanks.

Jennifer looked at the clock on the far wall. Less than six hours before the party began, six hours to the start of a dream for her parents. Expanding the *Riverboat Inn* was something they had talked about for many years. Jennifer remembered when they bought the property behind the restaurant. It was an old run down crab picking plant that had been closed as long as she could remember. The piers were in disarray and the buildings weren't much better. Besides, they were full of asbestos. Just bringing the place up to code would cost a fortune. When the packing house had declared bankruptcy, the city repossessed the property because of back taxes still owed. They immediately put it on the auction block but pulled it off after the first auction because the bids were way below what they felt it was worth. Again, the issue was the cost of asbestos removal. Local officials spent the next year looking for a *behind the scenes* buyer, someone who would close the gap between dollars wanted versus dollars willing to pay.

The Blackstones kept a close eye on all this. Even though the place was run down, it was well hidden behind the restaurant. Under those circumstances, it had neither a positive nor negative impact on their business. Their wish was that whoever took it over would do something productive with the area.

The more time that passed, the more worried the Blackstones became about the property. While the city official assigned to the place denied it, David Blackstone heard through others that he was under a lot of pressure from the mayor to unload it. In the meantime, the *Riverboat Inn* continued to thrive, growing to be the number one restaurant in the region several years running.

Jennifer remembered the discussion that turned the tide on the whole thing. All three were having breakfast one Sunday morning. Jennifer was eating a bowl of cereal listening to her parents debate whether they should go ahead and buy the property before someone else did.

"But what are we going to do with an old crab picking plant?" her mother exclaimed.

To which Jennifer looked up and said, "Tear it down and finish the boat."

Her suggestion was the catalyst that sealed the deal. The Blackstones paid more than they wanted. The City of Annapolis received less than they felt the land was worth. However, all parties went away from the settlement table feeling pretty good. The crab plant was torn down and a small public park was built until the time came for the expansion to begin. Then the problems started regarding building permits… until recently when these roadblocks suddenly disappeared. The expansion of the *Riverboat Inn* into a full-sized riverboat was a reality. All they had to do now was build the thing.

Jennifer looked at the clock again. It was less than six hours before the party. There was still a lot to do, yet very little required of her. The gears were greased. Preparations in the kitchen were on track. The dining room was ready. The staff was busy focusing on their individual areas of responsibility. So far, the weather was cooperating. Turnout was expected to be high. The only thing Jennifer had yet to decide was the entertainment for the evening. She had a DJ on standby. All the area bands were booked because of the holiday weekend.

Jennifer wished April could be there to play the piano. She hadn't wished for anything so hard in a long time. She chuckled. If she was a really good Catholic, she'd run to the nearest church and light a few candles. What she needed was a miracle.

With Cliff and the *Mona Lisa* back in town, April remained secluded aboard *Hamilton's Bench*. She insisted she was not ready to see anyone. Cliff claimed her time out on the bay had been positive, but he said she still had a lot of things to work through. Jennifer and her parents knew that pushing the time line on this would be detrimental to April and would potentially lead to another running away episode. April needed time. Still, it would be nice if she were there to play at the party.

Jennifer turned her thoughts away from April to the others. The sheriff, well he was a real waste of a man. He evidently had been a good sheriff, even surviving the death of his wife. He just couldn't accept that his only son was paralyzed, or accept that it as an accident. Jennifer wondered how he was going to accept a long term in federal prison. He had been charged with two counts of kidnaping with other charges pending. This was enough to keep him locked up without bail. Hamilton told her there was a potential for a plea bargain, but that would only reduce the number of years he spent behind bars. If nothing else, he'd have plenty of time to mull over the trouble he had caused.

As for the sheriff's dog, like Cliff, Jennifer had never seen a seasick animal before. However, once they reached land, the dog recovered quickly. The question became what to do with the animal. Without the sheriff around, the dog seemed quite docile. He showed no aggression towards April and responded positively to Eddie once he sniffed him a bit. Eddie thought about keeping him, but quickly realized this would be impractical. Everyone was in quandary until Jennifer came up with the idea to call Bobby, the governor's bodyguard. His wife would know what to do since she was a dog breeder. Bobby solved the problem quickly by simply coming and getting the dog. He said his wife would evaluate the canine physically and emotionally. Then an appropriate placement could be decided. What was especially interesting to Jennifer was George Hamilton's concern and compassion for the dog. He had never spoken about animals one way or the other that she could recall. Yet, here he was worried about a police dog. It was the opposite reaction of his concern for the sheriff.

Jennifer's thoughts turned to the sheriff's son. Eddie Richmond had changed. Physically, he was now a paraplegic and would be confined to a wheelchair the rest of his life. There was also a drastic change in his personality. Unlike his father, Eddie took full responsibility for what happened the night of the dance. He admitted without hesitation that April had never touched the gun. The gun's firing was an accident—an accident set up by his own inappropriate and inexcusable behavior. (His words, by the way.) This barrier, a significant one broken down during his many hours of therapy, helped him through the depression that had set in and delayed his physical rehabilitation. Once on the road to recovery, Eddie finished his high school requirements at the hospital and was now studying for his GED, which he expected to pass in another month or so. He even talked about going to college.

That is, he said, if he had time. As the new maître d' for the *Riverboat Inn*, he was going to be pretty busy the next few months. That job opportunity actually came about on a comment from April who said that deep down, Eddie was really a good person and was good with people. Jennifer talked the idea over with April, Cliff and her parents who all thought it was worth taking the chance on him. The maître d' position was created just for that purpose.

Danny was another story. To everyone's surprise, especially his father who always assumed he'd one day take over Worthington Industries, Danny announced he had accepted a position as a reporter for the Worthington newspaper. Also, to everyone's surprise, Samuel Worthington didn't object. On the contrary, he was quite supportive and happy to see his son show an interest in something productive. Jennifer learned this took the pressure off the elder Worthington to keep the business in the family. Seems he had received a very lucrative offer from one of the big three auto companies to sell out. Jennifer also learned that the new owners agreed to keep the plant open for at least five years, thus giving Worthington Industries's employees some peace of mind. Sam Worthington also assured Eddie that even though blackmail was no longer a part of the equation, he'd see to any medical bills that might crop up. His generosity, his attentiveness to his wife, his support of Danny's decision to not enter the family business and the fact that he made sure his employees were taken care of in the event of a sale, caused Jennifer to reconsider her thoughts about the man.

Danny's stepmother—April's mom—kept her promise of sobriety and was anxiously awaiting the reunion with her daughter. She and April talked on a daily basis. However, April insisted there be nothing more until she was ready. Jennifer suspected that would happen soon. Jennifer herself was anxious to meet the aunt she never knew. She was just as anxious to have her father reunited with his sister after all these years. April told Jennifer she thought her mother would now be able to find true happiness in her life.

The only other loose end was the bounty hunter. Since he failed to hold up his end of the bargain by finding April, Hamilton set the dogs on him. Besides being charged with accessory to kidnaping, his name was added to the civil suit filed on April's behalf. The only problem was he had disappeared. Hamilton had little doubt, however, he'd turn up soon. All his assets were frozen, so he had nothing to live on. He was now a fugitive from the law. The hunter had become the hunted. A fitting end for yet another scum bag, Jennifer thought.

Jennifer refocused on the computer screen. Why was there so much going on around her, yet she couldn't convert that to writing? Why was she so motivated with the *Riverboat Inn* and April, yet so unmotivated to do for herself what she really liked—to write? It just didn't make sense. Maybe it was time to put the past in the past and find something new to write about.

She cursed beneath her breath and placed her fingers on the keyboard. Maybe if she just typed what she was thinking, it would help. She got out a couple of words before her mind went blank. She cursed again.

And then the phone rang.

She thought about ignoring it, but decided it might have something to do with the restaurant. She picked up the receiver on the third ring. "Jennifer here."

"Good afternoon, sweetheart." It was George Hamilton.

She sat up straight and absently ran her hand through her hair. He always brought a much needed smile to her face. "Hey."

"I didn't expect to find you in your apartment."

"I just came up here to take a little break."

"What are you doing?"

"Taking a little break."

Hamilton laughed. "Well, break's over."

"How's that?"

"I need you to come over for a few minutes."

"Now?"

"I have a potential pianist for tonight I want you to hear."

"You do?"

"Yes, but they want to audition first."

"You can do it, can't you?"

"I don't know if I'm a very good judge of music," Hamilton teased.

Jennifer laughed. "I'll take your word," she said. The last thing she wanted to do was go over there now. Well, that wasn't exactly true, either. The last thing she needed…

"Say about a half hour?" Hamilton said, breaking her train of thought.

"But…"

"Thirty minutes then." The line went dead.

177

Jennifer muttered a few curses under her breath as she closed the door to her apartment. There were only five hours left before the party, so the last thing she needed was to be called over to *Hamilton's Bench*. As she put her keys in her pocket, she told herself to be more truthful. She wasn't actually *called over*. She was invited. She continued to curse Hamilton under her breath. The problem was that when Hamilton called, he had such a persuasive way about him; you listened and ultimately did what he wanted. But that was okay, she told herself. Maybe a short distraction would do her good. The key was *a short time*. As much as she might be tempted, she couldn't stay long. While things appeared to be all in order for the party, she knew it didn't take much to change a restaurant's rhythm. She also knew the last thing the staff needed or wanted was for the boss to be prancing about nervously. That's why she had gone up to her apartment in the first place. Actually, she had been chased up there by Martha who threatened an immediate unionization vote and subsequent labor strike if Jennifer didn't quit breathing down their necks. The thinking was done. Plans were finalized. It was time to allow the staff to set it all in motion. The only thing left was to find entertainment for the evening. She had a DJ ready, but she wanted April. If only—

She cut the thought off. Maybe there was a good reason for going over to *Hamilton's Bench*—to audition a pianist.

"For just a few minutes," she muttered softly. Her thoughts continued as she headed down the outside stairs. One of the first things that struck her about George Hamilton was the mysterious cloud that hovered over him. She initially pictured him as a man who sat high upon a pedestal overlooking the world. As she got to know him, she quickly realized he wasn't as mysterious as he was private. People around him put him on a pedestal, but in actuality, he was very down to earth. To see this, you just had to break through the shell surrounding him—a shell very hard to crack. *Hamilton's Bench* reeked of boldness, luxury and success. Her owner could put on a show of being outgoing and gregarious. However, Jennifer learned early on he was just as content sitting in his office reading a good book, listening to classical music or both. He never denied how hard he worked nor how hard he played, both symbolized by the luxuriousness of his yacht. However, what he liked to do best was play quietly.

Sometimes that meant alone, sometimes that meant with Jennifer. It seemed, at least the past week or so, the more they were together, the more he wanted her with him. She certainly didn't mind the attention. She was often able to find time to run over to the boat for a short visit. He even popped in on her on occasion, which was a whole new experience for Jennifer. She never had a man call on her. She always went to their place or they met someplace neutral. George Hamilton, however, had no qualms about coming right into the restaurant to see her, if only for a moment to inquire how she was doing and to get a bowl of oyster stew which he had grown to enjoy. It was a new experience for her. It was a new experience for her parents as well. Jennifer avoided discussing her personal relationships with her folks. She very seldom brought anyone home to even meet them. This sudden change took some adjustment on everyone's part. There were raised eyebrows, especially from her mother, but both David and Elizabeth Blackstone remained supportive and kept their opinions to themselves. Her father did tease on a couple occasions that maybe there was hope for their daughter yet.

Jennifer, on the other hand, kept telling herself not to read more into this than a lonely man looking for companionship, and a lonely girl looking for the same. She knew, however, at least from her end, it was rapidly becoming much more. She was falling for him big-time. She also knew this was very dangerous. Falling big meant falling hard, and that was something she could little afford. The question was what to do. She didn't want to hurt him, or herself, but she had some doubts about their blossoming relationship. She decided she would wait a couple more days before broaching the subject. He did say he wasn't sure how much longer he was going to stay in Annapolis. Maybe that would be a good time to broach the subject.

She reached the bottom of the steps and went through the back door of the restaurant into the kitchen. She hadn't made her daily visit to Old Man Hooper and she felt guilty about that. She also felt bad about the little time she spent with him lately. He was accustomed to her sitting and chatting awhile. Lately, however, it was more of a drop and run. She just didn't have time to sit and chat, and while he always said he understood, she knew deep down he was hurt. She remembered something he once told her: "a calloused hand could still feel pain if cut with a knife."

She hurriedly fixed his lunch and headed out the door, telling herself she'd start spending more time with him once the celebration was over.

In the meantime, she tried to figure out what Hamilton wanted. He told her he had a pianist for her to hear. He said the person wanted to audition before playing at the *Riverboat Inn*. Jennifer thought that strange, but Hamilton had a way of adding a pinch of mystery to a lot of things he did in life. Like with other things, she told herself to be patient. She'd find out soon enough.

178

Louis was waiting for her at the head of the gangplank. As usual, he had a bright smile on his face. "So nice to see you again, Ms. Blackstone."

"Thank you, Louis," she replied. "Am I late?"

"No. They're all waiting for you, though." He was so diplomatic.

Before she could ask what he meant by the word *all*, he turned and led her to the entrance into the main salon. Even though the blinds had been raised and the room was brightly lit from the sunlight, Jennifer still had to pause to let her eyes adjust to the change. She took off her sunglasses and instinctively ran her hand through her hair to make sure there were no loose strands dangling across her face.

She took two steps forward and came to a sudden halt. Her mouth dropped open as she scanned the room. The moment ago question about *all* was quickly answered. Her parents were sitting across the salon on the large leather couch. Eddie Richmond was in his wheelchair, dressed in his tuxedo all ready for the evening. Danny Worthington sat on the floor next to Eddie. Against the back wall were several other chairs that had been set up for the occasion. One was occupied by Danny's father. The other by a lady Jennifer had never before met. She recognized her from the old photographs as Danny's stepmother—Jennifer's long lost aunt.

So she wouldn't stare at Mrs. Worthington or any of the others for that matter, Jennifer quickly crossed the room to where her mother sat. She leaned forward and gave her a kiss on the cheek. Their eyes met. Mother and daughter communicated silently. Her mother's expression told Jennifer she didn't know what was going on either. Jennifer looked at her father, who rose to his feet and gave her a hug. He led her over to his sister. "Jennifer, I'd like you to meet your aunt… my sister."

There were tears in the woman's eyes, so Jennifer leaned forward, gave her a kiss on the cheek and said, "You'd better not stay away so long next time." The woman smiled.

Jennifer turned her attention to Samuel Worthington. Eye contact was made. No words were exchanged. The message was clear, however. From Jennifer to Worthington, "You're still a snake." From Sam Worthington to Jennifer, "Yes, but I'm trying."

Jennifer turned and looked over at Eddie. "Well, Mr., don't you have anything better to do than be over here messing around? You've got a party to put on."

Eddie laughed. "I sure do, but I'm only doing what I was told."

"I'll vouch for that," her father said.

Jennifer's father went back to his seat. He and his wife split apart to make room for their daughter. Jennifer shook her head, instead plopping down beside Danny. She gave him a gentle punch on the shoulder. "You should have told me you were going to be here. I would have dressed better."

Danny laughed. "If I knew you were going to be here, I would have been dressed up like Eddie here."

"What's this all about?" Jennifer inquired softly.

"Hell if I know," Danny whispered back. "But I can guess."

Their conversation was interrupted by George Hamilton who entered from the back of the room. An elderly, balding, short man followed behind. Hamilton's pace was quick and rapid. His guest was a few steps slower. Hamilton wore a red Polo shirt and khaki pants. The man wore a starched white shirt, conservative print tie and a blue sports jacket. Hamilton stopped beside the piano where he turned and faced the audience.

He made quick eye contact with everyone as he began to speak. "First off, I'd like to apologize for calling this gathering on such short notice. Secondly, I'd like to thank all of you for coming on such short notice." He paused, again making eye contact with the people in the room. Then he turned his attention to the man standing beside him. "I'd like to introduce our special guest this afternoon, Professor Alexander Winfield. For those of you who do not know, Dr. Winfield is both an accomplished pianist and a world renowned composer. He also happens to be the Dean of Admissions for the Peabody Conservatory of Music in Baltimore, where he holds a full-time faculty position. As you can imagine, he is a busy man and I am very pleased that he accepted my invitation this afternoon."

"I also had relatively short notice," Professor Winfield said, getting a polite laugh from the crowd. There was obvious tension in the room as no one admitted that they knew what all this was about.

Jennifer wasn't well versed in classical music, but she recognized the name Professor Winfield. The goings on at the Peabody conservatory were well covered by the Maryland media, and whenever Peabody was mentioned, Winfield's name wasn't far behind. He was the unofficial spokesperson. He had been a world renowned pianist early in his career. However, a small stroke a few years back left him with residual weakness in his left hand. If Jennifer remembered the details correctly, he was still a superb pianist, but no longer at the top of his game. He had already been on the visiting faculty at Peabody, so the conservatory wasted little time signing him as a full-time faculty member. He not only proved to be an excellent teacher, he was also a savvy politician. In the academic world, that meant a proficiency for raising money. Now, here he was standing beside George Hamilton. Jennifer was sure the question *why* would be answered momentarily.

She was correct.

Hamilton continued. "Again, Dr. Winfield has graciously agreed to come here today... for an audition."

Jennifer's jaw dropped open. The last thing she expected was to have a world renowned pianist play at the *Riverboat Inn's* ground breaking party. She started to speak, but her mouth was bone dry. Anticipating her concerns, Hamilton said, "So, Professor, if you'd be so kind as to take a seat, the audition will begin."

A second surprise, the pianist-teacher-academic politician did not head toward the piano. Instead, he went and sat on one of the empty chairs with the others. Hamilton then looked toward the rear of the room. He nodded and April entered the room.

179

April was wearing a tan pants suit—stylish but conservative. Her hair had been recently cut and was now just below her shoulders. She looked frail, her face thinner and more drawn than before. But through it all, she was still beautiful. She stared across the room looking only at George Hamilton who gave her an encouraging smile. Eye contact was broken as a loud sob filled the room. As much as she may have tried, she was unable to avoid looking in that direction. A moment later, April was in the arms of her mother. Mother and daughter were reunited after almost two years of separation. No words were exchanged. There was no need for that at the moment. There'd be plenty of time for conversation later.

Jennifer looked over at Hamilton who was leaning against the piano watching the scene unfold before him. If she didn't know any better, she'd swear she saw tears in his eyes. There were a few other wet eyes in the room as well. Hamilton looked at Jennifer and mouthed silently, "I'll fill you in later."

"Thank you," she mouthed back with a big smile.

April broke away from her mother. She turned, scanned the room quickly and found who she was looking for. Danny was already on his feet. April hugged and held him a long moment, then pushed away slightly so she could see the person beside him.

The room went dead silent. Their eyes met. Eddie's remained fixed on her, not darting around like in the past. It was obvious both she and Eddie were at a loss for words. But not for long as Eddie announced, "No, this isn't the same tux I had on the last time we were together."

There was another moment of silence. "I liked the other one better," April said.

Eddie grinned, April managed a smile, and the room filled with laughter. It was a nervous type of laughter, but it was laughter. After all this time, after all that had happened to them, they were smiling at one another. Jennifer had no doubt there'd be times in the near future when the smiles would be gone and the conversation more intense. But for now, for this moment, for the first time they'd seen each other since the night of the dance, they were smiling.

And that was good, Jennifer decided.

Eddie picked up a small bouquet of flowers from his lap. "I've been told flowers are supposed to be given at the end of a performance. But as you know, I don't always conform to tradition." He handed her the bouquet.

She took them gingerly. It was obvious she was fighting back tears. "Thank you."

"My pleasure," he said with sincerity.

She smelled them, hesitated a moment and said, "Will you hold them for me please?"

Eddie broke into a wide smile.

Wanting to keep things on track and not wanting the festive atmosphere to deteriorate, Hamilton coughed and then began to speak. "The reason behind this get together is twofold. The first has been to reunite April with her family. She's back, and has assured us plans to stay that way." There were a few chuckles as April blushed. "The second reason…"

Dr. Winfield rose to his feet and took a quick step towards Hamilton. "Mind if I take over from here, George?"

Hamilton gave his friend a wide grin. "Still can't resist the opportunity to be on stage, can you?"

Professor Winfield returned the facial expression. He motioned around the room. "A wonderful stage and a wonderful audience it is." He reached into his pocket and pulled out a business envelope. Jennifer could see the *Hamilton's Bench* logo in the upper left corner. Holding it out for everyone to see, the professor said, "For those who don't know him very well, George here loves to play what he calls *a game of friendly wager*. This doesn't mean going to the casinos or playing the ponies, nor does he play poker in a smoke-filled room. It means that he makes friendly bets with friends and colleagues about various things happening around him. Sometimes these bets can be quite unusual." The professor looked around the room. "While I wouldn't depict today's gathering as strange, it has obviously been very full of surprises." In afterthought, the professor added, "Hopefully, the surprises will keep coming." He held the envelope a little higher. "I received a recent visit and follow up call from George who invited me here today for lunch. He also asked if I might be interested in a little wager. Naturally, I asked for details and naturally he complied." Winfield looked directly at April who had turned around and was now standing by Danny. "George told me your story, April. Quite frankly, I was moved and impressed. George also told me you're quite the pianist, and throughout your ordeal, have managed to keep up with your music. That's impressive as well. Now, while I put a lot of faith in my friend's judgment of music, it is my duty to challenge even the most ardent critic's ear. That duty, the enticement of a friendly wager, and another phone call later in the day coaxed me here."

He laid the envelope he was holding on top of the piano. "The wager, for those of you who might be interested, is quite simple. After April's audition, which is going to happen in a moment, one of two things will happen." He tapped the envelope sitting on the piano. "Either I will leave here with a check—a very generous check, I might add—from George Hamilton made out to the Peabody Conservatory of Music, or…" He reached into the other side of his coat pocket and pulled out another envelope and held it up for everyone to see. This one had Peabody's logo on it. "Or I will leave behind an invitation for April Blackstone to attend the Peabody Conservatory of Music, and do so on a full scholarship." Murmurs naturally went through the small crowd. He pointed to the single envelope atop the piano. "The choice is mine with no strings attached… and no, I can't have both; I already asked." There was more nervous laughter. He put the second envelope back into his pocket and moved toward his seat. He added, "I did put one condition on the audition, that there be other people besides myself present. At the Peabody, it's more than an audition; it's a performance under immense pressure." Scanning the room, he said, "I think we've met those criteria today." Sitting down, he looked at April. "April, please come forward. The stage is yours."

180

April looked around the room nervously. Danny gave her a soft nudge in the back. Eddie muttered a couple words of encouragement. She stepped toward the piano, her mind trying to think of a way to stall for time. She was ready. The people in the room were ready. It was just that Cliff was missing, and she wanted him there. And he promised he'd be there.

She was just about to curse him under her breath when there was a noise outside the salon. The door slid open and Cliff popped through the entrance. He looked haggard and he looked rushed. The first was often his normal appearance. The latter was unusual. He ran his hands through his hair. "Am I late?"

There were chuckles around the room. "No, everyone is just waiting for you," Jennifer quipped.

Professor Winfield rose to his feet and stepped towards the new arrival. "Mr. Davidson, so nice to see you again… and thank you so much for your call yesterday."

April's eyes went back and forth between the two men. Jennifer's eyes did the same. "You two know each other?" they said simultaneously.

Cliff shrugged his shoulders. Professor Winfield said, "Only recently, but yes. Cliff here is one of the finest new artists I've seen in a long time." Anticipating the barrage of questions that were sure to come, the professor quickly added. "However, discussion about that is for a later time. Right now, let's get on with the audition. I understand there's a big celebration planned for tonight, and the clock's ticking."

The reminder of the rapidly approaching grand opening drew Jennifer's attention away from her many questions. "Sounds good," she said. She looked at April. "Break a leg… isn't that the good luck thing they say?"

"Not coming from an old emergency room nurse," Cliff chirped.

Everyone laughed. Those still standing found seats. April slid onto the piano bench. She adjusted the seat slightly as the room went silent. Her hands rose above the keyboard; she bowed her head and closed her eyes. Her hands dropped onto the keys. The first notes of Beethoven's *Moonlight Sonata* flowed forth.

Jennifer glanced around as the music filled the room. Eddie sat in his wheelchair, a smile on his face. He seemed very comfortable in the environment in which he unexpectedly found himself. It was evident he was a changed person. It had to be tough, seeing April after all this time. Danny sat with a touch of a smile as well. He was slouched back and had one leg crossed over another. His left arm was draped over the back of Eddie's wheelchair. Both boys seemed to be taking it all in stride. Jennifer's mother and father sat with hands folded in their laps. Jennifer was sure her father wanted to explode in glee at finally seeing his sister and meeting his niece after all these years.

The sonata ended a lot sooner than Jennifer remembered. Then she realized April must have played a short version, if such a thing existed. There was a momentary pause as if people didn't quite know what to do. Then Danny and Eddie started applauding. Others quickly joined them. Except for Mr. Winfield, who sat motionless in his chair. His expression remained unreadable. His stare remained forward.

April looked out over the top of the piano. She blushed and smiled, then looked back down at the keyboard. Her hands rose much further off the keys this time as the next piece for her audition started. Jennifer learned later it was a piece by Tchaikovsky.

Jennifer focused on her cousin. While Beethoven's *Moonlight Sonata* was played with emotion and charm, this piece was played with surprising ferocity and power. One would never meet April on the street and guess she could make a Tchaikovsky piece come so alive. Jennifer looked around the room. George Hamilton usually kept his emotions close to his chest. Today, he glowed with a happiness Jennifer had never seen before. Somehow, someway, he had masterminded a brilliant plan, and that plan was coming together right before his eyes. The thing that really struck Jennifer, George Hamilton would get absolutely nothing out of this ordeal. He was doing it all because he was a great guy. For whatever reason, he had picked April out as someone special, and he was doing everything in his power to ensure she had an opportunity for a bright future. Jennifer stared at the man a long time. Her earlier thoughts about their relationship evaporated. She realized at that moment she was falling in—

She snapped her head away from the Hamilton and looked over at April's mother and stepfather. Mr. Worthington seemed squeamish at first. It was obvious he was uncomfortable with what was happening. It was just as obvious he didn't like surprises. The first expression that crossed his face when April walked into the room was one of fear. He recovered quickly, and once he saw the expression on his wife's face, seemed genuinely happy to see April. Jennifer noticed he was especially attentive towards his wife, who was simply beside herself with joy. She never stopped crying the whole time. Even now, while her daughter played, tears rolled silently down her cheeks. Of everyone in the room, she was the most affected by what was happening. Jennifer couldn't blame her. The bond between mother and daughter was the strongest bond of any human relationship.

Jennifer glanced over at her own mother who was looking her way. She smiled and nodded in agreement, almost as if she were reading her daughter's thoughts—for the moment, everything was just peachy!

The Tchaikovsky piece ended. This time there was no hesitation before the applause started. The next piece was a short work, more of a song than a classical piece. After that, April went right into a more classical piece that produced a deep dark, almost depressing sound. It was relatively short as well. She paused only a moment before beginning the next selection, which Jennifer recognized as Chopin's *Polonaise*.

Jennifer looked toward the professor. He hadn't budged. His eyes remained fixed on April. He was obviously concentrating greatly, almost as if he were in a trance.

When the piece was over, there was more applause. April looked up and found Hamilton's face. He was clapping and beaming widely. Jennifer noticed he also gave his crew member a slight nod. Jennifer had no doubt the nod from the ship's master meant more to April than all the noise reverberating around the room.

When the applause died, the room fell silent. Barely moving his head, Professor Winfield spoke. "A great performer is always prepared to give his or her audience more than what was printed in the program. This is known as an encore. Are you, April, prepared to give us an encore?"

April, who was now looking at the professor, looked back toward Hamilton. He nodded again. Without breaking eye contact with April, Hamilton said, "Isn't it true Dr. Winfield, that all great performers also have a signature piece?"

"That is correct, but we usually don't see that developing in our students for several years."

Hamilton again nodded at April, and the first trill from George Gershwin's *Rhapsody in Blue* filled the room.

Twelve minutes later April played the final run notes to loud applause. Those who could, were on their feet cheering loudly. Danny and Eddie threw in a few cat calls and whistles. April simply sat and stared at the keys. It was a long moment before she looked up. She rose from her seat and bowed to the crowd. As the applause faded, the room filled with an eerie silence as everyone waited. They weren't sure for what, but they waited.

Dr. Winfield rose to his feet and walked to the piano. He leaned forward, whispering something to April. Her head bobbed up and down and Jennifer heard her say, "Here is okay."

The professor turned and faced the crowd. "I asked April if she wanted my comments in private of if she wanted me to share them with all of you as well. She chose the latter. So here goes." He paused. "First, April, I want to acknowledge the poise which you showed here today. I have sat through hundreds... probably thousands of auditions in my life, but never one quite like this. It required a unique set of skills to rise to the occasion, and you met those demands without hesitation. Second, I want to compliment you on your selection of music. You demonstrated both depth and diversity in your repertoire, and that's a very good thing to do. I would like to ask you about the two short pieces you played in the middle of the set. I did not recognize either of them, so I assume they were your own works?"

April nodded.

"Are they titled?"

April got a confused look on her face.

"Do they have names?"

"Yes," April said. "The first is a song I wrote for my mother a few years back. It's called *Happy Birthday Bouquet*. The second piece..." She hesitated and looked over at Cliff.

Cliff spoke up. "She didn't name it, but I call it *Trilogy in G Minor.*"

"Very good. I like it."

"You do?" April said, the surprise showing in your voice.

"The title, dear." Dr. Winfield smiled. "The piece needs some work."

Hamilton spoke up next. "Remember, Professor, she's had no formal training in music or music composition."

"I'm well aware of that," Winfield said. "However, as a critic, it is my duty to be open and honest. The first piece I liked a lot, but it was just that, a song. The trilogy piece..." He looked at April. "*Trilogy in G Minor* shows creativity and good use of a minor key, but again, it needs some work. That's all I have to say for now regarding your composing."

Faces around the room began to drop as everyone prepared for what they were sure was coming next. The great professor didn't torture the crowd too long. "As for my opinion of April as a pianist..."

Professor Winfield again whispered something to April. Keeping his back to everyone, he seemingly readjusted his sport coat. He straightened up and stared April in the eye. There was a wink that only April could see. Then he turned and walked out of the room.

All eyes snapped towards April. She had her hands up to her mouth. Tears poured down her face. She was staring at the top of the piano where two business envelopes lay side by side.

181

Sometime during the course of their lives, most people complain about those things they couldn't control. These usually deal with events surrounding other people or acts of nature. A common and frequently asked question: why did that happen to me and why did it happen now? Seldom does one give credit to this unseen force when something good happens. Jennifer Blackstone was no different than most. She was quick to ask the above questions. Why was life treating her so? Why did what happened at Annapolis General happen to her? Why did Daniel Baker have to die? Why couldn't she write her book like she wanted? Why was a member of her family involved in such a messy situation that took almost two years to resolve?

Why? Why? Why?

On this night, however, things were different. More than once over the past hour she said a short prayer to the man above. The day started out with a few problems. All had been solved with minimal effort. Her biggest wish for the evening had come true. April was there to play the piano. She hadn't yet been able to ask George Hamilton how he had convinced April to do the audition in such a fashion. Professor Winfield explained it as the need to prove herself under pressure. No one could challenge April on that. The young Blackstone came through with a vengeance and played brilliantly. In doing so, she earned a full scholarship to one of the most prestigious music conservatories in the world… and was reunited with her family at the same time! Not bad for thirty minutes of work. Jennifer smiled to herself. She felt a deep inner pride. All doubts she had about traveling to Worthington Valley in the first place were erased the moment she saw April enter the main salon of *Hamilton's Bench* and give her mother a hug. There wasn't a dry eye in the room.

The experience also changed Jennifer's attitude about George Hamilton. On the way over to *Hamilton's Bench*, she was thinking about pulling back. Walking back to the *Riverboat Inn*, she realized that would be a mistake. For that afternoon, while April was auditioning, Jennifer fell in love with their host.

"Miracles do happen," her mother said on the walk back to the restaurant.

And now, yet another miracle was happening right before her eyes. It was less than three minutes to sunset. Cliff told her the day before not to worry when she was complaining that the sunset was going to be obstructed by the clouds. The changing of the guard still occurred. "Just because you can't see something doesn't mean it's not there," he said. It was a profound statement from such a young person. (Jennifer later learned the lesson had originally come from his uncle.) It was a statement she had actually thought about walking back from *Hamilton's Bench* a short while ago. It was a statement she was thinking about now. She looked around the room. What was there that she couldn't see? Her eyes stopped on George Hamilton. He caught her look, smiled and blew her a soft kiss. She swore she could actually feel it land on her cheek. What couldn't she see in this brilliant man whom she had fallen in love with this very afternoon? What was he not telling her? Was it good or bad?

She told herself to think about that another time. *Now* should be her focus. She broke eye contact from Hamilton and looked out the window. A cloud covered sunset was not on the menu tonight. The sky was totally clear. The view out the restaurant windows was spectacular. The sun had nearly completely submerged below the western horizon. Its brilliance, however, still spread a majestic blanket of orange light across the clear blue sky. The dining room and bar, packed to the gills, had been a bee hive of activity and noise only moments before. Now with everyone holding a glass of champagne, all eyes were turned toward the west. All conversation had stopped. Even the wait staff seemed smitten by what was happening.

Jennifer stood along the back wall with her parents. Bertha had also come from the kitchen to watch. She had a glass of bubbly in hand, waiting for the okay to guzzle it down and return to her tasks. Danny was there, his eyes darting around the restaurant, wondering just what was going on. He had mentioned more than once just how chaotic everything looked, yet how smoothly everything was actually running. Jennifer responded with the same comment each time. "That's the food service industry at its best."

Eddie wheeled over to the group. He had two unopened bottles and several glasses in his lap just in case someone had been missed. "Everything okay?" he asked.

Everyone nodded in the affirmative. Things were just perfect. Maybe they were more than perfect. Jennifer looked around the room again. Something was different. The place looked spectacular, but…

Jennifer suddenly realized there were large baskets of multicolored flowers strategically placed around the room. She leaned over and whispered to Eddie, "Where did all those flowers come from?"

Eddie started opening a bottle of champagne. "You told me to make sure the place looked festive. What's more festive than beautiful people and beautiful flowers?" The cork popped and he poured a glass of bubbly.

"So, you have an expense account already," Jennifer teased.

"Not at all. Consider them a gift from me to you."

"For?"

"For giving me my life back. It was you that found me, right?" He handed her a glass of champagne. "Thank you."

Jennifer took the glass. While she was able to keep her hand from shaking, she was unable to hold back the tears. "You're welcome."

Just then, the old ship's bell that sat on the bar rang out loudly. Right on cue, the bartenders counted down the last ten seconds and when the sun completely disappeared from view, everyone raised their glasses in the air. The champagne was swallowed and the place erupted in a round of applause. Jennifer wanted her father and the governor to say a few words. However, much to her surprise, both men declined the opportunity. She wasn't surprised at her father's response. He was never one to get up in front of a crowd. The governor, however, was never known to be shy in public. On this occasion, however, he insisted this not to be perceived as a political event. He wanted it to be just what it was, a celebration for the Blackstone family and their guests.

So instead of speeches, April started playing the piano. The first run of *Rhapsody in Blue* began just as the applause died down. The place immediately erupted in a loud cheer. April looked up and appeared stunned at the response. There were few in the restaurant who didn't know April's story. Those who didn't when they walked in had surely been briefed by then. Many had already heard about the audition earlier in the day. The story was fueled by April's mother to anyone who happened by.

April looked over at Jennifer. The elder cousin gave her a big smile. The pianist then looked at the table closest to her. George Hamilton was beaming and applauding loudly. April's mother had her hands up to her mouth as tears ran down her face. She really hadn't stopped crying since seeing her daughter earlier that afternoon. Sam Worthington stared at April. He had one hand around his wife's shoulders; the other was clapping against the table. He'd been carrying an expression around that took Jennifer awhile to figure out. She finally realized it was the look of relief. Except for the sheriff, he knew more of the truth than anyone. Right or wrong, because of the whole blackmail thing with the sheriff, he had been unable to share what he knew about Eddie. That burden was lifted, and it showed. Danny even made a comment to Jennifer earlier that his father seemed like his old self. Jennifer wasn't sure of her willingness to erase the man off her shit list yet, but as she watched his reaction to April and his attentiveness to his wife, Jennifer knew it wouldn't be long before it happened.

Jennifer looked again at April's mother. She still seemed to be shell-shocked at seeing her daughter. At the same time, she seemed to relish in the energy filling the room. Much of it was due to the festive atmosphere of the grand opening, flowers included. Much of it was created by the music filling the air. Much of it was being the mother of a star—a lost star that had now been returned to its rightful place in the universe.

Jennifer smiled. Her parents had put her in charge of the celebration. They let her do the job without a lot of interference, too. Except for advice when asked, they pretty much sat back and let their daughter do her thing. Jennifer was sure they were pleased. She certainly was. She couldn't have asked for better weather, a better turnout or better entertainment. She hoped the rest of the evening went as smoothly. She was just about to think things couldn't get any better when Martha came up and told her there were a couple guests in the front who asked to see her.

"They aren't on the reservation list, so I didn't know what to do," Martha explained. "I suspect you'd want to know about 'em, though," she quipped. Before Jennifer could demand an explanation, she was gone.

Jennifer made her way to the front. It took her a second to find who Martha was talking about, but there he was, all dressed up in a tie and sports coat. He had even combed his hair. While she always thought him attractive before, he looked especially handsome tonight.

"Cliff, if you don't look…"

Cliff gave her a hug and kissed her on the cheek. "If I don't look what?"

"I was going to say handsome, but I didn't want your head to swell," she said. She stepped back so she could get a better look. "Anyway, you clean up real good."

"So do you," Cliff said raising and lowering his eyebrows in a flirtatious motion.

"You like my dress?" She was wearing a plain yet formal and very stunning long yellow dress, cut low in the front—too low for her mother's taste but not for the guys at the bar. Her parents had given her a single carat diamond necklace when she graduated from nursing school which now hung around her neck. She had thought about having her hair done. However, thanks to George Hamilton's surprise party, she ran out of time. Her aunt was able to help her pin it in a bun. Everyone said she looked beautiful tonight, and that made her feel really good about herself. She thought Hamilton was going to trip over his own feet when he first saw her. Naturally, she was pleased about that. However, for reasons that weren't really clear, it was Cliff's approval she sought the most.

Cliff broke her train of thought. "My invitation didn't say one way or the other, but I didn't think you'd mind. I brought somebody."

"You brought somebody!" Jennifer belted out almost too loudly.

Cliff nodded towards his left. Jennifer's eyes followed the motion. The next instant her eyes swelled with tears. "Mr. Hooper!"

"Evening, Jennifer," the old man replied. He stepped forward and gave his favorite gal a hug.

"Well, if you don't look a sight," Jennifer said accepting the greeting. He wore a light blue dress shirt and blue blazer. He also had on freshly pressed khaki pants. No tie though, and he had on his old boat shoes.

"Your friend here blackmailed me," Mr. Hooper said, poking Cliff in the side.

"He did, did he?"

"He said he was going to tell your mother that I no longer liked her oyster stew and that she shouldn't bring it over anymore."

Jennifer laughed and returned the hug. "We know better than that, don't we?" She kissed him on the cheek. "Anyway, thanks for coming. It means a lot to me."

The old man blushed.

"By the way," Jennifer added, "where'd you get the threads?"

Cliff laughed. "That's why I was late for April's Audition. He and I went clothes shopping. He couldn't make up his mind what to get."

"It was you couldn't make up your mind," the old man protested.

Cliff laughed again. "It was me fighting with you to get a tie."

Mr. Hooper grabbed the lapel of his sports jacket. "You may have gotten me into this, but I ain't ready to be hanged yet."

Jennifer laughed, too. "Anyway, come on in. Mother'll probably faint when she sees the two of you."

And she almost did, too.

182

April lay in her cabin aboard *Hamilton's Bench*, staring at the ceiling, one hand across her chest, the other holding the envelope from Professor Winfield. She was exhausted, yet she was wide awake. Part of her wanted to do nothing except sleep. Part of her wanted to stay awake so the day would never end. It was the day of her dreams. A day she was reunited with her family. A day she could stop running. A day she could look beyond the next meal, the next task aboard *Hamilton's Bench*, beyond the next bend in her moment-to-moment life. A day she could put all bad things in the attic and start looking to the future. She could again face the world as April Blackstone. She had lived day by day for so long, she knew nothing else. Now here she was with absolutely nothing to fear, no place to run, no need to run. It was as if time had come to a standstill. It felt strange, but it felt good. She was reunited with her mother, with Danny, with her stepfather, and in a very weird way, with Eddie. Maybe weird wasn't even the correct word, but it didn't matter. She was glad he was alive. She was glad he was okay. She was glad they had been able to talk; or rather, she listened as he poured out his soul to her. He took full blame for what happened over the past two years and apologized numerous times. At the end of the conversation, which took place a short time after the audition on the bow of *Hamilton's Bench*, he asked that she please keep an open mind so that one day she might forgive him.

It was a different Eddie than she had ever experienced. The cocky teenager was now a mature, humble young adult. The sharp tongue was now mellow and softer. He looked her in the eye for more than a second, no longer worrying about who else might be in need of his attention. He spoke slowly, he spoke with newfound wisdom, and he brought her beautiful flowers. Things had obviously changed for him. He had a whole new perspective on life. He claimed he was a much better person. He confessed he had conflicting feelings about his father. A natural instinct April understood only too well, especially now that she and her mother were reunited.

It definitely was a strange conversation. He was so sincere. His was focused on more than… more than…

Chicks, April finally decided. He was now more than a chick magnet.

As far as forgiveness, she'd have to think about that. But her initial impression was positive.

None of this, however, answered the question of how she was going to handle her own future. Cliff suggested she take one day at time—get her feet back under her so to speak. Jennifer told her not to even worry about it for a while. Her newfound cousin suggested she spend some time with her family. Mr. Hamilton, on the other hand, suggested a completely different approach. He said she should immediately start thinking about not only the next week or month, but the rest of her life. He said the quicker she focused on that, the quicker she'd be able to put the past behind her. He said dwelling on what had happened would only drag her down an unwanted path of craziness. He claimed, with a smile, that she was already crazy enough. She asked him what he had in mind. He suggested she think about something she had dreamed about all her life. She told him that playing Carnegie Hall was her favorite. He insisted that was a good goal, only it would take some work getting there. She laughed.

So the audition happened, not in front of Beethoven like she dreamed. Then again, maybe he was in the room with her. Maybe he was watching over her, guiding her, giving her the confidence she so desperately needed. She could only hope he would continue to be with her.

It had been a busy afternoon, but she did have a chance to talk to Danny a few minutes and learn that he was never in cahoots with Sheriff Richmond. It turned out he never actually saw the sheriff on the boardwalk at Atlantic City. He thought he did, but as fate would have it, a group of bicyclists got in his way. By the time they passed, the sheriff was gone. He figured it was simply his subconscious playing games. April told Danny that he did indeed see the sheriff, and that at one point they were a mere stone's throw apart.

April played at the *Riverboat Inn* party and was a huge hit. She normally drew a lot of applause aboard *Hamilton's Bench*, but nothing like she received at the *Riverboat Inn*. On a couple of occasions, the crowd applauded for nearly a minute. They didn't fuss too much when she took a couple short breaks, but they refused to let her stop at the end of the evening. April played an hour longer than planned. Her cousin came over and told her she'd be compensated for the extra time. April held up the Peabody envelope still in her possession and said that she'd already been paid enough on that day.

April rolled onto her side and faced the bulkhead. She buried her face in her pillow, imagining she could once again smell the smoke from her mother. It had been a long time since she experienced that sensation. It was something she missed, something she longed for. She read her scholarship letter over and over again. She was going to Peabody. Everyone in her family, including her stepfather, was ecstatic and supportive, although her mother said she was already having reservations about being separated from her daughter again. Her stepfather assured her that wouldn't be a problem. He'd already arranged for a real estate agent to find suitable housing in Baltimore. He promised his newly sober wife there would be frequent visits. While April had always dreamed of becoming a concert pianist, she never thought much about how she was going to get there. Dreams work that way. Reality, however, was a much different story.

She thought about all that had happened and all the people who helped her get to where she was—free and not running. She certainly owed a lot to Mr. Hamilton for what he did and continued to do, but there were others deserving of her gratitude as well. Near the top of the list was Jennifer. She had gone out to Worthington Valley and took a job as a nurse, just to get more information about what happened the night of the dance. It was Jennifer who discovered the cover up, and it was Jennifer who found out that Eddie was alive. From listening to the story, as told by Mr. Hamilton the first night April was back aboard *Hamilton's Bench*, there were many times Jennifer could have simply given up. But she didn't. She was determined to solve the mystery behind the cousin she never knew. And she did.

April wondered where she'd be today if Jennifer hadn't seen her the day she came out to greet Mr. Hamilton and the governor. She figured she'd either be working aboard *Hamilton's Bench* or back on the run. Without Jennifer, she'd still be separated from her mother and other family members.

And she would have never met Cliff.

Cliff… here was a guy she didn't know, who got involved purely out of his friendship with Jennifer, who had actually risked his life for her. One might think that pushing her over the side of the *Mona Lisa* was a strange way of helping, but April understood from the moment it happened exactly why he did it. The reason she ran when she got to the beach was so the sheriff would think she drowned and would let Cliff go. It wasn't until she saw the story in a local newspaper, including the sheriff being in jail, that she returned to Annapolis. Besides, Chessie refused to leave her side and April felt an obligation to return the dog to her rightful owner.

It seemed she had been running her whole life. April's first recollection was her and her mother running from her father. Then she was running from the boys in woods. Then she was running from Eddie's initial advances, and then on the night of the dance, she began a marathon.

Now it was over. There was only one more race to finish. There was only one more person to thank.

Of everyone, Cliff was the one who confused her the most. She didn't understand why he did what he did for her. Of everyone, Cliff got the least in return. Mr. Hamilton, sure, he did a lot for her too, but that was only after she hired on as a crew member. And he did get a pianist. Jennifer and the rest of the Blackstone family, well, they were just that. Family obligations run deep. Plus, there was this whole thing between her uncle and her mother. That was now on the way of being resolved. But Cliff unselfishly risked his life…

She felt a deep urge to see him. She jumped to her feet and stared at the back of her door. She hoped he was aboard the *Mona Lisa*. She hoped he would welcome her aboard. After all, she hadn't spoken to him all that much since the audition. She remembered she hadn't really thanked him properly. That would be a good excuse to go over now.

She changed clothes, combed her hair and checked herself in the mirror. Her face flushed from an embarrassing wave traveling down her spine. It had been a long time since she'd been worried about her looks for a boy.

She left the cabin and hurried up on deck.

September was officially here and the night temperature had dropped significantly from the heat of the day. She wrapped her arms across her chest and headed for the city docks. She was surprised how many people were still out and about. The party at the *Riverboat Inn* was just breaking up and she imagined many of the people were from there. She bent her head down to the ground so no one would recognize her. She didn't want to be antisocial, but she was on a mission. She had someone to thank.

There was also something else she'd been thinking about. It was a strange idea, she knew, and since it involved Cliff, she was anxious to discuss it with him.

183

Cliff took a sip of beer as he laid the dull pencil down and picked up a fresh one. He stared over the top of the bottle at the scene before him. The drawing was of the *Riverboat Inn* as seen from the bow of *Hamilton's Bench*. He had taken the photographs the day before. He wanted to give the drawing to Jennifer as a thank you and to let her know they were indeed still friends. Their agreement was intact.

He had watched her during the party. She was friendly towards him when she wasn't running around solving another crisis. Most of her free time, however, was spent at George Hamilton's side. There was no doubt her interest was more than friendship. Cliff's keen eyes for details told him the feeling was mutual. He told himself he shouldn't be upset and jealous. He and Jennifer were friends, nothing more. They had talked about that. They had their fling. It was good for both of them. Now it was time to move on. His guy genes would never allow him to admit it, but he needed Jennifer as a friend more than anything else. Truth be told...

He laughed. "The whole truth," he mouthed softly. Another carrot had been thrown into the soup known as his life. When he first agreed to meet with April in the hospital, he never imagined anything more would come of that. He made a visit out of his friendship with Jennifer. When Chessie saved April that night in the storm and he agreed to take her away from Annapolis it was the same thing. He was just helping a cousin of Jennifer's. Well, April quickly changed from being just a cousin of Jennifer's to April Blackstone, alias April Whiterock. She had a personality of her own and a life of her own. It didn't take Cliff long to realize she was a very unique and special person. The more time he spent with her, the more he got to know her. The more he learned of her story, the better he liked her. He tried to control the progression of these feelings—these emotions—but like most people's, they had a mind of their own. They chose their own path, ignoring any obstacles along the way. April went from being just a long lost cousin of Jennifer's, to the April who had somehow escaped from the hospital and ended up in the Annapolis Harbor, to April the cute, intuitive, strong survivor and pianist, to April the person he now saw as a soul mate. He didn't quite know what soul mate meant. He did know it was an entirely new experience for him. The more he got to know her, the more he wanted to know. The longer they were together, the more time he wanted. He was angry at the sheriff for interrupting this time, especially when their relationship was about to enter a new level. He was angry at the sheriff for what he had done to April these past two years. The lies, the fears, the forcing her to run and then chasing her like a dog—all this played on Cliff's opinion of the man. But in somewhat of a convoluted fashion, Cliff thanked the sheriff. He had chased April right into Cliff's arms.

The hardest part was not finding April on the Tolchester beach when he went back. It took him a long time to understand why she had run again. After all, didn't she feel the same about him? It was Danny Worthington who explained it in a way Cliff understood. April ran because she knew nothing else. It was a reflex she had developed starting the night of the shooting. Like a wild animal who feared for its life, the first choice was always to escape. She ran from the beach because of fear. Ingrained reflexes did not allow her the mental fortitude to wait around and see what happened. For all she knew, it would be the sheriff who came looking for her.

Once she was back aboard the yacht, it was George Hamilton who took the time to tame the wildness in her. He was the one who convinced her she no longer had to run. He was the one who gave her her future back. Through all this, Cliff's respect for George Hamilton grew rapidly and his feelings towards April grew stronger.

The question now was where to go with all this? He and April really hadn't had a chance to talk since she and Chessie came back to Annapolis. He was with her during the morning of the audition, only to help her mentally prepare for what was going to happen that afternoon. Initially he thought it would be hard to get her to do the audition, especially in front of family and friends. She agreed under one condition—he had to be there with her. While he was late, he was there. And she played wonderfully. However, all that didn't answer his big question. Cliff just hoped they had a chance to talk more before she went away to Baltimore. The start of the fall semester was less than a week away. The question then became what would he say? How would he say it? People always told him he was good with words. Still, he wondered. He remembered something a customer told him once—a little old lady in a mink coat to be exact. She told him to shoot straight in life. Isn't that what Jennifer had done? In spite of it not being what Cliff wanted to hear, it was the right thing to do... the agreement, that is.

"Shoot straight," he mouthed. But time was of the essence.

Cliff focused on the unfinished drawing before him. He wanted to get it done tonight so he could give it to Jennifer in the morning. He figured he had spent enough time in Annapolis. He needed to get back on the bay and continue working on new material. He had a lot of orders to fill. Between his commitments to the governor and Ms. Syzeman for the capital improvement project, and to his agreement with the Adamses in Philadelphia, Cliff figured he'd be busy for a long time. Besides, Jennifer told him he'd be a major part of the *Riverboat Inn* renovation. And like she said before, she wanted him to focus on the people of the bay, arguing that it was the people that made the Blackstone business so successful. Cliff did several drawings of Jennifer on the boat, but he had not drawn a close up of a human form since.

He thought of the drawing he did several years before of his uncle working the pots aboard *Rose Bud*. He forced the sadness aside, reminding himself the drawing won an award. It was good. He was good. He could do this, he told himself. And he would, especially for Jennifer. Then he remembered the drawings of April he had yet to complete.

There was also a secret drawing commissioned by Jane Syzeman of the capitol building. It was due by election night and would be presented to the governor by his staff as a gift on the night of his reelection. Cliff told himself all was good. He was determined to shake off the pressure and concentrate on quality.

A smile crossed his face. His career was off and running, much quicker and faster that he expected. Everyone seemed to like his work. Everyone gave him high praises. Still, he continued to harbor a doubt. Friends and family were always going to say good things. The true test came with objective eyes—the true critics of the world. Cautiously, he felt he was passing the test. The Adamses, George Hamilton and Maryland's Governor gave him high marks, but the two people whose comments meant the most were first, Professor Winfield. Mr. Hamilton bought one of the drawings of the Bay Bridge, telling Cliff it was for an old friend. He invited Cliff to go with him to Baltimore for the presentation. It was a hot August day, too hot to work, so the artist accepted. Professor Winfield was pleased with the drawing and went on and on about the quality of Cliff's work, saying that if Cliff could write music as well as he could write art, he could have a go at Peabody. The visit was short, during which time George Hamilton made the initial invitation for the professor to visit *Hamilton's Bench*.

The second person whose comments meant a lot to Cliff was Old Man Hooper. To Cliff, his blessing was a Godsend. Unbeknownst to Jennifer, Cliff stopped by Old Man Hooper's boat at least once a day, usually during one of Chessie's walks. While he never said much, Cliff could tell the old man liked the visits. He always seemed to perk up when Chessie bounded aboard and went right to the man for a back rub. The dog loved exploring the various nooks and crannies of the *Windskater*. The old man didn't seem to mind as Chessie did her exploring without being destructive. She was a gentle happy dog. One day, at Mr. Hooper's request, Cliff brought over several drawings for the old man to see. Cliff picked two of the Annapolis Harbor and one of the Bay Bridge as seen from the northern approach. Old Man Hooper examined Cliff's work without comment. He simply stared at the drawings placed at his feet. Cliff noticed that his hands stopped working the hole in the net. The old man studied the drawings for several minutes. Then he gathered them up and placed them carefully back in their folder. He leaned the folder against the bench beside him and went back to work on his net.

Cliff unwrapped three peanut butter and jelly sandwiches. He set one on the deck for Chessie. He laid one on the bench for Mr. Hooper. The third was his. The old man tied a few more knots then grabbed the sandwich and started chewing the bread.

"Best peanut butter and jelly I ever ate," the old man said with his mouth full. He swallowed and took a sip of the coffee Cliff brought. "You can't make coffee worth a damn though, boy."

Cliff laughed, his own mouth full of food. "I'll work on it."

"You do that."

They finished their meal in silence. Cliff cleaned up the trash and rose to his feet. He leaned forward across the bench for the drawings. The old man reached out and grabbed the artist's arm. Cliff could feel the rough callouses against his skin. "Jennifer takes care of all my financial affairs," Mr. Hooper said. "You let her know what I owe her for these three drawings. You be fair to yourself, too. Understand?"

Cliff straightened up. It took him a moment to comprehend what just happened. There was a sense of shock, followed by a sense of gratitude and pride.

Yes, the old man's opinion was very valuable.

Inspired by his thoughts, Cliff brought his eyes back into focus. The artist's pencil started to move.

184

Cliff certainly wasn't a non-religious person. At the same time, he wasn't overzealous about the issue either. His uncle was the same, teaching Cliff that you didn't have to go to church on Sunday to be a believer. For his uncle, church was the water; the altar, the wheel of *Rose Bud*. That worked for Cliff, although he admitted his faith had been severely rocked by his uncle's death. According to Uncle George, lightning was the angels in heaven practicing their spear tossing. Cliff wanted to know why they had to toss such a spear at his uncle. It was bad enough when both his parents were killed. Did they have to take his uncle, too?

This battle had raged more times than he cared to admit, but Cliff realized he was fortunate in so many ways. He had been raised right. He had good people looking over him while he was living at *Loafer's Glory*. And now he still had people watching out for him and giving him good advice. He had been given an artistic talent few others possessed. He had also been given something perhaps as valuable—opportunity. He was determined to make the most of these gifts. He just wished April was there with him. He seemed to work better in her presence, having grown accustomed to her being on board.

He was about to refocus on the drawing before him when he heard footsteps outside, followed by a tapping on the side of the boat.

"Anybody home?" A soft voice came from out in the darkness.

Chessie, who was half asleep under the table, awoke quickly. She jumped up, recognized the voice and bound out the hatch. Stunned, Cliff dropped his pencil and slid from behind the table. He looked up through the hatch at the night sky. "Thank you, Mr. Twain," he mouthed.

He went topside to greet April who was standing on the catwalk, her arms folded across her chest. "Hey," he said.

"Hey back to you," she returned.

"The party over?"

"Finally."

"Wow." He held out his hand to help her over the safety wires.

"Why'd you leave so early?" April asked, taking his hand and stepping onto the boat.

"Two hours was enough for me. Besides, I had some work I wanted to do, and I wanted to make sure Mr. Hooper got home okay."

"I didn't mean to ignore you. It was just that…"

"I understand," Cliff said.

They went into the cabin. While he didn't mind the cool air, Cliff realized April was chilled. He closed the hatchway. Grabbing a beer, he said, "Want something?"

She hesitated. "Yeah, why not?"

"What would you like?"

April pointed to what he was holding. Cliff pointed to the beer as well. She nodded.

"Damn," he said, pulling out another beer. "You do feel like celebrating, don't you?"

"Why not?" she said. "It's been a big day."

"I'll say." They slid into the booth across from one another. Cliff watched as she took a sip of the beer. She tried not to make a face as the liquid teased her throat. She failed. She swallowed it quickly and took another. This one went down easier.

"As you acquire a taste, you'll get used to the bite."

"Drinking this is fun?" she said, sitting the bottle on the counter.

Cliff shrugged his shoulders. He knew better than to get into such a debate. The frown on April's face slowly faded.

"So everything went well tonight, huh?" Cliff asked.

"The whole day went well."

"An understatement," Cliff suggested.

"I made over three hundred dollars just in tips! That doesn't count what Jennifer gave me. That's twice what we make on the boat in a week."

"That's great," Cliff said. "But…" He hesitated.

"But what?" April challenged.

"Don't get too excited about the money. That's how it is in this business. An artist, regardless of the type, lives feast or famine. You have to be disciplined when you're feasting so the famine periods aren't so bad."

April shrugged her shoulders. "I've learned that skill being poor most of my life."

Not wanting to dampen the mood, Cliff said, "Well, you certainly have a bright future." He raised his bottle in a toast. "Here's to the newest student at Peabody."

She reluctantly clicked his bottle with hers. "I guess so."

Cliff set his bottle down on the table. "Am I detecting a hint of self-doubt?"

"I don't know. Peabody's a big step. You know I've had no formal training."

"Thank God."

"Why do you say that?"

"That might have ruined you."

April laughed. "I doubt that," she insisted.

"Your brother Danny seems pretty smart and obviously has a big impact on you," Cliff said. "What's he think about all this?"

"We haven't had much time to talk. Eddie recruited him to help in the dish room. He was still there when I left."

"What do you think he'd say?" Cliff asked.

"It would probably have something to do with me being out in the wilderness," she replied. "He relates everything to that."

"Very symbolic," Cliff suggested.

"I guess."

"The wilderness—where in spite of all the dangers around you, you're the boss," Cliff said. "It's like if all the sudden I had to leave the *Mona Lisa* and go to Baltimore to art school. While that would be a great opportunity, I'd lose control of my life. I haven't really been on the run, but..." He stopped.

April leaned forward and reached for Cliff's hand. "We've both been on the run most of our lives."

"What have I been running from?" Cliff asked curiously.

"Only you can answer that, darling," April replied.

"How do you know I've been running?"

"Intuition, for one," April said. "For another, you understand it all too well. I mean, now look at you. You're all alone out here on the boat. Not a whole lot of friends, all absorbed in your work. There must be a reason?"

Cliff pondered the question. "I look at it more as a journey, like I'm running towards something, not running away."

"Then what are you running towards?" April challenged.

"Being a successful artist and..." he paused. His eyes dropped to the table.

"And?" April encouraged.

Their eyes locked. "To have the opportunity to meet someone as remarkable and special as you."

April blushed and looked away, eventually breaking the silence that ensued. "How in the world did you get Mr. Hooper to go to the party tonight?" she asked.

"I threatened him."

"With what?"

"I said I was going to tell Ms. Blackstone that he didn't like her oyster stew anymore."

April laughed. "He believed you?"

"No," Cliff laughed back. "He just fussed about not having anything to wear. I told him I was in the same boat so we went clothes shopping together."

"That was really nice of you."

"He helped me too," Cliff insisted.

"You help a lot of people," April said. "I can't figure it all out, but you do."

"What can't you figure out?"

April took a couple small sips of beer. She no longer made a face with each swallow. "I really shouldn't drink this."

"You feeling okay?"

"I really don't feel anything."

"Good. I certainly don't want to get you drunk."

She tipped her head to the side. "Isn't that what you guys try and do?"

Cliff's eyes widened. "That's mean."

"Sorry," she said immediately. "Maybe I am starting to feel something."

"Maybe you're just starting to relax. You've had a hectic few days."

"An understatement." She took another sip of beer.

"Anyway, what can't you figure out?" Cliff nudged.

April paused. "Why did you go so far to help me?"

"Help you, how?"

"Damn it, Cliff, you saved my life. Actually, you did it twice."

"Actually, it was Chessie the first time."

"Regardless, you know what I mean."

Cliff looked away. "It started out simply being a favor for a friend."

"You mean Jennifer?"

Cliff nodded. "She didn't want to go to the hospital herself because she used to work there. I guess she didn't leave under the best of terms. So I went in her place. And that was that until you decided to go for a swim in the middle of a storm."

"Why didn't you just call the police or something?"

"Because you asked me not to, and because you asked me to take you away."

"That's what I mean. Why did you do that? There was a bad storm going on, you know."

He used a drink of beer as an excuse to gather his thoughts. "I guess I sort of… sort of found you interesting."

April laughed. She followed Cliff's lead with the beer. "Interesting… how?"

"Maybe intriguing is a better word. Jennifer told me about her father and his sister—your mother—and how the two families had never really been in contact with one another. Her father felt bad about this and always said he was going to rectify the situation one day. Only, time passed and it never got done. Then you show up in Annapolis for reasons totally unclear to anyone and your uncle finds out that you're officially listed as missing, only you're really not. You're right here in the big A. Then you show up alongside my boat in the middle of a storm half drowned. I guess I kind of got caught up in the mystery behind the whole thing like everyone else."

"So I was only an adventure for you?"

"You're more than that," Cliff blurted out.

April glanced away.

Cliff wrapped his fingers around her hands. "Listen April, from the first time I met you, I was… I was…" He struggled to find the right word. "I was smitten."

April chuckled at his choice of words.

Cliff continued. "That feeling has only grown stronger the more I've gotten to know you. I understand you have a lot of things on your plate right now, and I know a lot of this has to do with things that have happened in the past. I'm not trying to add to your burden. I would never want that. It's just that…" His words faded away. He pulled back his hand and sat up straight. "You asked, and that's it."

There was a long moment of silence as Cliff looked around the cabin while April stared right at him. Finally, she said, "What if I told you that whatever we have together is something I need and depend on, rather than it being a burden?"

"That would make me very happy."

"Then be happy," she said. She paused and gave him a wide smile. "Thank you," she added. "Thank you for everything you've done for me."

"It works both ways," Cliff said.

April paused as she sat across the table from a person who played an important part in her regaining her freedom. He was her savior. He was her friend, her confidant, and—

She cut the thought off. No, she told herself. She couldn't go there. She wasn't ready for that. Her head began to spin. She felt lightheaded. She looked down at her beer. It was half-empty. So this is what it feels like, she thought. She looked at Cliff. This is what it feels like, she repeated. She blamed it on the alcohol. Then she blamed herself for drinking the beer. She should have known better. A wave of nausea passed, but the lightheadedness continued. She suddenly felt trapped.

"You no longer have to run," she reminded herself silently. However, old habits were hard to break. She slid out from behind the booth. "I gotta go," she muttered.

And she did.

185

Cliff watched as she went up the galleyway and listened as she quickly stepped off the boat. He could hear her footsteps as she walked up the short finger pier. Then there was silence. He looked over at Chessie who was curled up on the floor beside the couch. "I don't know what just happened, girl," he said. "It's beyond me."

He stared through the open hatchway, trying to figure it out. Failing, he pulled the artist's pad toward him and focused on the drawing he had been working on earlier. He grabbed a sharp pencil to continue. He worked a few minutes, only he had trouble concentrating. He thought about calling it a night, but wanted to get this drawing finished so he could give it to Jennifer in the morning. He looked down at Chessie again. He told himself he obviously had perception and reality all screwed up. His ability to read people had failed him.

"It's beyond me," he repeated. "Chessie, you have any ideas girl, you let me know. Meantime, I'm going to take a shower and try and wake up."

The dog whined as if she understood. Cliff laughed and slid out from behind the table. "Better yet, girl, I wish you could bark some sense into her. Maybe you can go figure out what's going on." He reached down, rubbed the dog on her back and headed for a shower.

186

As she left the *Mona Lisa*, April picked up her pace and headed across the near empty parking lot. She tried to hold back the tears. She failed. The salty fluid ran down her cheeks into the corners of her mouth. She struck at the tears with her tongue. There were only a few people around and they were far enough away, she didn't have to worry about being recognized. She still kept her head low. Turning the corner at the head of Ego Alley, she cursed under her breath. She had been talking to Cliff about not being on the run anymore, and here she was doing just that. She stepped onto the concrete pavement and increased her pace. She looked to the left and was able to pick out the lights from *Hamilton's Bench*. She planned to climb into her bunk and stay there for the next week. She was that disappointed with herself.

She thought back to when she first returned to *Hamilton's Bench*. Mr. Hamilton offered her one of the guest staterooms instead of her cubbyhole cabin up forward. She asked if she had been fired as a member of the crew to which Mr. Hamilton answered, "Certainly not."

"Thank you," she responded. "In that case I'd prefer to stay with the rest of the crew."

The tears became heavier. Her chest filled with sobs. As she rounded the top of Ego Alley, she stopped and sat down on the curb. She buried her face in her arms.

Time passed—a little or a lot? She didn't know. She didn't care. She felt drained and sad. Just when she thought things were looking up. What happened all of a sudden? Why did she leave Cliff's boat? Why did she feel compelled to run again? What was the matter with her? What was she afraid of? Was she running solely as a reflex, or was there something else? When she returned to Annapolis with Chessie, Mr. Hamilton told her it was time she got on with her life as a way of helping her deal with the past. She feared, however, that when she stopped running, she'd lose control. Then again, did she ever have control? Maybe it was time to put everything behind her and focus on the future like Mr. Hamilton said. Maybe it was time to face her fears... to answer some questions... to experience—

The tears suddenly stopped. A moment ago she was feeling sad. Now, she had a sense of fear. Something was wrong. Her sixth sense kicked in. Something was nearby. A fox? A bear? It was like she was out in the woods again. She sat up straight and opened her eyes. She started to scream, but recognized the dog in time to muffle the sound.

Catching a breath, she said, "Chessie, what in the world are you doing out here this time of the night?" Realizing the dog's master was probably close by, she wiped her eyes and ran her hand through her hair. Chessie moved closer and started licking the tears from her face. April waited for the dog's master to call the dog off. Only the command didn't come. April leaned forward and gave the animal a hug. "You all alone, girl?"

Chessie accepted the affection then backed up and started barking. April held her hand out and said, "Be quiet, girl. You're going to wake up the whole neighborhood."

The dog turned slowly in circles. "Isn't Cliff with you?" April asked again.

The dog barked back.

April rose to her feet. "I guess not." She hesitated. Was she ready to face her fears, to answer the questions? "No," she said aloud. She started towards *Hamilton's Bench*. Chessie followed at her side. "No, girl, you can't go with me. You need to go back to the *Mona Lisa*." April pointed in that direction.

After several failed attempts to get Chessie to head back toward her own boat, April said, "So no's the wrong answer, huh?" She hesitated. "Come on girl, I'll take you home… again."

187

Cliff sat on the shower seat, his head bent forward, the warm water trickling down his neck. He had already done the cold shower routine to wake up. Now it was time to loosen up the muscles. His neck was especially tight, which usually happened when he was bent over his drawing pad for long periods of time. Tonight, however, it was worse. He reached back and made the water a few degrees warmer. He ran his fingers around the waistline of his bathing suit to loosen the material. He had eaten a lot and still felt bloated. Between Mr. Hooper and himself, they must have devoured at least a half-gallon of oyster stew—and that was just the beginning. Fried oysters, oysters Rockefeller, fried shrimp, steamed shrimp, shrimp scampi… The list went on and on—all seafood of course! He hadn't seen that much food in one place in a long time. A flash from the past crossed his mind. The Labor Day picnic at his uncle's. Food everywhere. People everywhere—smiling, laughing, and moving from table to table. No one sad. No one confused. No one running. Just like the celebration at the restaurant earlier.

Steam rose from the floor. He inhaled deeply to help clear his lungs… and his mind. He was starting to feel better. A few more minutes, then he'd get back to work on the drawing for Jennifer.

He started to stand, only the boat rocked at the same time, causing him to plop back down. He listened for the sound of a boat engine, figuring it was a Cigarette boat running in and out of Ego Alley. The fuel would be wasted this time of night as there was no one to show off for. There were certainly no babes on the bow. Cliff waited for the rocking to stop and then started to stand up again. This time he was stopped by a tapping on the bathroom door. He figured it was Chessie's wagging tail hitting the door. It was her way of telling him to hurry up as she wanted to go out for a walk. She seemed to always wait until he was in the shower. He opened the door a crack to tell her he'd be out in a minute.

Only it wasn't Chessie tapping.

His mouth dropped open. He blinked several times. He pushed the hair out of his face.

"Hey," April said.

"Hey," Cliff returned.

"I came back," she said.

"I see."

"You're not mad, are you?"

"No," Cliff said. "I'm glad."

"Sure?"

Cliff nodded. "What made you come back?"

She pointed to where Chessie was lying on the top step of the hatchway.

"Chessie?" Cliff said.

"She made me come back. She started barking… It's the middle of the night."

Cliff grinned. "Good dog."

"Smart dog."

"In more ways than one," Cliff said. He made a mental to give his best friend a special treat in the morning.

"Besides," April said, "I forgot, I don't have to run anymore."

"Good feeling, isn't it?"

"You decent?" she asked, her eyes dropping down. She pushed the door open a bit more.

"I've got my swimming trunks on. I do that sometimes when I take a shower to wake up."

"Oh," April said. She was wearing a long sleeve tee shirt and jeans. "Can I come in?"

Cliff took a step back. "Sure."

April kicked off her shoes and stepped over the threshold. Cliff took her arm so she wouldn't slip on the fiberglass floor. "You feel cold," he said.

"It's chilly out," she replied. "Besides, you're in here in the hot steam." She pulled the door closed behind her. "So what are you doing besides waking up?"

"Sitting here thinking, I guess."

"What were you thinking about?"

Cliff pulled her toward him so she could get under the stream of water. "You." Cliff took the shower nozzle from its hook and reached over the back of her head. With the water wetting her hair, he gently massaged her scalp and the nape of her neck. As the hot water ran across her arms, the coolness was replaced with a warm glow. She bent her head forward, letting some of the water run over her head. It spilled down her front, causing her to shiver at first, but as the material of her shirt warmed, so did she. She leaned forward and rested her head on Cliff's chest.

"That feels good," she said softly.

She wrapped her arms around his waist. Cliff sensed a hesitation in her voice and in her movements. "So besides Chessie and not having to run anymore, why else did you come back?" he asked.

"Just because I don't have to run doesn't mean everything is finished." She chuckled. "I guess I have my own painting to complete."

Cliff pressed the water nozzle into the small of her back and moved it up and down her spine. "What's not finished?"

A pause ensued. "I thought once the Sheriff was put away and I could see my family again, everything would be okay."

"And it's not?" Cliff said. He brushed some water out of her eyes.

"There's this thing with Eddie and his father," April said.

"I don't think you have to worry about that man anymore."

"I'm not talking about that."

"Then?" Cliff gently encouraged. He sensed she wanted to talk.

She explained what she had been thinking about earlier that needed Cliff's blessing. When she was finished, she added, "And there's one last piece of unfinished business."

April pushed away and looked up. Cliff brushed a strand of wet hair from her face. She did the same to him, the tips of her fingers moving softly across his forehead. He quivered at her touch. A sharp chill shot up his spine.

"I want to find out what it's like not to run," April said. "I wanted to find out what it's like…" She looked away.

Cliff took the shower head and laid it atop her head. The water spilled down across her neck and onto the front of her shirt. The material clung to her body, causing yet another shot of electricity to shoot through Cliff's spine.

He pulled his eyes away and said, "Life is like the road leading into the marina where I bought the *Mona Lisa*. It's full of potholes… big pot holes. And even when you think you know the road well, there's always a new hole trying to gobble you up. The key is to realize there are going to be potholes and to confront them as they appear. It helps…" He paused.

"Go on," April encouraged.

"It helps if you have someone to navigate the road with you."

"I want to find that someone," April said. "Someone who cares about me, the person… not just…" Her words faded.

Cliff leaned over and kissed her atop the head. The water, mixed with the scent of her hair, felt good against his lips. He moved his mouth to her left ear. Softly, he said, "Well, April, you do have a nice body. But—" He got the *but* in before she could say anything in protest. "Your mind is just as beautiful."

She stared deep into his eyes. "Do you really think so?" There was a touch of pleading in her voice.

"Yes, you do have a beautiful mind. You're a beautiful person. Matter of fact, you're one of the most fascinating persons I've ever met."

"That's nice. Thank you. You know, Cliff, you're the first person I've ever been with who…" She struggled to find the words. "Who I can really trust. I want to be with somebody who wants to be with me in the same way I want to be with them… like you said earlier, to navigate the potholes together." She paused. "I know there's more to a relationship than physical stuff. Just like your art. There's more to one of your drawings than a bunch of pencil marks on a piece of paper."

"Or musical notes on a piece of paper," Cliff added.

"Exactly."

"I understand," Cliff said.

"Do you?"

Cliff nodded. "I think the issue is we're both worried about what's going to happen tomorrow, and then the next day, and then the day after that. It's the unknown that bothers us the most. But whatever tomorrow may bring, I want it to be with you. I don't really care in what manner. I just want us to be together. If that means a strong emotional relationship with a physical relationship consisting of taking showers with our clothes on, that's fine. I don't have all the pieces put together in my own mind, but…" He continued struggling to find the right words. "I've worked all my life to find you. I'll work the rest of my life to keep you."

"Oh, Cliff," she said. The space between them evaporated.

He pulled her tightly to him. She responded by pressing into him. She extended her ankles to make herself taller until their lips met. She was inexperienced. He was gentle. The kiss was perfect.

Their lips parted, as did their bodies. "How do we get past our fears?" April said.

"Together," Cliff said.

She put her hands on his chest and pushed him back until he was forced to sit.

She straddled his legs and sat on his knees. She reached down and grabbed the bottom of her shirt with both hands. There was a moment's hesitation. Cliff watched her chest rise and fall as she took a deep breath. Then she pulled the shirt up over the top of her head. "Be gentle with me," she said softly.

"We should be gentle with each other," Cliff said.

And so they were.

188

David Blackstone leaned back in his chair and pushed his hands through his hair. The piece of paper he was holding brushed against his ear. In disgust, he rolled it in a ball, dropping it in the trash can alongside his desk. The paper was a letter from the Salvo Produce Company, the main produce supplier to the restaurant. David Blackstone had used them for many years because their quality had always been high and their prices fair. The letter was stating that effective immediately, there was going to be a significant increase in the price of produce across the board. Now the *Riverboat Inn's* CEO didn't have a problem with price increases. They were a common and expected part of the business, normally occurring secondary to bad weather. But this price increase had nothing to do with the weather. Matter of fact, David Blackstone had read that crops were good this year. The issue was that the *Riverboat Inn* was expanding and projected to do a booming business. And Salvo wanted to get in on the action.

In addition, they recently assigned a new salesman to the *Riverboat Inn* account. Blackstone had met him once. He was new, green and right out of college. He thought he knew everything about anything. David Blackstone had always been tolerant with salespeople. He understood that everybody needed to earn a living. He even had the reputation of helping new people out with tips on how to do a better job.

However, this case made him livid. This was not a price increase secondary to normal business trends. It was price gouging. Salvo's new guy thought he could get away with it because the closest competition lacked the same quality. That was true before, but now that the restaurant was projected to do more business, more distant suppliers were coming to court the Blackstones. There was one in particular who also had a relatively new salesman. Only this young man did not have the know-it-all attitude and sold by properly and accurately presenting his product line. He was persistent without being pushy—just the way David Blackstone liked them.

David Blackstone opened the top desk drawer and pulled out this man's business card. He was about to make the call when there was a knock on his office door. "Come in," he said loud enough for anyone on the other side to hear, even someone with dead hearing aid batteries.

The door opened and George Hamilton walked in. Blackstone rose to his feet.

"Have a minute?" the yacht owner said.

"Sure. Come in," the *Riverboat Inn* owner said, making sure his tone of voice was softer. He also made sure to hide his surprise. "Have a seat. Want some coffee?"

"I'm fine for now," Hamilton said. "Thanks, anyway."

The two men took seats facing one another. "So what can I do for you?" David Blackstone said.

Unusual for Hamilton, there was a brief hesitation. "I want to talk to you about Jennifer."

"You mean April?"

"No, I mean Jennifer."

It was David Blackstone's turn to hesitate. "Then, Mr. Hamilton, fire away."

The yacht owner did.

189

Old Man Hooper's fingers moved slowly but steadily as the hole in the net gradually disappeared. A cigarette held loosely in his mouth bobbed up and down with his breathing. His only other movement was his fingers guiding the nylon twine across the net's defect. Eyes remaining focused on the task before him, he ignored the looks of the crowd that passed in a seemingly non-ending stream. He was reaching for the scissors when he noticed someone in the stream had stopped. He was about to ignore him, too, when he noticed something else. The fine fabric in the suit pants caused him to look up.

"Good afternoon, Mr. Hooper," the man in the suit said with a smile.

"Afternoon," Mr. Hooper said.

"My name's George Hamilton. I met you at the party last evening. Remember?"

"I remember," Old Man Hooper said.

George Hamilton scanned the length of the old skipjack. "I bet she was beautiful under full sail."

The old man lit another cigarette. "That she was."

"Not too many like her left."

The old man said nothing.

"It'll be a sad day for the Chesapeake when she finally goes to her grave."

"I suspect that'll be sooner than later," the old man said. "The pumps are having trouble keeping up with her bleeding heart."

"Doesn't have to be that way," Hamilton said.

Old Man Hooper paused in his inhalation of smoke. "I don't take no handouts, Mr."

Hamilton's expression turned serious. "I don't give them either." He smiled and held out a brown paper bag. "Cliff Davidson... you know him, right?"

Hooper nodded.

"Anyway, he said that if I wanted to get on your good side, I should bring you some of Mrs. Blackstone's oyster stew, and—" Hamilton glanced over his shoulder to make sure the wrong people weren't watching. "And some cigarettes." He held out the paper bag he was holding.

"That Davidson's a smart boy," the old man said.

"Hell-of-an artist, too."

The old man nodded in agreement. There was another moment of silence. "What do you want?" the old man said.

"Two things. The first is to see *Windskater* back out on the bay again."

The old man laughed and choked on a lung full of smoke. "That would take quite a lot of money."

Hamilton simply shrugged his shoulders. "I think it would be well worth the investment. Don't you?"

Hooper started to argue, but found he had nothing to say. "What's in it for you?"

"I'd be honored to be aboard as she leaves the harbor."

"That's it?"

"Maybe I could have a turn at the helm when she's out in the open water."

"I doubt that," the old man said.

George Hamilton laughed.

The old man cocked his head to the side. "You're bloody nuts, you know that?"

"I've been called worse."

The old man took another drag of his cigarette. "You said two things. What's the other?"

Hamilton answered the question.

Hooper's eyes widened. "Now I know you're off your rocker."

Hamilton laughed again. "Permission to come aboard?"

The old man failed to hide a smile. "Hurry up, would ya? There's nothing I hate worse than cold oyster stew."

190

George Hamilton admitted to Jennifer on a couple of occasions that a lot of important meetings had occurred in his office aboard *Hamilton's Bench*. Some turned out in favor of the yacht owner; a few, the opposite. Some were cordial, others involved heated discussion. None, however, were as unusual as the one on this Labor Day weekend. The room was initially occupied by Louis, Eddie Richmond and Sam Worthington. Also present was a man by the name of Jonathan Mitchell, the assistant state prosecutor assigned to Sheriff Richmond's kidnaping case. Louis made the introductions and then left them alone to wonder why they had been summoned on short notice to *Hamilton's Bench*. The wait wasn't long, however, as the far door opened and three other people entered. Cliff was first, followed by April and then George Hamilton himself. The yacht owner motioned for them all to take a seat around the conference table. He offered beverages which they all declined. He nodded to Louis who returned the gesture and exited quietly.

When he had everyone's attention, Hamilton spoke. "First of all, let me thank each of you for coming this morning on such short notice. Second, let me make sure everyone knows each other. Have you all met?"

Glances were exchanged. Heads nodded in the affirmative. Hamilton continued. "Then let's get started. I'm sure you know April is back with us safe and sound, for which we are thankful. She's also been reunited with her family and friends, and has actually met some new family she never knew she had. As for her future, she'll be starting at the Peabody Conservatory of Music in a couple of weeks. Not to put any pressure on her, but she will undoubtedly be one of the world's foremost pianists."

Hamilton paused as heads nodded in agreement. April blushed.

"Eddie Worthington has also come in out of the cold so to speak. I never knew him before the other day, but I can tell you that the man who sits before us now has a bright future ahead of him."

Smiles and nods all around.

"He has landed a position at the *Riverboat Inn* and will be starting college online as soon as he gets the paperwork done… which is going to be in the next couple days. Right, Eddie?"

Eddie laughed nervously. "Yes, sir."

Hamilton continued. "In short, there have been a lot of loose ends tied up here the past few days. However, there's one still remaining. April has been reunited with her family, but Eddie has not. As you know, Sheriff Richmond is still in federal custody."

Everyone looked at Eddie as the smiles disappeared. His lips started to quiver as he fought back the tears.

"And to quote April here, that's unacceptable."

The lip quivering stopped. Eddie looked over at April who gave him a faint smile.

Hamilton looked directly at Jonathan Mitchell. The prosecutor was the only one dressed in a suit. Everyone else was dressed casually. "Jonathan," Hamilton said. "What do you plan as the foundation of your case against Sheriff Richmond?"

"On the kidnaping charges?" the prosecutor said.

Hamilton nodded.

The man hesitated, trying to decide if he was at liberty to talk about this or not. Deciding there was no harm, "The testimony of Cliff and April, naturally."

"What happens if they refuse to testify?"

"They could be held in contempt."

"Put that aside a moment."

The prosecutor's mouth dropped open. "You know as well as I, there would be no case."

"Well…" Hamilton looked around the table. "That's what's going to happen… that is, if certain conditions are met." He continued before anyone could object. "Cliff and April want to drop all charges against Sheriff Richmond if he agrees to the following. First, he must undergo intense behavioral counseling. Second, he must agree to remain in the city of Worthington Valley, not to leave her borders without permission from you, Jonathan. Third, he must resign as sheriff, which is actually a moot point as that has already occurred by way of his arrest. Fourth, he must give up his right to bear firearms of any kind, which is also a given. Fifth, he must apologize in writing to the town of Worthington Valley, to April and to his son—this apology to be printed in the local paper. Sixth, he must meet Eddie who will be the sole determinant as to whether the sheriff is capable of holding up his end of the bargain. If Eddie says yes, the sheriff is to be released and the above deal is made. If Eddie says no, then the prosecution moves forward. If Eddie agrees, but at a later time the sheriff reneges on any part of the deal, including leaving the perimeters of Worthington Valley without permission, the deal is off and he will be taken back into federal custody. Finally, the sheriff must agree that if the latter does occur, all options for a plea bargain are waived."

"Now, this all sounds simple, and may even seem farfetched in some people's minds, but in reality will take a lot of legal maneuvering on everyone's part. I think Jonathan here will concur that it is possible. Again, it will depend on the sheriff's willingness and on Eddie's assessment of his father's ability to comply now and in the future. Agree, Jonathan?"

Jonathan Mitchell was obviously taken aback by the ramifications of what Hamilton was saying. In reality, he was looking forward to the publicity and subsequent advancement of his career this case was sure to bring. "What about the federal charges—the piracy issues in general?"

"They are only there to shore up the kidnaping charges and to give wiggle room if a plea bargain is considered," Hamilton said.

The prosecutor hesitated. He saw his premier case rapidly slipping away. "I'm sure you've done your homework, George. So I won't even begin to disagree… so long as that's what April and Cliff want. However…" He paused for effect, unable to avoid the spotlight, if only for a moment. "We just got calls yesterday from Atlantic City. There may be additional charges coming up. Seems the sheriff was a little rough in his investigative techniques. I don't have any authority there."

"I know the people involved in Atlantic City," April said. "I'm sure something can be worked out there. Money talks big in that town." Her voice softened. "Our families have been torn apart too long. It's time we start putting the pieces back together, Eddie's included."

All eyes turned to Eddie who was now in a full-fledged act of pouring out tears.

"Thank you,' he said.

April smiled fully for the first time since entering the room.

191

Jennifer stared eastward towards the mouth of the Severn River. The temperature had dropped a few degrees and a light breeze had picked up. The sky remained crystal clear. The moon, in all its glory, stood guard over the thousands of stars shining down on Annapolis. There were stars she had not seen in a long time. For all Jennifer knew, there were stars she had never seen. It was one of the most spectacular skies she'd ever witnessed. She turned toward the *Riverboat Inn*, soon to be the *Riverboat Inn Restaurant and Resort*. The restaurant was still lit up in all its splendor. As you faced the front, you swore you were looking at an old Mississippi riverboat. A magnificent sight, Jennifer thought. She wondered what it would look like when the complex was finished. They did have a basic architectural sketch, but a model wasn't planned until the final design was finished. She was sure it would be spectacular.

She used to wonder why her parents were going to all this trouble. After all, the restaurant itself was more than enough to support their family, and keep all three of them busy. The business had its up and downs, but the revenue stream was steady, and almost every year showed at least a small growth. Her parents could easily retire on the property value alone if they so desired. They certainly didn't need the headaches, the red faces or her father's occasional sailor's vocabulary. Nor did they need the health risks associated with such a high stress project.

It took Jennifer a long time to figure out the real reason behind it all. Then one day it sort of struck her—the boat wasn't finished. A simple, yet profound thought… an idea floated forth several years before by Jennifer herself.

Her eyes scanned the complex. The actual waterfront of the property had a slow smooth curve to it. The architects incorporated this curve into the design so that the finished complex would sit on the property in such a way that the whole south side of the boat could be seen from the harbor and from across Ego Alley. In addition, the back part of the building, or the stern of the boat, would actually sit several feet higher than the bow and original restaurant. Jennifer came up with the idea of a real working paddle wheel in the rear, giving the illusion that the boat was underway and heading right into the Annapolis Harbor. The paddle wheel would turn through a large pool of water that would serve as part of the mixing and filtration system for the planned swimming pool. The pool itself would be landscaped to look like the shores of the Mississippi River.

So in a lot of ways Jennifer was glad the St. Michaels project fell through—at least for the time being. Her father insisted that once word got out how impressive the *Riverboat Inn* expansion would be, St Michaels's town council would be clamoring for action. And since David and Elizabeth Blackstone owned the only piece of undeveloped waterfront property in the harbor, how sweet it was. It all reinforced Jennifer's belief that her father had this whole thing planned from the beginning.

"It certainly is a beautiful sight." George Hamilton's voice startled her as she didn't hear him come onto the bridge of *Hamilton's Bench*.

Jennifer turned and faced him. "The whole harbor is beautiful. Annapolis is spectacular by day. It's even more so at night," she said.

"Especially when it is serving as the backdrop for such a beautiful woman," Hamilton said. Jennifer felt herself blush. She still wasn't used to such compliments, compared to what came from the gang at the bar. "Thank you," she managed to chirp.

He held out a glass for her. "Here you go."

She took the long stem crystal. "What is it?"

"It's called crème royal," Hamilton replied. "It's a combination of champagne and Chambord."

Jennifer took a sip. It was sweet, yet still had the bite of champagne. "Very good. Thank you."

"It's festive yet it will still warm you up on a cool night like tonight."

"It does do that," Jennifer agreed. She could feel the liquid working. She wondered if it was from the liquor… or perhaps something else was warming her.

"You cold?" Hamilton said, taking a drink from his own glass.

"Not now," Jennifer replied.

"Autumn comes quickly to the Chesapeake Bay, doesn't it?" Hamilton commented.

"That's why they call it fall. It sort of drops right on top of you." Jennifer took another sip. "Seems like clockwork. The second night in September and summer's gone. Don't worry; it'll get warm a couple more times before it finally stays cold."

"Chesapeake Bay weather has a history of being chaotic," Hamilton said.

"In more ways than one," Jennifer agreed.

Hamilton chuckled. "Symbolic of life in general around here."

"It's not always like this," Jennifer defended. "Hopefully, things will settle down soon."

"Annapolis is the hub of Maryland's political machine," Hamilton said. "There will always be a certain amount of chaos here. That's one of the things that draws people like you and me to this town. You never know how strong the wind's going to blow, or from which direction."

"People like you and me?"

"People who thrive on chaos. We complain about it, yet we love it. It's almost an addiction."

"Makes non-chaotic times more meaningful," Jennifer said.

"Exactly."

"Seems like the non-chaotic times are getting less and less," Jennifer bemoaned. "I used to spend a lot of time with Mr. Hooper. Lately…"

"I'm sure he understands," Hamilton said.

"You don't know him."

"I—" Hamilton stopped short. "I'm certainly glad I decided to stop in Annapolis."

"You are?"

"Yes. Two good and one bad thing came from my visit." He didn't wait to be asked for an explanation. "The bad is that I'm going to lose a great pianist and crew member. A good thing is that April now has the future in music that she deserves. She's a special person with an exceptional talent."

"She is that," Jennifer agreed.

"To think, all she's been through, yet in the end to still be concerned about Eddie. That takes… Well, that's a rare commodity in today's world."

"Speaking of Eddie, how did the visit with the sheriff go this morning?" Jennifer asked.

"Surprisingly well. Eddie said his piece. The sheriff listened. The prosecutor laid the deal out on the table. The sheriff seemed genuinely surprised. He asked whose idea it was to let him off so easily. When the prosecutor told him it was April, I thought the man was going to fall off his chair. The sheriff asked why and Eddie said he would have to ask her that himself sometime. The sheriff said he would like that."

"Do you buy it?" Jennifer asked.

"Not entirely." Hamilton continued. "The sheriff can be quite intimidating. That's how he was able to keep Eddie's condition a secret. He intimidated the hell out of everyone at both hospitals. As you know, he blackmailed Danny's father, a form of intimidation in itself. That's a difficult trait to shake. Yet, I do think the sheriff will try. He's too smart to do otherwise. I also think he's on the road to accepting Eddie back into his life—vice versa as well. So it's a start—another flower in your vase of a very special weekend."

Jennifer shook her head in agreement and took another sip of her drink.

"Anyway, chaos or not, the entire weekend was a huge success. The party last night was great. The ground breaking ceremony today went off without a hitch. All and all, I'd say you did a terrific job." Hamilton paused and looked across the water. "You should really be proud of yourself. Your father filled me in on the details of the plans for the expansion. I like the idea of *finishing the boat*. Sounds terrific. I can't wait to see what it looks like when it's complete."

"Me, either."

"Your father gave you credit for coming up with the basic concept."

"We did it as a family," Jennifer insisted.

"Take credit where credit's due," Hamilton suggested gently.

"Whatever."

Hamilton stepped forward and placed his arms on her shoulders. "The *Riverboat Inn* is going to be almost as beautiful as the resort's manager."

Jennifer tipped her head as she blushed again. "You're so nice."

"It's easy to be nice to someone like you."

"It works both ways, you know," she said.

"I try."

Jennifer squinted as she looked up at Hamilton. "By the way, you said there were two good things that happened when you came to Annapolis. You only told me about April."

She watched him smile in the moonlight. "I met you," he said.

Jennifer chuckled. "Is that good or bad?" She didn't give him a chance to respond. Instead, she focused on something he said a moment before. "Wait a minute, you said *my father told you*. When did you meet with…?"

She didn't notice where it came from, but his right hand suddenly contained a small black box. Holding the box out to her, Hamilton said, "To answer your second question, I met with him this afternoon. As to your first question, it's been very good. I just hope it's been the same for you."

Jennifer stared a long moment. Her hands shook. She gasped for air. Her knees threatened to buckle. He had caught her totally off guard again. She ignored all this as the genes unique to single females took over and reminded her that this would not be a good time to faint. She took a deep breath and opened the box.

The city surrounding the yacht was lit up, engulfing the bridge of *Hamilton's Bench* in shadows. There was enough light, however, that the reflection off the single solitaire diamond was as bright as the night sky.

Hamilton took her hands in his. "Jennifer, I'd be honored if you would be my soul mate. I'd be even more honored if you'd be my wife. Will you marry me?"

Jennifer's mouth opened and closed several times without a sound. She was in a state of shock. Most young women dream of this moment many times as they are growing up, but dreaming, even practicing what you'd say, never prepares one for the reality of the moment—especially when the moment comes as a total surprise.

Hamilton continued. "Before you say anything, especially something I might not want to hear, I want to say a couple of things. First, I love you, Jennifer, with all my heart. I have never truly loved anyone before. I know it seems rather quick, but when the truth smacks you in the face, you either accept it or ignore it. I choose the former.

"I know we were just talking about chaos, and I know our marriage would contain its fair share. To start, we each have our careers—and let me say right away, I would never ask nor expect you to give up yours in order to marry me. One of the things that attracts me to you is just that—your ability to manage the many things in your life—the chaos, so to speak. And you do this all with such a pleasant disposition.

"Only there's a lot more to you than that. You're one of the most compassionate people I've ever met—compassionate in caring for others as well as passionate about sticking to what you believe in. You told me that's why you left your job at the hospital. You refused to sacrifice quality of care for budgetary reasons. You showed the same characteristic when you didn't give up on the face you recognized that day aboard *Hamilton's Bench* that turned out to be April." He took a deep breath. "However, that's all neither here nor there. It will be a challenge for each of us, I know. But I think that's good. We'd be bored out of our minds if it were any other way."

Jennifer finally stopped shaking. Stability returned to her knees. The fog started to lift. She was filled with questions. She cursed beneath her breath. Why did that have to happen? Why were there always so many questions? She shook her head in hopes they'd go away. Some did. Others remained. "My parents," she said. "What will they say?"

"Your father gave me his full blessing," Hamilton said.

"He did?"

Hamilton smiled. "I assured him I would love and care for you the rest of our lives." The smile widened. "I also promised I would not take you away from the restaurant."

"And he said okay."

This time Hamilton laughed. "He's already talking about the reception." The man paused. "And for the record, I spoke to Mr. Hooper, too."

"Mr. Hooper! What did he say?"

"He thought I was nuts tackling someone as feisty as you."

"No he didn't!"

Hamilton laughed, "He did start mumbling about having to get all dressed up again."

Jennifer's face turned serious. "There are so many things…"

"Exactly," Hamilton said. "These many issues are what will keep us strong."

"I don't know, George. I don't know."

Hamilton tipped his head to the side. A wide smirk grew across his face.

"What's the matter?" Jennifer said.

The smirk resolved. "Nothing, Blackstone. That's the first time you ever called me by my first name."

"I guess that's right." She smiled. "It won't be the last, either."

George's eyebrows rose. "Does that mean…?"

Her head bobbed ever so slightly up and down.

"Please, let me hear you say it," George said.

"Yes."

192

September 3rd was a beautiful day in Annapolis. The sky remained cloudless throughout the night. The guard had changed. The duty of watching over the earth was now in the hands of the sun, which was just waking up in the eastern sky. There was the hint of a cool breeze, a reminder that summer was over and fall was on its way. A flock of seagulls, some in the water, some sitting on pilings, stood watch at the end of Ego Alley. A red SUV drove around the circle in the center of town twice before heading up Main Street toward the capitol.

"Obviously a tourist," Jennifer thought as she wrapped her arms across her chest in response to the breeze. She stood in the crosswalk and chuckled as she watched the SUV speed up the road. Her life had certainly been spinning in circles lately. She shivered as a chill ran up her spine. Was she going in the right direction? Was she going too fast? What was the speed limit for this sort of thing?

"More damn questions," she cursed. She laughed again. But as she and George agreed, they would tackle each of these issues one at a time.

They spent the night on the bridge of *Hamilton's Bench*, drinking champagne, munching on potato chips and talking. Several times George offered to go inside where it was warmer. Each time Jennifer asked to remain where they were. She didn't want the night to end. So they stayed on the bridge, huddled together under a blanket, and talked. It was one of the most memorable evenings of Jennifer's life.

What do couples who just get engaged talk about? Everything and anything; some of it important, some not; some related to short term plans, some long term. Jennifer Blackstone and George Hamilton were no different. In the end, the blueprint for at least the next several years of their lives was rather simple. Jennifer would stay in Annapolis and run the *Riverboat Inn and Resort*. George would continue his practice as before. In that a lot of his work was done from *Hamilton's Bench* anyway, he'd spend as much time in Annapolis as possible. And when he wasn't in Annapolis, Jennifer would visit him whenever possible. Each agreed it would take a special effort, yet each agreed it could and would work.

"With a good dose of chaos," Jennifer mouthed silently.

Questions continued to cross Jennifer's mind during this time. One was money, to which George responded. "Your father and I already talked about that. I assured him I was not marrying you for your money and said I would sign a prenuptial agreement if he so desired."

Jennifer laughed, "That's not quite the way I was talking about."

"Then let's quit talking about it."

But perhaps the most compelling question to cross Jennifer's mind that night was why… why had George picked her? He surely had many other choices over the years. Why her? And why now?

Never one to avoid an issue, Jennifer asked him about that. Not one to avoid an issue himself, George responded with a straightforward response. "It's quite simple actually. Besides falling madly in love with you, you're the first person who has focused on *me* and not *mine*."

"I don't understand," Jennifer said.

"*Me* represents George Hamilton the person. *Mine* represents what George Hamilton has."

"Well, I think what a person has says a lot about who they are," Jennifer said. "More importantly, it's what they do with what they have. That's what impressed me so much about you. I also imagine that your success hasn't changed you all that much."

"I have a bigger boat," George boasted, teasingly.

"You know what I mean."

Then he kissed her. It was the first time he'd kissed her all evening.

Jennifer slowed as she rounded Ego Alley. The normal flock of seagulls were scattered atop the pilings. Most were asleep. A few, however, raised their heads as she passed. As if recognizing a familiar face, they buried their heads back beneath their wings without further ado. Turning the corner, Jennifer picked up her pace. She was anxious to get home to tell her parents. The sun was on the rise so her father would be up moving about. He was probably already at the restaurant making sure everything was going okay for the start of the day. Her mother would be in the kitchen doing the same.

Jennifer smiled. For the first time she could remember, she was going to be the one doing the summoning. "Got a minute?" she would simply say.

She continued toward the *Riverboat Inn.*

Before she went up to the restaurant, however, she had two stops to make. She slowed at the *Windskater.* The main hatch was closed indicating the old man was still asleep—a bit unusual for him. Then again he had a busy couple days… and a few too many beers each day as well. She was really glad Mr. Hooper was out and about again. It was the first time he had gone out other than to take care of basic essentials in many years.

They made a strange pair, Jennifer thought. Cliff and Old Man Hoper, that is. Who would have *thunk* it? Then again, why not? In so many ways they were so much alike. Caring, compassionate, dedicated to the bay, living the life many could only dream of. So why not? After all, Cliff was going to be spending a lot more time in Annapolis over the next year. He had a lot of work to do with the new *Riverboat Inn.* Plus, several other people had approached him about doing work for them. And there was the governor. He had big plans for Cliff as well. So Cliff was on his way of reaching his goal of supporting himself as an artist. And Mr. Hooper was well on his way to making a new friend. They were good for each other, Jennifer decided.

Their friendship was good for her as well.

She moved down the dock and stopped at the *Mona Lisa.* Not surprisingly, Cliff was sitting in the cockpit, his head bent down—one hand holding a drawing pad, the other a pencil. She stood there a full thirty seconds before he noticed her.

"Hey," he said somewhat surprised. He quickly closed the pad. "What are you doing up so early?"

"I could ask you the same."

"I'm working."

"I'm not," Jennifer quipped.

Cliff sat the pad aside. "Come on aboard."

"Thanks." She stepped over the safety wires and sat down across from him. Motioning towards the drawing pad, "What are you working on?"

"Just some stuff."

"Stuff?"

"Yeah."

Jennifer laughed. "You could be more specific, you know."

Cliff smiled. "I'm working on a drawing for you."

"Me!"

"Yes."

"When can I see it?"

"When it's finished."

"Clifford!"

"Be patient," Clifford instructed.

Jennifer gave him a stern look.

"Want some coffee?" the artist asked.

"Sure," she smiled.

Cliff disappeared below and returned with two steaming mugs. "It's a lot cooler this morning."

"It is September," Jennifer said. She took a sip of coffee. It was strong as usual, but good. The liquid warmed her as it poured into her stomach. She wrapped her hands around the cup.

"What are you doing out this time of the morning?" Cliff repeated.

Jennifer hesitated. "I was over at the boat."

"*Hamilton's Bench*?"

She nodded.

"You spent the night?" Cliff egged. He wasn't sure if he wanted to know more.

"We sat up on the bridge all night and talked."

"I'll believe that when the sun sets in the east."

"We did, for real."

"What did you talk about?"

Jennifer hesitated again. "Mainly our future."

"*Our* future."

"George asked me to marry him."

Cliff stared at her in silence. He didn't show the surprised look Jennifer expected. "Is that what you want?"

"Yes."

"Is that what you *really* want?"

"Yes."

"What did you tell him?"

She held out her hand for him to see the ring. He let out a soft whistle. "It's pretty, I guess."

Jennifer laughed. "It's beautiful."

"Okay, then it's beautiful."

"That's better."

Cliff stared into her eyes a long moment. "He's a very lucky guy." He took a sip of coffee. "I just hope he ain't the jealous type."

"Why's that?"

"You and I will still be best buds, won't we? After all, we do have an agreement."

A big grin crossed Jennifer's face. She was getting the support she so badly needed, and badly wanted. "Always. Matter of fact, he's going to ask you to be in the wedding."

"Me!"

"You dressed up good the other night. You can do it again."

"But that was only because of Mr. Hooper."

"He's going to be in the wedding, too."

"The sun is going to set in the east."

Jennifer laughed. Then she paused as her expression turned serious. "Are you happy for me?"

"Why wouldn't I be? You're my best friend, remember."

"What about you?"

Cliff smiled and swallowed a laugh. "I'll be okay."

"You sure?" A wave of concern abated as Jennifer noticed a noise below deck. She heard footsteps and then April's head popped up through the galleyway. "April!" Jennifer said, surprised at seeing her cousin.

April shielded her eyes from the sun. "Oh, hi Jen. I thought I heard voices."

Jennifer stared at her cousin and saw a hint of a blush. It was something another woman would notice. The blush was slight, the meaning enormous.

"What about me?" Cliff said, interrupting the moment.

April looked in his direction. The blush was gone. "Oh, you're here, too?"

"Smart ass," Cliff said.

"*I'm the best,*" April snickered. Another *woman to woman* message was passed silently. "Anybody want anything? More coffee?"

"I don't know about you two, but I'm hungry," Cliff said.

"Let me brush my teeth and I'll fix breakfast." April disappeared below deck.

It was the perkiest Jennifer had seen her cousin since they met. It reinforced the meaning behind the blush. "*I'm the best...*" she repeated. She felt a momentary surge of jealously which she quickly subdued. Her thumb caressed the underside of the new piece of finger jewelry.

Cliff laughed. "Nothing gets by you, does it?"

"I can say the same about you."

"Say the same about what?" April said, her head back in the hatchway.

"Oh, nothing," Cliff said. "Just banter between friends. Come here. Jennifer's got something to tell you."

"Give me a minute." April returned with a pot of coffee and a plate of breakfast rolls. "The eggs'll be done in a little bit." She sat down next to Cliff. "So... what's the news?"

Jennifer reached for a bun with her left hand. The sun hit the diamond and sent a sharp sparkle across the boat.

"Oh, my God, Jen. Where'd you get that?"

"George gave it to me last night."

"Mr. Hamilton?"

Jennifer shook her head.

"Is that what I think it is?"

The older cousin's head shook harder.

"Oh, Jennifer," April said. She stood up and gave her cousin a big hug. "I'm so happy for you. I'm happy for Mr. Hamilton, too."

The hug completed, Jennifer said, "I'd like you to be my maid of honor."

"Me!"

"Yes. I have this because of you."

"Me!"

"Yes."

There was a pop from the grease in the skillet below. "I'll go finish," Cliff said. "You two keep talking."

The *Mona Lisa's* captain returned a few minutes later with four plates piled high with toast and scrambled eggs. The food was passed out along with a plentiful supply of napkins. There was a minute or two of near silence as the food was eagerly consumed. The only sound was Chessie lapping her own plate clean. She was not the quietest diner in the world.

"I have a question," Cliff said.

"What?" Jennifer replied.

"What does Mr. Hamilton… George, do, anyway?"

Jennifer and April looked at one another. The older cousin nodded to the younger who spoke next. "He's an attorney."

Cliff looked across the waterway at *Hamilton's Bench.* "He must be a good one."

"One of the best in the country in his specialty."

"What's that mean?"

April continued. "I guess lawyers specialize like doctors. Mr. Hamilton's business is suing other businesses."

"What do they sue each other for?"

"All sorts of stuff."

"Must be big business," Cliff quipped.

Jennifer picked up the explanation. "It is. A lot of it has to do with copyright and patent infringements. He does other stuff, too. For instance, he told me last night he was going to be working for a client who was thinking about buying the hospital here in town."

"A person buying a whole hospital?" Cliff said.

"Not a person… a hospital group out of Richmond, Virginia."

"Oh."

Jennifer didn't add George reassured her that a golden parachute would not be part of any deal.

"Anyway," Cliff said. "How does he do all that from his boat?"

"Thanks to the Internet, that's where he spends most of his time. He also has other attorneys who work for him. They do most of the onsite prep work. Then when he needs to be there—wherever that is—he goes."

"Just how good is he?" Cliff asked.

Jennifer laughed. "Governor Wilson told me he is one of the most revered and feared corporate attorneys in America. If he's on your side, he's revered. If not…"

"And you're marrying this guy?" Cliff teased.

"I guess I'm on the right side."

"What about the name of his boat?" Cliff queried.

"*Hamilton's Bench*," Jennifer continued. "Most people assume the name symbolizes his office, his work bench. It's that plus more. The name is also partly in response to something that happened several years ago. A couple of Fortune 500 CEOs who had lost their shirts to George on several occasions and were in the process of losing again, came up with the idea of getting him appointed to the Federal Bench. That way he'd be out of their hair. He's smart enough. He certainly has the credentials, and he knows the right people. Most likely, it would have been a shoo-in. It's a real honor to be appointed to such a position. It's also a stepping stone to the Supreme Court, which was also mentioned. But George turned it down."

"You mean he could have been a federal judge?"

"Yes," Jennifer answered. "He found out about the CEOs' plot, and actually went along with the idea right up to the day before the Senate confirmation hearings. Then he withdrew his name from consideration. He said he still had too many hot pokers to strategically place in the backsides of crooked corporate leaders."

"The real reason," April injected, "was that he couldn't work from the boat. That is his judge's *bench*."

There was a pause as additional food was consumed. "Very good," Jennifer said.

"It is," April agreed. "Aunt Elizabeth may make the best oyster stew, but Cliff, you make the best eggs."

"He does," Jennifer added.

"Only the best for my friends."

Jennifer turned her head to the side. "We are friends, aren't we?"

Cliff and April nodded.

"A trio of friends," April said.

"A trilogy," Cliff said. "In G minor," he added.

April laughed. "Anyway, Jennifer, you're going to stay in Annapolis and run the restaurant?"

"That's the plan."

"*Hamilton's Bench* would be a great platform to write from," Cliff pointed out.

"That's true, I guess," Jennifer agreed.

"You're a writer?" April said.

"A wannabe writer," Jennifer corrected.

"A writer with tremendous potential, but a bad case of writer's block," Cliff said.

"The same kind of thing has happened to me with music," April said. "Sometimes I just can't seem to get through a piece. I kind of get stuck… just like you."

"How do you get unstuck?" Jennifer asked.

"I put that piece aside and start on something new… usually something entirely different—a new beginning so to speak."

"Very symbolic," Cliff said.

"A new beginning for all of us," Jennifer vocalized. "But I really don't have anything else to write about. I'm just an amateur author trying to write her first book. I don't have a repertoire of music like you, April."

Cliff said through a mouth full of eggs, "There's a book sitting right here."

"What do you mean?" Jennifer inquired.

"A book is like a drawing or painting," Cliff said. "It has to have a good background, good characters and a little bit of intrigue to keep the viewer interested. Art, in its own way, tells a story, just like a book."

"I still don't understand," Jennifer said.

"He's saying to write about the three of us," April laughed.

"We're a pretty interesting trio," Cliff boasted.

"What would I call this masterpiece?" Jennifer laughed.

"Trilogy in G Minor," Cliff said.

"About the three of us?" Jennifer said. She cleaned the remaining eggs off her plate with a piece of toast. "You're serious?"

The nods continued. Chessie even let out a bark.

"You want me to start a whole new book called *Trilogy in G Minor*?" Jennifer said.

"Why not?" Cliff said.

And so she…

And so I did.

Dorsey Butterbaugh has his undergraduate degree from the Johns Hopkins University and a MBA from Loyola College in Maryland. He has worked as a physician assistant for over 36 years. He has also been in management and consulting in the medical field. He has been involved behind the scenes in local politics in Baltimore and is the chairman of a local campaign in Baltimore County. He is also a political speech writer. While his hobbies include boating and fishing, he has always been an avid reader and writer.

He has written several books. Behind Bars, with James Willey, is his first published novel. Trilogy in G Minor is the second published novel. He has several other projects in the works.

Born and raised in Baltimore, he and his wife will soon be fulltime on the eastern shore, at which time he plans to devote more time to his writing. He also hopes to become more involved in the Guild.

Also by Dorsey Butterbaugh (with James Willey):

Dr. Adam Singer is a world famous surgeon who is faced with his greatest challenge—the ability to move on with his life after facing a terrible tragedy. He meets Bobby, a local bartender in Fenwick Island, Delaware, and soon begins to experience a different culture from his norm. He learns we all have bars in our lives we have to deal with. He also learns how to love again.

A fantastic tale of humor and intrigue set in the context of your local bar. With characters reminiscent of your neighbors, you will surely not put his book down.
- Brian Desaulniers, MD

Butterbaugh and Willey offer a plot that's an easy guide into a specialized field of medicine and into the Delmarva beach communities. Their characters are as memorable as their true to life anecdotes focusing on beach or bar life. Behind Bars is a fun book. Take it to the beach, the airport or an easy chair with your favorite refreshment. I'll take a Bud Lite.
- Frank Minni, President, Rehoboth Beach Writers' Guild.

Mr. Butterbaugh and Mr. Willey have created a beauty of a book here about the truth of human experience. Their characters are not the shiny false placeholders we've come to accept in literature today, but people drawn so real you feel as if you'll run into them if ever you sit down at Smitty McGee's. It's a lovely story of the resilience of the human spirit and the renewal of a person's soul.
- Kerry Forrestal, MD
- Author of *Club Hell* and *The Chronicles of the Myst-Clipper Shicaine*

Made in the USA
Charleston, SC
25 January 2014